READER'S DIGEST
SELECT EDITIONS

The condensations in this volume
are published with the consent of the authors
and the publishers © 2006 Reader's Digest.

www.readersdigest.co.uk

The Reader's Digest Association Limited
11 Westferry Circus Canary Wharf London E14 4HE

For information as to ownership of
copyright in the material of this book,
and acknowledgments, see last page.

Printed in Germany
ISBN 978 0 276 44224 7

**SELECTED AND CONDENSED
BY READER'S DIGEST**

THE READER'S DIGEST ASSOCIATION LIMITED, LONDON

CONTENTS

E ver since *The Day of the Jackal* burst onto the book scene in 1971, Frederick Forsyth has been writing dazzling international thrillers that provoke and entertain. *The Afghan*—the story of a daring mission to thwart an Al Qaeda plot against the West, by sending in a carefully trained lookalike to pose as an Afghan—displays all his classic hallmarks: impeccable research, political insight, breathtaking suspense.

S et in 1931, this unusual detective story takes private investigator Maisie Dobbs from her office in Bloomsbury to the beaches of Dungeness in Kent, and to the heart of London's art world. Former soldier and controversial artist Nick Bassington-Hope has been found dead on the eve of his eagerly awaited new exhibition, and it's Maisie's job to discover why. A thought-provoking story that paints a vivid picture of England in the thirties.

M ichael Connelly, who has been called the 'best crime writer in the world', seems to get better with every book. *Echo Park* features his much-acclaimed series character, Harry Bosch, who is once again in the LAPD cold case department, investigating an unsolved crime committed thirteen years ago. But the focus switches to Bosch himself when a colleague suggests that a clue he missed has allowed a serial killer to roam the streets.

Sitting bumper-to-bumper in a traffic jam, pressing into a crowded train, or waiting in a queue for the bus that never comes . . . such experiences—the very essence of the 9-to-5 routine—often trigger dreams of escape and a certainty that somewhere out there is a more natural way of life. Journalist Guy Grieve was quite convinced of the fact and went beyond the dreaming to a point where he gave up his job and took temporary leave of his wife and his two sons (seen below) in order to pit himself against the elements in Alaska. Did the gamble pay off? What did he learn from the experience?

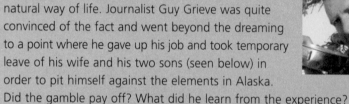

CALL OF THE WILD

GUY GRIEVE

153

CALL OF THE WILD
MY ESCAPE TO ALASKA

You'll need to read his book to find out, but here's what he told Reader's Digest very recently, from his home on the Isle of Mull: 'I gave way to nature for one year and, in so doing, I found my place on this earth. I learned to banish the ticking clock and to ignore the tail-chasing self-importance of those who rush confidently all over the globe, seeking nothing more than status or cash. The wilderness taught me to look at

the world around me in a manner that allowed me to draw strength from it. I learned to laugh at myself, and at almost anything else. Humour and the pursuit of happiness is every-thing—especially if one is tiny in the face of it all.'

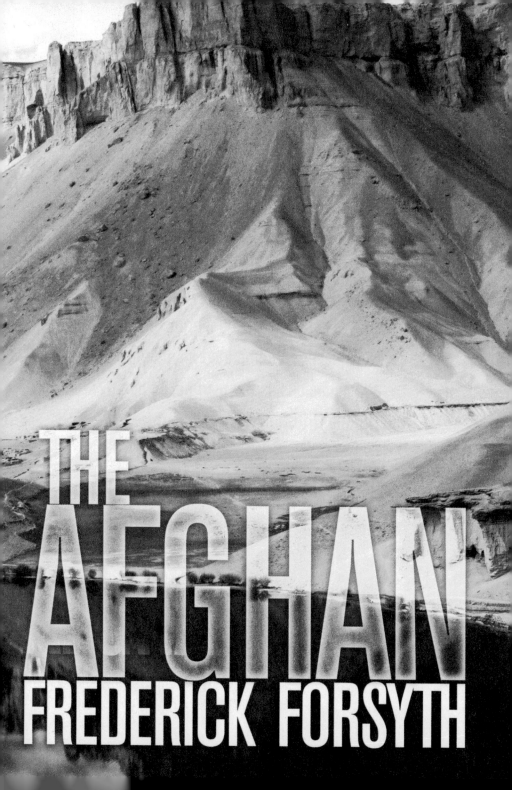

THE AFGHAN

FREDERICK FORSYTH

SAS veteran Colonel Mike Martin has been in
many of the world's toughest war zones,
pitted against the most dangerous of enemies.
But he's never contemplated anything as risky
and audacious as the plan put to him by
the US and British security services in 2006...

CHAPTER ONE

I f the young *Talib* bodyguard had known that making the cellphone call would kill him, he would not have done it. But he did not know, so he did and it did.

ON JULY 7, 2005, four suicide bombers let off their haversack bombs in Central London. They killed fifty-two commuters and injured about 700, leaving at least 100 crippled for life.

Within twenty-four hours, the bombers had been identified. Three were British born and raised, but of Pakistani immigrant parentage. The fourth was Jamaican by birth, British by naturalisation and a convert to Islam. He and one other were still teenagers, the third was twenty-two, and the group leader, Mohammad Siddique Khan, was thirty. Three of the bombers had been traced to various residences in and around the northern city of Leeds; indeed all had spoken with varying strengths of Yorkshire accent.

During the scouring of their homes and possessions the police discovered a small treasure trove that they chose not to reveal. There were four receipts showing that one of them had bought buy-use-and-throw cellphones, tri-band versions usable almost anywhere in the world, each containing a pre-paid SIM card. The phones had been bought for cash and all were missing. But the police traced their numbers and 'red-flagged' them all in case they ever came on stream.

It was also discovered that Siddique Khan and his closest intimate in the group, Shehzad Tanweer, had visited Pakistan the previous November and spent three months there. Weeks after the explosions, the Arab TV station Al-Jazeera broadcast a defiant video made by Siddique Khan as he planned his death, and it was clear this video had been made during that visit.

It was not until September 2006 that it became known that one of the bombers took one of the 'lily-white' untraceable cellphones with him and presented it to his Al-Qaeda organiser/instructor. Whoever this AQ high-up was, he seems to have passed on the gift to a member of the elite inner committee grouped round the person of Osama bin Laden, in his hideaway in the mountains of South Waziristan, which run along the Pakistani–Afghan border west of Peshawar. It would have been given for emergency purposes only, because all AQ operatives are extremely wary of cellphones, but the donor could not have known that the British fanatic would be stupid enough to leave the receipt lying around on his desk in Leeds.

There are four divisions to Bin Laden's inner committee. They deal with operations, financing, propaganda and doctrine. Each branch has a chieftain and only Bin Laden and his co-leader Ayman al-Zawahiri outrank them. By September 2006, the chief organiser of finance for the entire terror group was Zawahiri's fellow Egyptian, Tewfik al-Qur.

For reasons that became plain later, he was under deep disguise in the Pakistani city of Peshawar on September 15, not departing on an extensive and dangerous tour outside the mountain redoubt, but returning from one. He was waiting for the arrival of the guide who would take him back into the Waziri peaks and into the presence of the Sheikh himself.

To protect him during his brief stay in Peshawar he had been assigned four local zealots belonging to the Taliban movement. The men were technically Pakistanis but tribally Waziris, from the Northwestern Mountains. They spoke Pashto rather than Urdu and their loyalties were to the Pashtun people, of whom the Waziris are a sub-branch. All were raised from the gutter in a *madrasah*, or Koranic boarding school of extreme orientation. Given a task to do by their clan chief, they would die for it.

It was after the midday hour. It was too dangerous to emerge to go to the local mosque, so Al-Qur had said his prayers along with his bodyguards in their top-floor apartment. Then he had eaten and retired for a short rest.

One of the four Talib youths was Abdelahi, and his pride and joy was his cellphone. Abdelahi's brother lived several hundred miles to the west in the equally fundamentalist city of Quetta, and their mother had been ill. He wished to enquire after her so he tried to get through on his cellphone. But the phone would not work because its battery was flat. Abdelahi saw the spare phone lying on the Egyptian's attaché case in the sitting room.

It was fully charged. Seeing no harm, he dialled his brother's number and heard the ringing tone far away in Quetta. And in an underground warren of connecting rooms in Islamabad that constitute the listening department of Pakistan's Counter-Terrorism Centre, a small red light began to pulse.

MANY WHO LIVE in it regard Hampshire as England's prettiest county. At its heart lies the quiet valley of the river Meon, a gentle chalk stream along whose banks lie villages that date back to the Saxons. One single A road runs through from south to north, but the rest of the valley is a network of winding lanes edged with overhanging trees, hedges and meadows. This is farm country the way it used to be, with few farms larger than 500 acres. Most of the farmhouses are of ancient beam, brick and tile, and some of these are served by clusters of barns of great size, antiquity and beauty.

The man who perched at the apex of one such barn had a panorama of the Meon valley and a bird's eye view of his nearest village, Meonstoke, barely a mile away. At the time, several zones to the east, that Abdelahi made the last phone call of his life, the roof-climber wiped the sweat off his forehead and resumed his task of carefully removing the clay peg tiles that had been placed there hundreds of years earlier.

It would have been faster and safer to clad the barn in scaffolding and to have had a team of expert roofers do the job. But it would have been much more expensive. And that was the problem. The man with the claw hammer was an ex-soldier, retired after his twenty-five-year career, and he had used up most of his bounty to buy his dream: a place in the country to call home. Companies specialising in barn conversions had produced estimates that took his breath away. Hence the decision to do the work himself.

In his mind's eye he could see the roof restored to its former leak-proof glory, with nine-tenths of the original tiles retained and the rest replaced with reclaimed tiles from a salvage yard. The rafters of the hammerbeam roof were as sound as the day they were hacked from the oak tree, but the cross-battens would have to come off, to be replaced over modern roofing felt.

He could imagine the sitting room, kitchen, study and hall he would make far below him where dust now smothered the last old hay bales. He knew he would need professionals for the electrics and the plumbing, but he had already signed on at Southampton City College for courses in bricklaying, plastering, carpentry and glazing. Each night, camping in the paddock, he went over the figures and reckoned that with patience and hard work he could just survive on his modest budget.

He was forty-four, olive-skinned, black-haired and -eyed, lean and very hard of physique. And he had had enough. Enough of deserts and jungles, malaria and leeches, of freezing cold and shivering nights, of garbage food and pain-racked limbs. He would get a job locally, find a Labrador or a couple of Jack Russells and maybe even a woman to share his life.

The man on the roof removed another dozen tiles, kept the ten whole ones, threw down the broken ones, and in Islamabad the red light pulsed.

As ABDELAHI'S CALL was taken by his brother in Quetta, he began to use transmission time on the Paktel radio mast just outside Peshawar.

With a pre-paid SIM card in a cellphone, there is no future billing for the purchaser and user. But unless the phone is used only within the confines of the transmitting area where it was bought, there is still a settling-up to be accomplished between the cellphone companies, and their computers do it.

So the Paktel computer began to search for the original vendor of the cellphone in England; its intent was to say, electronically, 'One of your customers is using my time and airspace, so you owe me.' But the Pakistani Counter-Terrorism Centre had for years required Paktel and its rival Mobitel to patch through every call transmitted or received by their networks to the CTC listening room. And, alerted by the British, the CTC had inserted British software into its eavesdropping computers with an intercept suite for certain numbers. One of these had suddenly gone active.

The young Pashto-speaking Pakistani army sergeant monitoring the console hit a button and his superior officer came on the line.

The officer listened for several seconds, then asked, 'What is he saying?'

'Something about the speaker's mother,' the sergeant replied. 'He seems to be speaking to his brother.'

'From where?'

'The Peshawar transmitter.'

The CTC major doubted that it would be possible to locate the sender in one short phone call. But he pressed three buttons and by speed-dial a phone trilled in the office of the CTC Head of Station in Peshawar.

Years earlier, the Pakistani Inter-Services Intelligence department had been deeply infiltrated by fundamentalist Muslims of the Pakistani army. But President General Musharraf had listened to the USA's strongly worded 'advice' to clean up his house. He ordered the transfer of extremist officers out of ISI, and the creation of the elite Counter-Terrorism Centre, staffed by a new breed of young officers who had no truck with Islamist terrorism. Colonel Abdul Razak, formerly a tank commander, was one such. He commanded the CTC in Peshawar and he took the call at half past two.

He listened attentively to his colleague, then asked: 'How long?'

'About three minutes, so far.'

Colonel Razak had the good fortune to have an office just 800 yards from the Paktel mast, within the maximum radius—1,000 yards—needed for his direction-finder to work efficiently. With two technicians, he raced to the flat roof of the office block to start the DF sweeps of the city that would seek to pin the source of the signal to a smaller and ever smaller area.

In Islamabad the listening sergeant told his superior, 'The conversation has finished.'

'Damn,' said the major. 'Three minutes and forty-four seconds. Still, one could hardly have expected more.'

'But he doesn't appear to have switched off,' said the sergeant.

In a top-floor apartment in the Old Town of Peshawar, Abdelahi had made his second mistake. Hearing the Egyptian emerging from his private room, he had hastily ended his call to his brother and shoved the cellphone under a nearby cushion. But he forgot to turn it off. Half a mile away, Colonel Razak's sweepers came closer and closer.

Both Britain's Secret Intelligence Service (SIS) and America's Central Intelligence Agency (CIA) have big operations in Pakistan, one of the principal war zones in the struggle against terrorism. Part of the strength of the Western alliance has been the ability of the two agencies to work together. There have been spats, especially over the rash of British traitors such as Philby, Burgess and Maclean in 1951. Then the Americans became aware they too had a rogues' gallery of traitors working for Moscow and the inter-agency sniping stopped. The end of the Cold War in 1991 led to the asinine presumption among politicians on both sides of the Atlantic that peace had come to stay. That was the moment that the new Cold War, silent and hidden in the depths of Islam, was having its birth pangs.

After 9/11 there was no more rivalry and even the traditional horse-trading ended. The rule became: if we have it, you guys had better share it. And vice versa. Contributions to the common struggle come from a patchwork quilt of other foreign agencies but nothing matches the closeness of the Anglosphere information gatherers.

Colonel Razak knew both the Heads of Station in his own city. On personal terms he was closer to the SIS man, Brian O'Dowd, and the rogue cellphone was originally a British discovery. So it was O'Dowd he rang with the news when he came down from the roof.

At that moment Mr al-Qur went to the bathroom and Abdelahi reached under the cushion for the cellphone to put it back on top of the attaché case where he had found it. With a start, he realised it was still on, so he switched it off at once. He was thinking of battery wastage, not interception. Anyway, he was too late by eight seconds. The direction-finder had done its job.

'What do you mean, you've found it?' asked O'Dowd. His day had become Christmas and several birthdays rolled into one.

'No question, Brian. The call came from a top-floor apartment of a five-storey building in the Old Quarter. Two of my undercover people are slipping down there to have a look and work out the approaches.'

'When are you going in?'

'Just after dark. I'd like to make it later, but they might fly the coop . . .' Colonel Razak had been to the Army Staff College at Camberley in Britain on a one-year Commonwealth-sponsored course and was proud of his command of idiom.

'Can I come?' asked the Irishman.

'Would you like to?'

'Is the Pope Catholic?'

Razak laughed. 'As a believer in the one true God I would not know,' he said. 'All right. My office at six. But it is mufti. And I mean *our* mufti.'

He meant there would be no uniforms and no Western clothes either. In the Old Town, and especially in the Qissa Khawani Bazaar, only the *shalwar kameez* assembly of loose trousers and long shirt would pass unnoticed. Or the robes and turbans of the mountain clans.

O'Dowd was there just before six, in his black Toyota Land Cruiser, which was the preferred vehicle of local fundamentalists and would pass unnoticed. He had brought a bottle of Chivas Regal whisky. It was Abdul Razak's favourite tipple. He had once chided his Pakistani friend on his taste for the alcoholic tincture from Scotland.

'I regard myself as a good Muslim but not an obsessive one,' said Razak. 'I do not touch pork, but see no harm in dancing or a good cigar. Wine was widely drunk during the first four Caliphates and if, one day in

Paradise, I am chided by a higher authority than you, then I shall beg the all-merciful Allah for forgiveness. In the meantime, give me a top-up.'

It was perhaps strange that a tank corps officer should have made such an excellent policeman, but such was Abdul Razak. He was thirty-six, married with two children and educated. He also embodied a capacity for lateral thought and quiet subtlety. He wanted to take the apartment at the top of the block of flats without a raging fire-fight, if he could.

Peshawar is an ancient city and no part is older than the Qissa Khawani Bazaar. For many centuries, caravans travelling through the Khyber Pass into Afghanistan have paused here to refresh men and camels. It is multi-ethnic and multilingual. The accustomed eye can spot the turbans of the Afridis, Waziris, Ghilzai and Pakistanis from nearby, contrasting with the Chitral caps of the tribesmen from further north and the fur-trimmed winter hats of Tajiks and Uzbeks.

In this maze of narrow streets and lanes are the shops and stalls of the clock bazaar, basket bazaar, moneychangers, bird market and the bazaar of the storytellers. In imperial days the British called Peshawar the Piccadilly of Central Asia.

The apartment identified as the source of the phone call was in one of those tall, flat-roofed buildings with intricately carved balconies and shutters. It was four floors above a carpet warehouse.

Colonel Razak led his team on foot. He sent four men, all in tribal clothes, up to the roof of a building four houses down the street. They walked calmly from roof to roof to the target building, where they waited for their signal. The colonel led six men up the stairs from the street. All had machine pistols under their robes save the point man, a heavily muscled Punjabi who bore the rammer. When they were all lined up in the stairwell, the colonel nodded to the point man, who drew back the rammer and shattered the lock. The door sprang inwards and the team ran inside. Three of the men on the roof came down the access stairs; the fourth remained aloft.

The attack squad had no idea what they would find inside. It could have been a small army; it could have been a family sipping tiffin. In fact, they found four young men watching TV.

For two seconds the attack group feared they might have raided a perfectly innocent household. Then they registered that all the young men were heavily bearded, all were mountain men and one was reaching beneath his robes for a gun. His name was Abdelahi and he died with four bullets from a Heckler & Koch MP5 through the chest. The other three were smothered and held down before they could fight.

The presence of the fifth man was announced by a crash from the bedroom. The Punjabi had dropped his rammer but his shoulder was enough. The door came down and two CTC hard men went in, followed by Colonel Razak. In the middle of the room they found a middle-aged Arab, stooping to gather up the laptop computer he had hurled to the tiled floor in an effort to destroy it. He realised that there was no time, turned and ran for the open window. Colonel Razak screamed, 'Grab him!' but the officer missed his grip. The Egyptian was naked to the waist because of the heat, and his skin was slick with sweat. He went straight over the balustrade and crashed to the cobbles forty feet below. Bystanders gathered round the body within seconds but the AQ financier gurgled twice and died.

The street had become a chaos of shouting and running figures. Using his cellphone, the colonel called up the fifty soldiers he had positioned in black-windowed vans four streets away. They came racing down the alley to seal the apartment block. In time Abdul Razak would want to interview every neighbour and, above all, the landlord: the carpet-seller at street level.

The corpse was surrounded by the army and blanketed. A stretcher would appear, and the dead man would be carried away to the morgue of Peshawar General Hospital. No one had the faintest idea who he was. All that was clear was that he had preferred death to the attention of the Americans at Bagram Camp in Afghanistan, where he would surely have been horse-traded by Islamabad with the CIA Station Chief in Pakistan.

Colonel Razak turned back from the balcony. The three prisoners were handcuffed and hooded. There would have to be an armed escort to get them out of here. This was 'fundo' territory; the street would not be on his side. With the prisoners and the body gone, he would scour the flat for every last clue about the man with the red-flagged cellphone.

Brian O'Dowd had been asked to wait on the stairs during the raid. He was now in the bedroom holding the damaged Toshiba laptop. Both knew that this would be the crown jewel. All the passports, cellphones, papers, all the prisoners and the neighbours—the lot would be taken to a safe place and wrung dry for anything they could yield. But first the laptop . . .

The dead Egyptian had been optimistic if he thought denting the frame of the Toshiba would destroy its golden harvest.

'Pity about Whoever-he-was,' said the SIS agent.

Razak grunted. He would prepare a statement for the public that an unknown criminal had died in a fall while resisting arrest. Until the corpse was identified. If he turned out to be an AQ high-up, the Americans would insist on an all-singing, all-dancing press conference to claim the triumph.

'You'll be pinned down here for a while,' said O'Dowd. 'Can I do you the favour of seeing the laptop safely back to your HQ?'

Fortunately Abdul Razak possessed a wry humour. In the covert world only humour keeps a man sane. It was the word 'safely' that he enjoyed.

'That would be most kind of you,' he said. 'I'll give you a four-man escort back to your vehicle. Just in case. When this is all over we must share the immoral bottle you brought over this evening.'

Clutching the precious cargo to his chest, the SIS man was escorted back to his Land Cruiser. The technology he needed was already in the back. His driver, a fiercely loyal Sikh, drove him to a spot outside Peshawar, where O'Dowd hooked up the Toshiba to his own bigger and more powerful Tecra; and the Tecra opened a line in cyberspace to the British Government Communication HQ at Cheltenham, deep in the Cotswold hills.

Within a few seconds, Cheltenham had acquired the entire contents of the Toshiba's hard disk. It had gutted the laptop as efficiently as a spider drains the juices of a captured fly.

The Head of Station drove the laptop to CTC headquarters and delivered it into safe hands. Before he reached the CTC office block, Cheltenham had shared the treasure with America's National Security Agency at Fort Meade, Maryland. As the planet rolled on into another day and another night, experts at GCHQ and NSA began to reveal document after document that Al-Qur thought he had obliterated from his private files.

Brian O'Dowd had alerted his superior, the Head of Station in Islamabad, before accompanying Colonel Razak on the raid. The senior SIS man had informed the CIA Station Chief. Both men were waiting avidly for news.

Colonel Razak returned from the bazaar at midnight with his treasure trove in several bags. The three surviving bodyguards were in cells in the basement of his building. Islamabad now had their names and was no doubt haggling with the US Embassy, which contained the CIA station. The colonel suspected they would end up in Bagram for months of interrogation, though he doubted they even knew the name of the man they had been guarding.

The telltale cellphone had been found and identified. It was slowly becoming clear that the foolish Abdelahi had only borrowed it without permission. He was on a slab in the morgue with four bullets in the chest but an untouched face. The man who had been resting next door had a smashed head but the city's best facial surgeon was trying to put it back together. When he had done his best a photo was taken.

Like all counter-terrorist agencies, the CTC of Pakistan has a huge gallery of photos of suspects. Colonel Razak spent the night flashing this gallery of faces from his computer to a big plasma screen in his office, and he kept coming back to one face.

It was already plain from the captured passports, eleven of them, all forged and all of superb quality, that the Egyptian had changed his appearance for travelling. Yet this one face—of a man who could pass unnoticed in a bank's boardroom in the West—seemed to Colonel Razak to have something in common with the shattered head on the marble slab.

He rang O'Dowd with ill-concealed excitement, catching him having breakfast with his American CIA colleague. Both men left their scrambled eggs and raced over to CTC headquarters. They too stared at the face and compared it with the photo from the morgue. And both men had one priority: to tell Head Office that the body on the slab was none other than Tewfik al-Qur, the senior banker of Al-Qaeda.

Midmorning a Pakistani army helicopter came to take it all away. The prisoners, shackled and hooded, went. So did the two dead bodies and the boxes of evidence recovered from the apartment. Thanks were profuse but Peshawar is an out-station; the centre of gravity was moving, and moving fast. In fact it had already arrived in Maryland.

In the aftermath of the disaster now known simply as 9/11, one thing became clear. The intelligence about what was going on was there all the time—not in one beautiful gift-wrapped package but scattered all over. Seven or eight of the USA's nineteen primary intel-gathering or law-enforcement agencies had the bits. But they never talked to each other.

After 9/11 there was a huge shake-up. There are now six principals to whom everything has to be revealed at an early stage. Four are politicians: the President, Vice-President and the Secretaries of Defense and State. One of the two professionals is chairman of the National Security Committee, who oversee the Department of Homeland Security and the nineteen agencies. The other is the top of the pile: the Director of National Intelligence, John Negroponte.

Among the giants of the US intelligence community, the National

Security Agency at Fort Meade is the biggest, in budget and personnel, and the most secret. It listens to everything, decrypts everything, analyses everything. But so impenetrable is some of the stuff that is overheard, recorded, downloaded, or translated that it has to use 'out of house' committees of experts. One of these is the Koran Committee.

As the treasure from Peshawar came in, other agencies also went to work. Within twenty-four hours the FBI confirmed that the man who went over the balcony was indeed the principal finance-gatherer for Al-Qaeda, head-hunted by Ayman al-Zawahiri.

Two of the eleven passports seized had never been used, but nine showed entry and exit stamps all over Europe and the Middle East. The Federal Aviation Administration checked out plane tickets and passenger lists, and pretty much pinpointed the flights that Al-Qur had taken.

Slowly but surely it began to come together. Tewfik al-Qur had seemingly been charged to raise large sums of untraceable money to make unexplained purchases, but as there was no evidence he had made any himself it was concluded that he funded others to make the purchases themselves. The US authorities would have given their eye teeth to learn precisely to whom he had delivered funds. These names, they guessed, would have rolled up an entire covert network across Europe and the Middle East. The one notable target country the Egyptian had not visited was the USA.

It was at Fort Meade that the train of revelation finally hit the buffer. Seventy-three documents had been downloaded from Al-Qur's Toshiba. Some were just airline timetables; some were public-domain financial reports. Most were in English, some in French or German. It was known that Al-Qur spoke all three languages fluently. The captured bodyguards, up in Bagram Air Base and singing happily, had revealed that the man spoke halting Pashto, suggesting that he had spent some time in Afghanistan, though the West had no trace of when or where.

It was the Arabic texts that caused the unease. Apart from the classical language of the Koran and academia, Arabic is spoken by half a billion people in many different dialects. It is often a flowery language, using a great deal of imagery, flattery, exaggeration, simile and metaphor, and it can be very elliptical, with meanings implied rather than openly stated.

Because Fort Meade is basically a vast army base, the NSA's commanding officer is always a four-star general. It was to this soldier that the chief of the Agency's huge Arabic translation department reported.

'We have focused on the last two documents,' said the linguist. 'The first seems to have the word patterns of Ayman al-Zawahiri, as taken from his speeches and videos. The reply seems to be from Al-Qur, though we have no text on record of how he writes in Arabic. As a banker he wrote mainly in English. Both documents have repeated references to passages in the Koran, invoking Allah's blessing on something. Now, I have many scholars of Arabic, but the language and subtle meanings contained in the Koran are special. I think we should call on the Koran Committee to take a look.'

The general nodded. 'OK, professor, you got it.' He glanced up at his ADC. 'Get hold of our Koran scholars, Harry. Fly them in. No delays, no excuses.'

CHAPTER TWO

There were four men in the Koran Committee. None was an Arab but all had spent their lives steeped in the study of the Koran and its thousands of attendant scholarly commentaries.

One was resident at Columbia University, New York, and a military helicopter was dispatched to bring him to Fort Meade. Two were based in Washington, DC: one was with the Rand Corporation and the other with the Brookings Institution. Army staff cars were detached to collect them.

The fourth and youngest was Dr Terry Martin, on secondment to Georgetown University, Washington, DC, from the School of Oriental and African Studies, part of the University of London.

In terms of the study of matters Arabic, the Englishman had had a head start. He was born and raised in Iraq, the son of an accountant with an oil company operating there. His father had sent him to a private academy that schooled the sons of the elite of Iraqi society. By the time he was ten he could, linguistically at least, pass as an Arab boy. But with his pink face and ginger hair he could never *completely* pass as an Arab.

The Martins had lived through tumultuous times in Iraq—the slaughter of the young King Faisal and his pro-Western premier Nuri Said, the execution of his successor General Kassem and the arrival of the Ba'ath Party. That in turn had been toppled, but it returned to power in 1968. For seven years Martin senior watched the growing power of Vice-President Saddam

Hussein, and in 1975 decided it was time to leave. He obtained a good post with Burmah Oil in London, and he and his wife and two sons, Mike and Terry, then thirteen and ten, were back in the UK by Christmas.

Terry's brilliant brain had already been noted. It was presumed that a series of scholarships would carry him through senior school and Oxbridge. But he wanted to continue with Arabic studies, so he applied to SOAS and joined as an undergraduate in 1983, studying History of the Middle East. He sailed through a first-class degree, then put in three more years for his doctorate, specialising in the Koran and the first four Caliphates. He took a sabbatical year to continue Koranic studies at the Al-Azhar Institute in Cairo, and on his return to SOAS was offered a lectureship. He was promoted to a readership at thirty-four, earmarked for a professorship by forty. The day that the NSA came to Georgetown seeking his advice, he was forty-one and spending a year there as a visiting professor.

The emissary from Fort Meade found him in a lecture hall concluding a talk on the teachings of the Koran as relevant to the contemporary age.

The hall was packed. Terry Martin made his lectures feel like a long and civilised conversation between equals, seldom referring to notes, jacket off, pacing up and down, his short, plump body radiating enthusiasm. He always gave serious attention to any point raised from the floor, and kept the body of the lecture short with plenty of time for student questions. He had reached that point when the spook from Fort Meade appeared in the wings.

A red plaid shirt in the fifth row raised a hand. 'You said you disagreed with applying the term "fundamentalist" to the terrorists. Why?'

'Because it is a misnomer,' said the professor. 'The word implies "back to basics". The planters of bombs in trains, malls and buses are not going back to the basics of Islam. They are writing their own new script, then seeking to find Koranic passages that justify their war.'

In the wings, the man from Fort Meade tried to attract Dr Martin's attention. The professor glanced sideways and noted the young man with the short hair, button-down shirt and dark suit. He had 'government' written all over him. The man tapped the watch on his wrist. Martin nodded.

'Then what would you call the terrorists of today? Jihadists?' It was an earnest young woman further back.

'Even jihad is the wrong word. Jihad is either a personal struggle within oneself to become a better Muslim, or it means true holy war, armed struggle in the defence of Islam. But it has rules. For one thing true jihad can only be declared by a legitimate Koranic authority. Bin Laden and his acolytes are notorious for their lack of scholarship. Further, it is forbidden to attack and kill those who have done nothing to hurt you. It is forbidden to kill women and children. It is forbidden to take hostages, or to mistreat, torture or kill prisoners. The AQ terrorists and their followers do all four. And they have killed far more fellow Muslims than Christians or Jews.'

The man in the wings was becoming agitated. A full general had given him an order. He did not wish to be the last to report back.

'Last question, I'm afraid.'

There was a gathering of books and notes. A hand shot up at the front. Freckles, white T-shirt advertising a student rock group.

'All the bombers claim to be martyrs. How do they justify this?'

'Badly,' said Dr Martin. 'It is perfectly feasible to die a *shahid*, or martyr, fighting for Islam in a truly declared jihad. But again there are rules. The warrior must not die by his own hand, or know the time and place of his own death. Suicide bombers do exactly that. They are destined for hell, not paradise. The false preachers who trick them down this road will join them there. And now, I fear, we must rejoin the world of Georgetown and hamburgers. Thank you for your attention.'

They gave him a standing ovation and, pink with embarrassment, he took his jacket and walked into the wings.

'Sorry to interrupt, sir,' said the man from Fort Meade, 'but there's a flap on and the Koran Committee is needed at the Fort. The car is outside.'

The car was the usual dark sedan with the telltale aerial on the roof. Dr Martin climbed into the back while the driver held the door open. His escort took the front passenger seat and they began to drive through the early-evening traffic out to the Baltimore highway.

FAR TO THE EAST the man restoring his own barn stretched out by the camp fire in the orchard. He was perfectly happy like that. If he could sleep in rocks and snow drifts he could certainly sleep on the grass beneath the apple trees.

Camp-fire fuel was no problem. He had enough rotten old planks to last a lifetime. His billycan sizzled above the red embers and he prepared a mug of steaming tea. He had taken the afternoon off from his lofty task up on the roof and walked into Meonstoke to buy provisions for the weekend.

The dark-haired single man who had bought the barn was, so ran the growing belief in the village, a good sort. According to the postman, he received little mail save a few official-looking buff envelopes, which he asked to be delivered to the Buck's Head public house to save the postman the haul up the long, muddy track. The letters were addressed to 'Colonel' but he never mentioned that when he bought a drink at the bar or a newspaper or food at the store. Just smiled and was very polite. The locals' appreciation of the man was, however, tinged with curiosity. Who was he, where had he come from, and why had he chosen to settle in Meonstoke?

That afternoon, on his ramble through the village, he had visited the ancient church of St Andrew, and fallen into conversation with the rector.

The ex-soldier was beginning to think he would enjoy life where he had decided to settle; pedalling his rugged mountain bike to the produce market, exploring the myriad lanes he could see from his roof and sampling the ale in the old beamed pubs they would reveal.

But in two days he would attend Sunday matins at St Andrew's and, in the quiet gloom of the ancient stone, he would pray. He would ask for forgiveness of the God in whom he devoutly believed for all the men he had killed and for their immortal souls. He would ask for eternal rest for all the comrades he had seen die beside him; and he would pray that one day he too could expiate his sins and enter into the Kingdom.

Then he would come back to the hillside and resume his labours. There were only another thousand tiles to go.

FORT MEADE, one of the largest military bases in the USA, is home to around 10,000 military staff and 25,000 civilian employees, and has all the facilities of a small city. The sedan bearing Dr Martin glided through the sprawling base with no hindrance until it came to the security zone containing the National Security Agency's complex of buildings. At the main gate passes were examined and faces peered at before the sedan was waved through. Half a mile later the car drew up at the main block, where there were more checks; thumbs placed on keypads; iris recognition; admission.

After a marathon of corridors, Dr Martin found himself at last among faces he knew. The room had no windows but air conditioning kept the atmosphere fresh. There were a circular table and padded upright chairs, on one wall hung a screen, and small tables stood to the side with coffee urns.

The hosts, two intelligence officers, introduced themselves with give-nothing-away courtesy. One was the Deputy Director of the NSA; the other was a senior officer from Homeland Security in Washington.

And there were three academics. Terry Martin greeted Doctors Ludwig Schramme from Columbia, New York, Ben Jolley from Rand and 'Harry' Harrison from Brookings. The oldest and therefore the presumed senior was Ben Jolley, a great bearded bear of a man. Before agreeing to be co-opted onto the Koran Committee, they had known each other vicariously from their published works and personally from seminars, lectures and conferences. Now they were friends, as well as colleagues.

The Deputy Director cut straight to the heart of the reason for the convocation of the scholars. He distributed files to each man. These contained copies of the Arabic documents teased out of the AQ financier's laptop, and translations by the in-house Arabic division. The four men read the Arabic versions in silence, and finished more or less at the same time.

Jolley looked up at the two intelligence officers. 'Well?' he asked. 'What is the problem that has brought us all here?'

The Deputy Director leaned over and tapped a portion of the English translation. 'The problem is that. There. What does it mean?'

All four of them had spotted the Koranic reference in the Arabic text. Each had seen the phrase—here used four times in total—many times in scholarly texts, and had studied its possible various meanings.

'Al-Isra?' said Dr Jolley. 'It must be a code of some kind.'

'Forgive my ignorance,' said the man from Homeland. 'What is Al-Isra?'

'It refers to a revelation in the life of the Prophet,' said Terry Martin. 'He was asleep one night, a year before his emigration from his birthplace of Mecca to Medina, when he had a dream. Or a hallucination. Or a divine miracle. For brevity let me stick with "dream". In his dream he was transported from the depths of what is now Saudi Arabia across deserts and mountains to the city of Jerusalem, then a city holy only to Christians and Jews. There he found a tethered horse, a horse with wings. He was bidden to mount it. The horse flew up to heaven and the Prophet confronted Almighty God himself, who instructed him in all the prayer rituals required of a True Believer. These he memorised and later dictated to a scribe as what became an integral part of the six thousand, six hundred and sixty-six verses. These verses became and remain the basis of Islam.'

'Al-Isra is the journey,' Jolley cut in. 'A magical journey. A divine journey, undertaken on the instructions of Allah himself.'

'So what would a modern Muslim and a senior operative in Al-Qaeda mean by it?'

This was the first time the academics had been given an inkling as to the source of the documents. Not an intercept, but a capture.

'Was it fiercely guarded?' asked Harrison.

'Two men died trying to prevent us seeing it.'

'Ah, well, yes.' Dr Jolley studied the table. 'I fear it can be nothing but a reference to some kind of project, some operation. And not a small one. For devout Muslims Al-Isra changed the world. If they have code-named something Al-Isra, they intend that it should be huge.'

'And no indication what it might be?'

Dr Jolley looked round the table. His three colleagues shrugged.

'Not a hint. Both the writers call down divine blessings on their project but that is all. That said, I think I can speak for us all in suggesting you find out what it refers to. They would never give the title Al-Isra to a mere satchel bomb, a devastated nightclub or a wrecked commuter bus.'

The two intelligence officers would spend that night preparing their joint report. The report would leave the building before dawn, sealed and couriered with armed guard, and it would go high—as high as it gets in the USA, which is the White House.

IN MARYLAND the sun set. In the same time zone it was setting over Cuba, and on the peninsula known as Guantánamo a man spread his prayer mat, turned to the east, knelt and began his prayers. Outside the cell a GI watched impassively.

The man who prayed had been at Camp Delta, Guantánamo Bay, for nearly five years. He had tolerated the early brutalities and privations without a sound, but his tormentors could read the implacable hatred in the black eyes above the black beard, and so he was beaten the more. But he never broke.

In the files kept by the interrogators, there was much about the man who prayed that night, but almost nothing from him. He had civilly answered questions put to him years earlier by one interrogator who had decided on a humane approach. That was how a passable record of his life existed at all. But none of the interrogators understood a word of his native language and had always relied on the interpreters, or 'terps'. But the terps had their own agenda. They received favours for interesting revelations, so they had a motive to make them up. He had neither denied nor confirmed them.

After four years, the man was dubbed 'non-cooperative', which simply meant unbreakable. In 2005 he had been transferred across the Gulf to the new Camp Echo, a permanent isolation unit. Here the cells were smaller and exercise was only at night. For a year the man had not seen the sun.

No family clamoured for him; no government sought news of him; no lawyer filed papers for him. He just stayed silent and read his Koran. Outside, the guards changed while he prayed.

'Goddam Arab,' said the man coming off duty.

His replacement shook his head. 'He's not Arab,' he said. 'He's an Afghan.'

TERRY MARTIN SHARED a limousine with Ben Jolley on the ride back to Washington. It was bigger than the sedan in which he had come, with a partition between front and rear compartments. Through the glass they could see the backs of two heads: the driver and their youthful escorting officer.

The gruff old American stared out at the passing scenery, a sea of the russet and gold of autumn leaves. The younger British man stared the other way and also lapsed into reverie.

In all his life he had only really loved four people and he had lost three of them in the past ten months. At the start of the year his parents, who were both over seventy, had died almost together. Prostate cancer had taken his father and his mother was too broken-hearted to want to go on. She wrote a moving letter to each of her sons, then took a bottle of sleeping tablets.

Terry Martin was devastated, but survived by leaning on the strength of two men. One was his partner of fourteen years, the tall, handsome stockbroker with whom he shared his life. And then on one wild March night there had been the drunken driver going crazily fast, the crunch of metal hitting a human body, and the awful funeral. Terry had contemplated ending his own life then, but his elder brother Mike had seemed to sense his thoughts, moved in with him for a week and talked him through the crisis.

Terry had hero-worshipped his brother since they were boys. Mike had always been everything he was not. Dark to his fair, lean to his plump, hard to his soft, fast to his slow, brave to his frightened. When the moment came to tell his brother that he was gay, Terry had been seized by gut-wrenching fear. The older man, by then an officer in the Paras, thought about it for a moment, cracked his mocking grin and handed back the final line by Joe E. Brown in *Some Like it Hot*.

'Well, nobody's perfect.'

From that moment, Terry's hero-worship of his brother knew no limits.

'So, what do you think of our problem, Terry?'

It was Ben Jolley, wrenching him out of his daydream.

'Doesn't sound good,' Terry Martin replied. 'We only confirmed what our two spook friends had suspected, but they were not happy when we left.'

'No other verdict, though. They have to discover what this Al-Isra is.'

'But how?'

'Well, spooks have a lot of ways: sources on the inside, turned agents, eavesdropping, over-flying. They'll figure it out and stop it somehow.'

'Maybe they could slip someone inside Al-Qaeda,' Martin suggested.

The older man shook his head. 'Come on, we both know that's impossible. A native-born Arab could be turned and work against us. As for a non-Arab, forget it. All Arabs come from extended families, clans, tribes. One enquiry of the family or clan and the impostor would be exposed. Besides, he would have to look the part, speak the part and, most important, play the part. One syllable wrong in all those prayers and the fanatics would spot it.'

'True,' said Martin. 'But one could learn the Koranic passages and invent an untraceable family.'

'Forget it, Terry. No Westerner can pass for an Arab among Arabs.'

'My brother can,' said Terry Martin.

In seconds, if he could have bitten off his own tongue, he would have. But it was all right. Dr Jolley grunted, dropped the subject and studied the outskirts of Washington. Neither head, beyond the glass, moved an inch. Martin let out a sigh of relief. Any mike in the car must be turned off.

He was wrong.

THE FORT MEADE report on the deliberations of the Koran Committee was ready by dawn of that Saturday and destroyed several planned weekends. One of those roused during the following night at his home in Old Alexandria was Marek Gumienny, Deputy Director (Operations) at the CIA. He was bidden to report straight to his office in Langley without being told why.

The 'why' was on his desk when he got there. Pre-dawn on a Sunday is not an easy time to rustle up piping hot and aromatic black coffee, the way he liked it, so he brewed his own. While it perked, Gumienny started on the package on his desk, which contained the slim, wax-sealed file.

The file contained all the documents downloaded from the AQ financier's computer, but the two letters were the stars. The DDO spoke fluent street

Arabic, but reading script is always harder, so he repeatedly referred to the translations.

The report of the Koran Committee offered no surprises. To Gumienny it was clear the references to Al-Isra, the magical journey of the Prophet, could only be the code for some kind of important project.

That project now had to have an in-house code name. He checked with file-cryptography. Code names come out of a computer by a process known as random selection, the aim being to give nothing away. The CIA naming process that month was using fish; the computer chose Stingray, so Project Stingray it became.

The last sheet in the file had been added during the night. It came from the hand of a man who disliked wasting words, the Director of National Intelligence, and was on the DNI's headed paper. It said in capital letters:

WHAT IS AL-ISRA?
IS IT NUCLEAR, BIOLOGICAL, CHEMICAL, CONVENTIONAL?
FIND OUT WHAT, WHEN AND WHERE.
TIMESCALE: NOW. RESTRAINTS: NONE. POWERS: ABSOLUTE
JOHN NEGROPONTE

There was a scrawled signature. There are nineteen primary intelligence-gathering and archive-storing agencies in the USA. The letter gave him authority over them all.

There was a tap on the door—a junior staffer with another delivery. Gumienny signed the clipboard and waited until he was alone again.

The new file was a courtesy from the colleagues at Fort Meade. It was a transcript of a conversation held by two of the Koran eggheads in the car on the way back to Washington. One of them was British. Someone at Fort Meade had underlined his last line in red, with a brace of question marks.

The British code-named the CIA 'the Cousins' or 'the Company'; the Americans called the London-based Secret Intelligence Service 'the Friends' or 'the Firm'. For Marek Gumienny, one of those friends was a man he had shared good times, not-so-good times and downright dangerous times with when they were both field agents. Now Gumienny was pinned to a desk in Langley and Steve Hill had been pulled out of the field and elevated to Controller Middle East at the Firm's Vauxhall Cross headquarters.

Gumienny decided a conference might yield some good. The Brits, he knew, would have just about everything he had. They too had transmitted the guts of the laptop from Peshawar to their own listening and cryptography HQ at Cheltenham. They too would have printed out its contents and analysed the strange references to the Koran contained in the coded letters.

What they didn't have was the bizarre remark by a British academic in the back of a car. He punched up a number on the console on his desk.

A number rang in a modest house in Surrey. Eight a.m. in Langley, one p.m. in London; the house was about to sit down to Sunday lunch.

'Steve? Marek.'

'My dear chap, where are you? Over here by any chance?'

'No, I'm at my desk. Can we go to secure?'

'Sure. Give me two minutes . . .' And in the background: 'Darling, hold the roast.' The phone went down.

At the next call the voice from England was tinny but uninterceptable. 'I wondered when you'd call,' said Hill. 'I expect you have much the same stuff as I have out of Peshawar?'

'I guess so. But I have something you may not have, Steve. We have a visiting professor over here from London. He made a chance remark Friday evening. I'll cut to the chase. Do you know a man called Mike Martin?'

Steve Hill dropped all banter. Oh, yes, he knew Colonel Mike Martin. Back in the first Gulf War, Hill had been one of the control team in Saudi Arabia when he had slipped into Baghdad and lived there as a humble gardener under the noses of Saddam's secret police while transmitting back priceless intelligence from a source inside the dictator's cabinet.

'Could do,' he conceded. 'Why?'

'I think we should talk,' said the American. 'Face to face. I could fly over tonight. I have the Grumman. Be in London for breakfast.'

'OK. I'll arrange it with Northolt.'

The CIA has its own very private airfield near Langley and a small fleet of executive jets. Marek Gumienny's all-powerful piece of authority paper secured him the Grumman V, on which he slept in perfect comfort on the flight over. Steve Hill was at the RAF airfield west of London to meet him.

He took his guest not to the green and sandstone ziggurat at Vauxhall Cross on the south bank of the Thames by Vauxhall Bridge, home of the SIS, but to the much quieter Cliveden Hotel, formerly a private mansion, not thirty miles from Northolt. He had reserved a small conference suite.

There he read the analysis of the American Koran Committee, which was remarkably similar to the analysis from Cheltenham, and the transcript of the conversation in the back of the car.

'Damn fool,' Hill muttered when he reached the end. 'The other Arabist was right. It can't be done. It's not just the lingo, it's all the other tests. No stranger, no foreigner could ever pass them.'

'So, given my orders from the All-High, what would you suggest?'

'Pick up an AQ insider and sweat it out of him,' said Hill.

'Steve, if we had the faintest idea of the location of anyone that high in Al-Qaeda, we'd take them as a matter of course.'

'Wait and watch. Someone will use the phrase again.'

'My people have to presume that if Al-Isra is to be the next spectacular, the USA will be the target. Waiting for a miracle that may not happen will not pacify Washington. Besides, AQ must know by now we got the laptop. Chances are they will never use that phrase again, except person to person.' He paused. 'Could your man Martin really pass for an Arab among Arabs? Is he really that good?'

'He used to be,' grunted Hill and passed over a file. 'See for yourself.'

The file was an inch thick, in standard buff manila, and fronted simply with the words: COLONEL MIKE MARTIN.

The Martin boys' maternal grandfather had been a tea-planter in India, between the two world wars. While there he had done something almost unheard of. He had married an Indian girl. The boys had seen pictures of their grandfather, Terence Granger, tall, pink-faced, blond-moustached, pipe in mouth and gun in hand, standing over a shot tiger. And there were pictures of Miss Indira Bohse, gentle, loving and beautiful.

The young couple were posted to the wilds of Assam, up on the Burmese border. There Susan was born in 1930. By 1943 war had rolled towards Assam, the Japanese advancing through Burma to the border. Terence Granger volunteered and in 1945 he died crossing the river Irrawaddy. Two years later came more trouble; India was being partitioned and violent fighting broke out between Muslim Pakistan and the mainly Hindu India. Fearing for her daughter's safety, Indira Granger sent Susan to stay with her late husband's younger brother, an architect in Haslemere, Surrey. Six months later Mrs Granger died in the rioting.

At twenty-one, Susan Granger applied to be a stewardess with the British Overseas Airways Corporation. BOAC put her on the London–Bombay route because of her fluent Hindi. There was a crew-change and stopover at

Basra, southern Iraq, where, at the country club in 1951, she met oil company accountant Nigel Martin. They married in 1952. There was a ten-year wait until the birth of the first son, Mike; three years later came second son Terry. The two boys were like chalk and cheese.

Marek Gumienny stared at the photo in the file. Not a suntan but a naturally saturnine complexion, black hair and dark eyes. He realised the genes of the grandmother had jumped a generation to the grandson; he was not even remotely like his brother the academic in Georgetown.

Gumienny skipped through the rest of the boyhood. Both boys had gone to the Anglo-Iraqi school and learned also from their *dada*, or nanny, a plump, gentle girl from up-country. There was a reference that could only have come from an interview with Terry Martin: the older boy in his long, white Iraqi dishdash, racing about the lawn of the house in Saadun suburb, Baghdad, and his father's delighted Iraqi guests laughing with pleasure and shouting, 'But, Nigel, he's more like one of us.'

More like one of them, thought Marek Gumienny. He recalled Dr Ben Jolley's comments: any infiltrator with a chance of getting away with it inside Al-Qaeda would have to look the part and speak the part. Well, it seemed that Martin looked the part and could pass for an Arab in Arabic. Surely with intensive schooling he could master the prayer rituals?

The CIA man read a bit more, then he needed a break and a coffee.

'He could do it, you know,' he said when he came back from the toilet. 'With enough training and back-up he really could. Where is he now?'

'Apart from the two stints when we borrowed him and he worked for us, he spent his military career between the Paras and the Special Forces. Retired last year after completing his twenty-five. And no, it wouldn't work.'

'Why not, Steve? He has it all.'

'Except the background. The parentage, the extended family. You don't just walk into Al-Qaeda except as a youthful volunteer for a suicide mission; a low-level low-life; a gopher. Anyone who was able to get near the gold-standard project in preparation would have to have years behind him. That's the killer, Marek. Unless . . .'

He drifted off into a reverie, then shook his head.

'Unless what?' asked the American.

'No, it's not on the table,' said Hill.

'Indulge me.'

'I was thinking of a ringer. A doppelgänger. A man whose place he could take. But that's flawed too. If the real object were still alive, AQ would have him in their ranks. If he were dead, they'd know that too. So no dice.'

'It's a long file,' said Marek Gumienny. 'May I take it with me?'

'It's a copy, of course. Eyes only?'

'You have my word.'

Gumienny flew back to Langley, but a few days later he phoned again. Steve Hill took the call at his desk in Vauxhall Cross.

'I think I should fly back,' the DDO said without preamble.

'No problem, Marek. Do you have a breakthrough?' Steve Hill was intrigued. With modern technology there is nothing that cannot be passed rapidly from the CIA to the SIS in complete secrecy. So why fly?

'The ringer,' said Gumienny. 'I think I have him.'

TERRY MARTIN was still sleepless a week after his meeting at Fort Meade. That stupid remark. Why could he not keep his mouth shut? Why did he have to brag about his brother? Supposing Ben Jolley had said something? Washington was one big, gossiping village, after all. Seven days after the remark in the back of the limousine he rang his brother.

Mike Martin was lifting the last clutch of unbroken tiles off his precious roof when he heard his mobile phone ringing. It was in the pocket of his jerkin, hanging from a nail nearby. He inched across the rafters to reach it. The screen said it was his brother.

'Hi, Terry.'

'Mike, I've done something stupid and I want to ask your pardon. About a week ago I shot my mouth off.'

'Great. What did you say?'

'Never mind. Look, if ever you get a visitation from any men in suits—you know who I mean—you're to tell them to piss off. What I said was stupid. If anyone visits—'

From his eagle's nest, Mike Martin could see the charcoal-grey Jaguar nosing slowly up the track that led from the lane to the barn.

'It's OK, bro,' he said gently, 'I think they're here.'

THE TWO SPYMASTERS sat on folding camp chairs and Mike Martin on the bole of a tree that was about to be sawn up for camp-fire timber. Martin listened to the pitch from the American and cocked an eyebrow at Steve Hill.

'Your call, Mike. The British government has pledged the White House total cooperation on whatever they want or need, but that stops short of pressuring anyone to go on a no-return mission.'

'And would this one fit that category?'

'We don't think so,' Marek Gumienny interjected. 'And if we discovered the name and whereabouts of one single AQ operative who would know what is going down here, we'd pull you out and do the rest.'

'But I don't think I could pass for an Arab any more. In Baghdad fifteen years ago I made myself invisible by being a humble gardener living in a shack. This time, with someone who has supposedly been in American hands for five years, there'd be intensive questioning.' Martin tapped the file on the man in the Guantánamo cell. 'This is an Afghan. Ex-Taliban. That means Pashtun. I never got to be completely fluent in Pashto. I'd be spotted.'

'There'd be months of tutorials, Mike,' said Steve Hill. 'No way you'd go until you felt ready. And you'd be staying well away from Afghanistan. Afghan fundos hardly ever appear outside their own manor. Could you talk Arabic with the accent of a Pashtun of limited education?'

Mike Martin nodded. 'Possibly. But if they bring in an Afghan who really knew this guy?'

As the two spymasters fell silent, thinking about what would happen to an agent unmasked at the heart of Al-Qaeda, Martin flipped open the file on his lap. What he saw caused him to freeze.

The face was older, lined by suffering and looking ten years more than his calendar age. But it was still the boy from Qala-i-Jangi.

'I know this man,' he said quietly. 'His name is Izmat Khan.'

The American stared at him open-mouthed. 'How the hell can you know him? He's been cooped up at Gitmo since he was captured five years ago.'

'I know, but years before that we fought the Russians in the Tora Bora.'

The men from London and Washington recalled Martin's file. Of course, that year in Afghanistan helping the Mujahideen in their struggle against Soviet occupation. It was not unfeasible that the men had met. For ten minutes they asked him about Izmat Khan to see what else he could add.

Martin handed the file back. 'What is he like now, Izmat Khan?'

The American from Langley shrugged. 'He's tough, Mike. Very, very hard. He arrived with a bad head wound and double concussion. Injured during capture. This was early December 2001, just after 9/11. Treatment was . . . not gentle. Then it seemed nature took its course and he recovered enough for questioning.'

'And what did he tell you?'

'Not much. Just his résumé. Resisted all third degree. But from others we understand that he has passable Arabic, learned from years in a *madrasah*.'

As Martin studied the file, Marek Gumienny rose and wandered around the outside of the barn. 'Quite a project you have taken on here, Mike. I'd have thought this was a job for a crew of professionals. You doing it all yourself?'

'As much as I can. For the first time in twenty-five years I have the time.'

'But not the dough, eh?'

Martin shrugged. 'There are scores of security companies out there if I want a job. Professional bodyguards make more in a week working for your guys in the Sunni Triangle than they made in half a year as soldiers.'

'But that would mean back to the dust, the sand, the danger, the too-early death. Didn't you retire from that?'

'And what are you offering? A vacation with AQ in the Florida Keys?'

Gumienny had the grace to laugh. 'Americans are accused of many things, Mike, but not often of being ungenerous to those who help them. I'm thinking of a consultancy at, say, two hundred thousand dollars a year for five years. Paid abroad, no need to disturb the taxman. No need actually to show up for work. No need to go into harm's way ever again.'

Mike Martin's thoughts flitted to a scene in his all-time favourite film, when Auda abu Tayi is seduced into joining T.E. Lawrence in the attack on Aqaba, not for the money, but 'because it is his pleasure'. He stood up.

'Steve, I want my home shrouded in tarpaulins from top to bottom. When I come back I want it just the way I left it.'

The Controller Middle East nodded. 'Done,' he said.

'I'll get my kit. There's not much of it. Enough to fill the boot, no more.'

And so the Western strike-back against Project Stingray was agreed under apple trees in a Hampshire orchard. Two days later a computer by random selection dubbed it Operation Crowbar.

If challenged, Mike Martin would never have been able to defend himself. But in all the briefings he later gave them about the Afghan who had once been his friend, there was one detail he kept to himself.

Perhaps he thought that need-to-know was a two-way street. Perhaps he thought the detail too unimportant. It had to do with a muttered conversation in the shadows of a cave hospital at a place called Jaji.

CHAPTER THREE

The decision in the Hampshire orchard led to a blizzard of decision-making in Washington and London. Mike Martin's first condition was that no more than one dozen people should ever know what Operation Crowbar was about. His concern was understood. If fifty people know anything that interesting, one will eventually spill the beans. So Martin's condition was acceded to at once.

In Washington, DNI John Negroponte agreed with Gumienny that he alone would be the repository, and gave the operation the go-ahead. Steve Hill dined at his club with one man in the British government and secured the same result. That made four.

But Gumienny and Hill could not personally be on the case twenty-four hours a day. Each needed an executive officer. Marek Gumienny appointed a rising Arabist in the CIA's Counter-Terrorism Division: Michael McDonald dropped everything, explained to his family that he had to work in the UK for a while, and flew east as Marek Gumienny returned home. Steve Hill picked his own deputy on the Middle East Desk: Gordon Phillips. Colleagues at Langley and Vauxhall Cross were told that the men were on career-improving sabbaticals and would be away from their desks for about six months.

The two men were installed in a safe house out in the countryside. When they had unpacked and convened in the drawing room, Steve Hill introduced them to each other and told them what Crowbar was going to try to do.

McDonald and Phillips went very silent.

Hill tossed them both a thick file. 'You have twenty-four hours to commit this to memory,' he said. 'This is the man who is going to go in. You will work with him until that day, and for him after that. This'—he tossed onto the coffee table a thinner file—'is the man he is going to replace. Clearly we know much less. But that is everything the US interrogators have been able to secure from him in hundreds of hours of interrogation at Gitmo. Learn this also. Finding an ops HQ starts tomorrow.'

When he was gone, the two younger men asked for a large pot of coffee from the household staff and started to read.

AT THE TIME the ten-year-old Mike Martin was capering round his father's garden at Saadun, Baghdad, to the delight of the Iraqi guests, a boy was being born 1,000 miles away.

West of the road from Peshawar to Jalalabad lies the range of the Spin Ghar, the White Mountains, dominated by the towering Tora Bora. These bleak mountains are like a great barrier between Pakistan and Afghanistan, always tipped with snow and in winter wholly covered.

Running down to the rich plains around Jalalabad, on the Afghan side, streams carry the snow-melt off the Spin Ghar, forming upland valleys where small patches of land may be planted, and flocks of sheep and goats graze. Life is harsh for the Pashtun communities that live here.

In 1972 there was a hamlet in one of these upland valleys called Maloko-zai. The village headman was Nuri Khan, and it was round his fire that the men gathered on a summer evening to sip hot, unmilked tea, and wait.

When the sun had dropped far to the west, a midwife came scurrying from the shadows. She whispered in the ear of Nuri Khan and his face broke into a flashing smile. '*Allahu akhbar!* I have a son,' he cried.

His male relatives and neighbours rose as one and the air crackled with the sound of their rifles firing up into the night sky.

'I shall call him Izmat after my own grandfather, may his soul rest in eternal peace,' said Nuri Khan. And so it was when an imam came to the hamlet a few days later for the naming and the circumcision.

There was nothing unusual about the raising of the child, though his father was the richest man in the village in the only way a man could be rich: in cows, sheep and goats. There was no need to leave the village, so for the first eight years of his life Izmat Khan did not. The five extended families that made up the village shared the small mosque, and joined each other for communal worship on Fridays. Izmat's father led the prayers. He was devout but not fanatical.

Beyond this mountain existence, the government of Afghanistan was Communist and heavily supported by the USSR. In terms of religion, this was an oddity, because the people of the wild interior were devout Muslims for whom atheism was unacceptable. But the Afghans of the cities were moderate and tolerant. Women were educated, few covered their faces, singing and dancing were commonplace and the feared secret police pursued those suspected of political opposition, not religious laxity.

The hamlet of Maloko-zai had two links with the outside world. One was the occasional party of Kuchi nomads passing through with a mule-train of contraband, avoiding the patrols along the Khyber Pass. They brought news of faraway Kabul and the world beyond. And there was the radio, a treasured relic that squawked and screeched but uttered words they could understand. This was the BBC's Pashto service, bringing a non-Communist view of the world. It was a peaceful boyhood. Then came the Russians.

Maloko-zai neither knew nor cared that their president had displeased Moscow because he could not control his bailiwick. What mattered was that the Soviet army had rolled in from Uzbekistan and taken Kabul.

Izmat Khan's education had been very basic. His father had taught him the rudiments of reading and writing, but only in Pashto. He had also taught him the Koranic verses necessary for prayer and the rules of the Pukhtunwali, the code by which a Pashtun must live. Honour, hospitality, the necessity of vendetta to avenge insult: these were the rules of the code. And Moscow had insulted them.

It was in the mountains that the Resistance began, and they called themselves warriors of God, Mujahideen. But first the mountain men needed a conference, to decide what to do and who would lead them.

They knew nothing of the Cold War, but they were told they now had powerful friends, the enemies of the USSR. That made sense. He who is the enemy of my enemy . . . First among these was Pakistan, lying right next door and ruled by a fundamentalist dictator, General Zia-ul-Haq. Despite the religious difference, he was allied with the Christian power called America, and her friends, the Angleez, who the Pashtun had defeated in the mountains 150 years before.

AFTER A STINT in the Falklands as a patrol commander with Three Para, Mike Martin had tasted action and knew he enjoyed it. He did a tour in Northern Ireland, but the conditions were miserable and the patrols were boring, so in spring 1986 he applied for the SAS. His papers went through the Regiment's records office at Hereford, where his fluent Arabic was noted with interest and he was invited to a selection course, which he passed.

In the late summer of 1986 Martin started with 22 SAS as a troop commander with the rank of captain. His first assignment was with the Saudi National Guard in Riyadh, training the personal bodyguards of the country's rulers. But in summer 1987, he was called home.

'I don't like this sort of thing,' said the CO at the Regiment's Hereford

HQ. 'But the green slime wants to borrow you. It's the Arabic thing.'

He was using the occasionally friendly phrase reserved by fighting soldiers for intelligence people. He meant the SIS—the Firm.

'Haven't they got their own Arabic speakers?' asked Martin.

'Oh, yes, desks full of them. But this isn't just a question of speaking it. They want someone to go behind the Soviet lines in Afghanistan and work with the Resistance, the Mujahideen.'

With the help of aid pouring in from America, the Tajik Ahmad Shah Massoud was doing real damage to the occupiers. The trouble was getting aid to him. His territory was up in the north.

'The key word at every stage, Captain,' the SIS man told him at the Century House headquarters near Elephant and Castle, 'is deniability. That is why you have to—just a technicality—resign from the army. Of course, when you come back you'll be reinstated.'

Mike Martin noted that he was nice enough to say 'when', not 'if'.

'We need someone to slip into Afghanistan through the Khyber Pass,' the mandarin continued, 'to secure a local guide and be brought north to the Panjshir Valley, where Ahmad Shah Massoud operates.'

'Bringing gifts?' asked Martin.

'Only tokens, I'm afraid. But later we might move to mule-trains and a lot more kit, if Massoud will send his own guides south to the border. It's a question of making the first contact, you see.'

'And the gift?'

'Snuff. He likes our snuff. Oh, and two Blowpipe surface-to-air tubes with missiles. You'd have to teach his people how to use them. I reckon you'd be away six months from this autumn. How do you feel about it?'

BEFORE THE INVASION was half a year old, it was clear that the Afghans would still not do the thing that had always been impossible for them: unite. After weeks of arguing in Peshawar and Islamabad, the number of rival Resistance groups was reduced to seven. These became known as the Peshawar Seven.

To legitimise themselves in the eyes of the world, each warlord formed a political party, of which he was leader. Only one of the leaders was not Pashtun: Burhanuddin Rabbani, who, like his charismatic war commander Ahmad Shah Massoud, was a Tajik from the far north. Three of the others rarely if ever entered occupied Afghanistan, preferring to remain in safety abroad. Two, Abdul Rasul Sayyaf and Gulbuddin Hekmatyar, were cruel and vindictive leaders, and fanatical supporters of the Muslim Brotherhood of ultra-Islam.

Mullah Maulvi Younis Khalis controlled the province of Nangarhar, where Izmat Khan had been born. The oldest of the seven at more than sixty, Younis Khalis was a scholar and preacher, who had a twinkle in his eye that spoke of kindness. When he was not in occupied Afghanistan personally leading his men, his war commander was Abdul Haq.

By 1980 the war had come to the valleys of the Spin Ghar. The Soviets were streaming through Jalalabad below the mountains and their air force had started punitive raids on mountain villages. Nuri Khan had sworn allegiance to Younis Khalis as his warlord and been granted the right to form his own *lashkar* or fighting yeomanry. He could shelter much of the animal wealth of his village in the natural caves that riddled the White Mountains and his people could shelter in them too, when the air raids came. But he decided it was time for the women and children, accompanied by his own elderly father, to cross the border to seek refuge in Peshawar.

Fighting back tears at the shame of being sent out like a child, eight-year-old Izmat Khan was embraced by his father and brother, took the bridle of the mule bearing his mother, and turned towards the high peaks and Pakistan. It would be seven years before he returned from exile.

Outside Peshawar a rash of tented cities had sprung up under the auspices of something called the United Nations, though Izmat Khan had never heard of it. The UN had agreed that each warlord, now masquerading as leader of a political party, should have a separate refugee camp, and that all refugee boys should be educated at the Koranic school, or *madrasah*, in their own camp. They would not learn maths or science, history or geography. They would just learn to recite the verses of the Koran. And they would learn about war.

The imams of these *madrasahs* were in the main provided, salaried and funded by Saudi Arabia and many were Saudis. They brought with them the only version of Islam permitted in Saudi Arabia: Wahhabism, the harshest and most intolerant creed within Islam. Thus, within sight of the Red Cross workers dispensing food and medications, a whole generation of young Afghans was about to be brainwashed into fanaticism.

Nuri Khan visited his family as often as he could, two or three times a year, leaving his *lashkar* in the hands of his elder son. But in 1987 when he arrived he looked lined and drawn. Izmat's elder brother had been killed ushering others towards the caves during a bombing raid and now his father bade Izmat return, join the Resistance and become Mujahid.

The fifteen-year-old who came back to Nangarhar Province was different and the landscape he found was shattered. The Sukhoi fighter-bombers and the Hind helicopter gunships had devastated the valleys from the Panjshir Mountains to the north, where Ahmad Shah Massoud had his fighting zone, down to the Shinkay Range. But though they could be intimidated by the Afghan army or by the Khad secret police, the people of the mountains were intractable and, as it turned out, unconquerable. The Soviet losses were mounting relentlessly. The roads were not safe from ambush, the mountains unapproachable save by air, the Muj deployment of American Stinger missiles had forced the Soviets to fly too high for their firepower to be accurate.

It was a savagely cruel war. The mountain clans took few prisoners and the quickly dead were the lucky ones. The Soviet response was to bomb, rocket and strafe anything that moved: man, woman, child or animal. They seeded the mountains with millions of air-dropped mines, which eventually created a nation of crutches and prosthetic limbs. Before it was over there would be a million Afghans dead, a million crippled and 5 million refugees.

Izmat Khan was big for fifteen, and the mountains soon hardened him. He knew all about guns from his time in the refugee camp. The favourite was of course the Kalashnikov—the infamous AK-47. It was a supreme irony that this Soviet weapon was now being used against them. But the Americans were providing them for a reason: every Afghan could replenish his ammunition from the packs on a dead Russian.

Izmat Khan had been back home for a year when his father summoned him. There was a stranger with him—face burned dark from the sun, black-bearded, wearing a grey woollen *shalwar kameez* over stout hiking boots and a sleeveless jerkin. On the ground behind him stood a huge backpack and two tubes wrapped in sheepskin. On his head was a Pashtun turban.

'This man is a guest and a friend,' said Nuri Khan. 'He has to take his tubes to Shah Massoud in the Panjshir, and you will guide him there.'

The young Pashtun stared at the stranger. 'Is he Afghan?' he asked.

'No, he is Angleez.'

Izmat Khan was staggered. This was the old enemy. More, he was what the imam in the *madrasah* had condemned with constant venom. He must be *kafir*, an unbeliever, a Christian, destined to burn for all eternity in hell. Yet his father had called him friend. How could this be?

The Englishman tapped his forefingers lightly on his chest near the heart. '*Salaam aleikhem*, Izmat Khan,' he said in Arabic.

'*Aleikhem as-salaam*,' Izmat acknowledged. His imam had spoken only his native Saudi Arabic, so Izmat had a good working knowledge. 'How do you call yourself?'

'Mike,' said the man.

'Ma-ick.' Izmat tried it. Strange name.

'Good, let us take tea,' said his father.

They were sheltering in a cave mouth about ten miles from the wreckage of their hamlet.

'We will sleep here tonight. In the morning you will go north. I go south to join Abdul Haq, for an operation against the Jalalabad to Kandahar road.'

They chewed on goat and nibbled rice cakes. Then they slept. Before dawn the two heading north were roused and left on their journey.

BAD LUCK STRUCK them on the second day out. They had left night-camp before dawn and just after first light found themselves forced to cross an exposed expanse of rock-and-shale to find the cover of the next spine of steep-sided hills. To wait would have meant delaying until nightfall, so they crossed the mountainside in daylight. Halfway across they heard the growl of gunship engines.

Both man and boy dived for the ground—but not in time. Over the crest ahead, menacing as a deadly dragonfly, came the Soviet Mil Mi-24D, known simply as the Hind. One of the pilots must have seen a flicker of movement or perhaps the glint of metal, for the Hind turned from its course and headed towards them. The roar of the two Isotov engines grew in their ears, as did the unmistakable *tacka-tacka-tacka* of the main rotor blades.

Mike Martin risked raising his head for a quick glance. The two Soviet pilots, sitting in their tandem seats, with the second one above and behind the first, were staring straight at him as the Hind went into attack mode.

He glanced round. A hundred yards away was a group of boulders, just big enough to shelter behind. With a yell to the boy he was up and running, leaving his rucksack where it was but carrying one of the two tubes.

He heard the running feet of the boy behind him, the roaring of his own blood in his ears and the snarl of the diving Hind. Something about the gunship had given him a flicker of hope. Its rocket pods were empty and it carried no under-slung bombs. He hoped his guess was right. It was.

Pilot Simonov and his co-pilot Grigoriev had been on a dawn patrol to harass a narrow valley where agents had reported that Muj were hiding out. They had dropped their bombs from altitude, then gone in lower to blast the rocky cleft with rockets. A number of goats had pelted from the crack in the mountains, indicating there had indeed been human life sheltering in there. Simonov had shredded the beasts with his 30-mm cannon, using up most of the shells.

He had gone back to a safe altitude and was heading home when Grigoriev had spotted a tiny movement on the mountainside. When he saw the two figures far below start to run he flicked his cannon to 'fire' mode and dived. At 2,000 feet, the twin barrels of the cannon shuddered and the shells poured out. Then stopped. Simonov swore. Here were Muj to kill and he had no cannon shells left. He lifted the nose and turned in a wide arc, and the Hind clattered out over the valley.

Martin and Izmat Khan crouched behind their pitiable cluster of rocks. The Afghan boy watched as the Angleez rapidly opened his sheepskin case and extracted a short tube. He was vaguely aware that someone had punched him in the right thigh, but there was no pain. Just numbness.

What the SAS man was assembling as fast as his fingers would work was one of the two Blowpipe missiles he was trying to bring to Ahmad Shah Massoud in the Panjshir. Lighter and simpler than the American Stinger, it was styled 'command to line of sight', which meant that the firer had to guide the rocket all the way to target by sending radio signals to the movable fins via a tiny control stick.

Martin pushed the missile into the launching tube, fired up the battery and the gyro, squinted through the sight and found the Hind coming straight back at him. He steadied the image in the sights and fired. With a whoosh of blazing gases the rocket left the tube on his shoulder and headed blindly into the sky. It now required his control to rise or drop, turn left or right. He estimated the range at 1,400 yards and closing fast.

Simonov opened fire with his chain gun. In the nose of the Hind the four barrels hurling out a curtain of finger-sized bullets began to turn. Then the Soviet pilot saw the flickering flare of the Blowpipe coming towards him. It became a question of nerve.

Bullets tore into the rocks, blowing away chunks of stone in all directions.

It lasted two seconds but at 2,000 rounds per minute some seventy bullets hit the rocks before Simonov panicked and slewed the Hind to its left.

The Blowpipe had jettisoned its first stage and was going supersonic. Martin tweaked the trajectory to his right just before Simonov swerved. It was a good guess. As it turned out the Hind exposed its belly and the warhead slammed into it. At 1,000 mph, even a five-pound warhead has a terrific punch. It cracked the Hind's base armour, entered and exploded.

Drenched with sweat on the icy mountainside, Martin saw the beast lurch with the impact, start to stream smoke and plunge towards the valley floor.

When it impacted in the river bed the noise stopped. There was a silent peony of flame as the two pilots died, then a plume of dark smoke. That alone would bring attention from the Russians at Jalalabad.

'Let's go,' Martin said in Arabic to his guide.

The boy tried to rise but could not. Then Martin saw the smudge of blood on his thigh. He put down the Blowpipe tube and went to fetch his Bergen.

He used his Ka-Bar knife to slit the trouser leg of the *shalwar kameez*. The hole was small but it looked deep. It was only a fragment of cannon shell casing, but he did not know how near the femoral artery it might be.

'Are we going to die, Angleez?' asked the boy.

'*Inshallah*, not today, Izmat Khan. Not today,' he said.

Martin was in a quandary. He needed his Bergen and everything in it. He could carry either the Bergen or the boy, but not both.

'I must come back with another guide,' he told the boy as he rummaged for shell dressings. 'You must tell him where to come. I will bury the bag and the tubes.' He opened a flat steel box and took out a hypodermic syringe.

So be it, thought Izmat Khan. If the infidel wishes to torture me, let him. I will utter no sound.

The Angleez pushed the needle into his thigh. Izmat Khan made no sound. Seconds later, as the morphine took effect, the agony in his thigh began to diminish. Encouraged, he tried to rise. The Englishman had produced a small, foldable trenching tool and was digging a furrow in the shale among the rocks. When he had done, he covered his Bergen and the two rocket tubes with stones, memorising the shape of the cairn. If he could be brought back to this mountainside, he could recover his kit.

The boy protested that he could walk, but Martin hoisted him over one shoulder and began to march slowly down to the valley.

The plume of smoke from the downed Soviet aircraft had attracted a small party of Muj from another valley, eager to strip the wreck of anything that might be of use. They saw each other 1,000 feet above the valley floor.

Izmat Khan explained what had happened. The mountain men broke into delighted grins and started slapping the SAS man on the back. Martin insisted that his guide needed transportation and a surgical hospital. One of the Muj knew a man with a mule, only two valleys away, and went to get him. It took until nightfall. Martin administered a second shot of morphine.

With a fresh guide and Izmat Khan on a mule at last they marched through the night, just three of them, until at dawn they came to the southern side of the Spin Ghar and the guide stopped. He pointed ahead.

'Jaji,' he said. 'Arabs.'

He also wanted his mule back. Martin carried the boy the last two miles. Jaji was a complex of 500 caves, which the so-called Afghan-Arabs had been deepening, excavating, and equipping into a major guerrilla base. Though Martin did not know it, inside the complex were barracks, a mosque, a library of religious texts, kitchens and a fully equipped hospital.

As he approached, Martin was intercepted by the outer ring of guards. Martin thought it unwise to utter a word. With sign language he indicated that his friend needed emergency surgery.

Izmat Khan was operated on within an hour. A vicious fragment of cannon casing was extracted from the leg.

Martin waited until the lad woke up. He squatted, local-style, in the shadows at the corner of the ward and no one took him for anything other than a Pashtun mountain man who had brought in his friend.

An hour later two men entered the ward. One was very tall, youthful, bearded. He wore a camouflage combat jacket over Arab robes and a white headdress. The other was short, tubby, also in his thirties, with a button nose and round glasses. He wore a surgical smock.

The tall man spoke in Saudi Arabic. 'And how is our young Afghan fighter feeling?'

'*Inshallah*, I am much better, Sheikh.' Izmat spoke back in Arabic, giving the older man a title of reverence.

The tall man smiled. 'Ah, you speak Arabic, and still so young.'

'I was seven years in a *madrasah* at Peshawar. I returned last year to fight.'

'And whom do you fight for, my son?'

'I fight for Afghanistan,' said the boy.

Something like a cloud passed across the features of the Saudi.

'And I also fight for Allah, Sheikh,' Izmat added.

The gentle smile came back. The Saudi bent down and patted the youth on the shoulder. 'The day will come when Afghanistan will no longer have need of you, but the all-merciful Allah will always have need of a warrior like you.' He turned to the doctor. 'How is our young friend's wound healing?'

'Let us see,' said the doctor and peeled back the dressing.

The wound was clean, bruised round the edges but closed by six stitches and uninfected. He tutted his satisfaction and re-dressed the suture.

'You will be walking in a week,' said Dr Ayman al-Zawahiri.

Then he and Osama bin Laden left the ward. No one took any notice of the Muj squatting in the corner with his head on his knees as if asleep.

Martin rose and crossed to the youth on the bed. 'I must go now,' he said. 'The Arabs will look after you.'

'Be careful, Ma-ick,' said the boy. 'You are *kafir*, unbeliever. These Arabs are like the imam in my *madrasah*. They hate all infidel.'

'Then I would be grateful if you would not tell them who I am,' said the Englishman.

Izmat Khan closed his eyes. He would die rather than betray his new friend. It was the code. When he opened his eyes the Angleez was gone.

AFTER HIS SIX MONTHS in Afghanistan, Mike Martin made it home via Pakistan with fluent Pashto added to his armoury. He was sent on leave, remustered into the SAS, then posted to Northern Ireland again, working with the 14th Intelligence Company. In a dark-of-night shootout in an IRA leader's house, Martin took a bullet. He was lucky. It was a flesh wound in the left bicep but enough to see him flown home and sent for convalescence at Headley Court, Leatherhead. That was where he met the nurse, Lucinda, who was to become his wife after a brief courtship.

Reverting to the Paras in the spring of 1990, Mike Martin was posted to the Ministry of Defence in Whitehall. Having set up home with Lucinda in a rented cottage near Chobham, Martin found himself for the first time a commuter in a dark suit on the morning train to London. He worked in the office of MOSP, the Military Operations, Special Projects Unit.

On August 2 that year, Saddam Hussein of Iraq invaded neighbouring Kuwait. Within a week plans were in furious preparation to create a multi-national coalition to free the oil-rich mini-state. Even though MOSP was at full stretch, the influence of the Secret Intelligence Service was enough to trace Martin and 'suggest' he join a few of the 'friends' for lunch.

The meeting was in a discreet club in St James's and his hosts were two senior men from the Firm. Also at the table was a Jordanian-born analyst brought in from GCQH. He conversed with Mike Martin in rapid Arabic.

Finally the analyst nodded at the two spooks. 'I've never heard anything like it,' he remarked. 'With that face and voice, he can pass.'

The senior mandarin turned to Martin. 'We would be damnably grateful if you would go into Kuwait and see what is going on there,' he said.

The army grumbled again, but let him go. Weeks later, Martin slipped over the Saudi border into Iraqi-occupied Kuwait. On the plod north to Kuwait City he passed several Iraqi patrols but they took no notice of the bearded Bedouin nomad leading two camels to market.

In several weeks inside Kuwait, Martin contacted and assisted the fledgling Kuwaiti Resistance, taught them the tricks of the trade, plotted the Iraqi positions, strong points and weaknesses, then came out again.

His second incursion during the Gulf War was into Iraq itself. He went over the Saudi border in the west and caught an Iraqi bus heading for Baghdad. His cover was a simple peasant clutching a wicker basket of hens.

Back in a city he knew intimately, he took a position as a gardener in a wealthy villa, living in a shack in the garden. His mission was to collect and forward messages, using a folding, parabolic dish aerial whose 'blitz' messages were uninterceptable by the secret police but could reach Riyadh.

One of the best-kept secrets of that war was that the Firm had a source high in Saddam's government. Martin never met him; he just picked up the messages at dead-letter boxes and sent them to the US-led Coalition HQ. Saddam capitulated on February 26, 1991, and Mike Martin came out.

He rejoined the Parachute Regiment and after a spell at the Army Staff College at Camberley he went back to the Ministry, Military Operations directorate, but as a major. Chafing at the lack of any chance of action, he spent two years commuting again from the suburbs to London.

Officers who have served in the SAS can return for a second tour, on invitation. Martin got his call from Hereford at the end of 1994.

His marriage was under strain. There had been no baby. Lucinda had been offered a big promotion, the chance of a lifetime, but it meant going to work in the Midlands. Mike Martin's orders were to command B Squadron, 22 SAS, and take them covertly to Bosnia, ostensibly to be part of the UN's peace-keeping mission, in fact to hunt down war criminals. He was not allowed to tell Lucinda the details, only that he was leaving again.

It was the final straw. She presumed it was a transfer back to Arabia and she quite properly put to him an ultimatum: you can have the Paras, the SAS and your bloody desert, or you can come to Birmingham and have a marriage. He thought it over and chose the desert.

CHAPTER FOUR

On the morning of February 15, 1989, the general commanding the Soviet 40th Army, the army of occupation in Afghanistan, had walked alone back across the bridge over the Amu Darya River into Uzbekistan. His entire army had preceded him. The war was over.

Most analysts predicted that the victorious warlords would form a stable government and take over. But the government of President Najibullah hung on, backed as it was by the Afghan army and the Khad secret police. More to the point, the warlords simply disintegrated into a mêlée of snarling, feuding, self-serving opportunists who, far from uniting to form a stable government, created a civil war.

None of this affected Izmat Khan. With the help of neighbours, he and his family rebuilt the hamlet of Maloko-zai. Stone by stone and rock by rock, they cleared the rubble left by the bombs and rockets and remade the family compound by the mulberry and pomegranate trees.

With his leg fully healed, Izmat had returned to the war and taken command of his father's *lashkar* in all but name. When peace came, his guerrilla group seized a huge cache of weapons the Soviets could not be bothered to carry home. These they took over the Spin Ghar to Parachinar in Pakistan, a town that is virtually nothing but an arms bazaar. There they traded the Soviet leftovers for cows, goats and sheep to restart the flocks.

If life had been hard before, starting over was even harder, but Izmat Khan enjoyed the sense of triumph that Maloko-zai would live again.

The Kuchi nomads passing through brought grim tales from the plains. The Afghan army still held the cities, but the warlords infested the countryside and they and their men behaved like brigands. Tolls were set up on main roads and travellers were stripped of their money and goods or badly beaten.

Pakistan's ISI Directorate was backing Gulbuddin Hekmatyar to become controller of Afghanistan, and in the areas he ruled utter terror existed. Izmat Khan thanked Allah that he was spared the misery of the plains.

With the end of the war the Arabs had almost all gone from the mountains. Some five hundred had stayed behind but they were not popular; they were scattered far and wide and living like beggars.

When he was twenty, Izmat Khan was visiting a neighbouring valley when he saw a girl washing clothes in the stream. Before she could cover her face he had made eye contact. She fled in alarm and embarrassment. But he had seen that she was beautiful.

Izmat did what any young man would do. He consulted his mother. She was delighted and soon two aunts joined her in happy conspiracy to find the girl and persuade Nuri Khan to contact the father to arrange a union. Her name was Maryam and the wedding took place in the late spring of 1993. There was a feast and the bride came from her village on a decorated horse. For one day Izmat rejected his strict Wahhabi training and he danced in the meadow and the eyes of his bride followed him everywhere.

Three months later, it was clear that Maryam would bear a child in the snows of February. As she carried Izmat's child the Arabs came back. The tall Saudi was not among them, but he sent a great deal of money with which to set up training camps, and volunteers from across the Arabic-speaking world came to train for war. Izmat Khan learned that it was all because the Sheikh, as his followers called him, had declared jihad against his own government in Saudi Arabia and against the West.

But Izmat Khan had no quarrel with the West. The West had helped defeat the Soviets with arms and money, and the only *kafir* he had ever met had saved his life. It was not his holy war, not his jihad, he decided. His concern was for his country, which was descending into madness.

WHEN YOUNIS KHALIS DIED his party became wholly under the control of Hekmatyar, whose reputation for cruelty Izmat loathed. By the time Izmat's baby was born, in February 1994, President Najibullah had been succeeded by Professor Rabbani. The Tajik was not acceptable to the Pashtun, however, and outside Kabul, only the warlords ruled their domains. The real masters were chaos and anarchy.

After the Soviet war, thousands of young Afghans had gone over the border to complete their education in Pakistani *madrasahs*. Now they were coming back. Having been taught by barely literate imams, they were ill educated. They knew nothing of life, of women, or even of their own tribal cultures. Apart from the Koran, they knew only one thing: war.

In the summer of 1994, Izmat Khan and a cousin left the upland valley for Jalalabad. The two travellers came to a village that had refused to pay Hekmatyar any more tribute money, and found the menfolk tortured and slain, the women beaten, the village torched. In Jalalabad, Izmat Khan learned that what he had seen was quite commonplace.

Then something happened in the deep south. After the fall of the central government, the old official Afghan army had simply reassigned itself to the local warlord who paid the best. Outside Kandahar some soldiers took two teenage girls back to their camp and gang-raped them.

The village preacher, who ran his own religious school, went to the army camp with thirty students and sixteen rifles. They trounced the soldiers and hanged the commandant from the barrel of a tank gun. The preacher was Mullah Mohammed Omar. He had lost his right eye in battle.

The news spread. Others appealed to him for help. He and his group swelled in numbers and responded to the appeals. They took no money, they raped no women, they stole no crops, they asked no reward. They became local heroes. By December 1994, 12,000 had joined them, adopting this mullah's black turban. They called themselves the students. In Pashto 'student' is *talib*, and the plural is the Taliban. From village vigilantes they became a movement and, when they captured the city of Kandahar, an alternative government.

Pakistan, through its forever-plotting ISI, had been backing Hekmatyar, but as the ISI was infiltrated by ultra-orthodox Muslims it switched support to the Taliban. The new movement inherited a huge cache of arms, plus tanks, armoured cars, trucks, guns, six MiG 21 ex-Soviet fighters and six heavy helicopters. They began to sweep north.

In 1995 Izmat Khan embraced his wife, kissed his baby, then came down from the mountains to join the Taliban. He was twenty-three.

Too late he learned that there was a dark side to the Taliban. In Kandahar, even though the Pashtun had been devout before, they were subjected to the harshest regimen the world of Islam has ever seen. All girls' schools were closed. Women were forbidden to leave the house save in company of a male relative. The all-enveloping burka robe was decreed at all times. All singing, dancing, the playing of music, sports and kite-flying, a national pastime, was forbidden. Beards on men were compulsory. From being liberators, the enforcers in their black turbans became the new tyrants, their mission to destroy the rule of the warlords. The people acquiesced to the new strictness: at least there was law, order, no more corruption, no more rape, no more crime; just fanatical orthodoxy.

Having started his revolution by hanging a rapist from a gun barrel, Mullah Omar withdrew into seclusion in his southern fortress, Kandahar. The Taliban had no commanding general, no general staff, no officers, no ranks and no infrastructure. Each *lashkar* was semi-independent under its tribal leader, who often held sway through personality and courage. They acquired such a reputation for invincibility that opponents often capitulated without a shot fired. When they ran into real soldiers, the forces of Ahmad Shah Massoud, they took unspeakable losses. They had no medical corps, so their wounded simply died by the roadside. In all, 80,000 Taliban died in the fighting. But still they came on.

At the gates of Kabul they negotiated with Massoud but he refused to accept their terms and withdrew to his northern mountains. So began the next civil war, between the Taliban and the Northern Alliance of Massoud the Tajik and Rashid Dostum the Uzbek. It was 1996. Only Pakistan (who had organised it) and Saudi Arabia (who paid for it) recognised the new weird government of Afghanistan.

For Izmat Khan, who had joined a *lashkar* of men fighting from his own province in Nangarhar, the die was cast. His old ally Ahmad Shah Massoud was now his enemy. Far to the south an aeroplane landed. It brought back the tall Saudi who had spoken to him eight years earlier in a cave at Jaji and the chubby doctor who had pulled a chunk of Soviet steel from his leg. Both men paid immediate obeisance to Mullah Omar, paying huge tribute in money and equipment and thus securing his lifelong loyalty.

After Kabul there was a pause in the war. Almost the first act of the Taliban in Kabul was to drag the toppled ex-president Najibullah from his house arrest, torture and execute him before hanging his corpse from a lamp-post. That set the tenor of the rule to come. Izmat Khan had no taste for cruelty for its own sake. He had fought hard and risen to commander of his own *lashkar*, and word of his leadership spread until his *lashkar* became one of the four divisions in the Taliban army. Then he asked to be allowed to go back to his native Nangarhar where he was made provincial governor. Based in Jalalabad, he could visit his family, wife and baby.

He had heard much of a group now based in his country called Al-Qaeda and knew that it had declared global jihad against all unbelievers, especially those in a place called America. But it was not his jihad. He was fighting the Northern Alliance to unite his homeland once and for all.

On August 7, 1998, bombs exploded outside the American embassies in Nairobi and Dar es Salaam. Izmat knew nothing of this. Listening to foreign radio was now banned, and he obeyed. On August 20, America launched seventy Tomahawk cruise missiles at Afghanistan, from missile cruisers, destroyers and a submarine in the Arabian Gulf. They were aimed at the training camps of Al-Qaeda, and the caves of the Tora Bora.

Among those that went astray was one that entered the mouth of a natural and empty cave high in the mountain above Maloko-zai. The detonation deep inside the cave split the mountain and an entire face peeled away. Ten million tons of rock crashed into the valley below.

When Izmat Khan reached the village there was nothing to see. The entire valley had been buried. There was no stream any more, no farm, no orchards, no stock pens, no mosque, no stables. His entire family and all his neighbours were gone. His parents, uncles, aunts, sisters, wife and child were dead beneath millions of tonnes of granite rubble. There was nowhere to dig and nothing to dig for. He had become a man with no roots, no relatives, no clan.

In the dying August sun, he knelt on the shale and turned west towards Mecca, bowed his head to the ground and prayed. But it was a different prayer this time; it was a mighty oath, a sworn vendetta, a personal jihad against the people who had done this. He declared war on America.

A WEEK LATER, Izmat Khan had resigned his governorship and gone back to the front. For three years he fought the Northern Alliance. While he had been away, the tactically-brilliant Shah Massoud had caused huge losses to the Taliban. But on September 9, 2001, news flashed through the Taliban army that Shah Massoud was dead. The air above Izmat Khan's camp outside Bamiyan crackled with shots fired in a delirium of joy.

Massoud had been assassinated by two suicide bombers pretending to be Moroccan journalists, sent by Osama bin Laden as a favour to his friend Mullah Omar. The Saudi had not thought of the ploy; it was the far cleverer Egyptian Ayman al-Zawahiri who realised that if Al-Qaeda did this favour for Omar, he could never expel them for what was going to happen next.

On September 11, four airliners were hijacked over the American east coast. Two destroyed the World Trade Center in Manhattan, one devastated the Pentagon and the fourth, after its passengers invaded the flight deck to rip the hijackers from the controls, crashed in a field.

Within days the identity and inspiration of the nineteen hijackers had been established; within a few more days the new US President had given Mullah Omar a flat ultimatum: yield up the ringleaders or take the consequences. Because of Massoud, Omar could not capitulate. It was the code.

MIKE MARTIN WAS BACK in London, after a year in the West African hellhole of Sierra Leone, when life was temporarily interrupted by those unbelievable images on the TV screen of fully loaded and fuelled airliners flying straight into the Twin Towers.

A week later it was plain that the USA would be going into Afghanistan in pursuit of those responsible. London at once agreed to provide whatever was needed from its own resources and was asked for air-to-air refuelling tankers and Special Forces. The SIS Head of Station in Islamabad and the defence attaché in Islamabad also asked for help.

Mike Martin was taken from his desk at Para HQ Aldershot and found himself on the next flight to Islamabad as Special Forces Liaison Officer. He arrived four weeks after the destruction of the World Trade Center and the day the first allied attacks went in.

IZMAT KHAN WAS STILL commanding in the north when the bombs rained on Kabul. As the world focused on the capital, the US Special Forces slipped into the northeastern province of Badakhshan where the Northern Alliance, now led by General Fahim, had a small enclave.

Without ever taking off, Afghanistan's puny air force was vaporised. Its tanks and artillery, if they could be spotted, were 'taken out'. The Uzbek, Rashid Dostum, who had spent years in safety across the border, was persuaded to come back and open a second front in the northwest to match Fahim's front in the northeast. And in November the great break-out began.

Air strikes came from far south, where US Navy carriers hovered off the coast, or with A-10 tank-busters flying out of Uzbekistan. Unit by unit, the Taliban army was blown away. There was no medication, no evacuation, no doctors. The wounded said their prayers and died like flies.

Izmat Khan retreated as position after position was devastated and lost.

The Taliban army of the north began with over 30,000 soldiers, but were losing a thousand a day. Recruiting squads had pressed tens of thousands more into the ranks. And still Izmat Khan had to pull them back, each time convinced that he could not last another day. By November 18 they had reached the town of Kunduz.

By a fluke of history, Kunduz is a small enclave of Gilzai southerners, all Pashtun, in a sea of Tajiks and Hazaras. Thus the Taliban army could take refuge there. And it was there they agreed to surrender.

Among Afghans there is nothing dishonourable in a negotiated surrender and, once agreed, its terms are always honoured. The Taliban army surrendered to General Fahim and, to the rage of the US advisers, Fahim accepted.

Inside the Taliban were about 2,000 Pakistanis. After 9/11, General Musharraf had become a dedicated ally of the USA rather than continue to support the Taliban. The Pakistani volunteers were going to be a thundering embarrassment to Islamabad if they were discovered. So, over three nights, a secret air bridge exfiltrated most of them back to Pakistan.

The original army that surrendered was over 14,000 strong but their numbers were coming down. In another covert deal, some 4,000 prisoners were sold—for varying sums according to desirability—to the USA and Russia. The Russians wanted any Chechens and (as a favour to Tashkent) any anti-Tashkent Uzbeks. Finally the Northern Alliance announced to the world media that it had only 8,000 prisoners.

Then it was decided to hand over 5,000 of them to the Uzbek commander, General Dostum, who wished to take them to Sheberghan, inside his own territory. They were packed so tightly into freight containers they could only stand, straining upwards for the air pocket above their heads. Somewhere on the road west it was agreed to give them air holes. This was done with heavy machine guns that went on firing until the screaming stopped.

Of the remaining 3,000, the 600 Arabs—Saudis, Yemenis, Moroccans, Algerians, Egyptians, Jordanians and Syrians—were selected out. The rest stayed behind in Tajik hands and have not been heard of since.

Izmat Khan was spoken to by one of the selectors in Arabic. He replied in Arabic, so was thought to be an Arab. When he was pushed in a certain direction, filthy, hungry and exhausted, he was too tired to protest. Thus he ended up one of the twelve Afghans destined to be sent to Mazar-e-Sharif and into Dostum's hands.

By this time the Western media were watching, and the prisoners were given a guarantee of safe conduct by the newly arrived United Nations.

Trucks were found from somewhere and the 600 prisoners were loaded aboard for the journey west. But their final destination would not be Mazar itself, but a huge prison fortress ten miles further west.

So they came to the mouth of hell, but it was called Qala-i-Jangi.

SPECIAL FORCES from both allied countries were operational inside Afghanistan well before the first bomb fell. Mike Martin yearned to go with them but the British High Commission in Islamabad was adamant that it needed him on the spot to liaise with the Pakistani army brass.

Until Bagram. This vast ex-Soviet air base north of Kabul was clearly going to be a major allied base during the eventual occupation. It was captured in the third week of November and a team of Special Boat Squadron men moved in to stake the British claim. Mike Martin immediately hitched a lift from the Americans to go and have a look at the place, as he put it.

On the morning of November 26, the SBS unit CO told his men: 'There seems to be something going on at a place called Qala-i-Jangi, west of Mazar. Some prisoners appear to have risen in revolt, taken their guards' weapons, and are putting up a fight. I think we should have a look.'

Six Marines were chosen and two Land-Rovers allocated and fuelled.

As they were about to leave, Martin asked, 'Mind if I tag along? You might be able to use an interpreter.'

There was no objection. Martin boarded the second vehicle beside the driver. Behind him two Marines crouched over the .30-calibre machine gun. They headed north on the six-hour drive to the fort of Qala-i-Jangi.

The events that triggered the massacre of the prisoners at Qala-i-Jangi were disputed at the time and remain so. But there are compelling clues.

The Western media persistently called the prisoners Taliban. They were, in fact, except for the six Afghans included by accident, the defeated army of Al-Qaeda. They had come to Afghanistan to pursue jihad, to fight and to die, and were the 600 most dangerous men in Asia.

What met them at Qala were 100 partly trained Uzbeks under a desperately incompetent commander, Rashid Dostum's deputy, Sayid Kamel.

The fort of Qala is a huge, ten-acre compound containing open spaces, trees and one-storey buildings. The space is enclosed by a fifty-foot wall, which slopes inwards so that a climber can scramble up the ramp and peer over the parapet at the top.

This thick wall hosts a labyrinth of barracks, stores and passages, with another maze of tunnels and cellars beneath. The Uzbeks had captured it only ten days earlier and seemed not to know that there was a Taliban armoury and magazine stored at the southern end.

At Kunduz the captives had been relieved of their rifles and RPGs, but no one did a body search. Had they been frisked the captors would have realised that almost every man had a grenade or two hidden inside his robes. That was how they arrived in the motorcade at Qala.

The first hint came on the Saturday night of their arrival. Izmat Khan was in the fifth truck and heard the boom from 100 yards away. One of the Arabs, gathering several Uzbeks around him, had detonated his grenade, blowing himself and five Uzbeks to pemmican.

Night was falling. There were no lights. Dostum's men decided to do body searches the next morning. They herded the prisoners into the compound and left them, surrounded by armed but already nervous guards.

At dawn the searches began. The prisoners, still docile in their battle-fatigue, allowed their hands to be tied behind them. As there were no ropes the Uzbeks used the prisoners' turbans. But turbans are not ropes.

One by one the prisoners were hauled upright to be frisked. Out came handguns, grenades—and money. As the money piled up it was taken away to a side room by Sayid Kamel and his deputy. An Uzbek soldier, peering through the window, saw the two men pocketing the lot. The soldier entered the room to protest and was told to get lost. But he came back with a rifle.

Two of the prisoners saw this. They had already worked their hands free, and they followed the soldier into the room, seized the rifle and used its butt to beat all three Uzbeks to death.

Meanwhile, two CIA men, Mike Spann and Dave Tyson, had entered the compound. Mike Spann began a series of interrogations right out in the open surrounded by 600 fanatics whose only ambition before going to Allah was to kill an American. Then some Uzbek guard saw the armed Arab and yelled a warning. The Arab fired and killed him.

Izmat Khan was squatting on the dirt waiting for his turn. Like others he had worked his hands free. As the shot Uzbek soldier fell, others watching from atop the walls opened up with machine guns. The slaughter had begun.

Over 100 prisoners died in the dirt with bound hands. Others untied their neighbours' hands so that they could fight. Izmat Khan led a group of others, including his eleven fellow Afghans, in a dodging, weaving run through the trees to the south wall, where he knew the armoury was from a previous visit, when the fort was in Taliban hands.

Twenty Arabs nearest to Mike Spann fell on him and beat him to death. Dave Tyson emptied his handgun into the mob, killed three, heard the click of hammer on empty chamber and was lucky to make the main gate in time.

Within ten minutes the compound was empty except for the corpses and the wounded. The Uzbeks were now outside the wall, the gate was slammed and the prisoners were inside. The siege had begun. It would last six days. Each side was convinced the other had broken the terms of surrender, but by then it did not matter.

The armoury door was quickly shattered. There was enough for a small army—rifles, grenades, launchers, RPGs and mortars. Taking what they could, they fanned out through the tunnels and passages until they owned the fortress. Every time an Uzbek outside put his head over the parapet, an Arab, firing through a slit from across the compound, took a shot.

Dostum's men had no choice but to call for help. The general himself hurried towards Qala-i-Jangi with 100 more Uzbeks. Also on their way were four American Green Berets, one US Air Force man to assist in air coordination and six men from the 10th Mountain Division, whose job was to observe, report and call in air strikes.

By midmorning, coming up from Bagram Base north of Kabul were the two Land-Rovers bearing six British Special Forces from the SBS and an interpreter, Lieutenant-Colonel Mike Martin of the SAS.

Tuesday saw the Uzbek counterattack taking shape. Shielded by their simple tank, they re-entered the compound and began to pound the rebel positions. Izmat Khan had been given charge of one wing of the south face. When the tank opened up he ordered his men into the cellars. When the bombardment stopped they came back up again.

He knew it was only a matter of time. There was no way out and no chance of mercy. Not that he wanted it. He had finally, at the age of twenty-nine, found the place he was going to die, and it was as good as any other.

Then the US strike aircraft arrived. The four Green Berets and the airman were lying just outside the parapet at the top of the external ramp, plotting targets for the fighter-bombers. Thirty strikes took place that day and twenty-eight of them slammed into the masonry inside which the rebels were hiding, killing about 100. Two bombs were not so good.

The first landed right in the middle of the circle formed by the five

Americans. It was a JDAM, a bunker-buster, designed to penetrate deep into masonry. Landing nose-down in gravel, it shot forty feet down before exploding. The Americans found themselves on top of an earthquake, were hurled around, but survived, with shattered eardrums and some bone-breaks.

The second mis-hit was even more unfortunate. It took out the Uzbek tank and their command post behind it.

By Wednesday the Western media had arrived and were swarming all over the outside of the fort. Mike Martin lay on top of the ramp with the other Special Forces personnel, peering down into the compound. The bodies from the first days still lay there and the stench was appalling.

By that evening, Izmat Khan realised that he and his men could not stay above ground any longer. Artillery had arrived and down the length of the compound it was beginning to reduce the south face to rubble. The cellars were the last resort. The surviving rebels were down to under 300.

Some of these decided not to go below ground but to die under the sky. They staged a suicidal counterattack, which succeeded for 100 yards, killing a number of unwary Uzbeks. Then the machine gun on the Uzbeks' replacement tank opened up and cut the Arabs to pieces.

On Thursday, on American advice, the Uzbeks took barrels of diesel fuel and poured it down conduits into the cellars below. Then they set fire to it.

Izmat Khan was not in that section of the cellars, but he heard the *whoomf* and felt the heat. More died, but the survivors came staggering out of the smoke towards him, choking and gagging. In the last cellar, with about 150 men around him, Izmat Khan slammed and bolted the door to keep out the smoke. Beyond the door the hammering of the dying became fainter and finally stopped. Above them, shells slammed into empty rooms.

The last cellar led to a passage, and at the far end the men could smell fresh air. There was no way out, only a gutter from above. That night the Uzbek commander hit upon the idea of diverting an irrigation ditch into that pipe. After the November rains the ditch was full and the water icy. By midnight the remaining men were waist deep. Weakened by hunger and exhaustion, they began to slip beneath the surface and drown.

At ground level, the United Nations was in charge, surrounded by media. Through the rubble above them, the last rebels could hear the bullhorn ordering them to come out, unarmed and with hands up. After twenty hours, the first began to stagger towards the stairs. Others followed. Izmat Khan, with the six other Afghans left alive, went with them.

Stumbling over the broken stone blocks that had been the south face, the last eighty-six rebels found themselves facing a forest of pointed guns and rockets. In the light of Saturday dawn they looked like scarecrows from a horror film. Filthy, stinking, black from cordite soot, ragged, matted and hypothermic, they tottered and some fell. One of these was Izmat Khan.

Coming down a rock pile he slipped, reached out to steady himself and grabbed a rock. A chunk came away in his hand. Thinking he was being attacked, a nervous young Uzbek fired his RPG.

The fiery grenade went past the Afghan's ear into a boulder behind him. The stone splintered and a piece the size of a baseball hit him in the back of the head. He was wearing no turban. It had been used to bind his hands six days earlier and then lost. The rock ricocheted off, slicing the scalp and knocking him into a near coma. He fell among the rubble, blood gushing from the gash. The rest were marched away to trucks waiting outside.

An hour later, the seven British soldiers were moving through the compound taking notes. Mike Martin, as senior officer, although technically the unit interpreter, would have a long report to make. He was counting the dead, though he knew there were scores still underground. One body interested him; it was still bleeding. Corpses do not bleed.

He turned the scarecrow over. The clothing was wrong. It was Pashtun dress, and there were not supposed to be Pashtun present. He wiped the grime-smeared face. Something was familiar.

He took out his Ka-Bar, and cut into the trouser leg of the right thigh.

It was still there, puckered by the six stitches, the scar where the Soviet shell fragment had gone in over thirteen years before. For the second time, Martin hoisted Izmat Khan over one shoulder and carried him. At the main gate he found a white Land-Rover with the sign of the United Nations on it.

'This man is alive but injured,' he said. 'He has a bad head wound.' Duty done, he boarded the SBS Land-Rover for the drive back to Bagram.

The American trawl team found the Afghan in Mazar hospital three days later and claimed him for interrogation. They trucked him to Bagram, where he came to, on the floor of a makeshift cell on the US side of the base, cold and shackled but just alive, two days after that.

On January 14, 2002, the first detainees arrived at Guantánamo Bay, Cuba, from Kandahar. Izmat Khan was one of them.

United Nations records later showed that 514 Al-Qaeda fanatics died at Qala-i-Jangi and eighty-six survived, all injured. All went to Guantánamo

Bay. Sixty Uzbek Guards also died. General Rashid Dostum became Defence Minister in the new Afghan government.

Colonel Mike Martin returned to London in the spring of 2002 to spend three years as Deputy Chief of Staff, HQ Directorate of Special Forces. He retired in December 2005, and the following January he bought a listed barn in the Meon valley, Hampshire.

CHAPTER FIVE

Operation Crowbar's cover story was that it was an Anglo-American joint venture against the growing opium threat coming out of the poppy fields of Afghanistan. Heroin produced in the opium refineries of the Middle East was infiltrating the West both to destroy lives and to generate funds for terrorism. Crowbar, so the 'script' went, had been agreed by both governments as a specific, one-target operation prepared to use covert forces and the highest surveillance technology known to man to raid and destroy any factories found in any foreign country turning a blind eye to the trade. Even those working inside Crowbar would not know anything about infiltrating a ringer inside Al-Qaeda.

But Western intelligence did not intend to place all its eggs in the Crowbar basket. Between them the intelligence agencies had scores of informants inside the world of Islamic fundamentalism, and frantic efforts had been continuing to discover what Al-Isra referred to. It quickly became clear that Western informants knew the phrase's real significance. So the decision was taken to match secrecy with secrecy. There were clear advantages to letting Al-Qaeda believe that nothing had been harvested from the laptop of the dead banker at Peshawar.

The project's next chore was to find and establish a new headquarters. Marek Gumienny and Steve Hill agreed to base Crowbar somewhere in the British Isles, well away from London. After analysis of what would be needed in terms of size, lodgings, space and access, Gordon Phillips and Michael McDonald settled upon RAF Edzell, a decommissioned air base, in the county of Angus, on the southern threshold of the Scottish Highlands.

The base, when the two executive officers went up to visit it, served all their purposes. It was as remote as one could wish; it contained two good runways with control tower, hangars for storage, and all the mess halls, canteens, kitchens and accommodation they required for the resident staff. All they needed to do was add the 'golf-ball' domes hiding listening antennae and convert the former Ops block into the new communications centre.

Into this complex would be diverted links to GCHQ Cheltenham and NSA Maryland, direct and secure lines to Vauxhall Cross and Langley, and a permanent 'feed' from US space satellites, run by the National Reconnaissance office in Washington, DC.

With approval from their superiors secured, Phillips and McDonald got the 'works and bricks' people from the Royal Air Force working on a blitz assignment to bring Edzell back into commission. The good folk of Edzell village noticed that something was afoot, but with much winking and tapping of noses accepted that once again it would be hush-hush, like the good old days. The local landlord laid in some extra supplies of ale and whisky, hoping that custom might revert to the level he had enjoyed before decommissioning. Otherwise, nobody said a thing.

WHILE THE PAINTERS were running their brushes over the walls of the officers' quarters of a Scottish air base, the office of Siebart & Abercrombie, in a modest City of London street called Crutched Friars, received a visit.

Mr Ahmed Lampong had arrived by appointment following an exchange of emails between London and Jakarta, and was shown into the office of Mr Siebart, son of the founder. Had the London-based shipping broker known it, Lampong was an alias, though his passport in that name was flawless.

So was his English, and in response to Siebart's compliments he admitted that he had perfected it while studying for his master's at the London School of Economics. He was urbane and charming, and brought the prospect of business. There was nothing to suggest he was a member of Jemaat Islamiya, the terrorist organisation responsible for a wave of bombings in Bali.

His credentials as senior partner of Sumatra Trading International were in order, as were his bank references. When he asked permission to outline his problem, Mr Siebart was all ears.

Mr Lampong solemnly laid a sheet of paper in front of the British ship broker. The sheet had a list of forty-three names. It began with Alderney, one of the British Channel Islands, and ended with Western Samoa.

'These are all tax-haven countries,' said the Indonesian, 'and all practise banking secrecy. Some extremely dubious businesses shelter their financial secrets in such places. These'—he produced a second sheet—'are just as dubious in their way. These are merchant shipping flags of convenience.'

There were twenty-seven in this list, from Antigua to Vanuatu.

'Put the two together,' Mr Lampong continued, ' and you have fraud on a massive scale. And alas most prevalent in the part of the world where I and my partners trade. That is why we have decided in future to deal solely with ships of the British merchant fleet flying the Red Ensign, out of British ports under a British skipper and vouched for by a London broker.'

Siebart beamed. 'A wise choice, Mr Lampong. What cargoes do you want shipped?'

Matching freighters to cargoes and cargoes to freighters is what a shipping broker does, and Siebart & Abercrombie were long-standing pillars of the City of London's ancient partnership, the Baltic Exchange.

'We have been in discussion with this company: importers of British limousines and sports cars into Singapore,' said Mr Lampong, producing more letters of recommendation. 'For our part, we ship fine furniture timbers from Indonesia to the USA. It comes from North Borneo, but would be a part-cargo with the remainder being sea containers on deck with embroidered silks from Surabaya, Java, also bound for the USA. Here'—he laid down a final letter—'are the details of our friends in Surabaya. Clearly, this would be a triangular voyage. Could you find us a suitable UK-registered freighter? I have in mind a regular and ongoing partnership.'

Alex Siebart was confident he could supply Mr Lampong with a 'menu' of Red Ensign vessels of the needed tonnage for the double-cargo and the charter price. Mr Lampong, when he had consulted his partners, would provide desired collection dates at the two Far Eastern ports and the US delivery port. They parted with mutual expressions of good will.

'How nice,' sighed Alex Siebart's father when he told him over lunch at Rules, 'to be dealing with old-fashioned and civilised gentlemen.'

MAREK GUMIENNY had one simple question for the small office in Langley that runs and maintains the CIA's chain of 'safe houses': 'What is the most remote, obscure and hard-to-get-into-or-out-of facility that we have?'

The answer from his real-estate colleague took no time at all. 'We call it the Cabin. It's up in the Pasayten Wilderness of the Cascades Range.'

Gumienny asked for every detail and picture available. Within thirty minutes of receiving the file he had made his choice and given his orders.

East of Seattle, in the wilds of Washington State, is the range of steep, forested mountains known as the Cascades. Inside the borders of the Cascades are three zones: the National Park, the logging forest and the Pasayten Wilderness. The first two have access roads and some habitations, though in deep winter both areas close down because the snow makes most movement almost impossible.

East of the park and the forest, running up to the Canadian border, is the Wilderness. Here there are no tracks, only one or two trails and, in the far south, near Hart's Pass, a few log cabins. Winter and summer the zone teems with wildlife and game. The cabin owners tend to summer in the Wilderness, then disconnect all systems, lock up and withdraw to the city.

Years earlier a remote log cabin had come up for sale and the CIA bought it. It was an impulse purchase, later regretted but occasionally used by senior officers for summer vacations. In October, when Marek Gumienny made his enquiry, it was locked. He demanded that it be reopened.

The Cabin was almost inaccessible to start with. A very basic road went a few miles north of the tiny town of Mazama and then ran out ten miles short. Gumienny commandeered a Chinook helicopter from McChord Air Force Base south of Seattle to be used as a carthorse, and a build team from Army Engineers. Everyone was on a need-to-know basis and the legend was that the Cabin was being converted into an ultra-high-security research centre. In truth it was to become a one-man jail.

MIKE MARTIN could not show his face at Edzell Air Base. So Steve Hill called into play the array of contacts that exists in every business, and for a modest rent acquired a suitable venue nearby.

Martin flew from London to Aberdeen and was met by a former SAS sergeant, a tough Scot called Angus whom he knew well.

'How are you keeping, boss?' he asked, employing the old jargon for SAS men talking to an officer. He hefted Martin's kitbag into the rear and eased out of the airport car park towards Inverness. Half an hour later, the Land-Rover was turning across a river and up a long, winding private drive. Round two bends the stone bulk of an ancient castle sat on a slight eminence looking out over a stunning vista of wild hills and glens.

Two men emerged from the main entrance of the castle, came forward and introduced themselves.

'Gordon Phillips. Michael McDonald. Welcome to Castle Forbes, family seat of Lord Forbes. Good trip, Colonel?'

Mike Martin nodded. 'It's Mike.'

'Not a problem, Mike,' said the CIA man McDonald. 'Now, why not freshen up and after lunch we'll start the first briefing. A range of tutors are set to offer you their undivided attention for the next eighteen weeks.'

The regime started intensive and became more so. Martin was required to change out of Western clothes into the robes and turban of a Pashtun tribesman. His beard and hair were to grow as long as the time allowed.

Three members of staff had been allowed to stay on: the housekeeper, the gardener, and Angus, the former SAS sergeant, who was Lord Forbes's estate manager, or factor. Even if an interloper had wished to penetrate the estate, he would have been most unwise with Angus on the prowl.

For the rest, 'guests' came and went, save two permanent residents. One was Najib Qureshi, a native Afghan and former teacher in Kandahar, once a refugee given asylum in Britain, now a naturalised citizen and translator at GCHQ Cheltenham. He had been detached from his duties and transferred to Castle Forbes, as language tutor and coach in all forms of behaviour that would be expected of a Pashtun.

The other was Dr Tamian Godfrey: mid-sixties, iron-grey hair in a bun; she had been married for years to a senior officer in the Security Service, MI5, until his death two years earlier. Being 'one of us', as Steve Hill put it, she was no stranger to security procedures. Her expertise was the Koran; her knowledge of it was encyclopedic and her Arabic impeccable.

Even though he knew Arabic, Mike Martin realised what a staggering amount he had to learn. Najib Qureshi taught him to speak Arabic with a Pashtun accent. Izmat Khan's voice, speaking to fellow prisoners in Camp Delta, had been recorded secretly in case he had secrets to divulge. He did not, but for Mr Qureshi and his pupil the recording was invaluable. It was eighteen years since Martin had spent time with the Muj and he had forgotten much. Qureshi coached him in Pashto, even though it had been agreed that Martin could never pass as a Pashtun among other Pashtun.

But mostly it was two things: the prayers and what had happened to him in Guantánamo Bay. The CIA was the principal provider of interrogators in Camp Delta; so Michael McDonald flew back to Langley to spend days with three or four men who had had dealings with Izmat Khan there, draining them dry of every detail they could recall, plus the notes and tapes they had made. The cover story was that Izmat Khan was being considered for release under the NFD rules—no further danger—and Langley wanted to be sure. The explanation was not untrue, though it would require John Negroponte, as Director of National Intelligence, to request Donald Rumsfeld as Secretary of Defense, to 'have a word' with the military judges of the case in order to secure an acquittal and release.

All the CIA interrogators were adamant that the Pashtun mountain warrior and Taliban commander was the hardest man in detention. He had cooperated to the minimum, complained not at all, accepted all privations and punishments with stoicism. But, they agreed, when you looked into those black eyes, you just knew he would love to tear your head off.

McDonald flew back to brief Mike Martin on what he had discovered about Izmat Khan, and Tamian Godfrey and Najib Qureshi concentrated on the daily prayers. Martin would have to say them in front of others. The Koran was in classical Arabic and Izmat Khan was not a born Arab, so a one-word slip could be put down to mispronunciation. But for a boy who had spent seven years in a *madrasah*, an entire phrase was too much. So, with Najib rising and bowing, forehead to the carpet, beside him, and Tamian Godfrey (due to her stiff knees) in a chair, they recited and recited.

THERE WAS PROGRESS also at Edzell Air Base, where an Anglo-American technical team was installing and linking all the British intelligence services and those of the USA into one nexus. The accommodation and facilities were up and running. The RAF shipped in catering staff and the RAF Regiment took over perimeter security. No one doubted the base was becoming a listening post for opium-traffickers.

From the USA, giant Galaxies and Starlifters flew in with listening monitors that could scan the world. Arabic translations would be handled by GCHQ Cheltenham and Fort Meade, both of which would be in constant secure contact with Crowbar. Before Christmas, the twelve computer workstations that would be the nerve centre were brought on stream, fitted with ultra-secure ISDN telephone lines, and linked directly to the SIS at Vauxhall Cross, and the CIA Station in Grosvenor Square.

Then, to maintain its cover, Crowbar began to listen to every word spoken in the Arab world. Also piped into the Scottish air base were the images the NRO was picking up from its Keyhole KH-11 satellites and the yield of the increasingly popular Predator drones, whose high-definition images went back to the US Army Central Command HQ at Tampa, Florida.

Some of the more penetrating minds at Edzell realised that Crowbar was ready and waiting for something, but they were not quite sure what.

SHORTLY BEFORE CHRISTMAS 2006, Alex Siebart recontacted Mr Lampong at his Indonesian company office to propose a general-cargo freighter registered in Liverpool as suitable for his purpose. It was owned by McKendrick Shipping, a small family business that had been in merchant marine· for a century. The company chief was the patriarch, Liam McKendrick; who also captained the freighter. The *Countess of Richmond* was 8,000 tons, flew the Red Ensign, and would be available for a fresh cargo by March 1.

Unbeknown to either Siebart or McKendrick, Mr Lampong contacted someone in Birmingham, an academic at Aston University, who drove to Liverpool and took over 100 pictures of the *Countess*. A week later Mr Lampong emailed back. He apologised for the delay, explaining that he had been up-country examining his sawmills, but said that the *Countess of Richmond* sounded exactly right. His friends in Singapore would be in touch with details of the cargo of limousines to be brought from the UK.

In truth the friends in Singapore were fanatical Malaysian Islamists. They had been put in funds out of a new account created in Bermuda by the late Mr Tewfik al-Qur, and they fully intended to recoup their investment by selling the limousines, once their purpose had been served.

MIKE MARTIN'S LEG was healing nicely.

He had noted when he read Izmat Khan's slim file after that first meeting in the orchard that the Afghan had never described how he had acquired the scar on the right thigh. Martin saw no reason to mention it either. But when Michael McDonald arrived back from Langley he expressed concern that Khan's questioners had never received an explanation of the scar. If the existence of the scar was known to anyone inside Al-Qaeda and Mike Martin bore no such scar, he would be 'blown'.

A Harley Street surgeon with full security clearance was brought to Castle Forbes. It was all done with a local anaesthetic. The surgeon made an incision and excised a quantity of tissue beneath and around it, as if something had come out and created a concavity in the flesh. His sutures were large, clumsy, unstraight stitches, that looked like work done in a field hospital. There were six stitches.

'You must understand,' he said as he left, 'this scar is supposed to be over fifteen years old. A surgeon would probably spot that it can't be, but a non-medic should accept it. Especially if it has twelve weeks to settle down.'

That was in early November. By Christmas, nature had done an excellent job. The puffiness and redness were gone.

'IF YOU ARE GOING where I think you are going, young Mike,' said Tamian Godfrey one day as they walked the hills on the estate, 'you will have to master the various levels of fanaticism that you will be likely to encounter. At the core is self-arrogated jihad or holy war, but different factions arrive at this via different routes. They are not all the same by a long chalk.'

'It seems to start with Wahhabism,' said Martin.

'In a way, but let us not forget that Wahhabism is the state religion of Saudi Arabia, and Osama bin Laden has declared war on the Saudi establishment for dealing with the West, permitting US troops on its holy soil. Muhammad al-Wahhab was an eighteenth-century preacher who came out of the bleakest and harshest part of the interior of the Saudi peninsula, and whose interpretation of the Koran was once the harshest and most intolerant of all. But he has been superseded. Other prophets have arisen, even more intolerant of anything not Islamic, and they preach the duty of attack and destruction.'

'So who do you think I'll be meeting in my travels, Tamian?' asked Martin.

The scholar found a stone the size of a chair and sat down. 'There are numerous groups but two are at the core. Do you know the word "Salafi"?'

'I have heard of it,' admitted Martin.

'These are the back-to-the-beginning brigade. They really want to restore the great golden age of Islam. Back to the first four Caliphates, over a thousand years ago. Wild beards; sandals; robes; Shariah—the rigorous legal code: rejection of modernity and the West that brought it.'

'You're describing the Taliban,' Martin said.

'Among others. These are the suicide bombers, the simple believers; obedient to their spiritual guides, and believing that all their deranged hatred is going to please the mighty Allah.'

'There are worse?' asked Martin, as they resumed their walk.

'Oh, yes,' said Tamian Godfrey. 'The ultras, the real ultras, I would designate with one word. *Takfir*. Whatever it meant in Wahhab's day, it has changed. The true Salafi will not smoke, gamble, dance, accept music in his presence, drink alcohol or consort with Western women. But the *takfiri* will adopt every single custom of the West in order to pass as fully westernised. They are the ones to watch. Many are well-educated, clean-shaven, groomed, dressed in suits. These are the ultimate, prepared to become chameleons against their faith, and to achieve mass murder for it.'

They reached the castle. 'Thank heavens,' she said. 'My old legs are giving out. Time for midday prayers. Mike, you will utter the call.'

JUST AFTER THE NEW YEAR, an email was sent from the office of Siebart & Abercrombie to Jakarta. The *Countess of Richmond*, with a full cargo of crated Jaguar saloon cars for Singapore, would sail from Liverpool on March 1. After unloading at Singapore she would proceed in ballast to North Borneo to take aboard the hold cargo of timber before turning for Surabaya for the deck cargo of crated silks.

THE CONSTRUCTION CREW working inside the Pasayten Wilderness was deeply grateful when the job was done by the end of January. To keep up the work rate the men had chosen to overnight on site, and until the central heating came on stream they had been extremely cold. But the bonus was large and tempting. They completed on schedule.

From the outside, the Cabin looked much the same but larger. In fact it had been transformed. For a staff of two officers the bedrooms would suffice; for the extra eight guards needed to accomplish a twenty-four-hour surveillance regime, an extra bunkhouse and a refectory had been added. The spacious sitting room was retained, but another extension housed a recreation room with pool table, library, plasma TV and DVD selection.

The third extension looked like the others, but its exterior walls were in fact only clad with split tree trunks; inside the walls were stressed concrete and impregnable. The penitentiary wing was reached from the guards' quarters through a single steel door with food-service hatch and spyhole. Beyond this door was a single but spacious room. It contained a steel bed frame deeply embedded in the concrete floor, and shelving integral to the concrete. There were carpets on the floor, however, and heat came from skirting-level grills that could not be opened.

The room also contained a door opposite the spyhole and this the detainee could open or close at will. It led to an exercise yard whose ultra-smooth walls were ten feet tall. No man could get anywhere near the top, nor was there anything that could be propped against the wall or stood on.

For sanitation there was a recess off the sitting room/bedroom containing a single hole in the floor for bodily functions and a shower with controls that were in the hands of the guards outside.

Because all the new materials had come in by helicopter, the only visible exterior addition was a landing pad under the snow. Otherwise the isolated Cabin stood in its 500-acre tract, surrounded by pines, larch and spruce.

When they came, the ten guardians of probably the country's most exclusive prison were two middle-grade CIA men from Langley and eight junior staffers who had completed their training and were hoping for an exciting first assignment. Instead they got a forest in the snow.

THE MILITARY TRIAL at Guantánamo Bay began at the end of January and was held in one of the larger rooms in the interrogation block, decked out now for its judicial purpose. The proceedings were low in tone and orderly.

There were eight detainees being considered for release as of 'no further danger' and seven were vociferous in stating their harmlessness. One, a Taliban commander, maintained a scornful silence. His case was heard last.

'Prisoner Khan, into what language would you like these proceedings to be translated?' asked the colonel presiding. He was flanked by a major and a female captain. All three were from the US Marines legal branch.

The prisoner was hauled to his feet by two Marine guards. He shrugged gently, then he let his gaze rest on the wall above the judges.

'This court is aware that the prisoner understands Arabic, so that is the language the court chooses. Any objection, counsellor?'

The question was to the civilian defending attorney, who shook his head.

The Arabic interpreter positioned himself close to the Marine guards. The prosecuting counsel began and the terp translated.

The prosecutor did not take long. He stressed five years of virtual silence, a refusal to name collaborators in the war of terror against the USA and the fact the prisoner had been caught up in a jail uprising in which an American had been brutally beaten to death. Then he sat down. He had no doubt of the outcome. The man would remain in custody for years to come.

The defence attorney took a little longer. The prisoner had been fighting in an all-Afghan civil war at the time of the 9/11 atrocity, and had nothing to do with Al-Qaeda. As for Mullah Omar and the Afghan government sheltering Bin Laden and his cronies, that was a dictatorship of which Mr Khan was a serving officer but not a part.

'I must urge this court to admit the reality,' he wound up. 'If this man is a problem, he is an Afghan problem. There is a new, democratically elected government there now. We should ship him back for them to deal with.'

The three judges withdrew. They were away for thirty minutes. When they returned the captain was pink with anger. She still could not believe what she had heard. Only the colonel and the major had had the interview with the Chairman, Joint Chiefs of Staff, and knew their orders.

'Prisoner Khan, be upstanding. This court has been made aware that the government of President Karzai has agreed that if you are returned to your native land you will be sentenced to life imprisonment over there. That being so, this court intends to burden the American taxpayer with you no longer. Arrangements will therefore be made to ship you back to Kabul. You will return as you arrived—in shackles. That is all. Court rises.'

AS THE NEW YEAR holiday slipped into memory, a small protocol team that had been set up the previous summer in the British Foreign and Commonwealth Office in King Charles Street, just off Whitehall, resumed its task.

This was to coordinate with the Americans the details of the forthcoming 2007 G8 conference. The 2005 meeting of the governments of eight of the richest states in the world had been at Gleneagles Hotel, Perthshire, and had been a success up to a point. The point, however, was the crowds of protesters. At Gleneagles, the landscape had had to be disfigured by miles of chain-link fencing to create a complete cordon sanitaire round the estate.

The idea out of the White House, who would be hosting 2007, was acclaimed as simple, elegant, brilliant. A location sumptuous but isolated, unreachable, secure in total control. It was the mass of detail that concerned the protocol team—that and the advancement to mid-April. The British team accepted what had been agreed and got on with their task.

FAR TO THE SOUTHEAST, two huge USAF Starlifters came out of the sunset and began to drop towards the desert air base of Thumrait in Oman.

In their cavernous hulls the two aerial juggernauts contained an entire military unit. One had the living accommodation: everything from flat-pack, skilled-assembly hutments, generators and air conditioning to refrigeration plants for the fifteen-person technical team. The other carried two pilotless reconnaissance drones called Predator, their guidance and imaging kit and the men and women who would operate them.

A week later the aerial surveillance unit was set up, and patched through to Tampa, Florida, and Edzell, Scotland. On the far side of the air base the bungalows were up, the air conditioners hummed, the latrines were dug and under their hooped shelters the two Predators waited. Some day they would be told what they had to watch, photograph and transmit back. Until then men and machines waited in the heat.

MIKE MARTIN'S final briefing took three days and was so important that Marek Gumienny flew over in the Agency's Grumman. Steve Hill came up from London and the two spymasters joined their executive officers.

The point of the briefing was to show Mike Martin every piece of information in the possession of Western agencies concerning the faces he might meet. Over forty nations' agencies were pouring their discoveries into central data bases. Governments across the planet were sharing information on terrorists of the ultra-aggressive Islamist creed.

Martin stared at them all as they flashed up on the high-definition plasma screen. Some were face-on portraits taken in a police station; others were snatched with long lenses on the street. Possible variants were shown: with or without beard; in Arab or Western dress; long hair or shaven. There were mullahs and imams from extremist mosques; youths believed to be simple message-carriers; faces of those known to help with funds.

And there were the big players, the ones who had access to the very top, such as Saud Hamud al-Utaibi, new head of AQ in Saudi Arabia. Some were blanks, the outline of a head, black on white. These included the AQ chief from Southeast Asia, probably the man behind the latest bombings of tourist resorts in the Far East. And, surprisingly, the AQ chief for the United Kingdom.

'We knew who it was until six months ago,' said Phillips. 'But he quit just in time. He's back in Pakistan now. The ISI will get him eventually . . .'

'And ship him up to us in Bagram,' grunted Gumienny. They all knew that inside the US base north of Kabul was a very special facility where everyone 'sang' eventually.

'You will certainly seek out this one,' said Steve Hill as an elderly man, looking mild and courtly flashed on the screen, followed by a snatched shot on a quayside with bright blue water in the background.

They broke, ate, resumed, slept and started again. Only when the house-keeper was in the room with trays of food did Phillips switch off the TV screen. Tamian Godfrey and Najib Qureshi stayed in their rooms or walked the hills together. Finally it was over.

'Tomorrow we fly,' said Marek Gumienny.

Mrs Godfrey and the Afghan analyst came to the helipad to see him off.

'Take care of yourself, Mike,' said the Koranic scholar. 'Damn, stupid me, I'm choking up. God go with you, lad.'

'And if all else fails, may Allah keep you in his care,' said Qureshi.

NIGHT COMES FAST in the tropics and on the southeast coast of Cuba it was pitch black by seven. That was when four CIA men from 'special tasks' entered the cell of Izmat Khan. He rose, sensing something wrong. The regular guards had quit the corridor outside his cell half an hour earlier. That had never happened before.

The four men were not brutal but they were not taking no for an answer either. Two grabbed the Afghan, one round the torso pinioning his arms, the other round the thighs. The chloroform pad took only twenty seconds to work. The writhing stopped and the prisoner went limp.

He was put onto a trolley, photographed, then covered with a cotton sheet and wheeled outside. The crate was waiting. The cell block was devoid of guards. No one saw a thing. Seconds later, the Afghan was inside the crate.

From the outside it was just a large timber box such as are used for general freight purposes. But in the roof there was a small removable panel to replenish fresh air, though that would not be taken down until the crate was safely airborne. And inside there were two comfortable armchairs welded to the floor and a low-wattage amber light.

Izmat Khan was placed in one of the chairs and secured with restrainer straps. He was still asleep. Satisfied, the fifth CIA man, the one who would travel in the crate, nodded to his colleagues and the end of it was closed off. A forklift hoisted the crate a foot off the ground and ran it out to the airfield, where the Hercules AC-130 Talon was waiting.

Unexplained flights into and out of Guantánamo Bay are regular as clock-work; the tower gave a quick 'clear take-off' in response to the request and the Hercules was airborne for McChord Base, Washington State.

An hour later, a car drove up to the Camp Echo block and another small group got out. Inside the empty cell, a man was garbed in orange jumpsuit and soft slippers. Using the Polaroid print of the unconscious Afghan, a few minor adjustments were made to the beard and hair of the replacement. Then there were a few gruff farewells and the party left, locking the cell door behind them.

Twenty minutes later the guards were back, mystified but incurious. They checked the familiar figure of their prize prisoner and waited for the dawn.

THE MORNING SUN was tipping the pinnacles of the Cascades when the AC-130 drifted down to its home base at McChord. The base commander had been told that this was a CIA shipment, a last consignment for their new research facility up in the forests of the Wilderness. The Chinook stood by.

In flight the Afghan had come round. The roof panel was open and the air inside the hull of the Hercules fully pressurised and fresh. The escort smiled encouragingly and offered food and drink. The prisoner settled for a soda through a straw. He once bowed his face and murmured his prayers. Otherwise he was, as his escort would later report to Marek Gumienny, like a pussycat. No trouble at all.

Just before touchdown the roof panel was replaced and the waiting fork-lift driver had not the slightest suspicion he was not lifting an ordinary load of freight from the rear ramp of the Hercules across to the Chinook.

Given that it was mid-February, they were lucky with the weather. The skies were clear but freezing cold as the Chinook landed on the helipad outside the Cabin. The rear doors opened and the snatch team removed the back wall of the container.

The prisoner's hands and feet were shackled before the restraining straps were removed. Then he was bidden to rise and shuffled down the ramp into the snow. The ten resident staff stood in a semicircle, guns pointing. The Taliban commander was walked across the helipad, through the cabin and into his quarters.

Six guards stood round him in his cell as the manacles were removed. They left the cell backwards and the steel door slammed shut. He looked around him. They had told him he would return to Afghanistan. They had lied again.

IT WAS MIDMORNING and the sun was blazing down on the Cuban landscape when another Hercules rolled in to land.

In the prison block, a cell door swung open.

'Prisoner Khan, stand up. Face the wall. Adopt the position.'

The belt went round the midriff; chains fell from it to the ankle cuffs and another set to the wrists, held together and in front of the waist. The position permitted a shuffling walk, no more.

There was a short walk to a waiting truck that had a mesh screen between the prisoners and the driver, and black windows.

When he was ordered out at the airfield, the prisoner shook his shaggy head and blinked in the harsh sunlight. As his eyes grew accustomed to the glare, he gazed around and saw the waiting Hercules and a group of American officers staring at him. One of them advanced and beckoned. Meekly he followed him across the scorching tarmac. He turned to have one last look at the place that had held him for five miserable years. Then he shuffled up into the hull of the aircraft.

In a room one flight below the operations deck of the control tower two men stood and watched. 'There goes your man,' said Marek Gumienny.

'If they ever find out who he really is,' replied Steve Hill, 'may Allah have mercy on him.'

CHAPTER SIX

It was a long and wearisome flight. The Hercules flew via American bases in the Azores and Ramstein, Germany, and it wasn't until late the following afternoon that the C-130 dropped towards Bagram.

The flight crew had changed twice, but the escort squad had stayed the course, reading, playing cards, catnapping as the four sets of whirling blades drove them east. The prisoner remained shackled. He too slept as best he could.

As the Hercules taxied towards the huge hangars that dominate the American zone of Bagram Base the US major heading the escort unit looked at the the reception party and was gratified to see that the Afghans were taking no chances. Apart from the prison van, there were twenty Afghan Special Forces soldiers headed by the unit commander, Brigadier Yusuf.

The major trotted down the ramp to clear the paperwork before handing over his charge. Then he nodded to his colleagues. They unchained the prisoner from the fuselage rib and led him out into a freezing Afghan winter.

The Afghan troops enveloped the shivering man, dragged him to the prison van and threw him inside. The door slammed shut.

The US major threw up a salute to the brigadier. 'You take good care of him, sir,' he said. 'That is one very hard man.'

'Do not worry, Major,' said the Afghan officer. 'He is going to Pul-i-Charki jail for the rest of his days.'

Minutes later the prison van drove off, followed by the escort truck. Pul-i-Charki is a fearsome, brooding block of a place to the east of Kabul. During the civil war, several tens of thousands of prisoners failed to leave alive. On this occasion, the prison van never made it, because once darkness had fallen the van and the truck became separated in what would later be officially described as an unfortunate accident. The van proceeded alone.

Ten miles after the loss of the military escort, a pick-up truck took up station behind the van. When it flashed its lights, the van driver pulled off the road behind a clump of trees and the 'escape' took place.

The prisoner had already changed into the warm grey woollen *shalwar kameez* and boots provided. Just before the change-over he had wound round his head the feared black turban of the Talib.

Brigadier Yusuf now took charge.

There were four bodies in the open back of the utility, all fresh from the city mortuary. Two were bearded, and had been dressed in Talib clothing. They were construction workers who had been atop some scaffolding that collapsed and killed them both. The other two had been in car accidents. They were smooth-shaven and in prison service uniform.

The prison officers would be found with handguns drawn, but dead; the bullets were fired into the bodies there and then. The ambushing Taliban were scattered at the roadside, also shot with slugs from the pistols of the guards. The van door was savaged with a pickaxe and left swinging open. That was how the van would be found sometime the next day.

When the theatre had been accomplished, Brigadier Yusuf took the front seat of the pick-up beside the driver. The former prisoner climbed in the back with the two Special Forces men he had brought with him. All three wrapped the trailing end of their turbans round their faces against the cold.

The pick-up skirted Kabul City and cut across country until it intercepted the highway south to Ghazni and Kandahar. There waited, as each night, the long column of what all Asia knows as the 'jingly' trucks.

They all seem to have been built a century ago. They snort and snarl along every road of the Middle and Far East, emitting columns of black smoke. But they are the commercial lifeblood of a continent, carrying an amazing variety of supplies to the most isolated settlements.

The British named them jingly trucks many years ago. They are carefully painted on every available surface with images from religion and history, and caparisoned with ribbons, tinsel and even bells. Hence, they jingle.

The line on the highway south of Kabul contained several hundred, their drivers sleeping in their cabs, waiting for the dawn. The pick-up slewed to a halt. Mike Martin jumped from the back and walked to the cab. The driver had his face hidden by a *shemagh* of checked cloth.

On the other side, Brigadier Yusuf nodded but said nothing. End of the road. Start of the journey. As he turned away he heard the driver speak.

'Good luck, boss.'

That term again. Only the SAS called their officers 'boss'. Since the installation of President Hamid Karzai, the Afghan Special Forces had been created and trained at his request by the SAS.

Martin turned away and started to walk down the line of trucks. Behind him the pick-up headed back to Kabul. In the cab the SAS sergeant made a cellphone call to a number in Kabul. It was taken by the Head of Station. The sergeant uttered two words and terminated.

The SIS man also made a call on a secure line. It was 3.30 a.m. in Kabul, 11 p.m. in Scotland when a one-line message came up on one of the screens: 'Crowbar is running.'

On a freezing, pitted highway Mike Martin permitted himself one last glance behind him. The red lights of the pick-up were gone. He turned and walked on. Within 100 yards he had become the Afghan.

He knew what he was looking for but he was 100 trucks down the line before he found it. A licence plate from Karachi, Pakistan. The driver of such a truck would be unlikely to be Pashtun and so would not notice the imperfect command of Pashto. He would be probably be a Baluchi heading home to Pakistan's Baluchistan Province.

It was too early for the drivers to be rising, and unwise to rouse the driver of the chosen truck; Martin needed him in a generous mood. For two hours he curled up beneath the truck and shivered.

Around six there was a stirring and a hint of pink in the east. By the roadside someone started a fire and set a billy on it to boil. In central Asia, much of life is lived in the tea-house, the *chaikhana*, which can be created even with just a fire, a brew of tea and a group of men. Stowing his Talib turban in his bag, Martin walked over to the fire and warmed his hands.

The tea-brewer was Pashtun but taciturn, which suited Martin fine. With a fistful of his Afghanis he bought a steaming cup and sipped gratefully. Minutes later the Baluchi clambered sleepily out of his cab and came over for tea.

Dawn rose. Some of the trucks began to kick into life with plumes of black smoke. The Baluchi walked back to his cab. Martin followed.

'Greetings, my brother.'

The Baluchi responded, but with some suspicion.

'Do you by any chance head south to the border and Spin Boldak?'

If the man was heading back to Pakistan, the small border town south of Kandahar would be where he would cross.

'If it please Allah,' said the Baluchi.

'Then in the name of the all-merciful would you let a poor man trying to get home to his family ride with you?'

The Baluchi thought. His cousin normally came with him on these long hauls, but he was sick. This trip he had driven alone, and it was exhausting.

'Can you drive one of these?' he asked.

'In truth, I am a driver of many years.'

They drove south, listening to eastern pop music on the old plastic radio propped above the dash. The day wore on and they chugged on towards Kandahar. On the road they paused for tea and food, and filled the tank. Martin helped with the cost and the Baluchi became much friendlier.

There was an overnight stop north of Kandahar, for the Baluchi would not drive in the darkness. This was Zabol Province, wild country and peopled by wild men. It was safer to drive in daylight.

South of Kandahar he 'spelled' the Baluchi at the wheel, and it was still midafternoon when they came to Spin Boldak; Martin claimed he lived in the northern outskirts, bade his host a grateful farewell and was dropped off some miles before the border checkpoint.

Because the Baluchi spoke no Pashto he had kept his radio tuned to a pop station and never heard the news. At the border the queues were longer even than usual and when he finally rolled to the barrier he was shown a picture. A black-bearded Talib face stared at him.

He was an honest and hard-working man. He wanted to get home to his wife and four children. Life was hard enough. Why spend days, even weeks, in an Afghan jail trying to explain that he had been totally ignorant?

'By the Prophet, I have never seen him,' he swore, and they let him go.

Never again, he thought, as he trundled south on the Quetta road.

The staged murder scene had been discovered by patrols sent up the Bagram road when the prison van failed to arrive at the jail. The separation of the van from its military escort was put down to incompetence. But the freeing of the returnee from Guantánamo Bay was clearly by a criminal gang of Taliban leftovers. A hunt was put out for them, and there was nothing the CIA and SIS Heads of Station could do.

Though he knew nothing of this, Martin was determined to take no chances at border crossings. In the hills above Spin Boldak he hunkered down and waited for night to fall.

Before midnight, Martin stole quietly through the town and into Pakistan. Sunrise found him ten miles down the Quetta road. Here he found a *chaikhana* and waited until a truck that accepted paying passengers came along and gave him passage to Quetta. At last the black Talib turban became an asset and not a liability. So back on it went.

If Peshawar is a fairly extreme Islamist city, Quetta is more so, only exceeded in its ferocity of sympathy for Al-Qaeda by Miram Shah. These are within the Northwest Frontier Provinces, where local tribal law prevails. Though technically across the border from Afghanistan, the Pashtun people still abound, and a Talib turban is the mark of a man to be reckoned with.

The main highway south from Quetta heads for Karachi, but despite this Martin had been advised to take the smaller road southwest to the port of Gwador, which lies almost on the Iranian border at the extreme western end of Baluchistan. Once a sleepy fishing village, it has developed into a major harbour and entrepôt, contentedly devoted to smuggling, especially opium.

In Quetta, Martin found another Baluchi truck driver heading for Gwador, and he had also learned that there was a 5 million Afghani price on his head—but only in Afghanistan.

It was on the third morning after he heard the words 'good luck, boss' that he dropped off the truck and settled gratefully for a cup of sweet green tea at a pavement café. He was expected, but not by locals.

THERE WERE FOUR mosques in Gwador, but the Pakistani ISI had flagged the fourth and smallest as a hotbed of fundamentalist agitation. It had been created and was run by Imam Abdullah Halabi.

He knew his congregation well and from his raised chair as he led the prayers he could spot a visiting newcomer at a glance.

Later, before the black-bearded stranger could replace his sandals and lose himself in the crowds of the street, the imam tugged at his sleeve.

'Greeting of our all-merciful Lord be upon you,' he murmured in Arabic.

'And upon you, imam,' said the stranger.

He too spoke Arabic, but the imam noted the Pashto accent.

'My friends and I are adjourning to the *madafa*,' he said. 'Would you join us and take tea?'

The Pashtun considered for a second, then gravely inclined his head. Most mosques have a *madafa* attached, a more relaxed and private social club for prayers, gossip and religious schooling.

'I am Imam Halabi. Does our new worshipper have a name?'

Without hesitation, Martin gave the first name of the Afghan President and the second of the Special Forces brigadier. 'I am Hamid Yusuf,' he said.

'Then welcome, Hamid Yusuf,' said the imam. 'I notice you dare to wear the turban of the Taliban. Were you one of them?'

'Since I joined Mullah Omar at Kandahar in 1995.'

There were a dozen in the *madafa*, a shabby shack behind the mosque. Tea was served. Martin noticed one of the men staring at him. The same man then excitedly drew the imam aside and whispered frantically.

He would not, he explained, ever dream of watching television and its filthy images, but he had passed a shop with a set in the window. 'I am sure it is the man,' he hissed. 'He escaped from Kabul but three days ago.'

Martin did not understand Urdu, but he knew he was being talked about. The imam may have deplored all things Western and modern, but like most he found the cellphone damnably convenient. He asked three friends to engage the stranger in talk and not to let him leave. Then he retired to his own humble quarters and made several calls. He returned much impressed.

To have been a Talib from the start, lost his entire family and clan to the Americans, commanded half the northern front, broken open the armoury at Qala-i-Jangi, survived five years in the American hellhole, escaped the clutches of the Kabul regime—this man was a hero.

Imam Halabi may have been a Pakistani, but he loathed the government of Islamabad for its collaboration with America. The 5 million Afghani reward did not tempt him in the slightest.

He returned to the hall and beckoned the stranger to him. 'I know who you are,' he hissed. 'You are the one they call the Afghan. You are safe with me but not in Gwador. Agents of the ISI are everywhere and you have a price on your head. Where are your lodgings?'

'I have none. I have only just arrived from the north,' said Martin.

'I know where you have come from; it is all over the news. You must stay here, but not for long. Somehow you must leave Gwador. You will need papers, a new identity, safe passage away from here. Perhaps I know a man.'

He sent a small boy from his *madrasah* running to the harbour. The boat he sought was not in port. It arrived twenty-four hours later. The boy was still patiently waiting at the berth where it always docked.

FAISAL BIN SELIM was a Qatari by birth. He had been born to poor fisherfolk in a shack on the edge of a muddy creek near a village that eventually became the bustling capital of Doha. In his boyhood he had known poverty and automatic deference to the lordly white-skinned foreigners. But Bin Selim had determined he would rise in the world. The path he chose was what he knew: the sea. And he made himself prosperous by smuggling.

In his travels he saw many things that he came to admire: fine cloths and tapestries, Islamic art, ancient Korans and the beauty of the great mosques. And he saw other things he came to despise: rich Westerners, porcine faces lobster-pink in the sun, disgusting women in tiny bikinis, drunken slobs. The fact that the rulers of the Gulf States also benefited from money that simply poured in black streams from the desert did not escape him. As they also flaunted their Western habits, he despised them too.

By his mid-forties, twenty years before a small Baluchi boy waited for him at the dock in Gwador, Faisal bin Selim had saved enough money to buy a superb trading dhow called *Rasha*, the Pearl.

To the world he remained the courteous, frugally living, fastidious, devout master and owner of the *Rasha*, plying his trade along the entire Gulf coast and round into the Arabian Sea. But he had become a fervent Wahhabi. He did not seek trouble, but if a True Believer sought his help, he would do what he could.

He had come to the attention of Western security forces because a captured Saudi AQ activist let slip that secret messages destined for Bin Laden would occasionally leave the Saudi peninsula by boat. The emissary would be deposited on the Baluchi coast, whence he would take his message north to the unknown caves of Waziristan where the Sheikh resided. The boat was the *Rasha*. With the agreement of the ISI, the vessel was not intercepted, just watched.

Faisal bin Selim arrived in Gwador with a cargo of white goods—refrigerators, washing machines and televisions—from Dubai. He listened gravely to the small boy waiting for him, nodded, and two hours later, with his cargo safely inland without disturbing Pakistani Customs, left the *Rasha* in the charge of his Omani deck hand and walked sedately through Gwador to the mosque.

From years of trading with Pakistan, the courtly Arab spoke good Urdu and he and the imam conversed in that language. He sipped his tea, took sweet cakes and wiped his fingers on a small cambric handkerchief. All the while, he nodded and glanced at the Afghan. When he heard of the break-out from the prison van he smiled in approval. Then he broke into Arabic.

'And you wish to leave Pakistan, my brother?'

'There is no place for me here,' said Martin. 'The imam is right. The secret police will find me and hand me back to the dogs of Kabul. I will end my life before that.'

'Such a pity,' murmured the Qatari. 'So far . . . such a life. And if I take you to the Gulf States, what will you do?'

'I will try to find other True Believers and offer what I can.'

'And what would that be? What can you do?'

'I can fight. And I am prepared to die in Allah's holy war.'

The elderly captain thought for a while. 'The loading of my cargo of carpets takes place at dawn,' he said. 'It will take several hours. Then I shall depart, sails down. I shall cruise close past the end of the harbour mole. If a man were to leap from the concrete to the deck, no one would notice.'

After the ritual salutations he left. In the darkness Martin was led by the boy to the dock. Here he studied the *Rasha* so that he would recognise her in the morning. She came past the mole just before eleven. The gap was eight feet and Martin made it with inches to spare after a short run.

Faisal bin Selim greeted Martin with a gentle smile. He offered his guest fresh water to wash his hands and delicious dates from Muscat.

At noon the elderly man spread two mats on the broad coaming about the cargo hold. Side by side the two men knelt for the midday prayers. For Martin it was the first occasion of prayer other than in a crowd where a single voice can be drowned by all the others. He was word perfect.

THE FIRST OF THE TWO Predators had taken off from Thumrait forty-eight hours earlier. Flying in rotation, the UAVs kept up a constant patrol 20,000 feet above their surveillance area, out of sight, inaudible, radar-immune.

When an agent is way out in the cold, on a 'black' and dangerous job, his controllers at home are avid for some sign that he is still alive, still at liberty, still functioning. This indication may come from the agent himself, by a phone call, a message in the small ads column of a paper or even a chalk mark on a wall. After days of silence, controllers become very twitchy waiting for some 'sign of life', as it is called.

It was midday in Thumrait; breakfast time in Scotland; the wee small hours in Tampa. At Edzell Air Base there was a roar from the terminal operators in the ops room as they saw, clear as crystal, the Afghan saying his prayers on the deck of the *Rasha*. Seconds later Steve Hill took a call at his breakfast table and gave his wife a passionate and unexpected kiss. Two minutes later Marek Gumienny took a call in bed in Old Alexandria. He woke up, listened, smiled, murmured 'way to go' and went back to sleep. The Afghan was still on course.

WITH A GOOD WIND from the south, the *Rasha* hoisted sail and closed down her engine. The rumbling below was replaced by the lapping of the water under the bow, the sigh of the wind in the sail, the creak of block and tackle.

The dhow, shadowed by the invisible Predator four miles above her, crept along the coast of southern Iran and into the Gulf of Oman. Here she bore away to starboard, reset her sail as the wind took her full astern and headed for the narrow gap between Iran and Arabia called the Strait of Hormuz.

Through this gap, a constant stream of mighty oil tankers went past. Smaller boats like the dhow stayed closer to the shore to allow the leviathans the freedom of the deep channel.

The *Rasha*, being in no hurry, spent one night hove-to amid the islands east of the Omani naval base at Kumzar. Sitting on the raised poop deck in the balmy night, still clearly visible on a plasma screen in a Scottish air base, Martin caught sight of two 'cigarette boats' by the light of the moon and heard the roar of their huge outboards as they sped out of Omani waters with their illegal cargo of cheap cigarettes.

Faisal bin Selim smiled tolerantly. He too was a smuggler, but rather more dignified than these Gulf vagabonds he could hear in the distance.

'And when I have brought you to Arabia, my friend, what will you do?'

'I do not know,' admitted the Afghan. 'I know only that I am a dead man in my own country; Pakistan is closed to me for they are running-dogs of the Yankees. I hope to find other True Believers and ask to fight with them.'

'Fight? But there is no fighting in the United Arab Emirates. They too are wholly allied to the West. The interior is Saudi Arabia, where you will be found immediately and sent back. So . . .'

The Afghan shrugged. 'I ask only to serve Allah. I have lived my life. I will leave my fate in His care.'

'And you say you are prepared to die for Him,' said the courtly Qatari.

'If I can die *shahid*, in the service of His jihad, of course,' he replied.

The dhow master considered for a while. 'You are wearing the clothes of Afghanistan,' he said at last. 'You will be spotted in minutes. Wait.'

He went below and came back with a freshly laundered dishdash, the white cotton robe that falls from shoulders to ankles in unbroken line.

'Change,' he ordered. 'Drop the *shalwar kameez* and the Talib turban over the side.'

When Martin had changed, bin Selim handed him a new headdress, the red-flecked *keffiyeh* and black cord circlet of a Gulf Arab.

'Better,' said the old man, when his guest had completed the transformation. 'You will pass for a Gulf Arab, save when you speak. But there is a colony of Afghans in the area of Jeddah. Say that is where you come from, and strangers will believe you. Now let us sleep. We rise at dawn for the last day of cruising.'

The Predator saw them weigh anchor and leave the islands, sailing gently round the rocky tip of Al-Ghanam and turning southwest down the coast of the United Arab Emirates.

There are seven emirates in the UAE but only the biggest and richest— Dubai, Abu Dhabi and Sharjah—spring to mind. The other four are much smaller and poorer. Two of them, Ajman and Umm-al-Qaiwain, are cheek by jowl alongside oil-rich Dubai. Fujairah lies on the other side of the peninsula, facing east onto the Gulf of Oman. The seventh, Ras-al-Khaimah, lies on the same coast as Dubai but far up along the shore towards the Strait of Hormuz. Dirt poor and ultra-traditional, it has eagerly accepted the gifts of Saudi Arabia, including heavily financed mosques and schools. Ras-al-K, as Westerners know it, is the local home of fundamentalism and sympathy for Al-Qaeda. On the port side of the slowly cruising dhow, it would be the first to be reached. This occurred at sundown.

'You have no papers,' said the captain to his guest, 'and I cannot provide them. No matter, they are a Western impertinence. More important is money. Take these.' He thrust a wad of UAE dirhams into Martin's hand.

They were cruising in the fading light past the town, a mile away on the shore. The first lights began to flicker among the buildings.

'I will put you ashore further down the coast,' said Bin Selim. 'You will find the coast road and walk back. I know a small guesthouse in the Old Town. It is cheap, clean and discreet. Take lodgings there. Do not go out. You will be safe and, *inshallah*, I may have friends who can help you.'

It was fully dark when the *Rasha* slipped towards the shore. Despite the darkness, the thermal imager of the Predator at 20,000 feet saw the agile figure leap from the dhow to the jetty of a hotel, and the trader reverse her engine and pull back to the deeper water. The image went to the ops room at Edzell Air Base, and the Predator was instructed to stay with the figure walking along the coast road back towards Ras-al-K.

It was a five-mile hike but Martin reached the Old Town section around midnight. He asked twice and was directed to the guesthouse.

The proprietor was surly and suspicious until Martin mentioned Faisal bin Selim. That and the sight of a wad of dirhams cleared the air. Martin was bidden to enter and shown to a simple room. The room-keeper invited him to join him for a cup of tea before turning in.

Over tea, Martin explained that he was from Jeddah, but of Pashtun extraction. With his full black beard and the repeated references to Allah of the truly devout, Martin convinced his host that he also was a True Believer. They parted with mutual wishes for a good night's sleep.

THE DHOW MASTER sailed on through the night. His destination was the harbour known as the Creek in the heart of Dubai. Here the trading dhows are berthed side by side and the tourists come to stare at 'old Arabia'.

Bin Selim hailed a taxi and instructed it to take him three miles up the coast to the Sultanate of Ajman, smallest and second-poorest of the seven. There he dismissed the taxi, ducked into a covered souk and lost himself to any following 'tail'—should there have been one.

There was not. The Predator was concentrating on a guesthouse in the heart of Ras-al-Khaimah. The dhow master slipped from the souk into a small mosque and made a request of the imam. A boy was sent scurrying through the town and came back with a young man who was a student in the local technical college. He was also a graduate of the Darunta training camp run by Al-Qaeda outside Jalalabad until 2001.

The old man whispered in the ear of the younger, who nodded and thanked him. Then the dhow captain went back through the covered market, emerged, hailed a taxi and returned to his freighter in the Creek. He had done all he could. It was up to the younger men now. *Inshallah*.

THAT SAME MORNING, the *Countess of Richmond* eased out of the Mersey estuary and into the Irish Sea. Captain McKendrick had the conn and took his freighter south. In time she would clear the Irish Sea and Lizard Point to meet the Channel. Then her course lay south past Portugal, through the Mediterranean to the Suez Canal and thence to the Indian Ocean.

Below his decks, as the cold March seas flew up over the bow of the *Countess*, was a cargo of carefully protected and crated Jaguar saloons, destined for the showrooms of Singapore.

FOUR DAYS PASSED before the Afghan received his visitors. Following his instructions he had not gone out, though he had taken the air in the courtyard at the rear of the house, screened from the streets by tall double gates. Here various delivery vans came and went.

While in the courtyard he was seen by the Predator, and his controllers in Scotland noted his change of dress.

His visitors, when they came, did not come to deliver food, drink or laundry, but to make a collection. They backed the van close to the building's rear door, and while the driver stayed at the wheel the other three entered the house. They went swiftly to the appropriate door and went in without knocking. The seated figure, reading his Koran, rose to find himself facing a gun in the grip of a man trained in Afghanistan. All three were hooded.

Martin knew enough of fighting men to recognise that his visitors knew their business. The hood went over his head; his hands came behind his back and the plastic cuffs went on. Then he was marched out of his door, down the tiled corridor and into the back of a van. He lay on his side, heard the door slam, felt the van lurch out of the gate and into the street.

The Predator saw it, but the controllers thought it was another laundry delivery. In minutes the van was out of sight.

It took three days for the watchers at Edzell to realise that their man no longer appeared daily in the courtyard to give the sign of life. He had disappeared. And they had no idea which of the several vans had taken him.

In fact the van had not gone far. The hinterland behind the port and city of Ras-al-K is a wild and rocky desert rising to the mountains of Rus-al-Jibal. Nothing can live here but goats and salamanders.

The snatch squad took one of the many tracks leading up into the hills. Five miles up the track the van stopped and the leader, the one with the handgun, took powerful binoculars and surveyed the valley and the coast. When he was satisfied they weren't being tailed, the van turned and went back down the hills. Its real destination was a villa standing in a walled compound in the outer suburbs of the town. With the gates relocked, the van reversed up to an open door and Martin was marched back out and down another tiled passage.

The plastic ties came off his wrists and a cool metal shackle went onto the left one. When his hood came off, it was the kidnappers who had their heads covered. They withdrew backwards and the door slammed shut.

The cell was a windowless ground-floor room. A single bulb in the ceiling, protected by a wire frame, gave out a subdued but adequate light.

Martin's left wrist was in a stainless-steel shackle that linked to a chain and the chain went to a wall bracket. There was a camp bed and just enough slack in his chain to allow him to lie on it to sleep. Also in reach, but in different directions, were an upright chair and a chemical toilet. But he could not begin to reach the door through which his interrogators would enter, and a spyhole in the door meant they could check on him any time.

At Castle Forbes there had been lengthy and passionate discussions about one problem: should he carry any tracking device on him? There are now tracker transmitters so tiny they can be injected under the skin. Warmed by the blood, they need no power source. But there are ultrasensitive detectors that can spot them. Eventually the decision was: no planted bleeper. No signal-sender.

The kidnappers came for him an hour later. They were hooded again.

The body search was thorough. His clothes went first, and were taken away for searching in another room. A scanner was run over his naked body, inch by inch. At the mouth, it gave the bleep that meant it had discovered a non-body-tissue substance. They forced his mouth open and examined every filling. Then they returned his clothing and prepared to leave.

'I left my Koran at the guesthouse,' said the prisoner. 'I have no watch or mat, but it must be the hour of prayer.'

The leader stared at him through the eyeholes. He said nothing, but two minutes later he returned with mat and Koran. Martin thanked him gravely.

Food and water were brought regularly. Each time he was waved back with the handgun as the tray was deposited where he could reach it when they had done. The chemical lavatory was replaced in the same way.

It was three days before his interrogation began. For this he was masked, and led down two corridors. When his mask was removed he was astonished. The man in front of him, sitting calmly behind a carved refectory table, for all the world like a potential employer interviewing an applicant, was youthful, elegant, civilised, urbane and uncovered.

'I see no point in masks,' he said in perfect Gulf Arabic, 'nor silly names. Mine, by the way, is Dr Al-Khattab. There is no mystery here. If I am satisfied you are who you say you are, you will be welcome to join us. If not, then I am afraid you will be killed at once. So let us not pretend, Mr Izmat Khan. Are you really the one they call the Afghan?'

Martin stared back at the smiling Arab. He recalled the warnings of Tamian Godfrey. Never mind the wild-bearded screamers; watch out for the one who will be smooth-shaven, who will smoke, drink, consort with girls, pass for one of us. Wholly Westernised. A human chameleon, hiding the hatred. Totally deadly. There was a word . . . *takfiri*.

'There are many Afghans,' he said. 'Who calls me the Afghan?'

'Ah, you have been incommunicado for five years. After Qala-i-Jangi word spread about you. Some of our people have been released from Camp Delta. They spoke highly of you. They claim you never broke. True?'

'They asked me about myself. I told them that.'

'But you never denounced others? That is what the others say of you.'

'They wiped out my family. Most of me died then. How do you punish a man who is dead?'

'A good answer, my friend. So, let us talk about Guantánamo.'

Martin had been briefed hour after hour about what had happened on the Cuban peninsula. The arrival on January 14, 2002, hungry, thirsty, soiled, blindfolded, shackled so tightly the hands were numb for weeks. Beards and heads shaved, clothed in orange coveralls, stumbling in the darkness of the hoods . . .

Dr Al-Khattab took copious notes, writing on yellow legal notepaper with an old-fashioned fountain pen. Whenever he paused, he contemplated his prisoner with a gentle smile.

In the late afternoon he offered a photograph. 'Do you know this man?' he asked. 'Did you ever see him?'

Martin shook his head. The face in the photo was General Geoffrey D. Miller, successor as camp commandant to General Rick Baccus. The latter had sat in on interrogations but General Miller left it to the CIA teams.

'Quite right,' said Al-Khattab. 'He saw you, according to one of our released friends, but you were always hooded as a punishment for non-cooperation. And when did the conditions start to improve?'

They talked until sundown, then the Arab rose.

'I have much to check on,' he said. 'If you are telling the truth, we will continue in a few days. If not, I'm afraid I shall have to issue Suleiman, one of the guards, with the appropriate instructions.'

Martin was led back to his cell. His interrogator issued rapid orders to the guard team and left.

DRIVING A MODEST rented car, Dr Al-Khattab returned to the Hilton Hotel in Ras-al-Khaimah town. He spent the night and left the next day. He was wearing a well-cut cream tropical suit. When he checked in with British Airways at Dubai International Airport, his English was impeccable.

In fact Ali Aziz al-Khattab had been born a Kuwaiti, the son of a senior bank official. In 1989 his father had been posted to London as deputy manager of the Bank of Kuwait. The family had gone with him and avoided the invasion of their homeland by Saddam Hussein in 1990. Already a good English speaker, Ali Aziz was enrolled in a British school and left three years later with accentless English and excellent grades. When his family returned home, he elected to stay on. Four years later he emerged with a degree in chemical engineering from Loughborough University and proceeded to a doctorate.

In London he attended a mosque run by a firebrand preacher of anti-Western hatred, and became what the media like to call 'radicalised'. By twenty-one he was a fanatical supporter of Al-Qaeda.

A 'talent spotter' suggested he might like to visit Pakistan; he accepted, and went on to spend six months at an Al-Qaeda terrorist training camp. He had already been marked out as a 'sleeper' who should lie low in England and never come to the attention of the authorities.

Back in London he did what they all do; he reported to his embassy that he had lost his passport and was issued a new one that did not carry the telltale Pakistan entry stamp. If anyone asked, he had been visiting family and friends in the Gulf and had never been near Pakistan, let alone Afghanistan. He secured a post as lecturer at Aston University, Birmingham, in 1999. Two years later, Anglo-American forces invaded Afghanistan.

There were several weeks of panic in case any trace of him had been left lying around in the terror camps, but AQ's head of personnel had done his job. No evidence was found of any Al-Khattab having been there. So he remained undiscovered and rose to be AQ's commanding agent in the UK.

As DR AL-KHATTAB'S London-bound airliner was taking off, the *Java Star* eased away from her berth in the Sultanate of Brunei on the coast of North Borneo and headed for the open sea. Her destination was the Western Australian port of Fremantle, as usual, and her Norwegian skipper, Knut Herrmann, had no inkling that his journey would be other than routine.

He knew that these waters remain the most dangerous in the world, but not from riptides, rocks or reefs. The danger here is pirate attacks.

Every year, between the Malacca Strait in the west and the Celebes Sea to the east, there are over 500 pirate attacks on merchant shipping and up to 100 hijackings. Occasionally the crew are ransomed back to the ship owners; sometimes they are killed and the cargo sold on the black market.

If Captain Herrmann sailed with an easy mind on the 'milk run' to Fremantle, it was because he was convinced that his cargo was useless to the sea raiders. But on this trip he was wrong.

The first leg of his course lay north. It took him six hours to come round the northernmost tip of Sabah. Only then could he run southeast for the deep-water strait between Tawitawi and Jolo. South of the Sulu Archipelago it was a clear run down the Celebes Sea to the south.

His departure from Brunei had been watched, and a cellphone call made. The call referred only to the recovery of a sick uncle who would be out of hospital in twelve days. That meant: twelve hours to intercept.

The man who took the call, in a creek on Jolo Island, would have been recognised by Mr Alex Siebart of Crutched Friars, City of London. It was Mr Lampong, who no longer affected to be a businessman from Sumatra.

The twelve men he commanded in the velvety tropical night were members of Abu Sayyaf, an Islamist guerrilla group of the southern Philippines. The two speedboats they occupied put to sea at dawn, took up position between the two islands and waited. An hour later the *Java Star* bore down on them to pass from the Sulu Sea into the Celebes.

Captain Herrmann had taken the helm through the night, and as dawn came up he handed over to his Indonesian first officer and went below. His crew of ten Lascars were in their bunks in the forecastle.

The first thing the Indonesian officer saw was a pair of speedboats racing up astern, one each side. Dark, barefoot, agile men leapt from speedboat to deck and ran aft towards the bridge. He just had time to press the emergency buzzer to his captain's cabin before they burst through the door. Then there was a knife at his throat and a voice screaming 'Capitan, capitan . . .'

There was no need. A tired Knut Herrmann was coming topsides to see what was going on. He and Lampong arrived on the bridge together. Lampong held a mini-Uzi. The Norwegian knew better than to resist.

'Captain Herrmann . . .'

The bastard knew his name. This had been prepared.

'Please ask your first officer did he in any circumstances make a radio transmission in the past five minutes?'

There was no need to ask. Lampong was speaking in English. For the Norwegian and his Indonesian officer it was the common language. The first officer screamed that he had not touched the radio's transmit button.

'Excellent.' Lampong issued a stream of orders in the local dialect.

This the first officer understood and opened his mouth to scream again. The Norwegian understood everything when the pirate holding his Number Two jerked the seaman's head back and sliced his throat open with a single cut. The first officer kicked, jerked, slumped and died.

'Now, Captain,' said Lampong, 'for every minute you refuse to obey my orders, that will happen to one of your men. Am I clear?'

The Norwegian was escorted to the tiny radio shack behind the bridge where he selected Channel 16, the international distress frequency.

Lampong produced a written sheet. 'When I press "transmit" and nod, you will read this message, not in a calm voice, Captain; you will shout it with panic in your voice. Or your men die, one by one. Are you ready?'

Captain Herrmann nodded. He would not have to act extreme distress.

'Mayday, Mayday, Mayday. *Java Star, Java Star* . . . Catastrophic fire in engine room . . . I cannot save her . . . My position . . .'

He knew the position was wrong as he read it out. It was 100 miles south into the Celebes Sea. But he was not about to argue. Lampong cut the transmission. He brought the Norwegian at gunpoint back to the bridge.

Two of his own seamen had been put to work scrubbing up the blood on the floor of the bridge. The other eight had been marshalled in a terrified group out on the hatch covers with six pirates to watch them.

Two more of the hijackers stayed on the bridge. The other four were tossing life rafts, life belts and a pair of inflatable jackets down into one of the speedboats. It had extra fuel tanks stored amidships.

When they were ready, the speedboat left the side of the *Java Star* and went south. On a calm sea at an easy fifteen knots, they would be 100 miles south in seven hours, and back in their pirate creeks ten hours later.

'A new course, Captain,' said Lampong. His tone was gentle but the hatred in his eyes gave the lie to any humanity towards the Norwegian.

The new course was back towards the northeast, out of the Sulu Archipelago into Filipino water.

Parts of the Zamboanga Peninsula on Mindanao Island are no-go areas for Filipino government forces. This is the terrain of Abu Sayyaf. Here they are safe to recruit, train and bring their booty. The *Java Star* was certainly booty, albeit unmarketable. Lampong conferred in the local lingo with the senior pirate. He pointed ahead to the entrance to a narrow creek flanked by impenetrable jungle, and asked, 'Can your men manage her from here?' The pirate nodded. Lampong called his orders to the group round the Lascar seamen at the bow. Without even replying they herded the sailors to the rail and opened fire. The men screamed and toppled into the warm sea. Somewhere below, sharks turned to the blood smell.

Captain Herrmann was slow to react. Lampong's bullet took him full in the chest and he too tumbled back into the sea.

Half an hour later, towed by two small tugs that had been stolen weeks earlier, the *Java Star* was at her new berth beside a stout teak jetty.

The jungle concealed her from all sides and from above. Also hidden were the two long, low, tin-roofed workshops that housed the steel plates, cutters, welders, power generator and paint.

The last despairing cry from the *Java Star* on Channel 16 had been heard by a dozen vessels, but the nearest to the spot given as her position was a refrigerator ship loaded with fresh fruit for the American market. Her Finnish skipper diverted at once to the spot. There he found the bobbing life rafts, which had inflated automatically as designed. He circled once and spotted the life belts and two inflated jackets. All were marked with the name: MV *Java Star*. According to the law of the sea, which he respected, Captain Raikkonen cut power and lowered a pinnace to look inside the rafts. They were empty so he ordered them sunk. He had lost several hours and could stay no longer. There was no point.

With a heavy heart he reported by radio that the *Java Star* was lost with all hands. Far away in London the news was noted by insurers Lloyd's International and in Ipswich, *Lloyd's Register of Shipping* logged the loss. The *Java Star* ceased to exist.

CHAPTER SEVEN

The interrogator was gone for a week. Martin remained in his cell with only the Koran for company. But years in Special Forces had given him a rare gift: the ability to remain motionless for exceptionally long periods and defy boredom.

The operations room at Edzell Air Base, meanwhile, was becoming very tense. They had lost their man. The Predator was double-assigned: to look down on Ras-al-Khaimah in case Crowbar reappeared, and to monitor the dhow *Rasha*.

Dr Al-Khattab returned when he had confirmed every aspect of the story as it concerned Guantánamo Bay. It had not been easy. He had no intention of betraying himself to the four former British inmates who had been sent home. They had all declared repeatedly that they were not extremists and that they had been swept up in the American net by accident. Al-Qaeda could have confirmed they were telling the truth.

The little that Al-Khattab could glean from Afghanistan regarding the break-out from the prison van was that it had been genuine. He could not know that this episode had been accomplished by the Head of Station of the SIS office in the British Embassy. Brigadier Yusuf had acted out his rage convincingly and the agents of the by now resurgent Taliban were convinced. And they said so to Al-Qaeda enquiries.

'Let us go back to your early days in the Tora Bora,' Al-Khattab proposed when the interrogation resumed. 'Tell me about your boyhood.'

Al-Khattab could not know that the man in front of him, though he was a ringer, knew the mountains of Afghanistan better than he. The Kuwaiti's six months in the terrorist training camps had been among fellow Arabs, not Pashtun mountain men. He made copious notes, even listing the names of the fruits in the orchards of Maloko-zai.

On the third day of the second session the narrative had reached the date that proved a crucial hinge in the life of Izmat Khan: August 20, 1998, the day the Tomahawk cruise missile crashed in the mountains.

'Ah, yes, truly tragic,' he murmured. 'And a remarkable coincidence, for you must be the only Afghan for whom no family member remains alive to vouch for you. What was the effect on you?'

In Guantánamo, Izmat Khan had refused to talk about why he hated Americans with such a passion. But he had become an iconic figure in the Taliban army as the man immune to fear, and the story of his annihilated family, as whispered round the camp fires, was told to the interrogators by the other fighters who had survived Qala-i-Jangi and reached Camp Delta.

Al-Khattab gazed at his prisoner. He still had grave reservations, but of one thing he was certain: the man truly was Izmat Khan. His doubts were over another question: had he been 'turned' by the Americans?

'So you claim you declared a sort of private war? A very personal jihad? And you have never relented? But what did you actually do about it?'

'I fought against the Northern Alliance, the allies of the Americans.'

'But not until October and November 2001,' said Al-Khattab.

'The Americans first came in the autumn of 2001,' said Martin.

'True. So you fought for Afghanistan . . . and lost. Now you wish to fight for Allah.'

Martin nodded. 'As the Sheikh predicted,' he said.

For the first time, Dr Al-Khattab's urbanity forsook him. He stared at the black-bearded face across the table for a full thirty seconds, mouth agape. Finally he spoke in a whisper: 'You . . . have actually met the Sheikh?'

Al-Khattab had never met Osama bin Laden. He would have taken a meat cleaver and severed his left wrist for the chance of meeting, let alone conversing with, the man he venerated more than any other on earth.

Martin met his gaze and nodded.

Al-Khattab recovered his poise. 'Start at the beginning of this episode and describe exactly what happened. Leave out nothing, no tiny detail.'

So Martin told him. He told him of serving in his father's *lashkar* as a teenager. He told of the patrol with others and how they had been caught on a mountainside with only a group of boulders to shelter in.

He made no mention of any British officer, nor any Blowpipe missile, nor the destruction of the Hind gunship. He told only of the roaring gun in the nose of the aircraft; of the fragments of bullet and rock flying around until the Hind, praise be to Allah, ran out of ammunition and flew away.

He told of feeling a blow like a hit from a hammer in the thigh, and being carried by his comrades across the valleys until they found a man with a mule and took it from him. And he told of being carried to a complex of caves at Jaji and being handed over to Saudis who lived and worked there.

'But the Sheikh, tell me of the Sheikh,' insisted Al-Khattab.

'He said to me: "The day will come when Afghanistan will no longer have need of you, but the all-merciful Allah will always have need of a warrior like you."'

'Then what happened?' Al-Khattab said, taking down the dialogue word for word.

'He changed the dressing on the leg.'

'The Sheikh did that?'

'No, the doctor who was with him. The Egyptian.'

Dr Al-Khattab sat back and let out a long breath. Of course, the doctor, Ayman al-Zawahiri, companion and confidant, the man who had brought Egyptian Islamic Jihad to join the Sheikh to create Al-Qaeda.

He began to tidy up his papers. 'I have to leave you again. It will take a week, maybe more. You will stay here. Chained, I am afraid. You have seen too much; you know too much. But if you are indeed a True Believer, and truly the Afghan, you will join us as an honoured recruit. If not . . .'

Martin was back in his cell when the Kuwaiti left. This time Al-Khattab did not return to London. He went to the Hilton and wrote steadily for a day and a night. Then he made several calls on a new, lily-white cellphone, which then went into the harbour. Dr Al-Khattab was a careful man.

The calls he made arranged a meeting with Faisal bin Selim, master of the *Rasha*, which was moored in Dubai. That afternoon he drove his rental car to Dubai and conversed with the elderly captain, who took a personal letter and hid it in his robes. And the Predator kept circling at 20,000 feet.

Islamist terror groups have lost far too many senior operatives not to have realised that cellphone and satphone calls are dangerous. The West's interception and decryption technology is simply too good. Their other weakness is the transferring of sums of money through the banking system.

To overcome the latter danger they use the *hundi* system, which, with variations, is as old as the first Caliphate. *Hundi* is based on a total-trust concept: the payer hands over his money in cash to the *hundi* man in place A and asks that his friend in place B shall receive the equivalent minus the *hundi* man's cut. The *hundi* man has a trusted partner in place B, whom he instructs to make the money available, in cash, to the payer's friend.

Given that there are no computer records or checkable dockets, given that it is all in cash and both payers and receivers can use pseudonyms, the money movements are virtually impossible to trace. It works because any money-launderer who cheated his customer would soon be out of business—or worse.

For communications, the solution lies in hiding messages in three-figure codes that can be emailed or texted. Only a recipient with the decipher list can work out the message. This works for brief instructions and warnings. Occasionally a lengthy text must travel halfway across the world.

The West is always in a hurry. The East has patience. If it takes so long, then it takes that long. The *Rasha* sailed that night for Gwador. There a loyal emissary was waiting on his motorcycle. He took the letter and rode north across Pakistan to the small but fanatic town of Miram Shah.

There the man trusted enough to go into the high peaks of South Waziristan was waiting at the named *chaikhana* and the sealed package changed hands again. The reply came back the same way. It took ten days.

But Dr Al-Khattab did not stay in the Arabian Gulf. He flew to Cairo and then due west to Morocco, where he recruited four North Africans. Because he was still not under surveillance, his journey appeared on no one's radar.

WHEN THE HANDSOME cards were dealt, Mr Wei Wing Li received a pair of twos. Short, squat and toadlike, he had a football of a head and a face deeply pitted with smallpox scars. But he was good at his job.

He and his crew had arrived at the hidden creek on the Zamboanga Peninsula two days before the *Java Star*. Their journey from China, where they featured in the criminal underworld of Guangdong, had not involved the inconvenience of passports or visas, but the captain of the freighter they had boarded had been amply rewarded for his discretion.

Mr Wei had greeted his host, Mr Lampong, and the local Abu Sayyaf chieftain who had recommended him, inspected the living quarters for his dozen crewmen, taken the fifty per cent of his fee 'up front' and asked to see the workshops. After a lengthy inspection he pronounced himself satisfied. Then he studied the photos taken in Liverpool. When the *Java Star* was finally in the creek, he knew what had to be done and set about it.

Ship transformation was his speciality; over fifty cargo vessels plying the seas of Southeast Asia with false names and papers also had false shapes thanks to Mr Wei. He had been given three weeks, not an hour longer. In that time the *Java Star* was going to become the *Countess of Richmond*.

Mr Wei did not know that. He did not need to know. In the photos he studied, the name of the vessel had been airbrushed out. Mr Wei was not bothered with names or papers. It was shapes that concerned him.

There would be parts of the *Java Star* to cut out and others to cut off. There would be features to be fashioned from welded steel. But most of all he would create six steel sea containers, which would occupy the deck from below the bridge to the bow. From all sides and from above they would appear authentic, even at a range of a few feet. Yet inside they would form a long gallery with a hinged removable roof and access through a new door, which would be cut in the bulkhead below the bridge and then disguised to become invisible.

As Mr Wei fired up his oxyacetylene cutters, the *Countess of Richmond* was passing through the Suez Canal.

WHEN ALI AZIZ al-Khattab returned to the villa he was a changed man. He ordered the shackles removed from his prisoner and invited him to share his table at lunch. His eyes glittered with a deep excitement.

'I have communicated with the Sheikh himself,' he purred.

Clearly the honour consumed him. The reply had been confided verbally in the mountains to the messenger, who had memorised it. He had then brought it all the way to the Arabian Gulf. When the *Rasha* docked the message had been given word for word to Dr Al-Khattab.

'There is one last formality,' he said. 'Would you please raise the hem of your dishdash to mid-thigh?'

Martin did so. He knew nothing of Al-Khattab's scientific discipline; only that he had a doctorate. He hoped it was not in dermatology.

The Kuwaiti examined the puckered scar. It was where he was told it would be. It had the six stitches sutured into place in a Jaji cave nineteen years earlier by a man he revered.

'Thank you, my friend. The Sheikh himself sends his personal greetings. He and the doctor remembered the young warrior and the words spoken. He has authorised me to include you in a mission that will inflict on the Great Satan a blow so terrible that even the destruction of the Towers will seem minor. You will die gloriously, a true *shahid*. You and your fellow martyrs will be spoken of a thousand years from now.'

After three weeks of wasted time, Dr Al-Khattab was now in a hurry. A barber came to trim the shaggy mane to a Western-style haircut, but when he prepared to shave off the beard Martin protested. As a Muslim he wanted his beard. Al-Khattab conceded; it could be clipped to a neat Vandyke around the point of the chin, but no longer.

Suleiman, the leader of the men who had seized Martin, took full-face photos. Twenty-four hours later he appeared with a perfect passport for a marine engineer from Bahrain, a staunchly pro-Western sultanate.

A tailor came and took measurements, and reappeared with shoes, socks, shirt, tie and dark grey suit, along with a small case to contain them.

The travelling party prepared to leave the next day. Suleiman would be accompanying the Afghan all the way. The other two guards were 'muscle', locally recruited and dispensable.

As he prepared to leave, Dr Al-Khattab turned to Martin and shook his hand. 'I envy you, Afghan. You have fought for Allah, bled for Him, taken pain and the foulness of the infidel for Him. And now you will die for Him. Save a place for me in paradise. *Inshallah*.'

Then he was gone. He always parked his hire car several hundred yards away and round two corners. Outside the villa gates he crouched, adjusting a shoe so he could glance up and down the road. There was nothing but some chit of a girl 200 yards up, trying to start a scooter. But she was local, in *jilbab*, covering the hair and half the face. Still, it offended him that a woman would have any motorised vehicle at all.

He turned and walked away towards his car. The girl with the scooter leaned forward and spoke into something inside the basket above the front mudguard. Her clipped English spoke of Cheltenham Ladies' College.

'Mongoose One, on the move,' she said.

THE PICTURES from the two Predators over the UAE and the Arabian Sea were being sent back from Thumrait to Edzell Air Base, which knew exactly why, and US army CENTCOM at Tampa, Florida, which thought the British had simply asked for some routine surveillance. Consumed by the new atmosphere of cooperation, everyone at Tampa was trying to be helpful.

Whenever the Predators were over the Emirates, their images contained a teeming mass of Arabs and non-Arabs, far too many to begin checking out everyone. But the dhow called the *Rasha* and her master were known about. So when she was in dock, anyone visiting her was also of interest.

There were scores of visitors: she had to be loaded and unloaded, refuelled and victualled. The crewman exchanged pleasantries with passers-by on the quayside. Her skipper was visited by local agents and friends. When a clean-shaven young Gulf Arab in white dishdash and white filigree skull-cap conferred with Faisal bin Selim, he was just one of many.

Edzell's operations room had a menu of 1,000 faces of confirmed and suspected AQ members and sympathisers and every image from the Predators was electronically compared. Dr Al-Khattab did not trigger red flags because he was not known. So Edzell missed him.

The slim young Arab visiting the *Rasha* rang no bells in Tampa either, but the army sent the images as a courtesy to the National Security Agency at Fort Meade, which provided them as a service to their British partners at GCHQ Cheltenham, who had a good, long look, then sent them to MI5.

Here a young probationer, keen to impress, ran the faces of all the visitors to the *Rasha* through the Face Recognition data base. This data base stored the faces of convicted criminals, immigrants, legal and illegal, and protesters at demonstrations—over 3 million faces from all over the world.

The computer analysed the face of the man talking to the master of the *Rasha*, taking 600 different measurements, and began to compare.

Fast though it worked, the computer still took an hour. But it found him.

He was a face in a crowd outside a mosque just after 9/11, cheering the fanatical Al-Qaeda orator, Abu Qatada. The probationer took the photo to his superior. From there it went up to the Head of MI5, Dame Eliza Manningham-Buller, who ordered that the man be traced. No one knew then that the probationer had uncovered the chief of Al-Qaeda in Britain.

It took a bit more time, but another match came up: he was receiving his doctorate at an academic ceremony. His name was Ali Aziz al-Khattab, a highly Westernised academic with a post at Aston University, Birmingham.

He was either a successful long-term sleeper or a foolish man who in his student days had dabbled with extreme politics. Until it was proved otherwise, he would be put in the first category.

Further discreet checks revealed that he was back in Britain, at Aston. It was decided to put the academic under surveillance. A week later, Dr Al-Khattab booked a flight back to the Gulf. That was when the Special Reconnaissance Regiment was brought in.

The SRR is one of the best 'tracker' units in the world. Its headquarters remain secret and, if the SAS and SBS are discreet, the SRR is invisible. The Head of MI5 asked for them and got them.

When Dr Al-Khattab boarded the airliner from Heathrow to Dubai there were six from the SRR on board, scattered invisibly among 300 passengers.

Two hired cars and two rented scooters were available for the SRR team when it landed. While Dr Al-Khattab rented a small Japanese compact, they moved into position. He was tailed first from the airport to the Creek in Dubai, where once again the *Rasha* was moored after her return from Gwador. This time he did not approach the vessel but stood by his car 100 yards away until Bin Selim spotted him.

Minutes later a young man known to no one emerged from below decks on the *Rasha*, moved through the crowd and whispered in the ear of the Kuwaiti. It was the answer coming back from the man in the mountains of Waziristan. Al-Khattab's face registered amazement.

He then drove up the coast to Ras-al-Khaimah. There he went to the Hilton to check in and change, enabling the three young women in the SRR team to use the female washroom to change into the all-covering *jilbab* and get back to their vehicles.

Dr Al-Khattab emerged in his white dishdash and drove away through the town. Though he adopted several manoeuvres designed to shake off a 'tail', he had no luck. Since being assigned to the job, the team had been studying road maps of all seven emirates until they had memorised every highway. That was how he was tailed to the villa.

If there had been any residual doubt that he was up to no good, his tail-shaking antics dispelled it. Innocent men do not behave like that. Later that evening the SRR women followed him back to the Hilton, while the three men found a position on a hilltop that commanded a view of the target villa and kept vigil through the night. No one came or left.

The second day was different. There were visitors. The watchers could not know it but they brought the new passport and the new clothes. Their car numbers were noted and one would be traced and arrested later. The third visitor was the barber, also later traced.

At the end of the second day Al-Khattab emerged for the last time. That was when Katy Sexton, tinkering with her scooter up the road, alerted her colleagues that the target was on the move.

Back at the Hilton, the Kuwaiti academic revealed his plans when, speaking from his room, which had been bugged in his absence, he booked passage on the morning flight out of Dubai for London. He was escorted all the way home to Birmingham and never saw a thing.

MI5 had done a cracking job and knew it. The coup was circulated on a 'your eyes only' basis to just four men in the British intelligence community. One of them was Steve Hill. He nearly went into orbit.

The Predator was reassigned to survey the villa in the far desert-side suburbs of Ras-al-Khaimah. But it was midmorning in London, afternoon in the Gulf. All the bird saw were the cleaners going in. And the raid.

It was too late to stop the Special Forces of the UAE sending in their close-down squad commanded by a former British officer, Dave de Forest. The SIS Head of Station in Dubai, a personal friend anyway, called him up like a shot. Word was immediately put out on the jungle telegraph that the 'hit' had stemmed from an anonymous tip from a neighbour with a grudge.

The two cleaners knew nothing; they came from an agency, they had been paid in advance and the keys had been delivered to them. However, they had not finished and swept up in a pile was a quantity of black hair, some evidently from a scalp and some from a beard—the texture is different. Other than that there were no traces of the men who had lived there.

Neighbours reported a panel van, but no one could recall the number. It was eventually discovered abandoned, and revealed to have been stolen.

The tailor and the barber did not hesitate to talk, but they could only describe the five men in the house. Al-Khattab was already known. Suleiman was described and then identified from mug-shots because he was on a suspect list locally. The two underlings were described but rang no bells of recognition. It was the fifth man that De Forest, with his perfect Arabic, concentrated on. The SIS Station Chief sat in.

No one in that room knew about any Afghan; they simply took a description and passed it to London. No one knew why London was becoming hysterical about a big man with shaggy black hair and a full beard. All they could report was that he was now neatly barbered and possibly in a dark mohair two-piece suit.

But it was the final snippet that came from the barber and the tailor that delighted Steve Hill, Marek Gumienny and the team at Edzell: the Gulf Arabs had been treating their man like an honoured guest. He was clearly being prepared for departure. He was not a dead body on a tiled floor.

At Edzell, Michael McDonald and Gordon Phillips shared the same joy. After weeks of worry they had had their second sign of life. But had their agent discovered a single thing about Stingray, the object of the whole exercise? Where had he gone? Was there any way he could contact them?

THE TRAVELLING PARTY headed east, over the mountainous isthmus towards the seventh emirate, Fujairah, on the Gulf of Oman. They soon left the last metalled road and took to rutted tracks, which meandered through the baking brown hills of Jebel Yibir. From the col at the height of the range they descended towards the small port of Dibbah.

There is not much to Dibbah: just a cluster of white houses, a green-domed mosque and a small port for fishing vessels. Two creeks away, an aluminium boat waited on the shingle, its two-man crew was sheltering in the shade of a camelthorn tree.

For the two local youths this was the end of the road. They would take the stolen van into the hills and abandon it, then simply disappear. Suleiman and the Afghan, their Western clothes in bags to shield them from the salt water, helped push the cigarette boat out into waist-deep water.

With both passengers and the crew aboard, the smuggler craft idled its way up the coast almost to the tip of the Musandam Peninsula. The smugglers would only make the high-speed dash across the Strait in darkness.

Within twenty minutes of the sun setting, the helmsman opened up the power and the smuggler boat hurled itself towards Iran. In less than thirty minutes the first scattered lights of the Persian coast were visible to port and the smuggler raced east towards Gwador. This was the route Martin had covered under the sedate sails of the *Rasha* a month before. Now he was returning at ten times her speed.

Opposite the lights of Gwador the crew stopped to refuel the engines from tanks of fuel stowed in the hold. They were clearly going further. Dawn found them well inside Pakistani waters but close enough inshore to be taken for a fishing boat going about its business. There was no sign of officialdom and the bare brown coast sped past. By midday, Martin realised their destination must be Karachi. He had no idea why.

They refuelled at sea one more time and as the sun dipped to the west behind them were deposited at a reeking fishing village outside the sprawl of Pakistan's biggest port and harbour.

Suleiman may not have been there before, but Al-Qaeda had done its research, and he sought out the only vehicle for hire in the village. The fact that two strangers had come ashore from a smuggler craft raised not an eyebrow. This was Baluchistan; the rules of Karachi were for idiots.

The interior of the van stank of fish and body odour, and the misfiring engine could manage no more than forty miles per hour. But they found the highway and reached the airport with time to spare.

The Afghan was appropriately bewildered—he had only twice travelled by air, each time in an American C-130 Hercules and each time as a prisoner in shackles. He knew nothing of check-in desks, flight tickets, passport controls. With a mocking smile, Suleiman showed him.

Somewhere in the sprawling mass of pushing and shoving humanity that comprises the main concourse of Karachi International Airport, the Gulf Arab found the Malaysian Airlines ticket desk and bought two single tickets in economy class to Kuala Lumpur. He paid in cash, in US dollars.

The flight took six hours, plus three for time-zone changes, landing at nine thirty in the morning. For the second time, Martin offered his new Bahraini passport and wondered if it would pass muster. It did.

From international arrivals Suleiman led the way to domestic departures and bought two single tickets. They had just enough time to find a cloakroom and change into shirts and suits. Only when Martin had to proffer his boarding pass did he see where they were heading: the island of Labuan.

He had vaguely heard of Labuan. Situated off the northern coast of Borneo, and belonging to Malaysia, it had a reputation as an international offshore financial centre, whose no-tax free port, flag of convenience and smuggling activities attracted some extremely dubious clientele.

Martin realised he was being flown into the heart of the world's ship-hijacking, cargo-stealing and crew-murdering industry. He needed to make contact with base to give a sign of life, and he needed to work out how. Fast.

There was a brief stopover at Kuching, first port of call on the island of Borneo, but non-alighting travellers did not leave the aeroplane, and forty minutes later it took off again and headed northeast for Labuan. Far below the aircraft, the *Countess of Richmond*, in ballast, was steaming for Kota Kinabalu, capital of the state of Sabah, to pick up her cargo of timber.

After take-off the stewardess distributed landing cards. Suleiman took them both and began to fill them in, as Martin had to pretend he neither understood nor wrote English. Ostensibly they were a Bahraini engineer and an Omani accountant heading for Labuan on contract to the natural gas industry, and that was what Suleiman was filling in.

Martin muttered that he needed to go to the lavatory. He rose and went aft, where there were two. One was vacant, but he pretended both were in use, turned and went forward, beyond the curtain, into the business service.

Standing outside the door of the business-class toilet, he beamed at the stewardess who had distributed the landing cards, uttered an apology and plucked from her top pocket a fresh landing card and her pen. The lavatory door clicked open and he went in. There was only time to scrawl a brief message on the reverse of the landing card, fold it into his breast pocket, emerge and return the pen. Then he went back to his seat.

Labuan airport was a contrast to Karachi: small and trim. Martin still had no idea exactly where they were headed, but suspected the airport might be the last chance to get rid of his message and hoped for a stroke of luck.

It was only a fleeting moment and it came on the pavement outside the terminal concourse. Suleiman was scouring the access road, looking for a taxi when one appeared, heading towards the departures set-down point. It was occupied, but clearly about to deposit its cargo.

Two men alighted and Martin caught the English accents. Both were big and muscular; both wore khaki shorts and flowered shirts. One paid the driver, while the other emptied the boot of their luggage. There were two hard-framed suitcases and two scuba-diver's kitbags.

The man by the boot could not handle all four bags. Before Suleiman could utter a word, Martin helped the diver by hefting one of the kitbags onto the pavement. As he did so, the folded landing card went into one of the side pockets, of which all divebags have an array.

'Thanks, mate,' said the diver, and the pair of them headed for the check-in desk to find their flight to London, via Kuala Lumpur.

Suleiman instructed the Malay driver to take them to a shipping agency in the heart of the docks. Here at last someone was waiting to receive the travellers. Like the newcomers, he wore no ostentatious clothing or facial hair. Like them he was *takfir*. He introduced himself as Mr Lampong and took them to a fifty-foot cabin cruiser, tricked out as a game-fisherman, by the harbour wall. Within minutes they were out of the harbour.

The cruiser steadied her speed at ten knots and turned northeast. It had been a gruelling journey, with only catnaps on the aeroplanes, and soon both passengers fell asleep. The helmsman was from the Abu Sayyaf terror group; he knew his way home to the hide-out in the Zamboanga Peninsula. The sun dropped and the tropical darkness was not long behind. The cruiser motored on through the night, into Filipino waters.

THE SABAH PILOT eased the *Countess of Richmond* past the shoals and into her assigned berth by the quay at Kota Kinabalu. Captain McKendrick ran his bandanna kerchief round his wet neck once again and thanked the pilot. At last he could close all the doors and portholes and take relief in the air conditioning. That, he reckoned, and a cold beer would do him nicely. He could see his timber cargo under the lights of the dock. With a good loading crew he could be back at sea by evening.

MR WEI HAD FINISHED his commission before schedule and was already heading home to China. The results of his work were a to-the-rivet replica of the *Countess of Richmond*, fashioned from a ship of similar size, tonnage and dimensions. But Wei Wing Li never knew what the original ship had been called, nor what the new one would be. All that concerned him was the bulbous roll of high-denomination dollar bills drawn from a Labuan bank against a line of credit arranged by the late Mr Tewfik al-Qur.

Back in the creek off the Zamboanga Peninsula, working by floodlights from a platform hung over the stern, a skilled painter was affixing the last 'D' to the name of the moored ship. From her mast hung a limp Red Ensign. On either side of her bow and round her stern were the words COUNTESS OF RICHMOND and, at the stern only, the word LIVERPOOL beneath. Transformation complete, the painter descended and the lights flickered out.

At dawn a cruiser disguised as a game-fisherman motored slowly up the creek. It brought the last two members of the new crew of the former *Java Star*, the ones who would take the ship on her, and their, last voyage.

THE LOADING OF the *Countess of Richmond* began at dawn when the air was still cool. The dockside cranes were not exactly ultra-modern but the stevedores knew their business, and chained logs of rare timber swung inboard and were stowed in the hold by the crew that toiled below.

In the heat of midday even the local Borneans had to stop, and for four hours the old logging port slumbered in whatever shade it could find. The humidity was edging toward 100 per cent, and Captain McKendrick would have been happier at sea, but loading was not completed until sundown. It meant another night in the hothouse, so McKendrick sighed and again found refuge in the air conditioning below decks.

The local agent came bustling aboard with the pilot at six in the morning and the last paperwork was signed. Then the pilot guided the *Countess* out into the South China Sea. Like the *Java Star* before her, she turned northeast to round the tip of Borneo, then south through the Sulu Archipelago for Java, where the skipper believed that six sea containers full of eastern silks awaited him at Surabaya. He was not to know that there were not, nor ever had been, any silks at Surabaya.

THE CRUISER DEPOSITED its cargo of three at a ramshackle jetty halfway up the creek. Mr Lampong led the way to a longhouse on stilts above the water that served as a sleeping area and mess hall for the men who would depart on the mission that Martin knew as Stingray and Lampong as Al-Isra. Others in the longhouse would be staying behind. It was their labours that had prepared the hijacked *Java Star* for sea.

There were a mix of Indonesians from Jemaat Islamiya, the group who had planted the Bali bombs and others up the island chain, and Filipinos from Abu Sayyaf. One by one, Martin identified the crew and the special task of each of them.

The engineer, navigator and radio operator were all Indonesians. Suleiman revealed that his expertise was photography, and his job, before dying a martyr, would be to photograph the climax for transmission on the Al-Jazeera TV network.

There was a teenager who looked Pakistani, yet Lampong addressed him in English. When he replied it was clear that the boy could only have been British-born and raised but of Pakistani parentage. His accent was broad English north country; possibly from the Leeds/Bradford area. Martin could not work out what he was there for, except possibly as cook.

That left three: Martin himself; a chemical engineer and explosives expert; and the mission commander, whom they would meet later.

Midmorning, Lampong took a call on his satellite phone: the *Countess of Richmond* had left Kota Kinabalu and was at sea. She should be coming between the islands of Tawitawi and Jolo around sundown. The speedboat crews that would intercept her had four hours before they needed to leave.

Suleiman and Martin had changed from their Western suits into the trousers, flowered local shirts and sandals that had been provided. They were allowed down the steps into the shallow water of the creek to wash before prayers and a dinner of rice and fish.

All Martin could do was watch, understanding very little, and wait.

THE BRITISH AIRWAYS jet from Kuala Lumpur touched down at Heathrow at dawn. The two divers were lucky. Most of their fellow passengers were from Malaysia and had been diverted to the non-UK passport channel, leaving the few British easy access to immigration control. They grabbed their cases from the luggage carousel and headed for the nothing-to-declare Customs hall.

It might have been the shaven skulls, the stubble on the chins or the brawny arms emerging from short-sleeved flowered shirts on a bitter March morning, but one of the customs officers beckoned them to the examination bench. 'May I see your passports, please?'

It was a formality. They were in order.

'And where have you just arrived from?'

'Malaysia.'

'Purpose of visit?'

One of the young men explained that they had been diving the offshore reefs on behalf of the British magazine *Sport Diver*. The official's face remained impassive. He gestured to one of the divebags.

There was nothing inside but the usual scuba gear. As he was zipping the bag back up, he ran his fingers into the side pockets. From one he drew a folded card, looked and read it.

'Where did you get this, sir?'

The diver was genuinely puzzled. 'I don't know. I've never seen it before.'

Another customs man caught the rise in tension, and moved closer.

'Would you remain here, please?' said the first, and walked through a door behind him. Those ample mirrors in customs halls are not for the vain to touch up their make-up. They have one-way vision and behind them are the duty shift of internal security—in the case of Britain, MI5.

Within minutes, both divers, with their luggage, were in separate interview rooms. The customs men went through the luggage fin by fin, mask by mask and shirt by shirt. There was nothing illegal.

A man in plain clothes studied the card.

'It must have been put there by someone,' protested the diver.

By now it was nine thirty. Steve Hill was at his desk in Vauxhall Cross when his private and very unlisted phone rang.

'To whom am I speaking?' asked a voice.

Hill bristled. 'I think you may have a wrong number,' he replied.

The MI5 officer continued. 'I'm speaking from Heathrow, Terminal Three, internal security office. We have intercepted a passenger from the Far East. Stuffed into his divebag was a short handwritten message. Does Crowbar mean anything to you?'

Within five minutes Steve Hill's car swept out of the underground car park and headed towards Heathrow but disappointingly, after an hour's interrogation, Hill was sure that the divers were just innocent dupes. He secured for them a full with-trimmings breakfast from the staff canteen and asked them to rack their brains for a clue as to who had stuffed the folded note into the side pocket.

Finally one said: 'Mark, do you remember that Arab-looking fella who helped you unload at the airport?'

'What Arab-looking fellow?' asked Hill.

They described the man as best they could. Black hair, black beard. Neatly trimmed. Dark eyes, olive skin. About forty-five, fit-looking. Dark suit. Hill had had the descriptions from the barber and the tailor of Ras-al-Khaimah. It was Crowbar. He thanked them sincerely and asked that they be given a chauffeured ride back to their Essex home.

When Hill called Gordon Phillips at Edzell he read out the scrawled note: *If you love your country, get home and ring xxxxxxxxxx. Tell them Crowbar says it will be some kind of ship.*

'Pull out all the stops,' he said. 'Scour the world for a missing ship.'

CAPTAIN LIAM MCKENDRICK had chosen to hand over the helm to his first officer once they had cleared the strait between the islands of Tawitawi and Jolo, so when the speedboats swept up from astern, he was not on the bridge. As with the *Java Star*, the crew had no chance. Ten raiders were over the rails in seconds and running for the bridge. Mr Lampong, in charge of the hijack came at a more leisurely pace.

This time there was no need for ceremony or threats of violence unless instructions were obeyed. The only task the *Countess of Richmond* had to perform was to disappear, with her crew and for ever.

The six Indian crew members and the first officer were simply marched to the taffrail and machine-gunned down. Their bodies went straight over the rail. There was not even any need for weights to send them to the bottom. Lampong knew his sharks.

Liam McKendrick was the last to go, roaring his rage, calling Lampong a heathen pig. The Muslim fanatic did not like being called a pig and made sure the Liverpudlian was riddled but still alive when he hit the sea.

The raiders opened the seacocks and as the bilges began to flood, they left the *Countess* and bobbed on the water a few cables away until she reared on her stern, bow in the air, and slid backwards to the bottom of the sea. When she was gone the killers turned and raced for home.

FOR THE PARTY in the longhouse in the Filipino creek it was another brief call on a satphone from Lampong out at sea that triggered the departure. As they filed onto the cruiser moored at the foot of the steps, Martin realised that the ones being left behind were not showing any sense of relief, but only a deep envy; that for a suicide bomber a guaranteed passage to paradise vastly outweighed any residual love of life.

As they chugged slowly up the creek, the jungle closing in, he studied his companions and considered the depth of hatred that must be imbued in the *shahid* alongside the love of Allah. They all shared that hatred and counted themselves more blessed than any other True Believers on earth. And because they had offered themselves to die and been accepted, they believed they were going to strike at the Great Satan in a manner that would be spoken of for a thousand years. They, like the Prophet so long ago, were going on a great journey to heaven—the journey called Al-Isra.

Up ahead the creek split. The chugging cruiser took the wider branch and round a corner a moored vessel came into sight. Her deck cargo was apparently stored in the six sea containers that occupied her foredeck. And she was called the *Countess of Richmond*.

For a moment Martin toyed with the thought of escaping into the surrounding jungle. But he quickly realised that it was hopeless. Even with his jungle training, he would not make a mile without compass or machete. The hunting party would have him within the hour. He would have to wait for a better opportunity.

One by one they climbed the ladder to the deck of the freighter: the engineer, navigator and radio man, all Indonesians; the photographer and chemist, both Arabs; the Pakistani from the UK with the northern accent. In all the hours of studying faces of known suspects at Castle Forbes, Martin had never seen any of them. But when he reached the deck, and saw the man who would command them on their mission to eternal glory, the ex-SAS man recognised his face as belonging to one of the 'first division' in the rogues' gallery. He was staring at Yusuf Ibrahim, right-hand man of Al-Zarqawi, his homicidal fellow Jordanian.

The man was short and stocky, as expected, and the stunted left arm hung by his side. He had fought in Afghanistan against the Soviets and his left arm had stopped several shards of shrapnel during an air attack. Rather than accept a clean amputation he preferred to let it hang, useless. After the Soviet evacuation he had disappeared, and it was rumoured he was dead. But he reappeared after the 2003 Coalition invasion of Iraq, having spent the missing time as chief of security in one of the AQ camps.

For Mike Martin there was a heart-stopping moment in case the man remembered Izmat Khan from those Afghan days. But the mission commander just stared at him with expressionless, pebble-black eyes.

For twenty years this man had killed and killed. In Iraq, he had hacked off heads on camera and loved it, loved to hear them plead and scream. Martin gazed into the blank, manic eyes and gave the habitual greeting. *Peace be unto you, Yusuf Ibrahim, Butcher of Karbala.*

Shortly afterwards, the former *Java Star* emerged from the hidden Filipino creek. She headed into the Celebes Sea to join the south by south-west sea-track the *Countess* would have taken through the Makassar Strait.

CHAPTER EIGHT

By the end of March, spring had not even attempted to touch the Cascades mountain range. It was still bitterly cold and snow lay thick in the forest beyond the walls of the Cabin.

Inside, it was snug and warm. The enemy, despite TV, movies on DVD, music and board games, was boredom. Nevertheless the guard could always don skis or snowshoes and slog through the forest to keep fit and get a break from the bunkhouse. For the prisoner, the strain was that much greater.

Izmat Khan had listened to the judge at Guantánamo pronounce him free to go and was convinced that Pul-i-Charki jail would not have held him for more than a year. When he was brought to this lonely wilderness, so far as he knew for ever, it was hard to hide the screaming rage inside.

So he donned the kapok-lined jacket they had issued him, let himself outside and paced up and down the walled enclosure. Ten paces long, five paces wide. He could do it with eyes shut and never bump into the concrete.

The only variety was occasionally in the sky. Mostly it was of heavy leaden-grey cloud, from which the snow drifted down. But sometimes, when the skies were freezing cold but blue, he had seen aeroplanes. Some he knew were war planes like those he had seen turning into their bombing runs over northern Afghanistan. And there were the airliners in their different liveries. Many had the red maple leaf on the fin. They were always climbing and they always came from the north.

But what he liked most to watch were the birds, the eagles and ravens wheeling overhead. And the smaller birds that fluttered to the top of the wall and looked down at him, perhaps wondering why he could not come and join them in freedom.

IN A SLEAZY dockside bar in Port of Spain, Trinidad, two merchant seamen were attacked by a local gang with knives and left to die. By the time the Trinidadian police arrived, the witnesses had acquired amnesia and could recall only that there had been five attackers who had provoked the fight and that they were islanders. No arrests were ever made.

In fact the killers were local low-life, paid by a senior terrorist in the Jamaat-al-Muslimeen, the principal Trinidadian group on the side of Al-Qaeda. The money came from a line of credit set up by the late Mr Tewfik al-Qur, and the orders had come from an emissary of Dr Al-Khattab.

No attempt had been made to steal the wallets of the dead men, so the Port of Spain police could quickly identify them as Venezuelan citizens and deck crew from a Venezuelan ship then in port. Her master, Captain Pablo Montalban, was shocked and saddened to be informed of the loss of his crewmen, but he could not wait too long in harbour and so, while the Venezuelan consul arranged to ship the bodies back to Caracas, the captain contacted his local agent for replacement sailors. The agent asked around and came up with two polite and eager young Indians from Kerala who had worked their passage across the world and had perfectly good seamen's tickets.

The two were taken on, joined the other four seamen who made up the crew and the *Doña Maria* sailed only a day late.

Captain Montalban had no idea that his two new crewmen were working with Jamaat-al-Muslimeen, or that the two unfortunates in the bar had been killed deliberately to put the Indian matelots on his ship.

MAREK GUMIENNY chose to fly the Atlantic when he heard the report from the Far East. He brought with him a man from America's Bureau of Customs and Border Protection, merchant-marine division. Steve Hill came north from London accompanied by a colleague from the SIS's antiterrorism desk, maritime section.

At Edzell the two younger men met: Chuck Hemingway from New York and Sam Seymour from London. They were told they had twelve hours to come up with an evaluation of the threat and a game plan for coping with it.

Chuck Hemingway addressed the intel officers first. 'This is a search for a needle in a haystack,' he began. 'All we have as a target is something that floats. Maybe. Forty-six thousand merchant ships are now plying their trade on the world's oceans, half of them flying flags of convenience, and there are four thousand viable merchant ports around the world. You want to find a vessel, but you do not know her type, size, tonnage, contours, age, ownership, stern-flag, captain or name. To have a hope of tracing this vessel—this ghost ship—we will need a large dose of luck.'

There was a depressed silence.

'That's damn downbeat,' said Marek Gumienny. 'Sam, any ray of hope?'

'There might be, if we identify the kind of target the terrorists could be aiming at, then check out any ship heading towards that target and demand a gunpoint inspection of ship and cargo,' said Seymour.

'What kind of target could they be most likely heading for?' Hill asked.

'The oceans are a terrorists' playground and ship-hijacking is on the increase. Some has simply been to make money to fund terrorism's coffers. But there have also been events that defy logic. For instance the ten recent cases of pirates stealing tugs. They have no resale value. We think they could be used to tow a captured supertanker into a busy port.'

'And blow her up?' asked Hill.

'No need. Just sink her with her cargo hatches open. The port is closed for a decade.'

'OK,' said Gumienny, 'so . . . possible target number one. Take over a

supertanker and use her to close down a commercial port. This is a spectacular? Sounds pretty mundane, except for the port in question—no casualties.'

'There are other things that can be destroyed with a blocking ship with
vast damage to the world's economy,' said Chuck Hemingway. 'In his
October 2004 video Bin Laden said he was switching to economic damage.
The whole of world trade is geared to just-in-time delivery. The T-shirt
made in China sold in Dallas on Monday probably arrived at the docks the
previous Friday. Close down the Panama Canal, or the Suez Canal and the
whole global economy spins into chaos. You are talking damage in the hundreds of billions of dollars. There are ten other straits so narrow and so vital
that sinking a tanker broadside-on would close them.'

'All right,' said Gumienny. 'Look, I have a president to report to. Steve
has a prime minister. We have to propose concrete measures. So list the
likelihoods and suggest some countermeasures.'

Hemingway produced a paper he and Seymour had worked on earlier.
'OK, sir, we feel probability one is likely to be the taking-over of a large
vessel—tanker, freighter, ore-carrier—and sinking her in a vital marine
bottleneck. Measures to counter? Identify all such bottlenecks and post
warships at either end. All entering vessels to be boarded by Marines.'

'That will cause chaos,' said Hill. 'It will be claimed we are acting as
hijackers. What about the owners of the host waters? Don't they have
a say?'

'If the terrorists succeed, both the other ships and the coastal countries
will be ruined. There need be no delays—the Marines can board without
the freighter slowing down. And, frankly, the terrorists on board any ghost
ship cannot permit boarding. They have to fire back, expose themselves and
scuttle prematurely. I think the ship owners will see it our way.'

'Probability two?' queried Steve Hill.

'Running a ghost ship, crammed with explosives, into a major facility
like an oil rig and blowing it to pieces. It causes astronomical eco-damage
and economic ruin for years. Same countermeasure: identify and intercept.'

'We don't have enough warships,' protested Hill. 'Every sea island, every
seashore oil refinery, every offshore rig?'

'It need not be a warship, sir. If any interceptor vessel is fired on, the
ghost ship is exposed and may be sunk from the air.'

Marek Gumienny ran his hand over his forehead. 'Anything else?'

'A possible third is the use of explosives to cause a terrible massacre of humans,' said Seymour. 'The target would likely be a tourist facility crammed with holidaymakers by the seaside. It's a horrible prospect.'

Guimienny was silent. 'I am going to have to report all this to Washington,' he said at last. 'And they are not going to like it. And if countermeasures are taken there is no way we'll be able to keep the media out of this. We'll have to devise the best cover story we can to divert the bad guys' attention away from Colonel Martin. But we have to accept the reality. Chances are he's history.'

MAJOR LARRY DUVAL glanced out of the flight dispersal hut in the Arizona sunshine and marvelled as he always did at the sight of the F-15 Strike Eagle that awaited him. He had flown the F-15E version for ten years and reckoned it had to be the love of his life.

The fighter he would be flying that day up to Washington State was still being worked on, a swarm of men and women in overalls crawling over its burly frame. The plane had been at Luke Air Force Base for fundamental overhaul, and now had to be given a proving flight.

Larry Duval turned as his Weapons Systems Officer, Captain Nicky Johns, strolled in. In the Eagle the WSO, or wizzo, rides in tandem behind the pilot, surrounded by millions of dollars' worth of avionics. On the long flight to McChord AFB he would test them all.

The two aircrew were driven to the waiting fighter. Once on board they strapped themselves in, went through the pre-flight tests, and gave one last nod to the ground crew, who clambered down and headed back.

Larry Duval started the two powerful F-100 engines, the canopy hissed down and the Eagle began to roll. It turned into the light breeze down the runway, paused, received clearance and crouched for one last testing of the brakes. Then thirty-foot flames leapt back from its twin afterburners and Major Duval unleashed its full power.

A mile down the runway, at 185 knots, the wheels left the tarmac and the Eagle was airborne. Wheels up, flaps up, throttles back. At 30,000 feet Duval pointed her nose northwest towards Seattle. Below, the Rockies were clothed in snow and would stay with them all the way.

IN THE BRITISH Foreign Office, the final details for the transfer of the British government and its advisers to the April G8 conference were almost complete. The entire delegation would fly in a chartered airliner from Heathrow to JFK, New York, there to be formally met by the US Secretary of State. Together with the other non-American delegations they would remain 'airside' within JFK, a mile away from the nearest protesters, until an air bridge of helicopters transferred them to a second totally sealed environment. From there they would simply stroll into the venue of the five-day conference and be enclosed in luxury and privacy. It was simple and flawless.

'When you think about it, it's brilliant,' said one of the British diplomats. 'Perhaps we should do it ourselves one day.'

'The even better news,' muttered an older and more experienced colleague, 'is that after Gleneagles it won't be our turn for ages. Let the others cope with the security headaches for a few years.'

MAREK GUMIENNY was not long getting back to Steve Hill after his meeting with the six principals at the White House.

'They said much the same as before,' Gumienny reported. 'Whatever it is, wherever it is, find it and destroy it.'

'The same with my government,' said Steve Hill. 'No holds barred, destroy on sight. And they want us to work together on this.'

'No problem. But, Steve, my people are convinced the USA will be the target, so we have total priority on all our assets. If we locate the ghost ship elsewhere, OK, we'll divert assets to destroy it.'

The US Director of National Intelligence, John Negroponte, authorised the CIA to inform their British counterparts on an 'eyes-only' basis of the measures the States intended to take. The defence strategy would have three stages: aerial surveillance, identification of vessel and 'check-it-out'. They would monitor every ship within a 300-mile radius of Labuan that was steaming east towards any part of the American coast, including the Panama Canal. Any unsatisfactory explanations would generate physical interception. Any resistance would entail destruction at sea.

There was one procedural ally: major shipping lines now filed destination plans as a matter of routine, and seventy per cent of the vessels in the check-it-out zone would be on file. Their owners could contact their captains, who would use a code word if they were secure. Failure to use the agreed word could mean the captain was under duress.

It was seventy-two hours after the White House conference when the first Keyhole satellite rolled onto its track in space to focus on merchant-marine vessels within a 300-mile radius of Labuan. As it began photographing, the *Countess of Richmond* was sailing through the Makassar Strait, 310 miles south of Labuan. It was not photographed.

FOR LONDON, the White House obsession with an attack from the Pacific was only half the picture. It took a long personal call on the hotline between Downing Street and the White House to conclude an agreement on the two most vital narrows east of Malta. The Royal Navy, in partnership with the Egyptians, would monitor the southern end of the Suez Canal to intercept ships from Asia. US Navy warships would patrol the Strait of Hormuz. Here the threat would only be from a huge vessel capable of sinking itself in the deep-water channel in the centre of the Strait. The owning companies of such vessels were relatively few, and ready to cooperate.

As for threats two and three, every government in Europe with a major sea port was warned of the possible existence of a ghost ship under the command of terrorists. British Navy aeroplanes out of Gibraltar started to patrol the narrows between the Pillars of Hercules, between the Rock and Morocco, to identify anything coming in from the Atlantic.

ALL THE WAY over the Rockies, Major Duval had put the Eagle through its paces and it had performed perfectly. Below him the weather had changed.

The blue skies of Arizona betrayed first a few wisps of mares' tail cloud lines, which thickened as he left Nevada for Oregon. When he crossed the Columbia River into Washington the cloud below him was solid from tree-top height to 20,000 feet. The descent to McChord AFB would be through dense vapour, so 200 miles out he asked for a ground-controlled descent to landing. McChord asked him to stay out to the east, turn inbound over Spokane and descend on instructions. The Eagle was in the left-hand turn towards McChord when what was about to become the USAF's most expensive spanner slipped out of where it had lain jammed between two hydraulic lines in the starboard engine. When the Eagle levelled out, it fell into the blade of the turbofan.

The first result was a massive bang from deep in the guts of the starboard F-100 as the compressor blades began to shear off. In both cockpits a blazing red light answered Nicky Johns's yell of 'What the hell was that?'

Larry Duval's fingers flicked off one switch after another, fuel, electric circuits, hydraulic lines. But the starboard engine was blazing. The in-housing fire extinguishers operated automatically but were too late. The starboard F-100 was in what is known as 'catastrophic engine failure'.

Behind Duval, the wizzo was telling McChord, 'Mayday, Mayday, Mayday, starboard engine on fire—'

He was interrupted by another roar from behind him. Fragments of the starboard engine had torn through the firewall and were attacking the port side. More red lights blazed. The second engine had caught fire.

The pilot had switched the radio to 'transmit', so the air-traffic controller at McChord heard it all in real time. 'I have lost both engines,' said Duval, his voice calm and level. 'Stand by to eject.'

The wizzo glanced over his shoulder. The Eagle was a torch, flaming from end to end. He heard the same calm voice up front.

'Eject. Eject.'

Both men reached down for the handle beside the seat and pulled. With seconds to spare their bodies were hurled upwards through the shattering canopy and into the freezing stratosphere.

Both falling ejectors stabilised with tiny drogues and plunged through grey cloud towards the ground. The seats sensed when to release their charges. The restraining straps flicked open and the men, now a mile apart, just fell out of the seats, which dropped into the landscape below.

The parachutes were also automatic, deploying first with a small drogue to steady the falling men, then with the main canopy. Each man felt the heaving jerk as a terminal velocity of 120 mph slowed to around fourteen.

The major landed in a clearing, his fall cushioned by springy conifer branches lying flat on the ground. After several dazed seconds, he released the chute buckle at his midriff and stood up in the freezing gloom. Then he began to broadcast so the rescuers could get a fix on him.

Nicky Johns had come down in the thick of the trees. As he hit the branches he was drenched in the snow that fell off. He waited for the 'hit' of the ground, but it never came; his canopy was caught in the trees. He took a deep breath, hit the release buckle and fell.

He felt his left leg snap neatly at the shin as it slid between two stout branches under the snow. Knowing that cold and shock would eat into his reserve without mercy, he unhooked his transmitter and began to broadcast.

The Eagle had attempted to fly for a few seconds after its crew had left it. It turned its nose up, wallowed, tilted over, resumed its dive and, as it entered the cloud bank, blew up. The flames had reached the fuel tanks.

As it disintegrated, both engines tore themselves from their fixtures. Each engine, five tons of blazing metal, hit the Cascades wilderness below at 500 mph. One destroyed twenty trees. The other did more.

The CIA officer who commanded the garrison at the Cabin took two minutes to regain consciousness and pull himself off the floor. Dazed and feeling sick, he leaned against the wall of the log cabin amid the swirling dust and called names. He was answered by groans. When the condition of the twelve CIA staffers had been speedily established—two dead, three in need of hospitalisation, the other seven badly shaken—the uninjured survivors checked on the prisoner.

They burst into the Afghan's room, and saw that the door from the living area to the walled exercise court was open. The room itself, being of reinforced concrete, had survived intact.

The concrete wall of the compound was not so lucky. The falling F-100 jet engine had taken a five-foot chunk out of the wall before ricocheting into the garrison quarters. And the Afghan was gone.

CHAPTER NINE

As the great American sea-trap closed around the Philippines, Borneo and eastern Indonesia, all the way across the Pacific to the US coast, the *Countess of Richmond* slipped out of the Flores Sea, through the Lombok Strait between Bali and Lombok, and into the Indian Ocean. Then she turned due west for Africa.

Within seconds of the distress call from the dying Eagle the US Coast Guard unit up at Bellingham was standing by to triangulate on the positions of the downed crew.

Modern aircrew have a life jacket with a small but powerful beacon and a voice communicator. The beacons were picked up at once and the two crewmen located to a few yards. Major Duval was down in the heart of the state park; Captain Johns had fallen in the logging forest.

The cloud cover right on top of the trees would prevent extraction by helicopter, the fastest and favoured way. It would force an old-fashioned rescue. Off-road vehicles would take the rescue parties to the nearest point along one of the tracks; from there to the downed airmen it would be muscle and sweat all the way.

The sheriff of Whatcom County radioed to say he had deputies ready to move in with snowmobiles and quad bikes. But as the minutes ticked by, the body temperature of the airmen started to drop—slowly for Duval but faster for Johns, who was injured and could not move. The race was on to bring the two men gloves, boots, space blankets and piping hot soup before the cold beat them to it.

Nobody told the rescue parties, because nobody knew, that another man was out in the Wilderness that day, and he was very dangerous indeed.

THE SAVING GRACE for the CIA team at the shattered Cabin was that their communications had survived the hit. Just after 4 p.m. local time Marek Gumienny took the call at Langley.

He did not rant or rave. Before his junior colleague in the Cascades Wilderness had finished, Gumienny was analysing the catastrophe. The fugitive had to be hunted down.

'Can a helo get in there to reach you?' he asked.

'No, sir, we have cloud right to the treetops and threatening more snow.'

'What is your nearest town with a track leading to it?'

'Mazama. It's outside the Wilderness but there's a fair-weather track from the town to Hart's Pass. That's a mile away. No track from there to here.'

'You are a covert research facility, understand? You need urgent help. Raise the sheriff at Mazama, get him to come in there with anything he's got. Half-tracks, snowmobiles, off-roads as near as possible; skis, snow-shoes and sleds for the last mile. Meanwhile, can you stay warm?'

'Yes, sir. Two rooms are shattered, but we have three sealed off. The central heating is down but we're piling logs on the fire.'

'Right. When the rescue party reaches you, lock everything down, smash all covert comms equipment, bring all codes with you and come out with the injured. Get those men to hospital.'

'Sir? What about the Afghan?'

'Leave him to me.'

Marek Gumienny thought it was time the army earned its tax dollars. He rang the Pentagon and spoke with his contact at the Defense Intelligence Agency. Twenty minutes later he learned he might have had his first break of a very bad day.

FOUR MILES from McChord Air Force Base is the army's Fort Lewis. One corner of this huge army camp is the home of the First Special Forces Group, known to its few friends as Operational Detachment Group (OD) Alpha 143, a mountain company. Its Ops Commander was Senior Captain Michael Linnett.

When the unit adjutant took the call from a two-star general at the Pentagon, the team was involved in a simulated terrorist hunt on the slopes of Mount Rainer, a bleak pinnacle south of Tacoma. They were equipped for sub-zero rough-terrain operating, and had live ammunition. Captain Linnett was apprised of some kind of emergency while he was descending the mountain. A Chinook troop-carrier helicopter picked up the Alpha team from the empty visitor car park thirty minutes later.

The Chinook took the team as far north as the snow clouds would allow and set them down on a small airfield west of Burlington. A truck arrived from Fort Lewis almost at the same time. It was equipped for every kind of terrain, but progress was slow. Four hours later the exhausted driver crunched into the townlet of Mazama.

The CIA team was also exhausted, but at least their injured colleagues, doped with morphine, were already in real ambulances heading south for a helicopter pick-up and a final transfer to Tacoma Memorial Hospital.

The garrison commander told Captain Linnett what he thought was enough. Linnett snapped that he was security cleared and insisted on more.

'This fugitive, has he got arctic clothing and footwear?'

'No. Hiking boots, warm trousers, a light quilted jacket.'

'No skis, snowshoes? Night-vision goggles? Is he armed?'

'No, nothing like that. He was a prisoner in close confinement.'

'He's toast,' said Linnett. 'In these temperatures, ploughing through a metre of snow with no compass, going round in circles. We'll get him.'

He turned to his men. 'Saddle up,' he shouted, and the ODA climbed back in their truck. It would take them up the remainder of the track to Hart's Pass. After that they would be on skis and snowshoes.

As they left, the sheriff's radio brought the news that both airmen had been found and brought out, very cold but alive.

THE ANGLO-AMERICAN investigators of merchant marine who had taken over Operation Crowbar were still concentrating on threat one, the idea that Al-Qaeda might be planning to close down a vital world highway in the form of a narrow strait. For this, the size of the vessel was paramount.

The principal 500 ultra-large and very large crude carriers, the ULCCs and VLCCs, known to the public as supertankers, were checked and found to be unattacked. Then the tonnages were lowered in modules of 10,000 tonnes fully loaded. When all vessels of 50,000 tonnes and up were accounted for, the 'strait blockage' panic began to subside.

The Edzell team set up a direct line to *Lloyd's Register*, on whose advice they concentrated on vessels flying flags of convenience and those owned by suspect proprietors. A 'no approach to coast' label was slapped on over 200 vessels without their captains or owners being aware of it. But still nothing showed up to set the storm cones flying in the breeze.

THE MESSAGE from Langley was clear: under no circumstances must the fugitive reach Canada, nor must he reach a functioning telephone.

Captain Linnett knew his mountains, and he had few doubts. A man with no specialist footwear, trying to progress through snow over ground riddled with roots, cracks, ditches, gullies and streams, would be lucky to make half a mile per hour across country. Without a compass, he would wander in circles, and would stumble and fall at every second step. He could not see in the blackness under the trees where even the moon, had it not been hidden by 20,000 feet of freezing cloud, could not penetrate.

True, the man had a five-hour head start, but that would only give him under three miles of ground covered. Special Forces men could treble his speed on skis, and even using snowshoes they could double it.

From the truck's drop-off point at the end of the track, the twelve-man team reached the wrecked CIA Cabin in under an hour. The two bodies, rigid in the cold, were laid out in the now freezing refectory, safe from roaming animals, awaiting transport back, once the cloud had lifted.

Linnett's team sergeant, who was an expert tracker, scouted the ground outside. The threatening snow had not fallen; the area around the helipad and the front door, where the rescue team from Mazama had arrived, was a mush of snowshoe marks. But from the shattered compound wall a single trail of footprints led away due north.

Canada was twenty-two miles away. For the Afghan, forty-four hours of hiking. He would never make it, thought Linnett.

It took another hour to cover the next mile, on snowshoes. That was when they found the other cabin. No one had mentioned the other two or three cabins that were permitted in the Pasayten Wilderness because they predated the building prohibition. And this one had been broken into. The shattered triple-glazing and the rock beside the gaping hole left no doubt.

It took them less than a minute to ensure there was no one present, either in the cabin or the adjacent log store. But the signs of recent occupation were everywhere.

Captain Linnett turned to one of his comms sergeants.

'Raise the county sheriff and find out who owns this place,' he said.

THE NEW *COUNTESS of Richmond* took a route south of Java, passed Christmas Island and headed out into the Indian Ocean. For Mike Martin the onboard routines became a ritual.

Ibrahim remained mainly in his cabin and the good news was that most of the time he was violently ill. Of the remaining seven men, the engineer tended his engines, set at maximum speed regardless of fuel use. Wherever the *Countess* was going, she would need no fuel for a return journey.

The radio expert kept a listening watch and must have learned of a sea search taking place right across the Pacific and at the entrances to the Strait of Hormuz and the Suez Canal. He may have reported this to Ibrahim but made no mention of it to the rest.

The other five men took turns in the galley to produce plate after plate of cold tinned food, and also worked shifts at the wheel. The navigator set the heading—always west, then south of due west to the Cape of Good Hope.

As for the rest, they prayed five times a day, read the Koran and stared at the sea.

For Mike Martin the twin enigmas remained unanswered. Where was she going? And what explosive power lay beneath her decks? No one seemed to know, with the possible exception of the chemical engineer. But he never spoke and the subject was never raised.

Martin considered attempting to take over the ship. He had no weapon, just the chance to steal a kitchen knife, and he would have to kill seven men, one of whom, Ibrahim, he had to presume had a firearm. But if and when they came close to a clear target on shore, he knew he would have to do it. For now he bided his time.

He did not know whether his message in the divebag had ever been found, and he certainly did not know he had triggered a global ship-hunt.

'THIS IS DR BERENSON, whom am I talking with?'

They had had a lucky break. The owner of the cabin was a surgeon who had a pager in case of an emergency. This situation definitely rated as one.

Michael Linnett took the speaker from the set on the sergeant's back and lied. 'I'm with the sheriff's office at Mazama,' he said. 'Right now I'm in your cabin in the Wilderness. I'm sorry to tell you there's been a break-in.'

'Hell, no. Is there damage done?' asked the tinny voice from Seattle.

'He broke in by smashing the main front window with a rock, Doctor. That seems to be the only structural damage. I just want to check on theft. Did you have any firearms here?'

'Absolutely not. I keep two hunting rifles and a scatter gun, but I bring them out with me in the fall.'

'OK, now, clothing. Do you have a closet with heavy winter clothing?'

'Sure. It's a walk-in right beside the bedroom door.'

Captain Linnett nodded to his sergeant who led the way by flashlight, as the cabin's generator was closed down. The closet was full of winter kit.

'There should be my pair of arctic snow boots, quilted pants and a parka with zippered hood. Also skis and snowshoes.'

All gone.

'Any weapons at all? Compass?'

The big Bowie knife should have been hanging inside the closet door and the compass and flashlight should have been in the desk drawers. They were all taken. The fugitive had also ransacked the kitchen. An empty tin of baked beans lay on the worktop with two empty cans of soda. There was also an empty pickle jar that had been full of quarters, but no one knew that.

'Thanks, Doc. I'd get up here when the weather clears with a team for a new window, and file a loss claim.'

The Alpha leader cut the connection. He put the fugitive at two or three hours ahead, but now moving much faster. Swallowing his pride, Linnett decided to bring up some cavalry. He spoke to Fort Lewis again. 'Tell McChord I want a Spectre and I want it now. Engage all the authority you need; Pentagon if you have to. I want it over the Cascades and talking to me direct.'

The twelve men of Alpha 143 pressed on hard. The sergeant-tracker was at point, his flashlight picking up the marks of snowshoes in the frozen snow. They were pushing the pace, but they were carrying much more equipment than the Afghan. They had to be keeping up, but were they gaining?

Snow started to fall. It was a blessing and a curse. As the flakes drifted down the rocks and stumps became covered over, permitting a switch from shoes to the faster skis. They also wiped out the trail.

Linnett needed a guiding hand from heaven and it came just after midnight in the form of an AC-130 Hercules gunship, circling at 20,000 feet.

The Spectre gunship is, from the viewpoint of the enemy on the ground, about as nasty as it gets. The original Hercules transport plane has been gutted and its innards replaced with a cockpit-to-tail array of technology designed to locate, target and kill an opponent on the ground. Its infrared thermal imager can pick out any figure in a landscape that emits body heat. Nor is the image a vague blur; it is clear enough to differentiate between a four-legged beast and a two-legged one. But it still could not work out the weirdness of Mr Lemuel Wilson.

He too had a cabin just outside the Pasayten Wilderness. Unlike the Seattle surgeon, he overwintered up there, for he had no alternative home. He used a log fire for heat and kerosene lamps for lighting. Each summer he hunted game and air-dried the meat strips for winter. He cut his own logs and gathered in forage for his mountain pony. But he had another hobby.

He had enough CB equipment, powered by a tiny generator, to spend his winter hours scanning the wavebands of the sheriff, the emergency services and the public utilities. That was how he heard the reports of a two-man aircrew down in the Wilderness and professional teams struggling to the spot.

Hardly had the two airmen broadcast their plight, and the authorities replied with their exact positions, than Lemuel Wilson had saddled up and ridden out to rescue Major Duval, the nearer of the two.

His band-scanning equipment was too cumbersome to bring along, so he never heard that the aviators were rescued. But he did make human contact.

He did not see the man come at him. One second he was urging his pony through a snowdrift, the next a bank of snow came up to meet him. But the snow bank was a man in a silver space-age-material two-piece.

There was nothing space age about the Bowie knife, but it was very efficient. One arm round his neck dragged him off his mount; as he crashed down the blade entered his rib cage from the back and sliced open his heart.

A thermal imager is fine for detecting body heat, but Lemuel Wilson's corpse, dropped into a crevasse ten yards from where he died, lost its heat fast. By the time the AC-130 Spectre began its circling mission high above the Cascades thirty minutes later, Lemuel Wilson did not show up at all.

'Spectre Echo Foxtrot, calling Team Alpha, do you read me, Alpha?'

'Strength five,' reported Captain Linnett. 'We are twelve on skis down here; can you see us?'

'Smile nicely and I'll take your picture,' said the infrared operator.

'Comedy comes later,' said Linnett. 'About three miles due north of us is a fugitive. Single man, heading north on skis. Confirm?'

There was a pause, a long pause.

'Negative. No such image,' said the voice in the sky.

'There must be,' argued Linnett. 'He is up ahead of us somewhere.'

They emerged from the forest to a bare scree. His men looked like spectral figures in the darkness, white zombies in a white landscape. There was only one explanation for the lack of image: the Afghan had taken shelter in a cave. So they were closing on the fugitive.

The Spectre fixed Linnett's position to the yard. Twelve miles to the Canadian border. Five hours to dawn.

Linnett gave it another hour. The Spectre circled but saw nothing to report.

'Check again,' asked Captain Linnett. He was beginning to think something had gone wrong. Had the Afghan died up here? That would explain the absence of heat signature.

'I am scanning an arc subtending ninety degrees with you at the point,' said the imager-operator. 'Right up to the border. In that arc I can see six animals. Four deer, what looks like a marauding mountain lion and a single moose ambling north. About four miles ahead of you.'

The surgeon's arctic clothing was simply too good. Izmat Khan had actually lengthened his lead. The pony was sweating as it neared exhaustion and showed up clearly, but the man on top of it, leaning forward along its neck to urge it onwards, was so well muffled he blended with the animal.

'Sir,' said one of the engineer sergeants, 'it cannot be a moose. I'm from Minnesota and I know that moose do not move up into the mountains in weather like this. They come down to the valley to forage for lichen.'

Linnett called a halt. He stared at the falling snow ahead. How had the man done it? Another isolated cabin, maybe, with an overwintering idiot with a stable. Somehow the Afghan had got himself a horse.

Four miles ahead, back in deep forest, Izmat Khan, who had ambushed Lemuel Wilson, was himself ambushed. The cougar was old, a bit slow for deer, but cunning and very hungry. It came down from a ledge between two trees, and the pony would have smelt it but for its own exhaustion.

The first the Afghan knew, something fast and tawny had hit the pony and it was going down sideways. The rider had time to grab Wilson's rifle from the sleeve alongside the pommel and go backwards over the rump. He landed, turned, aimed and fired.

He had been lucky that the mountain lion had gone for the pony and not himself, but he had lost his mount. The animal was still alive, but it was not going to get up. He used a second bullet to finish its misery. The pony crumpled, lying across the torso and front legs of the cougar.

He unhitched the snowshoes from behind the saddle, fitted them over his boots, shouldered the rifle and moved forward. A hundred yards from him was a large rock overhang. He paused under it for a brief respite.

'Take out the moose,' said Captain Linnett. 'I think it's a horse with the fugitive on it.'

The operator studied his image again. 'You're right,' he said. 'I can see six legs. He's paused for a rest. Next circuit, down he goes.'

In the circling turn the Spectre dropped to 10,000 feet, and locked on with the Gau-12/U Gatling chain gun. This horror fires 1,800 rounds per minute and each round is a 25-mm slug, a single one of which will pull a human body apart. They fired the chain gun for ten seconds, loosing off 300 rounds at the body of the horse in the forest.

'There's nothing left,' said the imager-operator. 'Man and beast both gone.'

'Thank you, Echo Foxtrot,' said Linnett. 'We'll take over now.' The Spectre, mission accomplished, returned to McChord AFB.

The snow stopped, the skis made swift progress over the new powder, and the Alpha team came across the remains of the horse. Few fragments were bigger than a man's arm but they were definitely horse, not human.

Linnett spent ten minutes looking for pieces of arctic clothing, boots, femurs, skull. The skis were lying there, but one was broken, damaged by the falling horse. There was no rifle. No snowshoes, no Afghan.

Two hours to dawn and it had become a race. One man on snowshoes, twelve on skis. All exhausted, all desperate. As the sky lightened fractionally in the east, the team sergeant murmured: 'Border half a mile.'

They arrived twenty minutes later on a bluff overlooking a valley. Below was a logging road that formed the Canadian border and right across from them was another bluff with a clearing containing a cluster of log cabins.

Linnett crouched, steadied his forearms and studied the landscape through binoculars. Nothing moved. The light factor increased.

Unbidden, his snipers eased their weapons from the sleeves that had contained them throughout the mission, fixed their scopes, inserted one shell each and lay down to stare across the gulf through their telescopes.

'I have him, Captain,' the leading sniper whispered. 'He is in a phone booth.'

Izmat Khan had had little communication with his fellow inmates at Guantánamo, but he had spent many months in the same 'solitary' block with a hardline Jordanian who had been a trainer in the AQ camps. 'If you ever get out of here,' the Jordanian had told him, 'I have a friend. We were in the camps together. He will help a True Believer. Mention my name.'

There was a name. And a phone number. Izmat Khan did not know where it was. Nor did he know the overseas dial code out of Canada. So he punched in a quarter and asked for the operator.

'What number are you trying, caller?' said the Canadian telephonist.

Slowly, in halting English, he pronounced the figures he had so painstakingly memorised.

'That is a UK number,' said the operator. 'Are you using US quarters?'

'Yes.'

'That's acceptable. Put in eight of them and I will connect you.'

'Have you acquired the target?' asked Linnett.

'Yes, sir.'

'Take the shot.'

'He's in Canada, sir.'

'Take the shot, Sergeant.'

The sniper took a slow, calm breath, held it inside, and squeezed. The range was a still-air 2,100 yards on his range-meter, well over a mile.

Izmat Khan was pushing quarters into the slot. The glass front of the booth disintegrated into pinpricks of perspex and the bullet took away the back of his head.

The operator was as patient as she could be. The man down in the logging camp had inserted only two quarters, then left the handset hanging. Finally she had no choice but to hang up on him and cancel the call.

Because of the sensitivity of the cross-border shot, no official report was ever made. Captain Linnett reported to his commanding officer, who told Marek Gumienny in Washington. Nothing more was heard.

The body was found in the thaw when the lumberjacks returned that spring. The coroner could do little but record an open verdict. The man had no ID; no one recognised him locally.

Unofficially most people around the coroner's office presumed the man had been the victim of a tragic stray shot from a deer hunter, another death from careless shooting or ricochet. He was buried in an unmarked grave.

Because no one south of the border wanted to make waves, it was never thought to ask what number the fugitive had asked for.

In fact the number he wanted was that of a small apartment near Aston University in Birmingham. It was the home of Dr Ali Aziz al-Khattab, and the phone was on intercept by Britain's MI5. All they were waiting for was enough evidence to justify a raid and arrest. They would get it a month later. But that morning the Afghan was trying to call the only man west of Suez who knew the name of the ghost ship.

CHAPTER TEN

After two weeks, enthusiasm for the ghost-ship hunt was fading. Marek Gumienny was in London conferring with Steve Hill when the SIS expert in maritime terrorism, Sam Seymour, called up from the Ipswich HQ of *Lloyd's Register* and made matters worse. He said he had changed his mind. Hill ordered him to London to explain.

'The option of Al-Qaeda seeking to use a huge blocking ship to close down a vital sea highway to wreck global trade was always the likeliest option,' said Seymour. 'But it was never the only one.'

'What makes you think it was the wrong path to go?' asked Gumienny.

'Because, sir, every single vessel in the world big enough to achieve that has been checked out. They are all safe. That leaves options two and three, which are almost interchangeable but with different targets. I think we should now look at three: mass murder in a seashore city.'

'OK, Sam, convince me. Steve and I both have political masters demanding results or our heads. What kind of ship if not a blocking vessel?'

'For threat number three we don't look at the ship but at the cargo. It need not be large so long as it is deadly. Lloyd's have a hazardous cargo division—obviously it affects the premium.'

'An exploding oil tanker?' said Hill.

'Crude oil does not explode,' Seymour pointed out. 'A vented oil tanker will only cause eco-damage, not mass murder. But a quite small gas tanker could do it. Liquid gas, massively concentrated for transportation.'

'Natural gas, liquid form?' asked Gumienny.

'Liquid natural gas, known as LNG, is hard to ignite,' Seymour countered. 'It would have to leak into the atmosphere for hours before it became combustible. But there is one type that frightens the hell out of the boffins. LPG. Liquid Petroleum Gas. It is so awful that a small tanker, if torched within ten minutes of catastrophic rupture, would unleash the power of thirty Hiroshima bombs. It would be the biggest non-nuclear explosion on this planet.'

There was silence in the room. Steve Hill rose, strolled to the window and looked down at the river Thames flowing past in the April sunshine.

'How can a small tanker be worse than the entire Manhattan project?'

'With an atomic bomb, the damage comes in four waves: the flash, the heat, the shock wave and the gamma-ray radiation. An LPG explosion is all heat, but a heat so fierce that it will cause steel to run like honey. LPG is transported under pressure, in double-hulled tankers. When ruptured, the LPG will gush out and mix with the air. It is heavier than air, so it will swirl around the place it came from, forming one enormous fuel–air bomb. Ignite that, and the entire cargo explodes in flame, terrible flame, rising quickly to five thousand degrees Celsius. Then it starts to roll outwards from the source, a roaring tide of flame, consuming everything in its path until it has consumed itself. Then it gutters like a fading candle and dies.'

'How far will the fireball roll?'

'A small tanker of, say, eight thousand tonnes, fully vented and ignited, would extinguish all human life within a five-kilometre radius. But the explosion creates its own wind. It sucks in the air from periphery to centre, to feed itself, so even humans in a protective shell some distance away from the epicentre will die of asphyxia.'

Steve Hill had a mental image of a city after such a horror exploded within its harbour. Not even the outer suburbs would survive.

'The biggest importer of LPG is the USA,' Seymour continued. 'I know there's a mood in Washington that all this may be a wild-goose chase. But I think we should go the last mile. This is a very specialist market. The USA can check out every LPG tanker expected in her waters, and not just from the Far East. And stop them until boarded. From Lloyd's I can check out every other LPG cargo worldwide; from any point in the compass.'

Marek Gumienny took the next flight back to Washington. As he flew out of Heathrow, the *Countess of Richmond* rounded Cape Agulhas, South Africa, and entered the Atlantic.

SHE HAD MADE good speed, and her navigator, one of the three Indonesians, estimated the Agulhas Current and the north-running Benguela Current would give her an extra day and plenty of time to reach her destination.

High above, out of sight and mind, the satellites drifted across inner space, their cameras passing back to Washington the names on the sterns of all ships heading for Europe or North America. Each identification was checked out, and that included the *Countess of Richmond*, vouched for by Lloyd's and Siebart & Abercrombie as being a Liverpool-registered small freighter bringing a legitimate cargo from Surabaya to Baltimore. There was no point in probing deeper; she was thousands of miles from the American coast.

Within hours of Marek Gumienny's return to Washington, changes were made to the US precautions. In the Pacific the check-out-and-examine cordon was brought to a 1,000-mile band off the coast. A similar cordon was established in the Atlantic from Labrador to Puerto Rico and across the Caribbean Sea to the Yucatan Peninsula in Mexico.

Without fuss or announcement the emphasis was switched from the giant tankers and freighters (which by then had all been checked) to the scores of smaller tankers that ply the seas from Venezuela to the St Lawrence River. Every EP-3 Orion available was pressed into coastal patrol, flying over hundreds of thousands of square miles of tropical and subtropical sea looking for small tankers, especially for those bearing gas.

American industry cooperated to the full, supplying details of every cargo expected, where and when due. This data was cross-indexed with the sightings at sea and they all checked out. Gas tankers were permitted to arrive and dock, but only after taking on board a posse of US Navy, Marines or Coast Guards to escort them in under guard, from 200 miles out.

THE *DOÑA MARIA* was back in Port of Spain when the two terrorists she harboured in her crew saw the signal they had been briefed to expect.

The Republic of Trinidad and Tobago is a major supplier of petrochemical products to the United States. The *Doña Maria* was berthed at the offshore sea island, the tank farm where tankers could approach, take cargo on board and leave without ever approaching the city itself.

Along with two other small tankers, the *Doña Maria* was at a specially remote section of the tank farm. Her cargo after all was liquefied petroleum gas, and no one wanted to be too close during the loading.

It was late afternoon when she was finished and Captain Montalban prepared her for sea. There were still two hours of daylight left when she slipped her mooring lines and eased away from the jetty. A mile offshore she passed close to a rigid inflatable launch in which four men sat with fishing rods. It was the awaited sign.

The two Indians left their posts, ran below to their lockers and returned with handguns. One went to the waist of the tanker, where the scuppers were closest to the water and the men would board. The other went to the bridge and pointed his gun straight at the temple of Captain Montalban.

'Do nothing, please, Captain,' he said with great courtesy. 'There is no need to slow down. My friends will board in a few minutes. Do not attempt to broadcast or I will have to shoot you.'

The captain was simply too amazed to fail to obey. Minutes later the four terrorists were aboard and opposition became futile.

The last man out of the inflatable slashed it with a carving knife and it sank when the painter was released. The other three men had already hefted their canvas grips and stepped over the spaghetti-mix of pipes, tubes and tank hatches that define a tanker's foredeck as they made their way aft.

They appeared on the bridge seconds later: two Algerians and two Moroccans, the ones Dr Al-Khattab had recruited a month earlier. They spoke only Moorish Arabic, but the two Indians, still courteous, translated. The four South American crewmen were to be summoned to the foredeck and would wait there. A new sea course would be calculated and adhered to.

An hour after dark the four crewmen were coldly murdered and tossed overboard, with a length of chain wired to each body's ankle. If Captain Montalban had had any spirit to resist left in him, that was the end of it.

Through the night the *Doña Maria* steamed north, but no longer towards her scheduled destination of Puerto Rico. To her port side was the expanse of the Caribbean basin, unbroken all the way to Mexico. To starboard, quite close, were the two chains called the Windward and Leeward Islands, their warm seas alive with hundreds of small tramps and tankers that keep the islands victualled and alive for the tourists. Into this blizzard of coastal freighters and islands the *Doña Maria* would disappear and remain disappeared until she was logged overdue at Puerto Rico.

WHEN THE *COUNTESS of Richmond* reached the doldrums, Yusuf Ibrahim emerged from his cabin, pale and drained by nausea. He ordered the crew to bring out from its storage place in the engine room a twenty-foot inflatable speedboat. When it was rigid, it was suspended from the two davits above the stern.

It took six men, sweating and grunting, to bring up the 100-hp outboard engine from below and fix it to the rear of the speedboat. Then it was winched down into the gentle swell beneath the stern.

Fuel tanks were lowered and hooked up. After several false starts the engine coughed into life. The Indonesian navigator was at the helm and took the speedboat away for a fast circle round the *Countess*.

Finally, the other six men descended a ship's ladder to the inflatable, leaving only the crippled killer at the helm. It was evident this was a dress rehearsal. The point of the exercise was to allow Suleiman to be taken 300 yards from the freighter, then turn and photograph her with his digital equipment. When linked through his laptop to the satphone, his images could be uploaded to a website. Photography would continue until the boat and its seven men were wiped out. Only Ibrahim, it seemed, would stay at the helm.

But Martin could not know when and where, or what horror lay inside the sea containers. He considered one possibility: being first back on board, casting the inflatable adrift, killing Ibrahim and taking over the freighter. But there would be no such chance. The speedboat was so fast that the six men would be swarming over the rail in seconds.

When the exercise was over, the speedboat was swung empty from the davits, where it looked like any other ship's dinghy, the engineer increased power and the *Countess* headed northwest to skirt the coast of Senegal.

Recovered from his nausea, Yusuf Ibrahim spent more time on the bridge or in the wardroom where the crew ate together. The atmosphere was already hyper-tense and his presence made it more so.

All eight men on board had made their decision to die *shahid*. But that did not prevent the waiting and the boredom tearing at their nerves. Only constant prayer and the obsessive reading of the Holy Koran enabled them to stay calm and true to the belief in what they were doing.

IT HAD BEEN nearly four weeks since the discovery of the scrawled message on the landing card, and there had been no sign of life from Crowbar. Was he dead or alive? No one knew and some were ceasing to care.

Some muttered that he had done his job, been caught and killed, but had caused the plot to be abandoned. Only Steve Hill counselled caution and a continuation of the search for the source of the threat. In some gloom he motored to Ipswich to talk to Sam Seymour and the two eggheads in the hazardous cargo office of *Lloyd's Register* who were helping him.

Sam Seymour was exhausted. He had been saddled with a job that was looking every day more impossible to fulfil.

'Are these LPG tankers being checked out?' Hill asked him.

'Every one. The hazardous cargo team here is only two guys but they're good. In actual fact they are down to the last handful of LPG tankers. As for the general freighters, the sheer numbers mean that we had to cut off those under ten thousand tonnes. But every major port in the word has been apprised that Western intelligence thinks there may be a hijacked ghost ship on the high seas and they must take their own precautions.'

There was a tap on the door and a head came round. Young, pink-cheeked. 'Just got the last one in, Sam. *Wilhelmina Santos*, out of Caracas, bringing LPG to Galveston, confirms she's OK, Americans prepared to board her.'

'That's it?' asked Hill. 'Every LPG tanker in the world accounted for?'

'It's a small menu, Steve,' said Seymour.

'Still, it looks as if the LPG tanker idea was a blind alley,' said Hill.

'There is one thing that worries me, Mr Hill,' said the cargo egghead. 'Three months ago an LPG tanker was lost with all hands. No one actually saw her go down. Her captain came on the radio in high distress to say he had a catastrophic engine-room fire and did not think he could save his ship. Then . . . nothing. She was the *Java Star*.'

'Any traces?' asked Seymour.

'Well, yes. Traces. Before he went off the air he gave his exact position. First on the scene was a refrigerator ship coming up from the south. Her captain reported self-inflating dinghies, life belts, and various flotsam at the spot. No sign of survivors. Captain and crew have not been heard of since.'

'Tragic, but so what?' asked Hill.

'It was where it happened, sir. In the Celebes Sea. Two hundred miles from a place called Labuan Island.'

'Oh shit,' said Steve Hill and left for London.

WHILE MARTIN was at the helm, the *Countess of Richmond* crossed the Equator, heading north by northwest.

Those on board the *Countess* began their early preparations for the entry into paradise. This involved the shaving of all body hair and the writing of wills and last testaments of faith, which were read out to the camera lens.

The Afghan did his as well, but he chose to speak in Pashto. Yusuf Ibrahim, from his time in Afghanistan, had a few words of the language, but even if he had been fluent he could not have faulted the testament.

The man from the Tora Bora spoke of the destruction of his family by an American rocket and his joy that he would soon see them again while bringing justice to the Great Satan. As he spoke, he realised that none of this was going to reach any shore in physical form. It would all be transmitted by Suleiman in datastream before he too died and his equipment with him.

Given that the entire crew was surviving on cold tinned food, no one noticed that a steel carving knife with a seven-inch blade was missing from the galley. When he was unobserved, Martin quietly honed the blade to a razor edge with the whetstone in the knife drawer.

He thought of using the dead of night to drop over the stern to slash the dinghy. But he might be spotted, and although the loss of the dinghy would be a setback, it would not be enough to abort the mission. He dropped the idea but kept the rag-sheathed knife strapped to the small of his back. Each spell at the bridge he tried to work out which port they were going for and what lay inside the sea containers. Neither answer appeared, and the *Countess* steamed north by northwest.

THE GLOBAL HUNT switched and narrowed. After the tip from Ipswich, the origins and ownership of the *Java Star* were checked with a toothcomb. Because she was small, her owning company concealed itself behind a 'shell' company lodged with a bank that turned out to be a brass plate in a Far Eastern tax haven. Her builders were traced and provided plans. Computer imaging produced an exact replica of the tanker.

The government of the flag of convenience she flew when last seen was visited in force. But it was a Polynesian atoll republic and the checkers were soon satisfied that the *Java Star* had never even been there.

Was the gas tanker really dead? If not, where was she now? And what was her new name? The KH-11 satellites were instructed to narrow their search to something resembling the *Java Star*.

In the first week of April the joint operation at Edzell Air Base in Scotland was stood down. There was no more it could do that was not now being done far more officially by the main Western intel-gathering agencies.

With regret, Colonel Mike Martin was presumed to have been lost on mission. He had clearly done what he could, and if the *Java Star* or another floating bomb were discovered heading for the USA, he would be deemed to have succeeded. But no one expected to see him again. It had been too long since the note had been found in a diver's kitbag on Labuan.

Three days before the G8 meeting Marek Gumienny called Steve Hill on a secure line.

'Steve, I'm sorry. I'm sorry for you and even more so for your man Mike Martin. But the conviction here is that he's gone and he must have been wrong. We've checked out just about every tanker on the planet, all categories. Whatever this Al-Isra phrase meant, either we'll never find out or it has been long discontinued or . . . Hold on. I'll kill the other line.'

In a moment, he came back on. 'There's a ship overdue. Left Trinidad for Puerto Rico four days ago. Due yesterday. Never showed. Won't answer.'

'What kind of ship?' asked Hill.

'A tanker. Three thousand tonnes. Look, she may have foundered. But we're checking now.'

'What was she carrying?' asked Hill.

'Liquefied petroleum gas,' was the answer.

IT WAS A KEYHOLE KH-11 satellite that found her, six hours after the complaint from Puerto Rico to the head office of the oil company was turned into a major alarm situation.

Sweeping through the eastern Caribbean with its cameras and listening sensors checking a 500-mile wide swath of sea and islands, the Keyhole picked up a transponder signal from far below that its computer identified as from the missing *Doña Maria*. Various agencies were instantly informed, which was why Marek Gumienny's phone call was interrupted.

In not switching off the transponder, the hijackers were only following orders. With the transponder emitting, they gave away their name and position. With it switched off, they would have become immediately suspect as a possible rogue ship.

The small LPG tanker was still being navigated and steered by a terrified Captain Montalban, four days without sleep, save for a few catnaps before he was kicked awake again. She had slipped past Puerto Rico in the darkness, passed west of the Turks and Caicos Islands and lost herself for a while in the cluster of 700 islands that make up the Bahamas.

When the Keyhole found her she was steaming due west just south of Bimini, the westernmost island of the whole archipelago. At US Special Operations Command headquarters in Tampa her course was plotted and extended forward. It went straight into the open mouth of the Port of Miami.

Within ten minutes the small tanker was attracting real company. A P-3 Orion sub-hunter from the naval air station at Key West found her, dropped to a few thousand feet and began filming her from every angle. The US Coast Guard cutter operator out of Charleston, South Carolina, turned towards the hijacked fugitive and increased to maximum speed.

The word 'cutter' hardly does the *Mellon* justice; she can perform like a small destroyer at 150 metres in length and 3,300 tonnes deadweight. By the time the *Doña Maria* became a speck on the horizon, all the *Mellon*'s weaponry systems were crewed and ready. With the Orion above them, filming everything in real time and passing the images to Tampa, the *Mellon* came abreast of the tanker 200 yards off the beam. Then she called on the *Doña Maria* with her loudhailer.

'Unidentified tanker, this is United States Coast Guard vessel *Mellon*. Heave to. I say again, heave to. We are coming aboard.'

Powerful field glasses could pick up the figure at the helm holding the wheel, and two other figures flanking the man. There was no response.

The message was repeated twice. After the third message the captain gave the order for a single shell to be fired into the sea ahead of the tanker's bow. As the water spout erupted over the bow, those on the bridge of the *Doña Maria* must have got the message. Still she did not slow down.

Then two figures appeared from the door of the sterncastle, just behind the bridge. One had an M60 machine gun slung round his neck. It was a futile gesture and sealed the tanker's fate. He loosed off a short burst that went over the top of the *Mellon*, then took a bullet in the chest from one of the M16 carbines being aimed at him from the cutter's deck.

That was the end of negotiations. As the man's body slumped backwards, the captain of the *Mellon* asked for permission to sink the runaway. Permission was denied. The message from base was unequivocal.

'Pull away from her. Make distance now and make it fast. She's a floating bomb. Resume station a mile from the tanker.'

Regretfully the *Mellon* turned away, powered up to maximum speed and left the tanker to her fate. Two F-16 Falcons were already airborne out of Pensacola Air Force Base in Florida. They came out of the sunset in a clear darkling sky, locked onto the tanker west of Bimini and armed their Maverick missiles.

There was a clipped command from the element leader and both Mavericks left their racks beneath the fighters and followed their noses. Seconds later two 135 kilo warheads hit the tanker.

Even though her cargo was not air-mixed for maximum power, the detonations of the Mavericks deep inside the petrol jelly were enough.

From a mile away the crew of the *Mellon* watched her torch and were duly impressed. They felt the heat wash over their faces and smelt the stench of concentrated gasoline on fire. It was quick. There was nothing left to smoulder on the surface. The forward and stern ends of the tanker went down as two separate pieces of molten junk. The last of her heavier fuel oil flickered for five minutes, then the sea claimed it all.

Just as Ali Aziz al-Khattab had intended.

WITHIN AN HOUR, the President of the USA was interrupted at a state banquet with a brief whispered message. He nodded, demanded a full verbal report at eight the next morning in the Oval Office, and returned to his soup.

At five minutes before eight the Director of the CIA with Marek Gumienny at his side were shown into the Oval Office. The President and the other five of the six principals were there.

The formalities were brief. Keeping it short, Marek Gumienny reported on the exercise in counterterrorism known as Crowbar. He was aware that the President loathed long explanations. The rule of thumb was always 'fifteen minutes and then shut up'. Gumienny telescoped Crowbar into twelve.

There was silence when he stopped.

'So the tip from the Brits turned out to be right?' said the Vice-President.

'Yes, sir. The agent they slipped inside Al-Qaeda must be presumed dead. But he got the message out. The terror weapon was indeed a ship.'

'I had no idea cargoes that dangerous were being carried around the world on a daily basis,' marvelled the Secretary of State.

'Nor I,' said the President. 'Now, regarding the G8 Conference, what is your advice to me?'

The Secretary of Defense glanced at the Director of National

Intelligence and nodded. They had clearly prepared their go-ahead.

'Mr President, we have every reason to believe the terrorist threat to this country, notably to the city of Miami, was destroyed last night. Our advice therefore is that you go ahead with an easy mind.'

'Why, then, that's what I shall surely do,' said the President.

CHAPTER ELEVEN

David Gundlach reckoned he had the best job in the world. Second-best, anyway. To have that fourth gold ring on the sleeve or epaulette and be the captain of the vessel would be even better, but he settled happily for First Officer.

On an April evening he stood at the starboard wing of the huge bridge and looked down at the swarming humanity on the dock of the new Brooklyn Terminal 200 feet below him.

Pier Twelve on Buttermilk Channel is not a small dock, but this ship took up all of it. At 1,132 feet long, 135 feet in the beam and drawing 39 feet, she was the biggest passenger liner afloat by a big margin. The more First Officer Gundlach, on his first crossing since his promotion, looked at her, the more magnificent she seemed.

Far below he could make out the banners of the frustrated and angry demonstrators beyond the terminal buildings. New York's police had with great effectiveness cordoned off the entire area. Harbour Police boats skimmed and swerved round the terminal at sea level to ensure that no protesters in boats could come near. Even if they had, it would have done them no good. The steel hull of the liner towered above the waterline, its lowest ports more than fifty feet up. So those boarding that evening could do so in complete privacy.

Not that they were of interest to the protesters. So far the liner had only taken on board the lowly ones: stenographers, secretaries, junior diplomats and special advisers.

David Gundlach and his fellow officers had spent the day escorting scores of American Secret Servicemen over every inch of the ship. They all scowled in concentration, jabbered into their sleeves where the mikes were hidden and got their answers in earpieces. They found nothing amiss.

The backgrounds of the 1,200 crew had been vetted and not a shred of evidence found against any of them. The Grand Duplex Apartment set aside for the US President and First Lady was already sealed and guarded by the Secret Service, having been given an inch-by-inch search.

Gundlach checked his watch. Two hours to completion of boarding of the 3,000 passengers before the eight heads of state or government were due to arrive. Like the diplomats in London, Gundlach admired the simplicity of chartering the biggest and most luxurious liner in the world to host the biggest and most prestigious conference in the world, and to do so during a five-day crossing of the Atlantic from New York to Southampton.

The ruse confounded all the forces that sought to bring chaos to the G8 Conference every year. Better than a mountain, better than an island, with accommodation for 4,200 souls, the *Queen Mary 2* was untouchable.

Gundlach would stand beside his captain as the Typhoon hooters sounded their deep bass 'A' note to bid farewell to New York. He would give the required power settings from her four Mermaid pod motors and the captain, using only a tiny joystick on the control console, would ease her out into the East River and turn her towards the Atlantic.

FAR TO THE EAST, the *Countess of Richmond* was passing the Canary Islands, away to her starboard. She had two days in hand before her rendezvous with history. The Indonesian navigator had instructed his compatriot in the engine room to cut power to 'slow ahead', and she was moving at a walking pace through the gentle swell of an April evening.

The helmsman eased her a few more degrees to port, where, 1,600 miles away, lay the American coast. From high in space she was spotted yet again; and again the computers read her transponder, checked the records and repeated her clearance: 'Legitimate trader, no danger.'

THE FIRST GOVERNMENT party to arrive at the new terminal was the Prime Minister of Japan and his entourage. As the rotor blades slowed to a gentle twirl, the delegation was greeted by ship's officers and conducted along the covered tunnel to the entrance in the side of the hull; and from thence to one of the Royal Suites. Then the helicopters left for Kennedy to collect the Canadians, who had just arrived.

The Russians, French, Germans and Italians succeeded each other in smooth sequence and dusk fell as the British, owners of the *Queen Mary 2*, used the last flights of the helicopter shuttle.

The US President, who would be hosting the inaugural dinner just after eight, came in his dark blue helicopter on the dot of six. A Marine band on the quay struck up 'Hail to the Chief' as he strode into the hull and the steel doors closed. At six thirty the last mooring ropes were cast off and the *Queen Mary 2*, dressed overall and lit like a floating city, eased out into the East River.

Shortly after two escorting missile cruisers took up position and announced themselves to the captain. To port was the USS *Leyte Gulf* and to starboard the USS *Monterey*. The captain acknowledged their presence and thanked them. Then he left the bridge to change for dinner. David Gundlach had the helm and the command.

As the lights of Long Island dropped away, First Officer Gundlach increased the power to maximum cruise, and overhead the aerial escort appeared: one US Navy EC2 Hawkeye with radar scopes that would illuminate the surface of the Atlantic for 500 miles in any direction around the convoy. And an EA-6B Prowler capable of jamming any offensive weapons system that might dare to lock onto the convoy and destroying that source with its HARM missiles.

The air cover would be refuelled and replaced until it could be relieved by identical cover coming out of the US-leased base in the Azores. That in turn would continue until it could be replaced by cover out of the UK.

THE CONFERENCE met in full plenum the following morning. The Royal Court Theatre had been transformed to accommodate all eight delegations with, sitting behind the principals, their small army of minions.

Dinner that second night was hosted by the British Prime Minister in the 200-seat Queen's Grill. Those less eminent spread themselves through the huge Britannia Restaurant or the various pubs and bars. The younger diplomats favoured the Queen's Ballroom after dinner or the G32 nightclub.

High above them all, the lights were dimmed on the sweeping bridge where David Gundlach presided through the night. Spread out in front of him, below the forward windows, were plasma screens for every system in the ship. On the radar screen, he could see the blips made by the cruisers either side of him, and those of other vessels within twenty-five miles in all directions. He also had at his disposal an Automatic Identification System, which would read a ship's transponder and, using a cross-checking computer based on Lloyd's records, would identify not just who she was but her known route and cargo, and her radio channel.

Either side of the *Queen Mary 2*, also on darkened bridges, the radar men of the two cruisers pored over their screens with the same task. Their duty was to ensure nothing remotely threatening got near the huge monster thundering along between them. Even for a checked-out freighter the closeness limit was three miles. On the second night, nothing was nearer than ten.

The picture created by the E2C Hawkeye was bigger because of its altitude. The image was like an immense circular torch beam moving across the Atlantic from west to east. The Hawkeye could tell the cruisers what lay ahead of them. But being realistic, it put a limit of twenty-five miles or one hour's cruising on this projection.

Just before eleven on the third night, the Hawkeye posted a low-level warning. 'There is a small freighter twenty-five miles ahead, two miles south of intended track. It seems to be motionless in the water.'

THE *COUNTESS OF RICHMOND* was not quite motionless. Her propellers idled in the water, but there was a four-knot current, which gave her just enough way to keep her nose into the flow, and that meant towards the west.

The inflatable speedboat was in the water, tethered to her port side with a rope-and-plank ladder running down from the rail to the sea. Four men were already in it, bobbing on the current beside the hull of the freighter.

The other four were on the bridge. Ibrahim held the wheel, staring at the horizon, seeking the first glimmer of the approaching lights.

The Indonesian radio expert was adjusting the transmitting microphone for strength and clarity. Beside him stood the teenager of Pakistani parents born and raised in a suburb of Leeds. The fourth was the Afghan. When the radio man was satisfied he nodded at the boy, who nodded back and took a stool beside the ship's console, waiting for the call.

IT CAME FROM the cruiser plunging through the sea six cables to the starboard of the *Queen Mary 2*. David Gundlach heard it loud and clear, as did all on the night watch. The channel used was the common wavelength for ships in the North Atlantic. The voice had the drawl of the Deep South.

'*Countess of Richmond, Countess of Richmond,* this is US Navy cruiser *Monterey*. Do you read me?'

The voice that came back, had the flat vowels of Lancashire or Yorkshire. 'Oh, aye, *Monterey, Countess* 'ere.'

'You appear to be hove to. State your situation.'

'*Countess o'Richmond.* 'Aving a bit of overheating . . .' *Click, click.* '. . . prop shaft . . .' (Static.) '. . . repairing as fast as we can . . .'

There was a brief silence from the bridge of the cruiser. Then . . .

'Say again, *Countess of Richmond*, I repeat, say again.'

The reply came back and the accent was thicker than ever.

On the bridge of the *Queen Mary 2*, the First Officer saw the blip entering his radar screen slightly south of dead ahead and fifty minutes away. Another display gave all the details of the *Countess of Richmond* and confirmed that her transponder signal was genuine. He cut into the radio exchange.

'*Countess of Richmond*, this is *Queen Mary Two*. I read you have an overheat in the prop shaft and you are carrying out repairs at sea. Confirm.'

'That's reet. 'Ope to be finished in an hour,' said the voice on the speaker.

'*Countess*, give your details, please. Port of registry, port of departure, destination, cargo.'

'*Queen Moory*. Registered in Liverpool, eight thousand tonnes, general cargo freighter, coming from Java with brocades and timber, heading for Baltimore.'

Gundlach ran his eye down the screened information provided by the head office of McKendrick Shipping in Liverpool, brokers Siebart & Abercrombie in London and insurers Lloyd's. All accurate.

'Who am I speaking to, please?' he asked.

'This is Captain McKendrick. 'Oo are you?'

'First Officer David Gundlach speaking.'

The *Monterey*, following the exchange with difficulty, came back. '*Monterey, Queen*. Do you want to alter course?'

Gundlach consulted the displays. The bridge computer was guiding the *Queen Mary 2* along the pre-planned track and would adjust for any change in the sea, wind, current or waves. To divert would mean going to manual or resetting the programme and then returning to their original course.

'No need, *Monterey*. We'll be past her in forty minutes. Over two miles of sea between us.'

The *Monterey* would be closer than that, but there was still ample room. High above, the Hawkeye and the EA-6B scanned the helpless freighter for any sign of electronic activity. There was none, but they would keep watching until the *Countess* was well behind the convoy.

'Roger that,' said the *Monterey*.

IT HAD ALL BEEN heard on the bridge of the *Countess*. Ibrahim nodded that they should leave him. The radio engineer and the youth scuttled down the ladder to the speedboat and all six in the inflatable waited for the Afghan.

Convinced that the crazed Jordanian would attempt to ram one of the oncoming vessels, Martin knew he could not leave the ship. His only hope was to take her over after killing the crew.

He went down the rope ladder backwards. Behind the thwarts, Suleiman was setting up his photographic equipment. A rope trailed from the rail of the *Countess*; one of the Indonesians stood near the speedboat's bow, gripping the rope and holding her against the flow of the current.

Martin held the ladder fast, turned, reached down and slashed the grey rock-hard fabric over a six-foot length. The act was so fast and so unexpected that for several seconds no one reacted. The escaping air made a low roar and that side of the inflatable dipped downwards and began to ship water. Leaning further out, Martin slashed at the retaining rope. He missed but cut open the forearm of the Indonesian. Then the men reacted. But the Indonesian had released his grip and the sea took them.

Vengeful hands reached out at him, but the speedboat dropped astern. The weight of the great outboard pulled down the aft end and more water rushed in. Somewhere down-current in the blackness of the Atlantic night it sank. Martin saw waving hands on the water, then they too were gone. No one can swim against four knots.

He went back up the ladder. At that moment Ibrahim jerked one of the three controls the explosives expert had left him. As Martin climbed, there was a series of sharp cracks as tiny charges went off.

When Mr Wei had built the gallery masquerading as six sea containers along the deck of the *Java Star*, he had made the roof, or 'lid', out of a single piece of steel held down by four strongpoints. To these the explosives man had fitted shaped charges and linked all four to wires taking power from the ship's engines. When they blew, the sheet-metal lid of the cavern beneath lifted several feet. The power of the charges was asymmetric so that one side of the sheet rose higher than the other.

Martin was at the top of the rope ladder, knife in teeth, when the charges blew. He crouched there as the huge sheet of steel slid sideways into the sea. He put the knife away and entered the bridge.

The Al-Qaeda killer was standing at the wheel, staring forward through the glass. On the horizon, bearing down at twenty-five knots, was a floating city, seventeen decks and 150,000 tonnes of lights, steel and people. Right under the bridge the gallery was open to the stars. For the first time Martin realised that this was not a general freighter containing explosives; it was a tanker. Running away from the bridge was the cat's cradle of pipes, tubes, spigots and hydrant-wheels that gave away her purpose. Evenly spaced down the deck towards the bow were six circular steel discs—the venting hatches for the six cargo tanks below deck.

'You should have stayed on the boat, Afghan,' said Ibrahim.

'There was no room, my brother. Suleiman almost fell overboard. I stayed on the ladder. Then they were gone. Now I will die here with you, *inshallah*.'

Ibrahim seemed appeased. He glanced at the ship's clock and pulled a second lever. Six more charges detonated. The six hatches blew away from above the tanks. What followed was invisible to the naked eye: six vertical columns rose from the domes as the cargo began to vent. The rising vapour cloud reached a hundred feet, lost its impetus and gravity took over. The unseen cloud, mixing furiously with the night air, fell back to the sea and began to roll outwards, away from the source in all directions.

Martin had lost and he knew it. He was too late and he knew that too. He realised that he had been riding a floating bomb since the Philippines, and that what was pouring out of the six missing hatches was invisible death.

He had always presumed the *Countess of Richmond*, now become again the *Java Star*, was going to drive herself into some inner harbour and detonate what lay below her decks. He had presumed she was going to ram something of value as she blew herself up. For thirty days he had waited in vain for a chance to kill seven men and take over her command. No such chance had appeared. Now, too late, he realised the *Java Star* was not going to deliver a bomb; she was the bomb. And with her cargo venting fast, she did not need to move an inch. The oncoming liner had only to pass within three miles of her to be consumed.

He had heard the exchange between the Pakistani boy and the deck officer of the *Queen Mary 2*. The *Java Star* would not engage engines—the escorting cruisers would never allow that—but she did not need to.

There was a third control beside Ibrahim's right hand, a button to be hammered downwards. Martin followed the flexes to a flare-gun mounted just forward of the bridge windows. One flare, one single spark . . .

The city of lights was over the horizon. Fifteen miles, thirty minutes' cruising, optimum time for maximum fuel–air mixture.

Martin's glance flicked to the radio speaker on the console. A last chance to shout a warning. His right hand slid down towards the slit in his robe, inside which was his knife, strapped to his thigh.

The Jordanian caught the glance and the movement. He had not survived Afghanistan, a Jordanian jail and the relentless American hunt for him in Iraq without developing the instincts of a wild animal. Something told him that despite the fraternal language, the Afghan was not his friend.

Martin's hand slipped inside his robe for the knife. Ibrahim was first; the gun had been underneath the map on the chart table. It was pointing straight at Martin's chest. The distance to cross was twelve feet. Ten too many.

A soldier is trained to estimate chances and do it fast. Martin had spent much of his life doing that. On the bridge of the *Countess of Richmond*, enveloped in her own death cloud, there were only two: go for the man; go for the button. There would be no surviving either.

Colonel Mike Martin made his choice . . .

Ibrahim saw him coming; he knew the flicker in the eyes of a man about to die. The killer screamed and fired. The charging man took the bullet in the chest and began to die. But beyond pain and shock there is always will-power, just enough for another second of life.

At the end of that second, both men and ship were consumed in a rose-pink eternity.

DAVID GUNDLACH stared in stunned amazement. Fifteen miles ahead, where the world's largest liner would have been in thirty-five minutes, a huge volcano of flame erupted out of the sea. From the other three men on the night watch came cries of 'What the hell was that?'

'*Monterey* to *Queen Mary 2*. Divert to port, I say divert to port. We are investigating.'

To his right, Gundlach saw the US cruiser speed up and head for the flames. The *Countess* had clearly sustained some terrible accident. His job was to stay clear; if there were men in the water the *Monterey* would find them. But it was still wise to summon his captain. When the ship's master arrived on the bridge his first officer explained what he had seen. They were now a full eighteen miles from the estimated spot and heading away fast.

To port, the USS *Leyte Gulf* stayed with them. The *Monterey* was heading straight for the fireball miles up ahead. As the two men watched from the bridge, the flames began to flicker and die. The last blotches of flame upon the sea would be the remnants of the vanished ship's fuel oil. All the hyper-volatile cargo was gone before the *Monterey* reached the spot.

The captain ordered that the computers resume course for Southampton.

EPILOGUE

There was an inquiry, of course. It took almost two years.

One team took the real *Java Star*: from the laying of her keel to the moment she steamed out of Brunei loaded with LPG, destination Fremantle, Western Australia. It was confirmed by witnesses that Captain Herrmann was in charge and that all was well. She was seen by two other captains rounding the northeastern tip of Borneo shortly after that.

The recording of her captain's last Mayday message was played to a Norwegian psychiatrist, who confirmed that the voice was a Norwegian speaking good English, but that he appeared to be speaking under duress.

The captain of the fruit ship that had noted her given position and diverted to the spot was traced and interviewed. He repeated what he had heard and seen. But experts in fire at sea reckoned that if the fire in the *Java Star*'s engine room was so catastrophic that Captain Herrmann could not save her, it must have ignited her cargo eventually. In which case there would be no fabric-tented life rafts left floating on the water where she sank.

Filipino commandos carried out a raid on the Zamboanga Peninsula, ostensibly on Abu Sayyaf bases. They trawled and brought back two trackers, who reported that they had seen a small tanker in a narrow creek in the jungle being worked on by men with oxyacetylene torches.

The *Java Star* team entered its report within a year. It declared that the tanker had not been sunk by an onboard fire but had been hijacked intact; a lot of trouble had been gone to to persuade the marine world that she no longer existed. The crew was presumed dead, and this had to be confirmed.

Owing to need-to-know, all the arms of the inquiry were working on the various facets without knowing why. They were told, and believed, that it was an insurance investigation.

Another team followed the fortunes of the real *Countess of Richmond*. They proceeded from the office of Alex Siebart in Crutched Friars, London, to Liverpool, and checked out family and crew. They confirmed that all was in good order when the *Countess* unloaded her Jaguars at Singapore, and independent witnesses confirmed she was still in the command of her lawful captain when she took on timber at Kinabalu.

But a visit to Surabaya, Java, revealed that she had never taken on her second part-cargo of Asian silks. Yet Siebart & Abercrombie had received confirmation from the shippers that she had. So it was forged.

A likeness of 'Mr Lampong' was created and Indonesian Homeland Security recognised a suspected financial supporter of Jemaat Islamiya. A search was mounted but the terrorist had vanished.

The team concluded that the *Countess of Richmond* had been hijacked in the Celebes Sea. With all her papers, ID radio codes and transponder stolen, she would have been sunk with all hands. Next of kin were advised.

THE CLINCHER CAME from Dr Ali Aziz al-Khattab. The wiretaps on his phones revealed that he was booking a departure to the Middle East. After a conference at Thames House, home of MI5, it was decided that enough was enough. Birmingham police and Special Branch took down the apartment door of the Kuwaiti academic when the listeners confirmed he was in the bath, and he was escorted away in a towelling robe.

But Al-Khattab was clever. A search of his apartment, car and office, cellphone and laptop revealed not one incriminating detail about him.

He smiled blandly, and his lawyer protested, throughout the statutory twenty-eight days allowed to the British police for holding a suspect without preferring a formal charge. His smile faded when, as he stepped out of Her Majesty's Prison Belmarsh, he was rearrested, this time on an extradition warrant lodged by the government of the United Arab Emirates.

Under this legislation there is no limit of time. Al-Khattab went straight back to his cell. His lawyer lodged a vigorous appeal against extradition. As a Kuwaiti he was not even a citizen of the UAE, but that was not the point.

The Counter-Terrorist Centre at Dubai had, amazingly, come into possession of a sheaf of photos. These showed Al-Khattab conferring closely with a known Al-Qaeda courier, a dhow captain already under surveillance. Others showed him arriving at, and leaving, a villa in the outback of Ras-al-Khaimah, known to be a terrorist hideaway. The London judge was impressed and granted the extradition.

Al-Khattab appealed . . . and lost again. Faced with the dubious charms of HMP Belmarsh or an athletic interrogation by UAE Special Forces at their desert base in the Gulf, he asked to stay as a guest of Queen Elizabeth.

That posed a problem. The British explained they had nothing to hold him on, let alone try and convict him. He was halfway to Heathrow airport when he struck his deal and began to talk.

CIA guests who sat in on the sessions reported back that it was like watching the Boulder Dam give way. He blew away over one hundred AQ agents who until then had been lily-whites, unknown to Anglo-American intelligence, and twenty-four sleeping bank accounts.

When the interrogators mentioned the AQ project code-named Al-Isra, the Kuwaiti was stunned into silence. Then he started to talk again.

He confirmed everything London and Washington already knew or suspected, then added more. He could identify all the eight men aboard the *Countess of Richmond* on her final voyage except the three Indonesians. And he admitted that the *Doña Maria* and the men on board her had been a deliberate sacrifice, a diversion lest there be any hesitation for any reason in sending the American President to sea in a liner.

Gently the interrogators brought the subject round to an Afghan whom they knew Al-Khattab had interrogated in the UAE villa. In fact they did not know it at all; they suspected it, but Al-Khattab hardly hesitated.

He confirmed the arrival of the mysterious Taliban commander in Ras-al-Khaimah after a daring and bloody escape from custody outside Kabul. He claimed these details had been authenticated by AQ sympathisers in Kabul. And he revealed that it was the Sheikh, no less, who had verified the Afghan's identity on the basis of a conversation years earlier in a hospital cave in the Tora Bora. It was the Sheikh who permitted the Afghan the privilege of joining Al-Isra, and he, Al-Khattab, had despatched the man to Malaysia with others.

It gave his Anglo-American interrogators exquisite pleasure to wreck what was left of his life by telling him who the Afghan really was.

The Crowbar Committee concluded that Mike Martin had boarded the *Countess of Richmond*, still posing as a terrorist, somewhere after Labuan and that there was not one shred of evidence that he had got off in time.

The question of why the *Countess* blew up forty minutes prematurely was left open on the file.

IT IS CUSTOMARY in the UK for seven years to elapse before a person missing without trace can legally be presumed dead and a certificate issued. But when Dr Al-Khattab's interrogation reached its conclusion, the coroner for the City of Westminster was entertained to a discreet dinner in a private room at Brooks's Club, St James's Street. The three others present explained many things to the coroner when the stewards had left them alone.

The following week, the coroner issued a certificate of death to an academic from the School of Oriental and African Studies, a Dr Terry Martin, in respect of his late brother, Colonel Mike Martin of the Parachute Regiment, who had vanished without trace eighteen months earlier.

IN THE GROUNDS of the headquarters of the SAS Regiment outside Hereford stands an odd-looking structure known as the Clock Tower. Predictably, it has a clock at the top, but the points of interest are the four faces of the tower, on which are inscribed the names of all SAS men killed in combat.

Shortly after the issue of the death certificate, a memorial service was held at the foot of the Clock Tower. There were a dozen men in uniform and ten in civilian clothes, and two women. One of these was the Director-General of MI5, the Security Service, and the other the dead man's ex-wife.

The missing-in-action status had needed a bit of persuasion but the pressure came from very high indeed. When apprised of all the known facts, the Director, Special Forces, and the Commanding Officer of the Regiment had agreed that the status was justified.

The brief ceremony was held on a bleak February day, as the sun dipped behind the Black Mountains across the border to the west. At the end, the chaplain spoke the habitual words from the Gospel of St John: 'Greater love hath no man than this, that a man lay down his life for his friends.'

Only those grouped round the Clock Tower knew that Mike Martin, Parachute Regiment and SAS Colonel, retired, had done this for 4,000 complete strangers, none of whom ever knew he existed.

FREDERICK FORSYTH

Born: Ashford, Kent, August 25, 1938
Home: Hertfordshire
Former profession: journalist

RD: Is the audacious idea of sending in an undercover agent to pose as a member of Al Qaeda one that the security services might actually turn into reality some day?
FF: Impersonation is risky, but it has been tried successfully before. There are precedents. The same applies to infiltration under false colours. Sir Richard Burton posed as a Muslim and went into Mecca in the eighteenth century—his Arabic was that good—though he would have been killed if exposed. There are several British-born Anglo-Saxons who could pass among Arabs for an Arab.

RD: Would it be possible to survive such a mission?
FF: Certain conditions would have to be rigorously fulfilled. The impersonator would have to look, speak, act and pray like the doppelgänger. More, he could never meet anyone who could vouch for the real person he was pretending to be—exposure would be certain. Mike Martin was told never, ever, to mix with real Pashtun—they would spot the poor Pashto. But Gulf Arabs might be fooled. Finally—the mission should be short—in and out. Martin's mistake was to stay too long.

RD: What made you decide to reintroduce the character of Mike Martin, the retired Special Services officer who first appeared in *The Fist of God*?
FF: When I was researching *The Fist of God* over a decade ago I became pretty sure that the West had an 'asset' somewhere in Saddam's close circle. We were getting too much 'stuff' that could not have come from space cameras or eavesdropping. Therefore, someone must have gone in there to run the asset. Hence the idea of the fluent Arab-speaker who would dare to do that. Ten years later it seemed foolish to reinvent the character.

RD: You mentioned in an interview once that you think of yourself as a 'technopeasant', ie that you prefer not to use the Internet for research . . .
FF: I have no natural empathy with things technical or electronic. The Internet, as a research vehicle, is limited to bare facts and, in my experience, many are actually wrong. To get the 'flavour' of an episode or covert discipline, I find and talk to those who took part, those who have spent their active lives inside the world that

I am trying to research, and I persuade them to tell me what it is like.

RD: If you could alter one thing about modern life, what would it be?

FF: I would abolish political correctness. It began as a philosophy demanding greater tolerance and an end to bigotry. No problem there at all. But it has been perverted into a new bigotry of its own, a fascism of the mediocre against the ordinary citizen trying to enjoy his/her life without hurting anyone else.

RD: And what should be done to help speed an end to the 'war on terror'?

FF: The West can only form an 'alliance of the civilised' and work on the five fronts on which all covert or 'cold' wars are fought: diplomatic, financial, that of lethal action— and, most importantly, by using intelligence and psychological means, i.e. propaganda, persuasion, hearts and minds. You cannot defeat a modern, fanatical terrorist enemy without winning all five.

RD: What inspires or enthuses you about life today, and what, if anything, gets you down?

FF: I am inspired by reading of acts of courage, enterprise, daring, kindness, compassion and generosity. What depresses me is the reverse—the constant forbidding of human enjoyment by jacks-in-office, parasites on the tax payroll who substitute political correctness to compensate for their total lack of talent or common sense.

RD: Looking back over your life, is there anything or anyone who has profoundly influenced you, or changed the way you think?

FF: The greatest influence of my life was my father. He was not famous or rich or an intellectual. But he was the most decent, kindly, tolerant, genial, compassionate, generous and patriotic man I have ever known.

RD: Is there anything you wish you'd known when you were younger?

FF: I suppose I would have been wiser if I had learned earlier the levels of self-service, self-adoration and cynicism that can accompany the lust for wealth, power and fame. Only very rarely can anyone possessed of these appetites incite my respect or admiration.

RD: Does it get harder or easier to write as time goes by?

FF: The research can be strenuous, so with passing years one becomes less able or keen to undertake the slog and exhaustion that can accompany trips to weird and wonderful places to 'check things out'. But pounding away at keys is much the same as it always was—great when the words come flowing to the mind, a drag when the pauses are longer.

RD: And, finally, if we were to ask your family about your best and worst qualities, what would you guess to be their answer?

FF: Oh Lord . . . I hate self-analysis. Much better to ask my wife. But only when I'm out of the room, please.

CALL OF
THE WILD

GUY GRIEVE

Guy Grieve's life was going nowhere. Trapped in a job he hated, and up to his neck in debt, he decided to turn a long-cherished dream into reality: to live for a year in the harsh, unforgiving Alaskan wilderness.

His adventure was more testing than he could ever have imagined. Not only did he have to learn the hard way how to build a log cabin, hunt for food, survive extreme cold—he also had to watch out for hungry bears . . .

1

As I bend to hoist my overstuffed hiking bag onto my back, I see the impression of a large paw print in the cool mud. My heart squeezes a beat. I need no guidebook to tell me that, shortly before I landed on this beach, a grizzly bear stood on this spot. As I stare at the print, my tired brain adjusts to the reality of my situation: I am in the subarctic wilderness, a place where I could be overpowered and eaten by an animal weighing over a thousand pounds. I touch the deep holes where five claws have left their mark. Looking along the line of prints, I realise that the bear has disappeared into the same woods that I now plan to make my home.

Using a flood-bleached tree for support, I pull myself up the bank towards the trees. I am dripping with sweat and surrounded by buzzing black flies. The bag is too heavy to climb with, so I heave it over the lip of the bank and into a clump of thorny bushes before levering myself into the greenery.

I stand on the edge for a few minutes, looking down at my trail, reluctant to take the first step away from the safety of my boat and into the darkness of the woods. Night is coming and I know that I have over a mile of difficult passage through dense trees and undergrowth before I reach the lake where I will make camp. At this moment, I would joyfully undo everything, turn the clock back to a time when life was safe and predictable. Taking a deep breath, I turn away from the beach and walk towards the woods.

A LACONIC, world-weary but nevertheless warm voice answers the phone. '*Scotsman* Editor's office, Sonja speaking. Can I help you?'

I stutter into action like a rusty outboard on a wet day. 'Ah yes, um . . . could I possibly speak to Iain? This is Guy from downstairs.'

A slight pause. 'Can I ask what it's about?' She must be wondering what some hapless sod from the sales floor could possibly want with the editor of Scotland's most august newspaper.

I feel like telling her that it is about the fact that I am going stir-crazy and have finally reached the point of no return. That the only way I can see of freeing myself from the trap of office life is to head for one of the loneliest and wildest places on earth, where I will be alone and far from my family with a not inconsiderable chance of dying. Instead I say, 'Well, I'm just wondering if I could meet with him at some point?'

'Hold on.' There is a long pause as she checks his diary. 'Right—come up tonight after five thirty and wait. No guarantees, but I'm pretty sure you will be able to get a bit of time with Iain.'

I experience a surge of something quite foreign: hope. 'Thank you Sonja—I'll be there.'

I HAD BEEN WORKING in the commercial department of *The Scotsman* in Edinburgh for over five years. I had held a range of jobs, and had some success at coming up with new ways to get money into the company. In 2002, an indulgent managing director decided to see if I might be capable of holding a senior position within the company. I was duly promoted from lowly sales executive to the grand title of 'Head of Strategic Marketing', and given my own office on the top floor, where all the senior executives lurked. For a short period I found myself quite excited and began to feel that maybe this was the start of something. For weeks I plotted and planned and felt very professional and senior. I would swivel about in my chair and tap away ostentatiously at my computer. There were regular meetings held in my office, and I felt proud to offer people coffee and biscuits as they settled themselves around the faux mahogany meeting table.

As the weeks turned into months, the people on the top floor waited to see what the new lad was going to come up with. I was planning to launch a new reader loyalty scheme. In exchange for subscribing to *The Scotsman*, a gardening club would offer discounts at a range of horticultural retailers, and as an irresistible inducement I planned to offer every signed-up member a free porcelain 'digging dog' with a wind-activated wagging tail.

Each evening, I drove home with my head full of readers' incentives and digging dogs, unwinding as I left the city behind me and approached our home in the Scottish Borders. My daily commute added up to a three-hour round trip, but it seemed worth it to live in the country. I arrived home just in time to read a story to our two-year-old son, Oscar, before he fell asleep. Then Juliet and I would cram down a late supper and try hard to feel young and happy and full of life. The next morning I would get up early, slipping out as my family slept, knowing they would wake up without me.

The reader promotion launched and was an instant flop, and my office became a storeroom for over a thousand boxes marked DIGGING DOG. My management still clearly saw some benefit in having me around, and shuttled me back downstairs to the sales floor.

From there, I began to dream of escape. Juliet was shortly due to give birth to our second child, and our mortgage and credit-card debt was crippling us. I knew we were not alone—almost all of our friends were in the same situation—but I couldn't accept that this was the way we were meant to live. This debt gave me no choice but to continue my increasingly mournful journey through the corridors of cubicle hell. I was in the prime of my life, yet spending eight hours a day sitting down in an air-conditioned office, staring into a computer screen. Three further hours each day were spent sitting in my car. I felt trapped, and I was starting to panic.

During my lunch breaks I would set off round Arthur's Seat on a five-mile run. It was starting to save my soul. I began to smell the seasons as well as see them. Amid the trivia of office life, the run was offering me the chance to reconnect with the outdoors, and it was triggering a rebellion within me. At first whimsically but then with increasing seriousness, I began to yearn for a wild place, and a way of living that rejected the trappings of suburban life. No brands, no suppliers, no offices, no company cars or on-target earnings—just trees and space and a chance to rediscover what it is to be a man, as well as a new road to some kind of freedom for my family.

My wife tried hard to understand what this yearning was about. She also had concerns about our lifestyle. Our quality of life as a family was suffering—my long hours of work and commuting meant that she was alone for most of the week and raising the children virtually single-handed. Juliet felt deeply worried about my growing despair but was understandably anxious at the prospect of my turning my back on my career with nothing else to go to. She was also frustrated at my lack of ability to be happy with what, compared to many people, was a very fortunate life. A nice house, one healthy son and another child on the way, a good job—what more did I want? Yet inside she knew that it was not enough for either of us.

Over the next year, from 2003 to 2004, I spent every spare moment researching places that I might go to. Early on, Alaska emerged as the top contender, as one of the world's last great wildernesses, with an area of 1,477,270 square miles and a population of just 600,000. The far north had long been one of the landmarks of my imagination, given shape by Jack London and the poetry of Robert Service. Through the Internet and books I began to discover a vast and wild land where, to this day, few people dared to travel alone. I read lurid accounts of bear attacks and journeys across creaking ice, of a searing cold that turned men's faces white with frost as they battled with dog teams or toiled to build small cabins before the onset of winter. There were amazing stories of treks by moonlight across glittering expanses of ice and snow, of camps roughly made in the bend of a river, and of watching wood smoke curl into a clear sky while king salmon seared on iron and coffee boiled over charcoal. My heart skipped as I read of the loners who survived and learned the way of the land, reading the sky and stars and living carefully in the shade of the boreal woods.

During my journeys on the Internet I made contact with an Athabascan Indian woman who worked at the University of Alaska in Fairbanks, and she put me in touch with her brother, Charlie. He lived with his family in a small village on the Yukon river, in the wooded and sparsely populated Interior of Alaska, and made his way by fishing and working as a carpenter. He was willing to be my local contact.

Now I had only one major obstacle to making my dream a reality: money. Without a trust fund behind me, short of remortgaging the house (half-jokingly suggested at one point, but Juliet put her foot down) I had to find a source of funding. Juliet had left her job shortly before the birth of our second son, Luke, in May 2003, so responsibility for the family's financial security rested on me. Reminding myself that I was not alone in the need for sponsorship (from Columbus to Shackleton, throughout history expeditions have required commercial support), I put together some letters about my adventure and sent them out to potential sponsors.

The reactions of the people approached ranged from enthusiasm (though usually followed with a regretful shake of the head) to incredulity and outright derision. By early 2004 most of my potential sources of funding had come to nothing, and only one or two outside possibilities remained. I desperately searched for other solutions. Time was getting short, and I felt instinctively that if I couldn't pull it off this year it would never happen.

AT 5.30 P.M. I made my way to the editor's office. 'Take a seat, Guy,' Sonja said, smiling wearily. 'I'll just see if Iain is free.'

She replaced the handset and raised an eyebrow. 'Well, he's got five minutes. Off you go.' And she pointed to the door of his office.

I walked towards the door feeling sick with worry. For the first time, I was going to let my idea out into the public domain—or, more precisely, into the small and very gossipy world of *The Scotsman*.

Inside, Iain Martin raised a hand to indicate a chair for me. 'Guy—what can I do for you?'

I tried to think clearly. 'Right, um, OK. Now this might sound odd . . .'

'I am not faint-hearted.' He smiled. 'Try me.'

I took the leap. 'Iain, I think I am losing my mind.'

He laughed. 'So?'

'I have to change my life—I've had a searing vision of the future and I don't like it.'

I heard myself and thought of Billy Graham, imagining that the editor must be starting to worry about whether Security were still in the building. Yet he was looking at me seriously.

'I'm sorry to confront you with this—you must be busy, but . . .'

'Guy, don't waffle. What is it?'

I stood up. 'I'm going to leave my job and go to Alaska to build a cabin in the wilderness. Then I'm going to live in it through the winter.'

He blinked and opened his mouth. 'What?'

'I can't live my life sitting down any more. I have to go.' I sat down again.

'What about your kids—you do have a family, don't you?' He leaned back in his chair and looked hard at me.

'My wife knows that I have to do this—she supports me. And we can't carry on living as we are—hopefully this will change our lives somehow. Nothing belongs to us, our debt is crippling, and I hardly see my family anyway . . .' I opened my hands. 'Sorry, I'm going on a bit.'

He stood up and walked to a glass door that opened out onto a balcony, sliding it open. 'Do you smoke, Guy?'

I told him I would make an exception tonight, and accepted a cigarette.

Standing on the balcony we looked down at the dark wet streets, watching the rush-hour traffic circle Arthur's Seat. I felt elated. There was now no reason for nerves or tension—my boats had started to burn and I was enjoying the smell of fire. Iain put out his cigarette, then walked back to his desk.

'Build a cabin, you say? Where in Alaska?'

'The Interior, on the Yukon river.'

'Have you done this sort of thing before?'

'No,' I admitted. 'I have done a bit of shooting for the pot, so I'm not too worried about feeding myself. I'm not experienced at building, but I spent a few months working as a labourer, so I know I can work . . .'

He interrupted: 'Will you be on your own out there?'

'Yes.'

'What if something goes wrong—will you be able to get help?'

I tried to look dependable but failed, and raised my hands in surrender. 'I'll be on my own. I can't really say any more than that.'

He chuckled, shaking his head, and my nerves came back in a rush. He thinks I'm insane, I thought.

'Why have you come to me about this, Guy?'

'I need to earn some money while I'm away, and wondered if I could write a column for you.'

He sat in silence again. 'That Foreign Legion piece you wrote was all right, I suppose . . .' He fixed me with a hard look. 'It's a good story. OK, I'll take a weekly column from you, though God knows what will happen to you.'

I stuttered a thankyou and stood up feeling dizzy, knowing it was only partly due to the cigarette.

Iain walked me to the door and shook my hand, saying, 'We'll need about eight hundred words a week from you if you can pull it off. You'll have to figure out a way of getting it to us. Good luck.'

I stumbled out of his office in a state of complete disbelief. The dream was becoming a reality. The income from the column would help keep my family going while I was away. I still had to raise the money to finance the adventure itself, but I knew that I had crossed the first hurdle.

I ARRIVED HOME just as Juliet was drying Oscar and Luke, our second son who was nearly a year old, beside the fire.

'Well, how did it go?' she asked.

'It went well. He's offered me a weekly column.'

I met my wife's level gaze, and there was a silence between us. Her expression was quietly resigned, a sight that was hard for me to look at. The fire flickered behind her, reflecting on the warm wooden floor. I could smell our supper in the oven, and heard the murmur of the radio in the kitchen.

'Let's get the boys to bed, Guy, and then have some supper.'

As we ate and talked quietly about what lay ahead, for the first time it felt as if we were talking about something real. Juliet had already decided that, in the year I was away, she would rent our house out and take the boys to the Isle of Mull. Having grown up on the island, she had a strong network of family and friends there. She looked at me searchingly.

'Guy, are you sure you're prepared for this? I mean, there are the bears, then there's the cold in the winter, and building the cabin . . .'

I held her hand and tried to be reassuring. 'Somehow I just know it will be OK.' She fixed me with another steady look and I knew just what she was thinking. Only a week before I had spent a whole day wrestling with the assembly of a set of Ikea shelves for the boys' bedroom, and now I was planning to build my own cabin. In truth, I had no idea whether I could do this. But I was determined to give it a try.

I HAD A LOT TO ORGANISE. I couldn't leave until I'd found some more money from somewhere, and I had to sort out logistics, including a means of getting the column to the newspaper each week. I trawled through atlases and read through book after book. I contacted Charlie to tell him that I planned to arrive in the next few months. When we spoke I heard in his voice an understandable note of caution. It was clear that I had no experience of living in the subarctic, and he must have thought I was heading for disaster.

After this, things began to develop very fast: the pressure was on to pull the project together. One night I met up with a good friend who owns Graham Tiso Outdoors, a supplier of outdoor equipment and clothing. Over a beer in the Shore Bar in Leith, I told Chris of my plan.

He reacted immediately with enthusiasm. 'Guy, you've got to do this. Tell you what, I'll give you all the equipment you need, and I might come up with some money too if you need it. Do not give up!'

Encouraged by Chris's support, and in the knowledge that I had guaranteed income from the *Scotsman* column, Juliet and I agreed that there was no turning back. As we said our goodbyes each morning there was a feeling that our lives were on the brink of great change. Then one day I was called into the assistant managing director's office. He was doing what any good manager would have done, and making me redundant.

I came out of his office feeling oddly calm. The worst that could happen had happened. I wandered over to the sorry pile of paper, books, coffee cups and pens that was my workstation, with vague intentions of clearing my desk. Out of habit, I turned on my computer, and listened for the thousandth time to the irritating start-up jingle that summed up all that was dull and predictable about office life. There was an email headed HIGHLAND PARK. I opened it and read:

Hi Guy,
We have read over the information that you sent us about your Alaskan adventure, and we'd like to be involved. Can you call me?
Best wishes, Sharon McLaughlin

I read the message with a thudding heart. I could not quite believe what I was reading—on this of all days.

A few days later I met Sharon McLaughlin in Glasgow and discussed how Highland Park could get involved in my adventure. This was it now—I was definitely going, and as I journeyed back to Edinburgh on the train I felt overwhelmed by a mixture of emotions. I wondered what I had got myself into and what lay before me.

IT WAS EARLY SUMMER, and our little smallholding on the Rule Water Valley was blooming. The vegetable patch looked like an emerald hidden behind our home, and the strawberries were better than ever. And yet I felt numb as I came to terms with the fact that in a week's time I would be leaving it all behind. Our children, our home and the gentle country that surrounded us would soon be exchanged for people and a land that I knew nothing about.

Juliet and I tried to behave normally, but our impending separation hung over us like a black cloud. In the eight years that Juliet and I had lived together we had never been apart for more than a week, and now here I was leaving for one whole year. It was an appalling prospect.

My last few days were spent sorting out last-minute arrangements. I had spent a day at Tiso's the week before, sorting out my clothing and essential survival equipment. I had figured out how to get my column to *The Scotsman* each week, by sending emails via a laptop plugged into a satellite phone, and dashed down to London to see Inmarsat, who were giving me a satellite phone and free call time, and over to Glasgow to pick up an Apple iBook laptop from Scotsys.

A couple of nights before I was due to leave, a friend who is a local GP came over to show me how to insert an IV drip. It was an uncomfortable and bloody experience, but I emerged an hour later feeling confident that I could, if necessary, administer medication intravenously. The next morning I drove into Edinburgh and had a hurried meeting in a pub with another friend, a highly respected surgeon. He laid an impressive first-aid kit out on the table and gave me a potted lecture on how to treat everything from dog bite to appendicitis, while I frenziedly took notes.

On our last night together, when the boys were in bed, Juliet and I walked slowly away from our house, stopping to look at some trees that we had planted the previous summer.

'Well, this is it now, I suppose,' Juliet said in a quiet voice. 'I can't believe we won't see each other for so long.' Her voice tailed away.

'It feels very strange.' I couldn't say anything more, too choked to put my thoughts into words.

The next day I walked with Juliet, my mother and Luke towards the departure gates at Edinburgh airport. We were surrounded by people going on holiday, while we stood mute and in pain, about to enter two different worlds.

When it was time to say goodbye, I held Juliet in my arms and we sobbed beside a dreary shop selling shirts and ties. Hard times were coming for both of us. Juliet was facing her own challenge of looking after two little boys on her own, and I knew that she was going to carry an added daily burden of worry, as I took my first steps in a dangerous and unknown land.

2

A tiny passenger plane taxied towards the departure hut at Anchorage airport where I sat. Around me were seven other people who I could see were from the Interior. Most were indigenous Alaskans, and they were surrounded by boxes and bags packed with everything from tools to fresh fruit and peanut butter.

The co-pilot popped his head round the door—'OK, y'all. Let's saddle up'—and sauntered back towards the plane. Everyone stood up, gathered their possessions and followed him out onto the tarmac. I felt a pang of fear as I entered the tiny plane, made worse by the fact that there was no partition between the passengers and the pilots, and they both looked very young.

After a cursory safety announcement, we lifted off and circled into the air. It was cloudy, yet occasionally I would glimpse the massive, empty land below. From time to time I would catch one of those seven seasoned bush Alaskans staring at me. They didn't seem hostile—just curious. Maybe wondering why this tenderfoot was heading for one of the loneliest places on earth.

The cloud grew heavy and I saw nothing for the next two hours until we began our descent into Galena. This tiny village on the Yukon was home to Charlie, whom I had called a month earlier to confirm my arrival. He had sounded somewhat taken aback—I think he had dismissed me as a crackpot dreamer who needed to be humoured with an occasional phone call.

'All right everybody, let's think about seat belts,' the captain announced, and we banked steeply. As we neared the village landing strip, the clouds parted and a huge river revealed itself in a series of grand meandering curves. I saw brownish water braiding round huge wooded islands, and banks of sand stood out in places, exposed high above the stream.

I turned to the man seated by my side. 'Excuse me—is that the Yukon?'

He met my question with an unsmiling expression and a slow nod.

The plane landed and we clambered down the steps into a hot, humid atmosphere. I took a deep breath and smelt something familiar.

The man who had been seated beside me came past, and I said, 'Are people burning peat here?'

A wide smile opened across his face. 'No, been real big fire and now the ground's burning up too 'cause the trees are gone.'

He smiled and walked off while I waited for my bags. I looked up at the cloud, and my heart lurched: it was smoke. I had landed in the middle of a massive forest fire. What was this going to mean for me?

I grabbed my heavy bags and turned to walk towards the log cabin that was the airport for this village. As I drew near, a fit-looking native Alaskan man in a North Face jacket and yellow-shaded glasses stepped forward.

'Are you Guy?'

I let my bags down. 'Yes. Charlie?'

He smiled and nodded, then held out his hand. 'I'm Charlie and this is my son, Bubba.' He gestured towards a young man standing beside him, who slowly raised a hand in greeting. His dark eyes scrutinised me.

We walked towards a bashed-up 1960s pick-up truck, loaded my bags into the back and clambered in, then turned out of the airfield onto a bumpy dirt road heading for Charlie's home.

I cleared my throat. 'I hear there's been a fire here—has it been bad?'

'Yeah, fucking terrible. Everything burned up and very bad around here.'

'Right.' A flutter of panic passed through me.

'I want you to meet my father-in-law, then come and meet my family.'

'Thank you Charlie, I'm truly grateful.'

'Maybe you can stay at my father-in-law's place, maybe not.'

His sentence hung in the air, and my anxiety deepened.

We rattled down the dirt road, and I remembered that there were no true roads in the Interior: it was reachable only by river and air. We bumped along for a while, passing an occasional shack, then turned off into a wide gravel yard. Charlie pulled to a halt.

'This is where Don, my father-in-law, lives.'

I stepped out, and my eyes were immediately drawn to a gracious cabin made of entire trees or round logs, each around thirty-six feet in length. The cabin rested on stilts, and stood on a high bluff that looked out over a giant bend in the Yukon. The cabin seemed to glow; the logs had caught the light from the sun and shone like gold.

We walked up a flight of wooden stairs to a door at the side of the house. Inside, a large room opened up before me, the roof held up by entire, huge trees. A wide window looked down onto the mighty river, and beside the door there was a large wood-burning stove.

I stood uncertainly in the doorway. Seated at the dining table was a fearsome, wild-looking man, dressed in rough work clothing with an old pair of braces, dark glasses and a worn welder's cap. I guessed he was in his late sixties. Close by stood a native Alaskan woman, whom I took to be his wife.

The man rose to greet me. He shook my hand lightly and got straight down to business: 'Better tell you now—we been having one heck of a fire here lately. Charlie was planning for you to stay in my cabin out in the bush. Pain of it is, my cabin burnt to ashes.'

'It must have been some fire,' I mumbled, struggling to get my head round the consequences of this for my adventure.

'It sure was—three hundred thousand acres up in smoke. Coffee?'

I began to warm to him despite his intimidating looks. His eyes revealed intelligence and a quick sense of humour with a glint of cunning. But I was preoccupied with my own problems. I sat down, trying to muster up a feeling of positivity when I felt like a child on his first day at a new school— utterly at sea, away from everything that was familiar. Don introduced his wife and she smiled politely, her eyes giving nothing away. While she went to make coffee, Don and Charlie rooted around for some maps of the area. I sat looking out of the window. How could I have taken this risk? How could I have left my family and travelled 8,000 miles with no assurances that this was going to work out? Suddenly all my plans seemed unrealistic and stupid. Already I had hit a major hitch. I felt sure that Don and Charlie were building up to saying they couldn't help me, and that soon they would offer to drive me back to the airport. They sat down beside me, spreading some maps out on the table. Their commentary did nothing to raise my spirits.

'Nah—that bit's all been burned, right up to the margins of this lake.' Don pointed at a blue splotch on the map.

Charlie interjected: 'Actually Brownie flew that way yesterday and said it was burned clear up to here.' His hand indicated a vast swath of land.

They both looked full of doubt. Through the gloom, I felt a glimmer of determination: I couldn't give up at the first hurdle. I thought of my failed attempt to be selected for officer's training in the British army. A swaggering colonel had shouted: 'And remember—the first thing that always goes is the plan!' I repeated this internally like a mantra, until almost without knowing it I had said it out loud.

They stopped talking and looked at me. Charlie's eyes gave little away, but Don smiled ruefully and I could see that the maxim made sense to him.

'Yup, that sure is almost always the case with the bush.'

I decided to risk another positive thought: 'Yes and, um, maybe my coming here could be a good thing. Just when you have lost your cabin some oddball from Scotland comes to build another one.'

My words hung in the air for a moment.

'Hang on . . . Are you saying you want to build a cabin yourself?' Charlie leaned forward, looking incredulous.

'Yes—that is my plan.' I held his gaze, though I felt far from confident. 'I thought I had made that clear, but maybe . . .' I tailed off.

They looked at each other silently, and I watched as it all sank in. I could see that they were adjusting to a new and alarming reality: I was not just another tourist wanting a trip out into the wilderness; I was on a mission.

Don folded the maps, then said, 'Well, I ain't got no ideas right now. For the moment you can stay in a little place I got at the end of my yard there.'

Charlie led me out to a green shed on a little bluff overlooking the river. Inside it was painted white, and a handmade wooden bed stood in a corner.

As he left, Charlie said, 'I'll pick you up for dinner later. You just settle in here.' He jumped into his truck and drove off.

I wandered outside and sat on the edge of the bluff, looking down at the river. A light breeze drew gently through the needles of a white spruce tree beside me, and I caught my first whiff of the scent of its resin. I looked across the river at the huge expanse of wild country beyond, and thought of the lines by Robert Service:

> *This is the law of the Yukon, and ever she makes it plain:*
> *'Send not your foolish and feeble; send me your strong and your sane.'*

I hoped that I was going to prove to be in the latter category.

LATER THAT NIGHT I walked with Charlie along the dirt road to his house. We passed a few ramshackle wooden houses, and every now and then a beaten-up car would pass, leaving us in a cloud of thick dust. The village was rough and drab and everything seemed to be the colour of dirt, from the roads to the dust-caked scrub to the river that flowed sullenly to the west. I felt uneasy and depressed, and the conversation didn't help.

'Yeah, I take white men downriver every now and then,' Charlie said. 'We head out into some pretty lonely parts.'

'Oh right—you take them fishing, do you?'

'Yup, I take 'em fishing and make camp.' He fixed me with a complex look. 'Some they say to me, "Charlie, we've had enough now, we want to go home." They get scared pretty quick.' His eyes briefly met mine, and I saw the challenge in them. He was wondering how long I would last.

Ten minutes later we came to a small road that led down to the river. To my left there were stockpiles of raw timber and a battered mobile sawmill.

Charlie gestured towards it. 'We pull trees out of the river in spring for firewood, and we cut logs upstream and float 'em down for timber.'

Further on, we approached Charlie's house. It was surrounded by trucks dating back to the 1950s, a few motorbikes and a snow machine. I looked up at an impressive wooden house, which stood on stilts, surrounded by a wooden porch. It was two storeys high.

'Did you build this?' I asked.

Charlie nodded and motioned to me to go inside. I was met by his wife, Claudette, and their five children. Claudette was a tall, good-looking woman and her eyes were warm and welcoming. The three little girls whispered to each other. Beside Claudette stood Bubba. I guessed he was around seventeen years old, and he regarded me impassively. A younger boy, Jack, aged around ten, stood beside him, gazing at me in open wonder.

Claudette motioned for us all to sit at a large wooden table that was laid for dinner. Everyone bowed their heads as Claudette said a prayer, then lifted them again to stare at me. I raised a feeble hand in a kind of joke greeting.

Jack laughed, and came straight to the point. 'So, you have travelled all the way from Scotland to live in the bush?'

I nodded, trying to look confident. 'Yes, Jack, that's the plan.'

He leaned forward, furrowing his brow. 'Why?'

I fiddled with the cutlery, struggling to find an answer. 'Well, it's difficult to explain . . .' I glanced round the table: the whole family was waiting. 'What I mean is, there are many reasons behind what we do.'

Jack sat back in his chair; clearly he was not satisfied by my answer.

Claudette broke the silence, ladling a beautiful meat stew onto my plate. 'C'mon Jack, give him a chance to settle down—he just got here.'

The stew was wonderful, and I took the opportunity to change the subject. 'This beef is amazing—is it Alaskan?'

'It's moose,' Charlie said.

'Where did you buy it?'

Charlie smiled. 'We can't afford to buy meat at the store—it's too expensive. Everything in there has to come by air.'

'Of course.' I remembered that we were 300 miles from the nearest road. 'Jack shot this moose.'

I looked over at the bright young boy. 'Was it your first moose?'

He shook his head matter-of-factly. 'No.'

'He shot his first moose when he was seven,' Charlie said.

I regarded Jack with wonder, amazed that a seven-year-old boy could flatten the world's largest deer, which might weigh as much as 1,500 pounds. The family ate in silence, and my mind began hazily to search for any aspect of British life that might amuse or interest my hosts. An image came to mind, and I turned to my young inquisitor.

'Jack, have you ever heard of a game called cricket?'

He stopped eating and shook his head slowly from side to side.

I looked over to include the rest of the family. 'Well . . . cricket is maybe the only game in the world that you can play for five days without either side winning outright.' They all sat in stunned silence as I launched into an oratory on cricket—a curious choice for me, as I'm by no means an expert, but it seemed to help lighten the atmosphere.

After the meal, I thanked Charlie and Claudette for their welcome.

Charlie raised his hand. 'I will do my best to help you. But it's hard out there, and you really know nothing about this land, do you?'

I couldn't deny it. I shook my head.

'Don's cabin is gone, and we don't have another place where you can build one—do you understand?' He spoke slowly, as if to a child.

A hot feeling of panic returned, and I felt the blood thudding in my veins.

Claudette was looking at me too, and I could see the concern in her eyes. 'Guy, it is hard on your own here without family, and dangerous too.'

To them, I realised, it must seem strange that I had come all this way, leaving my family behind. I remembered how, in our early email exchanges, Charlie's sister had pointed out that native Alaskans value family and community above all else, and would never choose to go out into the bush alone. Yet I knew there was a long precedent for white men journeying on their own into wild places, and the ones who succeeded had almost always been those who had striven to forge bonds with indigenous people.

'I know what you're saying, Claudette,' I said, 'and I feel terrible about being away from my family. But this is important for all of us, and somehow I'm sure I will find a way of making it work.'

Charlie and Claudette stayed silent, and I felt their deep doubt.

I looked at my watch. 'Well, I think I should leave you all in peace.' Charlie stood up, ready to offer me a lift, but I held a hand up. 'Don't worry—I know the way. I can walk along the river.'

I walked out into the warm twilight and down towards the river. A dog shot out of a plywood kennel and barked shrilly at the end of its chain. He was a small, spry-looking dog with rich blond fur. I walked over and he raised himself onto strong hind legs and pawed at me, the barking replaced by eager friendliness and a frenzy of licking. I stepped back and the dog dropped again to all fours, resuming his high-pitched barking as I moved away.

I scrambled down the steep incline in front of the house and pushed through a thin screen of willow osiers until I reached the river beach. The water sucked greedily along the firm sand, and occasionally a tree passed swiftly by, carried by a powerful current. Behind me the rough little village of log cabins and shacks was settling down for the night. I thought of the leap of faith that this family was taking by letting me enter their home. I couldn't blame them for their cautious welcome. What did they know about me—except what I told them, and how did they know that was true?

As I walked along the beach, I cursed myself for having taken such a terrible gamble with my life and with my family's security. At Don's shed, I drew water from a storage jug and put it on the little camp stove to boil for tea. I saw the word LONDON on the box of tea, and thought of Juliet and her amazing ability to drink tea by the gallon. The memory brought on a bout of sadness, and I decided to forget about the tea. I folded sadly into the little wooden bed, feeling more alone and homesick than ever before in my life.

THE NEXT MORNING I woke early, and my homesickness hit me afresh as I thought of my children, who at weekends would drag me from sleep, shouting and bouncing painfully on top of me. I lay very still, trying to summon up some fighting spirit. After a few moments I got up and put on my clothes, then sat back down on the bed.

A light tap on the door brought me back to reality. 'Hey, you in there?'

Don stood on the doorstep. He looked sprightly and alert, and I could see that his eyes were perceptive and kind. I sensed that he had seen just about every type of man pass through the great wilderness that was his home.

'How're ya doing?'

'Oh, I'm OK,' I replied, hoping that I sounded more positive than I felt.

'You want a cup of coffee?'

I felt suddenly grateful that fate had led me to this man. Although I felt sure of nothing, he gave me hope. 'That would be great.'

'Son, it's just a cup of coffee,' he said wryly.

I nodded. 'Thanks for letting me stay here. Can I pay rent or something?'

He shook his head. 'Nah. Money does nothing for me.' I felt that if we had known each other better he would have said more, but he was still wary.

As we crossed his yard we saw a group of men standing round a battered old pick-up. One of them was Charlie. Beside the driver's door, a man was speaking fast, his deep-set, nervous eyes flitting about beneath his cap.

'I really need some help with my place,' he said. 'It's gonna fall into the lake and I kinda need to sort out my pilings. Can you help me, Charlie?'

Charlie shrugged. 'I'm real busy right now. I ain't sure what I can—'

The man interrupted, desperation in his eyes. 'Can ya just come an' see?'

Charlie gave me an almost imperceptible wink. 'OK, I'll come and have a look. You come along too, Guy.'

We jumped into the back of the old vehicle and rumbled along the dirt road until we reached a jumble of plywood and tin hovels. The man led us to his house, a windowless wooden box on stilts overlooking a dark, stagnant lake. The stilts on the downward side of the slope were in a state of collapse, and the whole rotting box seemed about to slide into oblivion. The man led us into his house, which was dark and messy and smelt bad.

Charlie looked around. 'You gonna stay here for the winter?'

The man nodded. 'Yeah, kinda hoping to.'

'But this place is gonna go into the lake any time now, you know that?'

'I know, but could you help me? Maybe we could figure some kinda payment plan?' He looked at Charlie pleadingly. 'See, I ain't got nothing.'

Charlie sighed. 'I'll see if I can get you some pilings.'

We turned and walked back towards Don's yard.

'Another crazy white man,' Charlie mumbled, shaking his head. 'He's the kind that comes here to die. The kind that drinks until he dies, gets lost in the snow or shoots himself—or worse still, someone else.'

I thought again of the many people who had come to Alaska on the tails of some dream. 'Have many people come unstuck here?'

Charlie smiled. 'Oh yeah, been many people who died out here and things gone wrong.'

'I imagine you must think I'm just another crazy white guy, hey?' I said.

He laughed. 'Well, where are you gonna build a cabin if the woods are burning? And who's gonna help you when we're all getting ready for winter ourselves? If you head out there on your own you could die very quick.'

His words hit me like an iron bar. I knew he was right.

'Yeah,' I muttered. 'I'm up the bloody Yukon without a paddle.'

I SPENT THE NEXT WEEK or so wandering around Galena, and found that, although it was rough, it had heart. 'Galena' is the chemical name for lead, and the village began life as a supply point for nearby lead ore mines that opened in 1918 and 1919. In 1920, Athabascans living upriver moved to Galena to sell wood to river steamers and to haul freight for the mine. A school was established in the mid-1920s, and during the Second World War an airfield was built. During the 1950s, the US air force developed a base around the airfield to use as an outpost during the Cold War, and the construction of these and other facilities caused the village to grow.

Today, the village is home to approximately 675 people, mostly

Athabascan, and boasts a shop, a post office and a motley selection of self-built houses. In 1993 the base was mothballed, and the empty buildings now sit silent and brooding. Part of the base is home to a residential school, set up to offer children from remote regions a chance to get some education.

I made no progress on finding a site where I could build my cabin, and as each day came to an end the chances of achieving my goal before winter seemed more remote. One morning I went in search of Don, and found him outside the old cabin that served as his workshop. He was welding the edge of a battered launch, wearing just a pair of sunglasses for protection from the sparks that poured off the metal. Behind him the walls of the cabin were festooned with lengths of chain and rope, along with axes, blocks, pipes and anchors. When he stopped, I pointed to some grappling hooks.

'What are those for?'

He looked, then bent back over his welding. 'Pulling bodies from the river.'

'Do many people drown in the Yukon?'

'Yeah.' He nodded. 'Many, many people drown in that water, and often we don't even find their bodies.' He stood up with a sigh, and I knew he must have lost people he loved. 'The water is so full of silt that their clothing fills up with sand. They sink fast and don't always come up again.' Don was silent for a moment, then said, 'Time is going on, and you got a lot to do.'

I shrugged helplessly. There seemed to be no way ahead here, and I was facing the prospect of going somewhere else in Alaska and starting all over again. I dreaded the thought.

He turned to me with measuring eyes. 'Maybe a guy could build a small trapping cabin somewhere away from the fire.'

My heart leapt at the thought. 'Yes, of course.'

'Go speak to Glenn,' Don said. 'He might be able to help you. You can borrow the bike.'

Glenn Stout was the Fish and Game biologist for the region, responsible for all matters relating to land use on State land. I had emailed him during my research and he had always been helpful. With a heart full of hope I leapt onto the old quad bike and charged down the dirt road towards the small wooden shack that served as his office.

Glenn was a big man with a long drooping moustache, and a face that would not have looked out of place in an old sepia print of a miner in a ten-gallon hat. Shaking my hand, he shyly offered me a plastic chair, then sat down behind his cluttered desk.

'Gee, I thought you were just gonna be the type that emails from time to time . . . And now here you are.'

I nodded. 'I know. Life sometimes moves fast, huh?' My gaze fell on a series of maps on the wall behind him. 'What part of the Interior is this?'

'Twenty-one D.'

'That's a romantic name. And you are the state's man for this region?'

He nodded.

'How big is it?'

He thought for a while. 'About twenty-nine million acres.'

I looked at him in stunned silence, then cleared my throat and got to the point: 'Don and Charlie were planning for me to stay in Don's cabin during the winter, but it's been burnt down. I am thinking that I would like to build a cabin myself. Can you think of anywhere I could do this?'

He shrugged. 'Well, you are not a resident, and homesteading is over, so I'm not sure.'

I felt hopeless and stupid. Our conversation stuttered along, with Glenn patiently answering my questions. When I left he shook my hand, wished me luck and said he would think about what could be done.

I drove slowly back to Don's yard, and found him talking to Charlie.

'Come on into the house,' Don said. 'We got an idea for you.'

Inside, I said hello to Carol, Don's wife, who gave me a guarded greeting, then walked over to the table to join Charlie and Don, who were examining maps. Don was tracing a route along a wide braid of the Yukon with his finger, counting off the miles as he did so. My eyes eagerly followed his finger along the ribbon of blue, past a river mouth and a mountain, and on in a series of sensuous curves until it stopped.

'A guy could maybe build a cabin here.' Don looked at me.

I kept still, scarcely daring to breathe.

His finger slid gently from the blue to the green. 'It's all forest below this mountain, and a cabin could maybe go up here by this lake.'

I let my breath out, trying not to get too hopeful. 'How far is it from here?'

'Oh, it's about three hours by boat.' Don's eyes stayed on the map. 'You'd have to cut portage from the slough to the site and clear a space for the cabin. When winter comes you'd need to break a good trail up the slough to the Yukon, otherwise you'd be cut off. For now you could use the river.'

I sat down, feeling faint with excitement and hope. 'And what then?'

Don threw Charlie a look that was a mixture of frustration and amusement.

'Then you fell trees, cut logs, peel 'em and build a cabin before winter shuts everything down.'

I sat in silence, as the enormity of the task that I had so boldly taken on sank in. Then a thought struck me. 'Do I have to get permission?'

'Well . . .' Don thought for a moment. 'You'll have to talk to Glenn about it, but it should be OK.' He paused again. 'Now, time ain't on your side. And I got a feeling you ain't got no idea how to build a cabin. Am I right?'

I nodded. There was silence in the room, then behind me Carol coughed.

'This is crazy,' Charlie said to Don. 'He's gonna kill himself.'

Don sat down, looking at the map, and I knew he was wrestling with contradictory thoughts. He looked up at me, his wise eyes seeming to size me up. Then he looked again at Charlie. 'We'll head down the river tomorrow and see if the woods is good enough for building in that part.'

Charlie nodded slowly, then looked at me with what I was sure was thinly veiled contempt.

Don folded the map and pointed it at me sternly. 'You got very little time,' he said. 'Ice-up is not far away. You can never tell how long Mother Nature is gonna give you. I'd say you got two months at the outside.'

'I'm sure I can do it—I have no choice. I've given up everything at home, and my family and future depend on it.'

'You know,' Don said, 'that is one thing that might just make the difference. Sometimes no choice is what you need in the bush.'

He stopped, and we sat in silence for a moment.

'First you gonna have to cut that portage. We will lend you tools and a boat, just as long as you pay for fuel.'

I was lost for words. I felt so grateful that fate had led me to these amazing people, as it was clear that without them I would have very little chance of making it work. I stood up, feeling dizzy with relief. I had a long way to go, but at least some kind of path was opening up ahead.

'Don, thank you for this, I cannot say how grateful . . .'

'Hey, don't thank me yet.' He held up a hand. 'We don't even know what it's like on the ground. Let's just hope the place works out, and that you can do it in time, 'cause it gets real cold here.'

'How cold?'

Charlie said, 'A few years back we went to minus eighty before wind chill.'

Don nodded. 'You can't beat the winter here—ever—and you shouldn't even try. A guy has just gotta pray and work hard and carefully.' He kept looking at me. 'You know there are plenty bears in the Interior, don't you?'

I nodded. 'Are they really that dangerous?'

'Sometimes, sometimes not. They're unpredictable and so you must be ready to look after yourself. You're gonna need a gun that can protect you as well as something for hunting.'

'What do you suggest?'

He shrugged. 'We'll just wait and see what comes along, but I can tell you now that a .22 will become a work horse for you—specially for chicken.'

'Chicken?'

He laughed. 'What do you limeys call 'em . . .? Grouse. Spruce grouse you find in the tops of trees. Then there's willow grouse that hang about on the sandbars and in birch and willow thickets. We call 'em chicken 'cause they taste good and they're plentiful.'

'Will I be able to hunt these for the pot?'

'Well, sure,' he chuckled. 'Now you be here good and early tomorrow.'

As I walked back to the green shed, I realised that my ideas of venturing out utterly alone and without help into the wilderness, fondly held from the safety of the UK, were foolhardy. In the depths of winter I would be on my own for long periods, so I had to try to learn all I could from these people, soak up every crumb of knowledge while I had the chance.

THE NEXT MORNING dawned bright and clear, as if the gods had decided to give the new boy an easy start. I found Don standing outside his cabin looking up at the sky.

'Gonna be a good day for looking about.' He pointed to the beach. 'Boat's down there—let's head on down and wait for Charlie.'

We turned and walked through a little grove of birch towards the beach. Don stopped and tightened his belt, where he carried a .44 magnum revolver and extra rounds held in leather loops.

'That looks like quite a cannon,' I said.

He patted the gun. 'Pretty much useless if a bear was actually after me. Not much can help in that case. Them critters move like cats.'

'Lovely.' I nodded sarcastically.

Don chuckled. 'Can't believe I'm heading downriver with a man that says "lovely".'

'And I can't believe that a .44 is pretty much useless.'

'Better than a stick.'

We both laughed, and I felt the tentative beginnings of friendship.

Charlie arrived, nodding a curt greeting. He and Don climbed into a sturdy aluminium launch, which I pushed off the beach before scrambling in. Charlie nursed it out into the main stream, then applied the power.

As we skimmed over the brown water, the treacherous nature of the Yukon began to be revealed. The river was laced with shoals, and Charlie guided the launch skilfully downstream, taking care to pick a route that would keep us from running aground. My nostrils caught the sharp scent of fire, and I looked up to see a treeless and charred landscape. We also had to look out for 'snags', which are the remains of flood-shattered trees that have been thrust deep into the riverbed. The strong current pulls the tops to the surface of the river, where they rise up at a sharp angle, ready to catch the bow of a boat and hold it until the vessel broaches and is sucked under.

After threading our way past a few large islands, we slipped into a slough—or side channel—that led off to the south. So great was the contrast between the Yukon and its offshoot, it felt as if we had left the ocean and made passage into a river. Yet the slough—as wide as the Thames in central London—was still formidable. We swerved from cut bank to cut bank, following as best as we could the route of the main current. Now at last I saw trees and scrub that had been untouched by fire, and the higher ground was swathed in white spruce trees. Closer to the water, beds of willow formed a dense undulating curtain of green.

The slough took us on a sinuous course, deeper into the wilderness. Every now and then we would pass the mouth of a small creek, and Don would crane his neck to look up the channels. Occasionally he would point, and I would catch sight of an immense moose standing up to its hocks in grey mud, or a cow and calf lumbering into the bush. I sat in silence, drinking it all in.

Eight miles after leaving the Yukon, the slough straightened. Ahead we saw a rounded mountain, its flanks covered in great stands of white spruce.

'That's Pilot Mountain,' Don shouted. He pointed to a good-sized river mouth on the southern side of the slough. 'That's Bishop Creek. It's gonna be good for fishing and not bad for water too—see.' He pointed at the two-tone water opposite the river mouth, where clear, peaty river water met the silty water of the Yukon.

The slough curved round Pilot Mountain and we passed a large sandbar and beach. Ahead the slough seemed to run on a straighter course, with cut banks on the south side and a large wooded sandbar to the north.

Don pointed to the southern bank, and Charlie steered the launch onto a black sand shelf. Don stepped out of the boat and tied the painter to a tree. The engine was cut, and there was silence. Charlie pulled off his windproof jacket and reached down to lift a heavy-calibre rifle onto his back. I rummaged around in my bag, pulled my pack on, and turned to look up the steep cut bank. Don and Charlie were gone.

You bastards! I thought, suspecting that they were giving me a little test. I followed their tracks in the muddy sand until I reached the edge of the bank. It was at my waist level, and beyond lay a tangle of thick bush above which tall balsam poplar, or cottonwood, soared. I could not see where they had gone. Then I noticed a dainty strip of bright red marker tape fluttering from the bough of an alder tree. I pulled myself up onto the ledge and walked into the thick undergrowth, pushing through sharp rose bushes and dainty clumps of red berries. I could not see more than a few feet in either direction. But ahead I saw another length of tape, and so, like a child following a trail of sweets, I moved further into the bush.

The air was thick with the smell of bark, rotting vegetation and greenery. I kept pushing through low-lying bush, willow and alder, following the tapes. Suddenly I heard a slashing sound followed by a sharp clang. I strained my eyes and saw Don through the trees, deftly cutting at the vegetal wall with a useful-looking tool. I pushed my way towards him.

'Charlie has gone up ahead,' he told me. 'We've found a game trail that'll lead to that lake.' He stood still for a moment. 'I love these woods.' Then he held up his cutting tool. 'You better learn to use one of these right—called a Sandvik. When you start cutting your portage you're gonna need one.' He slashed through an obstructive branch the size of a man's forearm in a single cut, then passed the tool to me. 'Now you go.'

I aimed and struck forcefully at another branch, only to hear the blade tinkle out of its slot as the branch swung away. I dropped to my knees and started searching. From the undergrowth, I heard Don laughing.

'Guy, you're gonna have a tough time.'

I stood up, holding the recovered blade, and said with some irritation, 'And do you know of many beginners who do everything right?'

I fumbled around, trying to slot the blade back into the handle, before two tough old hands deftly put the tool together again.

'This is how you do it—get your angle before you make the slash, and cut low, so that you don't leave a spear at eye level.'

He passed me the tool and I tried again. To my surprise it worked first time. I looked up proudly, expecting approval, but Don's face showed nothing but barely detectable amusement.

A few minutes later we were on our way, following the narrow trail deeper into the woods, with bushes up to our armpits. The trail twisted between the majestic grey trunks of a long strip of cottonwood trees, and above I could see shimmering leaves set against a blue sky. The trees filled the air with the rich scent of balsam.

After a few hundred yards the trail turned south, becoming gradually steeper. As we climbed, the vegetation changed, and we soon found ourselves pushing through a great tangle of alder, willow and every type of birch. The low-lying bushes, mainly roses and high-bush cranberry, became thicker.

'In this country it gets warmer the higher you get,' Don explained. 'That river is where all the cold air flows, so when you step up from that cold sink you get more plants.'

I stared into the impenetrable new layer of plants, and a shiver of fear passed through me. 'There are bears here, aren't there?'

'Well sure,' Don said, 'and they'll know you're here, like all the animals will. They'll see you a long time before you see them—*if* you see them.'

I looked around, wondering about the odds of being eaten by a bear. 'Not a good way to go, is it?'

Don laughed. 'No, them critters take their time over it. Still, no point worrying too much. If you're being hunted by a bear then you ain't got no chance anyway, so just relax.'

We walked on in silence until I noticed a large mound of blackened faeces dotted with red berries. 'Don, what's this?'

He didn't turn to look—clearly he'd noticed it already. 'Bear.'

'How old?'

'Yesterday.'

I swallowed, and said nothing.

We had now been walking for about twenty minutes, and the trail had taken us higher, into another change of plants and terrain. The air around us held the deep and complex scent of white spruce.

Don stopped and pointed up at a perfect swaying tree. 'Now that is a fine spruce. See how straight the timber is? This is where you'll get the wood to build your cabin.' He looked around. 'Yeah, some good wood here for building, and good firewood too.' He pointed to a dead tree that had been bleached grey by the sun and was perfectly air-dried. 'Standing dead spruce burns better than any wood on earth. Mix it with some green wood like birch, willow or alder, and your stove ain't never gonna let you down.'

I felt excitement at the thought of a stove crackling away in my log home, then I remembered how far I had to go before I reached that point. 'What about those cottonwood trees?' I asked. 'Can you use them for building?'

Don shook his head in humorous contempt. 'Why do you think we call 'em cottonwood? 'Cause the wood's like cotton, dummy.'

'Oh, right, yes. Does it have *any* use?'

'You'll use young cottonwood to catch beaver—that's where the tree comes in handy.'

'Beaver!' I exclaimed, and Davy Crockett strode into my imagination.

'Yup. Makes pretty good eating too.'

We had now left the spruce and passed into another layer of alder, birch and willow. The trail petered out and we descended over undulating ground before coming out through an opening in the woods. We entered a sunken open area, overgrown with thick white grass and isolated stands of willow. To the west it ran as far as I could see, bounded on either side by forest.

'Grass lake,' Don said. 'Held water once—now it holds grass.' He pointed down at some deep prints. 'Bull moose, maybe thousand pounds or more.'

I knelt and touched the deep print. 'Amazing . . .'

Don nudged the print with his boot. 'Yeah, them moose is great eating, but you know they kill more people than bears in this country—specially in fall when they're in rut.'

I stood up and gave him a twisted smile. 'Is the punch line always "kill" in this place?'

''Fraid so.' Don said sadly. 'There's a lot of death around here. Froze, drowned, got eaten, shot himself . . . there's a lot of ways to die in Alaska.'

We crossed through the strange grass lake, then pushed up a steep hill towards another stand of white spruce. Here we met Charlie, who raised his chin in greeting to me before turning to Don.

'This looks like good wood too.'

Don rubbed his chin. 'Yeah, kinda sheltered here, so they ain't got too much of a bow in them. How far is that lake now? Must be pretty close, huh?'

Charlie nodded. 'Five minute walk.'

We pushed on, into some thick vegetation covering a little ridge. Then, like free divers surfacing for air, we popped out of the woods onto a carpet

GUY GRIEVE

of luxuriant green grass, which ran down to a narrow lake, about half a mile long. We had been walking for about forty minutes, but had probably only travelled around two miles. The blue sky lit the glassy surface of the lake, and the tall trees along the ridge reflected out across the water. There was something mysterious and timeless about it, and I couldn't believe that this lost world would soon be my home.

Don pointed to a substantial mound of mud and branches that stood about halfway up the lake. 'Beaver house and pretty big. Be about ten of them varmints in there.'

I looked at the mound, then back at the woods from which we had emerged. 'So you think the cabin could be built up there?'

'Yup—but that water sure don't look too good. Full of beaver and otter piss and shit.'

'Oh, I've got something for purifying water.'

'Oh yeah—how much can it do in one go?'

My mind strained to recall the instructions. 'One litre, I think.'

Clearly unimpressed, he changed the subject. 'OK, so you gotta put your tent up quick as you can and cut a way from the river to here. Then clear your site and begin building the cabin. And you got very little time.'

I looked over at Charlie, and I could see that he held little belief that the tenderfoot could do it.

Don looked at the sky. 'We gotta go, it's getting late.'

And with that the old frontiersman turned back into the woods, with Charlie and me falling into step behind him. I looked into the darkening and silent woods, trying to imagine what it would be like to be here on my own.

IN THE HALF LIGHT of the evening, we at last pulled the launch up onto Don's beach. Charlie said his goodbyes and I walked with Don towards his cabin. I told Don that I was still determined to build the cabin, despite the obstacles that lay ahead.

He listened, then said, 'You gonna come and have dinner with me and Carol tonight. Come over in twenty minutes.'

That night we ate a beautiful meal of moose ribs, cornbread and beans. Carol was welcoming but I sensed she was still wary. She told me the tragic story of the night when she lost many members of her family when their boat capsized in the river. Whether in winter or summer, the Yukon was the cause of many deaths—on boats, snow machines, sled dogs or on foot.

We sat eating in silence for a while, then Don pushed back his chair. 'That place is gonna work out fine for you,' he said. 'It's got everything you need— OK water, wood for building and burning, and it's close enough for you to get onto the river for travel when the ice comes. You better check in with Glenn tomorrow to see if it's OK, then get on downriver soon as you can.'

I walked slowly back to my little shack, and sat on the step outside, thinking of the many tests that lay ahead. Charlie and Don took for granted that I could get the launch down the Yukon myself and find the beach where the trail started. They were also expecting me to defend myself against bears and moose and set up camp and find water and food. All this was challenging enough for someone who had never gone beyond basic camping in my own safe country. This, however, was just a starting point for the real task of building a cabin—something that called for technical ability and skills that I didn't possess.

I found my Inmarsat satellite phone, and hooked the whole thing together on the bluff overlooking the river, waving the dish about until I heard a little beep that told me that it had caught the beam of a satellite hovering above the Pacific. I dialled the number of my parents-in-law's house, where Juliet and the children were staying.

'Hello?' It was early morning in Scotland and Juliet sounded sleepy.

'Julsie, it's me.'

'Guy!'

I heard tearful joy in her voice, and imagined her sitting up in her warm bed. We spoke for a while, then I heard Oscar asking to speak to his dad.

'Hello, my big boy.'

'Dad?'

'How is everything? Tell me what you've been doing.'

Above the static beeps and interference I managed to follow most of what he was saying about living on the Isle of Mull, going to a new nursery school and making friends. It was painful to hear of this life that I was not a part of, but I was relieved that he sounded happy and well.

After a while I told him it was time to go. 'I am so glad things are going well for you. It sounds like you're being very brave.'

'Daddy?' I heard a new note enter his voice.

'Yes.'

'What are you going to do now?'

I told him that I was going to make some tea and go to bed. I knew he was trying to keep me talking a bit longer, and I realised that he was missing me in a way that was far deeper than I had allowed myself to predict.

'Have you seen any bears yet?'

'Not yet, darling—and I hope I don't.' I tried to sound cheery and positive. 'Now, can I speak to Mummy?'

'Yes, Dad.' His voice sounded very small now, and I knew he was wrestling with emotions that were too big for him.

'I love you, Oscar.'

'I love you, Daddy.'

Juliet came onto the line. 'Hi, Guy.' Her voice sounded flat and sad.

'Is he OK?'

'Not really.' I heard sobs in the background. 'He's gone to his room—I'd better go after him. We'll talk later.' The line went dead.

I sat in the darkness, swamped by a feeling of powerlessness. At one year old, Luke was too young to feel my absence, but Oscar was really suffering, making it even harder for Juliet. She was fighting conflicting emotions too—although she supported me, I knew she was coping with a lot and must feel resentful. As I shut down the phone, I felt a welling of sadness and loneliness. Just then I heard Don's footsteps approaching.

'Hey, you out there?'

'Yeah.' I started packing the phone away. 'Just making a call.'

'Man needs a dog in the bush—to keep him company and help look out for bears. Charlie's got a dog chained up in his yard. Why don't you take him?'

I remembered the yapping dog that I had encountered on my visits to Charlie's yard. I wasn't a big fan of dogs—I had always been more of a cat person—but I couldn't deny the logic. 'Well . . .' I looked up at Don and nodded. 'Do you think Charlie would mind?'

Don shook his head—he was already thinking of other things. 'And you're gonna need two types of gun out there. One for getting food and another for making sure you don't become food. Can you shoot?'

'I've used a shotgun.'

Don nodded. 'Well, that's good. Before you go we'll think about what you take for protection.' He turned to go.

'Don?'

'Yep?' He turned back towards me.

'Do you . . .' I hesitated, feeling vulnerable. 'Do you think I can do it?'

'Well, if you can't, you may as well find out now as later.' He paused as if he were going to say more, then decided not to. 'Good night.' He disappeared into the darkness.

I folded into my little wooden bed and lay with my eyes open, remembering the deep sobs of my oldest boy. Unable to sleep, I called Juliet again. The boys were playing outside and she was able to talk.

'Yeah, he's OK now. He's just missing you, like I am.'

'I know—I just felt so powerless there.'

I heard a sigh. 'You *are* powerless, Guy. That's the sad bit right now.'

There was a silence as we both felt the 8,000 miles stretch between us.

'Julsie, I'm heading downriver tomorrow. On my own.'

Another pause. 'Guy, please, please, be careful. We love you so much and we need you to come home.' I heard the anxiety in her voice.

'I will, don't worry.'

3

Early next morning, I placed my maps, compass, GPS and satellite phone in an unbreakable steel ammunition box, stuffed my hiking bag with my outdoor and camping equipment and loaded my medical supplies into another sturdy container. Outside I gathered the larger items: the petrol generator, which I would use for charging my laptop and satellite phone, a large water container and my stove, bulky but essential for both cooking and warmth. Outside I found a wheelbarrow, piled on as much of my gear as I could and made a couple of runs up and down to the beach. At the end of the second run I found Don beside Charlie's launch.

He pointed to a chain saw lying beside him. 'Any good with chain saws?'

'Well, I did use them occasionally back home for cutting firewood.'

Don lifted the chain saw into the boat. 'But I'm assuming you haven't felled trees, cut logs and made portages?'

'Sadly not.'

'Well, you better be damn careful in everything you do.' He looked at me very seriously. 'These saws'll kick back and rip into your face if you don't take care. Don't ever let this bit touch what you're cutting.' He lifted the chain saw and touched the top section of the saw tip. 'This is the kick-back zone.'

'Right, OK. I see it.'

'You're gonna have to work slowly. Don't rush. Take time on everything, and think about how each action is gonna turn out. Always second-guess yourself, and if it don't feel good don't do it. You are gonna be on your own out there and ain't no one gonna know if you get into trouble.'

I nodded, grateful, yet taken aback by the seriousness of the talk.

'Don't ever forget how big and dangerous this land can be. Respect it, and know that you can't ever beat it, just learn to work with it. And when things start to go right, get even more careful, 'cause it's when you're off guard that accidents will happen.'

'I understand.'

Don pointed to the bank side where the morning sunlight glinted dully on gunmetal. 'Charlie left these for you. You can choose what you want.'

'Hey, Don, I don't feel comfortable taking these. Can't I just buy—?'

A hand cut me off. 'Now this is a pump shotgun. It holds eight rounds in an extended chamber.' He passed the heavy gun to me. 'Loaded with buck or bear slug, it'll give a very big hit at up to fifty yards. With a bear, the most important thing to do is to stop him, and often it'll take more than one shot. Right, let's see how you do. Take a shot at that stump.'

I lifted the gun, fumblingly pumped a round into the breach and fired one slug. It blew a gaping hole through the half-buried stump.

'And again—jack another one in and fire a couple of shots.'

I fired three rounds, and in an instant a mess of shattered wood and splinters lay smoking across the black beach.

Don nodded in satisfaction. 'You can get a few lighter rounds in there too and use it for hunting duck.' Before he took the gun from me he said, 'Now, you must ensure that your breach is always empty, then when you need to shoot you jack one in and fire. Much faster than messing about with a safety catch, and safer. So when you're finished you empty the breach. OK?'

'Yes,' I said, trying to sound more confident than I felt.

'Now this is a 45/70 lever action rifle, and it fires four rounds.' He picked up a very short rifle. 'This has no scope, just steel sights, so that you can shoot at very close range. This one'll shoot with great stopping power at one hundred to one fifty yards or less. Not very long range for a rifle, but we are talking protection here, not hunting.' He passed me the little rifle and pointed at a paper plate he had nailed to a tree about a hundred yards away, with a tiny black dot in the centre. 'Lie down and take a shot.'

I levered a round in, lay down and took aim. The recoil was immense and the rifle roared as a round tore into the sand behind the untouched plate.

'You missed that target by a mile! You're flinching. Now, aim again. Centre the mark on all your sights, breathe gently and take your whole finger off that trigger—just leave the last bit of your finger lightly in place.'

I did as he said.

'When you're ready, hold the rifle tight into your shoulder, let your breath gently out and don't think of nothing but that target while your finger starts to squeeze the trigger. Don't expect the shot—be surprised when it happens.'

I fired four rounds, and when we strolled over to the target I was happy to see that two had knocked the dot out of the centre.

Don didn't comment, but said, 'Now you better get going. Keep that 45/70 on your back when you're out there.'

'Thanks, Don. I am grateful to you.'

I placed my belongings into the boat, along with a number of watertight bags and boxes full of provisions. I put in my wall tent, a heavy mass of folded white canvas that would become my home while I was building the cabin. Finally I lifted in my stove.

Don had disappeared while I was packing, and he returned with the dog, barking and jumping by his side. 'Well, here he is.'

My heart sank. The dog was covered in long hair and didn't look at all practical for the bush. He galloped excitedly up and down the beach, his golden fur flowing in the places where it was not knotted.

'What's his name?'

Don seemed to share my misgivings. 'Well, I think the pant-sniffer is called Fuzzy.'

'What sort of dog is he?'

'Half poodle and half golden retriever.'

As if on cue, the golden energy-ball stopped his charging and let out a shrill series of barks.

'Sounds like a poodle,' I muttered. 'Well, better get on with it. Fuzzy!'

He raced towards me, then got up on his hind legs and pawed at my shirt with a lolling tongue and an adoring look on his face.

I patted the side of the boat and commanded: 'Fuzzy, in!'

He dropped down onto all fours, and stood looking at me.

'In!' I repeated, patting the boat more forcefully.

He turned in a circle, whimpering.

'Get in!' I shouted.

Still he cringed, unable or unwilling to do as I asked. Exasperated, I bent and bodily lifted the dog into the boat. I gave Don a wave, pushed the boat out into the water then clambered in. As I did so, Fuzzy jumped out again.

'Fuzzy! No! Come here.'

He swam back to the little beach, where Don stood laughing. Swearing quietly I grabbed an oar and poled back into the beach, then jumped out and grabbed the dog. I dumped him back in the boat, this time tying him so he couldn't escape. He jumped and strained at the rope, barking shrilly.

'Shut up, you pain in the arse,' I muttered.

The outboard motor soon stuttered into life. I twisted the throttle up and aimed the nose towards the centre of the stream. As I moved swiftly downstream, I looked back to see Don still standing on the beach. Above him, on the high bluff beside the house, I saw Carol waving. I felt humbled by the kindness they had shown me, and profoundly grateful that fate had led me to a family who knew so much about the wilderness.

I turned to look downriver, then pulled a map from my breast pocket so I could keep tabs on where I was. Soon the little village was long behind me. Fuzzy was staring longingly at the distant river bank. Occasionally he stole a look at me, his whole body registering his resentment at his abduction.

Well, this is it, I thought grimly. I'm on my own.

Moving away from the centre of the stream, I steered the boat towards the far southern bank. The water grew choppy, and short, sharp waves came at us from every direction, slapping hard against the little boat and spraying us with water. Fuzzy looked even more unhappy, huddling into a ball and shaking himself overdramatically every so often. His brown eyes were now trained on me resentfully. 'Oh, don't start the blame game with me, pal,' I muttered, and he turned away with a wounded look.

On we travelled downstream, while I concentrated fiercely on looking out for snags and sandbanks. I passed Four Mile Point, so called because it marked a point four miles downstream from Galena. Rounding a bend, I looked along the wide channel ahead and saw four possible routes. I struggled to remember which way Charlie had gone, and looked from the bank to the map and back again, trying to find a landmark. Fuzzy let out a little whimper of anxiety before slumping lower in the boat. Clearly he had no confidence in my abilities as a boatman, and I couldn't blame him.

I finally worked out the route, and powered the launch towards a narrow, deep channel that passed to the south of a willow-clad island. I sped past sandbars and eddies and vicious snags that waved and bobbed in the stream like the gnarled fingers of foretellers of doom. At last I saw Pilot Mountain looming ahead, giving me a landmark to steer by.

The stream raced through the narrow mouth of Pilot Mountain slough, carrying the little boat along like a bath toy. Despite the force of the river, it felt reassuring to be in a narrower stretch of water. Still, we had eight miles to go, and as we motored deeper into wild country the stream meandered and twisted. The scent of hot vegetation hung in the air, and everything except the swift stream was still and quiet. I passed round another willow-covered island, and when I rejoined the main stream a great cloud of duck rose from a sandbar. Fluffy jumped up, yapping, as they flew across the water, rising and wheeling down the mouth of a creek.

We passed through the mouth of Bishop Creek and into an area of cold shadow beneath Pilot Mountain. The water grew choppy here as wind funnelled down the mountainside, then dropped again as we rounded the wide sandbar on the bend. A bald eagle sat on a gaunt cottonwood tree, staring down at us with a look of haughty disdain. Then I saw the long, straight stretch where I had stopped with Don and Charlie.

'So far so good,' I muttered to myself, breathing a long sigh of relief.

A movement caught my eye. In the shade of some willows growing along the sandbar, I saw a large white wolf stand up to look at me, while another lay nearby, watching. Fuzzy had also spotted them, and was letting out a low, threatening growl. My heart beat with excitement. Wolves are exceptionally wary of people, and it was surprising that they had not disappeared long before my noisy craft rounded the bend. In my current state of tension, everything seemed to be imbued with meaning, and I wondered if the sight—on my very first day alone in the wilderness—could be read as a sign. Perhaps welcoming me to live safely among the wild things of the woods, or, more ominously, warning me of the dangers to come.

I steered the little boat towards the black beach, and climbed out onto the sand. With some difficulty, I heaved the launch up the beach. The air was hot and humid, and I was surrounded by a cloud of black flies. The boat was full of kit and I thought with dread of the hours of carrying that lay ahead of me. Fuzzy was still sitting in the boat, regarding me balefully. I untied his tether and he reluctantly clambered out onto the beach. I tied him to a tree, afraid that he might desert me, then began unloading.

It was when I was heaving my heavy hiking bag onto my back that I caught sight of the bear tracks in the sand. They were recent—and huge. For the first time I faced the fact that I had arrived in a place where I could well be overpowered and eaten. I stood staring, loath to leave the relative safety of the beach yet aware of darkness approaching.

'Get on with it, Guy,' I muttered, and began climbing up the bank. I dropped my hiking bag on the lip of the bank, then slithered back down to get another load, and so on until the boat was empty.

After pulling the boat a bit higher up the beach, I untied Fuzzy, and clambered up to where all my belongings were piled. Remembering Don's advice that my priority should always be to set up camp, I sorted my stuff into two piles. One pile could remain stored by the river until tomorrow, and the other would be needed immediately. Onto the 'now' pile went the shotgun and rifle, and a blue plastic barrel holding five gallons of drinking water. Next to this I threw my hiking bag and a smaller bag containing water-purification equipment, ammunition, matches, tarpaulin and sleeping-bag, as well as my tent and stove pipes, which weighed well over fifty pounds. Finally I brought over my food boxes, my saw and my 'boys' axe'—a multipurpose axe with a twenty-four inch wooden handle and a two-pound blade. Fuzzy had climbed up the bank to join me, and lay slumped beside the generator, jerry cans of petrol, chain-saw oil and assorted tools that made up the 'later' pile.

My heart sank as I looked down at the immense heap of stuff that I had to haul along the game trail to the lake. It must have weighed nearly 300 pounds. I loaded the stove, my small bag, the shotgun and the boxes of food into a little plastic toboggan, and tied the kit down with rope. I heaved the big hiking bag onto my back and slung the 45/70 over my shoulder. One hand was left free to carry the five-gallon water barrel, and the other to pull the nylon line that towed the heavy toboggan.

I turned and walked heavily into the woods, pushing through sharp rose bushes that scratched and tore at my skin. My hand was already stinging from the tight nylon cord. Sweat began dripping down my chest in ticklish streams, but I pushed on. Then a thought stopped me in my tracks: I had left my fuel supplies sitting on the forest floor, easily within the reach of bears. Bears are powerfully attracted to all petroleum-based products. If a bear came across my petrol cans it would destroy them. I looked at my watch. It was midafternoon, and I was already worryingly late for setting up camp, but there was no way round it; I had to make my fuel safe.

I put everything down except the 45/70, and walked back down the trail, swearing profusely. Don's first lesson had already proved itself: work slowly, think about how each action is going to turn out—you'll save time. Fuzzy perked up, perhaps thinking we were heading for home, and trotted ahead.

Back at the river I cast about, looking for a way of getting the jerry cans out of a bear's reach. I'd left my rope back up the trail, and again cursed myself for not planning better. I sized up a tall, slender birch tree and saw a way to hoist up the fuel. All I needed was a means of tying the cans. My eye fell upon a dainty white spruce tree—a good source of cordage, I had read. I took my knife and dug away at the base of the tree, pulling up a few good lengths of root. I tied the withes to the handles of the two fuel cans, leaving a long tail, then began shimmying up the birch tree. The tree began to arch and bend downward. Birch is famed for having a superb strength-to-weight ratio. At about twenty feet up, the tree sagged down enough for me to reach the cans, and I timber-hitched the withes round the slender trunk. I then stepped off the tree, and stood back waiting for it to sail into the air. Instead it rose by about ten feet, then stayed put.

Cursing, I pulled the tree down again and untied a can. The tree sailed up high. I found another tree, and repeated the whole process with the second can and a few plastic bottles of chain-saw oil. I stood back in satisfaction, then remembered I had a long way to go. I trudged back up the trail, heaved on my load, and continued on my way.

Shortly I reached a place where the trail turned uphill, and bent my back to pull hard. Immediately, the sled hit a hummock and overturned, and my inadequate lashings broke free. I stood very still, looking at the upturned sled and its scattered load. Fuzzy flopped down beside the sled and yawned ostentatiously. Clearly he thought I was totally incompetent. All day, it seemed to me, he had been mocking my efforts, and the yawn was the last straw. My tiredness and frustration boiled over.

'Oh, you think you're so clever don't you—you little shit!' I said.

He stood up, his eyes widening as if in realisation that his new owner was not just hopeless but dangerous too, and slunk away.

I realised that I was using him as a kind of canine stress ball, and held my hands up. 'OK, I'm sorry.'

He gave me a wary look, then sat down again. As I bent to repack the sled, I heard the dog yawning again. I froze for a moment, battling to overcome my irritation, and heard him doing the same thing again—only louder. I whipped round to catch him in the act, and he snapped his jaws shut, looking away innocently. No sooner had I turned my back than I heard him yawning again. This time there was no doubt: he was deliberately challenging me.

I whipped round again. 'Right, that's it—go away.' I pointed down the trail. Fuzzy looked balefully back at me, his face registering disbelief.

'Yes, I mean it. Go away now.'

He looked along the tiny line of crushed vegetation, then back at me as if to say, Shouldn't we talk about this? I shook my head and continued to point down the trail. He turned and walked slowly away, stopping to look back occasionally as if waiting for me to change my mind.

'Good riddance,' I muttered as he sidled out of sight.

The trail seemed interminable this time, with my heavy load and the toboggan dragging unwillingly behind. About an hour after leaving the river, I crossed the grass lake, then struggled up a steep incline and through the second big stand of white spruce. When I finally reached the lake, I walked with relief onto the grass by the lakeside and stood very still for a moment, taking it all in. There was no time to waste, however, as I couldn't afford to be without shelter overnight. I walked back to the thickly forested site where I would build my cabin, then stacked my kit up beneath a spruce tree and looked around for a place to set up my wall tent. I needed two trees around eighteen feet apart. I soon spotted a large white birch tree and a spruce that would do nicely. I cleared a space between them, then found a young white spruce, its trunk about seven inches in diameter, that would make a perfect ridgepole. I used the handle of my axe to knock the small branches off the trunk, then I sawed the bare tree down and knocked off the remaining branches. I threaded the spruce pole through the heavy canvas of the tent, and pulled the unwieldy lump into position between the trees.

As I worked, it began to rain. I thought of Fuzzy and felt a pang of guilt. Where was he? The rain grew steadier and began to run down my neck, further lowering my morale. I made a crude ladder out of alder branches and used the rickety affair to reach high enough to tie up each end of the ridgepole. I now needed to cut six long, straight birch poles for the frame. I found these easily, quickly stripping off leaves and branches and leaning two poles in an 'A' shape against the ridge at either end of the tent. Between them, two more were tied at thigh level to run the length of the tent, and the canvas was pulled out and tied firmly to the poles. I then laid the spruce boughs I had cut earlier on the floor of the tent, creating a sprung floor.

Still I couldn't rest—I needed to set up my stove. I heaved it into the tent, placing it beneath the pre-made chimney hole in the canvas roof. I began to shove the sections of stove pipe together, only to discover I didn't have enough pipe to reach clear out of the roof. The only answer was to raise the stove. I cut a few lengths of spruce, which I hammered into the soft forest floor. Next I hammered some alder lengths onto the tops of the poles to make a rough cradle, into which I placed the barrel stove. The stove was now three feet higher and I was able to push the pipes clear of the tent.

I flopped down onto the fresh spruce and lay staring at the canvas, feeling cold, damp and exhausted. I wanted nothing more than to sleep. But there were still jobs that had to be done, so I forced myself up again.

Outside, the rain had stopped and an insipid setting sun threw very little light into the darkness of my campsite. I poured water from the five-gallon drum into a tin bowl and drank heavily, before turning my mind to the evening's chores. With night falling, the air was chilly, and the first job was to find wood for the stove. I felled a good-sized birch tree and set about sawing it into stove-sized logs. Then I split the logs on the birch stump. The echoes of my axe rang out through the great woods, and I thought of the animals around me, adjusting to the sounds of their new neighbour. When I had stacked the logs, I set about getting the stove ready to light, starting with some strips of bark, adding some pencil-sized twigs and the resiny white spruce boughs, and finishing with some sweet-smelling 'green' birch. I filled my coffee pot with water and placed it on the flat stove surface. Then I rolled a big log in front of the stove to act as a seat.

This was the first fire at my camp; it was time for a ceremony. I dug out a match, then closed my eyes and sent out a silent appeal to fate: *Give me strength and luck. Let me come out of this alive.* I lit the roll of birch and watched as it sparked into flame, the fire gathering strength as it reached the kindling and logs. Dense white smoke pulled through the wood, and I closed the door of the stove. It was dark outside now, and I pulled down the canvas door flaps, tying the opening shut. The stove was burning beautifully, and it was immensely cheering to feel its warmth. I lit my kerosene lamp and hung it from the ridgepole. Sheltered from the rain and dark woods outside, I was experiencing an ancient emotion, the feeling of security that comes from fire. For the first time that day, I was beginning to relax.

I took my wet clothes off, and hung them on a little line near the stove before changing into some dry clothes. The kettle was boiling, and I made my first cup of tea. I pulled a packet of air-dried king salmon from my bag, along with a little box of salt, and sat staring into the fire as I ate. When I had finished, I unrolled my heavy sleeping-bag and climbed inside. I lay back, listening to the occasional crack of wood in the stove.

I thought of my days in the office, and remembered the terrible feeling that my life was slipping away in that awful, grey, clerical world. I imagined what I might have been doing at that moment: in the car on my way to work, perhaps, sitting behind my computer or discussing brands or sales plans. Instead, here I was, in the Alaskan wilderness. I lay motionless, filled with joy at my escape, tempered with sadness at being away from my family.

I became aware of a faint sound carried on the wind. Sitting bolt upright, I strained to hear the noise again. For several minutes there was nothing, and I was just about to brew another cup of tea when I heard it again: the lonesome, unforgettable call of a timber wolf. My skin prickled, and I suddenly felt very small and weak. The wolf sounded close, but I had already learned that sound travels a long way in this realm of silence. I stood up, picking up the rifle, and stepped out of the tent. There it was again: another long, lilting call that curled up at the end, almost as if it were asking a question.

I looked up at the sky and saw a few faint stars as clouds pulled away from a crescent moon. I thought of Fuzzy, alone and vulnerable in the woods, and cursed myself for treating him so badly. 'Fuzzy!' I shouted. My voice echoed out into the darkness. 'Fuzzy!' I cried again, then stepped out of the circle of light around my tent and called again. I heard nothing.

Telling myself there was nothing I could do, I went back inside and stoked the stove. My sponsors, Highland Park, had sent me off with as much top-quality whisky as I could carry, and I decided it was time for some medication. As I poured a generous measure into my tin mug, I remembered Don's warning about never letting your dog wander.

'If a bear finds him, he's gonna run back to the only thing he knows in them woods,' he'd said, 'and that's you . . . with the bear following behind.'

Reflecting that, from a bear's point of view, the light from my tent was the equivalent of a neon roadside sign announcing GOOD FOOD 24 HOURS, I blew out my lamp and climbed into my sleeping-bag, the 45/70 propped within arm's reach. I tried to fall asleep, but I kept being wakened by an image of Fuzzy, sprinting through the undergrowth towards me, pursued by a thousand pounds of enraged predator.

All positive thoughts gone, I worried about everything from marauding bears to failing to build my cabin before winter. My cabin site, approximately half an acre and thickly wooded, would first have to be cleared—this alone was several weeks' work. Then I had to gather and prepare logs for building, and for that I needed the white spruce that grew at least a mile away back down the trail. The logs would weigh hundreds of pounds, and I would have to clear the portage before I could get them up to the site.

Exhausted by worry, I sank back into my sleeping-bag and was just on the edge of sleep when I heard a loud sniffing sound outside the tent. I froze, straining to hear above the wind. A few moments later it came again: unmistakably a sniff, and this time the animal pushed into the side of the tent slightly. I eased myself up, reaching cautiously towards the pump shotgun. I pumped a round into the chamber, and considered shooting through the canvas, but thought better of it. Suddenly there was a great scratching sound and clawing at the door of the tent. I brought the gun to my shoulder and aimed at the door. My finger was poised on the trigger as a black nose came into view, followed by a familiar golden head. Two almond eyes looked up at me nervously. Like a police negotiator, Fuzzy stayed very still, keeping his eyes firmly on mine as if to say: Take it easy, I'm a friend . . . Now slowly put down the gun.

I lowered the gun, deeply relieved. Fuzzy didn't move.

I cleared the breach. 'Good dog, Fuzzy—come on.'

He shrugged under the canvas, then sat just inside the door looking at me warily. He was soaking, and leaves were caught up in his coat.

I patted the floor beside the stove and said, 'Here.'

He cautiously approached the stove and sat down. I had to hand it to him for finding his way here. Clearly he was tenacious, and could look after himself in the bush. In his eyes, however, it was obvious that I had some making up to do. He lay down, one eye half open, watching my every move.

THE NEXT MORNING I woke up feeling disorientated. Then the memory of where I was returned, accompanied by the familiar wave of worry. Outside it was grey again, and the sight of the damp, forbidding woods did nothing to restore my morale. I stoked the stove, then made a jug of strong coffee. I fried some bacon and bread while staring out of the tent at the drab weather and claustrophobic vegetation surrounding the campsite. I wolfed everything down, while Fuzzy ate sparingly from the dog food I had given him, burying the rest. I could learn from him: he was making his food last.

After clearing up, I headed down the trail to collect the rest of my kit from the river bank. Up and down the trail I yomped, and gradually a pile of kit built up beside my tent. As the pile got larger, so the level of drinking water in my barrel dropped lower.

With everything finally back at camp, I found homes for tools on various handy branches and stored the rest of the kit tidily at the back of my tent. I then stood looking down the path of crushed vegetation that had to be transformed into a portage. The ground would have to be cleared of all obstructions. Fallen trees along the route would have to be removed, with no stumps or sharp points left behind. About a mile and a half long, the route down to the river went up and down several steep hills, and passed through thick vegetation. It would be no easy task. More immediately, I had to think about digging a hole for a latrine. Don had warned me of some bears known as 'shit-eaters', who are attracted by the scent of human excrement.

A feeling of panic rose once again. I looked at Fuzzy, who was tethered by the tent, staring at me sadly. It was late afternoon; to start my jobs now would be pointless. Four ducks flew low overhead, heading towards the river. That's it, I thought. I'll go and catch something for supper. I grabbed the shotgun, loading four number fives, and untied Fuzzy, who stood up on his hind legs and pawed me, tongue lolling.

'God, I hate dogs,' I muttered. 'Down!'

He dropped to all fours, looking up at me as if disappointed that I hadn't improved overnight. I heaved the 45/70 onto my shoulder and started to walk down the trail towards the river. Carrying both a shotgun and a rifle seemed like overkill, yet I was mindful of the risk of meeting a bear, and determined never to be caught unawares. As I walked I stopped to pick the odd high-bush cranberry. The beautiful, bitter-tasting, bright red berries took some getting used to, but I liked them.

A loud buzzing sound took my gaze down to a mass of flies sitting on a large, fresh-looking mound of bear droppings at my feet, peppered with high-bush cranberries. Clearly I wasn't the only one enjoying them. I scanned the undergrowth nervously, and began clapping my hands and singing noisily. The worst possible thing is to take a bear by surprise, and I had been told always to make as much noise as possible when moving in the bush. Most bears are as anxious to avoid an encounter as we are, and when they detect the presence of a human will move off in the other direction. A surprised bear, however, can be lethal, and may charge.

HAVING REACHED the river safely, I clambered into the launch and called Fuzzy to join me. Just as the day before, he turned in circles nervously, reluctant to get in.

'Come on,' I shouted. 'Get in!'

He steeled himself for the jump, then leapt, only to slip on takeoff and fall back onto the muddy beach. He tried again and failed, so I leaned over the bow and lifted him in. Once in the boat he shook himself violently, then looked at me in satisfaction. I was covered in specks of sticky river mud.

I stared at him angrily and pointed to the bow. 'Stay there!'

He turned his back on me and gazed sadly out at the river. I shook my head in exasperation. Fuzzy was nothing but a hindrance.

I started the engine and motored upstream along the slough, past the sandbar where I had seen the wolves and into the shadow of Pilot Mountain. Ahead on the right lay the entrance to Bishop Creek, where the peaty water changed colour as it clashed with the silty slough. As I approached the creek's mouth, the boat ran aground, and I had to punt off the mud and back into the stream. Finally I figured out a route through the sandbars.

The creek followed a sinuous course, bounded to the west by a forested ridge and to the east by a low bank that led out onto flat country still smoking from the fires. Rounding a bend, I saw four canvasback ducks lift and fly away. I dropped the tiller and fumbled the shotgun onto my shoulder, took aim and shot. To my amazement, a duck fell dead in the water while the others banked sharply and flew back over my head. I took a few more shots, but missed them all, and they whirred into the distance.

Ahead, the fat duck bobbed in the water. I steered towards it and killed the engine. Fuzzy was standing in the bow, staring intently at the bird.

'Fetch!' I said, pointing.

He did nothing except whine slightly as the bird floated past. Then he began barking shrilly, as if to tell me, Quick! Get it—it's floating away!

I lost my temper. 'Shut up!' I shouted, but he continued to bark. 'You bloody useless animal!' I yelled, and gave him a sharp clout on his rump.

The little dog whirled round, giving me a look of pure dislike. I sat back, knowing that I had again used Fuzzy as a stress outlet, and this time I had overstepped the mark. He turned away with surprising dignity, and stared intently over the side of the boat. Then he leaned back and wriggled his bottom before executing a perfect little jump into the water. He struggled momentarily against the current, then began swimming powerfully towards the shore. I watched him for a while, then steered downstream to pick up the duck. When I next looked up, Fuzzy was pulling himself out of the water.

'Fuzzy!' I shouted.

He turned to look at me defiantly. Then he let out a single, high-pitched poodle bark and trotted off into the woods. I had behaved badly, expecting him to carry out a task for which he hadn't been trained, and he'd had enough. Once more I regretted my impatience.

Back at camp I plucked and butchered the duck. I sealed the meat in bacon grease and added onion, garlic, dried mushrooms and rice to make an improvised risotto cooked over a fire outside. It was beautiful. As I ate, I stopped occasionally to listen to the sombre call of a great northern owl.

Suddenly I heard a branch snap in the woods behind me, and lifted my gun, only to see two familiar eyes shining back at me out of the darkness. Fuzzy walked slowly into the circle of flickering light. I said nothing, but scraped the remains of my meal into his feed dish. He looked warily up at me, sniffed at the bowl, then tentatively began eating, as usual stopping short of eating it all. Then he lay down between the roots of a large spruce and fell asleep. He must have travelled at least eight miles to get back to camp. I looked at him anew, feeling a growing admiration for his character.

THE NEXT MORNING I woke feeling ready for anything. It was a clear sunny day and I felt happy and hopeful. I looked around in vain for Fuzzy. Then I heard his characteristic yawn and saw that he had settled in the ashes of my fire. I was impressed at his initiative in finding a heated bed for the night.

I clapped my hands and Fuzzy shot over, jumping up and frantically licking me as usual. I pushed him down, saying, 'OK, fruitcake, enough,' and he dropped to the ground disconsolately. Then he let out another yawn, with the usual high-pitched ending that I found so irritating. 'Fuzzy, no. Please don't do that,' I said, and he stopped mid-yawn. Progress at last, I thought.

After breakfast, I filled my one-litre canteen with drinking water, then loaded the saw, the Sandvik and chain saw onto my little plastic sled. I slung the 45/70 over my shoulder and walked to where the portage would begin, fifty yards or so from my tent. 'Well, here we go,' I muttered.

With the Sandvik I began slashing at the undergrowth, feeling like a slave labourer on the River Kwai. Thorns embedded themselves in my hands and legs, and osiers whipped across my face. As I heaved rotten branches and tree trunks away from the path, I disturbed great clouds of midgelike flies, which added to my pain. On and on I went, cutting, pulling and stacking. Within minutes I was sweating heavily and getting very thirsty.

By midmorning I was soaked in sweat and covered in bites, cuts and scratches, yet when I surveyed my work it seemed as though I had achieved nothing. Beyond the few yards of portage that I had managed to clear, I could see the thin game trail continuing through dense bush leading off as far as the eye could see. I slumped down with my back against a tree, and drained the last few drops of warm water from my canteen.

I forced myself back to work, and by late afternoon I was exhausted and dreaming of water—I had very little left in my drum. I looked through the trees at the shimmering lake, and decided to inspect it more closely.

The water was still, and my hopes sank: it seemed to be just on the right side of stagnant. I knelt and gazed into the brown water, then jumped as something whacked the surface. Fuzzy barked, and I saw a brown animal swimming towards me. A large, grumpy, whiskered head broke through the water, and two outraged eyes fixed on mine. Then the beaver ducked, lifting his great flat scaly tail and bringing it down hard on the water.

Near the beaver house I saw a large, leafy branch moving across the water before it was pulled down into the grog. Four beavers were busily swimming to and fro. I waited to see what else might be using the lake, and shortly heard a series of chirping calls. Three otters were swimming swiftly alongside the reeds on the far side. Above me, a squadron of ducks banked and landed on the lake; while at the far end I could hear the honking of geese.

Fuzzy went to the edge of the water and drank heavily, reminding me of my own thirst. If only I had the constitution of a dog, I thought. But I couldn't afford to be fussy. I filled my canteen from the lake and returned to camp. My Miox water purifier works by mixing a sample of the suspect water with salt, then passing an electrical current through it. I managed to purify a pint or so in an hour, but it wasn't enough. In this heat, the intense physical work was making me incredibly thirsty, and I couldn't risk getting dehydrated.

OVER THE NEXT FEW DAYS I continued to clear my portage, working myself into a state of aching exhaustion. The water shortage was becoming acute, and I experimented with drinking water from the slough. This also had its problems. A source over a mile and a half away was not exactly convenient. The silty water was poor quality, and left an unpleasant film of sand at the back of my throat. I marvelled at my predicament: bears, wolves, ice, snow—all that I had been prepared for, but the last thing I had expected was thirst. All day long I fantasised about pure, ice-cold water, only to return to a warm, foul-tasting liquid that always left me wanting more.

During those early days of hard labour, I settled into a rhythm. Each morning I would wake early and cook up a good-sized breakfast. I would then walk along my newly cut portage until, like a miner at the coalface, I came to the end of the shaft. Working slowly and carefully, I would then progress through the bush, getting a little closer to the river with each day's work. By early afternoon I would be drenched in sweat and covered in dirt. At this point I would down tools and, bar of soap in my pocket, amble down to the swift, cool slough. I had found a perfect spot for washing, where a large cottonwood had fallen into the water at right angles to the bank. Hanging my clothes from its roots, I would walk along the tree until I was right out in the slough. I would then sink into the water on the downstream side, holding on to a branch while the swift current sluiced my tired and battered body. After a few minutes I would clamber onto a submerged bough and soap up. I would return to camp transformed.

About two weeks into my work, I sauntered down to the slough as usual. It had been a good day: I'd done a great deal of work, Fuzzy had been less irritating than usual and for once I was feeling optimistic about my chances in the race against winter. I undressed, then walked out along the tree, hanging the 45/70 on its usual root. Fuzzy was dozing in a cool spot on the river bank downstream. I lowered myself in, gasping at the cold, then sat up on the bough and soaped up. I rinsed off, then clambered back onto the tree.

I was sitting astride the tree, brushing my teeth, when I spotted a movement upstream. Looking again, I saw a large black bear standing up to its shoulders in the slough a hundred yards or so away.

For several minutes we stared at each other. Then I flicked my eyes across to the rifle, dangling uselessly in the sunshine fifty feet away. If the bear charged, would I have time to get the gun loaded before he reached me? The answer was undoubtedly no; he could easily reach the bank before me and come out along the tree, cutting me off from the gun. I looked back at him, standing motionless in the water, not taking his eyes off me for a second. Bears do not have good eyesight, and as I was downwind he would have difficulty getting my scent. It was important for me to broadcast the fact that I was a human, in the hope that he might decide to move on.

I raised an arm and waved it, shouting 'Hello! Goodbye! Not for lunch!'

The bear stiffened but did not move, and a fluttering of fear ran through me, mingled with a sense of the ridiculous as a frothy stream of toothpaste dribbled down my chin. Without taking my eyes off him, I began to pull myself slowly back along the tree towards the bank. The bear lifted his head and swung it from side to side, sniffing the air, and I began to move faster. I glanced over towards Fuzzy, who hadn't even noticed my predicament.

I reached the end of the tree, and with deep relief loaded a round into the breach. The bear dropped onto all fours and splashed out of the river, bounding along the bank towards me at considerable speed. I lifted the gun, but he dodged off into a patch of brush. I stared at the spot where he had disappeared, then he suddenly reappeared, considerably closer to me. I decided to play it cool—I didn't want to shoot him if I could avoid it—and began pulling my clothes on, chatting loudly. After a pause, the bear shuffled away into the thick willow. I finished dressing with shaking hands.

I walked back to camp lost in thought, a million miles from the happy-go-lucky boy who came down the trail an hour ago. It seemed that, just when I began to feel confident, nature had a way of bringing me back down to earth. This was my first encounter with an Alaskan black bear, and it worried me that he had seemed so curious. Black bears more commonly stalk and eat humans than their larger grizzly cousins. The bear was now aware of my presence, and might be bolder next time. At this time of year, bears are stocking up for winter, and determinedly seeking out all sources of food.

That night there was a strong wind, and I felt as though I was at sea as my lashings creaked, the ridgepole bucked and the canvas shivered like a sail under strain. I sat huddled beside the stove, looking anxiously up at the ridgepole and hoping it wouldn't fall down.

I looked at my watch: it was 10 p.m.—early morning in Scotland, and a good time to call home. The signal was a bit dodgy, but by holding my Inmarsat satellite phone up high in a particular corner of the camp I could hear reasonably well. On this occasion I hadn't called home for a couple of weeks. Both Juliet and I had to make it alone this year, and it would be easy to become over-reliant on phone contact. Now, though, I needed to hear Juliet's voice, and to be reassured that, at home at least, everything was safe.

'Julsie, it's me. Can you hear me?'

'Guy! Thank God it's you!' Her relief was palpable and I realised how worried she had been. 'Are you OK? What are you doing?'

My mind ran through the endless list of jobs that lay ahead of me, and I struggled to explain. 'Jules, I don't know if I can do this. Really, I think it might just be impossible. I have so little time—'

She interrupted me, her voice clear and strong. 'Tell me what you are doing now, Guy.'

'I'm cutting the portage. I have to clear the trail to the river so that I can drag logs up from the timber sites.'

'Oh. So how much longer will that take?'

I was about to answer when I heard Oscar in the background, pleading to talk to me. Juliet passed him the phone.

'Daddy! Hello, daddy!'

I felt a lump in my throat. 'Biggest boy! How is my biggest boy?'

'I'm OK, Daddy. We live on Mull now, do you know that?' He sounded excited and happy.

'I know. Are you having fun?'

He talked to me about the sea, and sailing in his grandfather's boat. It was painful to hear and I felt useless again, wishing that I could be with them all. I said my goodbyes and Juliet came on the line again.

'Oscar's crying. I've got to go. He wants to talk to you but it's too much for him. You'll have to call when he's asleep—he's got to get on with his life.'

'What do you mean?'

There was a pause. 'Well, he's doing fine, but every time you call he's reminded that his dad is gone and it hurts him. I think it would be better if he didn't speak to you for a while until things have settled down.' I heard her voice crack over the line. 'Call later, Guy—I love you.'

The phone went dead. I lit the pressure lamp, then rummaged for a piece of chocolate to cheer myself up, but was interrupted by a series of high-pitched barks from Fuzzy. I stepped outside.

'What is it, lad?'

He was staring into the darkening woods, emitting a low growl. I heard a branch crack and froze, but the trees were making so much noise in the wind that I couldn't be sure what had made the sound. I pumped a round into the shotgun and fired it above my head, hoping it would scare whatever it was away. Fuzzy didn't flinch, but after a few moments skulked off to his dry spot beneath the spruce and lay down, looking back as if to say, Well, that should have done it for now—let's sit back and see what happens. I settled into the tent for the night, glad that the little dog was keeping an eye out for me when all around the world seemed full of menace.

IT WAS MID-SEPTEMBER before I finished clearing my portage. It had taken almost a month and I was exhausted, and covered with cuts and grazes. I had also run out of provisions, and needed more tools, so I decided to go back to Galena. Any trip upriver would have to be done quickly, as the river would soon begin to run with ice and I would be cut off for a long time. During 'ice-up', travel becomes virtually impossible, as the river is too icy for boats, but the ice is not yet solid enough to bear any weight. I placed the remains of my food in a bag, which I hung from a high, thin branch, then strung up my fuel at the opposite end of the camp. The door of my tent I tied up tightly, though I knew bears would be undeterred by a couple of canvas flaps.

I walked down the new portage with Fuzzy at my heels, feeling excited at the prospect of seeing people again. The little aluminium launch was waiting at the beach like an obedient dog. I pushed it down to the river's edge and jumped in, calling Fuzzy who hopped in after a series of irritating half-jumps. As usual, he clambered clumsily all over me, covering every-thing with mud before sitting down in the bow of the boat.

'You tosser,' I muttered, then started the engine and pushed off.

The trip would take longer this time as we were heading upriver, against the current. On either side the land was preparing for winter: most of the green had turned to brown, and everything seemed to be shutting down.

Out on the Yukon we were hit by a stiff easterly wind. The bow of the boat banged against the waves, and Fuzzy rolled into a ball to keep out of the cold spray. The route was hard to define: there were no landmarks, just a low horizon and the river stretching ahead under a cold grey sky. After a few tense and uncomfortable hours, however, the village finally came into view. I strained my eyes to see Don's golden cabin, and when it appeared I aimed the bow of the boat towards it.

As I neared the mud I saw Don walking slowly down towards the beach. He raised a hand in greeting. 'Still alive, hey?'

'Yup.' I stepped out of the boat and pulled it up the beach.

'So, have you cut the portage?'

In answer I held out my battered hands.

He let out a coughing laugh. 'Ever heard of gloves?'

I fumbled in my pocket and pulled out my shredded gloves.

He laughed again. 'Them gloves'll do for England maybe, but—'

I interrupted. 'I think you mean the UK, Don.'

'Oh excuse me . . . the *UK*,' he said, affecting a fake English accent.

It felt good to have the piss taken out of me again, and I realised how much I had missed being with people.

Don turned and walked away, calling over his shoulder, 'Come for supper and we'll talk.' Halfway up the bank he stopped, shouting, 'Next time you cut yourself, plug the cut with spruce sap. The sap is like a second skin—waterproof and disinfectant all in one. Pretty damn clever is Mother Nature.' With that he turned and carried on up the hill.

THE NEXT FEW DAYS were spent buying and borrowing equipment and provisions: wood, tools, ropes, chains, pulleys, roofing iron, wire and a host of other bits and pieces. There was a limit to how much I could take, and I was faced with a few tough choices: a box of nails, for example, took precedence over an extra supply of flour. Don lent me two chain saws in addition to the one he'd already given me. He also gave me some peaveys, which are stout, old-fashioned tools designed for moving big logs by hand.

While I had been at camp, a postal delivery had arrived from Lehman's, an American mail-order company. The parcel contained a heavy two-bit axe, a Hudson Bay trapping axe and a pair of very solid Canadian snowshoes.

I held the shoes up to Don. 'Do you think I'm going to need these?'

He stopped his work and looked at me with a deadpan expression. 'Nah, it don't snow in the Interior.'

Between gathering supplies, I spent time with Don's family, who seemed keen to find out more about the stranger in their midst. They slowly seemed to accept me as a likeable if slightly odd outsider. They included me in family gatherings, and gently encouraged me in what I was trying to do, each member of the family offering invaluable advice and practical assistance.

Don's daughter Jenny gave me a stout pair of canvas overalls, which she assured me would take the toughest treatment. Moved by her gesture and knowing that payment would be refused, I looked for something to give her in return. With a heavy heart, I dug out an immense bar of Toblerone that Juliet had sent me. Jenny's eyes lit up with a kind of fanatical zeal, and I realised that I had found her weakness. As I packed the overalls into my bag, I noticed a little green ribbon attached to the zip, and asked her where it had come from. She told me that it came from the Stick Dance in Nulato, and that it would bring me luck. Without knowing it, she had discovered a weakness of mine: an inbuilt superstitiousness.

Jenny works as a biologist for the Alaska Fish and Wildlife Service, and is a tall, strong woman with an incisive mind. She shares her father's evil sense of humour. She and Claudette, Don's other daughter, both became almost like sisters to me, and despite their often savage teasing, their friendship lifted my morale. Don's support and the gradual acceptance from his family combined to somehow blunt the knife edge of sadness that cut into me each time I thought of my own little family.

WHEN IT WAS time for me to leave Galena, Jenny's husband Chris volunteered to take me back downriver. Down on the beach, he helped me to load my kit into his boat. It was a cold, steely day, and as we motored away from the warmth and friendship of Don's family all my worries began to return. I sat in silence, rubbing Fuzzy's ears and looking out across the river. The water level had dropped since I had come upriver, as if nature was huddling up in readiness for the cold, and Chris had to steer the boat with great care. We passed banks of grey mud that held pinpricks of gold where willow and alder leaves had fallen from the forest edge to stick like postage stamps.

As we passed Pilot Mountain, I saw a large black bear look up at us, then bound into the spruce.

'Sure hope those bears haven't ripped your tent up!' Chris shouted.

'Yeah, me too,' I replied, and fell back into gloomy silence.

We finally reached my familiar little beach, and pushed the boat onto the bank. I stacked my kit in a great mound on the edge of the bank.

'I better get going,' Chris said. 'Weather looks bad. Good luck.'

'Thanks.' I tried to make my voice sound calm. 'I hope I won't need it.'

I pushed the boat into the current and Chris turned upstream and powered away. He looked once and waved, and then he was gone.

I stood for a while, listening as the sound of the engine faded, until I could hear nothing but the wind in the trees, which were losing their leaves with each gust. The feeling of loneliness on that windy spot was greater than anything I had ever experienced before. I now had no way of getting upriver, and to walk back would be impossible.

With each day winter was coming closer, bringing with it temperatures too low to imagine. On a normal winter day in the Interior the temperature would be between −25 and −50° Fahrenheit, but I could regularly expect it to be much colder. A series of haunting calls made me look up. Hundreds of cranes were flying south, filling the cold air with their cries. Everything that could move was getting out, and here I was just moving in.

Forcing myself into action, I climbed the bank and began collecting my stuff. I pulled a .357 magnum out of my bag and strapped it round my waist as an extension to my bear defences. I started to talk to myself in a stiff-upper-lip, terribly British sort of way, and the tactic worked. My rock-bottom morale began to laugh back, at first out of politeness, like a commuter humouring a drunk on the last bus home, but then gradually warming up, as I heaved my gear along the portage.

'C'mon Grieve! Look lively! Chop chop—there's a boy!' My voice echoed out across the woods, and if anyone had seen me they surely would have slunk away to hide, as I must have looked insane.

All afternoon I trudged up and down the portage, lumping and heaving and dragging. I had expected to find my campsite in ruins, but to my relief it seemed to be undisturbed. At last the job was complete, and my kit sorted.

It grew dark earlier than I had expected, and a mean wind brought spits of rain that I knew would soon turn into a downpour. Grateful that I had left a good store of wood, I lit a roaring fire and warmed myself beside it, while looking through a box of books sent to me by family and friends. I reached for a slim paperback and smiled: *Heart of Darkness* by Joseph Conrad.

4

The nights were getting colder, and when I looked up from my lake to the side of the mountain I no longer saw a dense canopy of green. Every day, thousands more birds flew south. At night the tent swayed in the cold wind, and sometimes I would lie awake as eerie sounds stretched through the woods towards my little camp. At sunset, the long, lingering calls of the loon birds would float and hang in the trees like wood smoke.

The loons fascinated me. They are the oldest and most primitive water birds in the world, with legs flattened for propulsion through the water and set too far back for walking. They are reputed to have seventeen calls, each with a separate meaning. Many indigenous people believed that the loon carried messages from the other side, and I could understand why. Their cries echoed as they looped up into the cold sky, sounding as if they were calling, *Who are you? Who are you?* and making me feel even more alone.

Each day I worked hard on clearing the site for the cabin, but carrying out hard physical labour while living in a tent was difficult. At the end of the day, before I could even begin to relax, I had to cut wood for the stove and collect water. I had now resorted to boiling the water and treating it with iodine. This yielded a greater quantity than the purifier, but still it was always in short supply, and I felt permanently on the edge of dehydration.

Gradually the site began to clear, and as the dark forest gave way to light and air my spirits lifted. I was also looking forward to a visit from Don.

He arrived one cold, dry afternoon, having been dropped off at the slough by Charlie, and stepped into the clearing with a dry, 'Well, hullo.' He proceeded to inspect my camp, checking over my gear with an inscrutable expression. He picked up a piece of firewood. 'You need to cut your green birch thinner—your stove'll be too cool to burn big chunks. Come winter you'll have the stove on all day, so you can burn bigger green stuff.' Then he pointed at the five-gallon water barrel. 'Why's that water jug empty?'

'I just can't seem to clean up enough water for drinking.'

'Oh, really?' Don shook his head. 'Rig up your tarpaulin on some poles in the clearing, and angle it so the rain runs down into your dixie tin.'

It was so obvious I could have kicked myself. 'OK, I'll do that. But won't it fill with leaves and bits and pieces?'

'Get a clean T-shirt and tie it over the mouth of the tin—that'll be your filter. No need to clean it 'cause it's come from heaven. Where's your chopping stump?' I pointed and he walked over to it, gently lifting the axe from its place and dropping it onto a large, knotty log of spruce. He lifted the thick log onto the block, then held the axe up for me. 'Come and split this.'

Feeling uncomfortably under the spotlight, I took the axe and raised it high before bringing it hurtling down onto the log. The blade stuck in hard, hit a knot and went no further. I tried with all my might to free the axe, heaving and grunting and all the time aware of how inept I must look. When at last I managed to free the axe, Don took it from me.

'Now, you gotta learn how to cut wood properly, 'cause it'll be your only fuel. You work slowly so you don't waste energy and you don't sweat.'

'How can I work without sweating?'

'We wear layers out here. When you think it's gonna be hard work you take a layer off before you get hot, and when the work's done you put it back on.'

'Even at minus fifty?'

'Especially at minus fifty. When it's that cold, sweat will freeze into your gear, and then when you stop working *you* start to freeze. You got to avoid sweating at all costs.'

He raised the axe and brought it down lightly, tilting the blade so that it struck the wood at a forty-five degree angle. The axe wedged out a little chunk from the block. He pulled the wood round and struck again, working his way round until a neat circle of offcuts lay around the block ready for stacking. He picked a thick, knotty block from the pile and chopped, and the axe stuck. I cleared my throat. Don gave me a wry smile, then flipped the axe and jammed log into the air, spinning the handle deftly and bringing it down so that the back of the axe head came down first with the wood still on top of the blade. With a *clink* the log split obediently in two.

'See—that way you don't sweat hammering away at it,' Don said. 'Use this time to practise working like you will when it's cold.'

I started up the stove and got the kettle going, and Don resumed his lesson inside the tent.

'Let me show you a trick,' he said. 'Now you can stand up straight when you're right in the middle of the tent under the ridgepole, but'—he held out his arms—'you lose space at the sides. Now, come with me.'

I followed obediently as he lifted the Sandvik from the tool tree, then walked along the portage until we came to a belt of willow. He deftly cut some stout but springy osiers, each about eight feet in length. Back in the tent he pushed the osiers up over the ridgepole, letting them flex naturally so that they held the sides of the tent out. Instead of a mean sloping roof, I now had a wonderful light domed space above my head.

Don couldn't stay long because ice-up was coming, but in the space of a few hours he'd already taught me several life-saving lessons. And he could cook, too. Next he grabbed a pot and set about making a classic standby, 'bacon and beans', an archetypal frontier dish—bacon is easy to store if canned or salted, and beans are a great source of energy. The bacon becomes even more vital in the winter, when a fatty diet is essential.

When the dish was cooked we sat on logs outside. Don took an innocent-looking bottle of sauce from his bag and applied it liberally to his food.

'What's that?' I asked.

'Oh, just a little spicy stuff—want a taste?'

'Sure.'

I put my finger over the opening of the bottle and up-ended it, leaving a little red circle on my index finger. I sniffed it—it smelt of nothing—and then popped it into my mouth. The reaction was instantaneous: I felt a wave of stinging on my tongue, followed by a vicious prickling and burning on the inside of my cheeks. I made the mistake of swallowing, which sent a toxic bolus down my throat, burning all the way down. My eyes filled with tears and I went into spasms of coughing. Finally I stood up, my mouth and throat numb and my voice hoarse.

'This stuff is awful, Don, horrific. How can you eat it? It's insanity.'

Don couldn't hide his sadistic joy. 'You're right!' he cried. 'It *is* Insanity—here, look!' He held up the bottle.

I read: DAVE'S INSANITY SAUCE: THE HOTTEST SAUCE IN THE WORLD! I stared at the evil substance, amazed that pure torture could exist in a bottle.

'But why, Don? How can you taste anything?'

He laughed, and returned to his beans. That night, I tasted very little.

Later on, I offered Don some of my precious supply of Highland Park whisky, but he held up his hands. 'Ah, I just love whisky . . .' he said, 'but them days is over. I'll just have a little sip to be polite.'

I lifted a mug and was about to pour a dainty snifter, but before I could do so a rough old hand grabbed the bottle and Don drank straight from it.

'Yup, it's pretty good stuff you got over there in Scotland,' he said.

Later that night it began to rain, and from a corner of the tent I heard Don mumble, 'There's your water, dummy.'

I smiled to myself, thinking how strange it was that my hopes for the future had somehow become entwined with this sixty-eight-year-old backwoodsman, who had decided against all reason to help me.

The next morning, I headed straight for my rainwater traps and found them full to the brim with clear, clean water. I poured some into a tin and drank, but instead of the invigorating taste I expected it was flat and dull.

Don strolled over with one of my large dixie tins and said, 'You gotta put some air back in it.' He took a collecting drum and held it high up above the dixie, poured some water into it from a height, then back into the drum. After he'd repeated the process several times, he said, 'Try it now.'

I poured a cupful. The water was like a sample from a highland spring.

AFTER A FEW DAYS, the weather had grown much colder, with temperatures already dropping to the minus twenties and thirties at night. I had finished clearing the campsite, and was eager to lay the foundations of the cabin before Don left. We had felled some nearby spruce trees to make three twenty-four foot logs which would be the 'sill logs', each around two feet in diameter, that would make up the foundations. We worked companionably together, rolling the heavy logs using peaveys along lengths of cottonwood that acted as tracks, allowing us to slide the great lengths into position. Once the logs were in place, Don looked over at me and smiled.

'Now you're gonna have to find a way to handle your cabin logs without help. They're gonna be heavy, but once you get the centre of balance right you'll be able to move 'em about with a little finger.'

I leaned on my peavey and looked at him. 'How will I do that?'

He looked around, then pointed to a space in the clearing. 'That's where you should stack up your cabin logs. You roll 'em over to the cabin site with your peavey. Then you gotta be able to lift 'em up onto your floor, so that you can notch 'em and pin 'em in place for each round.'

I was already panicking about felling the trees, processing the logs correctly and getting them to camp. I was also beginning to worry about working with these great trees, completely cut off from help of any kind.

'This is going to be dangerous, isn't it? I could kill myself here.'

'You know that—I don't need to say it.' Don was looking at me with complete seriousness. 'Now you just use your head and let's figure this out, 'cause you ain't got no choice but to get this house built.' He looked up at two majestic spruce trees that stood on either side of the cabin site. 'You any good at tree climbing?'

'Umm . . . yes.'

'Good, 'cause you're gonna climb these trees and string up a high line over this cabin. Then we attach a coffin hoist to the centre, and fix the come-along onto that. So when it comes to liftin' the logs, you roll the log over to the cabin, hook up the come-along onto the centre of the log, and ratchet it up. If you lift it dead in the centre it'll come up straight and safe.'

'Brilliant idea!' I said, as always dazzled by his ingenuity.

I shimmied up one of the spruce trees and looped the wire round it at about forty feet. Then I climbed the tree opposite, carrying the other end of the wire over my shoulder. When I reached the required spot I wrapped my legs round the tree and rested like a koala bear. Don worked at ratcheting the cable tight, and I then cable-clamped my end, so that after a little work we had a tight cable passing high above the cabin site. By evening the coffin hoist and the come-along, a portable, hand-winched chain lever, had been secured onto the high line, ready for use.

That night, Don told me a little bit about his life, from his boyhood in the Sierra Nevadas to the wild parts of California, where he became a member of a group of men who found their freedom on motorbikes. Don rode with them for years, while earning his living as a heavy-equipment driver. After a while, heavy drinking and fighting progressed to drugs for the group, which later became the Hells Angels, and Don lost interest and moved north, looking for wilder and freer ways of living. He fished for some time in southwestern Alaska, before moving into the Interior, where he worked in construction during the summer and as a trapper in the winter months.

In the village of Ruby, Don met and married Carol, and when they had children they moved down the Yukon to Galena. Physically powerful and clever, Don soon earned a reputation as a man who should not be crossed, and throughout his life there had been fights with everything from fists to guns. Yet I knew that he was a good man, and that when his wrath fell it normally landed on the head of a man who deserved it.

As we spoke in our little circle of tented light, we heard the lake 'sing' in a series of lilting, rolling tinkles that came from the thickening layer of ice. We sat listening to the sounds, then stepped outside. The sky was clear and studded with stars. I looked towards the lake, where I could hear the occasional splash as the beavers dragged fresh sticks to their pile through a narrowing channel of water. The busy rodents worked ceaselessly, swimming back and forth from house to shore, where they clambered up the slope to gnaw away at various deciduous trees. Once felled, the trees would be cut up and dragged into the water. When the ice sealed the beavers in, they would rely on their stick pile as a winter larder, swimming from their house and resupplying whenever they needed food.

'Seems I could learn a thing or two from beavers when it comes to timber work,' I said.

Don laughed. 'Hell, I've come across a few of them critters trapped and dead under a tree that went wrong for 'em. Nature ain't perfect.' He shrugged. 'Mistakes are a natural part of what makes the world go round. One animal makes a mistake and another finds an easy meal.'

We stood a bit longer in silence, and then I asked Don about the people who lived wild in the Interior. I'd been told that very few people chose to live alone out in the bush through the winter. Those that did so in the past were usually trappers or prospectors, but today were mostly people who were opting out of life. Don told me about a man who had been murdered.

'I found him on the floor in his shack all covered in deep cuts and stabs. He was alive but the blood was running out of him. We could do nothing.'

'Who did it?' I felt a tingle of fear as I pictured the savage scene.

'A wild man with a crazy mind. I found him and held a shotgun at him till he dropped the knife. His family took him away.'

'Have you seen many dead men?'

'Yeah. Out here when a man dies there is no ambulance or police van to go get him—his family have to do it.'

'Have you ever had to do such a thing, Don?'

'Yeah.' He drew air into his lungs and let it out again. 'Three years ago my son died.' He went on to tell me about his son's death.

'I'm sorry,' I mumbled when he had finished his sad story, feeling the weight of Don and Carol's tragedy. I also realised afresh the extent of the favour they were doing for me. What had started out as an adventure from the safety of the UK, I now saw was a very dangerous indulgence.

'Don, I hope you know how grateful I am for your help. I don't know what I'd be doing if I hadn't run into you guys.'

'Well, I kinda like a challenge, and besides, you're a family man. If you was on your own I wouldn't give a damn.'

The lonely cries of a wolf pack started up in the distance, and I looked up towards Pilot Mountain, from where the sound seemed to be coming.

'There's a big family of wolves that have their den on that mountain,' Don said. 'When you hear 'em you know they're hunting in this area and they'll be around for a few weeks more—then they'll head off to another territory and come back again, chasing moose ahead of them all the while.'

As we settled in that night, Don told me that he would have to leave the next day, as ice was beginning to form on the river. Charlie was coming back out to pick him up. Don hoped that, while he was here, Charlie, a skilled joiner, would help us get the floor down.

CHARLIE ARRIVED looking unhappy, and the atmosphere at camp plummeted with the temperature. The river level had lowered, owing to ice forming further upstream, so Charlie had left the boat at the mouth of the slough and travelled the rest of the way on foot. While Don and I collected the tools and food, Charlie sprang into action, laying the flooring for the cabin with amazing skill. By midday the job was done, and we stopped for coffee.

'We gotta go, Don,' Charlie said. 'There's ice in the main channel.'

'Shit,' Don said. Then he looked at me. 'You better get working.'

'Sure, Don, I know.' I stood up and paced around nervously. 'Trouble is, I just have very little idea about what to do next. I mean—'

He held up a finger to silence me. 'Get your logs cut and up to camp. Use the chain-saw hoist to drag 'em in, then practise your notches with some finger-sized willow and build the cabin in small scale. When you're happy with it, do the same with the house.' He pointed at a huge log at the side of the camp. 'Now we're gonna cut that big log in half, and place one half at each end of the floor platform to make the start of the cabin. Then you'll notch and fit your logs from there. D'you follow me?'

'Yes . . .' I said uncertainly, 'but—'

'Don't worry—it'll make sense once you get goin'. Tip then butt, then tip then butt, till you got seven rounds up per wall. C'mon Charlie!'

I watched as the two of them set about halving the log. Between us all we carried the heavy timbers up to the floor platform, and placed them as Don had said, one at the north-facing end of the floor and the other at the south.

By the time the job was finished, the men were in a hurry to get away. We walked down my portage till we reached the slough, which was still navigable, but had ice edging in from the sides.

'It's coming,' Don muttered, looking up at the sky. 'It sure is coming.'

We walked a few miles further along the slough until we reached the boat. Don and Charlie pulled it down the beach, clambered in and started the engine. I stood watching as they disappeared into the grey half-light.

A very cold wind had come in from the northwest, and it ripped at my clothing. Fuzzy whined and cringed against me to keep out of the wind as we walked slowly back through the woods. As I neared the grass lake I heard a familiar fluttering and a few little tweeting calls. Pheasant? I thought. Surely not. I took a step forward and a large, grouse-like bird lifted up from no more than five feet away. I stepped forward again, and this time a whole covey lifted and whirred away—seven large birds. These could only be what Don called 'chicken', which was good news for me, as it seemed that every other edible bird had long since left the woods. At least I would have a chance of some fresh meat through the winter.

By the time I reached camp it was nearly dark, and I was grateful to be back inside my tent. As always at the day's end, my thoughts turned to home. I checked my emails, and saw there were several from Juliet. She had been sending me regular messages that I would download all at once when I logged on to send my columns. These three were titled IMPORTANT!, VERY IMPORTANT! and F****** IMPORTANT!! With a prickle of worry I opened the most recent one, and read:

Are you OK, Guy? I haven't heard from you for ages and my imagination is running riot. Please phone me IMMEDIATELY!!

'Shit!' I said aloud. I had been so wrapped up in my problems here that I had forgotten what really mattered, and I felt guilty that Juliet had been so worried. I unplugged the phone from the computer and dialled.

'Hello?'

'Julsie, it's me. I just got your email—I'm so sorry, Don's been here and we've been so busy.'

'Guy!' Her voice was strong and clear. 'We've been really worried.'

'I know, I'm sorry. I'm all in one piece.'

'How's it going with the cabin?'

'Well . . .' I searched for the words—I was longing to give her good news, but I couldn't. 'It's going slowly. I've got a floor, but so far that's it. Don and Charlie were helping me, but they've had to go because ice-up is coming. So I've got to just get on with it on my own, and I don't know if I'm going to build the cabin in time. It's so much harder than I thought it would be, Jules, and dangerous too. Even cutting down the trees could be deadly.' I regretted my words immediately.

'Oh God, Guy. Why are you doing this?'

'I'm not sure, actually.'

There was silence for a moment, then Juliet spoke in the clear, practical tone I knew so well. 'Well, you're there now—there's no point in regretting it. We need a plan. What are you going to do if you can't build the cabin?'

'Don said it is possible to live through a winter in a wall tent. I'll just put a tarp over it as a second layer and pile snow up the sides.'

A note of steel entered Juliet's voice. 'Guy, just get that bloody cabin built, because being in a tent all winter . . . just doesn't sound possible.'

'I'll try, Jules, I really will.'

'Look, you've always been pretty good at doing stuff at home, as long as you had the instructions . . .'

She said it seriously, but we both found ourselves laughing as we remembered my poor efforts at DIY. The laughter ended the call on a good note, but there was a note of desperation in both our voices as we said goodbye.

I HEADED DOWN to my portage the next morning to the first stand of spruce trees, pulling my sled, which contained the two chain saws, fuel and my two-bit axe. My mission was to cut fifty-two logs and get them up to the cabin site. I approached the first suitable-looking tree and sized it up as Don had instructed. I needed to get at least one eighteen-and-a-half foot log out of the trunk. The log had to be between nine-and-a-half and ten inches in diameter at the tip, and the trunk as straight as possible. Having made sure of all these points, I had to think about how the tree stood. In which direction did it want to fall? Satisfied on all fronts, I stepped forward and cleared all the sharp, dry branches from the trunk with my axe.

When the trunk was clear I positioned myself at ninety degrees to the direction that the tree would be taking when it fell. I looked up for any large dead branches that might fall on my head, then glanced behind me, looking for fallen wood or bushes that could delay escape if the tree fell the wrong way. Once satisfied, I fired up the saw, and began cutting.

My first two cuts were on the side of the tree that faced the direction in which I wanted it to fall, about three feet from its base. I made first one, . then a second diagonal cut about six inches deep, the incisions meeting so that a woody wedge fell from the trunk. I stood back and checked all was in order, then moved to the other side of the tree. I began cutting a straight line opposite the wedge and a little above it. The idea was that the tree would lean away from the cut, and the open chink on its other side would act as a hinge over which the tree would fall. When I had cut about four inches I heard a woody creak, and the cut opened a little as the tree leaned away. I pulled out the chain-saw blade and replaced it with the wedge of my boys' axe, so that the tree could not lean back. The creaks increased until with a final woody yawn the hinge gave way. The tree plummeted to the ground.

Using the axe, I chopped the boughs off the trunk, then hooked my logging tape to its base and measured eighteen and a half feet. I marked this spot on the bark, and used the chain saw to cut through the thick trunk. At last, my log lay at my feet. I glanced at my watch: it had taken far too long.

'One down, fifty-one to go,' I muttered.

FOR THE FIRST FEW DAYS I only managed a few logs each day, but as I became more confident I worked faster, until I was cutting around ten to fourteen logs per day. The work was dangerous, and demanded full concentration, yet constantly at the back of my mind was the pressure to work as quickly as possible. I would return to my tent tired and dirty. Cuts, bruises and splinters became so numerous that I ceased to notice them, and I used Don's trick of plugging cuts up with spruce sap.

For nine days I worked ceaselessly. A warm spell came, and for this I was grateful, as the still days made the felling easier. Even the slightest breeze could have a great effect on where a tree fell. Sometimes, after I had made my last cut, the giant timber would teeter in a state of deadly limbo. When this happened I would stand back, look up at the top of the tree and mutter a silent prayer. When the gust had passed, I would rush in and hammer a wedge in the cut to make it fall in the right direction before the next treacherous zephyr. Two or three times I got my last cut wrong, and was not fast enough at getting my saw clear before the tree sat back and trapped the blade under its immense weight. My only option then was to take the engine off the blade, and start the whole process again with my second chain saw, cutting a foot or so above the trapped blade. This meant working up close to a tree that was fundamentally unstable. It felt as though I was defusing a bomb, and when the tree fell safely away the relief was profound.

I also learned to trust my instincts. Once I felled a seventy-foot tree, which would give me two logs, in such a way that it caught on another tree, where it stuck fast. I cut a wedge in the supporting tree. Nothing moved, and all seemed well, so I began on the final hinge cut. But something stopped me. Looking up, I realised that the timber leviathan was not only placing great strain on the supporting tree but teetering directly above me. Moving slowly, I pulled out the chain saw and stepped gingerly away. My gut instinct told me to leave it alone for today, and I walked wearily back to camp. I heated up a jug of water on the outside fire and had a joyful wash. As I stood by the fire, drying, I heard a series of strong gusts coming in from the northeast, and I distinctly heard the leaning tree and its support fall heavily.

By mid-September I had felled fifty-three trees—wasting only one. It felt like a minor miracle, and I called Don, trying to sound casual.

'Well, you done good,' he said. 'Now, you know that draw knife I made for you?' Don had fashioned the knife, a heavy curved blade set between two handles, from the leaf spring of an old car.

'Yup.'

'Well, you better get to peeling them logs.'

'OK . . .' Don had talked me through log peeling when he gave me the draw knife, so I knew the basics.

'Just remember, keep an eye out for bears, be careful and work slow.'

'Thanks, I will.'

I sat back, wishing I could just build with the bark on. But logs must be peeled because the bark holds many little lives, such as the bark beetle, and if it is left on the cabin will soon be crawling with insects. The peeling process has to remove the bark and the cambium layer, leaving behind clean, bare wood. The cambium is a whitish, gut-like layer that lies beneath the bark and holds snugly to the wood. It is full of sugars, and if left on the wood it will mildew and rot, making the logs turn slowly black.

I DECIDED TO TAKE a day off to work on the camp. Some essential maintenance was needed, as well as some preparations for the bad weather to come. First I began reinforcing my tent, setting up a second stout ridgepole above the roof, slinging a tarpaulin over it and pinning it down outside the canvas, leaving an insulating space in between. I then set up a smaller tent and stored in it all the remaining tools, along with rolls of insulation for the cabin roof. I also had to think about my toilet arrangements. Up till now I had been digging small latrines every few days. What I needed was a proper khazi. I scrambled down the ridge behind the cabin site and found a flat area of ground where a belt of willow grew. Clearing the leaves and fallen wood, I discovered that the ground was firm and sandy, and set about digging.

An hour later I was standing in a decent-sized hole, and this spurred me to dig even deeper, until eventually I was flinging the earth high above my head to get it over the sides. I stopped. Fuzzy had walked to the lip of the shaft and was gazing down in bewilderment. I glanced up at the dank walls that surrounded me. Had I dug the hole so deep that I could not get out?

'Oh God—please, no,' I said aloud, wondering if the sides might collapse in on me. I could not think of a more ignominious and dreadful end. A headline came to mind: ALASKAN ADVENTURER DIGS HIS OWN GRAVE. The sheer stupidity of it amazed me—how did I let myself get into this situation?

I imagined a large bear arriving at the edge of the hole, unable to believe its luck. The vision shook me into action. I pulled my thicker knife from its sheath and cut foot holes in the crumbly soil all the way up one side of the bank. Slowly I began to climb, the holes providing just enough leverage to enable me to scrabble up the sides. I pulled myself out and lay face down on the ground, savouring my freedom. Fuzzy nudged a wet nose into the palm of my hand, as if to say, Get up—don't be so overdramatic.

Back in the tent, my thoughts turned to food. I had plenty of water: I had been chipping ice from the lake and melting it on the stove, yielding about two and a half gallons a day. But my food stores were low: I only had a couple of bags of rice and flour, some potatoes and dried beans. On the positive side, I had hundreds of tea bags and plenty of coffee, as well as ample supplies of cooking oil. I also had, bizarrely, three small portions of honey in bear-shaped bottles (why did I buy them?), one tin of condensed milk and a carton containing the juice of eight Sicilian lemons, sent to me by my mother, who was worried about me contracting scurvy.

I sat looking at my pathetic pile of staples. It would be some time before I could make a provision run to Galena, as I had to wait until after ice-up. I needed to do more hunting or I would soon run into trouble.

Night was coming on when I headed off along the portage with my .22 rifle, Fuzzy by my side. I scanned the trees and undergrowth for grouse. Nothing stirred. Where were they? Suddenly a loud aggressive chattering stopped me in my tracks. A little red squirrel sat on a spruce bough above me. Quietly I loaded the rifle and waited, and when the squirrel settled I fired. A heavy thud on the soft forest floor told me he had died quickly.

'Fetch!' I said to Fuzzy, and he looked at me uncomprehendingly. I trudged into the undergrowth and picked up the tiny creature, disappointed by the size of the meal to come.

Back at camp, I gutted and skinned the squirrel, chopped the haunches away and fed the rest to Fuzzy. I then removed the meat from the bone and fried it in olive oil with some garlic. I ate it with boiled rice, and tried to convince myself that it was delicious, but had to admit that it was a drab and rather sinister repast.

THE NEXT DAY I set off early after a meal of porridge and sweet black coffee. It was time to start peeling. Arriving at the nearest logging site, I straddled a log, leaned forward with the draw knife and dug the blade through the bark until it touched the wood. I tilted the blade towards me and pulled hard, and a thin strip of bark and cambium curled up, revealing the beautiful white wood beneath. A residue of thick, glutinous sap clung to my hands and clothes, and the air filled with the intoxicating scent of spruce. I could only peel off a strip about a foot wide before I had to reposition the log, and my hands and wrists took the strain as the blade repeatedly stuck on knots.

Day after day I peeled, until my hands were raw. The work was tedious and slow. During those solitary days in the lonely woods my moods altered wildly, and although I was occasionally happy, the tension and self-inflicted pain of my situation would often overcome me.

My spirits rose as the pile of peeled logs slowly grew. But the endless work was taking its toll. I was getting thinner, and one morning I noticed that my fingers felt numb, and when I made a fist and then opened it again two fingers remained clenched. During the following days I got used to straightening the digits out with the other hand before starting work.

One morning I was sitting in my tent, sipping coffee, when I heard a thud, followed a split second later by the retort of a rifle. I leapt to my feet, startled. I strained my ears for more shots, but heard nothing. Pocketing four extra rounds for the rifle, I ambled down the portage to my second logging site, where a dense stand of spruce stood darkly over rich, mossy ground. I had named this 'the enchanted wood', because of its serene quality. All around me logs lay ready to be peeled, and I picked one and started work. After some minutes I became aware of the sound of voices. I looked up to see two Indian men approaching. I raised a hand in greeting.

'Who cut the portage?' the larger of the two men asked, his voice neutral.

'Well, um . . . I did,' I replied.

He spat contentedly, showing teeth blackened by chewing tobacco. 'Well hey, you done pretty good job there.'

'Thanks,' I said, waiting for whatever was coming next.

There was a silence, during which both men scrutinised me, then the smaller one spoke. 'Your portage sure helped us get a moose.' He raised his chin towards the river. 'We can take him down to the river better.'

'Oh that's good—I'm glad.' I remembered the shot.

The big man took out a tin. 'You chew?' he asked.

'I wish I did,' I said. 'I've got whisky if you boys would like a drop.'

They held up their hands. 'Shit, no!' the big one said. 'We Indians go crazy on that stuff!' After another pause, he asked, 'What are you doing here?'

'I'm building a cabin up at the end of this portage.'

They nodded. 'You living in the woods?'

'Yes. Don Lowe up at Galena has been helping me—you know him?'

'Oh, yeah. Now he's one real good woodsman—you're lucky. Are you staying when the cabin is done?'

'Well, for the winter—then I have to get back to my family.'

'We need more white men like you here!' the big man said.

'Why?' I asked.

''Cause you come and make portage, build house and go home!'

We all laughed, and I turned back to my work.

As they left, the bigger man called, 'Hey, you see the bear sign around?' I looked up. 'No.'

'Well, you better be real careful, 'cause we seen lots of it on the portage down towards the river. Them bears is using your portage too, so watch out. We've cached a moose in a tree up there by the grass lake—tomorrow we'll come back with a four wheeler to collect it.'

They walked off, talking quietly. When it grew too dark to work I hung up my drawknife. I reckoned I had just a few more days of peeling to go.

The Indians' warning weighed on my mind as I walked back to camp, and I scanned the undergrowth warily. Suddenly Fuzzy stopped and stood dead still, a bloodcurdling growl playing out from behind bared teeth. My blood froze, and I stealthily unshouldered my rifle and chambered a heavy round. Fuzzy sneaked slowly forwards, sniffing the path as he went until he stopped at a great black mound of bear droppings, steaming in the chill air. Alarmed, I carried on slowly up the trail, shouting and clapping my hands to ensure that the bear heard me, and would perhaps move away.

I arrived at camp exhausted and deeply relieved to be home. Black clouds rolled overhead, bringing heavy drops of rain. I set up the tarpaulin for collecting water, and loaded BB shot and lead slug into the pump shotgun before settling into my night-time routine. Before going to bed I called Don to ask his advice about a technical point, and he passed me a message from his daughter, Jenny. She had been flying over the area, surveying for moose, and seen a big brown bear mooching about not far from my camp.

I found it hard to sleep that night.

I STILL FELT NERVOUS the next morning, and I returned to the purgatory of log peeling with the heavy 45/70 strapped across my back. Like all the animals around me, I was getting panicky about the coming cold, and I knew that the bears would be unhappy and tense, trying to cram in as much food as possible before the snow gave them the signal to hibernate.

Around midmorning the two Indian hunters passed by again, this time riding an ancient Honda FourTrax quad bike. I took a break and we sat chewing dried fish and talking about moose and bears before they headed off to the grass lake, where they had cached their moose kill.

Half an hour after they had gone, I heard a volley of shots echo through the woods. I sat still, listening. Another series of shots rang out. Assuming that the hunters were being attacked by a bear, I ran fast along the portage, and down onto the grass lake. I set out along the parted grass where the Honda had passed, and spotted a large pair of black shoulders in the bushes.

I stopped, and called out, 'Hey! Are you OK?'

In response, a large black bear turned round and fixed me with her small eyes. To my further horror, two large cubs trundled up. I had committed the cardinal offence: I had surprised a bear. Worse still, it was a mother and cubs.

I chambered a round into the rifle and rested my finger on the trigger just as the bear dropped and pushed through the bushes towards me. She stood up on her back legs and sniffed loudly, staring at me myopically. For a few seconds she stayed still, and I readied myself for the worst. Then she suddenly dropped again and charged away through the bushes, followed by the two cubs. I remained frozen where I stood, feeling weak with relief. With trembling hands I levered the round out of my breach to clear the chamber, but failed to catch the shiny brass cartridge. I stood staring in vain down at the ground, astonished that such a shiny piece of brass could disappear.

I was still moving the grass about with my boot when the two hunters appeared, with the moose meat tied to the front and back of the bike. They switched off the engine and sat looking at me respectfully. I realised they thought I was analysing the tracks of the troublesome bear. I raised a hand, deciding not to disillusion them by telling them I had simply lost a bullet. They stepped off the bike and walked slowly towards me.

'You seen anything?' the smaller of the two men asked.

I kept looking down. 'Well . . . one female over there.' I nodded sagely towards the bushes. 'Got two cubs.'

'Yeah, you right,' the bigger one said, clearly impressed. 'That big black bear was after the moose kill—they got a good bit of our meat.'

'Did you shoot at them?' I asked.

'Nah—we don't need no bear meat. Too much to carry.' As they turned to go, his gaze fixed on something on the ground. 'This yours?' he asked.

'Oh yeah—actually it is,' I mumbled. 'Thanks.'

A knowing smile spread across his face. He'd rumbled me, but thankfully he was merciful. 'Hey—thanks for coming to see if you could help.'

I smiled sheepishly. 'Don't quite know what I could have done, but I thought you might be in trouble.'

'So how you gonna get them logs up the trail?' he asked.

'Planning to use the chain-saw winch.'

'Shit, that's pretty slow.' He thought for a moment. 'You got rope?'

'Yes.'

'You got fuel?'

'Well, I've got a bit . . .'

'You can use this bike then. We don't need it till summer, 'cause soon it will snow and then we'll be using snow machines.'

'Are you sure?' I asked. I could hardly believe my luck.

'Hell yeah—we don't need it. You take it.'

They puttered down the portage with their load of moose meat. I walked behind them to the slough's edge and helped them load their boat. It was very cold, and Fuzzy leaned against my leg as though pushed there by the wind. We must have looked a sorry sight. I noticed the two men rummaging about in the boat, then the big one emerged with a box.

'Candy, beer, .22 ammo, fish sticks,' he said, passing it over the bow.

'Hey, thanks—that's great.' I accepted the box without protest. Any boost to my provisions was welcome.

He stood back and looked at me. 'You want a wife?'

I widened my eyes in amused surprise. 'Um . . . no thanks. I've got one.'

He tilted his head, raising an eyebrow. 'So?'

'So . . . Ah . . . Well thanks, but I'll be OK.'

He smiled, then disappeared into the wheelhouse before re-emerging with a copy of *Playboy* magazine. 'Here—you might run out of toilet paper . . .' He gave me a knowing look, then he pushed the boat off into the frigid brown stream before jumping back in.

'Thanks!' I shouted, and waved the lurid magazine above my head. 'Especially for this—it'll make perfect fire starter!'

They laughed and clapped before aiming the boat downstream and opening the engines out to power away.

I ambled slowly along my portage, reflecting on the fact that instead of the white man handing out his charity, here was I, gratefully accepting a box of goodies from two native Alaskans. Their offer of a wife came back to me, and I smiled, wondering what he would have come up with had I accepted. I looked at my gold wedding ring, which seemed especially bright against my cold, battered hand, a spiritual beacon—a reminder of what I had waiting for me at home, in case I ever got lonely enough to forget.

THE HUNTERS HAD LEFT me an extra twenty gallons of fuel, which I cached thirty feet up a slim tree. By early October, after five days of dangerous improvising, I had managed to drag all the heavy green logs up to camp. The logs weighed much more than the Honda, yet somehow the battered old quad bike did it for me time after time.

Each log had first to be dragged laboriously out of the thick undergrowth and onto the portage, using a rope. Once the log was on the portage I would charge up to camp at full speed, somehow gathering sufficient momentum to heave it over obstructions. Sometimes I would make it up to the brow of a hill, then the bike would lose power as the great log joined forces with gravity to pull me back down again. Just before I felt the backward slide begin, I would grab a wooden wedge and shove it under one of the front wheels. Then I would ease myself off the bike and attach the hook from my come-along to the bumper. I would then harness the winch to a tree, so that I could hand-winch the bike over the brow of the hill. Once in camp, I would lever the log up onto cottonwood rollers using a peavey.

On the night following my last log run, I sat on my bedroll, trying to read a collection of poetry. After a short while I threw it aside, too preoccupied to concentrate on anything that didn't relate to building my cabin. Tomorrow would be my first day of building.

The world outside my tent seemed quieter than normal, and I noticed that when the wood in my stove cracked I couldn't hear the usual corresponding echo in the woods. I parted the tent flaps. It was snowing. Great fat flakes were falling, and had already covered my camp in a thick white carpet.

I saw Fuzzy approaching. He had a thick layer of snow on his back, and as I looked at him he made a friendly growling sound.

'What's up, fruitcake?' I asked. He pawed at the tent, and I saw his meaning. I pointed to a spot by the stove: 'There.'

With a great show of respect he picked his way over to the stove and settled down. I wrote in my diary: *Must build house for dog . . . Maybe I can live in it too.* Fuzzy was making a soft growling sound, and I looked up to see two great loving brown eyes fixed on me.

'Good lad, Fuzz,' I said, and carried on writing.

A few minutes later the friendly growling returned, and I leaned over to give him a pat. This was a mistake, as he began to make a thumping noise with his tail. I tried to carry on writing, but the distracting noise continued. Finally I couldn't stand it any more, and said, 'Fuzzy! Shut up!'

Clearly embarrassed, he rolled up demurely. I turned back to my diary to continue my account, and then, just as I found my rhythm again, out of the corner of my eye I saw that Fuzzy was creeping slowly towards me. He froze like a prisoner caught by a searchlight.

'There!' I said firmly, pointing back to the warm spot by the stove.

He slunk back and lay down again, only to renew covert operations the moment I attempted to get back to work. The charade continued, until at last I gave up. I couldn't help admiring his determination. Don was right: having a dog around—however annoying—was good for morale. There is something so irrepressibly positive about a dog's spirit. I closed my diary and sat staring into the fire with my hands sunk deep in Fuzzy's rich fur.

The snow fell heavily all night, and the next morning I woke up with a deep sense of foreboding, half wondering if I should just call it quits. In fact, I knew full well that getting anywhere would be impossible until after ice-up, so there was nothing for it but to get on with it. I made a pot of porridge, which I ate as if it was a last meal. I looked down at Fuzzy, who gave my hand a firm nudge with his nose as if to say, C'mon! Get on with it!

'OK, boy,' I sighed. 'I'm coming.'

I opened the tent flaps and stepped out into a changed world. Everything had turned white, my camp rendered picturesque by its soft covering of snow. I stopped to look at my thermometer, which read −20°F, then ducked back into the tent to pull on my rabbit-fur hat and thick jacket. I wandered across to the cabin site, stopping to stare at the exposed cabin floor, covered in about four inches of snow. How am I going to do this? I thought.

I swept the layer of snow off the pile of peeled logs with a spare bough, then moved over to clear the floor platform. Next I began to peavey the first log along the cottonwood rollers towards the floor platform so that it came to rest alongside the ends of the sill logs. Round logs are difficult to work with. Each one has to be notched at either end in order to fit over the log beneath. I would have to use a log scribe to trace the contour of the bottom log onto the uncut log above, then, using chain saw and axe, I would cut out the round or 'saddle' notch. The theory was that you would flip the notched log over so that it fitted snugly over the bottom log.

Before I could even begin to cut notches, I had to raise the logs into position. First I had to get the log as near to the cabin as possible, hook the come-along chain round the centre of the log, then crank it up above the level of the floor platform. I would then push it gently along until it was above a round of logs, and when happy with its position gradually let out the come-along chain until the log came to rest. Then I would peavey and manhandle the timber into position over the supporting logs below, where it would rest precariously while I jumped down to stare along its length. This 'sighting' of the log allowed me to make minor adjustments to the log's position and ensure that its natural bow faced out before starting to cut a notch. Once I had one end where I wanted it, I would hammer in gadgets called 'log dogs', to keep it there while I wrestled with the other end.

Magically, if I could get the chain precisely at the log's centre of balance, I found I could indeed move it with one finger, as Don had said. But once the log was down, with its full weight resting on the timber below, I had to be very careful that it didn't roll off the cabin and onto the ground, or me.

Once the log was in place over its supporting round, with its tip resting on a butt—or thick end—and vice versa, it was time to cut the two saddle notches. Cutting a good notch was not easy, and my first mistake led to the total waste of a log. This was a disaster, as it meant going back into the woods to fell a new tree. As more snow fell, this would become increasingly difficult, and pretty soon impossible. As I stared down at the wasted tree, I wished fervently that I had more practical skills. Bleak thought added to bleak thought, until I could stand it no longer and walked over to the tent to brew some coffee.

It was midday and getting dark already. Inside the tent, I looked at my clothing and kit piled chaotically in one corner. Everything looked grey in the weak light. To make matters worse, a large shrew ran across my shoe in the direction of my meagre food stores. This wasn't the first time I'd noticed one of these invaders. It was time to improve my living conditions. I decided that I would make myself a bed, and a chair with a backrest so that I would no longer have to spend all my time perching on a log.

I set out to find suitable wood. The snow had stopped, and as I walked towards the frozen lake, Fuzzy following loyally behind me, it felt quite warm. I walked out gingerly across the ice, using my axe to test the strength of the surface before each new step. Using young birch and alder trees I was able to pull myself up the far bank and up onto the spruce-topped ridge. I found a game trail and followed it down across a little grass lake and up onto another ridge, where I found myself surrounded by paper birch and white birch trees. Their delicate white trunks, straight as flagpoles, were perfect for my furniture. I felled them and carried them home.

Back at camp, I made a simple bed and armchair, as well as a long shelf to keep my clothes and food off the floor. When the chair was finished I sat down warily to try it out. It gave a long creak and then held, putting an end to my days of perching like a parrot.

That night I slept in comfort, away from the freezing floor and the sooty-coloured shrews, who were prone to late-night arguments, and had even on occasion run rudely across my face. As I gently stretched myself out on the stout birch bed, I banished all tension relating to failed cabin projects. I closed my eyes and imagined my two little boys, their blond heads and small, capable hands, and thought of Juliet alone in her bed, reading as she always did before turning out the light. I thought of her laugh and her green eyes, her serenity and intelligence, and the long, lonely journey that she too was undertaking. As I fell asleep, the thoughts turned to dreams, and I was transported 8,000 miles back home.

The weather stayed warm over the next few days and the snow began to melt, turning my camp to a quagmire of slush. Freezing rain began to fall, covering the logs in ice and making them even more treacherous to work with. Despite this, the weather was giving me precious extra building time, and I was grateful. In the back of my mind was a faint hope that Don might make it out to check on my progress, and I called him.

'Yeah, we been thinking of you out there,' he said. 'You winning?'

'No, I'm losing.'

'You got them logs in camp?'

'Yes.'

'And you're making them notches?'

'Yeah. But badly—in fact, I'm worried I might waste every log here.'

A silence, then, 'I'm gonna talk to Charlie. You call tomorrow.'

I replaced the handset and prayed for the warmth to hold.

I WAS BUSY HAULING LOGS the next day when I heard a rifle shot from the direction of the river. My heart leapt, and I called Fuzzy, who had been chasing shrews. Together we charged down the portage to the slough. I sat on the black beach, straining my eyes downstream until I saw two men walking slowly towards me. I lifted my 45/70 and shot into the air, and the men waved. It was Don and Charlie, my guardian angels. As we greeted each other I had to restrain myself from hugging them.

'Well, you've lost some weight,' Don observed dryly, his eyes glittering.

Charlie stood behind him, his dark eyes framed by a hat made of marten fur. He followed my eyes. 'So what fur is your hat?'

'Well, um . . .' I took it off and looked at it. 'It's rabbit, actually.'

They laughed. Don shook his head. 'Comes to the Interior with rabbit fur on his head.'

'Well, what do you suggest?' I asked.

'Oh, you gotta get a beaver hat or marten. You need fur with guard hairs.'

We walked up the portage together, the men gently teasing me. When we reached camp Don inspected my work with a critical eye.

'Yup, you was heading in the right direction,' he said, 'but piss-poor slow.' He looked at Charlie. 'You gonna be able to stay long?'

Charlie shook his head. 'Nah, that river's running bad with ice, you know—it's no time for travelling.'

Don inspected my notches. 'Not too bad, but you been fucking up 'cause you haven't used a plumb line.'

Within minutes he had us organised and working efficiently as a team, achieving in a few hours what would have taken me the best part of a week.

That night Charlie headed back to the boat to sleep, and Don cooked up a great meal of eggs, bacon, beans and bread. I accepted my plate gratefully, but when he offered me the bottle of Insanity Sauce I firmly declined.

Afterwards he lay back on my birch bed. 'Yup, you're trying. Bed is badly made, but it works.' He leapt up and flew out of the tent, returning with a hammer and nails to 'make it better'.

I watched him, stunned by the man's energy. After he'd finished, he glanced around my tent, looking for something else to criticise. His eyes lit upon some clothes I had washed and was attempting to dry by the stove.

'Don't hang them clothes over the goddamn stove,' he said. 'One day a sock is gonna fall and you'll burn the place down.'

I went to move the clothes, and heard the bed creak as Don lay back.

'Now this bed'll do me,' he said. 'Where are you gonna sleep?'

'Oh, don't worry about me,' I said with just a touch of sarcasm. 'I'll sleep on the floor with the shrews.'

He sat bolt upright. 'Shrews! Did you say shrews?' He cast about wildly. 'Gimme that bowl and peanut butter—there's some in my bag over there!'

I watched as he put some peanut butter in the bowl, then placed it carefully in a corner of the tent with a little wood ramp leading up to its rim.

That night, when Don was finally satisfied with my living conditions and the lamp was off, we talked further, and I felt more relaxed than I had since coming out into the bush. I felt that at last I had a chance of completing the cabin. I was also keenly aware that these men, between them responsible for two households, had made a dangerous journey down the river to help me. I knew I could never even come close to repaying the growing debt.

THE NEXT MORNING we woke up to a bowl full of shrews, which I took off into the woods. The day was clear and sunny, but Don looked unhappy. He stood by the thermometer, casting worried glances up at the sky.

'Yeah, this is not the weather we need,' he said. 'We need snow, 'cause then it'll stay warm. This weather'll be making a lot of ice.'

We heard a shot echo in the woods.

'That'll be Charlie,' Don said. 'Let's get to work.'

I set about moving logs and notching, and Don bustled about, stopping from time to time to inspect my work or answer my inane questions. We worked well together, and with Charlie on site were making good progress.

However, I could feel a tension emanating from Charlie, and I became aware that it was aimed at me. As the day wore on, the atmosphere between us grew worse, and every remark seemed to be barbed.

At one point, I stepped forward to say something, only to be cut off by Charlie, who said, 'Shut up, or I'll kick you in the balls!'

I was momentarily stunned, but managed to laugh it off.

Later, we were cutting out a notch when Charlie dropped his chisel. Without looking at me he said, 'Get that now.'

I hesitated, then dropped to the floor platform and picked up the chisel, which he took without comment.

After a while he said, 'You go get me a pin from the tree.'

This was too much, I decided. I might be in his debt, but I wasn't going to be so rudely ordered around. 'No—you get it,' I said.

He stopped working. I watched as his jaw muscles moved beneath his dark skin, one hand clenching and unclenching while the other, holding a mash hammer, began to shiver. He slowly raised his head, and as I met his eyes I saw a different man staring at me, his entire body quivering with an uncontrollable fury. At last he exploded. 'Get off this fucking log!'

'What?' I said.

'You get away from me! Get off this fucking log!'

Out of the corner of my eye I saw Don looking up from his work.

'Charlie, what is wrong with you?' I said, my voice purposely quiet and calm. 'Don't order me around like your dog.'

I watched his clenched hand raise the mash hammer slightly, and saw his mouth opening and shutting as a torrent of abuse was unleashed.

Suddenly Don appeared between us. 'Hey, Charlie, calm down, goddamn it!' He glanced at me coolly. 'Guy, you come on and help me pull them logs over. You stay here, Charlie.'

'Just leave me alone,' Charlie said coldly. 'I don't want to work with him.'

I climbed down the ladder feeling shocked. Without Don's intervention we would have come to blows. I brooded over this as I worked on. In this wild part of the world there were guns everywhere, and fights could easily escalate until one or both protagonists was fatally injured.

A few hours passed, during which my anger ebbed away. I could understand Charlie's point of view: here he was, spending time away from his family helping some stranger who, as far as he was concerned, was wasting his time. And yet I hoped the cabin was going to be for their use after I left, so his work wasn't all for nothing, and he had been aggressive. I rehearsed both sides of the argument for a while, then decided it was time to try and build bridges. I walked over to where he was working.

'Charlie, whatever happened between us there . . . I'm sorry. Maybe we were both to blame,' I said. 'Perhaps I should not—'

He cut me off. '*Both* to blame?!'

'Yeah, well . . .' I paused. 'I'll happily get stuff for you, but I just won't be treated like a dog with it.'

He stared at me, his expression a mixture of rage and disbelief. 'Who do you think gave you all these fucking tools to use?' He gestured around at the camp. 'I gave you everything you need to build this cabin, so don't say I've been treating you badly.'

I swallowed hard, feeling miserable and ashamed. Again it came home to me what a massive favour he was doing. 'Charlie, I am sorry,' I said. 'I owe you an apology.'

'Oh, fuck that,' he said and climbed down from the log. 'Let's leave him,' he said to Don. 'I've had enough of this—I'm going.'

As I heard those dreaded words I looked up towards the two towering spruce trees and then out across the white lake. I felt surprisingly calm, like a man in the dock receiving his life sentence, happy that at least now the months of tension and uncertainty were over.

'C'mon, Charlie,' Don was saying. 'No one in this family lets a man down once we say we're gonna help.'

I felt for Charlie then, and clearly saw his predicament for the first time. The fact was that he did not like me, and now he was caught between his desire to see me fall flat on my face, and his duty to help and obey Don, his wife's father and a man he greatly respected. He reluctantly agreed to stay on, but after a short time he left, saying he was going back to the boat.

That night I kept going over the day's events. I then thought about the fact that in the beginning he had agreed to help me willingly. I knew that at heart he was a decent and generous man, but also—like many people out here—someone who was quite primal in his reactions. I called Juliet and wished with all my heart that I could be home. I felt isolated and vulnerable. Don said nothing, and I knew that he was purposely keeping out of it. I didn't blame him—I felt he was probably sympathetic to both parties, but his loyalty had to lie with Charlie, his daughter's husband.

After we had eaten, we sat by the stove. 'Guy, we're gonna have to ship out tomorrow, you know that?' Don said.

'Yes, I do.' I nodded, staring into the fire. 'Thanks so much for all of this.' I looked at the ground. 'I hope I haven't caused a lot of trouble . . .'

'Nah—it'll be fine.' His tone let me know that he didn't want to discuss it. 'Now, you should think about killing a beaver and getting him hung up for meat. Also, them grouse'll be easier to spot now the leaves are gone. Shoot them at night, and if you come across a lot get as many as you can, then hang 'em on your game pole. Soon you're gonna have a freezer that never breaks down.' He stood up. 'You got any chocolate?'

'No,' I said gloomily. 'All gone, I'm afraid.'

'Ha!' he said with satisfaction. He stood up. 'Well, here's one man who knows how to hold on to his treats.'

'Hang on . . .' I said. 'Have you been saving up your chocolate bars?'

'Yup,' he said triumphantly. 'And now I'm gonna eat 'em up real slow, right here in front of you.'

I shook my head ruefully. 'Don, you're bad. So where did you stash them?'

'Oh, in a little corner of that equipment tent of yours.'

He opened the canvas and stepped outside. A few minutes later I heard him swearing loudly. He came back into the tent bristling with rage. He threw me an empty Snickers wrapper, gnawed and slippery with frozen rodent spittle.

'SHREWS!' we both shouted at once, and I laughed and laughed.

THE NEXT DAY I walked down the portage to meet Charlie, and found him walking up through the poplars.

He gave me a curt nod. 'Hey, we gotta go today—that river is full of ice floes and if we don't go we'll be stuck.'

'I know,' I said. 'And thanks so much for coming out here. I know you took a risk.' I fell into step beside him. 'Listen, Charlie, I don't expect you to say anything, but I'm really sorry about yesterday.'

'Me too,' he said, glancing quickly at me.

'I want you to know that I've got a huge amount of respect for you, and without your help I would have been totally fucked out here—I know that.'

He nodded silently, still walking.

'I've been feeling under a lot of pressure out here on my own,' I said, 'and maybe I forgot my manners. So can we be friends?'

I stopped and held my hand out, and he took it immediately, a great wide smile passing across his face.

'You know, I think you're the Athabascan equivalent of Charles Bronson,' I said.

'Athabascan Charles Bronson . . .' He laughed. 'I like that!'

We walked on in companionable silence for a while, and I felt deeply relieved that we had made peace.

At camp, I stared at the two massive twenty-four foot purlins and ridge-pole. 'Now just remind me: how am I going to get those into place?'

Don stared at me in mock surprise. 'Just hoist 'em up like the cabin logs.'

'But won't they smash into the cabin and knock it to pieces?'

'Yeah, they will. So tie 'em off against one of the spruce trees, and just belay 'em out as you go up real slow. Once they're up you can put the roof on—you've got some tin cached down at the river, haven't you?'

'Yes, I do.'

Then Don shook my hand. 'You'll be OK. Just work slow, and be real careful, 'cause it's gonna be a while before anyone can get to you now.'

We walked together down the portage, across the snow-bound slough towards a narrow stream of open water that had remained unfrozen. As the men pulled on their waders, Charlie gave me a parcel and some letters.

'Good luck and be careful,' he said gruffly, stuffing a bar of chocolate into my pocket.

I watched as they moved off towards the main river where the boat waited. Soon they were gone, and the familiar silence descended upon me, accompanied by the equally familiar loneliness and anxiety. I looked at the parcels and letters with their British stamps, and the sight of Juliet's clear writing brought on a wave of homesickness. Fuzzy looked up at me and barked, wagging his tail. I took my glove off and stroked his deep fur.

'Well, Fuzzy,' I murmured. 'Now we really are up the creek.'

THE WEATHER was closing in, and I knew that I had just a matter of days to finish off the cabin. The conditions were horrendous, with freezing rain one moment, thick snow the next. My tent billowed in the cold, mean wind, making any idea of living in it through the winter seem ludicrous.

My first task was to complete the gable ends, which involved hoisting six logs on top of the walls, decreasing in length as they went up to form a triangle shape that would support the roof. Then it was time to begin the roof. Twenty sixteen-foot lengths of galvanised tin, weighing fifty pounds apiece, were buried deep in the snow beside the slough. It took a day to dig them out and stack them, then a further day to heave the wet, icy tin up to camp.

The next job was to raise the purlins and ridgepole, which would support the roof. This would be the most challenging job yet, and frightening, as the logs were so heavy. Before lifting each purlin, I timber-hitched a ship's warp round its centre and tied it securely to a spruce tree. I then stood on the log, using one hand to ratchet it slowly into the air, and the other to feed the rope out gradually from the tree that was anchoring the whole operation. Once each purlin was in place on the gables, I cut two notches into the log below. When I had finished, the purlins sat snug in the top of the gables, and the whole structure looked distinctly more solid.

To raise the ridgepole I repeated the whole process, holding the log carefully away from the cabin until it dangled exactly above the highest point on the gables. I slowly lowered it into place. To my relief, it held. I jammed a chock of wood on either side of it, then hammered a pin through each to keep them, and their captive, in place. I climbed down and took a good look—not perfect, but it would hold.

Now all that remained was to trim off the uneven ends of the gable logs, making a nice neat triangle shape for the roof. To do this I used a monstrous chain saw with a thirty-three inch long bar. The great saw had runners that allowed me to slot it onto a length of plank that I had tacked onto the gables as a cutting guide. It ripped through the logs as if they were marzipan, and I tried not to imagine what it would do to my head if it kicked back.

When it grew too dark to work I retreated to the tent, now sagging under a thick covering of snow. My body ached, and I climbed straight into bed, too tired to make a cup of tea. I reached for my grandfather's copy of *Henry V*, which I had brought for moments when I needed courage. A line leapt from the page: 'Hold hard the breath, and bend up every spirit to his full height!'

THE NEXT DAY I put the tin roof up, hammering it roughly straight onto the purlins and ridgepole, then slinging the tarpaulin from my tent over the top for extra protection. I had planned to build the roof properly, putting up a plywood ceiling first, then a layer of insulation between this and the tin, but time was running out. I tacked up some planks for a doorframe, and then made a crude door from a length of plywood, with a rope handle. I began shovelling the snow, which lay about three feet deep, out of the cabin, but the wood was covered in a thick layer of ice that was impossible to get rid of. I looked around the cabin, now as ready as it would ever be. The prospect of moving into that dark, frozen space was not inviting, yet as I returned for my last night in the tent, I knew it was a lot better than the alternative.

Diary, October 27th

A triumphant day! After three long months, I am finally in my cabin. Got up at 5 a.m. to let the stove go out so that I could move it across to the cabin. Threw the charcoals onto the snow and then with gloves lifted the stove outside. Watched as its hot sides melted the snow. When it was cool enough to touch, I moved the stove into the cabin, but panicked as I'd forgotten to make a hole in the roof for the stovepipe. Had a bright idea to use shotgun, so loaded it and shot at the ceiling. Bit brutal, but it worked—after eight rounds I had a perfect six-inch diameter hole! Fed the stove pipe sections through, then got the stove going to start warming things. Spent ages moving all my stuff across, until finally all my worldly goods are in my new home. Cooked my first meal in the cabin, and am now tucked up in bed with the stove burning red hot. Dripping wet as the ice melts, but I don't care. After all these months of worry and hard work, at last I feel safe.

A word formed in my head—one that sounded out of place in this empty wilderness. 'Home,' I said aloud as I sat in the cabin that first night.

The stove was burning like a jet engine, and the firelight flickered across the woody walls. Beside it there stood a tidy pile of logs, ready for burning, and in the corner a lamp hissed on a tree stump beside my new bed, made from a sheet of plywood standing on four slender birch logs. I had put up some rough shelves to hold my food and other essentials, and fashioned a crude loft space from some straight lengths of birch, where I slung up my extra gear. At last I would have good space for hanging up washed clothes.

It felt luxurious to move around the new home, which had miraculously come out at exactly sixteen feet square as I had intended, and to have a proper floor, albeit still covered in a dirty layer of ice. A deep scent of pine emanated from the drying logs. The only thing that diminished my joy was the lack of a companion with whom to share it. I wanted to celebrate: to shout and laugh, but there was no one to do it with.

I opened the door and called to Fuzzy, who padded quickly across the snow towards me. He looked up at me questioningly, and I gestured for him to come in. He glanced back towards the little log kennel I had made for him, and then, less than enthusiastically, stepped daintily inside and settled beside the stove. I emptied the dregs of my last bottle of whisky into a tin cup and sat down beside the furnace, savouring each sip. After a while, Fuzzy got up and sat by the door, clearly feeling overheated, so I let him out. I watched him scurry into the snow-filled darkness, then pulled the door tight shut and climbed into bed. Outside the wind howled above several feet of freshly fallen snow, and I shuddered to imagine what might have happened if I'd tried to live out the winter in that tent.

5

After a week of burning the stove at full blast, the cabin at last dried out. Until then, everything was wet. The walls ran with water as the ice thawed, and all my clothes were damp, though thankfully my bedroll was inside a canvas outer bag so it had remained dry. My rushed job on the roof meant that I had to work doubly hard to keep the cabin warm. If the roof had been insulated, the snow falling on it would have warmed the cabin further. Instead, the warmth of the cabin melted the snow on the roof.

I had imagined long, dark hours in my cabin, reading books or writing in my diary, but little did I know how hard I would have to work. With the short daylight and atrocious weather conditions, it took all my time just to survive. The stove had to be kept burning constantly, and gathering wood was an ongoing chore. Standing dead spruce were perfect for starting fires, and would help to light my green wood, such as birch, which would burn for longer. The frozen green wood was not difficult to work with; in many ways it was easier, as the ice in it created less resistance than water, and the brittle logs split effortlessly.

Another daily chore was collecting water for drinking. Each morning I would trek out along the lake searching for a berm of compacted, wind-blown snow. This firm, clean snow would be pummelled into my biggest pot and left on the stove, which I had banked up to burn slowly during the day. Once it had melted, I would use Don's trick of pouring it into a jug and out again several times, to aerate it and make it tastier to drink.

One morning, a week or so after I moved into my cabin, I pulled the blanket away from the door, and was concerned to see that the plywood was white with ice. I scraped it away and pushed the door out just enough for me to take a peek. It was snowing again, and where there had been bushes there were now just comical white mounds. I stepped gingerly out of the cabin and closed the door behind me.

Outside, the world was so quiet and still that I could hear nothing except my own breathing. I turned to pick up my rifle, taking off my glove to lever open the breach. The lever didn't budge; it was frozen shut and, worse still, my hand had stuck to the frigid steel. It was a schoolboy error, immediately followed by another one: I pulled my hand away and ripped the skin from my fingers. I pulled my glove back on, watching as the blood seeped through the light-coloured wool and then froze. Don's advice came to mind. I walked over to the fuel tree and washed the gun through with petrol, pouring the precious fuel into the working parts and down the barrel, before drying it with a cloth. I called for Fuzzy, who appeared at the end of a tunnel of snow that he had dug into the mound that now covered his rustic hovel. His home was lined with thick, dry grass and probably better insulated than mine.

We left the camp and walked along the portage. My boots sank into the snow with a satisfying sound, while behind me Fuzzy's little paws marked out their own arctic tattoo. The portage appeared as a pure, unbroken line of white meandering ahead through the black and white of the snowy woods.

We walked down to the slough and peered down at it, as it was now sunk about thirty feet below the bank. It had stopped snowing, but a strong wind was blowing fallen snow along the slough, whipping it up into a cruel, swirling ground blizzard. I felt as if Fuzzy and I were being given a rare glimpse of an impossible world where nothing could live.

As I walked slowly back to the cabin, I felt my feet getting cold: my boots were too tight for these conditions, and gave no space for movement. I felt a twinge of anxiety, until I remembered my mukluks, given to me by the women of Don's family. They were made out of canvas with moose-hide soles, stuffed with felt and tied with lengths of moose hide. I was greatly moved by the gift, but as I looked at the beautiful blue canvas with its bright gold stitching along the top, I had secretly wondered if they would ever be of any practical use. But they were to prove their worth.

By the time I got back to the cabin it was almost dark, even though it was only midday. I fed Fuzzy from a dwindling bag of dog feed, then watched him scurry into his cosy lair. Inside the cabin, the air temperature was warm, but the floor was so cold that I couldn't stand on it my socks. When I closed the door I could see nothing, as the cabin had no window. I fumbled about for matches, then lit a candle that gave me enough light to find the pressure lamp, which I pumped and lit. I took off my socks and rubbed the toes of one foot, which had taken on a sinister, white, waxy look that I knew was the beginning of frostnip. Frostnip can quickly develop into frostbite, and I cursed myself as my toes burned with pain. In the Interior it is seen as shaming to suffer from frostnip or frostbite, completely avoidable complaints.

Today had been my first proper encounter with winter, and I had been shocked by the severity of the conditions, which I knew would get much worse. All my worries about bears now seemed trivial in comparison to the much more sinister, powerful threat of the cold. If I fell, got hurt or made a mistake I would very quickly die.

IT WAS EARLY NOVEMBER, the days were dark and my food supply was getting leaner. The snow was four feet deep and still falling, and it was now impossible to walk without snowshoes, so I set out one morning to try them out. I strapped them on over my mukluks, and strode out with big, comical steps down towards the lake. I enjoyed walking easily on the surface of the fresh snow. The snowshoes felt like a magic carpet, taking me anywhere across frozen white clouds. I stared down at them, lost in the sight of the bright blue mukluks inside the creaking birch snowshoes. It reminded me of when we bought Oscar some new shoes with lights that flashed each time he put his foot down—he was so entranced that we had to remind him to look ahead while he ran. Tears welled up in my eyes. I was missing my family more than ever, but couldn't afford to give full vent to my emotions, which given the chance would overwhelm me.

I reached the steep, snow-covered bank on the other side of the lake, where I experienced the unique sensation of falling uphill. I placed one snowshoe on the incline ahead, and then, as I lifted the other leg, it slid back down the hill, creating a small avalanche, which resulted in me falling flat on my face in the snowy bank. I pushed my hands into the snow to lift myself up, only to find my arms sunk up to the armpits. Finally I rolled onto my back and used gravity to get myself upright. Clearly in this new world everything had to be relearned, including walking.

I walked up the bank at an angle, using the tops of small trees for leverage. Fuzzy walked behind me, using the compressed footprints of my snowshoes like steppingstones. I came across a few standing dead spruce, perfect for burning, then passed into a glowing stand of paper and white birch that stretched as far as the eye could see. I looked around in satisfaction: here I would find enough good-sized green logs to keep me going for a long time to come. I looked down at the ground and saw the marks of a small animal in the snow. Then I realised something exciting: all around my camp, I would be able to follow animal tracks in the snow. No man or animal would be able to enter my snowy domain without my knowledge.

Later on, Fuzzy and I walked along the portage and came across a set of large wolf prints. The prints followed the clumsy trail I had left on my first trip down to the slough, and led me through the grass lake. Then the tracks veered away from the portage, through some willow and alder and a stand of birch and poplar. The going was harder now, and I was snowshoeing through thick, snow-covered bush and fallen trees. Remembering Don's advice about not allowing myself to sweat, I stopped just before a stand of spruce and cut some branches to sit on. I reached into my outside pocket for my water bottle, and found it was frozen solid.

'Idiot!' I said aloud, resolving to carry the bottle under a few layers of clothing next time. But as I sat chewing on a fish stick, I felt relaxed, as I knew that the trail had taken me round in a rough circle, and I wasn't far from camp. For the first time in months I realised I felt happy. I thought back to my life in the office, and felt enormously privileged to have escaped to such a magical, unspoiled world.

I was shaken from my reverie by a great crashing and crunching noise. I stood up quickly and whipped the 45/70 into my hands, then leaned against a tree and stared into the woods. Fuzzy was growling, his lips curling. I peered into the murky light beneath the trees and strained my ears, but there was silence. Then the sounds came again: *CRASH! RRRIP! THWAAACK!* It was clearly a very big animal. I kept staring into the spruce forest, growing more frightened as the sound grew louder. Then I became aware that the animal was coming from the opposite direction, from the birch, willow and cottonwood belt I had just passed through. I whipped round.

'Be calm,' I muttered, as I levered a 500 grain round into the breach.

Suddenly, an immense, dark brown, shaggy bull moose broke through the screen of trees thirty yards away. It was a stirring sight. A brown eye rolled in a pool of vivid white as the bull raised its huge head, topped by immense antlers, to sniff the air. I remembered Don telling me that if ever I found myself being chased by a moose I should run round a tree until it got tired, bored and disorientated. At least I was near a tree. I looked closely at the animal's huge flank, judging that he must have weighed well over a thousand pounds, and his rack of horns looked at least four feet wide. Dog, man and moose all stood very still, until finally the leviathan engaged his reverse gear, and crashed back into the woods.

I stood in the same spot for a few minutes, feeling drained but incredibly excited at having met a member of the world's largest species of deer. It was dark, but the snow gave off some light, and I called Fuzzy, who trotted ahead, showing me the way home.

Visitors to Alaska are not permitted to shoot moose unless they shell out thousands of dollars for a guide, but in the past I could have shot that huge bull, and his meat would have guaranteed me sustenance through the winter.

When I got back to my cabin the stove had burnt low, and it was cold inside. I split some birch logs, and placed light lengths of spruce on the fire to get the blaze going. The thermometer read –40°F, my coldest night yet. The cabin gradually began to tick with warmth, and even the floor had lost its icy chill. Earlier that day I had piled up snow to a depth of four feet all round the cabin, and this had stopped the cold air getting in at the bottom.

I lay back on my bed. My body ached, and I knew that I was thinner than I had ever been. Although I enjoyed wearing my snowshoes, carrying out any task with the equivalent of a pair of tennis rackets stuck on one's feet was not easy. Yet I was warm and safe, and I reflected on how strange it was to be lying in comfort while a subarctic cold was sinking across the land. Outside it was utterly still, and I could hear nothing. My eyes gently closed.

Through my slumber I heard a loud noise, and jerked awake. What was it? I sat very still, listening. There it was again—a loud cracking sound—and it seemed to come from the cabin walls. I leapt up. Seeing nothing in the pitch darkness, I stood still, uncertain what to do. Another crack resounded from a corner of the cabin, followed by a high-pitched creak. It seemed as if an entire log had shifted, and I imagined the massive ridgepole coming loose, or one of the purlins rolling off while sheets of frigid tin sliced down on top of me. I fumbled about for a match and lit my candle. Then I realised what was happening: the intense cold was freezing the logs, and the cabin walls were contracting. After a while it stopped, but I could see my breath in front of me, and knew that the fire needed to burn hotter. I needed more wood, so I pulled on my mukluks and popped on my hat, feeling grateful that I had a good stack of logs beside the door.

Outside, the snow glowed blue-white under a full moon. The sky was studded with stars, and I saw my white breath fall away, ice instantly forming on my eyelashes. I was very, very cold but I had to stay for a moment to look around me. It was a wonderland: a place of exquisite cruelty, yet beautiful, like the honed blade of a sharp sword. I grabbed my heavy jacket, then walked down to the white lake, which glittered and glinted in the moonlight. I looked up, and saw to my amazement a ghostly curtain of brilliant, lime-coloured light shimmering in the eastern sky.

'The northern lights,' I whispered, watching entranced.

My head hung back until my neck ached, and I stood, enraptured by this awesome spectacle, until across the lake, out of the silence, a shot rang out. I jumped, and stood staring at the dark, spruce-clad bank. Another shot resounded, and I saw snow falling from a tree as if it had been shaken. The trees were contracting in the cold just as my cabin logs had done, and as the cold deepened I heard the woody cracks ringing out all over the forest.

As THE LIGHT FADED and the cold increased, I settled into a simple rhythm of existence. Each day I worked hard cutting wood and melting snow, gradually learning tricks to make my work more efficient. Before felling a tree, I cut the tops of little saplings and bushes, then laid them in a line where the tree would fall. The brush prevented it from falling too deep into the snow, making it easier to work with. As the days passed I grew more confident, and began to feel that I was learning the ways of the wild white land of the Interior. My life had been pared down to its barest essentials—the cold had long since stopped my watch, and I was keeping time by daylight and the slow, clockwise movement of the Plough round the Pole Star. The days passed slowly, mostly without event, and I savoured their simplicity.

To maintain my trails as more snow fell, each day I walked down the portage to the slough, my snowshoes packing the newly fallen snow onto the hard, previously compressed snow. Overnight the trail would freeze, and become harder as the depth of compacted snow increased. My wood-gathering and hunting trails across deep, powdery snow had also begun to harden down, and thus became increasingly useful. As the snow continued to fall it rose up on either side of my trails like English hedgerows, and increasingly the animals used my trails to get around.

The trees resounded with the shrill call of red squirrels, and their scampering footprints crisscrossed my trail. I followed the progress of the odd lone wolf or fox that used my trail as a short cut to the grass lake. The willow grouse left beautiful patterns, their wings slashing delicate lines into the snow as they whirred into the air. Whenever I saw these marks, Fuzzy and I would hungrily search the nearby trees in the hope of catching the birds unawares. In forested parts I often came across the neat prints of a marten. This voracious weasel feeds mainly on shrews, making it an ally of mine. Occasionally I would come across a moose track, and the great weight of the animal would leave irritating potholes in my trails. Like a grumpy local government roads contractor I would fill them in, wishing I had a means of imposing a weight restriction.

Sometimes I made one-off trails to scout for wood in new places, or hunt for grouse. Over a number of days I realised that some sort of animal was tracking me, not only along my established trails but also on my forays. The creature left a deep, regular print, kicked up at the front, as if the animal were flicking the snow as it moved. I called Don to ask him about it.

'He's been following all your trails? Long way from camp too?'

I thought about it. 'Yes. On the ridges away to the south.'

I heard him draw his breath in. 'That's doyon!' he said excitedly.

'Doyon?'

'It's another name for a wolverine. He's the biggest weasel in the world—real tough sonofabitch.'

'Amazing,' I said. 'Do you think I'll get a look at him?'

'Nah, he's very secretive. Have you seen his tracks near the beaver house?'

'Yes,' I replied, remembering.

'All the animals are hoping to catch a beaver. Them critters are full of fat and good meat.'

'I suppose I should think about trying to catch one.'

'Yeah, you'll need to.' There was a pause. 'You eating good?'

'Well . . .' I hesitated slightly: 'Beans, beans and more beans, with fried bread and grouse when I've got it.'

'You getting plenty of grouse?'

'Yeah, I am now. I'm also trying to snare some hare.'

'They make fine eating, but still not enough fat in them. What does their sign look like?'

I described it in great detail.

He said something to Carol that I didn't hear, then said, 'You finding any bits of spruce cone along those hare trails?'

'Yes actually, quite a lot. I didn't know that hare eat cones. Do they dig them up? They can't climb, surely?'

There was a silence, then laughter erupted on the other end of the phone. 'It's a squirrel, dummy—you've been trying to snare squirrel!'

I was smiling as I packed the phone away, knowing that I had supplied the man with another titbit that would amuse him for days. I had long since given up hope of maintaining any kind of pride where Don was concerned—the bargain between us meant giving him full access to my mistakes in return for his sage advice. But I never again confused a hare with a squirrel.

I WAS LOSING six minutes of light each day, and now had just one hour of daylight before the sun slipped out of sight far to the south. To make matters worse, I had run out of fuel for my pressure lamp, and was having to rely on the feeble, acrid kerosene lamp and candles, because all my battery-operated gadgets had run down in the cold. I tried to make the most of the short period of strange, lemony sunlight, but often found myself working in the feeble light provided by the moon and the stars.

I had been giving some thought to improving my toilet arrangements, and had decided to build myself an 'ig-loo'. Igloos are not normally built in this part of Alaska, as the snow is too dry and powdery, but I got round this by spending a few days mounding up snow with my shovel, so that the snow would lose some of its air content and become firmer. One morning I set about cutting igloo blocks from the mound, giving them a slightly bevelled shape so that they would lean inwards. I placed them in my hand sled and pulled it over to the latrine hole.

Using the principles of igloo-building, I laid the blocks so that they tapered up in a spiral. After several hours of labour my igloo had reached a height of about six feet, and I placed a 'king' block on the top. I cut two holes on either side, through which I slid two wood slats on either side of the latrine hole. Onto these poles I placed a portable loo seat, which I had been hoarding for just this opportunity. I also cut a cubby for a candle, and stuck a stick into the snow to form a kind of improvised toilet roll holder. The structure held perfectly. It protected me from the wind, and gave me an absurd sense of privacy. The whole thing seemed ludicrously civilised, and I laughed every time I sat within its hygienic walls.

The success of the 'ig-loo' lifted my spirits, but the next day things took a turn for the worse. I dropped my kerosene lamp and broke the glass, which meant that I had even less light, and was unable to read—a terrible blow as, along with my multivitamins, books had become essential to my world.

I was spending a lot of time hunting grouse to supplement my dwindling food stocks. To my joy, with just the minimum of training, Fuzzy had become a wonderful hunting dog and our partnership strengthened in our shared mission to find food. We would set out each day just after sundown, when there was still a little light, going off the trail and into the woods. Once I had spotted a bird, I would keep my eye fixed on it while stalking up to a suitable tree and steadying myself for the shot. I used a battered old .22 rifle called a Nylon 66, which was very accurate, and aimed for the bird's head. Fuzzy would be sitting tensely until the command 'Fetch!' set him loose, and he would bound, crawl, sink and then swim across the deep snow towards the hole left by the bird. Like a diver, he would launch himself head-first into the hole, retrieving the bird and then scrambling back out. Then he would power back towards me and place the bird into my hand.

Despite the grouse, the benefits of my hunting forays were dubious, as I had to snowshoe for miles to find a quarry, and this effort, combined with the cold, meant that I was using more calories than I gained. People living in these extremely cold conditions need forty per cent more body fat to keep warm, and I had used up all my fat reserves long ago. Gradually I was beginning to starve. I was feeling lethargic, and my brain was working slowly; each day it was harder to force myself to get up.

I had to get up every four hours through the night to feed the stove, and it was agony to have to pull myself out of my warm bag to creep across the icy floor. One night, I failed to wake up to bank the stove. Cold seeped rapidly through the log house, and at some point I must have sniffed in my sleep because my nostrils clung together, as though two icy fingers had closed a grip over my nose. I spluttered awake, and found that I could barely see the stove through a heavy cloud of cold air. As I walked to the stove, the white cloud swirled ominously around my legs, making me feel as if I was in an old horror movie. I knelt shivering by the stove, desperately blowing the feeble coals until at last the spruce caught light and I was able to shove some good-sized logs into the firebox. I clambered back into my bag, and lay trembling with cold until the cabin warmed up.

ONE MORNING after breakfast I checked my store of potatoes. My heart sank as I saw that I had just three. I placed them in a pot containing a whole grouse, which thankfully had a little layer of yellow fat. I added some beans and covered the whole thing with grouse stock that I had saved from my last meal. It looked delicious to my starved eyes.

Outside it was a whiteout, with snow thick in the air. At least it would be warmer, I thought. I decided to have a wash, for morale's sake. I warmed about two gallons of water, poured it into my wide tin washing bowl, then undressed and stepped in. After I had soaped and rinsed my body, I knelt beside the bowl and washed my hair, before towelling off and standing up to warm beside the fire. It felt wonderful to be clean and naked, after months of being enclosed in the same sour clothes. I hung the heliograph (a device for signalling by means of a movable mirror that reflects sunlight) from a nail and shaved, and for the first time in many months caught sight of my body in the mirror. The sight scared me.

I had arrived in the bush weighing sixteen stone, and I could see that I was nowhere near that now. I was pale, and the bones were showing through my skin. For the first time, I truly took on board the severity of my situation. What would I do once my provisions had run out? I lay back on my bed. To my surprise I didn't feel particularly panicky; rather I felt resigned, and had almost a sick curiosity as to how things would progress from here.

After a while I forced myself to get up, knowing that my passive state of mind could spell the beginning of disaster. I knew that my diminished phys-ical state had begun to weaken my judgment, and would seriously affect my ability to keep safe. I decided to stay in my cabin for the next few days. Fortunately I had stockpiled a week's worth of wood for an emergency, and I had a couple of grouse hanging outside which would keep me going.

That evening I tried to focus my mind on writing a column for the newspaper. I set the satellite phone up to send the article, knowing that I could only keep it on for a few minutes as I was low on fuel for my generator. After I had sent it I wrote an email to Juliet:

> I can't wait to be with you again and our little boys who are so precious to me. I am missing being a father badly. I keep telling myself that this whole thing will be good for us, and that we'll find a way ahead. I just hope I can make it.

'GUY! ARE YOU OK? I hear you've finished your cabin. That's great news!'

The urbane voice of Tom Roberts was winging its way across the world from the comfortable offices of his film-production company in London. He had sent two film-makers out to visit me back in the summer, and they'd taken some footage with a view to perhaps making a documentary. As we spoke, I wondered what he'd be having for lunch. I had begun to fantasise about food now. As Tom talked, my mind ranged over pies, chips, beer and pub lunches.

'Hello? Can you hear me?'

'Yes. Sorry, Tom.' I cleared my throat. 'What were you saying?'

'Just saying that we're hoping to do some more filming. Matt and Ashley are planning to come out next week—is that OK?'

'I suppose so, but warn them it's pretty grim out here, and very cold.'

'Sure, they know that,' he said. 'That's why they want to come now—to catch some of the winter. Now, they can get as far as Galena, but what I want to know is how will they get out to you?'

'Well . . .' I thought hard, as it had suddenly occurred to me that if Matt and Ashley were coming out they could bring food. 'They might be able to fly in and land on the lake,' I said, sounding much more enthusiastic.

'Is the ice solid enough?'

'I'm not sure, but I can check it out.'

'OK. Call me back tomorrow and let me know.'

I replaced the handset with mixed feelings. Half of me relished the thought of spending some time with people from home. Yet mingled with my anticipation was a reluctance to give up my solitary existence, and my routine. I pondered this for a while until my social side, and more importantly the lure of food, won out. I called Don to ask whether he thought a bush pilot might be able to land on the lake.

'Yeah, maybe. I'll get Brownie to take a look. You could hitch a ride back when they go, 'cause the ice is still not good on the river.'

It seemed that all my problems might have been solved at once, but still I felt a strange reluctance to give up my solitude.

OVER THE NEXT few days I was unable to feed Fuzzy more than just a handful of dog feed and the odd scrap of grouse, and one night when I called him he didn't come. Where was he? My mind raced, then settled morbidly on the wolf pack. That was it, I thought: he probably went further than he should have in search of food, and was ambushed by wolves. Guilt descended: I should have packed more dog food. I spent the rest of the night miserably wondering if I would ever see him again.

When I woke the next morning, I heard the unmistakable sound of Fuzzy's steps in the snow outside. My heart leapt with joy. He was back! I pulled on my clothes and stepped outside. It was very cold, and the thick, white, heavy air hung like fog about a foot above the ground. Fuzzy barked, and I looked around for him, peering in the murky half-light. When I saw him, I knew immediately that something special had happened, because his whole body radiated pride. One friendly, almond-coloured eye was fixed upon me, and as I watched him he glanced down at something lying in the snow before him, then back at me. Clearly he was waiting for my reaction. I walked closer and bent down to see the object of his pride. It was an entire moose leg. It was three feet long, the biggest dog bone I had ever seen. He sat with one paw resting proprietarily on the bone, looking up at me.

I stood back, laughing in admiration at the little dog's bravery and ingenuity. Then I examined the bone more closely and my admiration increased. It was truly enormous, with a good amount of fresh meat and skin still attached. By this time, Fuzzy had clearly decided that the viewing was over, and I followed him round the cabin to watch as he tried to get the bone into his snug. It took a few attempts, but finally he managed it, leaving just the end poking out of the door. I walked back to the cabin, shaking my head in disbelief. The moose leg must have been the remnants of a kill by our local pack of timberwolves, and Fuzzy would have known that he was risking his life as he sneaked up to the site and dug up that leg. He then had to negotiate the long, hard journey back to camp, dragging the heavy load.

I WAS ON THE RIDGE, loading birch logs into my sled, when I heard the distant sound of a small plane.

'This must be him, Fuzz!' I shouted, and he let out an excited yelp.

Brownie, a local bush pilot, had come out to check whether my lake was safe for landing. He buzzed the cabin before banking to the north, beginning a wide arc that would bring him in to land at the western end of the lake. I snowshoed fast to the edge of the lake. Then I saw him coming in over the tree tops, lining up over the middle of the lake and descending rapidly. His skis touched the surface, then he lifted back up again, made another arching turn, and flew back along the lake. I could see him tilting over and peering down at the lines of his skis.

I waved as the plane banked round for a third time, then watched as it skied along the surface, banging alarmingly on the ice. It hit a large lump of snow and catapulted into the air, before coming down thirty feet later and finally skidding to a halt. The pilot gunned the engine and the prop whirred as he taxied towards me. Fuzzy was jumping up and down with excitement.

At last the engine stopped, and there was silence. I stepped forward in anticipation. The door opened to reveal a middle-aged, bespectacled man who looked more like a family GP than an intrepid pilot.

'Hi, I'm Brownie,' he said. 'Is your trail good, or do I need snowshoes?'

'No, the trail's fine,' I replied. 'That was quite a landing!'

He grinned. 'Yeah, snowy landings in a new place are hard, 'cause there's no contrast from the air. All looks flat from up there 'till you come in to land, and then it's kinda late.' He leaned down and patted Fuzzy.

'Well, can I offer you some coffee?'

'Sure thing.'

We walked to the cabin and he bent his head to duck through the door. I rolled over a stump for him to sit on, and we sat by the stove with our coffee. Brownie listened as I talked, nodding patiently every so often.

'How long since you seen anyone?' he asked in a soft voice, when I finally stopped to draw breath.

'Oh, maybe six weeks or so—I've lost track.'

'See, I do a lot for folks in the woods.' He smiled. 'Now first off, like you, they get real chatty. It all kinda comes out at once.'

I blushed as I realised I'd been talking nonstop since his arrival.

He saw my embarrassment and raised a hand. 'Hey, I don't mind one bit—the chatty ones are fine.'

'What do you mean?' I asked.

'Well, after too long they stop talking.'

'Completely?'

'No—but they only talk when they need to. They get like animals: more inclined to listen and watch than to speak. You have to coax it out of them until they get into the way of being with people again. Out here we say they've gone "bushy".'

He put down his tin mug and looked at his watch, then said he would have to go. We walked back to the plane.

'I remember once picking up a couple to bring 'em back in midwinter,' he said. 'She started crying when we got into the plane—said nothing all the way, just kept on crying until we landed. She kinda seemed to have lost her mind.' He smiled and patted my shoulder. 'But you look OK to me!'

'Well, just get me out of here if you think I'm going bushy too, will you?'

We laughed, but I knew I had already skated close to the edge of insanity.

As Brownie climbed into the plane, he seemed to remember the point of coming out here. 'Oh yeah, two guys in Galena want me to bring them out tomorrow. That OK?' It was part of the etiquette here in the bush that you never broke in on a person's solitude unless asked.

'Sure,' I replied. 'It'll be good to see them. Have they got much stuff?'

'Yeah. Boxes of food, and I believe a case of whisky.'

'They've got whisky!' I had long since run out.

He looked at me quizzically. 'I think the food'll do you more good . . .'

I nodded sheepishly, remembering that he didn't know me, and might think I was an alcoholic. 'Yes, some grub would certainly be welcome.'

'You been living on beans and flour?'

I smiled weakly. 'How did you guess?'

He laughed. ''Cause that's what every cheechako lives on when he starts out in the bush.'

'Cheechako? Is that the same as tenderfoot?

'Yup. Now, after I've gone you flatten down that windblown snow and cut some spruce to mark out the runway. See you tomorrow.' With that he shut the door, then turned the plane and took off in the direction of Galena.

I walked back to the cabin feeling happy. The prospect of seeing people was growing on me. As Don had suggested, when the film-makers left I planned to hitch a lift back to Galena to resupply. I also wanted to see Glenn Stout, who had a dog yard and had offered back in the summer to help me get a dog team together. I wanted to be able to travel through the winter, and other than a snow machine, this was the only way to do it.

That night I put on my snowshoes and in the light of the full moon flattened the hummocks on the lake and marked out Brownie's runway with Christmas trees. This seemed appropriate, because I was looking forward to Matt and Ashley's arrival as eagerly as a child waiting for Christmas.

BROWNIE BUZZED THE CABIN the next morning at ten o'clock, the bush equivalent of ringing the doorbell. I stoked up the fire, then snowshoed out to the lake. He circled round in the grey sky, and landed neatly between my Christmas trees. Two smiling faces peered out at me, and I saw Ashley digging for his camera, ready from the first moment to start filming. I stepped forward to shake hands but was treated to a series of North London-style hugs before they stood back and scrutinised me.

'Shit! You've lost some weight!' Ashley said, looking suddenly serious. Behind us Brownie was beginning his take-off.

'Yeah, I know.' I felt rather vulnerable, remembering my image in the mirror. 'I haven't been able to make it back to the village to resupply, because the ice on the river is still bad.'

Matt looked at me closely. 'How's the mental state?'

'Oh, it's fine,' I said casually, loading their bags into my sled.

When Matt and Ashley last visited I hadn't even begun work on the cabin, and now as we approached the little building they stared in disbelief.

'We never thought you'd do it,' Matt said, touching a log.

'Well, it was a nightmare,' I replied. 'Without Don's help I wouldn't have pulled it off.' I couldn't help a smile. 'Sorry—I know it would make a much better film for you if everything went wrong.'

They had the good grace to smile back, and as we packed their gear into the cabin I thought of the months of darkness and hardship they had missed. I poured them some coffee, and Ashley produced a box.

'Hey, we brought you some stuff from home.'

I took the box eagerly, seeing Juliet's handwriting across the top. Inside I found chocolate, biscuits, honey and coffee, and from my mother there were some beautiful Southern Italian staples, including olive oil, sugared almonds and pine nuts. I was overwhelmed by the gifts and had to resist ripping them open immediately. I must have looked like a wild man on a desert island, having my first contact for years with civilisation.

Ashley pulled a little parcel from his bag. 'Here,' he said, passing it to me.

It was another packet from Juliet, with postcards showing the Isle of Mull. The pictures were incomprehensibly green and gentle, and brought back treasured memories of times we had spent there together when we first met. There was a drawing by Oscar. At the top he had written his name in big, wobbly letters with a felt pen. My eyes filled with tears, and for several minutes I couldn't speak. I bowed my head, and we sat in silence, two men from North London, sensitive and kind, and one undernourished mongrel.

After a few minutes Ashley slipped a bottle of Highland Park whisky into my hands. 'I think we could all do with some of this,' he said, 'especially Matt, who hates flying.'

Matt leaned forward in mock anger. 'No I don't!'

We all laughed, and I was relieved to move away from the painful subject of my family, whom I was missing deeply. I poured a healthy measure of whisky into a tin mug for each of us, then added a drop of water to each.

Matt raised his tin mug. 'Well, here's to Yukon snowmelt!'

Later that night they told me they'd brought a film that Juliet had been making for me. I watched it on one of their cameras, seeing the boys playing on the beach, with Juliet's voice occasionally calling out to one of the little scamps. Images that would have filled a parent with joy under normal circumstances now filled me with almost unbearable pain. At the end of the film I couldn't speak. I was in turmoil. The arrival of these two men had been wonderful, but had also brought forth a great mix of emotions, from reassurance at still being missed and loved to heartache at missing out on my children's lives. I felt as though they had opened the floodgates of my guilty heart, which I had worked so hard to keep under control.

FOR THE NEXT FEW DAYS they filmed on determinedly, dogging my every move as I cut firewood and melted snow round the clock to keep up with their fanatical washing and consumption. The arrival of new food stocks transformed my quality of life. Ashley was a fine cook, and seduced me with stacks of delicious pancakes drizzled in maple syrup. I returned the compliment, cooking up seared grouse breast on noodles flavoured with oregano and lemon juice. Matt's attempts at cooking, however, threw me into fits of unreasonable rage, because I had become fanatical about not wasting a morsel. Whenever he bravely offered to cook, I would subject him to close and often aggressive scrutiny, poring over his shoulder and muttering darkly. He soldiered on, and I grew to respect his endurance.

Soon it was time for them to go, and we all prepared for our trip back to the village. It was snowing heavily on the day of departure, and there was a strong, blustery wind. Brownie set off with Matt and the film equipment on the first trip, and I watched the little plane as it took off shakily and disappeared into the snowy sky.

I turned to Ashley. 'You know, I don't like the look of this weather.'

He stared at me, perplexed. 'Well, I'm going, whatever the weather,' he said. I could hear in his tone that he'd had more than enough rough living.

We sat in silence for a few minutes watching the snow falling.

'Well, I'll help you load up, at least,' I said.

An hour later, Brownie returned. 'OK guys, let's move it along here,' he said, when we'd finished loading the plane. 'This snow storm's getting worse.'

'Well, travel carefully,' I said.

Brownie stopped and looked at me. 'You not coming?'

'Sorry, Brownie, but no. Don't like the weather. Things are risky enough for me without adding to the list.'

He looked at me with an expression of wonder mixed with irritation. 'Do you think I would risk anything to come and get you all?'

'Ah . . . No.'

'Just get in, then, 'cause let me tell you—Brownie does not take risks.'

I stared at the tiny plane for a moment, then swallowed and got in. Fuzzy was stuffed into a locker in the tail compartment, where he packed himself into a tight, worried-looking fur ball.

Brownie ran through his checks, then said, 'OK, Guy, put your arm round my shoulders.'

I raised my hand. 'Thanks, Brownie, but I'm fine, really.'

He looked at me wryly. 'No, you need to do that during takeoff to keep the plane balanced.'

'Oh, right—OK.' I obligingly put my arm round him.

'Now brace yourself by holding on to that handle as we go, and don't touch that stick between your legs.'

With that we charged off at full tilt into the snow. After a series of bone-shaking jumps off the icy ridges, the skis were in the air. The plane shuddered as the wind hit it, and as we passed Pilot Mountain we bucked violently. I looked down, and saw nothing beneath us but mile upon mile of bleak, black and white land.

Half an hour after takeoff, the lights of the little village came into view, and we landed on the grass lake beside Brownie's house.

Brownie pulled the earphones from his head and looked at me with a smile. 'Well, you look like you're alive, and this'—he indicated the village— 'this sure don't look like heaven to me!'

6

Later that evening I walked through the snow-covered village to Chris and Jenny's house, where I was invited to a meal with the whole family. It felt wonderful to be surrounded by people, and in a warm, well-lit house. I particularly enjoyed the electric lights, and resolved never to run out of lamp oil again, as the past couple of weeks had been grim.

Chris and Jenny's four-year-old daughter, Tirzah, met me at the top of the stairs. 'Hey—what you doing back here?' She stared at me in mock seriousness with her clever dark eyes.

'Well, I couldn't miss out on the cooking,' I replied with a smile.

Her little brother Asa appeared. 'Guy! Guy!' he shouted, giving me a big hug, and then Tirzah ran to hug me as well.

Tears welled up in my eyes, and for a moment I felt unable to go through with this gathering of children and their loving parents.

Chris greeted me with a warm smile, and shoved a bottle of beer into my hand. I demolished it in a split second, and was given another. Soon Claudette and Charlie arrived with their family, and the noise of happy children filled the room. I sat quietly watching, not enjoying the experience of being a lone man in a family setting. Yet I was also happy to be there, comfortable and warm and surrounded by a family that I loved. The table sagged with the best cooking I had seen in a long time: moose ribs, pumpkin pie, salads, potatoes, grouse and corn bread. I stared at it, my mouth literally watering. The two sisters stood back and looked at me critically.

'Hey—you're looking thin,' Jenny said.

Charlie cut in. 'Yeah, and you smell of camp, that's for sure!'

The room filled with laughter, and it felt good to fall back into my familiar role. We had just sat down to eat when Don and Carol arrived.

'Well, look what the cat brought in,' Don said, looking at me with his familiar expression of wry amusement.

I smiled. 'It's really good to be back.'

'So what are you up to?'

'Well, I'm here to get some supplies, and I'm planning to learn to mush, so that I can get together a dog team.'

There was a sudden silence. I looked around, wondering what I had said.

Don shook his head. 'Kid gets the cabin built, and now he wants to get going with a team of pant-sniffers!' He raised his hands. 'Now, don't you come asking me to help. No way! I ran my trapline with a team of dogs, and was pretty happy when them snow-machines came along, I can tell you.'

Everyone laughed. Clearly this would be another source of amusement.

Before he headed home, Don said, 'I got an old snow machine that might come in handy when you get sick of dogs. It's called a Tundra II—real light and easy to move when you get stuck. You any good on a snow machine?'

I shrugged. 'Never been on one.'

He smiled. 'Well, there's a surprise.'

That night I settled back into the warm little cabin in Don's yard, and sank into the homemade bed and fell into a very deep sleep. After months of solitude I was exhausted by the effort of talking. I was also missing my family more than ever, and I was learning that in many ways being apart from them was even harder when I was with other people.

THE NEXT MORNING, when I walked into Glenn Stout's office, a broad smile crossed his long, morose face. 'Well, you're still alive, hey?'

'Just about.'

He looked me up and down. 'So, you ready to learn to mush?'

'Yes!' Clearly Glenn's promise to teach me held good.

'Come to my dog yard at midday and we'll get started.'

Later on, I walked over to where Glenn's house stood. He fired up his snow machine, and we drove together over to his dog yard.

'I got twenty-one huskies here,' he announced when we arrived, 'and I can give you six for your team.'

The dogs were running incessantly around the pegs to which they were tethered. Their eyes flashed white and blue, and the noise of barking and howling was alarming. I wondered why I had ever thought this was going to be easy. The dogs looked half wild, and their energy and power was intimidating. I remembered the reaction of the family last night, and wondered whether what I was doing was wise.

'Now, I've got your dogs from a whole bunch of mushers,' Glenn said, 'so we don't know much yet about their characters. Let's go ahead and hook up your six, just for the practice.'

He brought out a small birch sled, and unravelled the gang line ahead of it.

'First dog on is the lead dog,' he told me. 'He keeps the gang line straight, and if he turns you make sure he straightens out.'

'How do I do that?'

'Better to watch and learn—you'll see.'

We walked into the midst of the dog yard.

'These dogs are Alaskan huskies,' Glenn shouted over the canine cacophony. 'They can pull about two hundred pounds per dog when good and fit.'

He grabbed a wiry, dark-haired dog, which immediately jumped onto its hind legs. Its eyes were filled with fanatical zeal as it led Glenn to the sled.

'This is Bubbles—she's a good lead dog,' Glenn yelled.

He held the dog between his knees while he slipped the harness over her head, then pulled her legs through and let her go. She kept straining forwards, and everything in her body said, Let me run! The sled was held fast by a clawlike steel anchor that had been stamped deep into the snow. We walked back to get more dogs.

Glenn pointed to a small black and white bitch. 'You get that one there.'

I steeled myself and walked over. She ran shyly into her kennel, then re-emerged, jumping up and down with excitement. I unclipped her from the tether, and was taken aback by her strength as she pulled towards the sled, wheezing against her collar. I asked Glenn where he wanted her.

'Just put her anywhere for now,' he said. 'We'll be moving them around until we find the place that best suits each dog.'

I walked over to a harness and tried to hold her still while I yoked her up, but she was so excited that I couldn't get the confusing thing on.

'Hold her between your knees,' Glenn called.

In the end I got the dog yoked up. It didn't help that my fingers were freezing. I couldn't use big gloves, but working with bare hands at −35°F is no joke. I noticed that Glenn used woollen gloves for detailed work, then in between times sunk his hands into big beaver mitts that he wore strung round his back. Four dogs were now attached to the line and Bubbles held it tight.

Next Glenn brought me two big dogs, saying, 'Hold them for a moment.'

I took a firm hold of the dogs' collars. My right hand was attached to a thin, mean-looking red dog with a scarred face. He looked more like a dingo than anything else. He bucked violently in all directions, straining against my grip. My left hand held a very big brown dog, which also jumped up and down, yowling and barking. I held on to the dogs for dear life, watching Glenn, who was examining the feet of one of the dogs. Out of the corner of my eye I could see Matt and Ashley, who had appeared from nowhere to do some last-minute filming. Just then I heard a sinister growling, and realised it was coming from the dingo, who was staring fixedly at the dog on my left. His lips were wrinkled back over a jagged line of teeth, and he was drooling saliva. The brown dog tried to pull away but I held on to him, knowing that if I let him go even worse chaos would ensue.

'Glenn,' I called softly, trying to keep my voice low. He didn't hear me, and the dingo launched himself at the brown dog and tore into its shoulder. 'Glenn!' I yelled, but he couldn't hear me above the din of the dog team.

I tried to pull the dogs apart, but they were like two bits of steel colliding, and sparks of frozen blood were hitting the snow. I kicked the red dog, and my foot bounced off his rock hard flanks. In desperation I committed a musher's schoolboy error. I put my hand between the two dogs, and in an instant the red dog had sunk his teeth straight through my thick glove and deep into my left wrist. I looked on in a distracted way as my own blood joined that of the dogs' in the snow.

To my relief, Glenn appeared. He sprang into action and, holding the other dog by its collar, launched his whole body on top of the dingo, pushing it down hard into the snow. It let go of the brown dog, which stood shaking by my side, still bleeding copiously. Glenn dragged first the dingo and then the brown dog back to their tethers, before returning to examine my hand.

'You better go and get that dealt with at the clinic,' he said, concern showing in his eyes. 'I'll sort things out here.'

As I walked away from the crime scene, Ashley and Matt ran over to ask if they could help. I could see from their expressions that they had been treated to a filmic bonanza.

A FEW DAYS LATER I went back to see Glenn. He looked at me over his cowboy's moustache, his eyes passing from my face to my bandaged hand.

'How's that hand of yours?' he asked, and I smiled sheepishly.

'Oh, it's OK, thanks,' I said. 'Looks far worse than it is.'

'I sure am sorry, Guy. Kinda feel that red dog was not right.'

'Well, it wasn't your fault,' I said. 'I think I'll be OK for more training if you can bear it.'

'Sure I can,' he smiled. 'I'm real happy to see you ain't giving up. Come back here around five and we'll get going.'

IT WAS DARK when I returned, and very cold. We walked over to a fifty-five gallon drum that had been converted into a makeshift stove. Glenn lit a fire underneath it, and then lifted a tarpaulin from a massive pile of fish.

'Caught about twelve hundred green fish in the summer,' he said. 'Now I cook 'em in the dog pot every night. I chop in about half a fish per dog, then mix in some dog feed, rice and snow for water.'

We scooped in snow, and chopped the mix of pike, grayling and perch with an axe before adding the fishy bits to the steaming cauldron.

Glenn stirred the pot with a long stick. 'We leave this to cook up while we're out,' he said. 'That way, by the time we get back it'll be ready. Great grub for warming a dog. Now we give 'em some fishy water.'

He ladled some of the odious brew into a bucket, and carried it into the howling yard to scoop into each animal's dish. I stood watching the dogs leap and bark, their eyes glinting in the light from my head torch.

Glenn walked over to his snow machine, gesturing for me to sit behind him. 'Gonna show you the route that you'll learn on.'

The wind chill had picked up and the temperature must have been around −50°F, but I was well wrapped up. We passed out of his yard and along an icy gravel road, then over a high dyke that had been built to safeguard the village against flooding. Then we followed a snowy portage through willow and alder woods before crossing an open, hummocky area that led on towards the great frozen Yukon. When we reached the steep river embankment, we passed over it and down before turning sharp right. The narrow sled trail ran along the river for a mile or so before bending to the right, back up the bank and into the woods. There it snaked along, into hollows and up over wooded ridges, before finally returning to the dyke in a loop.

Back in the yard we readied the team, which I managed more easily, despite the difficulty of working with a bandaged hand. The dogs barked and yowled as we hitched them up, their breath forming a white cloud that rose above them, then froze and fell on their backs as frost.

'OK, Guy,' Glenn said when we were ready, 'I'm gonna be tied on behind you on the snow machine to slow 'em down as you go out. Put these on Bubbles's feet. She needs the protection.' He handed me four cloth 'booties'.

As I pulled them on the lead dog's feet, she licked my cheek. I gave her a pat and she looked at me briefly with intelligent and determined eyes, silent while behind her the whole team was at a fever pitch of barking excitement.

I walked back to the sled and stood in position on the runners. 'How do I stop this thing, Glenn?' I asked.

'That metal pedal there is the snow brake,' he replied.

I saw a piece of metal held between the runners by a thick piece of black rubber. On the underside there were three stout steel studs.

'You shout "Whoa", and push your foot down hard on the brake. On an icy trail it'll only slow the dogs down, but on snow it'll hold 'em good.'

'OK.' I hoped I sounded more confident than I felt. 'And how do I steer?'

'You shout "gee" if you want to go right, "ha" if you want to go left. "Hike" means go, and "whoa" means stop.'

'And they'll stop on voice command?'

'No, never. That command has to be backed up with the foot brake, then when they've stopped you stamp in the anchor.'

He showed me how to use the anchor, and to hold the team on the foot brake while throwing the anchor into a suitable spot and stamping it into the snow. Once the anchor was in, I would gently release the foot brake, with the idea that the team would strain forward, pulling the anchor in deep.

Glenn walked back to the snow machine and started the engine. 'OK,' he shouted. 'Pull the anchor!'

I did so, and it squeaked out of the snow. The dogs went silent, leaning into their harnesses and heaving the sled. We clattered out along the frozen road, then towards the dyke. The dogs streamed over the lip of ice, and we pulled along the snowy portage until we reached a straight section. Glenn shouted for me to stamp in the anchor. I did so, and the dogs came to a halt.

'You sure you got that anchor in good?' he shouted.

'Yes, I hope so,' I answered over my shoulder.

'Good, 'cause I'm gonna unhook you from the Tundra. OK?'

I raised a hand, although all my instincts told me I wasn't ready, and only pride was preventing me from saying so. Glenn unhitched the snow machine and the sled jerked forward. I watched the anchor line tighten as the claw bit deep into the snow. The dogs strained impatiently.

Glenn's voice came from behind me in the darkness. 'You go when you're ready, and remember: you're sending commands to the lead dog and not the others. You need to sound like you mean it. If they're going too fast shout "easy", and push the brake down for a bit to back that order up, or else stick your feet down into the snow.'

'OK, Glenn,' I replied in a feeble voice.

I put on my mask and goggles, took a deep breath, and pushed the brake down with my left foot while I leaned over and pulled up the anchor. The dogs responded to the sound of it squeaking up through the snow, and began jumping into their harnesses. The front of the sled lifted and all that now held them was my little foot brake. I let the brake go and jumped onto the runners, and in an instant we were off, tearing at full speed into the darkness.

For the first time I experienced the dogs' immense pulling power. The only sounds were the creaking of the sled and the swishing of the runners. We tore along the trail beneath a glittering arch of frosted trees, and although I felt utterly out of my depth I was captivated by the elemental power of it all.

I glanced behind me and saw the light of Glenn's snow machine following at a distance. Then I realised that we were charging straight for a series of hummocks and going much too fast. It was too late to do anything about it, and I held on for dear life. The dogs flew across the obstacles, sending the sled flying up into the sky. I just managed to hang on, and then saw the river bank approaching.

'Whoa!' I shouted, and jammed the brake down hard. We skidded to a halt, and I held the pedal down while I gathered my breath. The dogs didn't seem in the least tired, and looked back at me impatiently, eager to be off.

A few minutes later I let the brake off again, but this time more carefully, holding it half down as we neared the embankment. At the turn I let the brake off fully. They shot off again, and I held on desperately, then relaxed a little as the trail straightened out along the river. Just before the trail re-entered the woods Glenn came abreast of me and waved for me to stop.

'You're going too fast,' he shouted. 'Try to hold 'em back a bit more at tricky points, and when you make a turn, lean back on the sled and be very firm about your direction. Set your runners hard on the turn—don't try to muddle through.' He started the engine. 'Oh, when you go up that steep bank, get off and run behind the sled just to help 'em up the hill. When you get to the top, jump on again. When you're going downhill, put the brake on, otherwise you'll run into the dogs. Always keep the gang line tight.'

We set off again, and before I knew it we were approaching the steep bank, which was about ten feet high. I jumped off as instructed, and stumbled along between the runners, holding on tightly to the sled. When the front of the team was at the top of the bank, the speed picked up dramatically, and I leapt on just in time before we shot off again. We swerved through the forest, each turn almost finishing me, but by some miracle I hung on. Just when I thought I could take no more, we reached the end of the forest, pulling up the embankment before descending onto the road. We barrelled into the cul-de-sac in front of the dog yard and came to a stop.

Glenn shook my hand. 'You made it,' he said, 'well done.'

'Thanks.' I shook my head, feeling a mixture of shock and exhilaration. 'That was quite an experience.'

'Now we keep practising that trail, and when the dogs can pull you up that embankment we'll know they're fit enough to take you home.'

'What, you mean they're unfit?'

'Oh yeah, they're running real slow now—you'll see the difference when they're fit. Then you'll really feel the power.'

I looked over at the six dogs, panting in their harnesses, and wondered how I, a confirmed cat person, had found myself in this position.

GLENN WAS A PATIENT and determined teacher. I was learning not just how to mush, but also how to run a dog yard, and check their feet and treat common problems. We took the team out for a practice run each day, increasing from five miles to ten as their fitness improved, and they were rapidly growing stronger and faster. The cold weather was hardening the trail, making the runs faster still, and my confidence grew with each run survived.

We went out in all weather, even blizzards, and as I became more adept I began to relish the perks of travelling by dog. The best of these was being able to move in silence; instead of the relentless drone of a snow machine's engine the only sound was the swish of wooden runners on snow. Because I was not moving at the high speed of a snow machine I could look closely at the land I was passing through. I also knew I wouldn't break down, and as long as the dogs were fed and watered we would make it back home.

One morning Glenn said, 'You're ready to take them dogs out on your own.'

I froze with excitement and fear. 'Well, if you think so . . .'

'You're ready, and you'll need to start thinking about making trails down the river to your camp.'

'How do I do that?'

'Take a snow machine down to camp. It'll be tough, as there's been a lot of snow, but once that trail is there it'll freeze and you'll be able to get the dogs down. Now, where you planning to keep the dogs?'

'I'm going to cut a dog yard in the woods by my cabin.'

Glenn nodded. 'Make sure you cut it close to the cabin so wolves don't vacuum up your entire team. Put your most valuable dog nearest to the cabin and your least effective dogs nearer to the perimeter.'

I nodded, struck anew by the savagery of arctic life. My time in the village had begun to soften me. 'Won't the dogs kick up a fuss if wolves come?'

'Yes, and this'll give you a chance to do something about it. They'll bark at everything that comes into camp except a brown bear. Then they go quiet and sneak back into their boxes—you won't hear a thing.'

I thought about the horror of being visited in winter by a brown bear. Brown bears, unlike their black cousins, have sometimes been known to wander around the woods at the wrong time of the year.

'What else should I watch out for?'

'Well, moose'll be getting meaner as the winter goes on, and because a dog sled moves quietly you could surprise one on your portage.'

'What should I do then?' I asked.

'Well, that's when you need a gun, 'cause sometimes a moose'll stamp on a team of dogs, smashing 'em all to pieces.'

I looked closely at his face, wondering if he was trying to scare me, but then realised he was merely being practical. I felt a trickle of fear.

IT FELT ODD SETTING UP the team without Glenn around. The dogs strained against their harnesses, barking and whining as they looked back at me, pleading with their eyes to be let loose. I lifted the anchor and they rose like sprinters to the mark, then I let go of the brake. A split second's pause and we were off, hurtling along the hard, icy road.

Somehow I kept the gang line tight as they vaulted the embankment, and soon we were skimming through the woods towards the river. The sun was going down, and the western sky was lit by a cold, yellow light. I passed down onto the river, where I looked out across four miles of frozen white water towards the distant tree-lined bank. I looked up and caught the flash of a comet, spitting a bright little trajectory towards the northwest.

We rounded a sandbar covered in snow, and I noticed the dogs suddenly upping the pace while looking off to their right. In a stand of willow I dimly saw a moose calf standing in the deep snow. A split second later my eyes widened in horror as a dark brown lump rose up from the snow just thirty yards ahead. It was a moose—a great big cow, right in the middle of the trail.

'Oh shit,' I said desperately. 'Not a moose—please, no!'

The dogs barked furiously and sped up. I pushed the brake down, but the dogs were pulling so hard that it did nothing. I jumped on it again, and managed to hold it down long enough to stop the dogs. Then I quickly let a foot off to stamp in the snow anchor. Only by stamping repeatedly on it was I able to make it hold. The dogs had lost their minds with excitement.

The moose stood stock still, staring at us. My heart pounded. I had no rifle, and felt small and vulnerable. The moose dropped her ears and lowered her head in a threatening manner—then she stepped forwards and swung her great head over towards the other moose in the willows. Stalemate, I thought, and knew that I had to take action of some kind. I ripped the mask away and started to shout and swear. The cow looked at me in a shocked way. For a few minutes I continued to swear at her, until eventually, holding her head high in disgust, she stepped haughtily off the trail.

I waited until she was well out of the way, then pulled up the anchor and moved off fast. We entered the forest, passing along the narrow, twisting trail. Having survived the encounter with the moose, I was feeling wonderfully calm, and enjoyed our meandering journey through the icy, silent woods. At last we skittered back to the yard. The dogs were panting, their faces covered with frost, and I felt the beginnings of a partnership with the desperate half-dozen. As I stepped off the runners I felt a powerful sense of satisfaction: I had travelled ten miles on my own in the darkness and come home in one piece. I thought of the comet and my superstitious mind told me that it was an omen of good fortune. It was time to head back to camp.

'HELLO, HELLO, HELLO—can you hear me?'

'Yes, I can hear you,' Juliet's faint voice replied. 'Are you OK?'

'Yes, but I'm missing everyone badly. It's harder being in the village—it makes me miss you all even more. I need to get back to camp.'

There was a pause, and I could hear her saying, 'I'm talking to Daddy. Oscar, do you want to say hello?' I waited to hear his little voice, but instead Juliet came back on. 'He's busy—he says he'll speak to you later.'

Sadness welled up inside me. So this is what it feels like to lose touch with your children, I thought, feeling guilty and angry at the same time.

'It's normal for him to start being a bit distant, isn't it?'

'Well, he still loves you, Guy, but he's got to get on with it. If he'd kept missing you like he did in the beginning he couldn't have coped.'

'Do you think he'll be OK?'

'I'm sure he will, but right now you are in the background and that is good.' She changes the subject. 'You haven't forgotten that it's Christmas next week have you? What are you going to do?'

'I'm going back to my cabin.'

'I had an email from Claudette saying she'd like you to be with them.'

Claudette and Juliet had been emailing each other since my arrival in Alaska, and a connection had been established between the families.

'It would feel wrong to be with them while my own family is without me.'

'They've helped you so much, Guy, and they really want you to be there.'

'Yes, I know that, and I love them but—'

'Suffering alone in your cabin won't help us have a better Christmas—I think you should stay.' She paused. 'Besides, if you're in the village we can all relax and enjoy Christmas, knowing that you're safe for another week or so.'

'OK, let me think about it,' I said.

I packed away the little phone, then sat for a minute considering the two options: Christmas alone in my cabin, or in the midst of Don's wonderful family. There was no contest.

WHEN THE FAMILY gathered for the Christmas meal, the table groaned with delicious food, and children milled about, wide-eyed and happy and excited. Watching them, I felt my shaky defences crumble. I yearned for home. Juliet had sent a box of presents for the family, and the children ripped into the wrapping paper with true Alaskan ferocity.

'Where are your kids?' Tirzah asked, fixing me with her wide, clever eyes.

'Well, they're at home in Scotland,' I said. 'I'm going back in the spring.'

She inspected me narrowly. 'That's a long time.'

'Yes, it is.' I nodded slowly, feeling miserable, and she darted off.

Later when the meal was over, I walked back alone to the little cabin in Don's yard. I called home, and spoke first to Oscar, who was full of excitement and happiness. Then I talked to Juliet, who was quietly hopeful, feeling that we were on the home run. All too soon it was time to end the call. I lay back on the bed, feeling lower than I had ever been in my life. I knew my salvation lay in getting back to camp.

I STOOD BESIDE DON, looking out over the frozen river. It was snowing lightly, and I could see from the darkening sky that more snow was on its way.

'How difficult is it going to be making the trail back to camp?' I asked.

'Lot of snow this year.' Don looked downriver. 'Might take a bit of work. We'll come with you, as the more men you got breaking a trail the better. If the weather's not too white we'll head off tomorrow.'

That night, Don showed me how to keep the Tundra in good order. Snow machines can travel at speeds in excess of 120 miles per hour, and drivers get caught out by travelling great distances and then breaking down. Luckily my teacher was old school, the message was simple: always prepare for the worst. I packed enough food, clothing and kit for five days, and took my snowshoes everywhere. I was obsessive about carrying every possible means of starting a fire, and always had lighters, matches, flints and birch bark, as well as bottles of anti-freeze, which is a superb fire starter in any conditions.

The next morning, Charlie and Chris arrived on their powerful machines. We set off in a little convoy, with Charlie leading, followed by Don, then Chris and me at the back. I couldn't see how they were able to go so fast. I wobbled and bumped along in their wake, falling so far behind that more than once they had to stop and wait for me. On and on we travelled, the trail leading up and down steep hummocks of ice and windblown snow, rattling my bones on the jagged, rutted surface.

When we reached Four Mile Point, the trail dipped sharply down, and the white river stretched away for miles. It grew much colder now, as we were in the lowest part of the river basin. Finally we came to a stop and Don pointed across the river towards a snowy opening.

'That's the slough!' he shouted. 'Lots of snow there. Gonna be overflow.'

Now we were going to be breaking trail, which would be much harder. Don set off first. The rest of us followed one by one, and even though I had the benefit of the others' trails, the going was difficult. The snow was deep, and we had to go fast enough to stop the machines from sinking, yet slow enough to maintain control. Several times I got it wrong, and sank into the snow, whereupon the Tundra's belt clogged and stopped. Then I had to get off the machine and compact a snowy platform beside it, so that I could heave the machine onto the platform, climb back on and accelerate out of the hole.

Eventually we reached the mouth of the slough, and the four of us shot off across the deep snow that had blown down into the slough basin.

When breaking trail on a river, you aim to cross sandbanks or areas where there is likely to be little or no water. Falling through ice is the Arctic's greatest hazard, and whenever we were forced to cross an area of deep water we would do so as quickly as possible. The ice at the edge of the river is also likely to be thin, so you stay away from the bank.

On we travelled, with me still trailing behind but gradually mastering the snow machine. About three miles into the slough, I heard a shout. The three men had stopped about two hundred yards ahead, and were signalling for me to stop. I slewed to a halt and saw a terrible sight. The trail was steaming, and a long slender cloud followed its course for about fifty yards ahead. Where there should have been white, compacted snow, instead the trail was covered by a long streak of putrid water. That's river water, I thought, and realised I was about to have my first encounter with overflow.

Overflow occurs when the weight of the snow forces down the river ice, and water comes up over the edges and lies on top. There it remains liquid, insulated by the heavy snow, and invisible to the traveller. Those who do not go through fast enough may find their machines stuck to the river ice as the exposed water freezes. Rescue is very tricky, and can only be done by cutting poles and winching the machine out. The driver will invariably get wet, and wherever there is water there's a greatly increased danger of frostbite.

The men beckoned energetically—their message was clear: Charge!

Taking a deep breath, I gunned the throttle and charged along the trail. The machine hit the water, and immediately floundered, sinking backwards. I felt the steerage fail as the skis slewed about in the water. 'Come on!' I shouted, and threw my weight forwards to lift the belt from the fast-freezing water. The Tundra shot forward and planed across the rest of the water to safety.

At length we reached the little river beach at the end of my portage, and I was thankful that I had cut a siding through the embankment. We charged up it, then on up the portage, where the snow lay in deep drifts. When we reached the cabin, we found it was almost buried in snow, and everything inside was frozen solid. We took a break for a few minutes, then got back on our snow machines and set off back to the village.

Being last wasn't such a good position on the return journey, as by the time I reached patches of overflow the others had already broken the newly formed ice, meaning that I had to cross water again. It was dark now, and that sour fog looked even worse in the headlights of the snow machines. I knew there was no other option, however, so I swallowed my fear and charged. Twice the machine almost tipped over sideways. It was also harder to balance in the dark, as there was nothing ahead to fix on, and at one point I stuck out my right leg and to my horror felt water enter my boot. I felt foolish and didn't mention it to the others to begin with. But as we journeyed on I felt my foot growing colder and colder until I couldn't feel it at all.

The next time we stopped I told Don, and he immediately told me to get the boot off, and to rub my foot while they dried my sock on the carburettor of the snow machine. Frostnip had attacked one toe. I rubbed my foot and wondered whether I would lose my toe. My foot wasn't responding, and suddenly losing a toe seemed a good outcome compared to losing a foot.

Charlie took off his gloves and knelt down, massaging my clammy foot between his warm hands. Taking off your gloves in these temperatures is not recommended, and I was moved by what he had done.

'Thanks, Charlie,' I said, 'although my book says you should hold the foot against your bare stomach.'

'Hey, fuck you!' he said, flashing me a grin.

'The Athabascan Charles Bronson is back,' I said, and we all laughed.

Throughout the rest of the journey I tried to keep my foot moving, stopping and running up and down the trail occasionally to get the circulation going. At last we saw the distant lights of Galena, and half an hour later I was warming my frost-nipped toes by Don's fire. This had been my closest brush with disaster yet, and I knew I had been lucky.

IN THE VILLAGE I was being seduced by the lure of human company, and knew that if I was going to be able to cope on my own again I had to get back to my cabin fast. However, there was no way that I could take my dog team out to the cabin with the overflow situation, which was getting worse.

I blurted out my worries to Jenny one morning, and she listened patiently.

'Well, maybe Brad could help out,' she said. 'He goes all over in that little plane of his.'

Bradley Scotton was a colleague of Jenny's at the Alaska Fish and Wildlife Service. A spark of hope flickered.

'Brad's upstairs,' she said, 'go on up and ask him.'

I ran up the wooden stairs to Bradley's office and knocked on his door.

'C'mon in!' a voice answered.

I found Bradley Scotton sitting at his desk. In his mid-thirties, he was light and agile, with intelligent, humorous blue eyes and a bushy beard that gave him a rebellious look. He looked every bit the bush flyer.

'Hello—are you Bradley?' I smiled. 'My name's Guy.'

'Ah, yes, the cheechako from Scotland.' He nodded and leaned back in his chair, looking me up and down. Clearly my reputation had gone before me. 'I heard you were in the village. Enjoying them dogs?'

'Oh yeah. No disasters so far. Well, let me see, how can I say this?'

'You need a flight back to your camp, right?'

I nodded, wondering how he knew. 'It's the overflow—I can't take the dogs out till it hardens up, but I was thinking that if it was possible to get to the slough opposite my portage I'd be able to walk across it and on up to camp.'

'Well, we could give it a try, but overflow's no fun in a plane either. Possibly we could land on the sand-banked bits of the slough, then you could walk across from there.'

'How much will it cost?'

'Nothin' at all. I'll give you a call when this snow stops and we'll see what can be done.'

'Thank you so much, Brad—I'm really grateful.'

THE PLANE was a 1940 J-3 Cub, a superb machine, made of birch and canvas with a 125 horsepower engine, and perfect for the bush because it weighs only around a thousand pounds.

'You go there.' Brad pushed the front seat forward and I stuffed myself into the tiny space in the back. Somehow I managed to get in, but my shoulders filled the width of the plane and my knees were around my chin.

Behind me in a fetid cubby I had stuffed my bag, rifle and Fuzzy, who had wrapped himself into a ball and appeared to be asleep, although I suspected he was secretly wide awake and scared.

Brad walked over to the propeller and began to crank the plane's engine. After two impotent spins the engine turned over and spat deafeningly into life. He passed me a headset and pulled his flimsy door shut, and before I knew it we were charging for the trees, then up into the great blue sky.

At the sight of the great, clean expanse of the wilderness, my heart filled with joy. I was so happy to be going home again, where I could live simply as I had intended, free of all the conflicting emotions that had plagued me of late. Bradley flew low over twisting rivers and creeks, swooping and circling past huge moose lumbering through the snow. All along the slough I could see sickly yellow patches of overflow. And I was relieved to see the thin line of my trail, which still clearly existed despite the heavy snow.

When we reached a straight part of the slough, Brad began to circle sickeningly. 'OK, let's see what the landing is like,' he shouted, then he swooped down and ran the skis along the surface.

We lifted back into the air in a long, banking curve, then came back round again so that Bradley could examine his ski lines in the snow.

'Yeah, we'll put down there,' he said. 'It's over a sandbar—no overflow.'

We made another turn, and dropped down to land smoothly. We slewed to a gentle halt, and Bradley turned off the engine. He nipped out and shimmied along one of the skis. He draped a heat-retaining quilt over the engine, then jumped into the snow and sank to his chest.

'This is where I could have done with being just a bit taller!' he shouted.

I jumped out after him, also sinking immediately, and we both laughed. Fuzzy came next, landing with a *wumpf* and disappearing entirely. He barked in muffled alarm from the bottom of the hole, but soon managed to snow-swim up to the surface where he shook himself, looking happy to be back. I put on my snowshoes, heaved my kit onto my shoulders and said goodbye to Brad. He turned the little plane into the wind and tore into the cold sky, became a speck, and then disappeared. Silence descended.

I turned to walk across the slough, noticing as I did so that the snow was shallow, due to wind barrelling along its course, piling snow up along the sandbanks. I knew I was about to cross overflow and didn't want to get my snowshoes wet, as they would quickly freeze and clog with ice, making them unbearably heavy and virtually impossible to get off. I took them off, feeling grateful for my US army vapour-barrier boots, or 'bunny boots', which I knew would remain watertight. Jenny bought them for me after my near frostbite experience. They are made of two layers of rubber and you inflate them, thus creating a layer of insulating air in between.

My new padded overalls, a present from Don and Carol, locked over the high boots, ensuring that no water would seep through. I stepped onto the river ice, and immediately cracked through a thin layer on the surface, sinking down through about a foot of water before reaching solid river ice below. I had to keep telling myself that there was no danger of falling through that, as it was at least three feet thick. At last I reached the other side, and dried Fuzzy's legs with my handkerchief before strapping on my snowshoes and making my way along the trail. It was getting dark, and yet I felt unafraid, deeply relieved to be home.

Back at camp, I poured some food onto the snow for Fuzzy, then walked

THE CALL OF THE WILD | 263

over to the cabin. The door was frozen shut so tightly that I had to kick it open. My heart sank. The interior of the cabin was white, and looked like the inside of a freezer, with a layer of frost covering everything in cruel, icy sparkles. I dusted the frost off a bucket of kindling and bunches of birch bark and lit the stove, closing the door tightly behind me and hanging up the still-frozen blanket. Then I filled and lit the pressure lamp. It was clear that it was going to take a long time to thaw the cabin out. The temperature inside stood at $-18°F$. Our freezer at home was warm by comparison.

I made some tea, then climbed into bed. The logs in the cabin were starting to thaw and their sides were wet, so I pulled my bed into a dryer spot, only to find a steady drip falling from the melting frost on the tin above. I considered moving again, but decided it was pointless. Effectively I was defrosting a freezer while living in it, and the dripping would only increase as the logs warmed up. Nevertheless, I was glad to be back.

7

The weather grew colder over the next week or so, and it stopped snowing, which meant that the overflow would be less of a problem. I was keen to get my dog team out while I had the opportunity, and managed to hitch another ride with Brad back to the village.

When I got there, Don asked, 'How you gonna get all them dogs down there? I hope you're not expecting me to help.'

'No, not at all. Glenn says I can borrow the dog box,' I answered. 'Then all I need to do is tie it onto a big wood sled and tow them down in that.'

'OK, so whose wood sled you gonna use?' he asked with a look of resigned amusement in his eyes.

'Ah, now that is where you might come in. Perhaps I could borrow yours?'

'Thought so.' He nodded sarcastically. 'We go tomorrow.'

'We?'

'Yeah, we. Think I'm gonna let you trash my wood sled? But this is the only time I'm gonna help with them pant-sniffers. Goddit?'

'Of course, Don, but really . . .'

He walked away. This was a man who just couldn't let a friend down.

THE NEXT DAY, Don and I drove over to Glenn's yard to collect the dogs. While Don secured the dog carrier to his sled, Glenn and I tied the six dogs inside. Then we fixed on the lid, and on top of this lashed the dogs' boxes with their tether chains, bowls, dog feed and rice, as well as booties for their feet and extra lengths of rope for sled line repairs. I also tied on a shovel and rake for cleaning the dog yard, as well as buckets, ladles and a fifty-five gallon drum that I would use to make the dog pot. Once it was all tied up, Glenn placed the birch sled on top of the pile and bungee-corded it on.

Then he looked at me seriously. 'You be careful, go slow and keep yourself and these dogs in good shape, you hear?'

'I'll try, Glenn, and thanks so much for everything.'

He raised a hand to both of us and drove off on his snow machine.

'I just can't believe you got me doing this,' Don said. 'I sure hope no one sees me today—I'd be mortified if it got out that I'd become a musher.'

We set off, Don first, trailing the wood sled behind his snow machine, while I followed behind on the Tundra with Fuzzy nestled between my arms. Several hours later we stopped opposite my portage.

Don wiped the frost from his moustache. 'You hook 'em up,' he said, 'and I'll cache your stuff here.'

I unhitched the dog sled and anchored it in the snow. I then rolled out the gang line, straightening each tug line and harness ready for its dog.

I suddenly remembered Fuzzy. He had no idea about the arrival of the six new dogs. 'Oh shit!' I said. 'What about Fuzzy?'

'I don't know.' Don shrugged. 'I was kinda thinking the same.'

It is a well-known fact that sled dogs and pet dogs do not mix. Sled teams sometimes snatch pets as they run, chewing them up and spitting them out like a giant shredder. Yet I knew that Fuzzy was a careful dog, and obedient. I would have to impose a new and immediate rule, that whenever the sled was out Fuzzy would remain behind it. If he stayed beside the sled's runners and never came alongside the dogs, he would be out of danger.

'Yeah, might work,' Don said when we discussed the idea, 'and them sled dogs might also treat Fuzzy different. If they're chained up all day and he gets to walk around with you, in dog language that means he's the boss's dog.'

I led Fuzzy over to the runners and told him sit and stay. He sat obediently, looking up at me with eyes full of love and happiness. I opened the box, and it rocked about as the dogs scrabbled and clawed at the sides, barking and yowling. One dog stood quite still, gazing up at me with determined, incisive eyes. It was Bubbles, my lead dog, and as usual she was showing her leadership abilities. I reached in and unclipped her, then leaned over to lift her clear. She licked the side of my face once, then hopped onto the snow and stood looking around her as I put her booties on and harnessed her up. Fuzzy, standing beside us, was in clear contravention of the rules.

'No!' I said firmly, dragging him back to the runners. 'Stay!' I said.

He sat down reluctantly, glaring at me indignantly as if to say, Why? And more to the point, who the hell is she?

Soon I had the whole team in place, and the river basin resounded with barks and howls. Fuzzy was now staying by the runners as instructed. I knew that this first run up the portage would be dangerous: Bubbles did not know the trail, which was sinuous in the extreme. I watched the dogs, leaping and howling and packed full of energy.

'Going to be very fast,' I said.

Don nodded. 'Them dogs is fit and they're raring to go. Over time you'll get them used to a steady working pace.' He shook my hand. 'Good luck.'

I pulled the anchor and we were off. We rocketed towards the cutting, and they surged up it effortlessly. The sled flew onto the narrow trail, and the cottonwoods passed in a blur as we shaved the high sides of the trail.

'Easy!' I shouted, and pushed my foot hard on the brake. To my relief Bubbles fell back into a trot, then gradually the whole thing cranked up again and we galloped on. It felt like taking a Ferrari along a mule track.

We shot up a little incline, then dropped down and turned so fast that I slipped off the runners and fell. I dragged behind the sled, holding on for dear life: to lose the dogs on their first outing was too terrible to contemplate. I tried to pull myself back onto the runners, but couldn't quite make it, and ran comically behind until the snow whipped my feet away again. Finally the sled ran off the trail and lodged in some snow-covered bushes. The dogs stopped, and I threw in the anchor and lay panting face down in the snow. Fuzzy barked at me, and after a moment I got up and straightened the sled. I stood back on the runners, lifted the anchor, and off we charged again.

Taking a tight corner on a sled in a woodland portage is one of the biggest challenges for any musher. The length of the team means that the dogs will have rounded a corner before the sled has reached it, and the musher's instinct will be to brake sharply. If he does so, the gang line suddenly goes tight between the slowing sled and the lead dog, and both sled and musher can be pulled off the trail. Instead of braking the musher must therefore lean back, and set his runners firmly at the outside of the bend, allowing the power of the team to rip him around the turn. I had to face this test time after time as we charged up the portage, but somehow we made it.

When we arrived at camp, I had to improvise a dog yard that would last until I was able to fetch the rest of the gear next day. The dogs would spend their first night outdoors, but snow was falling, so it would be relatively warm. I cut away the brush surrounding six alder trees behind the cabin. I then snowshoed around each tree until I'd made a solid surface, before cutting some spruce boughs for the dogs to lie on. I unharnessed the dogs and tethered them to the trees. They immediately began pacing in circles, stopping to mark their trees or sniff about. I poured them each some dog food, which they devoured in seconds, and watched them settle down on their spruce beds, curling up into little balls. I felt cold just looking at them, and resolved to get their boxes set up the next day, then groaned at the thought of manhandling the gear up to camp. But then I remembered I had dog power—my days as a human mule were over. I had six dogs, each with a pulling power of around 200 pounds. The idea was exciting, and with it came the realisation that I had moved on just a step.

BY NIGHTFALL the next day my cabin had thawed out, and felt like home again. The dogs' homes were in good shape too; each now had its own snug box. To make them extra warm I piled an insulating layer of snow around and on top of each one, and just behind the cabin I placed the dog pot. Keeping this going meant a dramatic increase in my wood consumption, so I spent days cutting eight-foot lengths of wood, and used the dogs to drag them back to camp. There I would spend endless hours cutting, splitting and stacking the logs ready for use. Once I had worked out a routine, the process became almost joyful, and the dogs made a huge difference to what had formerly been demanding work.

My day would start with hooking up the dogs and letting them charge out onto the lake, where I would run them for ten minutes to allow them to burn off their pent-up energy. When they had calmed down a bit, I would take them down to a suitable point on the lake and anchor them securely using two anchors. Then I would snowshoe up into the woods beside the lake, where there were many good-sized standing dead spruce. Even when working in temperatures as low as −50°F, I wore very little, and my spare clothes would hang over a nearby bough, waiting to warm me when the job was done. I would then shoulder the felled logs and snowshoe back to the sled, hitching on the logs and trailing them back to camp. The dogs were learning to work slowly and steadily, and seemed to enjoy their new role.

At the end of the day's work I would return the dogs to their tethers as I started piling up wood ready to light the dog pot. Once I'd lit the fire, I would shovel snow in, followed by ladles of rice, dog feed, chopped fish and scraps of grouse. The fishy smell of the pot would be driving the dogs crazy by this time, and the air would be reverberating with their barks, yelps and howls. The pot would be like a black, fire-belching demon, lurking beneath a great white cloud of hot air and bitter smoke.

When it was ready, I would ladle the thick broth into a large bucket, then stir in some snow so as not to scald the animals. The dogs would hang back, darting in and out of their boxes while I ladled the stew into their dishes, then pounce on it as soon as I had moved on. Unlike Fuzzy, they didn't make the meal last, and would lap up the liquid in seconds before devouring the chunks in single gulps.

As I crunched back to the cabin, a dog would occasionally start to howl, then gradually the others would emerge from their boxes to join in. Each dog would add a different call to the eerie song, some fading away as others rose high. Old-timers called this a 'howlankyou', and said that it came after a good meal, when the dogs felt safe and warm with heavy stomachs. In those great boreal woods, shivering beside my cabin beneath a sky full of stars, I could have cried as I listened. Their canine song of gratitude meant more to me than anything else in the world at that moment, as it told me the team was well and happy, and that tomorrow they would run and run and run.

WHEN I HAD CUT enough wood to see us through a few weeks, my thoughts turned to making a winter portage. My old portage was too sinuous for the dog sled, so I worked out a new, straighter route down the grass lake, giving me a straight run towards the slough, with only about half a mile of woodland to pass through towards the end. Each day I snowshoed down the lake towards the willow woods at the far western end, dragging my chain saw, axe and Sandvik in the hand-pulled sled, while Fuzzy loyally trailed behind me. Overnight my tracks would freeze hard, and the next day I would retrace my steps, compress newly fallen snow and widen the trail. After a few days the portage through the grass lake had a good icy surface.

One particularly dark, moonless night, I was on my way home when I was stopped in my tracks by a strange sound coming from the direction of my cabin. It was a continuous low murmuring, which rose every now and then as if about to crescendo. It had to be the wolf pack. I looked down at Fuzzy, who was standing rigid with his hair on end. This was a new sound from the wolves; it had a malevolence that I had never heard before.

'Oh shit! The dogs!' I said, remembering they were alone and unguarded.

Glenn had told me how wolves would attack sled dogs, ripping them off their tethers, and I started snowshoeing as fast as I could. The murmuring was growing louder as I got nearer to camp, and I entered the dog yard with dread. To my relief they were unmolested, and I heard no more of the wolves that night, yet they must have been very close by. Midwinter was a hard time for animals in the Interior, and I felt vulnerable, knowing that my camp was emitting an irresistible scent.

NOW THAT MY TRAILS were solid I set about getting the dogs fitter. If they were to be useful, they needed to be able to travel long distances, and certainly as far as the village thirty-five miles away. I used the slough trail as a training ground, venturing a little further each day until I reached the Yukon proper. The dogs enjoyed these journeys, and came back into camp each day with their tails wagging.

The dogs wanted to work for me, and although they liked me and knew that I liked them, they were also just a little bit scared, knowing that I could be very stern. Glenn had taught me it was vital to assert my dominance from the start, and when any of the dogs had been caught dawdling or not concentrating they were quickly disciplined.

From the start, Bubbles and I had got on well. I called out her commands very gently, and when we traversed tough sections of trail I would encourage her in a high, light voice. With each petite call a forwards surge would ripple through the team, in contrast to occasions when I had shouted or been too strident, when the dogs seemed to lose heart and give up.

Next to Bubbles ran Sprite, a pure white dog with a positive attitude and a seemingly inexhaustible supply of energy. Her character was fresh and fun, and she never gave up, even in deep snow, a head wind or a blizzard.

Behind Sprite and Bubbles ran the 'team' dogs, Spot and Lefty. Running on the left was Spot, who was the youngest in the team and had much to learn. He had incredible strength and endurance, but was incapable of trotting, by far the most economical gait for long distances, and would endlessly gallop, jerking the whole team. Yet I had a soft spot for him, as he had great heart and was still very much a puppy. On the right ran Lefty, the veteran of the team. He fascinated me with his composure: while the other dogs yelped and barked he would pace wisely, his mouth tight shut beneath a few silvery whiskers. When I unhooked him he would pull towards the sled in anticipation, and once harnessed he would lean hard on the tug line, looking ahead unflinchingly. Lefty had run the Yukon Quest, one of the longest sled races in the world, three times. I was deeply impressed by him, and yet on the odd occasion when I attempted to pet him he would shrink away.

Behind Lefty ran my two 'wheel' dogs, Blackie and Brownie. The wheel dogs' position is a hard one, as they run nearest the sled, acting like canine shock absorbers and taking the strain as the sled jars over miles of uneven trail. Blackie was tiny, slight and shy, yet when she was hooked up she transformed into a hard pulling dog, and never, ever gave up. Brownie was the biggest dog in the team and the most striking, with fearsome, dramatic eyes. Like Spot he never trotted. Unlike Spot he didn't have the excuse of youth or inexperience. When the anchor was lifted he would charge off, galloping in great long strides. This was worrying, and he turned out to be what mushers call a 'one day dog', meaning that on the first day he ran well but on the second flaked out completely.

One night, as we returned from a run up the slough, Brownie was running sideways and letting the tired team drag him along. I could do nothing about it—if I put him on the sled he would probably do it the next day, hoping for another lift. I stopped the sled and let them rest for a moment, but saw that this would not help the others, who all stared at me in disgust. We carried on, but then Brownie collapsed completely. I rested them again, giving Brownie a good rub and stretch while whispering encouragements. When we finally made it back to camp, the other dogs barked for their dog pot while he stood quiet and exhausted in his run. I felt sorry for him, yet knew that for him to have any future he would have to improve.

Bubbles was showing real ability as a lead dog, and although Glenn told me she was just starting out it was clear that she was skilled. If we came to a fork where we usually went left, for example, and I cried out 'Gee!' for a right turn instead, she would at first instinctively head in our usual direction. 'No!' I would say firmly, then give a few light but insistent calls of 'Gee, gee, gee!'. She would then look right, clearly showing that she had understood. Then I would shout 'Gee!' one more time and off we would go to the right. As we got to know each other she began to make these adjustments faster and faster, so that eventually she just had to look the wrong way, and a quiet 'No' from me would set her on the right course. As the lead dog she was the most important in the team, and was always given slightly more rations than the others because her workload was the greatest.

Our training sessions also benefited Fuzzy, who would run tirelessly between the runners of the sled. The meals from the dog pot were also doing him a lot of good, and his great shaggy blond coat shone. Sometimes I would stop to rest the team and walk along the gang line, patting each dog. Fuzzy would stay at a safe distance, leaning casually against the sled and chewing ice from his paws, regarding the team with thinly disguised scorn.

Once, he sneaked into Brownie's run. I was about to retrieve him, then decided he had to learn for himself that messing with sled dogs was not a good idea. I heard growls, scuffles and a high-pitched squeal. To my surprise I saw Brownie retreating into his box and Fuzzy growling victoriously. He puffed up his chest and walked calmly towards me, as if announcing to the whole yard: That's right. I'm the boss's dog. And don't you forget it.

After a few days, our daily runs were up to around sixteen miles, and Fuzzy often proved his worth as tail-end Charlie. Once we were skittering fast over a bumpy section of trail when one of my snowshoes fell off the sled. I braked, but the pedal just slid over the ice. Eventually the brake just held, but I couldn't risk the anchor, as the holding wasn't good. I looked back at the snowshoe, which lay about fifty yards behind us, then down at Fuzzy. 'Fetch', I said, and he dashed back, then spent a few minutes trying to balance the snowshoe in his mouth, before galloping back to me.

I took the shoe from him and said, 'I love you, Fuzzy, do you know that?'

He answered with a loving growl. From then on, he would collect things without even being asked, passing them to me when we were on the move. There's no doubt about it, without my canine companions my life in the subarctic would have been much the poorer.

THE COLD KEPT her grip tight over my forest home throughout January. Each time I left camp I armed myself with a cloak of caution, knowing that she would kill me at the slightest chance. A big area of high atmospheric pressure had moved in, and the temperatures dropped as low as –60°F. I was losing weight again in the harsh cold, and realised it was time to start hunting for fatty meat, which could only mean beaver. In this weather that meant snaring, as hanging around outside for too long was not a good idea.

Through the winter months, when the beavers were trapped by ice and had to live full time in their house, they swam to the stick pile whenever they needed to, grabbing a tasty branch and bringing it back to the house. When they had gnawed off all the bark, the beavers would deposit the left-over stick on their refuse pile, known as the 'boneyard'. I spent many hours thinking about how I might intercept them in their routine. They were intelligent animals, and catching one presented quite a challenge.

One morning, with Fuzzy beside me, I set off to collect my 'bait'. I dug away the snow surrounding a delicious-looking cottonwood sapling, and sawed it as near as possible to its base. I then cut a three-foot spruce pole and threw everything into my hand sled, which I dragged over the lake towards the beaver house. Above the snug white house a thin trail of heat was rising from the apex as if a fire burned within. It was caused by the heat of their bodies in the upper chamber. It made me feel guilty, as if I were a killer lurking at the gate of a little cottage, planning to murder the family seated cosily round the fireplace. Then I thought of the glorious beaver stews I would cook up, and it hardened my resolve.

I tried to work out the location of their stick pile. I was planning to sink the tasty sapling between the pile and the house, hoping to tempt a passing beaver with a fresh bit of bark. The idea was that in swimming for the branch it would place its head through a wire snare that hung in front of the bait. The beaver's flat tail becomes a drag if it tries to swim backwards, so it would have to plunge forwards, pulling the snare tight round its neck.

I identified a likely spot for the stick pile, and started to shovel snow. Four feet of hard, wind-packed snow lay on top of the ice, and it was heavy work. I dug slowly and methodically until I reached a layer of crunchy ice that had been overflow. I shovelled a clear area around this, then used the heavy ice pick to chip a hole roughly three feet in diameter. After a foot or so I reached a layer of much harder, clearer ice—the lake ice proper. On and on I picked, my arms and shoulders aching and my hands numb with cold. Three feet later my pick finally broke through, and I was glad that I had tied it to my hand, or it would have sunk without trace.

Brown water sucked and gushed into the hole, filling the air with the stink of a sewer. I chipped on, making the hole wider, and stared down through the noxious steam. I saw a branch float up, and as I reached into the hole with the ice pick I realised that I was right over the stick pile. My heart sank—there was no way a snare would work with all those sticks around it.

It was dark by the time I had finished cutting the next hole, not so close to the stick pile. I sunk the cottonwood sapling down, leaving just the end poking above the hole, and then looped two snares onto the spruce branch, which I laid across the hole in front of the bait. I fiddled about, lowering the loops down through the dark water. The first attack was in place.

The next day, when I checked the trap, the hole was buried in windblown snow, and I could just see the top of my bait stick poking out. I scooped the snow out of the way, then cleared the ice that had grown over the hole. I was looking for bubbles or chips of bark that would have been evidence of a beaver working away at the bait stick, but I saw nothing. I trudged a little way off to dig a second set. Once I had decided on a spot, I began the tiresome job of digging, shovelling and ice-picking all over again. When I had set the bait and snares, I returned to the first hole. One of the crafty rodents had indeed gone for my bait, and nibbled its way round the outside, removing the side branches and leaving the main stem intact. I was stumped. I cut another branch and reset the snare, then walked back to the cabin feeling doubtful about the whole enterprise.

Over the next week or so I tried every combination of sapling and snare, but always returned to find a nibbled bait and useless dangling loop of wire. With each day, both my determination and my hunger grew. One morning I walked back to my cabin clutching a gnawed bait branch. I pumped the lamp to shine brightly, and stared at it. The beavers were taking my bait and somehow missing my snares. Maybe the snares were at the wrong depth. Then I realised that the beavers' neat line of trimming on the bait sticks could show me the exact depth at which they were approaching my bait. I went back to the hole and reset the trap.

When I returned the next day, I brushed the snow away from the frozen-over hole, and for the first time saw something that hinted at food. In the pane of ice, little chips of bark hung round a burst of frozen bubbles. I chipped round the wire of my snare until it hung free of ice. The wire felt tight, and the snare was heavy. I had caught something. Fuzzy had picked up on my excitement and was whining in anticipation. I chipped out the rest of the ice, grabbed the snare and pulled. I couldn't budge it. I lifted the spruce pole to which the snare was attached, leaned back and pulled with all my strength. Still it didn't move, and I began to wonder if it might be a log. I then took a length of discarded bait and poked it gently into the hole, following the snare wire down into the dark water and feeling around. The end of the stick struck something that yielded and had a soft covering.

'It's a beaver!' I shouted to Fuzzy, who bounded around in circles. I realised that the creature was stuck fast to the underside of the ice. The only way to get it out would be to cut round it through the ice.

Two hours later I managed to free the incredibly heavy beaver, which was weighed down by water and ice. It shot up head first through the slushy dark water, and made me jump. I stared down aghast as two huge and very yellow front teeth glinted in the gloom, framed by a pair of sharp-clawed paws. As soon as I had it on the ice I cut away a fleshy rear paw, throwing it to Fuzzy. I hauled the beast into my sled with some difficulty; it was about four feet long and must have weighed fifty pounds at least.

The beaver was frozen solid by the time I reached the cabin and I needed to hang the carcass up somewhere warm. The only warm place was inside, and with a sinking heart I strung the giant rodent from the purlin nearest the stove, placing my sled underneath to catch the drips as it thawed. That night, as I sat down to eat my beans, I had to work hard to keep my appetite, distracted by the sight of those yellow teeth.

The beaver took three days to thaw. As it dried out it became less ghastly, and I admired the rich brown colour and incredible thickness of its fur. I hung it from a tree outside, then made a cut from its lower lip to its vent. I neatly cut out its dark liver and placed it in Fuzzy's bowl, where he fell on the meal. I threw the rest of the innards into the dog pot. Then I used snow to clean out the internal cavity, and brought the beaver back into the cabin. Determined not to waste anything, I skinned away the pelt, glad to see the animal's thick layer of fat. I stretched the pelt out on a board, hammering in little nails and leaving it flesh-side-out to dry. I had cut off the wide, scaly tail and added it to the dog pot. I hung the animal up on my game pole outside, knowing it would freeze solid and I could saw off portions of meat as required.

OVER THE COMING WEEKS I caught a few more beaver, and began to see the benefits of the fatty meat for myself and the dogs. I had come up with a few good recipes, particularly for beaver ribs, which I would fry up with paprika and dried onion shavings. Once they were browned, I would add some dried split peas, and cover it all with grouse stock. The result was delicious.

I was now feeling very comfortable living on my own in the wilderness, but my dreams were full of Juliet and the children, almost as though my subconscious was reminding me of where my true home was. One night I plugged in my laptop to see if I had any messages, and found one from Juliet titled CALL ME NOW!! I looked at the date and saw it was yesterday's, then dialled without reading the message.

'Hello, it's me,' I shouted. 'Is everything OK?'

'Yes . . .' Juliet sounded hesitant, but even through the crackly line I could hear she was excited. 'At least I think it is. I've sold the house!'

'You've what?' I thought I must have misheard her.

'I've sold the house! I'm sorry, Guy, I hope it's OK, but I had to make a very quick decision and I couldn't get hold of you.'

A series of images of our little house ran through my mind, and I thought sadly of my vegetable garden, which it seemed I would never see again. Still, this is what happens if you leave your wife to run the ship alone, I thought. I could hardly protest.

'Well . . . what are we going to do then?' I asked, feeling confused.

'We're going to live on Mull! You know we've discussed it so many times, Guy, and it was just too good an opportunity. The boys absolutely love it here, and it would be very hard for them to leave after all this time. We'll make things work here—I know we will.'

I was speechless but she was right, and as I put down the receiver at the end of the call I felt happy. Now there was no going back to our old life, whatever happened. Assuming, of course, that I made it home in one piece.

THE DOG TEAM was working like a crack squad of legionnaires, and one night in particular they proved their worth. I was travelling along the Yukon, having overruled my instinct to stay in as it was threatening snow, when the blizzard began. I had about six miles to go to the mouth of the slough, then eight miles further to my portage. I was having enough trouble following this well-worn path, and the trail would be much less distinct when I veered off the main channel. The snow grew heavier and pretty soon I could see nothing: I was caught in a white-out in the middle of the night. I mentally kicked myself for being so stupid.

The Eskimo solution is to stop and wait for the storm to pass, and I knew that if necessary I could build a snow shelter. Yet I also knew that it might well snow nonstop for days, and the idea of being holed up in a shelter for a long time so far from home was not appealing. My main concern was finding my turn-off from the main Yukon trail. I decided to proceed carefully, hoping that Bubbles would pick up the turn. After a while I felt the team swing confidently to the left, and a few minutes later I was just able to make out a prominent bank of willow that marked the mouth of the slough. She had done it, and I felt deeply grateful to the clever little dog.

A mile or so later the blizzard grew dramatically worse. These were conditions to die in: nobody in their right mind would travel in such weather. Even Bubbles wasn't up to it, and once or twice she wandered off the trail, pulling the team into the soft, powdery snow. On both occasions I managed to salvage the sled, untangling the harnesses more by feel than sight, but Bubbles was clearly tired. Through the gloom I saw Lefty glancing back at me casually as if to say, OK, boss, let me take it from here.

I took Bubbles off her harness and put the iron-hard veteran in her place, deciding I had no option but to put my trust in him. He pulled the line out beautifully, and I walked along the line of friends, patting each dog and speaking soft words of encouragement. Tails wagged, and they shook the snow from their backs in readiness. We set off, not as fast as under Bubble's leadership, but at a slow, steady trot. The wind and snow barrelled into us, and the dogs' heads hung low, yet they continued to pull steadily.

Two hours later I glimpsed the high bank of cottonwoods near the entrance to my winter portage, and I knew the old boy had done it. He led us up the portage in his economic way until we reached the cabin. I stepped off the runners with deep relief, and warmly congratulated each of the dogs. When I got to Lefty, he looked up at me with a tired expression that seemed to say, Yeah, yeah—less of the talk, get on with that dog pot.

WITH RELENTLESS predictability, the snow cleared, and the temperature plunged to a brutal –60°F. It hovered there for the next few weeks. It seemed extraordinary that the dogs could survive these conditions. As they ran around their tethers they would sometimes lift a paw and hop along on three legs, then drop it and lift another, warming a pad for a moment by keeping it off the frozen ground. One morning I walked through the yard and saw that Blackie had not emerged from her box. I called her, and she sweetly scurried out to nestle her head between my gloved hands. I looked at her closely, then peered into the box. Inside there were two little puppies, completely frozen. Glenn had told me she was pregnant, but it hadn't showed and I thought she must have miscarried. I sat for a while slumped beside the box, holding the two frozen little puppies in my lap, my fragile defences under siege. Of all the places for a new life to begin, an Alaskan dog yard in the depths of winter had to be one of the worst.

I buried them in the snow not far from the cabin, and as I snowshoed home knew that it wouldn't be long before an animal emerged from the woods to dig them up again. I sat beside the stove, feeling morose and belittled by the harshness of it all. I longed for softness, gentleness and compassion, things that didn't exist in this brutal order of things.

FRIGID WEEKS PASSED BY, and I was kept busy in my daily routine of wood cutting, hunting and dog mushing. Then, around the beginning of March, I noticed that the world had begun to change. Gradually, almost imperceptibly at first, the days were lengthening, and each day the sun held a little more warmth. Winter was giving way at last. Although still usually in the minus twenties, it felt positively balmy by comparison to what had gone before.

The thaw was still some way off, though, and my trails remained hard. Most days I would travel up the slough, and we often stopped at a particular place opposite Bishop Creek, near a long belt of willow osiers. Here the air was filled with the sweet scent of rising willow sap, and I would breathe deeply, relishing the smell of spring.

One day, as we neared the spot, I saw two moose calves, sitting close together in the snow right in the middle of the rust-coloured osiers. I braked, and to my surprise the calves did not lumber off, but simply lay there chewing contentedly on the sugary willow. The sight captivated me. Bubbles suddenly leapt into the air and whined, and I saw their huge mother appear on the bank above the willows. She looked at me angrily and advanced with a snort of aggression, and I lifted my foot and we shot off.

Each day as I passed the willow belt the calves were there, sitting like chocolate-brown boulders in snow that shone blue in the sunshine. I always stopped for a moment, and would disappear when the mother looked threatening. My yearning for my own children had grown to a point where I needed an outlet, and those calves became a kind of touchstone for me that was keeping the fathering instinct alive.

One night I heard the wolves, and knew that they were back in their territory to hunt. The next day I passed by the willows as usual and looked about for the calves' mother, but she was not there, and when I passed by later there was still no sign of her. Days passed, and I grew seriously worried, as the calves had not moved. I felt sure that the mother must have been taken by wolves, and I felt helpless, knowing they were alone and defenceless.

One afternoon I made camp on the sandbar, a mile or so from the willows. I tethered the dogs out along my wire and built a quinzee, or snow shelter, to sleep in. First I piled snow into a ten-foot-high mound, compressing it by jumping on the mound with my snowshoes. Then I cut foot-long lengths of willow, which I inserted into the mound until their ends were flush with the outside surface. Next I hollowed out an opening, and started to dig snow out from inside the mound, stopping whenever I reached the end of one of the sticks, to ensure that my walls were thick enough. Inside the quinzee I dug a cold well in front of the door, and at the far end created a shelf for sleeping, where I laid spruce boughs and my sleeping-bag. Cold air would drop into the cold well, and Fuzzy would make a superb pillow. If it grew very cold I could take the whole team in, and in fact old-timers used to talk of 'four dog nights' or 'six dog nights', meaning the number of dogs you would need in your shelter to keep you warm.

That night I fed the dogs cold food and cut spruce for each one to lie on. As I lay inside the perfect little snow house, I heard the wolves again. There was no howling, but instead I heard that strange humming, which I now knew was the sound that wolves make after a kill.

The next morning the sun was its brightest yet, and reflected dazzlingly off the wind-polished snow. I hooked up the dogs and headed along the slough towards the calves, and a chill gripped me when I saw that the trail was covered in wolf prints, all leading in the direction of the willows. Sleek black ravens had gathered in the cottonwoods.

I anchored the sled, put on my snowshoes and walked into the willows. There were wolf prints everywhere. I parted the osiers and looked down to see the remains of the two calves. Everything that could be eaten had been, and all that was left apart from bones was the frozen contents of their stomachs. I stood looking at the scene feeling hollowed out with sadness. I knew that I shouldn't have allowed myself to become so attached to the two little calves, and I knew that the wolf pack had to live, yet it hurt me in a way that was not rational. It was yet more evidence of the harshness of the Interior. And what really rubbed salt in the wounds was the fact that my trail had led those wolves quickly and directly to the calves.

As I turned back towards the sled, I heard a crunching noise behind me. I spun round, rifle at the ready, to find Fuzzy snacking on a dainty rib. He gave me a nonchalant look, and crunched on.

IT WAS MID-MARCH, and there were days of perfect sunshine when I put all tasks aside and sat with my back to a tree, soaking it up and feeling rewarded for the hardships of winter. Yet I knew each warm day brought me closer to the end of my journey. I had achieved my goal of living through the winter, and it was time to start thinking about packing up camp. I was full of conflicting emotions: desperate to be reunited with my family, but reluctant to say goodbye to this place that had become my home.

It was clear that travel would soon be impossible, as the snow was becoming thick and wet. Even walking was difficult, as my snowshoes sank through the surface to a slushy layer underneath, clogging the shoes and making them impossibly heavy. The hard work I had done on my trails really began to pay off, however, as the layers of compressed snow lasted well into the thaw. Gradually the snow levels on either side of the trails dropped down, leaving them standing sometimes three feet proud of the surface, and instead of hedged country lanes they now appeared like raised highways. I had to travel with great care—if we fell off the trail we would sink into deep slush.

The rivers, too, had to be treated with immense caution, as the ice was becoming unreliable. At the mouth of the slough a large lead had opened up. I couldn't avoid the river, as I had to get the dogs back to the village before the trails melted altogether. I decided to make the journey the following morning, before sunrise, when everything that had melted during the day would be refrozen and relatively safe. Once I had returned the dogs, I would use Don's old snow machine to ferry tools and equipment back to Galena.

I called home later and Juliet sounded happier than she had for months. 'Guy! We're counting the weeks. I can't believe you're coming home!'

With a sense of unreality we discussed flights and timetables. I talked to each of the boys, knowing that to them I had become an abstract notion rather than a real father. Luke particularly could have no memory of me at all, as he had been just one year old when I left.

'Daddy,' he said, 'Oo coming home?'

His sweet, pure voice almost brought me to my knees, and my voice was shaking when Juliet came back on the phone. 'What have we done?' I asked, no longer bothering to hide the tears.

'I know—it's been so hard.' She, too, was crying. It was as if now that time was short we could afford to let go.

'Are we going to be OK, do you think?'

'Yes, of course we will—our lives will be so much better. The boys love living on Mull, and we can go to the beaches and fish and camp all summer. We'll have lots of time to catch up.'

'Do you think Luke will accept me as his father?'

She paused. 'Well, it'll be strange for him at first, but he'll see how Oscar and I are with you and I'm sure it won't take long.'

My throat felt numb, and I hoped I would be able to find my way into that little boy's heart. 'I'd better go,' I said, 'I'm taking the dogs back to the village tomorrow—all the snow's melting.'

'Be careful, Guy—please be careful. We need you to come home.'

THE NEXT MORNING I woke in pitch darkness at 4 a.m. I felt both sad and excited about the journey, and as I placed each dog in its harness I felt proud that they were so strong. We scythed off through the dark woods, and kept going straight past the winter portage turn, as I wanted to travel along my old portage on our last journey. Soon we were on the slough, and I let the dogs open up a bit as we flew along the frozen trail.

Just before we reached the slough mouth, Bubbles suddenly pulled the team to a stop. I anchored the sled and walked forward with my axe to see that five yards ahead the trail had collapsed, leaving just a thin sheet of ice below which I could see water. I tapped the ice and water gurgled through. Bubbles must have smelt the river water—yet again these dogs had saved me from serious trouble. I strapped on my snowshoes and walked round the little lead, prodding ahead of me with my axe. Then I walked back again, to compress the new trail. I got back on the sled, lifted the anchor and called 'Ha!' The team bucked their way round the lead, until we rejoined the firm trail.

As we proceeded, the sun rose in the sky, and it was so warm that I took off my hat and jacket. Close to Four Mile Point I looked out across the glittering expanse of the Yukon to see a silver mirage, wavering and shifting in a vast curtain that stretched across miles of river ice. I could smell green everywhere, and it was good to be able to breathe the invigorating air instead of hiding below layer upon layer of material.

In no time at all we were on the outskirts of the village and clattering along the road. When we reached Glenn's dog yard I braked, and a stream of ice and snow shot up behind me as we slithered to a stop. I held the dogs on the brake, wanting to prolong our last journey for just a moment longer. They looked back at me questioningly, tails wagging and tongues lolling as if to ask, What next, but I knew our journeys had come to an end.

I cooked up some dog pot and fed the dogs, giving them extra portions as a reward for their long journey. Then I shuffled over to the edge of the yard to look at them one last time. Bubbles sat quietly amid the chaos of the yard, looking at me with steady, intelligent eyes. In all the journeys we had made together she had never let me down, and she was the bravest, most willing dog I had ever known. I raised a hand and said goodbye, then turned away. As I walked through the quiet village our silvery sled lines were all melting into the earth, but I knew they would be forever etched in my heart.

8

I spent the next couple of weeks ferrying borrowed tools and equipment back to the village using Don's old snow machine. The river was thawing fast, and I travelled either at night or in the early morning to make the most of the cold, towing the wooden sled behind me. After many repetitive journeys I finally got everything back to the family and then returned to see out my last few weeks.

Life was distinctly less arduous, as I had acclimatised to cold temperatures and thus consumed much less wood. At −15°F I would wander about in not much more than a T-shirt. For water I would simply amble down to the slough and dig until I reached the layer of clean thawed snow that lay between the river ice and the snow above. I was feeling relaxed and comfortable, and had forgotten Don's words of warning about being overconfident.

Searching for relief from the monotony of beaver and grouse meat my mind turned to fishing, and one morning I decided to head down the slough to look around. I came down off the bank and onto the river, and immediately had an incredibly strong urge to turn back—so strong that I actually turned the Tundra. Overruling my instincts, however, and telling myself not to be stupid, I completed the circle and carried on. Geese lifted from little pools of snowmelt as I charged along the slough, following the faint outline of a trail that I had not used for months. Suddenly the snow machine slowed down, and I felt a kind of juddering. I looked back, and where my tracks should have been I saw dark, sinister water opening up. I knew immediately that this was river water, and that it would be deep.

THE CALL OF THE WILD | 281

'Shit!' I shouted, realising that the ice had been breaking behind me, and I hadn't heard it over the roar of the engine.

Then, before I could do anything, the ice ahead of me gave way and the machine and I plunged into the water. The Tundra lurched forward, turning to the right. With a sickening jolt I realised that it was going to be swept beneath the ice, taking me with it.

I let go of the snow machine and jumped towards the unbroken ice, feeling my ankle give a painful click. The ice broke under my weight, and I fell into the freezing water. The shock hit me hard, and I felt the strong current pulling at my legs. Holding on desperately to the edge of the ice, I reached down to grab my knife from my pocket, and, stretching as far away as possible, jabbed it firmly into solid ice. Then I pulled my second knife out and did the same. With immense effort, I pulled myself up, spreading my weight. When I was finally lying flat on my stomach I lay still for a moment, shocked and sodden, before gradually starting to slither away.

When I reached solid ice, I turned to see the snow machine bobbing on its side on the fast current. It had caught on the downstream end of the hole, but I knew it would soon sink. I had to release my snowshoes, which were tied to the machine, so I slithered carefully over and cut them free. I put them on, wincing when I tried my weight on my ankle, and limped over to the more solid ice in the middle of the slough. Fortunately I was carrying my pack of survival essentials, including a change of clothing. I changed into dry clothes, teeth chattering and shaking as I did so, then dug out my little stove and brewed tea. All the time I was cursing myself for being so stupid. I had done exactly what Don had told me never to do, and travelled close to the river edge, where the ice was thin and likely to break first.

When I had drunk some tea I dragged myself up the steep, snowy river bank, then cut some lengths of cottonwood to use to lever the machine out. Returning to the hole, I slipped them under the heavy machine and heaved, but it just wouldn't budge. I gave up, eventually, and pushed a few more boughs underneath to ensure that the Tundra wouldn't sink. Then I started the long, painful walk back to camp.

Five hours later I finally made it home. My ankle was swollen to the size of a grapefruit, but I knew I'd got off lightly. I felt terribly guilty about Don's snow machine, and set up the satellite phone to call him. Waves of shame washed over me as I explained what had happened.

'We'll come out tonight when it's all frozen up,' Don said calmly.

'God, I'm so sorry about all this,' I groaned, 'and about the Tundra—I hope it'll be OK.'

'Ain't nothin' more important than living,' he said. 'I don't give a shit about that machine as long as you're in one piece.'

It was snowing when Chris arrived. I jumped onto the back of the machine and we drove down to the slough where Don was waiting. Not once did either of them make me feel guilty, and I realised this was because their priorities were right. Life came before anything else. We managed to get the machine out and loaded onto a sled behind one of their machines.

'You came close to buying the farm there,' Don said.

'I know.' I dropped my head, feeling ashamed again. 'I really chuffed up.'

'Well you were travelling in exactly the wrong place on the river. You never travel along the sides—that's where the bad ice will be.' He reached into his pocket and brought out a chocolate bar, which he pushed into my hand. 'Now don't beat yourself up about it,' he said. 'You know what?'

'What?' I said sadly.

'We've all done it. And I'll tell you something else, those that have lived to tell the tale have never travelled on the ice hoping for the best since. You've been lucky enough to learn a lesson through experience—now don't you ever forget it.' He shook my hand in his iron grip then turned back to Chris. 'Let's move!' he shouted, and they were off into the snowstorm.

I turned and started hobbling home, knowing that I had miles of shuffling ahead, but I didn't care. Then I heard the sound of a snow machine, and Chris pulled up behind me.

'Hey, I forgot you,' he said. 'Hop on—I'll take you up the portage.'

I climbed on, and we shot off towards the cabin in a whirl of snow.

That night I thought again about Don and his family, wondering what lucky star had led me to them. Today's events had proved once again that friendship was an essential ingredient of survival in the lonely Interior. As well as adding greatly to my whole experience, Don, Chris and Charlie had taught me almost everything I knew. Never again would I ignore my instincts, or forget how utterly small and insignificant I was.

A WEEK OR SO LATER my ankle had healed, and it was time to close up the cabin. I collected the rolls of insulation and plywood that I had stored for the roof, and piled them inside the cabin, knowing that some day Charlie would put on a proper roof. It was early April, and bears were much in evidence again. I knew that my thawing camp was emitting a range of smells that would be a magnet to bears. I had to get some bear boards up, or pretty soon they would come knocking at my door. I also had to get back to the village before it thawed any more, as soon the river would be impossible for travel.

Bear boards are simply lengths of wood with scores of long nails sticking through. They are fixed over the windows and doorways of vacant cabins with the nails pointing outwards, in the hope of deterring curious bears from breaking and entering. If bears ever do manage to get into a cabin, they trash the place. First they eat everything—from packets of sugar to soap—and then they defecate all over the cabin before ripping the place to bits. The sickly smell of a bear is almost impossible to get rid of, and sometimes there's no choice but to abandon the cabin altogether after such a visit.

I nailed the bear boards securely up, then stepped back to look at the place. One thing was certain, there could have been no more final way of saying goodbye to my little log home.

I had decided that a fitting end to my time here would be to spend one last night alone beneath the stars. I snowshoed across the lake and walked on until I reached an area of black spruce trees beneath the mountain. I found a suitable spot where two thin trees grew close together, forming a natural doorway. I half cut one tree at about four feet, then bent it across and tied it to the other before snowshoeing my length back from the doorway to create a floor. I covered the floor with spruce boughs, then set up a ridgepole, which rested on top of the bent tree. Next I attached two purlins, which stretched back from the doorway, and laid sticks all over the frame. Finally I thatched the shelter with spruce boughs, and finished it off with a layer of snow. The result was a snug A-frame shelter.

In front of it I laid a platform of green boughs, and lit a slow-burning fire on top. That night I snuggled into my green shelter and, despite a temperature of −20°F outside, slept only in my bivvy bag. A yellow moon hung low, and as I blew out my candle a gentle wind sighed through the trees and owls hooted mournfully. A great sense of privilege again washed over me.

I woke early the next day to see the spring sunshine streaming across a perfect blue sky. I packed and headed for the slough. When I reached my lake, I walked up to my cabin to say a last goodbye. I stood staring at the honey-coloured logs, thinking that each round told a story. I remembered the months of hard work and the times of fear and hopelessness, and also the moments of utter freedom and joy when I knew that I had discovered the ideal existence for my spirit. There was no denying it: I had built a cabin in the wilderness, the dream had become reality and I had survived.

I drove slowly down my portage, savouring every sight and sound and trying to fix it in my mind for ever. As I went I thought of the well-known lines by Robert Frost:

Two roads diverged in a wood, and I—
I took the one less travelled by,
And that has made all the difference.

IT WAS THE END of April, and I spent my final week in Alaska mooching about from house to house. Playing with the children was less painful now, as I knew I would soon be reunited with my own. It was also good simply to sit in the sun besides Don's smokehouse, watching the birds returning and filling the sky with their calls where so recently there had been frozen silence.

On my last day, when I was all set to leave, Don asked what I was going to do about Fuzzy, who sat with his tongue lolling, ready for orders.

'Can I leave him with you?' I asked.

Don nodded slowly. 'Yeah, he can have Pancho's old box till I get another.' He smiled. 'Fuzzy sure had a great time out there with you. Kinda won his spurs, wouldn't you say?'

'He certainly did.' I gazed down at the little dog sadly, wishing I could take him with me. 'Do you think I could come back and fetch him?'

'Well, sure, you know we'll always be here. And if it all goes pear-shaped, you know you've got a place here too.'

I looked over at the grizzled, kind man, who had taught me more than he would ever know, and felt bereft. I wished the world were smaller.

I called Fuzzy over and he shot across, looking up at me excitedly as if to say, Right, boss, what next? Are we going downriver? I'm ready!

'Not this time, Fuzzy. I'm sorry,' I said. I knelt down and sunk my hands into his blond shaggy coat and said, 'Well, fruitcake, I'm off. You behave and I'll see you soon if luck allows it.'

I stood up slowly, keeping my eyes fixed on his, then took a step back. He jumped up and barked shrilly. Tears pricked and I turned quickly away to load my bags onto the back of Don's pick-up. Leaving Fuzzy felt like a betrayal, after all we had been through together. I felt terrible. And as I drove out of the yard, I could still hear his high-pitched barking.

At the airstrip I met Charlie, who shook my hand. 'Well, you sure made it,' he said. 'You done good!'

We laughed, and I thanked him sincerely for all he had done. I would see Don and the rest of the family for the last time in Anchorage the next morning, as they were all going to a family wedding and would be passing through the airport while I was waiting for the connecting flight.

The plane that had once felt so small now felt immense in comparison to Brad's tiny canvas Cub. It lifted up high over the great brown river, and I looked out over thousands upon thousands of square miles of wilderness, which had looked so alien when I first arrived, but now were familiar.

The next morning I checked in for the flight to New York, then went to find the family beside the airline desks. As I walked towards them I felt I was going to be unable to say goodbye. I hugged Claudette and Jenny, two women who I wished could have been my sisters, then Carol, whose stern exterior concealed a heart of gold. I said goodbye to the children in turn, and with each one the pain welled higher, until last of all I came to Don.

'Good luck,' he said, pressing a piece of river-washed jade into my hand.

I hugged this man who had become a father and friend in that lonely wilderness. Then I turned and walked away fast towards the check-in. I found Chris walking alongside me. He had become like a brother in the past few months, and when we said goodbye I hugged him too.

I closed my eyes as the plane lifted and thought of home, thanking fortune that I had survived. I thought of the huge, silent, wild place that had been my home, and told myself that it was over, over, over.

AT NEW YORK AIRPORT I felt stunned by the sheer hectic chaos of it all, yet far from resenting the large numbers of people swarming around me, I was enthralled. For seven hours I sat on a shiny steel chair in an airport café, smiling at anyone who looked my way. In the bathroom I turned on the tap, smiling at the luxury of hot water without having to cut wood or gather snow. I stared into the mirror and saw that I was still the same, intact, and nothing had been lost except the part of me that believed he knew it all. That residue of certainty from my childish years had gone, but somehow I felt stronger as a result. How lucky I was that the reality of Alaska had held far more than my dreaming mind could ever have predicted.

That night I left America as Juliet drove with the children through the Highlands to Glasgow, where my plane would be landing at 7 a.m. the next day. I sat by the window, replaying image after image of my adventure, and remembering the ups and the downs with equal clarity.

The next morning I lifted the plastic window screen as the sun was rising from the east. Dark clouds were still strewn across a pale, duck-egg-blue sky.

'Good morning, ladies and gentlemen,' said the pilot. 'We are now approaching Scotland. Those on the left of the plane will have a good view of the islands of the Inner Hebrides, particularly Mull, which is below.'

I couldn't believe it—I was coming home at last. I craned my neck to look down on the island, and saw the Ross of Mull lying purple in a sea that was being touched by the pale dawn light.

At Glasgow airport I walked through to the arrivals lounge in a daze, and they were waiting for me. Oscar was standing with his arms round Juliet's leg, watching eagerly for the first sight of me, and in her arms was Luke, chubby and curious and waiting to see this 'daddy' that Oscar kept talking about. They looked excited, happy and just a bit anxious, and like the most beautiful thing I had ever seen. Only as we embraced, and Oscar and Luke clung to me with all their strength, did I know that we were safe again. My days as a loner were over, and I knew I was exactly where I should be.

We got in the car and drove towards the Highlands, passing through the grey Glaswegian commuting traffic, then on through landscape that grew more beautiful and remote. At Oban we boarded the ferry for Mull. We sat in silence, and I held the boys in my arms and buried my nose in their hair, breathing in their warm smell and digesting the fact that I was a father back in his proper place. I looked at Juliet and saw the woman I remembered but also a woman who had grown more confident. She too had come to the end of a long hard test and had pulled through with the same conclusions about how we should live our lives.

The ferry cut a sparkling white trail past Lismore Lighthouse across a fresh blue sea. This was our home now, and I knew that the pain and sacrifice had all been worth while. We would never return to the lives we had before, as we had passed from one way of looking at the world to another and had dropped our artificial career-related goals in favour of other, slower values that would stand us in greater stead than any amount of money or status. Sometimes, just sometimes, it pays to refuse to be rational and to turn our backs on everything that society says we should do. Whether our destiny lies halfway across the world or in the next room, what is certain is that we only have one life and it must belong to us.

I WRITE THESE LAST LINES looking out over a sea loch on the island, from the windows of a hut where I write each morning. Often the wind whistles hard and I see grey, foam-topped waves beat against the shore, reminding me never to forget the simplicity of life. Mull feels gentle and safe by comparison to where I have been, but there is still plenty of wildness to keep my soul alive. One morning I walked out during a gale that touched Force 12 on the Beaufort scale, and came across a stag and his harem sheltering in a stand of birch trees and bracken. Sometimes I pluck up the courage to swim across the loch, and often a seal follows in my wake, popping his head up as if hoping for a conversation. How life has changed: eighteen months ago, all I saw were grey lines of traffic and the hardened faces of frustrated commuters. I was lost and going nowhere, living a half-life.

It is now six months since I came home from Alaska, and I still cannot clearly explain why I went. The reasons are complex, and do not come fast enough for some people, who get impatient when I cannot give quick answers to the question 'Why?' What I am able to talk about more lucidly is what I learned: that, if I forgot how frail and insignificant I was, I would die quickly. Humility helped me to deal with the pain, loneliness, hardship and hunger, as I believed I deserved nothing more. Every animal had a hard time in the winter, so why should I be any different?

My journey was not based on anything rational, which is why I can't fully explain it. My time in the woods was the result of a daydream that gradually became an obsession, until I had no choice but to follow it. What is certain is that I was unhappy before I went into the wilderness, and now I am happy. Sometimes, perhaps, the route to happiness cannot come from our ordered mind or the seemingly sensible world that surrounds us; instead, clues lie hidden deep within our subconscious.

I would not recommend my course of action to every person, but I would always ask: is most of you happy? And if not, how can you change things? I am not sure what will come next or where life will lead us. Life does not reveal itself to us all in one go, and why should it? Better to seek out happiness now than to waste time scrimping and saving for a future that may not exist and can never be tamed.

GUY GRIEVE

Inspiration: *The Call of the Wild* by Jack London
Literary ambition: 'To continue writing until
the day I die.'

RD: The first question we have to ask is, are you still living on Mull?

GG: Yes, we are still happily tucked away on the Hebridean Island of Mull and intend to stay here!

RD: Was it difficult to adjust to family life after being alone for so long?

GG: Thankfully, it went well. It felt good to be back where I belonged. Thoughts of my family had kept me going for many long months. For them, if for no one else, I knew that I had to make it back. I think it's essential to have something in life that is many times more important than oneself. My family gave me hope.

RD: What did your children think of your adventure?

GG: My youngest boy, aged one when I left, was too young to really understand it all. My older boy, however, knew that I was far away. Paradoxically, the sheer oddness of my journey made it easier for him to handle my absence. It was as if I had stepped into one of his bedtime storybooks. He'd heard of bears and ice and great rivers full of fish, and knew that when the winter came his dad would travel about by dog team and live in a house made from trees. Strangely, he would probably have found a more conventional absence tougher to deal with. How, for example, would he have handled being told that I was working as a chartered accountant in Dubai for tax reasons?

RD: Are you still in touch with Don?

GG: I talk regularly with Don and his family on the telephone, and I miss them very much. Don became like a father to me in that silent, merciless place. I miss his two daughters and their wonderful husbands, too. I heard that when I left Don got himself a puppy. What does that tell you?

RD: Have you any plans to visit Alaska with your family?

GG: Yes, but sadly our lack of a trust fund gets in the way! I dream of being able to take my boys on a dog sled and I know that those whom I love in that part of the world would greatly enjoy meeting my family. They would all set about happily teasing me as usual—except this time they would be reinforced by my wife and two very sparky boys!

RD: What happened to Fuzzy?

GG: Fuzzy is back in his dog box overlooking the great silty Yukon. I wanted to take him home with me, but in the end I had to come round to the sad fact that he belonged to Don's daughter and was not my dog.

RD: Do you feel that the experience has changed you a great deal?

GG: One of the first things my wife said to me was that I had not changed. She was relieved that I had not come back as some hardened 'man of the North'. I asked why she felt that I had not altered greatly and she answered, 'Well, you must have always had it in you to do it—you didn't have to become another person to get through.' She has always been much brighter than me, I think!

RD: Now that you are back at home, what is your biggest indulgence?

GG: To sleep as late as possible and make sure my wife cannot escape to do anything useful. Then to cook up the kind of breakfast that would make a doctor faint: pancakes, bacon, eggs, black pudding, toast, fried bread and tomatoes, finished off with black coffee.

RD: What are your plans for the future?

GG: I hope to keep writing and not to forget some advice from Henry Thoreau: 'How vain it is to sit down to write when you have not stood up to live.'

RD: And are there any more adventures planned?

GG: Yes, but that would be telling!

'From the start, even though he drove me nuts, I knew Fuzzy was a dog of character.'

'Somehow it was up. Note the planks hammered up to keep the gables from wobbling about.'

MESSENGER
OF TRUTH

JACQUELINE WINSPEAR

On a cold November afternoon, in London's Fitzroy Square, Georgina Bassington-Hope hesitates before the entrance to one of its elegant buildings. Will the renowned Maisie Dobbs, private investigator, be able to help her to uncover the truth about her brother's apparent suicide?
As if in answer, the door opens and a tall, striking figure steps out into the chilly air.

PROLOGUE

Romney Marsh, Kent, Tuesday, December 30th, 1930
The taxicab slowed down alongside the gates of Camden Abbey, a red-brick former mansion that seemed even more like a refuge as a bitter sleet swept across the grey, forbidding landscape.

'Is this the place, madam?'

'Yes, thank you.'

The driver parked in front of the main entrance and the woman respectfully covered her head with a silk scarf before leaving the car.

'I shan't be long.'

'Right you are, madam.' He watched the woman enter by the main door, which slammed shut behind her.

'Rather you than me, love,' he said to himself as he picked up a newspaper to while away the minutes until the woman returned.

THE SITTING ROOM was warm, with a fire in the grate, red carpet on the stone floor and heavy curtains at the windows to counter draughts. The woman, now seated facing a grille, had been in conversation with the abbess for some forty-five minutes.

'Grief is not an event, my dear, but a passage, a pilgrimage along a path that allows us to reflect upon the past. At times the way is filled with stones underfoot and we feel pained by our memories, yet on other days the shadows reflect our longing and those happinesses shared.'

The woman nodded. 'I just wish there were not this doubt.'

'Uncertainty is sure to follow in such circumstances.'

'But how do I put my mind at rest, Dame Constance?'

'Ah, you have not changed,' observed the abbess. 'Always seeking to *do* rather than to *be*. Do you really seek the counsel of the spirit?'

The woman began to press down her cuticles with the thumbnail of the opposite hand. 'I know I missed just about every one of your tutorials when I was at Girton, but I thought . . .'

'That I could help you find peace?' Dame Constance paused, took a pencil and small notebook from a pocket within the folds of her habit and scribbled on a piece of paper. 'Sometimes help takes the form of directing. And peace is something we find when we have a companion on the journey. Here's someone who will help you. She was at Girton too, though she came later, in 1914, if my memory serves me well.'

She passed the folded note through the grille.

Scotland Yard, London, Wednesday, December 31st, 1930
'So you see, madam, there's very little more I can do in the circumstances, which are pretty cut and dried, as far as we're concerned.'

'Yes, you've made that clear, Detective Inspector Stratton.' The woman sat bolt upright on her chair, brushing back her hair with an air of defiance. For a second she looked at her hands, rubbing an ink stain where her middle finger always pressed against the nib of her fountain pen. 'However, I cannot stop searching because your investigations have drawn nothing. To that end I have decided to enlist the services of a private enquiry agent.'

The policeman rolled his eyes. 'That is your prerogative, of course, though I am sure his findings will mirror our own.'

'It's not a he, it's a she.' The woman smiled. 'A Miss Maisie Dobbs. She's highly recommended.'

Stratton nodded. 'Indeed. I'm familiar with her work. She knows her business. In fact, we have consulted her here at Scotland Yard.'

The woman leaned forward, intrigued. 'Really?'

Stratton inclined his head. 'Miss Dobbs has certain skills, certain . . . methods, that seem to bear fruit.'

'Would it be overstepping the mark if I asked what you know of her background? I know she was at Cambridge—Girton College—a few years after me, and that she was a nurse in the war and was wounded in Flanders.'

Stratton looked at the woman, gauging the wisdom of sharing his knowledge of the private investigator. 'She was born in Lambeth, went to work in service when she was thirteen.'

'In *service?*'

'Don't let that put you off. Her intelligence was discovered by a friend of her employer, a brilliant man, an expert in legal medicine and a psychologist. When she came back from Flanders, she worked for a year in a secure institution, nursing profoundly shell-shocked men. She completed her education at the Department of Legal Medicine in Edinburgh and went to work as assistant to her mentor. She learned her business from the best, if I am to be honest.'

'And she's never married? How old is she, thirty-two, thirty-three?'

'Yes, something like that. And no, she's never married, though I understand her wartime sweetheart was severely wounded.' He tapped the side of his head. 'Up here.'

'I see.' The woman paused, then held out her hand. 'I wish I could say thank you for all that you've done, Inspector. Perhaps Miss Dobbs will be able to shed light where you have seen nothing.'

Stratton stood up, shook hands to bid the woman goodbye and called for a constable to escort her from the building. As soon as the door was closed, while reflecting that they had not even wished each other a cordial Happy New Year, he picked up the telephone receiver and placed a call.

'Yes?'

'You'll be pleased to hear that I've got rid of that bloody woman. She's going to a private investigator.'

'Anyone I should worry about?'

Stratton shook his head. 'Nothing I can't handle. I can keep an eye on her.'

'Her?'

'Yes, *her.*'

Fitzroy Square, London, Wednesday, January 7th, 1931
Snow had begun to fall once again in small, harsh flakes that swirled around the woman as she emerged from Conway Street into Fitzroy Square. She pulled her fur collar up and thought that, even though she did not care for hats, she should have worn one this morning. There were those who would have suggested that she probably wanted to draw attention to herself, what with that thick copper-coloured hair cascading in damp waves across her shoulders. But the truth was that, despite drawing glances wherever she went, on this occasion, she really didn't want to be seen.

She crossed the square, walking with care lest she slip on the slush-covered flagstones, then halted alongside the iron railings that surrounded the winter-barren garden. The enquiry agent Dame Constance had instructed her to see worked from a room in the building she now surveyed. She had been told by the investigator's assistant that she should come to the first-floor office at nine on Monday morning. When she had cancelled the appointment, he had calmly suggested the same time on the following day. And when, at the last minute, she had cancelled the second appointment, he simply moved the time by twenty-four hours. She was intrigued that an accomplished woman would employ a man with such a common dialect.

As she stood, wondering whether today she would have the courage to see Maisie Dobbs, she looked up and saw a woman in the first-floor office, standing by the floor-to-ceiling window looking out, simply contemplating the square. Sweeping a lock of windblown hair from her face, it struck the visitor that this was the person she had come to see: Maisie Dobbs. She wondered if that window was her place to stand and think. Shivering, she pushed her hands deep inside the sleeves of her coat and began to turn away. But then, as if commanded to do so by a force she could feel but not see, she looked up at the window once more. The woman was staring directly at her now, and raising her hand in a manner so compelling that the visitor could not leave, could do nothing but meet the other woman's eyes. And in that moment, as Maisie Dobbs captured her with her gaze, she was filled with confidence; it was as if, in lifting her hand, the figure in the window had promised that, from the first step in her direction, she would be safe. She began to move forward, but faltered again as she looked down at the flagstones. Turning to leave, she was surprised to hear a voice behind her.

'Miss Bassington-Hope?' It was a sharp voice that exuded strength.

'Yes?' Georgina Bassington-Hope turned back and looked up into the eyes of the woman she had just been watching in the window.

'Come.' It was an instruction given in a manner that was neither sharp nor soft, and Georgina found that she was mesmerised as Maisie Dobbs, holding a pale blue cashmere wrap round her shoulders, led her across the threshold and through the door, alongside which a nameplate bore the words MAISIE DOBBS, PSYCHOLOGIST AND INVESTIGATOR. And she instinctively understood that she had been directed well, that she would be given leave to describe the doubt-ridden wilderness in which she had languished since that terrible moment when she knew in her heart—knew before anyone had told her—that the one who was most dear to her was dead.

Chapter One

'Good morning, Miss Bassington-'ope. Come on in out of that cold.' Billy Beale, Maisie Dobbs's assistant, stood by the first-floor office door as Maisie allowed the visitor to ascend the stairs before her.

'Thank you.' Georgina Bassington-Hope glanced at the man and thought his smile to be infectious, his eyes kind.

'I've brewed a fresh pot of tea for us.'

'Thank you, Billy, that will be just the ticket, it's brassy out there today.' Maisie smiled in return at Billy as she directed Georgina into the room.

Three chairs had been set by the gas fire and the tea tray placed on Maisie's desk. As soon as her coat was taken and hung on the hook behind the door, Georgina settled in the middle chair. There was a camaraderie between the investigator and her assistant that intrigued the visitor. The man clearly admired his employer, though it did not appear to be a romantic fondness. But there was a bond, thought Georgina Bassington-Hope, her journalist's eye at work.

She turned her attention to Maisie Dobbs, who was collecting a fresh manila folder and a series of coloured pencils. Her black wavy hair had probably been cut in a bob some time ago but was now in need of a trim. She wore a cream silk blouse with a long, pale blue cashmere cardigan— the same shade as the wrap—a black skirt with kick pleats, and black shoes with a single strap. It was a stylish ensemble, but one that marked the investigator as someone who set more store by comfort than fashion.

Rejoining Georgina, Maisie said nothing until her assistant had seen that the guest had tea and was comfortable.

'I'm much obliged to you for agreeing to see me, Miss Dobbs. Thank you,' Georgina said. 'I have come to you in the hope that you might be able to help me . . . You have been recommended by someone we both know from our Girton days.'

'Might that person have been Dame Constance?' Maisie smiled.

'However did you know?' Georgina seemed puzzled.

'We rekindled our acquaintance last year. I always looked forward to her lessons at university, and especially that we had to go to the abbey to see her.' Maisie allowed a few seconds to pass. 'So why did you visit Dame Constance?'

'I must say, I would have had teeth pulled rather than attend her tutorials. However, I went to see her when . . .' She swallowed. 'My brother, Nick, died several weeks ago, in early December. A verdict of accidental death has been recorded.' She stared into the gas fire. 'He is—was—an artist. He was working late on the night before the opening of his first major exhibition in years and, it appears, fell from scaffolding that had been set up at the gallery to allow him to construct his main piece.' She paused. 'I needed to speak to someone who might help me navigate this . . . this . . . doubt. And Dame Constance suggested I come to you. I have discovered that there was little to be gained from badgering the police, and the man who was called when my brother was found seemed only too pleased when I told him I was going to talk to an enquiry agent.'

'And who was the policeman?' The investigator held her pen ready to note the name.

'Detective Inspector Richard Stratton, of Scotland Yard.'

'Stratton was pleased to learn that you were coming to see me?'

Georgina was intrigued by the faint blush revealed when Maisie looked up from her notes, her midnight-blue eyes darkening. 'Well, yes. I think he was heartily sick of me peppering him with questions.'

Maisie made another note before continuing. 'Miss Bassington-Hope, perhaps you could tell me how you wish me to assist you—how can I help?'

Georgina sat up straight in the chair, and ran her fingers back through thick, damp hair that was springing into even richer copper curls as the room became warmer. 'I believe Nick was murdered. I believe someone pushed him, or caused him to fall deliberately.' She looked directly at Maisie. 'My brother was a passionate artist. His work drew both accolades and disgust. I want you to find out how he died.'

Maisie nodded, frowning. 'I take it there is a police report?'

'As I said, Detective Inspector Stratton was called. It was early and he was the detective on duty, apparently,' said Georgina. 'By the time he'd arrived, the pathologist had made a preliminary inspection . . .'

'But I am sure Detective Inspector Stratton conducted a thorough investigation. How do you think I might assist you?'

Georgina tensed. 'I thought you might say that. Devil's advocate, aren't you?' She leaned back, showing some of the nerve for which she was renowned. Georgina Bassington-Hope, intrepid journalist, became infamous at twenty-two when she disguised herself as a man to gain a closer view than any other reporter of the lines of battle in Flanders. She brought back stories that were not of generals and battles, but of the men, their bravery, their fears, and the truth of life as a soldier at war. Her dispatches were published the world over and, like her brother's masterpieces, her work drew as much criticism as admiration.

'I know what I want, Miss Dobbs. I want the truth and will find it myself if I have to. However, I also believe in using the very best tools when they are available—price notwithstanding. And I believe you are the best.' She paused to reach for her cup of tea. 'And I believe—because I have done my homework—that you ask questions that others fail to ask and see things that others are blind to.' Georgina Bassington-Hope looked back at Billy briefly, then turned to Maisie again, her eyes unwavering. 'Nick's work was extraordinary; his views were well known, though his art was his voice. I want you to find out who killed him, Miss Dobbs—and bring them to justice.'

Maisie closed her eyes, pausing for a few seconds before speaking again. 'You were very close, it seems.'

Georgina's eyes sparkled. 'Oh, yes, we were close, Miss Dobbs. Nick was my twin. He worked with colour, texture and light, I work with words.'

Maisie nodded, then stood up, moved away from the fire and walked across to the window. Billy smiled at their guest and pointed to the teapot, indicating that perhaps she might like another cup. He had been taking notes throughout the conversation.

Finally, Maisie turned from the window.

'Tell me, Miss Bassington-Hope: why were you so reluctant to keep your appointments? You cancelled twice.'

Georgina shook her head. 'I have no proof. I have nothing to go on and I am a person used to dealing with facts. I would be the first to admit that this looks like a classic accident, a careless move by a tired man balancing on a rather precarious ledge.' She paused. 'I have nothing except this.' She pressed her hand to her chest. 'A feeling here, right in my heart, that this "accident" was murder. I believe I knew the very second that my brother died, for I experienced such an ache at what was, according to the pathologist, the time of his death. And I did not know how I might explain such a thing.'

Maisie approached Georgina and gently laid a hand on her shoulder.

'Then you have most definitely come to the right place. In my estimation, that feeling in your heart is the most significant clue and all we need to take on your case.' She looked at Billy and nodded. 'Now then, let us begin. First of all, let me tell you about my terms and the conditions of our contract.'

MAISIE DOBBS had been in business as a psychologist and investigator for almost two years, having previously been apprenticed to her mentor since childhood. Dr Maurice Blanche was not only an expert in legal medicine, but a psychologist and philosopher who had provided a depth of learning that might otherwise have been unavailable to his protégée. Now, with a steady stream of clients, Maisie had cause for optimism. Although the country was in the grip of economic depression, there was still plenty of business for an investigator with a growing reputation.

Once the contract had been signed by both Maisie and Georgina Bassington-Hope, Maisie suggested the trio move to the table by the window to continue the conversation.

Later, after the new client had left, Maisie and Billy would unfurl a length of plain wallpaper across the table, pin the edges to the wood, and begin to formulate a case map of known facts, thoughts, feelings, hunches and questions. As the work went on, more information would be added, with the mosaic eventually yielding up previously unseen connections.

Maisie had already jotted some initial questions on an index card, though she knew that many more would come to mind with each response from her new client. 'Miss Bassington-Hope—'

'*Georgina*, please. I would rather dispense with the formalities.' The woman looked from Maisie to Billy.

Billy glanced at Maisie in a way that made his discomfort obvious.

Maisie smiled. 'Yes, of course, as you wish. And you may call me Maisie.' Both women now looked at Billy, who blushed.

'Well, if you don't mind, I think I'll stick to your proper name.' He looked at Maisie for guidance, then turned to the woman again. 'But you can call me Billy if you like, Miss Bassington-'ope.'

Georgina smiled, understanding the predicament she had placed them in. 'All right, then, Billy—and how about just "Miss B-H" for me.'

'Right you are. Miss B-H it is.'

Maisie cleared her throat. 'Georgina, first I want you to tell me as much as you know about the circumstances of your brother's death.'

The woman nodded. 'Nick had been preparing for this exhibition for over a year. His work was becoming very well known, especially in America—there are still a fair few millionaires buying up everything from poor old Europe, it seems. Anyway, Stig Svenson of Svenson's Gallery in Albemarle Street—he's more or less Nick's regular dealer—offered him a special exhibition that comprised both earlier and new works. Nick jumped at the chance, especially as he thought the gallery would be the ideal place to unveil a piece he has been working on, one way or another, for years.'

Maisie interjected with a question. 'Why was it perfect for his work? What did the gallery have that made him so excited?'

'Nick needed a certain amount of room for the new pieces.' Georgina held out her arms to help describe the gallery. 'Essentially, there are two huge bay windows at the front with a door in between, so you can clearly see in from the street. Svenson has, as you might imagine, a very modern, Scandinavian idea of how to use space. He's had the latest electric lighting installed, which directs beams in such a way as to create shadows and light to draw buyers in.' She paused. 'At the far end there is one huge blank wall almost two floors high for larger pieces, then on both sides there's a galleried landing. You can go to either side, up stairs to the landings, but there are screens to divide the room in sections so that you never actually see the whole pièce de résistance—if there is one—until the end.'

Maisie tapped her pen against the palm of her left hand. 'Would you describe his "pièce de résistance" for us?'

Georgina shook her head. 'Actually, I can't. No one had seen it in its entirety. He was very secretive about it. That was why he was at the gallery until late—he wanted to construct it himself.' She paused thoughtfully. 'The only thing I know about it is that it was in several pieces. When he died he was working on scaffolding, placing the anchors that would secure the pieces when he brought them in. He had them in storage in London—frankly, I have no idea where.'

'Who would know where? Svenson?'

She shook her head. 'No one can find the key, and no one knows the address. We just knew he had a lockup. He wanted it all to be kept under wraps until the last moment so that it would draw even more attention.'

'I see, and—'

'The trouble is,' Georgina interrupted, 'he had already promised most of the collection—except that main piece—to a collector, sight unseen.'

'Was it a significant offer?'

The woman nodded. 'Tens of thousands of pounds, to my knowledge.'

Maisie's eyes grew large; glancing at Billy, she thought he might pass out.

'For some paintings?'

Georgina Bassington-Hope shrugged. 'It's what people will pay if they think the work will dramatically increase in value. The buyer has already paid a deposit, which Svenson retains until delivery.'

'Who *was* the buyer?'

'A man called Randolph Bradley. He's an American living in Paris, though he also has a home in New York.'

Billy rolled his eyes. 'I think I'll put the kettle on again.' He stood up and left the room, taking the tea tray with him. Maisie understood his annoyance at such amounts of money passing hands in such troubled times. She made small talk, a series of barely consequential questions, until he returned.

'Several pieces? So, was this "pièce" like a jigsaw puzzle, Miss B-H?' Billy set a cup of hot tea in front of Georgina and the customary tin mug in front of Maisie. Maisie was relieved that he had been thinking as he made tea, and not just fuming with resentment.

Georgina nodded. 'Yes, you could say that. Before the war, Nick was studying art in Belgium where he became interested in the triptych form.'

'Triptych?' Maisie and Billy spoke in unison.

'Yes,' continued Georgina. 'A triptych comprises three parts, a central main panel with smaller panels on either side. The stories depicted on the smaller panels give more detail to the scene in the main panel.'

'Bit like the mirror on a dressing table, eh, Miss B-H?'

The woman smiled. 'Yes, that's right—though a stained-glass window in a church might be a better description. Triptychs are often religious in nature, though many are quite gory, with scenes of war.'

'Yes, I've seen some in the museums.' Maisie paused, making a note to come back to Nicholas Bassington-Hope's background. 'So, let's continue with Nick's death—he was at the gallery . . . what happened, as far as the inquest revealed?'

'There was scaffolding against the main wall. All the smaller, less important pieces had been placed, and Nick was working on the main wall. The scaffolding was there so that he could situate the pieces correctly. His friends Alex and Duncan helped.'

'Alex and Duncan?' Maisie glanced at Billy to ensure that he remained attentive. If they both took notes, then nothing would be missed as they studied the cache of information later.

'Alex Courtman and Duncan Haywood. Both artists, Nick's neighbours in Dungeness, where he lived. His other friend, Quentin Trayner, had a twisted ankle and couldn't help. He'd fallen while bringing a boat ashore.' She paused briefly. 'The four of them always helped one another out.'

'And they all lived at Dungeness—in Kent? It's a bit bleak and isolated, isn't it?'

'There's quite an artists' haven there, you know. The local railway sold off some carriages for ten pounds apiece, and a few artists bought them to set up as cottages and studios on the beach.' Georgina paused and her voice cracked, just slightly. 'I called it "the place where lost souls were beached".'

'What do you mean?' asked Maisie.

Georgina leaned forward. 'Nick, Quentin, Duncan and Alex forged a strong friendship at the Slade. And they had all seen service in France. Nick was wounded at the Somme and was sent to work in propaganda after he'd healed. Alex worked there too. Then Nick was sent back over to Flanders as a war artist.' She shook her head. 'It changed him for ever, that's why he had to get away after the war, to America. He said he needed space around him.'

Maisie nodded and flicked back through her notes. 'Look, Miss— Georgina—I suggest we complete our notes on the actual events of your brother's death today, then let us make another appointment to talk about his history. That will give you time to gather other items that might be of interest to us—journals, sketchbooks, letters, that sort of thing.'

'All right.'

'So . . .' Maisie stood up and walked to the other side of the table to look out at the snow-covered square. 'Your brother, Nick, was working late, preparing the gallery's main wall to hang his art. At what time did he arrive to do this work? Who else was with him? And what time, according to the pathologist, did he die—and how?'

Georgina sipped her tea, set her cup down again. 'He had been there since dawn, hanging the pieces. They had set up the scaffolding later in the day, according to Duncan and Alex, who said he told them to return to my flat around half past eight—it wasn't unusual for Nick to bring friends to stay at my flat. My home is a convenient London bolt hole.' She took another sip of tea, and went on, 'The gallery caretaker, Arthur Levitt, said that he told Nick around nine that he was ready to go home. Nick replied that he would lock up.'

There was silence, a hiatus that Maisie allowed to linger in the air.

'Detective Richard Stratton from Scotland Yard was on my doorstep at eight the following morning, with the news. He was on duty when the alarm was raised by Mr Levitt when he came in and found Nick . . .'

Maisie spoke softly. 'Can you tell me how he described finding your brother?'

'On the floor below the scaffolding. Part of the rail was broken and it looked as if Nick had leaned back a bit too far while checking the position of some anchors. His neck had been broken and it is thought that he died instantly when he hit the stone floor, probably around ten-ish, according to the pathologist.' She shook her head. 'If he hadn't been there alone . . .'

'Georgina, let's summon a taxicab to take you home.' Maisie placed a hand on her shoulder. 'We'll speak again tomorrow—and perhaps we should meet at the gallery. Would ten be convenient?'

Georgina nodded. Billy stood up and pulled on his overcoat before making his way out to hail a taxicab.

As Maisie helped Georgina into her coat she said, 'Everything you've described points to an accident. However, when we meet tomorrow, I would like to know if you are aware of anyone who might harbour an intensity of feeling about your brother, or his work, which might have led to a desire to see him dead.'

'Yes, I've been thinking about that, I—'

'Good. Now then. One final question today—may I have details of your family? I will need to meet them.'

'Of course, though they do not share my feelings and would be horrified if they knew I had come to an enquiry agent.' She buttoned her coat. 'My parents live on an impossibly large estate just outside Tenterden in Kent. Noelle—"Nolly"—my older sister, lives with them. She's forty now, lost her husband in the war. She's a Justice of the Peace at the local magistrates' courts, sits on all sorts of local committees. And she heartily disapproves of me. My brother Harry is the baby, the child who came along when everyone least expected it, according to Emsy—that's Emma, my mother. Harry is twenty-nine now and a musician. Much to Nolly's dismay he plays the trumpet in dark places where people have fun and enjoy themselves.'

Billy came into the room, a coating of fresh snowflakes across his shoulders. 'Taxicab's outside, Miss B-H.'

'Thank you, B . . . Mr Beale.' Georgina Bassington-Hope shook hands with Billy, then addressed Maisie. 'See you at ten tomorrow morning at Svenson's Gallery in Albemarle Street.'

Maisie nodded. 'Georgina, forgive me—one last question. You were obviously close to your brother, but were you on good terms when he died?'

The woman's eyes reddened. She nodded. 'We were close, so close that we never had to explain ourselves to each other. We just *knew* about each other, what the other one was thinking, even when we were miles apart.' Georgina Bassington-Hope looked at Billy, who opened the door to accompany her downstairs to the waiting taxicab.

When Billy came back to the office, he was shaking his head. 'Well, what do you think about all that, Miss?'

Maisie was now seated at the paper drawn across the table to form the case map, working with coloured pencils on a growing diagram. 'It's too soon to say, Billy.' She looked up. 'Come and help me pin this paper on to the table.'

Billy studied his employer's preliminary notations as he worked. 'What do we do next?'

Maisie smiled. 'Well, here's what we'll be doing this afternoon—we're off to the Tate to learn a bit more than we know already about art.'

'If you say so, Miss.' Billy patted the case map as he pressed in the last pin, then collected Maisie's coat, which he held out for her.

Chapter Two

Maisie and Billy left Fitzroy Square at half past nine the next morning, each wrapped up in a heavy coat, scarf and hat.

'Nippy, innit, Miss?'

Maisie's eyes watered. 'Yes, and the so-called central-heating system in my flat is not working properly.'

Billy stood aside for Maisie to go through the turnstile at Warren Street tube station before him, then they stepped on to the wooden escalator.

'P'raps the main boiler weren't put in right, what with the builder goin' bust like 'e did.'

Maisie turned around to continue the conversation as the escalator clattered down to the platforms. 'Wouldn't surprise me. Thank heavens there's a gas fire!'

When the train arrived, they clambered aboard the nearest carriage, each taking a seat before Billy continued. 'Doreen's 'ad the fires goin' nonstop. I don't think that coal smoke is good for you at all, but our little Lizzie is a bit poorly now.'

'What's wrong with her?' Maisie had a soft spot for the Beales's youngest child, who was barely two years old.

'Doreen thinks it's a bit of a chill. Poor scrap, even turned 'er nose up at a bit of bread and drippin' for 'er tea yesterday.'

The train slowed to a halt, and as they alighted to change trains for Green Park, Maisie instructed Billy, 'Look, when we're finished here you should go home early to give Doreen a hand. And keep an eye on Lizzie's cold—there are some nasty things going round. Keep the windows closed and put some Friars' Balsam in a bowl of hot water next to her cot.'

'Right you are, Miss.' Billy looked away. Lizzie was the apple of his eye and he was clearly worried about her.

As they walked down Albemarle Street, their talk was of the terrible state of London traffic and how it was easier now to ride by tube. They came to a halt alongside Svenson's Gallery and Maisie looked both ways, anticipating the arrival of Georgina Bassington-Hope. She turned to Billy. 'Look, I want you to find your way to the back of the building—there must be an entrance for deliveries. See if you can locate the caretaker. I want you to get to know him, see if you can get some inside information regarding Svenson, and the night of Nicholas Bassington-Hope's death.' She paused, reaching into her case. 'You might need a few shillings to oil his vocal cords, so take this—' Maisie handed Billy several coins.

Billy nodded. 'Consider it done, Miss. I'll come back to the front 'ere to find you when I'm finished.'

As she watched him continue on down Albemarle Street, Maisie saw him bear the weight of concern for his daughter. She knew the East End of London to be a breeding ground for disease, with its proximity to the filth of the Thames and with houses standing almost on top of one another. She knew, too, that Billy would be worried about the cost of a doctor. Not for the first time, she was thankful she was able to employ him—he might be in a line at the assistance office if the situation were different.

'Good morning, Maisie!' A taxicab screeched to a halt, and Georgina

Bassington-Hope was calling to Maisie from the open window.

'Ah, good morning, Georgina. How was your journey?'

The woman alighted onto the pavement, paid the driver and turned to Maisie. 'You wouldn't think it would take so long to get from Kensington to Albemarle Street. Heaven only knows where the traffic comes from.'

Maisie nodded and held out her gloved hand towards the gallery. 'Let's go inside.'

Georgina placed her hand on Maisie's arm. 'Just a moment—' She bit her lip. 'Look, it would be best if Stig isn't told who you are. It will give him the Viking vapours if he thinks I've asked a professional to look into Nick's "accident". We'll let him think you are an interested buyer.'

Maisie nodded. 'All right.'

The two women entered the gallery and were met by Svenson. He was impeccably turned out in a blue blazer and grey trousers. He ran his fingers through his silver-blond hair as he walked towards them. 'Georgie, darling, how are you bearing up?' He leaned to kiss Georgina on both cheeks.

'I'm as well as can be expected, Stig.' She turned to Maisie. 'This is an old friend, Miss Maisie Dobbs.'

Svenson leaned towards Maisie, and pressed his lips to her right hand.

'Delighted to meet you, Mr Svenson.' She looked around at the paintings exhibited, chiefly landscapes. 'Your gallery is most impressive.'

'Thank you. Are you a collector, Miss Dobbs?'

Maisie smiled. 'Not a collector, as such, though I have recently moved and have a few bare walls to do something with.'

'Then I am sure I can help you fill them; however, this entire collection was purchased yesterday.'

'The whole collection? Goodness me!'

'Yes, as fast as the old families are selling off their collections, so the American new money is buying them up.'

'Is it usual for one person to buy a whole collection, Mr Svenson?'

'Yes and no.' He smiled at Maisie in a way that suggested he had embarked upon such conversations many times. 'Yes, in that once a collector becomes enthusiastic about a given artist, he or she will look out for more examples of their work, especially if that artist is on the cusp of a wider fame.' Svenson turned to Georgina. 'Such as our dear Nicholas, Georgie.' He brought his attention back to Maisie. 'However, there are also complete collections from certain families that are of great interest when they come onto the market—such as the Guthrie collection here.'

'What makes this one valuable?' Maisie was genuinely interested.

'In this case'—he swept his hand around all the paintings in the gallery—'it is not only the name of the collector, but the interesting blend of pieces. Lady Alicia and her late husband, Sir John Guthrie, never had children and both inherited substantial collections. Lady Alicia's solicitors have persuaded her to sell to support their Yorkshire property.'

'Is Nick's work safely in storage now?' Georgina changed the subject.

Svenson nodded. 'Yes, indeed, although not for long. A buyer—another American—wants to view and purchase other works not previously exhibited. He's even interested in sketches and partials, and is very keen.'

'Does he think he's getting a chance to purchase the triptych?'

'Ah, a thorny subject, especially as we don't know the whereabouts of that main piece. I also think our friend Mr Bradley should have first refusal.'

Georgina nodded. 'Let me discuss it with the family this weekend. I think they may be interested, though I do not wish to include the triptych.'

'Georgie, I must advise you—'

'No, Stig. No triptych. When we find it, I will decide what to do with it.'

Maisie spoke up, asking a timely question to diffuse the situation. 'Mr Svenson, how many pieces were there in Nick's exhibition, all told?'

'Counting the sketches and fragments there were twenty pieces.'

'And all in the same style?' Maisie wondered whether she was using the correct terminology.

'Oh, no, that was the interesting thing about this exhibit. It comprised works from all stages of Nick's life as an artist and demonstrated the arc of his artistic gift.'

'I see. Of course, I know about Nick's paintings from Georgina's descriptions, but have never seen any exhibited.' She turned to Georgina. 'I do hope this is not too difficult for you, dear.'

Georgina smiled, understanding that Maisie had spoken with such intimacy so that Svenson would not doubt the authenticity of their friendship. She replied in the same vein. 'Oh, no. In fact, it's rather lovely, talking about Nick's work when all I have thought about is that terrible accident.'

'So, Mr Svenson,' Maisie continued. 'I'd love to hear more about the work that was on display before the accident.'

'Yes, of course.' He directed his full attention to Maisie. 'First there was his interest in those artists from the Low Countries whom he studied in

Belgium. What is fascinating is that it was not the technique that interested him as much as the crafting of stories told in a painting.'

'Did he employ the triptych form even then?'

'No, that came later. What he did was to paint fragments of stories on one canvas, so that he achieved a rather avant-garde effect. That phase caused a stir when first exhibited.'

'Interesting . . .'

'Then, sadly, the war intervened and—as you know—Nick enlisted and was sent to France. I still believe it was his good fortune to have sustained an injury serious enough to bring him home. However, I was rather upset when I heard that he had accepted the work of war artist at the front. Mind you, it was an offer that was probably not up for discussion.'

'No . . .' Maisie said only enough to keep Svenson talking.

'That, of course, was when he grew up, when he became not just a man, but—I am sad to say—an old man.' He sighed, as if genuinely pained. 'But his work at that time proved to be more than a record. It became a reflection of the very soul of war, of death.'

'Did his technique change? I have not seen those works, so I am trying to imagine them.' Maisie was aware of Georgina watching her.

'There were elements of the old work, images superimposed, death a shadow in the background. Nick's work needed no explanation. You could feel his emotions, see what he had seen . . .' Svenson turned to Georgina and placed a hand on her shoulder. 'Just as Georgina recreated what she saw with her words, so Nick could do the same with colour and texture.'

'What came next, from your perspective?' Maisie asked.

'As you know, Nick left the country almost as soon as he received his demobilisation papers. America was, frankly, the obvious place for him.'

'Why do you say that?'

'The sheer enormity of the place. The space.' Svenson held out his arms to emphasise an expanse he could not describe. 'And the possibilities.'

'Possibilities?'

'Yes, his techniques became so influenced by the geography of the country. Look at his sketches, and you will see the bold landscapes, the use of muted and vivid colours blended to achieve a quality of light. He went alone to canyons, to valleys, across prairies. And that's where he began to experiment with the mural, an extension of his interest in the triptych form.'

'And all these different styles'—once again, Maisie hoped she had chosen the correct term—'were on display here when he died?'

'Yes, that's right.'

'Would you call his work offensive in any way, or controversial?'

Svenson laughed. 'Oh, yes, it was most certainly controversial in the art world, and in the world outside. Nick drew the onlooker into his world with his paintings. He could lull you by a landscape, then challenge you with a man screaming his way into death, impaled on the bayonet. He confused people, he threatened.' He shrugged, his hands upturned.

Maisie looked at her watch. 'Oh, goodness, we should be getting on, shouldn't we, Georgina? But I would love to look at the upper galleries.'

'Please, be my guest.' Svenson gave a short bow then turned to Georgina. 'Georgie, a moment of your time, perhaps?'

Maisie made her way to the galleried landing, to the wall where Nicholas Bassington-Hope was to have exhibited his masterpiece. She leaned forward, squinting to see where anchors had been placed in the plasterwork, anchors that had now been removed. Fresh repairs were visible, and Maisie wondered whether the damage had been due to the scaffolding, which must have dented the wall as it collapsed when the artist fell—if he fell. How high might the scaffolding have been, and which level had Nick Bassington-Hope been working from? The wall must be some twenty-five feet high, not a height that would necessarily cause a life to be lost as a result of a fall. *And if someone had pushed . . .*

'Oi, Miss!'

Maisie looked around. She could hear Billy, but could not see him. 'Where are you?' She kept her voice low.

'Over 'ere.'

Maisie walked towards a painting at the far end of the landing. Much to her surprise, the painting moved. Billy Beale poked his head round what was, in fact, a door. 'Come and 'ave a dekko at this 'ere trick door, Miss.'

Maisie followed Billy, stepping as quietly as she could. 'What is this?'

'I've been down there talking to the caretaker, man by the name of Arthur Levitt. Nice enough bloke. Anyway, I found a staircase, came up it and then along this 'ere corridor. They must use this for bringing up the art from where it's delivered. There's one on the other side, too.' He crooked his finger again, closing the door that led on to the balcony. 'Look through 'ere.'

Maisie leaned forward to the point in the door indicated by Billy. 'Oh!' She stepped back. 'You can see most of the gallery from here—as well as having access to the balcony that extends along three sides of the room.'

'Do you reckon it's impor—' Billy stopped speaking when raised voices were heard coming from below.

'I told you, Stig, you were to deal with me only. My sister Nolly has no business poking her nose into this. She knows nothing about art.'

'But she does have a right, after all, as joint executor—'

'I'll speak to Nolly today. In the meantime, I will not allow the piece to be sold with the rest of the collection. Absolutely not. And if I even think of selling the remaining sketches and incompletes, I will let you know. You can keep your rich buyers hanging on for a day or two if they're that interested.'

'But—'

'That is final, Stig. Now, I had better find my friend.'

A door below slammed.

Maisie leaned towards Billy and whispered, 'Right. I want you to pursue your usual lines of enquiry with your newspaper friends in Fleet Street. I'll see you back at the office around three.'

THE TWO WOMEN departed the gallery, Svenson cordially thanking them for visiting, though perhaps not with the theatrical flourish of his greeting.

'Let's walk along the street here—I have several requests to make, in order to commence with my investigation.'

'Of course.' Georgina fell into step with Maisie.

'First of all, I want to meet your family, so please arrange for us to visit, using the pretext of our both being at Girton.'

'All right.'

'I would like to see where Nicholas lived in Dungeness,' Maisie continued. 'Perhaps you would be so kind as to furnish me with keys and his address. And I will need financial records of all previous purchases of your brother's paintings. I want to know who was collecting his work.'

'Of course.'

'I want to see his friends, the men he was closest to. Was he courting, do you know?'

Georgina shook her head, and gave a half laugh. 'Let's just say that Nick was better with his finances than with his romantic life.'

'I see.' Maisie knew from experience that the more personal aspects of a person's life were seldom understood by immediate family.

The women stopped when they reached Piccadilly, where each would go their separate way. 'Oh, and one last question for you.'

'Yes?' Georgina turned to face Maisie.

'When a person close to the victim suspects foul play, they usually have a suspect or two in mind. Would that be true of you, Georgina?'

She blushed. 'I'm afraid it isn't. As I told you yesterday, it was just that feeling here.' She touched her chest. 'That's all I can say.'

Maisie nodded, then smiled. 'I'd like to go down to Dungeness tomorrow, so perhaps you can let me have keys at your earliest convenience. Then perhaps we can meet your parents in Tenterden on Saturday?'

'Of—of course.' Georgina paused, somewhat flustered. She reached into her handbag and took out an envelope. 'This is a photograph of Nick, taken in the summer at Bassington Place, my parents' estate.'

Maisie took the envelope and removed the photograph halfway, studying the man whom the lens had caught leaning in an easy manner against a tractor. Using the size of the tractor as a guide, Maisie thought he must have been about six feet in height, with hair that was a barely controlled mop of curls. He wore wide trousers, a collarless shirt with rolled-up sleeves and an unbuttoned waistcoat. His smile was expansive.

She placed the photograph in her bag and nodded to Georgina. 'Good. Now then, I must be on my way. Please telephone me as soon as you can so that we can confirm arrangements.' Maisie held out her hand, which Georgina took in a manner that suggested she was regaining some of the resolve that had propelled her somewhat infamous reputation.

Chapter Three

Having already nurtured contacts among the newspapermen who gathered in Fleet Street pubs—and many of those men, reporters, compositors and printers alike, were at the bar by midmorning following a night shift—the cost of a pint often proved to be a good investment, as far as Billy was concerned. Following the meeting at Svenson's Gallery, Billy procured information from newspaper reports pertaining to Nicholas Bassington-Hope's death. For her part, Maisie returned to the Tate Gallery to meet the helpful curator with whom she had consulted the previous day. Now they were back at the Fitzroy Square office.

'The obituary didn't say anything that wasn't known to us already. It was all along the lines of "a rare talent lost"—you know, that sort of thing.' Billy stifled a yawn. 'Mind you, there was a line or two in one of the papers about the sibling rivalry. In the *Sketch*, it was. The reporter sayin' that the B-Hs had always competed to see who could get more attention.'

'That doesn't mean that there was anything untoward in the competition, though. That sort of thing often happens, I believe.'

'Too right, Miss. You should see my boys go at it sometimes.'

Maisie smiled and was about to speak again, when Billy continued. 'Now, Brian Hickmott, one of the reporters what I know, did mention the younger brother, 'arry.' Billy read through his notes. 'The boy might be able to carry a tune with that trumpet of 'is, but 'e 'as a reputation for carryin' on with all sorts of people—you know, girls on the game. And 'e keeps the villains entertained while they get up to no good. The press 'ad their eyes on 'im when the police raided a club one night.'

Maisie was thoughtful. 'Since Miss B-H first mentioned him, I have had a sense that all was not well with the brother. I want to know where he is, who he works for, who he consorts with and, if he's on the edge of the underworld, so to speak, whether he's in any trouble.'

Billy nodded.

Maisie had been staring out at the square, seeing only the closing hours of the dead man's life, rather than the trees, or people walking across the square. She turned to Billy again. 'There is much to gather, Billy. Let's be ready to put our backs into the case again tomorrow.'

He nodded, then asked Maisie whether her second visit to the Tate had been fruitful.

'Yes, I think it was. I wanted to find out more about the artist as a person. What character traits define someone who takes on that kind of work—'

'Work?' Billy was frowning. 'I can't say as I would call dabbling around with brushes and paints *work*.'

Maisie leaned back against the table and regarded Billy for what must have felt like an age to him, though it was only seconds. 'I think you had better get what's gnawing at you off your chest, because if there is one thing we cannot afford in our work, it's jumping to conclusions about the moral worth of our clients. We must accept who they are and get on with it, putting our personal feelings and beliefs aside.'

Billy's lips formed a tight line. He said nothing for some time, then blurted out his words. 'It was when that man yesterday, you know, 'im at the Tate, was tellin' us about that bloke who spent almost 'alf a million—'alf a bleedin' million—on a picture last year. What was 'is name? Duveen or somethin'? There's men out of work and children wantin' for a good meal—' He bit his lip. 'It makes me seethe, it does.'

Maisie nodded. 'Point taken, Billy. And it's a good one.' She paused, allowing her agreement to soften her assistant's temper. 'But there is something to remember, when this sort of thing comes up and makes you angry: that in our work we come across injustice. And sometimes we can put right an injustice against someone who stands accused. To accomplish this, we have to face aspects of life that are not always palatable.'

'What you're sayin' is, I've just got to swallow it and get on wiv me job.'

Maisie nodded, then looked at her watch. 'Time to go home to your family.'

Billy gathered his coat and cap, and left the office with a 'Thanks, Miss'.

SOME THREE HOURS LATER, having seen two more clients, one man and one woman seeking not her skill as an investigator but her psychologist's compassion and guidance, Maisie made her way home. Home, to the new flat that was quiet and cold, and that did not have the comforts to which she had become accustomed while living at the Belgravia residence of Lord Julian Compton and his wife, Lady Rowan Compton. Lady Rowan had been her employer and the sponsor of her education, and now, in her senior years, she was something of an ally. These days, however, she spent more and more time at her estate in Kent rather than Belgravia.

Maisie's flat was in Pimlico, which, despite the proximity of neighbouring Belgravia, was considered less than salubrious. However, for Maisie, who was careful with her money and had squirrelled away savings for years, the property was affordable, which was the main consideration.

She had travelled by underground railway earlier in the day, instead of driving her MG, so she returned the same way this evening. The cold and thick yellow smog conspired to nip at her ears, gloved fingers and even her toes, so she pulled her hat down even lower, navigating her way from the station to the new block of flats by following the flagstones underfoot.

The four-storey building housed some sixteen flats. Each end of the building was curved to reflect a fascination with ocean travel fashionable in the 1920s. Enclosed service stairwells to both the right and left of the building were made brighter by porthole windows, and in the centre, a column of glass revealed an inner spiral staircase for use by residents and guests.

Turning her key in the lock, Maisie entered the ground-floor flat. It was deceptively capacious. A corridor gave way to a drawing room with plenty of space for a three-piece suite and, at the far end, a dining table and chairs—if, of course, Maisie had owned a three-piece suite and dining table with chairs. Instead, an old Persian carpet half-covered the parquet floor, and two Queen Anne chairs with faded chintz covers were positioned in front of a gas fire. There were two bedrooms to the left of the hallway, one larger than the other and separated by a bathroom. Only one bedroom had a bed but, fortunately, the flat was already equipped with some new Venetian blinds.

Maisie sighed as she felt the radiator in the corridor, then made her way to the living room without taking off her coat. She took a matchbox from the mantelpiece and lit the gas fire, then moved to the windows and pulled down the blinds.

The compact kitchen, which was situated to the left of the area that would one day accommodate the dining table and chairs, was already fitted with a brand-new Main stove. The deep white enamel sink had one cupboard underneath and Maisie opened it, took out another box of matches and lit the gas ring under a tin kettle. As the heat filtered upwards from the kettle, she held her hands open to the warmth for comfort.

'Blast, it's cold in here!' Though she could rise above many deprivations, as she had in France during the war, Maisie found the cold hard to ignore. Even as she set about making tea, she would not take off her coat until after she had sipped the first cup. Reaching into the cabinet again, she pulled out a tin of oxtail soup, which she poured into a saucepan. Admonishing herself for not going to the grocer's, she gave thanks for a half-loaf of bread and wedge of cheddar cheese.

Later, with the drawing room warmer and a hearty supper inside her, Maisie sat back to read before going to bed. She picked up *A Portrait of the Artist as a Young Man*, a book borrowed from the lending library. She flipped open the cover, pulled her cardigan around her and began to read. Distracted, she only read for a page or two before setting the book down and leaning back to gaze at the white-hot gas jets. Amid the activity of the day, she had neglected to write to Andrew Dene, the man she had been walking out with for more than six months. She knew full well that she had failed to write because she was bothered—by what she should do next.

Dene was an orthopaedic surgeon at All Saints Convalescent Hospital in Hastings. He was a good person, full of humour and energy, and she knew he wanted to marry her, though he had not proposed. There were those—including her father and Lady Rowan—who thought that, perhaps, her heart still ached for that first love, for Simon Lynch, who lived through each day in a comalike shell of existence, the result of wounds sustained in the war. But Maisie's independence was gained early, more by default than design, and as time went on, like many women of her generation, her position, her quest for financial security and professional standing, were paramount. Since the war, her work had been her rock, giving structure to life. To marry now would be to relinquish that work for a life in the home.

It was clear to her that she must call a halt to the relationship, allow Dene to meet another. She knew that he would ultimately want more than she might ever be willing—or able—to give.

Maisie and Billy arrived at the office at exactly the same time the following morning.

'Mornin', Miss. All right?'

Pulling her scarf down to her chin so that she could be heard, Maisie stamped her feet on the front step, put the key in the lock and pushed open the door. 'Yes, thank you, Billy. How's Lizzie?'

Billy closed the door behind him and replied as they made their way upstairs, 'Still not well, Miss. Runnin' a temperature. Doreen bought a bit of brisket yesterday, put it in a soup to go round everybody, and Lizzie wouldn't even take some of the broth.'

'"Go round everybody"?' Maisie hung her coat on the hook behind the door, as did Billy. 'You make it sound like a tribe!'

'Aw, it's not any more than anyone has to put up with these days.'

Maisie stood in front of Billy's desk as he placed his notebook on the polished oak surface and reached into his inside jacket pocket for a pencil.

'Look, I know it's not my business, but are you stretched a bit?'

Billy would not sit down until Maisie had gone to her desk and taken a seat. He shook his head, then explained, 'Doreen and me always thought we were lucky, you know, with a two-up, two-down for just the five of us. The nippers've got a bedroom, we've got a bedroom, and, with cold runnin' water, we don't have to walk down to the pump.' He reached for the tray, ready to make a pot of tea. 'Doin' well, I am, thanks to you, so we've even been able to afford a few extras—a bit of beef every now and again, a toy each for the kids at Christmas . . .'

'What's happened?'

'A few months ago, my brother-in-law—that's Doreen's sister Ada's husband, he's a carpenter—lost 'is job. They 'ad to move out because there weren't money for the rent and they were feedin' their boy and girl on bread and Oxo water—and there's another one on the way, y'know. So, Jim reckoned there'd be work in London, and they turned up wantin' somewhere to live. Now they're sleepin' in one bedroom, the five of us are in the other, and it's like sardines, it is. Jim still 'asn't got work and, to tell you the truth, Miss, it's a stretch, puttin' food on the table for nine people every day. Not that Jim's idle, no, 'e's walkin' round all day tryin' to get work.'

'Is there anything I can do?'

'No, Miss, I'm managing, it's just tight, that's all. It'll be better when Jim gets on 'is feet.' He paused. 'Poor man fought for 'is country, and now look at what 'e's bein' treated like—it's not good enough, Miss.'

'No . . . Billy, have you been in touch with the nurse, to see Lizzie?' asked Maisie. It was common for a nurse, instead of a doctor, to be summoned to see the sick, simply because of the greater cost of a physician.

'No. Fool's choice, really, Miss. We thought she'd be over it by now.'

Maisie checked her watch. 'I'm driving down to Dungeness later this morning. I'll detour and go to the house first to have a look at Lizzie.'

Billy shook his head. 'Nah, Miss, don't you go out of your way—we'll get the nurse round later if Lizzie's not any better by this evening.'

Maisie took several pencils of different colours from a jar on the table. She knew Billy's pride and did not want to push. 'All right, but the offer's there, you know. And if things get any more troublesome . . .'

Billy simply nodded, so Maisie moved on to the Bassington-Hope case. She nodded towards the table by the window where the case map was laid out. 'Come on.'

Billy slumped into the chair alongside Maisie, who was already studying the map.

'Right then, let's look at where we are. It's your job to find out more about the gallery, Nick B-H and that mysterious lockup of his. See what you can sniff out. And also see if you can uncover more about the younger brother.' She paused. 'In the meantime, I'll be having a quick cup of coffee with Detective Inspector Stratton this morning before I set off—I'm curious to know why he was so keen to support Georgina's decision to seek my help.' Reaching out onto the case map, she linked several notes, creating circles which she joined with arrows. 'On Monday I'll be doing some background research on Miss B-H and her family, by which time I'll have some impressions from my visit to the house.' Maisie consulted her watch. 'The morning post should be here soon and I am expecting to hear from her.'

Billy nodded. 'And when're you goin' to see the family?'

'I am to join her at Bassington Place on Saturday.'

The doorbell rang. Billy left the room, returning to the office less than three minutes later. 'Messenger turned up at the same time as the postman, so you've got one thick envelope'—he passed a bulky package to Maisie—'and a few letters from the postie.'

Maisie placed the letters on the table and reached for an opener to slit the seal securing the envelope delivered by messenger. As she pulled out the letter, a second envelope fell onto the table along with a key.

'Hmmm, looks like I will definitely be going alone to Dungeness, much as I suspected. Interesting . . .' Maisie allowed her words to fade as she began to read the accompanying letter aloud.

Dear Miss Dobbs,

I must beg your pardon for the swift communiqué. I am attending a banquet this evening and have much to do. The attached map and directions will see you safely to Nick's carriage-cum-cottage in Dungeness. Should you encounter a problem with the key or lock, Mr Amos White, a fisherman, lives in the old cottage to the right of Nick's carriage as you are facing it, and I am sure he will help. Duncan and Quentin returned to Dungeness this morning, so do look out for them. I believe they will only be there for a day or so.

I will meet you outside Tenterden station at three o'clock on Saturday afternoon, as we agreed. It's best that we meet there and then go together to the house.

You will also find enclosed an invitation to a party at my flat on Sunday evening. It's just a few friends. I thought it might give you a chance to meet some of Nick's pals. Do come.

'Gosh . . .' Maisie put down the letter. 'An invitation to a party at Georgina B-H's flat on Sunday evening.'

'That'll be nice, Miss.'

Maisie shook her head. 'I don't know how nice it will be, but I will most certainly go.'

'Take Dr Dene along—you know, make an evenin' of it.'

Maisie reddened. 'No, just me, Billy. It's business.'

Billy regarded her carefully, his attention drawn to the slight edge in her voice. Though they would never discuss Maisie's private life, Billy could see it was quite clear that Andrew Dene's intentions were towards marriage, whereas Maisie's responses had become generally lukewarm. Now she was going to a party alone, which wasn't something that a woman on the cusp of an engagement might do, work or no work.

THE CAFÉ in Oxford Street where Maisie was to meet Richard Stratton was a rather down-at-heel establishment. She had already packed her case for the journey to Dungeness, and it was in the car. She had decided to make her way to her father's cottage in Chelstone for the evening, then visit Andrew Dene in Hastings on Saturday morning. It wouldn't take long to drive from Hastings to Tenterden in the afternoon.

The detective was waiting at a table by the window and had just sat down. Having removed his hat and coat, he was smoothing back his dark hair, which was peppered with grey at the temples. He wore dark grey gabardine trousers, with a black waistcoat, grey tweed jacket, white shirt and black tie. Though he was not a young man—Maisie had thought him to be about thirty-eight or forty—an olive complexion and dark eyes meant that he was often the subject of a second glance from strangers.

Stratton had already bought two cups of strong tea and a plate of toast and jam.

'You could stand a spoon up in that tea.' Maisie sat down as Stratton pulled out a chair for her, and smiled. Though they had crossed words on several occasions, there was a mutual respect that had led Maisie to be called to Scotland Yard to consult on cases where her particular skill and insight was thought to be of use in the investigations.

'Keeps you going on a day like this, though. It's been very chilly this past week, hasn't it?'

Their eyes met. Maisie sipped her tea and nodded. 'Gosh, that's better.'

Stratton looked at his watch. 'You wanted to see me, Miss Dobbs?'

'Yes.' She placed the plain white cup in the saucer, then paused as she reached for a slice of toast and jam. 'I wanted to speak to you about the death of Nicholas Bassington-Hope. Of course, I must thank you for supporting his sister's plan to engage my services so that certain doubts might be put to rest; however, I hope that you can tell me more about the event, from your perspective.' Maisie inclined her head, then bit into the toast.

Stratton allowed a few seconds to elapse, then said, 'There was—is—no doubt in my mind that Mr Bassington-Hope fell from the scaffolding he had constructed. It hadn't been put up by a builder or other person used to such a task. It was quite amateurish—in fact, he was asking for trouble.' He sipped from his cup. 'Terrible waste.'

Maisie placed a half-eaten crust on her plate. 'I'm not an expert at this sort of thing, but I would have thought that, being an artist, he would have been used to setting up all sorts of exhibits, and, seeing as he worked on fairly large pieces, of actually getting at the canvas to paint. I mean, the man wasn't a fool, he'd been a soldier, had a certain dexterity—'

Stratton shook his head. 'That artistic temperament—seen it a lot in my time. He was a soldier over thirteen years ago now, so I am dubious about any lingering practicality that might have been drilled into him at the time. And he was fiercely secretive about his work—as you probably know, they can't even find half of it! No, for his own reasons, he wanted to do everything himself, which led to his death.'

'Do you think there might be even the merest scrap of merit in Miss Bassington-Hope's belief that her brother was the victim of a crime?'

Stratton sipped again from his cup. Maisie smiled. *He's playing for time.*

'To tell the truth, I'm only too glad she came to you, otherwise she would be nipping at my heels. That woman is one of those terrier-like people who, once they have something to chew on, do not let go.' Stratton sighed. 'She did not accept that her brother was the victim of his own ineptitude and seemed set to make a nuisance of herself, just as she did in the war.'

'But I thought she did something quite brave in the war in order to obtain background information for her dispatches?'

'Oh, dear Miss Dobbs, I do hope you haven't fallen under the spell of the charismatic Georgie Bassington-Hope. She uses her buoyant charm to get what she wants, even if that is access to dangerous places she has no right to even contemplate entering—and all to write a story.'

Maisie raised an eyebrow. 'To write the truth.'

Stratton shook his head. 'She was a troublemaker, her "stories" undermined the government's decision to—'

'Detective Inspector Stratton, if I am to keep Georgina Bassington-Hope out of your way, I should say you owe me a bit more than a few minutes. I have a few questions for *you*, if you don't mind.'

Stratton looked round at the counter. 'I think they've just brewed up a fresh urn of tea. Another cup?'

Maisie nodded. Stratton picked up the cups and walked to the counter. She checked her watch, noting that if she left London by half past eleven, she could feasibly be in Dungeness by half past two.

'This is a bit better.' He set two cups of tea on the table.

'Thank you.' Maisie reached for her cup. 'Now then, I want you to tell me anything you can about Mr Bassington-Hope's death.'

'I anticipated that you wanted to see me regarding this case.' He reached into the large inner pocket of his mackintosh and pulled out an envelope from which he removed several sheets of paper. 'You can't take this with you, but you can peruse the post-mortem notes.'

Maisie reached for the sheets of paper proffered by Stratton, then took several moments to read them carefully. Determined not to rush, she opened her document case, removed a few cards and set them on the table. She placed the report in front of her and flicked through a few pages again, then reached for a pencil in her case and proceeded to take notes.

'I say, I haven't got all day, you know.'

'Just a moment longer, Detective Inspector.' Maisie completed her notes, then leaned back. 'The broken neck, caused by a fall at an awkward angle. Death almost instantaneous, according to the examiner. Now, how about the bruises to the side of the head and to the upper arm? Is the pathologist sure that these indications of trauma are in keeping with the nature of the fall?'

'Second-guessing the doctor, are you?'

'I should not have to remind you that I was a nurse.'

'The bruises were, as the pathologist concluded, in keeping with the nature of the accident. Miss Dobbs, I would not have closed the case had I any doubt—'

'Wouldn't you?' Maisie did not allow the question to linger, and ensured only that it had been voiced. 'If I seem confrontational, it is only because my brief from my client requires me to ask such questions. Indeed, I do believe I could point out several anomalies.'

'May I?' Stratton reached for the document. 'Now, I'm sure you have more questions, but if I had the time to answer—or saw reason to answer—then

I wouldn't have closed the case.' Stratton returned the report to the envelope. 'I've got to leave now. Busy day as I'm leaving work early today.'

Maisie knotted her scarf and stood up as Stratton pulled out her chair. 'Going away for the weekend, Inspector?'

Stratton shook his head. 'No, just an evening out. A banquet, actually.'

They left the café, shaking hands before they went their separate ways. Maisie felt compelled to turn and look back as she walked towards her motor car, and as she did so, she saw Stratton crossing the road in the direction of a waiting black Invicta. It was at that moment that she noticed another car parked behind Stratton's, and though she could not be sure, she thought that the second motor was the sort used by the Flying Squad. A man wearing a black hat and black overcoat, who had been leaning on the door of the car, threw a cigarette stub on the ground, then walked over to Stratton. They spoke briefly, before shaking hands and climbing into their vehicles.

Reaching her MG, Maisie checked her watch. Yes, she would be in Dungeness before half past two. As she drove—confidently, despite the sleet—she replayed the meeting with Stratton. There were questions to be asked, centred on Stratton's delight that she was working for Georgina Bassington-Hope. Did he really want the woman occupied lest she pen some controversial piece regarding police procedure for a newspaper? Had he reason to continue his investigation into the artist's death without the knowledge of either Maisie or the next of kin?

Maisie used the back of her hand to wipe condensation from the inside of the MG's windscreen while thinking about the meeting between Stratton and the man in the black hat and coat. Of course, collaboration between men with different police responsibilities—one dealing with murder, one with gangs and robberies—should not be suspicious; after all, their paths must cross all the time.

As she left the outskirts of London and crossed the border into Kent, Maisie looked out across the Weald, the wintry white swath of land interspersed with patches of green where sheep and cattle clustered. Despite that calm, Maisie was unsettled, the image of Stratton and the other man giving rise to more questions. Then Georgina and Stratton came to mind. Might they be attending the same function this evening? Together, perhaps? As she changed gears to negotiate a turn, she wondered if there was a plan already in progress, and whether she could be a pawn in the game. But if so, whose pawn might she be?

Chapter Four

Maisie arrived in Dungeness at two o'clock, having made good time. The flat expanse of shingled land, a promontory that reached out into the western limits of the Straits of Dover, seemed to extend from the village of Lydd to the sea. She thought the word 'windswept' must have been invented for Dungeness, positioned at this southernmost point of the Romney Marshes.

She made her way at a low speed along a worn shingle track. After she had crossed the narrow-gauge lines of the Romney, Hythe and Dymchurch railway, she held Georgina's map against the steering wheel and looked down for a second or two as she continued driving. It seemed that most of the old railway-carriage cottages were to the south, so she turned right past the lighthouse and maintained a crawling pace until she reached the former railway carriage that was the home of Nicholas Bassington-Hope.

Maisie parked, pulled her scarf round her, then opened the MG's door, which she had to hang on to, fearing that it would be swept back by the wind. Once she reached the carriage, she fumbled with the key and gained entry after only one false turn in the lock. She pressed all her weight against the door to close it again against the freezing winter weather, then secured it behind her.

'Nothing like the marshes to brittle your bones!' Maisie said aloud, as she pulled back her scarf, removed her hat and looked around.

Without taking off her coat—it was still far too cold—she walked round the room. She found matches next to an oil lamp on the sideboard, and, placing the document case she had brought with her on the table, she removed the flue to light the wick. She was rewarded by a warming light as she re-placed the column of glass and then a yellow globe shade.

'That's better.' As neat as a pin, the room had been thoughtfully deco-rated, retaining the more attractive elements of railway-carriage design. The rich wooden bulkhead walls at either end had been stripped, varnished and polished to a shine, as had the floorboards underfoot. Side walls had been painted in a pale cream distemper, and there were dark linen blinds against windows that faced the sea. Two leather armchairs, the sort one might find in a gentlemen's club, were positioned close to a wood-burning stove. A stack of dry driftwood had been placed on one side of the red-tiled hearth, and on the other was a large kettle filled with water, alongside several fire tools. A wood-framed bed was set lengthways against the other bulkhead, with a rich burgundy counterpane hanging low over the sides. Opposite the sideboard stood a dresser with upper cupboards and shelving for crockery and an open space underneath for jars and a bread bin. Two more cupboards below held a frying pan, saucepan, and various dry goods and tins of soup.

Opening a second door, Maisie found that the accommodation was not one carriage, but two, positioned parallel to one another. A house-sized door had been installed, leading to a small vestibule that had been built to connect the two carriages. Windows on this long side of the carriage had been painted white, then decorated with a mural. Maisie did not linger to consider the story depicted in the series of paintings, instead continuing her survey of Nick Bassington-Hope's home. The vestibule gave on to a studio and bathroom, though there was no running water or plumbing. The bathroom consisted of a wooden washstand with a tile splashback and marble top. A jug was placed on top of the washstand, while underneath a chamber pot was covered with a plain white cloth.

Upon investigation, a small wardrobe in the vestibule held several items of clothing: three shirts, a pair of corduroy trousers, a woollen jacket and another made of heavy waxed cotton. Reaching further into the wardrobe, Maisie felt the rough texture of heavy wool and drew the sleeve of another garment towards her. Nick Bassington-Hope had kept his army greatcoat.

Pulling the coat from the wardrobe, Maisie walked into the studio with it to take a closer look. There was still a speckle of mud across the hem of the coat, and then she noticed a broad, aged stain on the sleeve that she knew to be blood. *My God, he kept it all this time.* Maisie closed her eyes and gripped the coat to her, the smell of death lingering among the folds of fabric, as if the garment had absorbed something of what the artist had seen as a young subaltern.

It was almost dusk now and Maisie had barely dented the task she had set for herself this afternoon. She returned the coat to the wardrobe, picked up the lamp and moved on.

On the wall that paralleled the first carriage, a special wooden case had been fitted to store the artist's paints. Each wooden pigeonhole held tubes and small pots of paint in many hues. Jugs in varying sizes had been set on a painted wooden tea trolley to hold a collection of brushes. An easel stood by the bulkhead close to the bank of windows, and a chest of drawers held papers of different weights as well as wood for frames and sections of unused canvas. There was also a deep, cushioned armchair by the window, and alongside the chair a small table with untouched sketchbooks and pencils.

'But where's your work, Nicholas?' Maisie asked the silent studio.

She opened the bottom drawer of the paper chest. Bundles of well-used sketchbooks were stored there, so, still with her coat on, she set the lamp on the floor, sat down beside it and began to leaf through the books. She was lost in thought when there was a loud thump on the door.

'Oh!' Maisie was startled at the intrusion, but clambered to her feet and, lamp in hand, went to unlock the door. Outside stood a thickset man wearing a long jacket of rubber-covered cloth and a woollen cap over his greying red hair, which was drawn back in a thick ponytail. His trousers of the same rubbered cloth were tucked into boots that had been turned over at the top.

'You must be Mr White,' she said before he had could open his mouth.

He stared at her, taken aback by her forthright manner. 'Just thought I'd look in, don't want strangers looking into Mr 'ope's matters.' He spoke with the rounded brogue of a Kentish fisherman.

'I'm not a stranger, Mr White. I am a friend of Mr Bassington-Hope's sister Georgina. She asked me to look in as I was in the area.'

'Funny area to be in, not a place you pass through, Dungeness.'

'No, I know, it was just a bit out of my way.' Maisie smiled. 'I know the Marshes and was going to Hastings, so it seemed a good opportunity to help Miss Bassington-Hope.'

He shook his head. 'Strange lot, them 'ope's. You'd've thought they'd've been down a bit more, not just the one visit. Three of 'em just came in, then left as soon as they got 'ere. Funny lot.' He shook his head. 'You'd be best to move that little motor car be'ind the carriage, out to the back. Come mornin' you won't 'ave a roof on that thing, what with the wind.'

'Well, I didn't expect to stay very long.' She checked her watch. 'Gosh, I really should be on my way.'

Amos White turned, speaking as he walked away. 'Just remember to put that little motor to the lee of the cottage.' Then he was gone.

Maisie closed the door behind her and shuddered. Perhaps she ought to stay here in Dungeness, especially as she had barely started her search of

Nick's property. There was little time, and already more questions were lining up. *Who were the three family members? Could it have been Georgina and her parents? Or perhaps the three bereaved siblings?*

It was when Maisie stepped into the centre of the room again that she allowed herself to push all questions to the back of her mind and studied the mural painstakingly crafted on the former railway carriage windows. Each window depicted a scene that was pure Romney Marsh, from the trees forced to lean inland by the wind, to isolated churches set in flat hedge-divided fields, with sheep grazing and, above the water meadows, silvered clouds scudding across a grey sky.

As Maisie's eyes moved from left to right, she saw that the story told in the mural was one that had been part of the coast's history for centuries. In the middle of the tale, day had drawn into night and the scene was of a fishing boat beached. Men were unloading their catch by lantern light. Atop a black horse with wild eyes, a man in a tricorn hat wielded a pistol while watching over the haul, which was not cod, nor plaice, but barrels bursting open to reveal a bounty of gold and spices, silk and rum. Moving along the mural, the men had taken flight towards the church with their booty, where a welcoming vicar bade them enter. The next scene saw dawn break and the excisemen—as feared today as in ancient times—searching for the smugglers, to no avail. In the final scene, daylight had returned to the marshes. Sheep were grazing, and the thunderous sky had given way to blue.

Maisie stood back to look at the mural in its entirety. The infamous eighteenth-century Kent gangs given life by the hand of the artist. Nick Bassington-Hope was indeed talented.

She checked her watch again and sighed. It was already past four and dark outside, but she decided that she could not leave until she had conducted a thorough search of the cottage.

She went outside again and moved the MG to a place behind the second carriage, where a surprisingly strong lean-to had been constructed and sheltered, not only a carefully stacked pile of driftwood, but a barrel where water was collected from a clever gutter system. It would seem that this was one artist with a very practical streak.

Locking the cottage door behind her again, Maisie closed the blinds and made up a fire in the cast-iron stove and put the kettle of water on to boil. As the room warmed, she looked again at the home that Nick Bassington-Hope had created. No, none of this was the work of a man who would have had a slapdash attitude towards the construction of a scaffolding platform.

Returning to the sketchbooks she had been looking at when Amos White banged on the door, she saw they contained work from the artist's early days—charcoal drawings and watercolours that lacked the mature interpretation of later years—and also some recent work.

Unlike the contents of the rest of the cottage, the sketchbooks had not been kept in any order, and Maisie concluded that they had been worked through quite recently. Nick's early sketches were pastoral, horses in Kentish fields, cattle ambling towards the milking shed in late afternoon and women gathered outside farm buildings, their jackets secured by string. There were detail sketches, a face here, a nose there, a child's dimpled hand held by the worn, working hand of her father. And then came the war.

Maisie could barely bring herself to look at these sketches, and she turned instead to work completed in the time following Nick's return from France, when, still recuperating from his wounds, he was called upon to work on designing propaganda literature. This time the sketches inflamed Maisie. A small boy sitting on his father's knee, and the words: WHAT WAR STORIES WILL YOU TELL, FATHER? A young man with his sweetheart, the woman looking away towards a man in uniform: ARE YOU STILL HER BEST BOY? Then another, a German soldier breaking down the door of a family's home: YOU CAN STOP HIM NOW!

At first Maisie felt anger towards the artist. She had seen the posters herself in the war, but had never questioned who might have drafted each idea that had compelled those at home to service. Then she found herself wondering if Nick Bassington-Hope had had a choice, and, if not, how he might have felt, knowing the ultimate, deadly outcome of his work. What remorse, if any, might have shadowed his every day.

The sketches from his time in America were most interesting to Maisie, because they revealed a man who seemed to have found peace of mind. Magnificent canyons backlit by the sun; trees of such grandeur that she could barely imagine walking through the forest; then the plains—she could almost smell the heat, the breeze pressed against fields of corn. Again, Nick Bassington-Hope had drawn segments in detail, water rushing across a single rock, or part of an eagle's wing. And there, pencilled into the corner of a single page, the artist had written: *I can dance with life again.*

As Maisie closed the sketchbook, she realised that tears had fallen, and that the work of an artist she never knew was touching her deeply. She dried her eyes and took up a collection of sketchbooks marked CONSTRUCTS. It appeared that not only had the artist planned his murals and triptych pieces with utmost care, but he had anticipated each step involved in exhibiting them. But the details here were of past exhibits. There was nothing pertaining to the unveiling at Svenson's Gallery.

Maisie pushed the books to one side, rose to her feet and walked through to the main room, where she placed her hands on the back of first one chair, then the other. As she touched the chair on the left of the fireplace, it felt warm against her fingers—and as she rested her hand on the leather, Maisie knew it was Nick Bassington-Hope's preferred seat. She sat in his place, closed her eyes and an image came to her of Nick sitting there. Though it is a bright day, he is wearing the greatcoat, drawing it round him as he sketches, as he struggles with the emotion his work inspires. He stops and puts his work to one side, then takes a piece of paper from his pocket. He looks at the paper for just a moment, then puts it . . . The picture becomes blurred and he is gone.

The sound of seagulls screeching and wheeling overhead brought Maisie back to the present. Opening her eyes, she rubbed her temples and looked at her watch. Half past seven! She stood up and moved as if to go to the studio, but suddenly stopped, for it struck her that to hear seagulls whooping was unusual at this hour of darkness. Her weekend visits to Andrew Dene's home in Hastings Old Town had given her a sense of the rhythms of coastal life. She stepped to the window, and, as she did so, extinguished the lamp.

Maisie drew back the blind a little. Lights went back and forth, and there was a flurry of activity close to the shingle bank where a fishing boat had just been drawn up. Maisie watched as men—there must have been three, perhaps four—unloaded a haul. There were no nets, as far as she could see, no barrels for the fish, and in any case it was late for the catch to come in. A rumbling, heavy sound distracted her as a lorry appeared, backing up as far as the driver could take the vehicle to the shingle bank. Perhaps it *was* a late catch. Shadows could be misleading.

Maisie returned to Nick's living room, where she relit the lamp, then washed the cup and saucer and placed them on the dresser. She damped down the fire, pulled on her hat and coat, then waited until the only light on the beach came from the lighthouse. Then she extinguished the lamp, picked up her document case and crept back to the MG. The engine seemed loud, but—she hoped—was probably drowned out by crashing waves as she again made her way slowly along the track to the main road.

Her route was one that took her across Kent towards Chelstone, and her father's cottage. But it was as she left the marshes that her headlamps illuminated, just for a second or two, the back of a lorry as it pulled off the main road and down a lane. It was the same vehicle she had seen at the beach. She made a mental note of the place where the lorry had turned, and, as she drove along in the darkness, she knew she would be back.

MAISIE HAD ARRIVED LATE at Frankie Dobbs's home in the Groom's Cottage on Lady Rowan's estate. Yet, despite the time, father and daughter sat together until the small hours of the next morning, speaking of Maisie's work or talking of the past. Frankie had lived in Kent since 1914, but his dialect was easily recognisable as harking from within the sound of the tolling bells of Bow, marking him as a true Cockney.

'There you are, fresh eggs this morning and two rashers of bacon!' he said to Maisie later that morning. 'That'll keep you going, my girl.'

'You spoil me, Dad.' Maisie admonished her father as he sat down to tuck into his own hearty breakfast.

Frankie looked at the clock. 'I've got to get out to the horses a bit sharpish. I tell you, we're doing well, with another mare due to foal soon. Spend all my time makin' sure the stables're warm.'

'As long as you're not overdoing it, Dad.'

Frankie shook his head. 'Nah. All in a day's work.'

After breakfast, Maisie kissed her father and waved him off, watching him walk slowly down the path. Frankie hated to see his daughter drive away, so she had expected him to leave before she departed the cottage. It would not be long before he retired, and Maisie was grateful for the fact that Lady Rowan had assured her that the Groom's Cottage would be her father's home for the rest of his life; she had never forgotten that Frankie Dobbs had saved her horses from requisition in the war.

After tidying up the kitchen, Maisie packed her belongings and left before nine, with the intention of reaching Hastings by ten o'clock. In the solitude of the journey down to the Sussex coast, she would consider the case of Nicholas Bassington-Hope against the cold light of day. And it was most certainly cold and bright, for a clearing wind had swept across the south, leaving blue skies but frosty ground.

As she drove, she reflected upon the fact that she was only just beginning to fill in the outline of Nick Bassington-Hope's life. She had first to sketch in her landscape, then, as she uncovered new information, she would add colour and depth to her work. Maisie liked to work methodically through a case, while at the same time allowing for intuition to speak to her, for truth to make itself known.

As she pulled into the narrow road that led to the outer edge of Hastings Old Town and along to the houses that commanded views across the Channel, she knew she had a list of detailed sketches to create: the Bassington-Hope family; Nick's friends and associates; those who collected his work and those who hated it; the mysterious lockup.

It was early days yet, she thought as she parked the MG near Andrew Dene's house. Only three days had passed since the first meeting with Georgina Bassington-Hope.

'Maisie! By golly, I thought I would never see you again—and why, might I ask, are you sitting in your little red car staring out to sea?'

Maisie shook her head. 'Oh, sorry, Andrew, I was miles away.'

Dene opened the door of the MG, took Maisie's hand and pulled her to him as she stepped out. 'You've been avoiding me, I think,' he said teasingly.

Maisie smiled and blushed. 'Of course I haven't. Don't be silly.' She turned her head towards the sea. 'Let's go for a walk. I have to leave at about two o'clock, you know, so let's not waste the morning.'

For just a second Dene's expression revealed his disappointment, then he smiled in return. 'Grand idea, Maisie. Come on in while I put on my coat.'

IT TOOK ONLY fifteen minutes to amble down to the High Street and then on to Rock-a-Nore towards the tall fishermen's net shops at the Stade, where the couple stopped to watch a boat being winched ashore.

Strolling along, Maisie and Andrew Dene watched as the womenfolk of the Old Town sold fish, winkles and whelks to winter day-trippers from London. All around them conversations could be heard, but little passed between the pair. Dene was about to try to start a conversation, when he noticed Maisie looking across the Stade at one of the fishing boats. She was holding a hand across her forehead to shield her eyes from the light.

'What is it, Maisie? Seen one of the boys unload a fish you'd like?' quipped Dene.

She barely moved, still staring in the direction of the boat, then looked back at him. 'Sorry, Andrew, what did you say? I was rather preoccupied.'

Dene replied in a clipped manner. 'If you don't mind me saying so, Maisie, you have been rather preoccupied since you arrived.'

Maisie did not address his comment, but instead asked a question. 'Do you know the fishermen here, Andrew? Are their names familiar?'

Dene suspected that Maisie had barely even heard him. 'I—I . . . yes, I do, Maisie. I know most of the families round here.' He felt tension rise as he spoke, a mixture of annoyance at her avoiding his observation and fear that she might speak of her feelings—feelings he wasn't sure he was ready to hear. He was relieved when she laced her arm through his and continued to walk in the direction of the men she'd been watching.

'Come on, let's wander back to the tea shop. I'd love a cup before I leave for Tenterden.'

With that she smiled, though Dene was quick to notice that her attention had now been drawn to three fishermen standing alongside their boat. They were deep in discussion, backs against the wind. As the couple passed by, Dene saw the men look up in unison, then turn back to resume their talk. Maisie was facing him, as if she did not want them to know she had seen them. They crossed the road.

'So, do you know who those men were, Andrew?'

Dene sighed. 'I don't know the one in the middle with the red ponytail, but the other two are brothers. The Drapers: Rowland and Tom. They run *Misty Rose*, the boat they were all leaning against.'

Maisie walked faster now, unentwined her arm and faced Dene again. 'Do you know anything about smuggling along the coast?'

Dene laughed, shaking his head as they reached the tea shop. 'Oh, the things you ask, Maisie.' Placing coins on the counter for two cups of tea, Dene waited until they were served and they had secured two seats at a table before replying. 'Smuggling has flourished along the coast from the Middle Ages, you know. Once upon a time it was cloth, fine wool or silk. Spice was valuable enough to be smuggled, then alcohol. It's all a bit cloak-and-dagger and Dr Syn-ish.'

'Dr Syn?'

Dene picked up his cup and took a sip of his tea. 'You should read a few more adventure stories, Maisie, then perhaps you wouldn't look for trouble.' He paused to see if she would rise to the bait, but she continued to listen, without comment. 'Dr Syn, the Romney Marsh vicar and smuggler—a tale of devil riders and witches, me 'earties!' He mimicked the voice of a pantomime pirate and was delighted when Maisie laughed at his joke.

'And what about now? What do they smuggle now?'

Dene leaned back. 'Oh, I don't know if there is smuggling nowadays.'

Maisie was thoughtful. 'But if you had to hazard a guess, what do you think people might smuggle?'

Andrew shrugged. 'I suppose people smuggle things that are hard to get, and that you can get a good price for. I'm not sure that means alcohol any more, or spices, silks and wools.' He thought for a moment. 'People probably smuggle things for different reasons . . .' He paused, shaking his head. 'Now you've got me at it, Maisie. Speculating over something of little consequence.' He consulted his watch. 'You'd better be getting on if you want to arrive at your appointment in Tenterden on time.'

They reached the MG in silence. Maisie turned to Dene before taking her seat and starting the engine. 'I'm sorry, Andrew. I don't seem to be able to give you what you want, do I?'

'We're probably the kind of people who end up wanting the same thing at different times.' He smiled at her, though his shoulders sagged.

Maisie touched his cheek with her hand but did not kiss him. It was just as she was about to drive away, her face framed in the side window of the car, that Dene leaned down and kissed her. He drew back, then spoke again. 'Oh, and about those smugglers—I would imagine that the only reason for smuggling now is if someone is prepared to pay handsomely for something they desire. There are people who will do almost anything for something they really want, you know.' Dene patted the roof of the car, then stepped back to watch Maisie drive off.

There are people who will do almost anything for something they really want, you know. Maisie repeated the words as she drove to Tenterden. The third man at the Stade, the one Dene didn't know, was Amos White, the Dungeness fisherman.

Yes, she had seen them all before, and so had Nick Bassington-Hope. She knew that now.

THE SKY HAD BECOME lightly overcast by the time Maisie reached Tenterden. The conditions were ideal for ice on the roads, perhaps snow later. She had allowed more than enough time to drive from Hastings, so there would now be an opportunity to accomplish an errand.

The local bookshop was run from premises with limited space. She was curious to see a copy of *Dr Syn*, the book mentioned by Andrew Dene. There were two copies in stock, and Maisie picked one of them and settled into a chair to read a few pages. If the novel had in some way inspired the artist, Maisie wanted to know more. Before leaving the shop, she made a notation or two on an index card, then slipped it into her shoulder bag.

'Maisie!' Georgina Bassington-Hope waved to Maisie when she saw her pull up at the station, then walked over to the passenger side of the MG, opened the door and sat down. 'I cajoled Nolly into giving me a lift.'

Maisie checked the road and began to pull out.

'No, don't let's go yet, I'd like to have a word first.'

'Of course.' Maisie turned off the engine, then reached for the scarf and gloves she'd pushed behind her seat. 'Only you won't mind if we walk rather than sit here?'

Georgina agreed, but appeared rather taken aback.

'What do you want to talk about?'

'Well, first of all, Nick's cottage. Did you glean much from your visit?'

Maisie nodded, composing her reply as they walked. Georgina seemed afraid, perhaps regretful of her decision to delve into the cause of her brother's accident. Maisie considered that such feelings on Georgina's part could have come as a result of some new information received.

'I came away with more questions than answers, to tell you the truth. Mind you, that's not unusual at this stage in an investigation.' Maisie paused. 'Nick was a most interesting artist, wasn't he?'

Georgina took a handkerchief from her pocket, which she dabbed against her brow. 'Yes, he was interesting, and innovative. But, in what way did *you* discern that he was "interesting"?'

'I noticed in one or two pieces that Nick depicted people he knew—in scenes that they couldn't have posed in. I thought it interesting that he would do such a thing. I assumed that a painter will disguise the real person in a given scene. Nick seems to have gone out of his way to do the opposite.'

'Which pieces are you referring to?'

'The mural on the walls of his cottage.'

'The smugglers?'

'Yes. It appears he used the fictional character, Dr Syn, from the books by Russell Thorndike, to inspire an illustrated story. Yet when you look at the faces, they are clearly men known to him.'

'Oh, of course! You know, I think he only did that the once. I remember him saying that fishermen have such weatherbeaten faces, like rocks chiselled by sea over the years, so he wanted to paint them in an historical context of smuggling in the area. Then, of course, he read that book and was inspired to depict the story as a decoration for his carriage.'

Maisie nodded. 'Yes, I thought it was rather clever. But, I was curious about one thing.' She turned to Georgina as they walked back to the MG.

'Oh, what's that?'

Maisie took her seat and leaned across to open the door for Georgina. She started the engine, then continued. 'I've placed the three fishermen who inspired the smugglers in the mural, but not the face behind the character of their fearless leader on his charger.' She let the comment hang in the air, looked both ways to check the road, then pulled away from the station.

Chapter Five

The entrance to Bassington Place was flanked by two snow-clad pillars from which rusted iron gates hung open. Maisie thought the gates had probably not been closed for years, judging by the ivy tethering them in place. There was a one-storey sandstone lodge, to the left, also covered in ivy.

'Gower, our gamekeeper, lives there with his wife, the housekeeper. Frankly, I wonder why we still have a gamekeeper, but Nolly is determined to raise funds by opening the estate to shooting parties.' Georgina pointed to the right. 'Turn right, over there, by that oak tree.'

Making her way along a drive bordered by snow-dusted rhododendrons, Maisie drove slowly to avoid ruts in the road. She slowed the MG even more on the approach to the grand country house, so that she could study the property. A little down-at-heel, it appeared as though three houses had been joined together, so numerous were the pitched roofs; there were even some ornate candy-twist Elizabethan chimneys. Despite its size, however, the ivy-clad house seemed warm and welcoming.

As she parked the MG, the heavy oak door opened and a tall man of about seventy approached them.

Georgina clambered from the car, walked towards her father and kissed him on the cheek. 'Hello, Piers, darling, let me introduce my old friend from Girton, Maisie Dobbs.'

Though Georgina had portrayed her parents as being somewhat eccentric, Maisie was surprised when the woman used her father's Christian name. Piers Bassington-Hope held out his hand to Maisie, who immediately felt his warmth and strength. He was over six foot in height, and still walked with the bearing of a younger man. His corduroy trousers were well kept, if slightly worn, and along with a Viyella shirt and a lavender tie, he wore a brown cable-knit pullover. His ash-grey hair, which matched that of his eyebrows, was combed back, and his steel-grey eyes seemed kind.

'Delighted to meet you, Miss Dobbs. We're so glad you've come and that you've agreed to help Georgina here.'

Bassington-Hope's smile of welcome was genuine but could not camouflage a grey pallor that pointed to the man's sorrow at losing his eldest son.

'Come along, Mrs Gower has put up a tea the like of which we have not seen in years! Your favourite this weekend, Georgie—Eccles cakes!' He turned to Maisie. 'Our children may well have grown, but Mrs Gower feels a need to fill them up with their favourite foods when they make a weekend visit.' The man stood back to allow the women to enter before him.

In the entrance hall, Maisie found the decor at once stimulating and a little alarming. Each wall was painted a different colour, and not only that, someone—perhaps a group of people—had left their mark by adding a mural of a garden of flowers and foliage growing up from a green skirting board: it appeared as if ivy had snaked in from the exterior of the house. On another wall, a rainbow arched over a doorway. Avant-garde tapestry wall hangings and needlepoint pillows of red with yellow orbs, or orange with green parallel lines, added to the confusion of colour.

The drawing room seemed to be named more for the activity that went on there than as a place to which guests would withdraw for tea or drinks. The walls were painted pale yellow, the picture rail in deep maroon, while the skirting boards and doors were hunter green.

Georgina's mother turned from her place in front of one of two easels set alongside French windows, wiped her hands and came to welcome Maisie. Her grey hair was pinned on the top of her head in a loose braid, with wisps coming free at the back and sides. A paint-splashed blue artist's smock covered her clothing, but Maisie could see the lower half of a deep red embroidered skirt. She wore hooped earrings, and silver and gold bangles.

'Thank heavens Georgina found you. We thought Nolly might insist on completing her errands first before running Georgie to the station to meet you. We were worried you'd be left in the lurch.' Emma Bassington-Hope clasped Maisie's hands. 'Come along, let's sit down to Mrs Gower's magnificent tea and you can tell us all about yourself.'

Becoming comfortable on a settee covered in floral fabric, she beckoned Maisie and patted the place next to her. Georgina and her father seated themselves in armchairs.

'Emsy, Maisie is here on business, remember. She will have to ask you some questions.'

Maisie smiled and raised a hand. 'Oh, that's all right, Georgina. Later. There's plenty of time.' She turned to Emma Bassington-Hope, and then to Georgina's father. 'You have a lovely house, so interesting.'

Georgina poured tea and offered cucumber sandwiches. Emma continued the conversation with Maisie.

'Well, it is a wonderful house for people who love to paint. We're surrounded by the most exquisite countryside and we have all this space to experiment with.' She pointed at her daughter. 'Why, when Georgie was a child, she would compose whole stories on the bedroom walls, then Nick would come in and illustrate them—we still have them, you know.' She reached for the edge of the painter's smock and pressed it against her eyes.

Piers Bassington-Hope stood up, opened the French windows and walked outside. For her part, Georgina studied her hands and made no move to comfort her mother, whose shoulders moved as she sobbed into the smock. After some moments Maisie reached across, taking the older woman's hands in both of her own. 'Tell me about your son, Emma.'

The woman was quiet for a while, then sniffed and shook her head. 'I've been lost, quite lost, since the accident. Nick was so much more like me, you see. Georgina's like her father—he writes, you know. But Nick was an artist even in boyhood. His work was so sophisticated for a child. I remember thinking that not only could the boy draw a man working in a field, but he seemed to draw the very thoughts the man held within him.' She choked on a sob, then leaned forward towards her knees, her forehead now touching Maisie's hands as they continued to clasp her own. Maisie rested her cheek against the back of the grieving woman's head. Some moments later Emma Bassington-Hope raised her head. 'Goodness me, I . . . I . . . do excuse me, I . . .'

Maisie spoke, her voice soft. 'Say nothing, there's no need.' She paused. 'Would you like to show me some of Nick's work, tell me more about him?'

IT WAS PERHAPS an hour later that Georgina's mother and Maisie returned to the drawing room. During that time, Maisie had received a tour of the house, seen that every room was decorated in a different colour and style and had concluded that this family seemed to typify everything she had associated with the word 'bohemian'.

More of Nick Bassington-Hope's work was on display around the house, though Emma pointed out that Noelle had sold a few pieces, gifts to his parents, even before Nick's death. The parents had acquiesced at the time, realising that the family trust was presently more than a little underfunded.

Maisie and Emma returned to the settee, where Emma was talking about Nick's wartime service, explaining how he had felt the need to 'do his bit' for King and country and had joined the Artists' Rifles at the outset of war in 1914.

'Of course, we were against it—after all, Nick was a sensitive boy.' She smiled. 'Now if they had given a rifle to Noelle or Georgina, I might not have worried, but then Georgie went in, anyway. And as for Nolly—'

'"As for Nolly" what?' The door slammed, and a tall, fortyish woman wearing a tweed skirt, brown leather shoes and a brown woollen jacket strode into the room. Pulling a beret from her head and running her fingers through mousey-brown hair cut in a sharp bob, she cursed the snow that had begun to fall again as she helped herself to tea and a scone.

'Go on, Mother, "as for Nolly"—what?' With features more pointed than Georgina's, Noelle Bassington-Hope appeared terse and inflexible.

'Oh, don't be boring, Nolly. Miss Dobbs is our guest.' Georgina fumed at Nolly as she and her father entered the drawing room through the French windows.

Maisie held out a hand to Noelle. 'Mrs . . .'

'Grant. You must be Georgie's enquiry agent, not that there's anything to enquire into.' She took a bite from her scone, set the plate back on the table and held out her hand. Her nonchalant flippancy revealed a lack of confidence, and something else. *She's afraid of me.*

'A pleasure, Mrs Grant.' Maisie paused. 'I've been looking forward to meeting you.'

'Hmmph!' Noelle sat down next to her mother, in the place just vacated by Maisie. 'I'm surprised a woman of your intelligence would get involved in this sort of thing—after all, our family was bereaved by an accident. Mind you, the things that women of supposed intelligence are wont to get up to always did flummox me, eh, Georgie?' She looked across at her sister.

'Oh, for God's sake, Noll.' The younger sister rolled her eyes.

Maisie did not want to become embroiled in sibling arguments. 'Mrs Grant, I realise that Georgina's decision to enlist my services must have come as a shock to you, but you have broad responsibilities as a Justice of the Peace here and also in managing your parents' estate; I would very much like to speak to you, especially as, in your role as a JP, you are familiar with the need for detail—is that not so? I would value your opinions on a few matters.'

'Well . . . I . . . I suppose . . .'

'Good.' Maisie held out her hand towards the garden. 'Let's go for a stroll. It's not as cold as it was and it's only just started to snow lightly.'

'Righty-o.' Noelle Grant set down her cup, clearly warming to Maisie. 'Just a tick while I grab a scarf and gloves.' She stopped by the window as she looked out. 'I'll find you some gumboots.'

Noelle led Maisie to the gun room, which smelt of wet dogs, rubber boots and stale pipe smoke. Once furnished with outdoor clothing, Noelle took two walking sticks from an old clay pot and handed one to Maisie before opening the door and striding forward into the gently falling snow.

'Hmmm, I hope this doesn't settle, or I'll have to get old Jenkins out with his horses to clear the drive in the morning.' She went on, barely glancing at Maisie as she spoke. 'The man has a brand-new tractor in his barn and still maintains the shires do a better job.'

Maisie kept up stride for stride. So far as she was concerned, it would have to be a quick walk if she were to get on the main road before the weather made the going difficult for her low-slung MG.

'Mrs Grant, I—'

'Call me Nolly, everyone else does.'

'Nolly, I wonder if you could tell me about your brother Nick.'

'I don't think Nick was ever as much of a flibbertigibbet as Georgie. They were twins, but Nick was always more single-minded.' She paused for a second. 'Now, I know you asked about Nick, but we have to talk about them both, for they were twins. Georgie can be a bit of a will-o'-the-wisp, a new idea every five seconds—such as hiring you, if you don't mind me saying so.' She paused to negotiate a fallen branch. 'Nick had all Emsy's emotion, all that intensity, but it was tempered by something from my father, a solidity, I suppose you could call it. Piers has a bit more—Lord, what would you call it?' Nolly stopped and looked up.

'Practicality?' suggested Maisie.

'That's it! Yes, Piers may be a creative individual, but he also has a practicality about him. Now, if you take me—I am all practicality. Nick, as I said, was both. But as boy and man he could and did sail close to the wind.'

'Just like Georgina?'

'But in a different way. Georgina sprayed her bullets with abandon; Nick always had a target before he took aim. And don't get me wrong, I admired him terribly. I just think certain sleeping dogs should be allowed to lie.'

'The war?'

'Yes, the war, for a start.' Nolly looked across the land now covered with soft, white snow. 'We'd better be walking back soon. It's getting dark and this snow is set in for the night now.'

The women walked on for a while, talking about Nolly's plans for Bassington Place and the surrounding land. Though it was obscured by snow, there were meadows and woodland where, Maisie imagined, primroses, bluebells and abundant white wood anemones bloomed in spring.

She continued her questioning as they made their way back to the house. 'So, tell me about the war and Nick.'

'He joined up straight away, dragging his arty friends with him. They were all sent to different regiments following their training with the Artists' Rifles, so it was rather a surprise when Godfrey and Nick found they were serving together.'

'I was sorry to learn that your husband was lost in France.'

Nolly Grant shook her head. 'Nothing *lost* about it. He was *killed*, buried over there. My husband died a hero on a battlefield, fighting for his country—and proud of it! I get so fed up with all this pussyfooting around the truth. People die, they don't get lost and they don't pass anywhere!'

Maisie raised her eyebrows. 'I understand that Nick was close to him when he died.'

'Nick was wounded shortly after Godfrey died. I received the telegram informing me that I was a widow, then looked after my brother as soon as he was brought home. Kept me busy. No time to think about it, you know.'

'Of course.' Maisie nodded. 'Nolly, did you approve of Nick?' she asked as they came into the stable yard.

The woman sighed. 'What did it matter whether I approved or disapproved? This family does what it wants when it wants. And if they don't let me go ahead with plans for the estate, we'll all be at the doors of the poorhouse!' She paused. 'I'm the only one with any sense of the money it takes to run the place or how to deal with the tenant farmers—Godfrey was a sort of de facto manager after we got married and before he went over to France. Now I want to draw visitors in. And visitors will never come if two of the Bassington-Hopes—make that three, if Harry has his way—manage to rub people up the wrong way. So, did I approve? No, I didn't.' She looked at Maisie. 'Did Nick and Georgie really think they could stop a war with their pictures and words? Frankly, someone should have stopped them long ago.'

The women removed boots and coats, and before entering the main part of the house, Nolly looked out of the window to cast judgment on the weather. 'Well, Maisie, I don't think you'll be going anywhere but a guest room tonight. From here I can see that the avenue down to the main road is barely passable now.'

'But I must—'

'Please don't argue. We never allow guests to leave impaired by wine or weather. Now at least Piers can impress you with his 1929 elderflower!'

'NOLLY'S ABSOLUTELY RIGHT, you must stay, mustn't she, Emsy, Piers?' Georgina looked at her mother and father while Nolly poured glasses of sherry from the tray just brought into the room by Mrs Gower.

Maisie acquiesced. 'Thank you for your hospitality.'

'The good news is that, according to Jenkins, who came to the door after you left, this little lot should shift with ease tomorrow morning. He'll be over with Jack and Ben to clear the avenue first thing.'

'Not with the tractor?'

'No, the horses.'

'That silly man!' Nolly cursed.

Maisie moved the MG to a spare stall in the stable block, which was home to four hunters. Returning to the house, she was shown to a wood-panelled guest room by Georgina.

'Good, the fire's already been lit. Mrs Gower will make up the bed and bring fresh towels for you. Here, let me show you, there's a bathroom next door. I'll bring along some nightclothes for you, and a dress for dinner, though it may be a bit big. Nolly likes to keep up appearances.' Georgina smiled, waving as she left the room. 'Drinks in about half an hour, then we'll have dinner. I think it's roast duck this evening.'

PIERS LED EMMA to one end of the dining-room table, made sure she was comfortable, then waited for the women to be seated before taking his place opposite his wife. Emma was wearing a deep red velvet gown.

'Now you'll be treated to Daddy's wines!' Georgina reached for her table napkin, then turned to Piers. 'What are we having this evening to grace the duck, Daddy?'

Piers smiled. 'Last year's damson.'

'Fruity with an oakish balance,' added Georgina.

'Utter tosh!' Nolly reached for her glass, as Gower, now dressed in formal attire, served a rich blood-red wine from a crystal decanter. 'Not the wine, Daddy, but Georgina's description, as usual trimmed with lace!'

'Girls, please! Let's not bicker in front of our guest.' Piers reached out to place a hand on the hand of each daughter. 'They may be grown women, Maisie, but together they can be like cats!'

'And when Nick was here, why—'

Maisie looked from Emma to Piers. The head of the Bassington-Hope household had released his daughters' hands and was shaking his head.

'Oh, darling, I'm sorry, I shouldn't have,' Emma said. 'It was the wrong moment, with us all together here, and with company.'

'If you would excuse me—' Piers placed his table napkin next to his still-full wineglass and left the room.

Nolly pushed back her chair, as if to follow her father.

'Noelle!' Emma used her elder daughter's Christian name. 'Allow your father to have a moment. We all feel grief, and we never know when it might catch us.' She turned to Maisie and smiled. 'I understand that you are good friends with Lady Rowan Compton, Maisie. Did you know she and I were presented at court in the same year?'

Maisie held her wineglass by the stem and leaned aside as Mrs Gower served pea soup from a tureen. She smiled at her hostess. 'What a coincidence! No, I didn't know. I bet she was quite a firebrand in her day.'

'My goodness, yes. Of course, she went off and married Julian Compton—

he was considered quite the catch. And I, thank heavens,' continued Emma, 'found an artist who saw the world from eyes like mine, *and* who also had a name, much to my parents' delight.'

'Talking about how fortunate you were to bag me, eh, Emsy?'

'Darling, yes, I am!' Emma Bassington-Hope's eyes glistened as her husband entered the room once again, taking his place at the head of the table.

'Here we go, ready for a walk down memory lane, Piers?' Nolly rolled her eyes in a conspiratorial fashion.

'A finer walk could not be had—if our new friend could bear to join us.' Piers looked to Maisie.

'Of course. And I must say, this is an exquisite wine.'

'Yes, and hopefully there will be more of it—where's Gower?'

Two more decanters of Piers Bassington-Hope's wine tempered the family's tensions and, thought Maisie, made them sparkling company. By eleven o'clock they were lingering over the cheese course and the two sisters were finally at ease with each other.

'Do let's tell Maisie about the big play. You remember, when Nick almost drowned dear little Harry in the river.'

'Should've held his head down a bit longer!'

'Oh, Nolly, come on!' Georgina tapped her sister playfully on the hand, and they both began to laugh. She turned to Maisie. 'I think Nolly must have been sixteen, because Harry was only four.'

'I *was* sixteen, silly—it was my birthday!'

Piers laughed. 'Sweet sixteen and we invited everyone we knew for the weekend. How many sixteen-year-olds have two MPs, three actors, a clutch of poets and writers and I don't know how many artists at her party?'

Georgina took up the story. 'We decided to do a river play—all of us.'

Maisie raised her eyebrows. 'What's a river play?'

'A play on the river! We had to compose a play that could be acted from the rowing boats. There we were, in boats, all dressed up in our finery and acting, when Nick decided, on the spur of the moment, to bring some realism into the play. Harry had been cast as a court jester—he was always either the dog or the court jester—' Georgina could hardly speak for laughing.

Nolly continued where her sister left off. 'So, Nick picked Harry up, saying, "I shall cast yonder servant into the sea!" and threw him in the river. But Harry couldn't swim and went down like an anchor. Nick leapt into the water, which wasn't that deep, and pulled out the poor, spluttering boy.'

Georgina was still gasping with laughter. 'I remember poor little wet Harry screaming, "I hate you, Nick! Just you wait until I grow up!"'

The laughter subsided and Emma suggested retiring to the drawing room for coffee. As they relaxed in front of the fire, she brought out photograph albums, telling detailed stories of this or that event. Soon, however, the wine that had aided such mirth an hour earlier rendered the group a little soporific.

Maisie returned to her room, which was warm and cosy. She undressed, put on the nightgown left by Georgina and snuggled under the covers. It was clear to her that Nick Bassington-Hope had been the blue-eyed boy of the family. And, despite their differences, Maisie detected a respect between Noelle and Georgina. Though Noelle might have disapproved of her sister's way of life, she was proud of her sister's accomplishments as a journalist. For her part, Georgina may well be frustrated by her sister's bossy behaviour, but she was filled with compassion for the woman who had lost her husband to war, the young man she had clearly adored.

Noelle had been completely honest with Maisie about her ambitions for the estate, and it was evident that she considered both Nick and Georgina 'troublesome' and Harry a lost cause. *A musician, if you please!*

What was it that Georgina's father had said about his younger son, when they were looking at photographs taken of the children in the summer of 1914? It was when he pointed out the photograph of Noelle, Georgina, Nicholas and Harry, who was about twelve at the time, some ten years younger than the twins, and about half Noelle's age. 'And there's Harry, bringing up the rear. Always behind, always on the edge, that's Harry.'

Burrowing under the covers, Maisie pondered the words before sleep claimed her: *Always behind, always on the edge, that's Harry.*

Chapter Six

An early-morning thaw, together with the efforts of Jenkins, the tenant farmer, and his shire horses, meant that the avenue leading to Bassington Place was cleared of snow by eleven, allowing Maisie to leave at noon—with Georgina, who had claimed a lift back into London. The women conversed comfortably throughout the drive, though Maisie found herself questioning the source of an unease in Georgina's company that had dogged her from the time the woman had first come to her office in Fitzroy Square.

It was as they drove across the Weald that a single word came to Maisie with such power that she almost said it out loud: doubt. Her sense of confidence was being undermined by doubt, though she did not know whether it was her ability that she doubted, or her relationship with Georgina and the other Bassington-Hopes, or the case itself.

When they reached London, Maisie dropped Georgina outside her flat and then drove home. On entering her own flat, Maisie was delighted to find that the radiators were now warm to the touch.

Sitting in an armchair, her legs curled to one side, she rested a notebook on her knees and jotted some notes. Despite thoughts and feelings that had assailed her earlier in the day, there was nothing to convince her that Nick Bassington-Hope's death was anything but an accident. However, if she assumed foul play, she might make progress swiftly. She must look for evidence, motive and a killer.

LATER THAT DAY, the clock on the mantelpiece in Maisie's sitting room struck the hour. It was six o'clock, time to get ready for Georgina Bassington-Hope's drinks party. Maisie was dreading it. The truth was that she knew she would feel ill at ease. For her, such events usually meant an hour or two holding up the wall, a barely sipped drink in her hand, before leaving without even locating a host to thank. Despite the passage of time along with academic and professional success, she had never managed to garner confidence in such social situations.

Dressing in her black day dress along with her pale blue cashmere cardigan and matching stole, Maisie brushed out her hair, rubbed a little rouge on her cheeks and added a sweep of colour to her lips. Checking her watch, she took her navy coat from the wardrobe in her bedroom and collected her black shoulder bag.

It was not possible to travel at more than a crawl along the Embankment, so dense was the ochre smog that enveloped buses, horses and carts and pedestrians alike—not that there were many out on a murky Sunday evening. Pulling on close to the red-brick mansions, Maisie was grateful to secure a parking spot from where she could see people enter Georgina's flat. She didn't want to be the first to arrive. It was cold, so she pulled the stole up round her neck and blew across her fingers as she waited.

After a while, when it was clear that several guests had gone inside, Maisie reached for her bag and was just about to open the car door when another motor car pulled up, followed by a second which she recognised immediately. She hoped that, under cover of the smog and the darkness, her MG could not be easily recognised from the front of the building. As she watched, Stratton stepped from the Invicta, whereupon he approached the first car just as the man she had seen him speaking to on Friday alighted onto the pavement. A young woman, dressed for a party, followed the man from the first motor, and as both Stratton and the man spoke to her, she nodded. Maisie suspected the woman might be one of the new female recruits to detection working at Scotland Yard. She waited. Soon the woman entered Georgina's building, whereupon the two men returned to their respective vehicles and departed.

Maisie waited as two more cars, both chauffeur-driven, deposited party guests at the mansion. Then a man came out of the smog, walking along the street. He was swinging a cane, his gait that of a young man. He wore no hat, and his overcoat was open to reveal evening attire, with a white dinner scarf hanging rakishly around his neck. Maisie suspected that this was Harry Bassington-Hope. As he walked up the steps to the front door, another car emerged and drove slowly past, much as a predator tracked his prey. But just as a lion might stalk just for the sport, so the driver seemed only to be following, in no hurry to make his move. *At least, not yet.*

'LOVELY TO SEE you, so glad you're here.' Georgina linked her arm through Maisie's. 'Let me introduce you to a few people.' She turned to a waiter and took two glasses of champagne, passing one to Maisie, before tapping a man on the shoulder. The family likeness was instantly evident. He was the man Maisie had seen walking along the street, cane in hand.

'Harry, I want you to meet Maisie Dobbs.'

The young man reached out to shake hands. 'Charmed, I'm sure. Always good to meet one of Georgina's Amazons.'

'Amazons?' asked Maisie.

'Oh, you know, accomplished independent new women and all that, a fellow marauder abroad. Likes to cut off a man in his prime.'

'Don't make me sorry I asked you to come, Harry.' Georgina led Maisie through the crowded room towards three men standing close to the fireplace.

'Come and meet Nick's old friends.' As they approached the men, Georgina gained their attention. 'Gentlemen, I'd love you to meet an old friend from Girton: Maisie Dobbs. Maisie—allow me to introduce Alex Courtman, Duncan Haywood and Quentin Trayner.' Georgina glanced back into the room, then extricated herself from the group.

They watched Georgina vanish into the gathering throng. Maisie was the first to speak. 'So, you've known each other for years, I understand.'

Duncan pressed a half-smoked cigarette into a silver ashtray. He was shorter than his friends, with a wiry build, quick in his movements. His features were sharp, with a small slender nose and light brown hair swept back from his forehead. Maisie thought he looked like a vole. He was about to reply when Alex responded to Maisie's question.

'Yes, since before the war. Duncan, Quentin, Nick and I met at the Slade.' Alex nodded towards his two friends. 'And when the powers that be learned that I was a bit on the young side to have joined up—wanting to follow my compatriots into the fray but thwarted when my mother insisted I was to be sent home—I was put to work at the ministry. Nick turned up after he was wounded and we both ended up drafting pictures to shake the populace out of its midwar torpor.'

'I see.' Maisie thought Alex painted an almost romantic picture of the friends' wartime exploits. Tall and lanky, he seemed to be something of a romantic figure himself, with dark brown hair combed into place in such a way as to remind her of a poet. His eyes seemed to narrow into half-moons when he smiled, which was often. Quentin, who was of medium height, with light brown hair and deep, hooded eyelids, seemed to stand apart, looking across at other guests as Maisie conversed with Duncan and Alex. She felt he wanted nothing more than for her to leave the three in peace.

A waiter approached with a tray of glasses filled to the brim with champagne. Alex handed fresh glasses to his friends, while Maisie raised hers to indicate that it was still half full.

'And now you all live down in Dungeness?'

Once again Alex was the first to reply. 'We're all moving on now, aren't we chaps?' He didn't wait for a response. 'Duncan has recently married his long-suffering fiancée, so he's moved to an idyllic cottage in Hythe. And Quentin's in the process of moving.' He turned to Maisie and said in a mock whisper, 'To live with his thrice-wed paramour in Mayfair.'

'That's quite enough.' Quentin's voice signalled a warning.

As the conversation listed towards matters of property in London, Maisie wondered how she might orchestrate a meeting with each man alone. For now it was enough to have made the acquaintances necessary to reintroduce herself within the next few days.

She chatted to the men for a little longer, then excused herself, claiming a need to catch up with an old friend. As she walked towards the young woman she had seen with Stratton earlier, she knew that Nick's fellow artists were waiting until she was out of earshot.

'Oh, hello, I think we've met before, haven't we? Was it at the Derby last year?' Maisie addressed the woman just as she was reaching for an hors d'oeuvre offered by a waiter.

'I—I—yes, I do believe we have. And yes, it must have been the Derby.'

Maisie smiled. 'Hadn't you just backed a horse called Murder Squad?'

'Oh, crikey!' The woman all but choked on a vol-au-vent.

'Don't worry, your secret is safe with me, but next time, don't agree to having seen someone at a place you haven't visited. Best to admit that you don't recognise them. A downright lie will always catch you out.'

'Who are you?'

Maisie smiled as if she really were chatting to an old friend. 'I'm Maisie Dobbs. Are you working for Stratton?'

She nodded. 'I can't tell you anything. Look, I should be going.'

'No, don't give up now, you'll likely lose your job. Does our hostess know who you are?'

'No.' The woman sighed. 'I latched on to one of those men over there when I came in.' She signalled discreetly across the room. 'I was ordered to come here by Stratton, and also Vance, from the Flying Squad.'

'And who are you watching?'

'Harry Bassington-Hope. I'm just here to report back on what time he arrived, who he spoke to, what time he leaves, and whether he takes a taxi.'

'What's your name?'

'Doris Watts. Will you tell Stratton you saw me?'

Maisie glanced round the room to locate Georgina, then replied, 'Yes, I probably will, but I will also tell him that you were acting quite inconspicuously and that I would only have guessed that you were with the Yard because I saw them drop you off—now that *was* amateurish.'

Doris Watts was about to speak again when there was a commotion at the door as Georgina welcomed another guest into the party. The hubbub of conversation died down and people began looking at the new arrival, stepping back as their hostess manoeuvred the man into the centre of a group standing by the window. Maisie turned away, for she had grown cold.

'Oh, my goodness, look who it is.' Doris Watts placed her hand on Maisie's arm. 'It's Mosley,' she whispered. 'Wait until I tell D.I. Stratton that she knows Oswald Mosley.'

As the man began to speak to the group, more guests edged nearer to him. And with his immediate circle burgeoning to become an audience, what was at first an intimate conversation began to develop into a speech. Maisie saw Alex, Duncan and Quentin move away, each of them frowning.

Oswald Mosley, the former Labour MP, was a suave, almost hypnotic orator, with black hair accentuating his piercing dark eyes. Maisie found him cobralike, with a power to beguile that mesmerised those present as he expounded his views on the future of the country.

'The New Party will lead the way, friends. There will be no more unemployment, which has only been increased by our Labour Party's policies. There will be new friendships forged with our former enemies, and never, ever will we march again to die on foreign lands in defence of our soil.'

The cheers and shouts of 'Hear, hear!' and 'Hurrah!' escalated around him, with men and women reaching out to touch the charismatic politician. Maisie decided to take her leave and went in search for her hostess to thank her and to say good night. The hall was empty as Maisie turned the corner, in time to hear raised voices coming from a room off to the side. Now, as she crept closer, she heard Georgina's voice, followed by that of her younger brother.

'For God's sake, Georgie, you're getting more like Nolly every day.'

'If asking you what in heaven's name you think you're doing is making me like Nolly, then so be it. Do you think I can keep handing over more money to pay off your debts?'

'Come on, Georgie. This is a matter of life and death.'

'Don't be dramatic, Harry.' As Georgina spoke, Maisie heard paper rustle. 'There you are. It's all I can let you have at the moment.'

There was a pause in the conversation, then Harry Bassington-Hope spoke again. 'Nick might have nagged the stuffing out of me, but there was always a bit more in my pocket after the upbraiding.'

'Well, I'm not Nick! The least you could do is say thank you.'

Maisie heard the door open wider and stepped back. The front door slammed behind Harry, who had not even bid his sister good night.

'Georgina, I'm leaving now, I—'

'Must you go?' Georgina appeared tired, but in the manner of the true hostess began the pretense of being put out by the departure of her guest. 'Well, I hope you had a good evening, Maisie, dear.'

Maisie nodded. 'Yes, indeed I did. Though I was rather surprised to see Sir Oswald Mosley here—do you know him?'

'My dear, everyone who's anyone knows Oswald. Future PM, just you watch. We're lucky to have his like among us.'

Nodding again, Maisie changed the subject. 'I'd like us to confer tomorrow morning as early as possible. I have some more questions for you.'

'Right you are, but let's hope you don't mean too early. How about ten?'

'Of course. Can you come to my office?'

'All right. Ten o'clock at your office.'

Maisie smiled. 'Thank you for inviting me to the party.'

MAISIE SLIPPED into the driver's seat of the MG and sighed. Despite earlier misgivings, which had remained uppermost in her mind, she had seen a vulnerability in Georgina Bassington-Hope. She was still on her guard, but that did not preclude the compassion she had felt for her client when she'd overheard the conversation with manipulative Harry Bassington-Hope.

She started the motor, turned on the lights and pulled out into the street. The smog was even thicker, if that were possible, and once again rendered any speed in excess of a crawl dangerous.

Leaning forward as she drove, Maisie stopped at the junction with the Embankment before turning right to continue her journey. It was then that she saw an unexpected movement by the river wall, an activity that sparked her suspicion and caused her to pull over and turn off the MG's lights. In the murky light shed by gas streetlamps, she saw two men talking to a third man who had his back to the wall. One of the first two poked the third man repeatedly on the shoulder, until he reached into his pocket and pulled out something that he passed to the second man, whereupon he and the first man stepped into a waiting car and drove off. The man with his back against the wall took a few moments to compose himself, then he turned and ambled off along the Embankment. The man was Harry Bassington-Hope.

At first, Maisie thought she should offer him a lift, but then decided against such a move. She did not want him to consider that she might have seen what had just transpired, the passing on of money taken from his sister.

And she thought that he was probably safe now, seeing as the piper had been paid. But who was the piper?

At length, Maisie parked in her customary place, close to her flat. As she closed and locked the car door, a physical sensation of fear enveloped her. The feeling increased as she approached the door. Maisie took the flat key from her shoulder bag, then looked towards the brightly illuminated centre stairway and the silhouette of a man pacing back and forth. Now she understood the root of her dread. The appearance of Billy Beale waiting for her late on a Sunday night could mean only one thing.

MAISIE WAS SO INTENT upon getting to Billy's house that she took chances she would never otherwise have taken. Barely missing a horse and cart, she turned into Billy's street with a screech of tyres.

Billy's wife stood at the already open door as Maisie leapt from the MG, reached behind the seat for what she called her 'medicine bag' and rushed into the house.

'We've got her downstairs, Miss Dobbs.' Doreen Beale had been crying but followed Maisie as she made her way along the narrow passage through to the kitchen at the back of the house. A pregnant woman sat holding Lizzie Beale, who was whimpering and, it seemed as her eyes rolled back, was on the brink of unconsciousness.

'Clear the table, and set a blanket on it for me—and Billy, bring over that lamp so that I can see her.' Maisie reached for Lizzie, cradling her in one arm as she pulled open the shawl that swaddled her. 'She's burning up and fighting to breathe—and you say you couldn't find the nurse or the doctor?'

Billy shook his head as Doreen laid out a blanket across the table and topped it with a clean sheet. Maisie set Lizzie down.

'No, Miss,' replied Billy shaking his head. 'And every time we tried to pick Lizzie up, she screamed, so I knew we'd never get 'er to the 'ospital.'

Maisie reached into the bag that Billy had set on a chair next to her and pulled out a white cotton mask which she placed over her nose and mouth, then secured with ties knotted behind her head. She reached into the bag again and took out a thermometer, along with a wooden tongue depressor. She also unpacked a small, narrow pan which she set on the table and filled with hydrogen peroxide, a makeshift form of disinfection. Taking up the thermometer, she shook it before placing it between the folds of skin under Lizzie's armpit. Then, leaning closer to Lizzie's face, she gently opened the cherry-red lips a little wider, and pressed down on Lizzie's tongue.

'She's been sick for about four or five days now, hasn't she?' Maisie reached for the thermometer, leaning towards the oil lamp to study the result.

Billy and his wife nodded, then Doreen spoke. 'We thought she was getting better, then she started to get worse.' She pressed a handkerchief to her mouth. 'What do you think's wrong with her, Miss Dobbs?'

Maisie looked up. 'She has diphtheria, Doreen. She has a temperature like a furnace and she must be taken to the fever hospital immediately. There is no time to lose.' She turned to Billy. 'If I'm right, I think the nearest is in Stockwell. Doreen, come with me. I have room for only one passenger, and you're the child's mother. We'll use this blanket to wrap Lizzie.' She took off her mask and disinfected the instruments. 'Now, here's the important thing: you have got to disinfect this whole house. Take all the sheets and blankets and boil them in the copper—and I mean a rolling boil with disinfectant. As soon as you can, get all the children up and into a tin bath with disinfectant. Scrub yourselves, the children, everything and everyone. You'll probably have the inspector around tomorrow, and they may take the children in as a precaution.'

It was almost midnight when Maisie sped off once again, this time balancing regard for the comfort of her passengers with the need to get Lizzie to the hospital. She knew only too well that Lizzie's chances would have increased greatly had she been admitted to hospital three days ago.

Parking the car in front of the hospital, Maisie put her arm round Doreen's shoulders as they rushed into the dour Victorian building. A doctor was summoned, Maisie gave details of symptoms and Lizzie Beale was taken away.

'Oh, my precious Lizzie. My precious girl.' Doreen Beale broke down in Maisie's arms, tears coursing down her face. 'I blame myself.'

'It's not your fault, Doreen. Some children don't display the usual signs until the disease has progressed. It must have looked just like a cold to start with.' As she clutched the woman to her, she concentrated on pouring strength into the mother who would need every ounce of resolve in the hours ahead. 'Look, Doreen, Billy should be here with you and Lizzie. The doctor will be out as soon as he has some news, and after he's seen you, they'll likely advise you to leave. I'll go and get Billy, and'—she reached into her shoulder bag—'here's the money for a taxicab home.'

Doreen began to object, but Maisie countered immediately. 'Please, Doreen, take it. I'm too tired to argue.'

The woman nodded, still sobbing, and Maisie left.

Later, having dropped Billy at the hospital, with an instruction to send word if there was anything else she could do, Maisie returned home. The cold silence of the drawing room barely touched her, for she was as numb now as she had ever been when faced with the prospect of death. She should have insisted on coming to see Lizzie earlier.

When, finally, she slipped into her cold bed, pulling the blankets round her, Maisie could not sleep. The emotion that weighed heavy upon her was anger. She appreciated that her view of the world was blighted by the events of the evening, but when she considered the seeming inequity of a society where people would spend thousands on a painting, while a child could die for want of a few pounds' worth of medical attention, she was left with a sour taste in her mouth. And wasn't it just plain unfair that there were those who had the wherewithal to paint all day, when others knew only the bitterness of unemployment, the gnawing hunger of want?

MAISIE WAS NOT in the best of moods when she arrived at the office the following morning. Having risen early, she'd left the house before six, planning to visit the Beales. As she drove down the narrow cobblestone street, she saw a grey fever ambulance outside Billy and Doreen's house. She parked behind the vehicle in time to see three children being brought out.

Billy followed them. He seemed as grey as the vehicle into which his middle child had been placed, along with Doreen's sister's two children. Turning to go back into the house, he saw Maisie.

'What's happening, Billy? Do you have news of Lizzie?'

'I came 'ome a couple of 'ours ago; Doreen stayed. She weren't leavin' with our Lizzie so ill.' He rubbed his eyes. 'Took out 'er tonsils. And she's been given injections of antisomething or other.'

Maisie nodded. 'What do they say?'

'It's touch and go. They say they're surprised she's still alive. Said they thought they'd lost 'er in the operatin' theatre, but she started to pick up again. And now they're takin' the others, all except the eldest, who's not showin' any symptoms.' Billy shook his head.

'Do you want a lift back to the hospital, Billy?'

'But what about my job, Miss? Can't afford to be out of work, can I?'

Maisie shook her head. 'Look, let's not worry about that now. I'll drop you at the hospital. Come back to work when you're ready.'

Later, as Billy was about to get out of the MG at the fever hospital in

Stockwell, he turned to Maisie. 'There's many an employer would 'ave put me on the street for this little how-d'you-do. I won't forget it, y'know.'

'It's not important, Billy.' She sighed. 'Just keep imagining Lizzie at home, back to her old self. Don't see the sickness. See the life in your child. It's the best thing you can do.'

As MAISIE MADE her way round London she could see men on their way to join the lines for assistance, or queues at factories where it was said a man could find work. Many of the men wore the expression of those embattled to a point where any last vestige of optimism had been lost. These were men—and women—whose country had needed them but who were now without a means to support themselves.

Slamming the door of her office, Maisie was in high dudgeon as she picked up the telephone receiver and dialled Scotland Yard. She asked to be put through to Detective Inspector Stratton.

'Yes!' The detective sounded rushed.

'Detective Inspector Stratton, I'd like to have a word with you this morning. Can you be at the usual caff, at around half past eleven?'

'All right. I assume it's something important?'

'Important, Inspector? Well, you can tell me when we meet whether Harry Bassington-Hope is important or not.' She did not wait to hear a response before setting the black telephone receiver back in its cradle.

Chapter Seven

'Lovely to see you at the party, Maisie. I feared you might have had more than enough of us.' Georgina eased into a chair by the fire.

'It was a colourful evening—a lot of fun,' replied Maisie, as she placed the woman's coat on a hook behind the door. 'I had an opportunity to speak to Nick's friends, and to meet Harry. Thank you for inviting me, Georgina. Would you like tea?'

'No, thank you.' Georgina looked around. 'Where's your man today?'

Maisie seated herself close to her client. 'His children are rather ill, so it seemed only right that he should be with his family.'

'Oh dear. I am sorry . . . Now then, to Nick.'

'Yes, *Nick*.' Maisie was surprised that the plight of Billy's family had been brushed off so quickly. 'I'd like to ask some more questions, if I may.'

'Fire away.' Georgina fidgeted in her seat and crossed her arms.

'First of all, I'd like to have a more detailed picture of Nick's relationships with those he was closest to and those who had an effect on his life. Let's start with his work, and Stig Svenson.'

Georgina nodded. 'Yes, indeed, Stig. He was a supporter of Nick's work right from the beginning. He believes in nurturing new talent along with close hand-holding, and always encouraged Nick to develop his range. He's very good at his job, steering his clients towards works that not only reflect their tastes but that prove to be lucrative investments. He knows his market and he understands his artists.'

'So, Svenson has done quite well out of his relationship with Nick?'

'Oh, yes, I'll say, very well indeed.'

Maisie nodded, stood up and paced to the window, then back to the fireplace, where she leaned against the mantelpiece to continue the conversation. 'Georgina, it's important for me to have a true sense of who your brother was in his heart.' She touched her chest as she spoke. 'I know the war affected him deeply—how could it not? But I would like you to recall conversations, perhaps, that might lead me to have a greater understanding of him. If I am to establish a motive for murder, then I must inhabit the victim, as far as that might be possible.'

'Yes, I know.' Georgina Bassington-Hope paused. 'To say that Nick lost an innocence in France would be too light an observation, but the description serves to explain what happened to him.'

Maisie spoke softly. 'Yes, I understand. Very well. Go on.'

'It wasn't so much that first time, when he was wounded—though that was bad enough. But going back disturbed him deeply.'

'Tell me about the wounds first.'

'To his shoulder, a shrapnel wound that effectively gave him a "blighty"— a wound serious enough to get him away from the front. He was also gassed, and . . .' She paused. 'He wasn't unbalanced, but he was *disturbed*. Then they drafted him to work in propaganda.'

Maisie was thoughtful. 'Does anything stand out from your conversations immediately following his repatriation?'

'What stands out was his silence, though within that reserve, there were stories here or there, if you happened to be with him.' Georgina's eyes narrowed as if she were looking into the past. 'As an artist, Nick saw events as messages, if you know what I mean. He would see a man killed and at the same time, in the mêlée, look up and see the dot that was a skylark overhead. It was something that intrigued him, the reality of that moment.'

Maisie said nothing, waiting for the woman to continue her reflection.

'He told me that he had seen overwhelming acts of terror and, on the other side of the coin, acts of compassion that touched him to the core.' She sat forward. 'Shortly after Nick joined his regiment, a soldier completely lost his mind after a battle, running here and there, uncontrollable. Nick said that he thought there would be compassion for him, but no, something quite different happened.' She paused again, as if choosing her words with care. 'Someone called him a shirker, then another said, "What shall we do with him, boys?" It was decided that he would be sent out alone in broad daylight to check the wires. So the man staggered out towards the line and in short order was cut down by an enemy sniper.'

Maisie shook her head and was about to speak when Georgina went on.

'And that's not the end of it. His body was brought back and hung from a post above the trench, whereupon the soldiers used the dead man's remains for target practice, having daubed the letters "LMF" on his back. Now that's the sort of thing you'll never hear about in an official record.'

'LMF?'

'Low Moral Fibre.'

Maisie tasted the salty saliva that flooded her mouth. She swallowed before continuing. 'Georgina, did Nick know the men who committed this dreadful act, or their commanding officer?'

Frowning, Georgina replied, 'I believe he must have, because I can just remember him saying that war could bring about a sort of anarchy where soldiers—human beings—would do something out of fear.'

'Fear?'

'Yes, that fear we have of someone who was one of us, but who has now changed. Nick said that's what scared people—people like those men— seeing something terrible that could so easily have been them, so they have to destroy it.'

'Did he paint this scene?'

'I'm sure he did. I looked for it when I went to the carriage after he died. In fact, I looked for work that depicted some of his stories and found only those general war sketches that you must have seen.'

'Yes.' Maisie checked her watch, taking a seat next to her client once again. 'And what about compassion? Did he draw those episodes?'

'I believe there's a whole body of work that we haven't seen, to tell you the truth, and that Nick kept those pieces away from view because they were like a rehearsal for the big show.'

Picking up her notes, Maisie knew she must make progress. 'Had Nick had any arguments with anyone lately? I know I have asked this before, but I must ask again.'

'Well, though they all lived in Dungeness, the boys—Quentin, Alex and Duncan—weren't quite as close as they once were.' She paused. 'And Nick was distancing himself from everyone, it seemed, though that isn't unusual for an artist preparing for a major exhibition.'

'And within your family?'

'Nick had argued with Harry. Harry gambles with a nasty losing habit, so he's come to both Nick and me for help. No good going to Nolly. Nick took him to task last time he got into big trouble.'

'And Nick could help?'

'He had reached a position where his art commanded a good price. Since Nick died, Harry has come to me twice for help.'

'Where does he work?'

'Various clubs, you know—the Kit Kat, the Trocadero . . .'

'I'd like to talk to him, Georgina. May I have a list of the clubs, perhaps?'

'All right, I'll scribble a few down.'

Maisie flicked through some notes. 'Now, how about Nick and Nolly?'

Georgina sighed. 'As you know, Nolly can be terribly difficult, though she hasn't always been like that. She adored Godfrey, her husband, and is bent upon cherishing his memory as a war hero.'

'Yes, she said as much to me.'

'He was a delightful chap, but a bit bland. We all joked that it was her quest to breed some common sense into the line. Being a Bassington-Hope must have been so terribly hard on her, when I think of it. Mind you, she and Nick were very close when he came back. She visited him just about every day in hospital, then remained in London with him, just to make sure he was all right when he started work at the Office of Information. I think the fact that he was with Godfrey when he died—'

'Nick was with Nolly's husband?'

'Didn't you know? I was sure . . . well, anyway, he was with him when he died. Godfrey was in the regiment that Nick joined.' Georgina looked at Maisie, frowning. 'It's just sad that Nolly and Nick fell out and didn't really put their differences behind them.'

'What were their differences?'

'I'm trying to think when things deteriorated. I do know that she took an intense dislike to his work, said that he should forget the war, that it was idiocy to dredge it all up just for the sake of a picture.'

'When was that?'

'They were on the outs just before he went over to America. Daddy agreed with her—mind you, Daddy always tries to see Nolly's side of things. She's the eldest and he's really rather protective of her.'

Maisie was pensive for a moment. 'And how about you and Nick? Were you on good terms when he died?'

'Of course. I mean, we had our little differences of opinion, but Nick and I were terribly close, not fighters.'

As she spoke, Maisie watched as Georgina systematically pressed down the cuticle of each finger with the thumbnail of the opposite hand.

'Now then, just two or three more questions today. Was Nick seeing anyone, did he have a sweetheart?'

Georgina smiled. 'Such an old-fashioned term, "sweetheart". Nick played the field in a "dark horse" sort of way. There was always a girl here or there, if he wanted someone with him, but certainly no one I can remember.'

'What do you know about Randolph Bradley?'

Georgina shrugged, and as she looked away, Maisie noticed the faintest colour rise to her cheeks. 'Typical American businessman. Pots and pots of money. He began collecting Nick's work some time ago. I understand he has a gallery at his house dedicated to Nick's work. I've heard that he will stop at nothing to get a piece he wants.'

'And he wants the triptych?'

'Yes, but when it's found we're not selling. Nick didn't want to. After he died, Nolly thought it would be a good idea to get rid of everything. Which is strange, as at one point she wanted to have all of Nick's work hidden away. As I said, she hated Nick's war work, said that it shouldn't be allowed to hang anywhere in Britain or Europe.' Georgina looked directly at Maisie. 'Do you think he *was* murdered?'

'There is compelling evidence to support the pathologist's conclusion that his death was an accident, though I have a feeling—as you do—that the truth is not quite as straightforward. I will be leaving for Dungeness again on Wednesday, but I would ask you not to tell anyone else that I will be there. I plan to go to the gallery again, and to pay a visit to Mr Bradley.'

'And what tack will you take in these meetings?'

Maisie tapped the index cards with her pen. 'If Nick sought to illustrate personal or universal truths, there are many who must have been touched by his work. People do not always like to see themselves reflected in the brutal honesty of the artist. I'm curious to know how he touched his immediate audience—friends and associates—with his work. You see, if Nick was the victim of a crime, it is more than possible that he knew his killer. Which means that you are likely to be known to that person too.'

'INSPECTOR, I'M SORRY I'm late. My first appointment of the day went on a bit.' Maisie took off her scarf and placed it on the back of the chair facing Stratton, who was already sipping tea. 'Another cup?'

'No, thank you, this will do.'

'Then you won't mind waiting while I just fetch myself some.'

Maisie returned with a cup of strong tea and a plate of toast and jam.

'So, Miss Dobbs, what is it this time?'

'Inspector, as I said before, I am grateful to you for supporting Miss Bassington-Hope's decision to seek my help. However, what has become clear to me is that something else is going on. You must have known that I would stumble across the fact that you—and the Flying Squad chappie—have an interest in the activities of Harry Bassington-Hope.'

Stratton shook his head. 'I told them you would find out.'

'And whose idea was it to deliver Doris to her place of surveillance without regard for who might be watching?'

Stratton sighed. 'All right, so you know there's been an interest in Harry.'

'You're going to have to tell me more than that, Inspector.'

Stratton took a sip of tea. 'Harry Bassington-Hope, as you probably know, has got himself involved with some undesirable people. The gambling habit, together with the types he meets in those clubs, led him deeper into debt with people one should never be indebted to.'

'How does this all connect to his brother?'

'We doubt if there's a direct connection, apart from the elder Bassington-Hope bailing out the younger. No, the reason for a collaboration between departments is that a small-time punter one step shy of crooked—another Harry Bassington-Hope type—was found dead a couple of months ago, we believe murdered by the same men that Harry is indebted to.'

'Harry's the mouse to catch the big cat, is that it?'

'Yes. We are simply watching and waiting.'

'So, again, Inspector, the connection—or not—to the death of the artist?'

'Nick Bassington-Hope tripped over his feet on scaffolding, *as we know*. However, the last thing we wanted was that hotheaded sister running amok in search of a killer and ruining months of solid police work in the process.'

'I see. But what if there was no accident?'

'You mean our criminal element? No, they would have no interest in Nick Bassington-Hope. Art isn't their game. They make a lot from the clubs—protection, that sort of thing. They're fencing jewellery—diamonds, gold. They are involved with bank robberies. The crime barons of London, you could call them.'

'I see . . . it's clearer to me why you kept things quiet, though I do wish you had told me more a week ago.'

Stratton sighed. 'Well, I must say, you're doing a good job of keeping that woman quiet.'

'Am I, Inspector?' Maisie took one last sip of tea, finished the toast, then reached for her scarf. 'By the way, how is Doris?'

'Well, I don't think we'll be using women in detection for a while. Wasn't quite up to the job.'

Maisie stood up, her chair scraping against the floorboards. 'Oh, I wouldn't write off the likes of Doris just like that, Inspector. You never know what a woman might uncover that you've missed completely.'

MAISIE FOUND BILLY and Doreen Beale in the waiting room of the fever hospital. 'What news of the children? And Lizzie?'

Billy had his arm round Doreen. Their faces bore the signs of strain. Billy shook his head. 'The eldest is at 'ome, with Doreen's sister, and the other nippers are all doin' all right. But Lizzie . . . we was just about to go in to see the little lass again, and they turfed us out, said there was an emergency. The poor little mite is in trouble all over 'er body. I reckon they've shoved some more of that antiwhatsit into 'er.' Billy faltered.

'I'll see if I can find out anything more for you.' Maisie placed a hand on Doreen Beale's shoulder, nodded at Billy, and went in search of a nurse. She had barely reached the door when a doctor came into the waiting area.

'Are you Mrs Beale?'

'No,' replied Maisie, 'I am Mr Beale's employer. I was a nurse, so I have an understanding of the situation. How is Lizzie?'

The doctor sighed. 'I wish I had better news. How that child is still alive beggars belief. As you know, we proceeded with an immediate tracheotomy, tonsillectomy and adenoidectomy, so the risk of infection is high. There's little more we can do except watch and keep her as comfortable as possible.' He paused. 'I can't promise she'll still be with us by this time tomorrow.'

Maisie felt the lump in her throat grow. 'And the other Beale children?'

'Got it in time, so they are expected to make a full recovery.'

'Can the parents see Lizzie? They are grasping for a shred of hope. Why not allow them to be together, just for a few minutes?'

The doctor shook his head. 'Strict rules. Matron would have my entrails for garters. But . . . oh, all right. Go and get them, then come with me.'

He led the Beales along the corridor, into an anteroom where they were instructed to wash their hands and put on masks, then into a ward where the most serious cases were quarantined in austere, iron-framed cots, each with just a sheet and rough blanket to cover the feverish body of a child.

Maisie spoke to the couple. 'Don't be afraid to touch Lizzie. Hold her hands, tell her you're there, rub her feet. Let her feel you. It's important.'

She departed the hospital half an hour later and drove to the Ritz, to call on Randolph Bradley. She decided that a visit to Svenson's Gallery would be more effective before her visit to Dungeness on Wednesday. She didn't want to arrive at the coast too early. No, she needed to be there at dusk. To wait.

THE DESK CLERK, with perfectly oiled, swept-back hair, pushed a pair of tortoiseshell spectacles to the bridge of his nose and peered at Maisie's calling card. 'Mr Bradley is not expecting you?'

'No, but I am sure he will see me.' She reached for the card. 'Look, let me scribble a quick note for him on the back.'

Maisie wrote on the card, then passed it back to the clerk, along with a coin. 'I'm sure you can arrange for him to receive this directly.'

The man executed a short bow. Twenty minutes later, as Maisie stood waiting in the lobby, a tall, distinguished man walked towards her. She estimated him to be about six foot two and probably forty-five years old. His suit was impeccably tailored, his smile was engaging and his blue eyes sparkled. He had one hand in a trouser pocket as he walked across the lobby and waved to the clerk with his free hand. This was a successful man, a man who seemed to excel at cultivating Englishness.

'Miss Dobbs?' The man had taken the hand from his pocket, and now held it out to her. 'Randolph Bradley.'

Maisie smiled. 'It's very good of you to see me, Mr Bradley.'

The American looked around, clearly searching for a place conducive to private conversation. 'We'll have coffee in there.' He pointed to the dining room, where it appeared the waiters were preparing for lunch. Undeterred, Bradley strode to a table, stood as a waiter pulled out a chair for Maisie, then took a seat, ordering a large pot of fresh coffee as he did so.

'So, Miss Dobbs. You want to know more about my interest in Nick Bassington-Hope's work?'

'Yes. When did he—and his work—first come to your attention?'

Bradley reached into the inside pocket of his jacket and pulled out a packet of cigarettes and a lighter. 'Let me ask a question before I say anything. Are you helping the police?'

'No, I am not. I work privately, as I said in my note, and as you can see from my card.'

'So, who're you working for? Who's paying you?'

'I have been asked by Georgina Bassington-Hope to conduct a limited investigation into her brother's death. She felt that there were a few unanswered questions.'

'So are you investigating me?'

Maisie smiled. 'Mr Bradley, you are an avid collector of Mr Bassington-Hope's work, so he obviously spent time with you. Any artist would be anxious to keep the buyer happy, is that not so?'

Bradley nodded. 'Nick was nobody's fool, and knew where his bread and butter came from. He may have had his garret on the beach but he knew how to sell his work.'

'What do you mean?'

The American acknowledged a waiter who came bearing a silver coffee pot, setting it on the table. He did not speak until the waiter had left the table after pouring coffee for Maisie and himself.

'A lot of these artists have no idea when it comes to selling their work. They have an agent, and they leave it all up to him.' Bradley took a sip of coffee. 'But Nick wanted to meet me, and we talked a lot, got to know each other.'

'I see.' Maisie set her cup in its saucer. 'I've been trying to build a picture of who Nick Bassington-Hope was. He was an artist, and yet a most sensible person. He had seen unspeakable things in the war, yet he did not draw back from depicting them. And he wasn't afraid to use real people in his work either.' Maisie did not miss a beat. 'So, when did you first learn of his work? How did you go about building the collection?'

Bradley stubbed out his cigarette. 'Svenson came to see me, oh, must have been in 1922. Nick had a few pieces in an exhibition at the gallery—of course, it was a much smaller outfit then. I reckon Svenson has made a mint off Nick Bassington-Hope, and those old masters he buys from Europeans on the brink of ruin. Anyway, he tipped me off early, and I saw, right away, that this was an artist I could appreciate.'

'Why?'

'It was just amazing! Nick didn't just serve up blood and guts, no, he could touch the . . . the . . . *essence* of the scene. He could touch the truth.'

'So you started buying?'

'There and then. And I wanted to see what he'd done before, and I wanted everything he painted that was for sale later.'

'So what about his latest collection? You've bought all but the main piece, I understand.'

'Yeah. Bought it all, didn't even have to see it.'

'But you didn't procure the main piece?'

'Nick didn't want to sell. But when they find it, I'll get it.'

'Do you know anything about it, apart from the fact that it's supposed to be more than one piece?'

'I believe that this piece, whatever it is, will distill—yeah, I reckon that's a good word—*distill* everything he thought and felt about that war. I think that once it was finished, he was ready to let the past be the past, you know, step forward to whatever was to come next. I predict that whatever he had moved on to would have been an example of . . . of . . .'

'Resurrection? Rebirth?' Maisie offered.

'Yeah, that sounds about right. I like that.' He looked around the room, now filled with guests taking luncheon, then at his watch. 'Any more questions, Miss Dobbs?'

'I'd like to know how long you've been doing business with Stig Svenson, and—I promise this is confidential—what he's like to deal with.'

'I've known Svenson since before the war, when we were both starting out. I'd made some money and I wanted to indulge myself. When I was a boy, an English *fellow*'—he grinned, checking that Maisie had caught the quip—'lived in our street. He wasn't rich, but he was dapper, as you would say. *Dapper* and I wanted to be like him. He worked in a factory. Not a fancy office, but a factory. And he spent money on art, all sorts of pictures from artists you'd never even heard of. I was only young, but I bought a couple I liked, cheap. So, that set me on my path, my love of art. I bought some pieces from Svenson in 1919. We kept in touch. My business boomed and I was over here as much as I was at home.' He looked directly at Maisie. 'Now, even though I've known Svenson awhile now, and we respect each other, I believe he'd take the shirt off my back if he could. He's sharp, understands what sells—and right now, that's European art, all your rich counts and princes selling off the family heirlooms. God only knows where he's getting it from—*and* he knows who wants to buy.' Bradley stood up and came round to pull out Maisie's chair for her. 'Nick knew Svenson could pull a buyer, but he watched him like a hawk all the same.'

Bradley accompanied Maisie into the lobby of the hotel.

'Thank you for seeing me, Mr Bradley. You have been most helpful.'

'My pleasure, Miss Dobbs.' He handed her a visiting card. 'Call me if you need any more information.' He laughed. 'In fact, call me if you find that darn painting. I'll pay the family whatever they want for it. Nolly Bassington-Hope knows that. In fact, she can't wait to get it out of the country!'

Maisie drew a breath to put another question to the American, but he had turned and walked away.

Chapter Eight

Nick's three closest friends, according to Georgina, were still in London; as far as she knew, Alex Courtman would be at her flat this afternoon. As Maisie travelled to Kensington, she was struck by the fact that all three men were moving on, with two of them appearing recently to have become financially better heeled.

She parked the MG and walked to Georgina's flat. A housekeeper answered, then showed her into the drawing room and went to summon Alex Courtman.

'Ah, Miss Dobbs. How delightful to see you again.' Alex held out his hand. He appeared even more youthful today, dressed in gabardine trousers, a white collarless shirt with the sleeves rolled up and a reddish-brown cable-knit pullover. His unruly dark hair appeared not to have had the benefit of a comb that morning.

'I wonder if you would be so kind as to oblige me with a moment or two of your time, Mr Courtman?'

'Of course.' He extended his hand towards an armchair, then sat down on the end seat of a chesterfield, close to Maisie, who glanced around her. There had been so many people at Georgina's party, she had hardly noticed the room, which now seemed quintessentially bohemian, though perhaps not as outlandish as the Bassington-Hope family seat. There were antique pieces that immediately suggested a connection to old money, but it was bright, with windows flanked by heavy swags of pale gold silk. In one corner a carved screen was draped with fabrics from Asia, and a collection of masks from around the world were displayed on a wall. There were three paintings by Georgina's brother, and others by artists unknown to Maisie.

'How may I help you, Miss Dobbs?'

'As you know, I am working on behalf of Miss Bassington-Hope to discover more about the circumstances of her brother's death. You were one of Nick's dearest friends, so I thought you might be able to'—she smiled—'paint a picture of him for me, by answering some questions?'

'Fire away!' He leaned back into the chesterfield.

'You're all moving on now. Duncan has his cottage in Hythe, Quentin's moving into a flat with his paramour, and you're spending more time here than in Dungeness. It couldn't have all been planned since the accident.'

Courtman answered calmly. 'Well, these things tend to happen all at once, don't they? It just takes one to step off the boat and everyone else gets itchy feet. I'll probably get my own flat soon.'

'You've all done very well with your work, haven't you?'

He shrugged. 'Nick's work sold very well, and I do believe we were affected simply by being associated with him, as if some of that stardust flaked off onto us. Svenson talks about the "Bassington-Hope" school.'

'You said at the party that you met some years ago.'

Courtman nodded. 'Yes, as I told you, we all met at the Slade, though I knew Duncan better than I knew Nick and Quentin, to tell you the truth. I'm a bit younger than the others. I was a latecomer to the group. It doesn't make much difference now, but in those days I was definitely the new boy. Then we joined the Artists' Rifles together, more or less, which sealed the friendships, though Nick, Duncan and Quentin are—were—something of an exclusive trio. But when it comes to a move such as the one to Dungeness and away again—it only takes one and we all fall in.'

'And who was the one?'

'Nick. He's the one who said that we ought to do our bit in the war. Seemed as if that's all people said then, you know, do your *bit*. Trouble was, it was a bit too much to have bitten off, if you ask me. Old men always tell the young to do their bit, and half the time it isn't anything they'd want to do themselves.'

'Indeed.' Maisie nodded, familiar with the stream of disillusion that formed an undercurrent to conversations concerning the war. She continued. 'Perhaps you can tell me about the Rifles. Was this where you got to know each other really well?'

'In training, not over in France. We were all assigned to different regiments there. Nick ended up in the same regiment as his brother-in-law, much to his dismay, though I understand he came rather to like the chap.' Courtman stared out of the window. 'He said in a letter that he'd always thought the man was a bit wet, but came to regard him as simply *kind*. Nick was quite shattered when he was killed.'

'Do you know the circumstances, specifically?' Maisie was intrigued enough to allow the man to reminisce.

Courtman turned to Maisie. 'Circumstances? You mean other than two lines of men with guns pointed at each other?'

'I meant—'

'Yes, I know what you meant. I was being facetious. How did Godfrey Grant die? As far as I know it was during a cease-fire.'

'Cease-fire?'

'It happened fairly often. In fact, it wasn't unusual for there to be a quick truce for both sides to whip out, collect their wounded and bury their dead. Imagine it, men like ants scurrying back and forth, trying to honour their own before some smart-aleck officer calls them all back to their own side for another round.'

'Nolly's husband was killed in a truce?'

'As far as I know. Probably didn't get back to his trench before they were under starter's orders again.'

'I see.' Maisie made note of the conversation on an index card. 'So, back to Nick. What was your training like? Did he continue with his work?'

'Never saw him without a sketchbook. Mind you, we're artists, we all had our sketchbooks, even though Nick's art was his exorcism, in a way. He painted the war out of his soul and into the open.'

'What do you know about the triptych?'

'If you know it's a triptych, then I know about as much as you.'

'Do you think it was his last war painting?' Maisie leaned forward.

Courtman was quiet for some moments, then he looked up at Maisie. 'You know, I believe it was. I hadn't thought about it like that before. Yes, very astute of you, Miss Dobbs.'

'No, not me. It was something suggested by Randolph Bradley, actually.'

'Hmmph! The American moneybags, eh? Well, he should know, shouldn't he? He all but bought Nick himself, the way he snapped up his work. He was furious about that triptych, or whatever it is. Furious! He came to the gallery when we were setting up Nick's scaffolding—and, let me tell you, we knew what we were doing, that scaffolding was solid, absolutely solid.'

'What did he want?'

'He called Nick aside. They started talking quietly, then the next thing you know, Bradley is saying, "I'll have that painting if it's the last thing I do—and if I don't, your career is dead, pal!" Makes you wonder, now that I think of it.'

'Then what happened?'

'Svenson came out in a bit of a lather and everyone calmed down. Bradley apologised to Nick, to Duncan and to me.'

'Did Nick say anything?'

'Oh, yes, that's when he really let the cat out of the bag.'

'Yes?' Maisie inclined her head.

'He smiled, as if he'd really got the upper hand now. Then he said, quite calmly—you know, I'm surprised Georgie didn't tell you this—'

'She knows the story?'

'For heaven's sake—she was there! Anyway—'

'She was at the gallery, when this was going on?'

'Well, she came with Bradley.' He grinned. 'Come on, you must have known about Georgie and Bradley?'

'No. I didn't.' Maisie paused for a moment, then was quick to go back to the conversation. She'd consider Georgie and the American later. 'But,

Mr Courtman, how did Nick let the cat out of the bag?'

'He announced his intention for the piece. He said that it would not grace a private home, but instead he was going to give it to the nation, to the Tate or the National. It was his gift to the dead of war and those who would have us go to war in the future, so that we may never forget who we are.'

'"Never forget who we are?" Did he say what he meant?'

'Yes, in fact, Bradley asked him. "And who the hell are we, goddamn it?" And Nick said, quite simply, "We are *humanity*." And then he turned back to the scaffolding, and Duncan and I just carried on with our work.'

Alex leaned back on the chesterfield and closed his eyes. He sat that way for some moments, until Maisie spoke in a soft voice. 'You've been most helpful, Mr Courtman.' She stood up, collected her black document case and checked her watch. 'I really must be going now.'

'Righty-o.' Courtman came to his feet. 'Hope I didn't put my foot in it, you know, spilling the beans about Georgie and Bradley.'

'No, of course not.' Maisie held out her hand to Courtman. 'I have one more question for you, if you don't mind?'

'Yes?'

'Were Georgina and Nick on good terms when he died?'

'Oh, lummy, here we go.' He sighed before answering. 'Nick was upset about the affair with Bradley—the American's married, you know, has a wife in New York—and said as much to Georgie. On the day we left to go and set up the scaffolding, I was in the guest room with Duncan and I heard Georgie and Nick yelling at each other.' He shrugged. 'I feel sorry for Georgie, actually. Must feel awful, now that Nick has gone. In fact, it's a wonder she came to you, really, isn't it?'

'Why?' Maisie had reached the door.

'Well, if I were a detective, I'd wonder about that temper of Georgie's.'

Maisie smiled. 'That's the interesting thing about detection, Mr Courtman. Things are rarely as they seem. I will keep our conversation in confidence and trust that you will do the same.'

'Absolutely! No problem there, Miss Dobbs.'

MAISIE PASSED the parked Austin Swallow upon her return to the flat that evening. Oh dear, she thought, as she manoeuvred the MG into its customary place. She locked the car, then turned to face Andrew Dene, who was walking towards her, his overcoat flapping. To smile was his way, and he did so as Maisie greeted him, though she could see tension in his hunched shoulders. He placed a hand on her arm and kissed her on the cheek.

'This is a surprise, Andrew.' Maisie searched for her keys, her hands shaking in anticipation of a looming confrontation. 'Come on in.'

Andrew Dene followed her into the hallway, then to her flat, where she selected a second key to enter. 'I thought it was about time we sorted things out,' he said, as she pressed the key into the lock.

Opening the door, Maisie turned and nodded, before placing her hat and gloves on a small table. She took off her mackintosh. 'Yes, of course, you're right. Here, let me take your coat.' She waited as Dene removed his overcoat and scarf. 'Shall I make a pot of tea?'

Dene sat down in one of the two armchairs and shook his head. 'No, thank you. I doubt I shall be staying long, Maisie.'

Maisie nodded as she made herself comfortable on the second armchair, kicking off her shoes and tucking her legs up.

'I thought we ought to talk about *us*, Maisie.'

She said nothing, allowing him to speak uninterrupted.

'I had hoped, when we first began seeing each other, that you might one day become my wife.' Dene swallowed deeply. 'I've been waiting for the right girl, someone who would have an understanding of my background, what it takes to move up, so to speak, from one's given station in life. And I thought that girl might be you.' His voice wavered briefly. 'I know your work is so very important to you, but I trusted that it might, in time, take a second place to our courtship. Now, I don't know.' Dene turned to her, his eyes glistening. 'I have to say, Maisie, that I was flummoxed by your manner when we last met. But even before that, buying this flat'— he swept his hand around—'it sort of put me in my place, even though I held out hope.'

Still Maisie said nothing, instead keeping her attention focused on the man in front of her, cradling in her heart a bittersweet ache of relief.

'So, before I say anything else, I want to know, Maisie, if there's any hope for me—for us, as a couple—if I propose?'

She said nothing for some seconds. When she spoke, her voice was soft, measured. 'Andrew, you are, and have been, a wonderful companion. But the truth of the matter is that . . . oh, this is so hard to explain.' She felt incompetent with words where personal matters were concerned. 'I feel that I have some . . . some sort of mastery over circumstance when I am working. And the fact is, Andrew, my business takes all the stamina I have—and you deserve more.' She cleared her throat. 'I have seen how the joys of our courtship have been compromised by my responsibilities to the people who come to me for help, and my choice has often been the source of great angst for us both.' She paused again. 'Even though you have journeyed to London every fortnight, and I have travelled to Hastings in between . . . it hasn't been conducive to a happy courtship, has it?' She did not wait for a reply, but continued, 'I have found myself fearing that as time goes on there will be pressures upon us to conform to the accepted role of a doctor and his wife, and that would mean I would have to choose between my work and you. So, I have chosen now, Andrew. Now, instead of later.'

Dene inspected the palms of his fine hands, the long fingers stretched out before him. 'Don't mind me saying so, Maisie, but you could have been more honest from the start. You must have known all this, and that I wasn't prepared to sort of drift along.'

With tears blurring her vision, Maisie interrupted Dene. 'I believe I have been responsible towards you, and respectful, I—'

'You haven't been honest with *yourself*—until now, I suppose. I have been a handy diversion for you, a weekend here, a dinner there.'

Maisie stood up, shaken. 'Andrew, I think it's time for you to go. I wish we could part on better terms, but I fear that isn't going to happen.'

Andrew Dene, now on his feet, responded in a tone laced with sarcasm. 'So be it, Miss Dobbs, psychologist and investigator.' He sighed, adding, 'I'm sorry, that wasn't called for.'

Maisie nodded, and without saying more she gathered Dene's coat and opened it for him. 'Drive carefully, Andrew. It's icy out there.'

'I'm in hospital digs tonight, I'll be all right.'

'Good luck, Andrew.'

'You, too, Maisie.' Dene turned, and walked away.

MAISIE WENT DIRECTLY to her bedroom, switched on the light and opened the wardrobe. At this point she did not want to think about Dene or consider the consequences of the end of their courtship. Having pulled out several items of clothing, she slumped on the edge of the bed, clutching her blue cashmere cardigan and stole. She pressed the soft fabric to her cheek and wept. In spite of the sense of relief, she already felt the cool breeze of loneliness. Knowing Andrew had been a barrier between herself and an isolation that seemed to so readily envelop her.

As her tears gradually abated, she confessed to herself that there was something else, a truth she may never have considered had she not met the Bassington-Hopes—and that she knew she would never find with Andrew Dene as her partner. She realised that she had come to love colour, both in the landscape of character and quite literally—on fabric, canvas, clay or a room. The world she had entered by dint of working for Georgina was bursting with something fresh: there was a potency that made her feel as if she were cracking open her cocoon and taking energy, life, from those who lived in a world of colour, of words, of artistry.

Maisie leaned back, exhausted, then she galvanised herself, drying her eyes and taking a deep breath. 'It was for the best,' she said aloud, thinking of Dene. Rubbing a hand across her eyes, she stepped in front of the mirror, wrapping the stylish blue stole around her. Yes, together with the black dress, it would do quite well for a woman out alone in the evening.

MAISIE LEFT THE FLAT at ten o'clock. It wasn't completely unusual for women to go out alone any more. In fact, it had become quite acceptable, especially as there were no longer enough men to accompany them.

Clutching her list of clubs, Maisie planned simply to pop her head around the door of each, act as if she were there to see her friend Harry Bassington-Hope, and then leave if she couldn't confirm his presence.

Chelsea for two of the clubs, Soho for another two, and one in Mayfair were on her list. By the time she arrived at Stanislav's, in Soho, Maisie thought she was becoming more accomplished in the act of nonchalantly walking into a club, sweet-talking the man or woman at the door, and then leaving when the reply was to the effect that Harry was expected later, or on another evening. Clearly he worked at different places each night.

She took a deep breath and pushed against the door, whereupon a well-built man stepped forward to hold it open. A young woman smiled from behind a black and silver counter framed by a series of square silver lampshades. Maisie blinked, then smiled in return at the woman, whose blonde hair was tied back into a small chignon. Her eyes were accentuated by kohl, her lips blood-red, and sequins sparkled along her collar and cuffs.

The woman greeted her cordially. 'Are you a member?'

'Oh, no. But I am a guest of Harry Bassington-Hope. Is he here yet?'

The woman inclined her head. 'I'll find out. Just a moment, please.'

She opened a door behind her, poked her head into a room that Maisie couldn't see, and said, 'Oi, is 'arry 'ere yet?' There was a delay of several seconds before she closed the door and addressed Maisie again, the cut-glass accent restored. 'He should be here at any moment, madam. Please follow me. We have a small table where you can wait.'

Maisie was relieved to see that the table was situated in a corner, close to the back wall, a perfect position from which to observe the comings and go-ings of people in the club. A waiter came to the table, and Maisie ordered a ginger beer with lime cordial. She settled back to observe the room.

A series of tables of varying sizes, seating from two to eight people, were placed several tables deep around three sides of a small parquet dance floor. A quartet had just started to play and already a few couples were dancing. Maisie tapped her foot, glancing up as her harmless cocktail was delivered. As she sipped her drink, she decided that it would be quite fun to come with friends to such a place. If one *had* a clutch of friends to come with, that is.

'Care to dance, Miss Dobbs?'

'Oh, my goodness, you made me jump!'

Alex Courtman pulled back a chair and sat down at the table. 'Well, I can't for a moment believe that you are here for anything but business, but, I must say, you look ravishing.'

Maisie raised an eyebrow. 'Thank you for the compliment, Mr Court-man. In actual fact I'm waiting for a friend.'

'I am sure your friend won't mind if I steal you for a dance, will he?'

'No, thank you, Mr Courtman. I'd rather not.'

'Come on! You don't go to a club unless you are up for a dance or two.' Courtman took Maisie's hand and led her, protesting, to the dance floor. The popular tune had drawn many more couples from their tables, so there was hardly room to move, but that didn't stop Courtman from swinging his arms from side to side with the beat. Maisie, too, began to swing her arms, following her partner's lead. Seeing her enthusiasm, Courtman took her by the waist and swirled her around. As the music reached a crescendo, a trumpet wheeled in with a high-pitched long note, to the accompaniment of piano, bass and drums. The dancers applauded as they continued to move around the floor. Harry Bassington-Hope had arrived.

Courtman claimed Maisie for two more dances before, breathless, she held up her hands in mock surrender and returned to the table, her partner following her.

'I say, you can dance when you like, can't you?'

Maisie shook her head. 'To tell you the truth, I don't think I've danced since . . . since . . . well, since before the war, actually.'

Courtman raised his hand to summon a waiter. 'Don't tell me, you danced with the love of your life and he never came home from France.'

The smile left Maisie's face. 'It's none of your business, Mr Courtman.'

He touched her hand. 'I'm terribly sorry. I didn't mean to offend.'

Maisie nodded to acknowledge the apology, withdrawing her hand. She changed the subject. 'So, are you a regular here?'

'I come occasionally. But especially when I'm owed money.'

'Harry?'

Courtman nodded. 'He tapped me for a few pounds on Sunday. Said he'd repay it in two days. I'm not exactly flush, so I want it back today.'

Maisie looked at Harry Bassington-Hope, his legs splayed, his bow tie pulled loose, as he leaned back, his trumpet held high, teasing another impossibly high note from the shining instrument.

'When does he stop, or take a break?' said Maisie.

'In about another fifteen minutes. You can leave a message with the waiter—along with the appropriate monetary accompaniment—and he'll pass it on to Harry, telling him to join you.'

When the waiter arrived with their drinks, Maisie followed Courtman's instructions, slipping a couple of coins into the waiter's palm as she gave him the folded piece of paper.

'Shall I wait until he comes?' Courtman smiled with such sincerity that she could almost forgive his lack of manners just a few moments ago.

'Yes, thank you, Mr Courtman. I am not really accustomed to such places, to tell you the truth.'

'I'm sure. Mind you, I'm only staying on one condition. I want to claim the first dance after trumpet boy gets back up there.'

HARRY BASSINGTON-HOPE swaggered off the stage and over to the bar, stopping on the way to shake hands with customers and to lean over and kiss women on the cheek. Maisie watched as the waiter approached him and whispered in his ear, whereupon Harry looked around to locate Maisie's table. He nodded to the waiter, reached for the drink that had already been placed on the bar for him, and made his way over to Maisie.

'Miss Dobbs, we meet again.' He pulled out a chair, turned it round and sat down, his arm resting on the chair back as he set his glass down on the table. He saw Maisie glance at the clear liquid. 'Soda water. Never drink anything stronger while playing, though I try to make up for lost time when I'm off duty.' He turned to Alex Courtman. 'Alex, old chap, still taking up room in my sister's flat? I would have thought the Yankee would have kicked you out by now.'

Alex Courtman stood up. 'Moving on next week, Harry, to new digs over in Chelsea.' He drained his glass and turned to Maisie. 'I'll be back to claim that dance when trumpet boy here starts playing again.'

Harry watched as Courtman strode towards the bar, then brought his attention back to Maisie. 'So, what can I do for you, Miss Dobbs?'

Maisie thought Harry Bassington-Hope did not look like a man who had recently lost his brother. 'As you know, Georgina has been unsettled regarding the police assessment of the circumstances of your brother's death and believes be may have been the victim of foul play. She asked me to look into the matter, and—in asking questions, of family and friends—I find that even a small recollection can shed light on the truth of the incident.'

'I suppose it's no secret, then, that my relationship with my brother—as dear as he was to me—was really rather poor.'

'Was it?' Maisie said only enough to keep Bassington-Hope speaking.

'I was still at school when Nick went into the army, so he was very much the big brother, and as for the girls, Georgie and Nolly, well, Georgie was off on her own adventure anyway, and Nolly barely noticed me. I was a sort of fly in the sibling ointment. Mind you, I rather liked Godfrey, Nolly's husband. He was always up for a game of cricket, you know.'

'And what about when Nick died?'

'Stupid accident, very stupid accident. If he'd just let his pals help him a bit more and hadn't been so secretive, then it wouldn't have happened.' He shook his head. 'No, I can't imagine anything but an accident.'

'Hadn't you and Nick argued over money?'

'Hmmph! I suppose that must be common knowledge.' He paused, checked his watch, then went on. 'Yes, I had hit a spot of trouble financially, and Nick helped me out. But with Nick there always had to be a bit of a lecture. God knows why, it's not as if his halo wasn't a bit tarnished.'

'What do you mean?'

'He just wasn't the blue-eyed boy that Georgina would have you believe. Didn't think twice about who he'd upset with his work.'

'Who did he upset?'

Harry looked away, towards the stage, where the other musicians were taking their places. He stood up and drained his drink before replying. 'You could start with the family. Father had to calm Nolly down a couple of times—to think he could upset her so much after all she'd done for him.'

'How did he upset—'

'Sorry, Miss Dobbs. I really have to go, the boys are waiting for me.' He turned and hurried around the perimeter of the room so as not to be waylaid by admirers and was up on the stage with a single leap, taking up his trumpet and coaxing another wail into the rafters. The dancers were up and moving, and as Maisie collected her bag, she felt a pressure on her elbow.

'Oh no you don't! You promised one more dance.' Alex Courtman had been sitting at the bar, waiting for Harry Bassington-Hope to depart.

'But—'

'No "buts"—come on.'

Chapter Nine

Though there was no rain, no sleet, the sky above Fitzroy Square was gunmetal grey, shedding a deep silver light. As she unlocked the front door, Maisie checked her watch. Even though she was a few minutes late, she knew she would be surprised if Billy were at the office. He would not come today. She moved towards the staircase and stopped. *Why am I even going up the stairs?* Then she turned, locking the door behind her again.

Rain had started to fall lightly as she made her way back to the MG. Maisie did not drive to the hospital in Stockwell, for she knew there was no point. Instead she drove straight to the Beales' home in the East End.

She saw that the curtains were drawn as she parked her car in the street outside the house, and, as she stepped from the driver's seat, she was aware that the fabric at the windows of other houses on the street had flicked back and forth, as neighbours watched. Maisie knocked at the door. There was no answer, so she knocked again. Eventually, the door opened and Doreen's sister, Ada, peered out.

'I came . . . I hope . . .'

The woman nodded and stepped aside for Maisie to enter, her eyes red-rimmed, the bulk of her pregnancy weighing upon her.

'They've been talkin' about you, Miss. They'll want to see you.'

Maisie touched the woman on the shoulder, and walked to the kitchen. Billy and Doreen Beale sat at the kitchen table, both with untouched cups of cold tea in front of them. Maisie entered and said nothing but, standing behind them, rested a hand gently on each of their shoulders.

'I am so sorry. I am so, so sorry.'

Doreen Beale choked, pulled her pinafore up to her eyes and wept. Billy bit into his lower lip and stood up, allowing Maisie to take his seat.

'I knew you'd know, Miss. I knew you'd know she was gone.' He could barely form words, his voice cracking. 'It's all wrong, all bleedin' wrong, when something as beautiful as our little Lizzie can be taken.'

'Yes, Billy, you're right, it's all wrong.' She silently petitioned herself to say the words that might soothe the bereaved parents. She had seen, when she entered the kitchen, the chasm of sorrow that divided man and wife. She knew that to begin to talk about what had happened was a key to acknowledging their loss, and that such acceptance would in turn be a means to enduring the days and months ahead.

'When did it happen?'

Billy swallowed as Doreen reached for the teapot. 'We're not mindin' our manners, Miss Dobbs. I'll put the kettle on.' She stood up and busied herself at the stove.

'We went back to the 'ospital yesterday evening, early-ish.' Billy said, slumping into a seat by the fire. 'Turns out she'd taken a turn for the worse, so we went in to see the poor little mite—there was nothing of 'er, Miss.' Billy paused and reached for the cold tea, just as Doreen turned to pick up his cup. She nodded for him to continue talking as she took the cup and washed it in the sink. 'The doctor was there, and the nurses, and they tried to make us leave, but we wouldn't go.'

Maisie whispered thanks as cups of fresh tea were set on the table and Billy's wife sat down again. Ada remained seated next to the fire.

Billy continued. 'Seemed to go on for 'ours, the waitin', but it was—can't remember the time now, to tell you the truth—'

'Eleven. It was eleven o'clock. I remember looking up at the clock,' Doreen interjected as she stirred her tea.

'Anyway, at eleven o'clock, the nurse comes to get us, and when we got to the ward, the doctor told us she was on 'er last. That there was nothin' more that could be done.' He closed his eyes.

They remained in silence for some moments, then Doreen sat up straight. 'They let me hold her until she was gone, Miss Dobbs, so that she didn't go alone.' She paused, then looked at Maisie. 'They said she never would've known anything, at the end. You were a nurse, Miss Dobbs. Do you think she knew we'd come, that we were there?'

Maisie reached for Doreen's hands, looked first at Billy, then his wife. 'Yes, she knew.' She paused, searching for words. 'I used to believe, in the war, that when someone died, it was as if they'd shed a thick woollen coat that had become too heavy. The weight those men released was a result of wounds caused by guns, by shells. Lizzie's weight was a disease that was stronger than her body and the fight was too much for her.' Maisie's voice cracked. 'I believe she knew you were there, that you'd come to hold her as she took off that heavy coat. Yes, she knew you'd come. And then her little spirit was free of the struggle and she slipped away.'

Doreen turned to her husband, who knelt down beside her. They clutched each other, weeping together, as Maisie quietly stood up, signalled to Ada that she was leaving and stepped lightly along the corridor to the front door. She turned to Ada as she opened the door.

'Tell Billy not to come to work until he's ready.'

'All right, Miss Dobbs.'

'When will Lizzie be laid to rest?'

'Not for a few days yet, might even be over a week, what with one thing and another.'

'Please send word to me. And if you need anything . . .' Maisie handed her a visiting card.

'Right you are, Miss. You've been good to Billy and our Doreen.'

Maisie smiled, then said goodbye. She left the East End with her hands firmly on the steering wheel, her attention on the road, her eyes smarting. But instead of going to Fitzroy Square, she was compelled to make her way towards the Embankment, where she parked the MG and walked down to the water. She leaned on the wall and watched the Thames. The damp smog had barely lifted and Maisie pulled up the collar of her mackintosh. She closed her eyes and remembered Lizzie Beale, felt her head in the crook of her neck when she had taken her in her arms on the day that Doreen had come into the office last year. Maisie folded her arms round her body, felt herself fighting the tears that she knew would come, if she succumbed. Then she opened her eyes again and stood looking out over the water for some moments longer, before turning to walk back to her car.

SLUMPED IN an office chair, Maisie looked at the cold, damp weather outside and felt a wave of fatigue wash over her. She leaned over to ignite the gas fire, then, sighing, she moved to her desk, reached for the telephone receiver and placed a call to Duncan at Georgina's flat. As luck would have it, he was there alone and agreed to see her in an hour. She was sure that Duncan and Quentin would recount their respective conversations with her to each other, so she took the liberty of enquiring as to where she might find Quentin and was directed to the Chelsea Arts Club, where he would most likely be playing snooker all afternoon.

As Maisie replaced the receiver, she wondered if Alex had confided details of their meeting to his friends. She was still uneasy upon recalling their conversation and the casual way he had shared confidences.

Turning the knob at the side of the gas fire, Maisie shut off the jets and looked round the office. Everything was tidy, all notes and files were neat. Closing the door, she secured the room, turning keys in two locks and checking the handle. As she stepped out into the square, the cold caught her cheeks and she slammed the door behind her, again taking care to check the lock—she might not come back to the office until tomorrow morning when, she hoped, Billy would return to work.

She looked at her watch and set off towards the MG, which she'd parked round the corner. Had she waited just one more moment, Maisie would have seen two men walk across the square to the building she had just left and open the door with ease.

DUNCAN HAYWOOD opened the door before Maisie had a chance to knock. As at their first meeting, Maisie thought he resembled a vole, quick in his movements and precise in manner. He wore a well-tailored but well-worn tweed suit, a clean shirt and tie and polished shoes.

'Miss Dobbs, lovely to see you again.' He took her hand.

'Thank you for agreeing to a meeting.' Maisie smiled and entered the flat, taking up the same seat as before, with Duncan settling onto the chesterfield in the same place that Alex had previously chosen.

'I take it that Alex and Georgina are both out today?'

'Yes, Alex is looking at a studio-cum-bed-sitting-room he's planning to rent, and Georgina is probably with Lord Bradley.'

'Lord Bradley?'

Duncan smirked. 'A joke, Miss Dobbs. It's a nickname we have for him, Quentin, Alex and I, and, of course, Nick, when he was alive.' He paused, as if to gauge her sense of humour. 'After all, the man is trying to be British to the core, what with his suits for the City, tweeds for shooting—and you should see him on a horse! Then, of course, he opens his mouth.'

Maisie thought the man's manner snobbish. 'Duncan, I wonder if you can tell me more about your relationship with Nick, and your life in Dungeness—even though you live in Hythe now, and are newly married.' She smiled. 'Congratulations, by the way.'

'Thank you.' He smiled in return, hesitating in a manner that suggested he was measuring his response to the question. 'I've known Nick since before the war, as you know—so I won't repeat old news.'

She inclined her head, acknowledging his subtle reference to her information gathering.

'I was as close as one could be to Nick, to tell you the truth. Georgina was his closest confidante, though a chap can't tell his sister everything, can he?' The question was rhetorical. 'We were all in the same boat. A bit broke, wanting some peace and quiet, and the coast provided exactly the environment we were looking for, plus there was the added attraction of railway carriages being sold off on the cheap and a community of artists coming together in Dungeness. Of course, Nick was coming back and forth a lot to London, as he began to enjoy a level of success that we three could only dream of. He was just getting to that point where the money was coming through in large quantities.'

'But I thought Bradley had been purchasing his work for years?'

'He had, but not only does Lord Bradley drive a hard bargain, Svenson also takes a cut, then there's all sorts of others to pay when you have an exhibition. And you obviously know that Nick was more or less bankrolling the activities of his brother.'

'I knew he helped him out.'

He smirked again. 'Oh, to have that kind of helping out!' Standing up, Duncan moved to the mantelpiece and kneeled down to light the paper, kindling and coals already set in the grate. Maisie noticed a packing crate had been put to good use as kindling, the black lettering still visible across one or two shards of wood. She read the word: STEIN.

The wood began to catch and, reaching for the bellows, Duncan turned to Maisie. 'Living out in Dungeness was an adventure, but I'd had my eye on Hythe for some time, and it seemed logical to move there permanently.'

'You were with Nick and Alex on the night of Nick's death, weren't you?'

'Yes—look, Miss Dobbs, you know all this already, so why are you asking me? Do you think I had something to do with Nick's death? If you do, then let's get it out on the table.'

'Do you think he was murdered?'

'Put it this way, he was not a careless person, and he had planned the exhibition down to the last nail in the wall. He was tired, he had been working feverishly hard, and he wanted this to be the best, the most talked-about art opening in London.'

'Would it have been?'

'I saw all but the main piece, and I thought it was brilliant. Bradley's got the bulk of the exhibit now, though.'

'Did Nick work on it in Dungeness?'

'If he did, I never saw it.'

'Did Nick ever receive visitors at his carriage?'

The man shrugged. 'I think I can count the times on one hand when we were all down there together in the past year, so, no, I cannot give you any information about his social life, I'm afraid.'

'Did Harry visit, as far as you know?'

'He came down a few times.'

'When was the first time?'

He shook his head. 'Can't remember.'

Maisie did not take her eyes off him, but kept up the pace of her questioning. 'Do you know the Old Town, in Hastings?'

'Been there. All jellied eels, whelks, Londoners on their days off.'

'Have you ever spoken to the fishermen? The Draper brothers, perhaps?' Maisie pressed, before he had time to conceal the shock his eyes revealed.

'I—I . . . well I have no idea what you are talking about.'

Maisie checked her momentum. 'Tell me what you know about the mural in Nick's carriage.'

He shrugged again. '*Dr Syn*. He loved the myths and legends of the Marshes, loved the stories of smuggling gangs, of devil riders.'

'What about the Draper boys?'

'What about them?'

'In the mural.'

Another shrug. 'I have no idea what you are talking about.'

Maisie paused before speaking. 'I wonder if you wouldn't mind explaining something else to me.' She leaned forward. 'At Georgina's party, when Oswald Mosley came into the room, he was almost immediately surrounded by admirers, yet you, Alex and Quentin all but turned your backs.'

Haywood lost no time in replying. 'That man makes me sick. Look at the way he postures, the rhetoric—and the fools can't see through him, any more than people can see through that tyrant in Germany, Herr Hitler. I cannot believe Georgina invited him or even thinks he can do half of what he says—the man's power-hungry.'

'I see. That's a strong opinion.'

'I have friends in Heidelberg, Munich and Dresden, and to a man they have the same opinions about Hitler.'

She smiled. 'Mr Haywood, thank you so much for your time, you have been an invaluable help to me.'

Maisie wound her scarf round her neck and stood up to warm her hands by the fire before plunging them into her gloves. 'Now, I had best be off. I'm hoping to catch Quentin at the Chelsea Arts Club.'

Duncan had risen to his feet as Maisie stood in front of the fire. 'Yes, quite.' Without adding further comment, he led her to the front door and bade her farewell. As the MG's engine rumbled to life, Maisie watched his silhouette move with haste to the telephone table.

She would go to the club, just in case, though she knew the purpose for her visit would have departed before her arrival. Even as she drove to Chelsea, Quentin would be apologising to his companions for deserting their game of snooker.

As SHE TURNED the corner into Fitzroy Square, Maisie was surprised to see Sandra, one of the maids at the Belgravia mansion of Lord and Lady Compton, waiting on the doorstep.

'Sandra, whatever are you doing here?' Maisie had always straddled a fine line when it came to addressing the staff at Lady Rowan's house. They knew of her days in service at the mansion when she was a girl before the war. Through trial and error she had forged a relationship, blending respect with amiability, with Sandra and her fiancé, Eric—the footman-cum-chauffeur being the one who was the most forthcoming. But now, with Sandra's ready smile gone, it seemed that something was amiss. 'Is everything all right?'

'I wondered if I could have a word with you, Miss.' She was twisting her fingers round the handle of the shopping bag she carried.

Maisie understood that it must have taken more than a spoonful of courage for the young woman to come to her. She turned to press her key into the lock, but was surprised when the door simply opened at a light touch. 'That's strange . . . one of the other tenants must have forgotten to lock the door.'

Sandra looked around. 'Probably those two men I saw leaving as I crossed the road.'

Maisie shrugged and smiled at Sandra. 'Come on, let's get into the office and you can tell me everything.' She led the way up the stairs. 'This is the first time you've seen our office, isn't it? Of course, my assistant—you remember Billy—isn't here at the moment. It's very sad, but—oh my God!'

There was no need for Maisie to turn her key in the lock upstairs. The door was already wide open, the lock forced for someone to gain entry. The office was strewn with paper. Drawers were pulled open, a chair was on its side, even a china cup had been broken as those who had gained unlawful entry had gone through in search of—what?

'Crikey, Miss.' Sandra stepped forward and reached down, unbuttoning her coat as she did so. 'This won't take—'

'Don't touch a thing!' Maisie surveyed the scene. 'No, leave everything as it is.'

'Shouldn't you call the police?'

Maisie had already considered that the two men might well have been police themselves, given Stratton's strange behaviour recently. She shook her head. 'I don't think I will.' She sighed, appraising the task ahead of her. 'Sandra, do you know anyone who could fit a new lock, someone handy?'

The young woman nodded. 'Yes. I do. Sort of why I came to you.'

'I'm sorry, Sandra. Look, let me deal with this first, then—'

'You stay right here, Miss. I'll be back as soon as I can. Eric don't work for the Comptons any more. He's working for Reg Martin at the garage now. He can turn his hand to anything, can Eric. He'll put in a new lock for you.' Sandra pulled on her gloves. 'And if I were you, Miss, I'd close this door and shove that desk in front of it until I get back.'

Maisie heard the door slam as Sandra left the building. Negotiating across papers strewn on the floor, she stepped over to the table where she had worked on the case map with Billy. Usually the map was locked away each time they left the office, but this time she had slipped up, leaving the diagram of their progress on the Bassington-Hope case laid out ready to resume work if Billy returned tomorrow. Now the map was gone.

BACK HOME inside her empty flat, Maisie collapsed into a chair without taking off her coat. The death of Lizzie Beale had taken its toll and now the burglary at her office had added to her fatigue. She reached to ignite the gas fire, then leaned back into the chair again.

She felt vulnerable, invaded. The image of the broken lock flashed through her mind; the memories of shredded wood where the door had been forced and the paper strewn across the floor conspired to unsettle her even further. *Who has stolen our case map?* Bradley, perhaps expecting to find a clue to the whereabouts of the triptych? Might it have been Duncan and Quentin whom she had so recently unsettled?

Or could it have been Nick Bassington-Hope's killer? Sandra said she had seen two men. Could Harry's gangland associates have taken the life of his brother? Maisie rubbed her eyes and slipped the coat from her shoulders, reaching behind her to drape it over the seat of the chair. *Sandra.* She'd never discovered why Sandra had come to see her. The young woman had returned with Eric, who had brought a bag of tools and a new lock. The door was soon repaired, and with every bone aching for rest, Maisie had returned home. It was only now, as she sat gazing at the gas jets, that she realised she hadn't discovered the reason for Sandra's visit.

MAISIE WAS ON HER HANDS and knees in the office the following morning when she heard the front door thump and Billy Beale's distinctive footfall on the stairs. She clambered to her feet as her assistant entered the office.

'Bloody 'ell . . .'

Maisie smiled. 'We've got our work cut out for us today.' She smiled and came towards him. 'Do you feel up to it, Billy?'

With the semblance of a man in his sixties, not his thirties, Billy nodded. 'Got to earn my keep, Miss.' He paused, taking off his coat and hanging it on the hook at the back of the door. A black cloth band stitched round the upper arm of his jacket signalled his state of mourning. 'And to tell you the truth, what with one thing and another, it's best for me, is this. Doreen's sister started with the baby this mornin'. Give something for Doreen to think about. The woman from up the road, the one who's there for all the babies round our way, was just comin' in the door when I was leavin'.'

'Is Doreen coping?'

'I should say she's keepin' 'er 'ead above the water, Miss. Just. It's all a bit strange. There we are, you know, just lost our little girl, and there's a baby about to come into the world. And what to? Me and Doreen've been talkin' and we've laid it out for ourselves, for our boys. We've decided. We're savin' up to emigrate. Mate of mine in the war, 'e went over to Canada afterwards. 'E says there's a good life for men like me, men what ain't afraid of a bit of 'ard graft.'

Maisie smiled. 'You're a good father, Billy. You'll do what's best. Now, unless you're planning to sail to Canada this afternoon, we'd better get on. I have to leave for Dungeness later, but I want to ensure this is all put away before I go.' She turned to the desk. 'Oh, and you'll need these—keys for the new lock.'

Billy caught the set of keys Maisie threw to him. 'Did we lose anythin' important, Miss?'

Maisie nodded. 'The case map.'

SOME TWO HOURS LATER, Maisie and Billy had brought order to the chaos and were now sitting at the oak table in front of a length of pristine white lining paper pinned to the wood.

'There, clean slate, Billy. We might see some links, some clues that have evaded us thus far.'

'I 'ope so, Miss. Bloomin' lot of 'ard work down the drain if we don't.'

Maisie took a red pen and began to draw a circle with Nick Bassington-Hope's name in the centre. 'I want to see Arthur Levitt, the caretaker at the gallery, this morning, Billy, and I also want you to talk to your Fleet Street friend this afternoon, if you can.'

'Right you are, Miss.'

'All right, then, let's get on.'

They worked on the map until ten o'clock, whereupon the length of paper was rolled up and secured with a piece of string. Both Billy and Maisie looked around the room.

'My old mum always said to 'ide somethin' in plain view, Miss.'

'Well, in my haste I already did that, and look where it got me! No, we need a very safe place.'

'I've got an idea, Miss.' Billy walked over to the fireplace and edged out the gas fire that had been fitted to stand in front of an original grate. 'Long as we don't weaken the old gas line by pulling the fire back and forth, this should work for us, the old "up the chimney" trick.'

'Seems a bit obvious to me, Billy, but it will have to do. Here you are.'

Billy pushed the case map behind the gas fire, moved the fire back into position and checked to ensure the fuel line was not compromised.

Then, scrutinising the door several times to check the integrity of the lock, the pair set off towards Albemarle Street in the MG.

SEEING BILLY'S ARMBAND, Arthur Levitt removed his flat cap. 'Everything all right, son?'

Billy pressed his lips together and Maisie could see him struggling. He shook his head. 'We lost our youngest, Mr Levitt.'

'I'm sorry, son.'

'We're not the first, and we won't be the last. My old mum lost four babies, all of 'em under two. Anyway, there's the boys to look after.' He changed the subject quickly. 'Arthur, this is Miss Dobbs, my employer.'

Maisie stepped forward, extending her hand. Levitt raised an eyebrow but was courteous. 'What can I do for you, Miss Dobbs?'

'Mr Levitt, I am conducting an informal enquiry on behalf of Miss Georgina Bassington-Hope into the death of her brother at this gallery. Miss Bassington-Hope feels that there are a few places where information regarding the events leading up to his death is rather thin.'

'Well, Miss Dobbs, I don't know.' He looked around. 'Mr Svenson isn't here, and he won't like it, I'm sure.'

'I've already spoken to Mr Svenson.' It was true enough, though Maisie was quite aware that her words suggested that he had given her leave to speak to his caretaker.

Levitt looked back and forth between Billy and Maisie, then sighed. 'If it helps Miss Bassington-Hope, there's probably no harm in it.'

'You liked Mr Bassington-Hope?'

He nodded. 'Very nice man. Always thoughtful, always respectful.'

'Yes, so I understand.' Maisie glanced at Billy, who was busy taking notes. She saw that his hands were shaking, and wondered when he had last taken food. Turning her attention to Levitt again, she continued. 'Mr Levitt, perhaps you could tell me what you remember about the day Mr Bassington-Hope died.'

The caretaker nodded. 'He was here early. Came in a van. He came on his motorbike, as a rule, kept it spick-and-span, he did, but he didn't use the bike that day because he had too much to carry, his tools and so on.'

'I see. Go on,' Maisie encouraged the caretaker.

'I was here before seven, so I reckon he came at about eight. There was a lot of unloading. He'd picked up Mr Haywood and Mr Courtman on the way.'

'How did they spend the day?'

'First of all they put up the main part of the exhibition, which was easy. I reckon it would've been a very good show, but there was nothing there for anyone to purchase, on account of Mr Bradley buying up the lot.'

'So I understand. Tell me about the scaffolding and what happened next.'

'Well, as soon as they had put up the works that had been brought over in the van, Mr Bassington-Hope went back to his lockup to collect more paintings, and the other two went out for a bit of something to eat. Mr Courtman did ask if he needed help, but he said that he didn't.'

'Were there visitors?'

'Well, yes. There was family dropping in throughout the day, and, of course, Mr Svenson was flapping a bit, giving everyone directions, Mr Bassington-Hope was meticulous about the scaffolding, measuring, testing the strength of the trestle. He knew that, once it was up, he'd be here on his own working on placing the pieces. He said to me, "Last thing I want is to break my painting arm, Arthur". Mind you'—he looked at Maisie to ensure she was listening carefully—'he also knew the scaffolding was temporary. But it was sturdy enough for the job, and with a barrier along the back, so he could lean—lightly, mind—and check the placing of the anchors and, of course, the paintings.'

'When did everyone leave?'

'The men worked until, oh, must've been eight o'clock. I leave at nine, as a rule, only I stayed a bit, but Mr Bassington-Hope said he'd lock up and I should get home, because the next day would be a long one. I asked if he was sure, what with having to lug the main pieces up the stairs on his own, and what have you—'

'Lug the main pieces up the stairs?'

'You see these staircases?' He pointed to a staircase at either side of the storage room, in the centre of which was a corridor that snaked through to the main gallery. 'They lead out onto the balconied landings in the gallery. There's a door at either side. He would have had to carry the pieces up these stairs, then lift them over the balcony to the scaffolding. Then he'd either hop on over or climb up from below. He wanted the downstairs door to the gallery locked, didn't want anyone coming in to disturb him.'

'And no one else came to visit between eight and the time you left?'

'Mr Svenson came in again, but he left before me. He was very anxious, but he trusted Mr Bassington-Hope.'

'Could anyone have entered the gallery?'

'The downstairs door was locked, definitely, but the upstairs door was unlocked, what with him having to go back and forth.'

'Did he pull the van in?'

'The van was in the street. And of course he hadn't collected the main pieces. He would have wanted to bring them in late, I would have thought, on account of him wanting to keep them a secret.'

Maisie paced back and forth. 'Mr Levitt, tell me about the morning when you found Mr Bassington-Hope.'

'It was long before seven, and I expected him to be here to make sure that no one could eyeball the exhibition before the opening. The van was parked in the street here and the outside door was unlocked, so that's when I thought he was already in. I put the kettle on'—he pointed to a small gas stove—'and I went down the corridor here, where the door was still locked, with the key in it on the other side. I banged on the door to let him know it was me, only there was no answer. So I went upstairs, hoping he'd left that door unlocked, and he had. But when I opened it and went out onto the balcony, that's when I saw the scaffolding had broken where the poor man had lost his balance and fallen back.' Levitt choked. Maisie and Billy were silent, waiting for him to settle into the story again. 'I ran downstairs as quick as I could to get to him. He was stone cold. I could see straight away that it was a broken neck. I telephoned the police from Mr Svenson's office. That's when Detective Inspector Stratton came to the gallery.'

Maisie cleared her throat. 'Do you know what happened to the van?'

'The chap he borrowed it from found out what had happened and claimed it from the police.'

'And what about a key or set of keys? Mr Bassington-Hope must have had a key to his lockup?'

Levitt shook his head. 'You'd be best to ask Miss Bassington-Hope. But to tell you the truth, I don't know if there was anything.'

'Why do you say that?'

'Well, I was standing there, talking to Detective Inspector Stratton while two other policemen were going through Mr Bassington-Hope's belongings, you know, patting down his body. And there was no key found.'

'Does that strike you as strange?'

The man sighed. 'I thought the whole thing was strange, Miss Dobbs. Something about it just didn't sit right with me. But there again, if you were there, you'd've probably thought it was an accident too.'

Maisie inclined her head. 'Would I, Mr Levitt?'

MAISIE AND BILLY took a brief sojourn in a pie-and-mash shop, where a hearty helping of eel pie, mashed potato and parsley brought some colour back to Billy's hollow cheeks. As they stood in the street ready to part company, he declared himself 'well up' for his trip to Fleet Street that afternoon.

As soon as she was back in the office, Maisie set about catching up with her work. There were some bills to prepare, and planning for the following week to complete. The post had to be dealt with, and she was pleased to see two letters of interest with regard to her services.

With about half an hour before she needed to leave for Dungeness, she moved to the table but did not remove the case map from its hiding place. She took a seat and doodled with a pen on a blank index card. She thought there might be something going on in Dungeness—based more upon her understanding of Nick's mural than anything else—that suggested knowledge on his part of some underhanded dealing. But how deep was his personal involvement? She felt that Haywood and Trayner had something to hide, but Courtman seemed on the periphery of the group, probably not part of an inner circle.

Harry Bassington-Hope? Her mind drifted back to the dilettante musician. She knew his type, had seen it before. Harry's actions had led him to the slippery slope, and she knew he would not draw back from dragging someone else down with him—be it a friend, a brother or a sister.

Maisie scraped back her chair and wandered to the window. She ran her finger across the condensation on the windowpane, then watched a rivulet of water drizzle down to the wooden frame.

Heavens, didn't everyone have something to hide? Maisie sighed and turned away from the window. She put on her coat, hat and gloves, and took up the black document case, along with her suitcase and shoulder bag. She left the office, double-checked the lock and made her way to the MG.

It was as she was about to slip into the driver's seat that Maisie saw Billy running along Warren Street towards her.

'Miss! Miss! Wait a minute!'

'You've built up a head of steam there, Billy. What's wrong?'

'Nothin' wrong, Miss.' Billy caught his breath and held his hand to his chest. ''Old on a minute.' He coughed, wheezing and looking around him as he did so. 'Right, then. This is what my mate down Fleet Street 'ad to say today. There ain't nothing on our 'arry B-H to report, nothing on Nick, or the sisters. Generally, it's all clean. So, I says to 'im, "So, what else 'as been comin' down the blower this week, mate?" and 'e says that the only thing 'e's got a lead on is that these 'ere villains that 'arry's been in cahoots with 'ave been suspected of gettin' into the minin' business.'

'Mining? What on earth do you mean?'

'Manner of talkin', Miss.' Billy grinned. 'Turns out that my mate is followin' a lead that they're into diamonds, as in the movin' around of the same. We're talkin' raw diamonds, brought in from somewhere else and fenced over 'ere.'

Maisie was silent for a moment or two. 'That's very interesting, Billy. I'm not sure how that might have anything to do with this case, but . . .'

'What, Miss?'

'Just a thought. Anything else?'

Billy shook his head. 'Nah, nothin' much. My mate says 'e's been keepin' an eye on what's goin' on over there on the Continent. Says that it's a bit more interestin' at the moment.'

Maisie settled into the MG, winding down the window as the engine grumbled to life. 'And what has been happening in Europe, then?'

'Well, my mate says, all the usual stuff. Been a few burglaries, old money's 'eirlooms bein' pinched, that sort of thing.'

'Good work, Billy—I'll consider everything you've said on my drive to the coast. Hold the fort until tomorrow afternoon, won't you?'

'Right you are, Miss. You can depend on me.'

Chapter Ten

Maisie made a snap decision that there was no need to begin her journey to Dungeness for another hour or two—she certainly didn't want to arrive *too* early. Much of the planning was based on supposition anyway. She had no firm evidence that this evening, under cover of darkness, she would find out if her suspicions concerning the activities of a few residents in the small coastal community were well founded; all she had to go on, truly, was a tale of derring-do, a colourful mural in a former railway carriage and the history of a desolate place.

She parked alongside the entrance to Georgina's flat and made her way to the front door, where she rang the bell. The housekeeper came within seconds, smiling when she recognised Maisie.

'Miss Dobbs. I'll tell Miss Bassington-Hope that you're here.' She showed Maisie into the drawing room as she spoke.

'Thank you.' Maisie removed her gloves and scarf and waited without taking a seat.

'Maisie, what a surprise. Have you news?' Georgina entered the room several minutes later. Her hair was drawn back in a loose chignon, which exposed her pale skin and the grey circles under her eyes.

'No, but I wanted to clarify my understanding of certain events leading up to the death of your brother.'

'Of course.' As she held out her hand towards the chesterfield, Maisie noticed a circular ink stain on the middle finger of her right hand.

'I see you've been writing, Georgina. Have I disturbed you?'

The journalist sank into a chair opposite Maisie. 'I wish I could say that you had. In fact, I welcome any disturbance, to tell you the truth. I've been assigned to write something about Oswald Mosley for an American journal, but I can't seem to get going.'

'Perhaps it's your subject, rather than your ability.'

'Hardly. The man elicits excitement wherever he goes, but I can't seem to describe the honesty, the integrity of his mission.'

Maisie smiled. 'Could that be because, in truth, such qualities are not truly present?'

'What do you mean?' Georgina sat up, erect with indignation. 'He is—'

'It was simply a question to consider. Have you experienced such an issue with your work before?'

'No.' She curled a stray wisp of hair behind her ear before leaning forward and resting her elbows on her knees. 'Sorry, that's a lie. To tell you the truth, even though I've done quite well—especially with the bound collection of my wartime reports—I haven't been inspired since the peace conference in 1919.' Georgina shook her head. 'I think I need a war to write about. I should really just leave the country and look for one.'

Maisie continued to smile, though it was not a smile of mirth but one that she knew was rooted in an emotion akin to that expressed by Billy when he first met the Bassington-Hope woman. Her resentment was growing, but she was mindful that even though she knew the woman a little better now, she was still a client. 'As I said, Georgina, I'd like to ask a few questions. First of all, are Nick's friends still with you?'

'No, Duncan left this morning. As far as I know, he and Quentin have gone down to Dungeness.' She paused, looking at Maisie. 'I thought you were going there again this week?'

'Yes, that's right.' She did not elucidate with more information. 'They've been staying here with you for a few days, haven't they?'

Georgina stood up and poked the fire, then replaced the cast-iron poker in the holder next to the coal scuttle. 'Yes, I think they were down in Dungeness for just a day about the time you visited. I remember thinking that it was a shame you hadn't met then. You must have just missed them.'

'Of course.' Maisie was thoughtful. *I am right.* 'Georgina, why did you not tell me of the encounter between Mr Bradley and Nick at the gallery on the afternoon before he died?'

'I—I—I forgot.'

Maisie pushed harder. 'Might it have anything to do with your relationship with Mr Bradley?'

Georgina cleared her throat and Maisie, once again, watched as she pushed down the cuticles of each finger. 'There was no "relationship", as you put it. There was an attraction. But we weren't close at the time of Nick's death.'

'And what about you and Nick? I understand that you went back to the gallery after the row in the afternoon—of course, it was a row during which you took Nick's part. I realise you supported his refusal to sell the triptych.'

'Yes, I supported his decision. We always supported each other.'

'And why did you go back?'

Georgina sighed, then continued, 'I went back to talk to Nick. We'd left under a cloud and I couldn't leave it on such terms. I wanted to explain.'

'What?'

'Nick knew that Randolph and I were attracted and he didn't like it. He heartily disapproved of our interest in each other—which, I have to say, was a bit rich, when you consider his peccadilloes.'

Maisie said nothing.

'He'd had an affair with Duncan's wife-to-be,' continued Georgina, 'and he'd had a bit of a fling with a married woman years ago, so he wasn't pure as the driven snow. But I went to Nick to make up, to let him know that I supported him, and I wanted him to accept me too.'

'And he didn't?'

'Not with Randolph, no.' She looked straight at Maisie. 'My brother could be pretty bloody-minded when he liked, Maisie. On the one hand you had a man with the morals of a vicar, and on the other, actions that fell shy of the sort of behaviour that Harry is capable of.'

'I see.'

'And he never forgot. Sometimes the things he saved in his mind turned up in his work. I imagined a mural of star-crossed lovers with my face depicted alongside Randolph's. So we had words on the evening of his death, and I left without saying good-bye . . .' Georgina began to weep.

Maisie said nothing, allowing the tears to fall.

'And you do not think that the argument might have rendered Nick so unsettled as to make an error of judgment with his step?'

'Absolutely not! Nick was too single-minded to allow such a thing. He had only one thought on his mind—exhibiting the triptych.'

Maisie reached for her scarf beside her on the chesterfield and stood up. 'You didn't see anyone else after you left the gallery that evening?'

'Well, Stig came back. I saw him turn into Albemarle Street as I left the gallery.' Georgina paused. 'Frankly, I didn't really want to see him and fortunately a taxicab came along at just that moment.'

'About what time was this? Had Mr Levitt gone for the day?'

'Yes.' Georgina closed her eyes, as if to recall the events. 'I went in through the front door. The back door was locked.'

'And did you leave by the front door?'

'Yes.'

Maisie sighed, allowing a pause in the questioning. 'Georgina, why did you not tell me about the affair with Bradley sooner? You must have known how important such information could be.'

Georgina shrugged. 'Having an affair with a married man is not something I'm proud of, to be perfectly honest with you.'

Maisie nodded thoughtfully and walked towards the painting above the cocktail cabinet. 'This is new, isn't it?'

Georgina looked up. 'Um, yes, it is. I'm looking after it, for a friend.'

'Lovely to have it for a while.'

She nodded. 'Yes. I hope it won't be too long, though.'

Maisie noticed a wistfulness about her client, a blend of sadness and regret that possession of the piece seemed to have brought with it. She continued to look at the painting, and as she did so, a fragment of the jigsaw puzzle that was Nick Bassington-Hope's life fell into place.

She did not question Georgina further, satisfied—for the moment—with her responses. She was dismayed, however, that she had not learned of the unlocked front entrance to the gallery before.

As the two women stood on the threshold, Maisie decided to throw a grain of possibility to the once-renowned journalist.

'Georgina, you mentioned that you needed a war to inspire your work. Well, you need look no further than the boundaries of the city in which you live. Mr Beale and his wife have lost their youngest child to diphtheria. In a house that barely contains one family, they have taken in a family of four—a new baby will be born before the end of the day—because his brother-in-law has lost his job. And the Beales are among those who consider themselves better off. The war is being waged, Georgina, only the war is here and now, and it is a war against poverty, against disease and against injustice. You would do well to consider igniting your pen with that!'

'I—I hadn't thought—'

'I'll be in touch, Georgina. Expect to hear from me within two days.'

Georgina nodded and was about to close the door when Maisie turned to her one last time. 'Oh, by the way, are you acquainted with a Mr Stein?'

Georgina frowned and shook her head rather too fiercely as she replied, 'No. The only Stein I know is Gertrude.'

DUSK WAS ON THE VERGE of night as Maisie drove from Lydd along the road to Dungeness. Though the land was barren, with few houses and a cold wind blowing up from the beach, she managed to park the car on the side of the road, where it was shielded by an overhanging tree. She wrapped her scarf round her neck, pulled her cloche down as far as she could, and picked up her belongings, then set off in the direction of the beach. She had taken a small torch from her shoulder bag, and now flicked it on every fifty or so yards to get her bearings. Finally, with salt-filled sea air whipping across her face, she came upon the front door of Nick Bassington-Hope's cottage, having taken care to move into the shadows as the lighthouse beam swung round onto the beach. Her gloved fingertips were numb as she removed the key from her coat pocket. She flashed the light to illuminate the lock, pressed the key home and gained entrance. Closing the door behind her, she moved to the windows to pull down the blinds.

Now Maisie inspected the cottage with the torch beam to see whether there were any signs that others had been there since her previous visit. The stove was as she had left it, the counterpane seemed untouched. She studied the mural once again. Yes, Nick Bassington-Hope was a talented artist, though she wondered what others had thought when they looked at the mural. What of Amos White? Could he have seen the mural? If so, he must have felt threatened. Nick told stories with his work, transposing images of those he knew onto his depiction of the myths and legends that inspired him. She thought of the triptych. *What if the story were true, and the faces known to others as well as to Nick?*

Maisie pushed one of the leather armchairs close to the window, then pulled the counterpane from the bed. She settled into the chair, wrapping the counterpane round her body, then reached into her bag and took out some cheese and pickle sandwiches. The set of the blind allowed the barest snip of a view out to the beach. She tucked into her food and waited.

Feeling the gritty sensation of fatigue, Maisie squirmed in the chair, pulling the counterpane closer. It was then that she heard the crunch of boots on the pathway. Moving to the gap between window and blind, Maisie squinted to see better. The shadowed figures tramped towards the shingle bank, drawn by an ever-brighter light that beamed up from the beach, then she heard the rumble of a lorry. It was time for her to make a move.

Replacing the counterpane and chair took barely a minute, then she left by the back door. Maisie stepped forward with care, using old barrels and the sides of other cottages to disguise her approach towards the activity, which was now illuminated by lanterns.

Leaning round the corner of an old shed to ensure her way was clear, she ran, stooping, to the side of an old boat. She caught her breath, the cold air razor sharp in her throat and chest, then looked out from her hiding place.

A large fishing boat had made landfall and been winched up the beach. On the boat, the Draper brothers from Hastings, together with Amos White, moved back and forth, easing large wooden containers from the deck onto the shingle, where Duncan and Quentin picked up the contraband and carried it to the waiting lorry. Barely a word passed between the men, though when a voice was raised, it was invariably that of the fourth man on the boat. The man whose face was depicted in the mural on the dead man's carriage wall. Maisie remained in place, observing, working out who was who. Clearly the fishermen were mere puppets, doing what many had done for centuries to augment a meagre income. The artists seemed confident, knowing exactly what they were doing, and the other man—what was his role? *He isn't the boss, but he does have power.* It was time to leave.

Maisie made her way back towards the path that led out onto the Lydd Road. Then she ran to the MG, unlocked the door and took her place in the driver's seat, her teeth chattering. She sat in silence, to ensure she hadn't been seen or followed, then started the car, setting her course towards the road the lorry had taken when she had observed it before.

She'd had no time to conduct an initial reconnaissance, depending instead upon her supposition that the route taken by the lorry would lead to a barn, or some other building where goods could be stored until later. Or perhaps the barn took the role of a clearing-house, where booty was divided. Again she chose a spot where the MG would be hidden by one of the leaning trees common to the Marshes, and made off on foot. The road was muddy and Maisie could feel the cold, wet earth squelch through her brown leather walking shoes. Her toes were beginning to tingle and her fingertips were numb. She lifted her hands to her mouth and blew warm air through her gloves. A dog barked in the distance, and she slowed her pace as she made her way along the farm road.

Though the night was pitch-black, she could ascertain the outline of a medieval beamed barn set among fields. She ran the last few yards to the side of the barn and paused. Rubbing her arms for warmth, Maisie knew she must find a hiding place before the lorry rumbled along the road.

Though double doors had been added at each end of the barn, Maisie located a smaller doorway, listened, then pulled it open. She closed the door and, flashing the torch once, she saw that an old delivery van was already hidden inside the barn. She stepped quickly towards the ladderlike staircase leading into the loft. Climbing up, she found a cubbyhole space under the eaves, alongside bales of hay from the summer's harvest. From her vantage point she would be able to see any activity at the far end of the barn where she expected the men to enter. She had gambled upon there not being anyone waiting for the containers to arrive and was glad to discover that she had been correct.

Silence. Maisie waited, her heartbeat slowing to a pace that was almost normal. Then, in the distance, the sound of an engine revving, a bump, a rumble: the lorry coming closer along the rutted road. The occasional roar as the driver accelerated to clear a mudhole suggested that the vehicle was being manoeuvred in reverse gear.

After some manipulation of forward and reverse gears, the lorry was brought into position, finally scrunching to a halt beyond the doors at the far end of the barn. Men's voices were raised, then the double doors were pushed open. The canvas flap at the back of the lorry was drawn back, and Duncan and Quentin jumped out.

The wooden containers were unloaded. As expected, each container resembled ones she'd seen at the back of Svenson's Gallery, where Arthur Levitt unpacked and shipped artwork.

'Right then, you two, we'll take what's ours and we'll be on our way. You know which one our stuff's in, so get a move on,' instructed the driver.

Quentin pointed to two of the containers and, as he did so, Maisie noticed that the top of each was numbered in black paint and also bore a name. She managed to read three names: D. ROSENBERG, H. KATZ, and another marked STEIN. Quentin took the crowbar that Duncan held out to him and ripped the slats of wood apart. He reached inside and pulled out what was clearly a painting, wrapped in a light linen cloth. Duncan helped Quentin to unwrap the work. They both hesitated for a moment as they caught a first glimpse of the painting.

The gang leader prodded Quentin. 'Get a move on. You can admire the fancy bits later.'

The artists exchanged glances and together laid first sackcloth, then clean linen on the floor to protect the painting, which they placed on top of the cloth, face down. Duncan handed a knife to Quentin. 'Be careful.'

'Of course.' Quentin leaned down, piercing the paper at the back of the painting with the knife, then proceeded to remove the backing. Maisie chewed her bottom lip as she watched the scene unfold before her. Quentin pulled out a small pouch from the back of the painting. He threw the pouch to the gang leader and then repeated the exercise with a second piece.

'There, you can tell your boss that that's the last one, Williams. There will be no more "deliveries". We've done all that we can.'

The man shook his head. 'Nah, you don't expect me to believe that, do you, my little artsy-fartsy darlings? Mr Smith don't like to be lied to. Anyway, that German fella ain't finished yet, no, not by a long chalk, so I reckon them heirlooms will keep on coming.'

Quentin shook his head. 'We aren't doing this any more, Williams. It was straightforward until you came along, and now it isn't. Makes it tricky for everyone—especially our friends in Germany and France.'

'Well, I ain't got the time to chinwag about this with you. But I'll be in touch.' He smiled, climbed up into his seat and nodded to his driver.

The two men left in the lorry, which rumbled away along the road.

In the barn, Quentin became agitated. 'Damn that stupid Harry. And damn Nick for telling him about what we were doing. He had no right—'

'All right!' Duncan held up a hand. 'The fact is that he did talk, and Harry got us into this. Now we have to get out of it. Bloody shame that we can't help out Martin and Etienne and their people any longer, though.' He sighed. 'Anyway, let's pack up and get out of here.'

Maisie watched as they repacked the opened crates. She made a mental note of the black numerals used for identification. Once the loading up was completed, Duncan stood by the doors while Quentin reversed the van out of the barn. The doors were locked again, though Maisie did not move until she was sure she could no longer hear the engine.

EASING HER WAY down the ladderlike staircase, Maisie brushed hay from her clothes. She took an index card from her bag and made a note of the identification markings she'd observed on the containers. It was as she began to pack away her pencil and notes that she ceased all movement, barely daring to breathe. Voices outside became louder, so she hurried towards the stairs again, but was only halfway up when the doors flew open and an Alsatian dog burst through. He made a beeline for Maisie, though the men who came behind the beast could not see his quarry. For her part, Maisie sat down on the middle step and closed her eyes. She relaxed every muscle, calming her mind and body so that she felt no fear. The bounding dog halted his gallop. Instead he stood before her, as if weighing instinct against training, then lay down at her feet, subdued.

The panting dog was soon joined by a man. 'And what have we here, Brutus?'

Another man, clearly more senior, given his manner and tone of voice, was close behind. He was dressed completely in black, with a black sweater and cap, and black leather gloves. In fact, as other men came into the barn, Maisie noticed that they were all dressed for stealth at nightfall, with two men in uniform, but it was not the uniform of the police.

'If you're mixed up with these little shenanigans, Miss Dobbs, you should be wrapping a worried look across your face.'

Maisie stood up, determined not to show any surprise that her name was known to the man. 'I am not involved in "these little shenanigans", though, like you, I was curious to know what was going on here.'

'Jones!' The man called over his shoulder to a colleague, currently searching the barn. 'Escort this young lady to HQ for questioning. And while you're about it, get this bloody useless specimen of a dog out of my sight and back into the training kennels. Brutus, my eye!'

Maisie was silent while being escorted to a waiting motor car. It would not have done any good to complain about lack of warrants or any other required documentation. The powers of Customs and Excise officers were well known and predated the founding of the police.

The officer ensured that she was seated securely, if not comfortably, in the van.

'Excuse me, sir, will you be able to bring me back here to collect my car?'

The man smiled, his grin eerie in flashes of light shed by torches and the headlamps of other vehicles. 'The little red motor? No need, Miss. We've already got an officer taking it in for you.'

'I see.' Maisie sat back in the van and closed her eyes. Even if she did not sleep, she must regain some energy for the inquisition that surely awaited her. And she knew she would have to be very, very careful. Without a doubt these men were operating independently of Stratton and Vance, who were probably themselves being manipulated so that their investigation did not interfere with that of Customs and Excise. She had to be the one to pull the strings in the hours ahead.

Chapter Eleven

Maisie was surprised. Instead of being led into a bleak, whitewashed cell for questioning, she was shown into a sitting room where she was served tea and biscuits. She was tired, which was hardly surprising, for it was now past three in the morning. Anticipating a long wait, she removed her shoes and lay down on the settee.

'Nice little forty winks, Miss?'

Maisie woke with a start, as an officer touched her shoulder.

'Time to see the boss, if you don't mind.'

Pushing her feet into the cold, mud-encrusted leather, she took time to tie her laces before standing to follow the officer.

'Ah, Miss Dobbs, do come in.' The man held out his hand towards a chair, then flicked open a folder from which he took several sheets of paper. 'Now, just a few questions for you, then, all being well, we can let you go.'

'Where's my motor car?'

'Safe as houses. Just needed to give it a bit of a once-over. Nice little car, cost a young woman like you a bob or two.'

Maisie did not rise to the bait, though she inclined her head and smiled at the man in front of her, who was clearly a senior officer. 'I believe it's not only my car that has been the subject of one of your once-overs, Mr . . . ?'

'Tucker. The name is Tucker.' The man paused, gauging his response. 'And you mean your office?'

'Yes, my office. Your men broke in and turned over my office with little consideration for my property.'

'Let's just say that you were keeping company with persons who were subject to investigation. In the country's interests, it was a good idea to see what you'd gathered. As you know, I do not have to explain myself to you.'

'You might have asked, instead of costing me a new lock.'

'And we might not.' He pulled a wad of folded paper from the file. 'I think we should start with this, don't you, Miss Dobbs?'

Maisie leaned back in the hard wooden chair, just enough to underscore her detachment from the outcome of the questioning. She didn't want this man to think she was concerned.

'I was thinking, while being brought here, that I might see that particular item again today.'

'So, what is it?' the man snapped.

Maisie cleared her throat. *Good, he's just a little off-balance.* 'It's what my assistant and I call a "case map".' She paused deliberately to exhibit an ease as she answered the questions put to her. 'We draw up a chart where we ensure that every single aspect of our investigation is available to us in this graphic form. Pictures and shapes, even if constructed with words, can tell us more than just talking back and forth.'

The man was silent for a moment or two. 'And what does this map tell you—what have your little patterns led you to?'

'I haven't finished yet,' she countered with an edge to her voice, which led to more fidgeting on the man's part. Her interrogator clearly wasn't used to the sense that control of a conversation was slipping from his grasp.

'Right then, what do you know, Miss Dobbs, about the activities of the boys down in Dungeness on dark and windless nights?'

'I should say you know more than I, Mr Tucker.' She shrugged. 'I was merely interested in the two men, given their relationship with Mr Bassington-Hope—Nicholas, not Harry, that is. You know that I was retained by his sister to corroborate the police finding.'

'Are you aware of what was going on in Dungeness?'

'Smuggling. But if you must know, I think Duncan Haywood and Quentin Trayner are a long way from being seasoned smugglers, and embarked upon the operation with only the best of intentions. However, the underworld element clearly found a means of using the situation to their advantage.'

'You know about the diamonds, then?'

'I guessed.' Maisie leaned forward. 'How long have you been watching them?'

Tucker threw his pen onto the desk, splattering ink across the manila folder. 'About three months—and you keep this under your hat, mind. I've looked into who you are, and I know which side you're on, though I wish you'd keep your nose out of it. I'm not interested in these little bits and pieces of art coming across.' He gave a cynical half laugh. 'No, we're after what you call the "underworld element", though we're waiting to catch the blighters red-handed. But we've been too slow about it.' He closed the file.

Now calmer, he explained that his interest was not in the artists, but in those who had taken advantage of the wayward Harry and his brother. For her part, Maisie explained that Nick would have done anything to keep Harry safe—even if it meant submitting to the demands of criminals. Tucker agreed, nodding as she spoke, whereupon Maisie shared her knowledge of the diamond-smuggling operation. When it was clear that there was nothing more to be gained by detaining her, she was allowed to leave.

Collecting her MG, she drove back to Dungeness. It was all falling into place. Soon every single clue would be set on the case map she carried in her head, the one that no one could steal.

MAISIE HAD NO FEAR of lighting the fire and warming water on the stove in Nick's cottage. If she were seen, it was of little import now. The former railway carriage was soon warm, and, as the kettle came to the boil, Maisie used a fork to toast her remaining sandwiches in front of the open stove. Once she had eaten, soothed by food and hot tea, fatigue enveloped her again. The blinds had remained closed against a winter sun just beginning its climb into the now clear coastal sky, so all Maisie had to do was draw back the counterpane and curl into Nick Bassington-Hope's bed.

It was past ten when she woke, rested and ready to set out on her quest to discover the location of the lockup. She was convinced that she would find the information she wanted here, in the artist's home. Using the jug from Nick's bathroom, she brought water from the barrel in the lean-to, shivering as she splashed her face. Refreshed, she stepped into the main room.

The image that had presented itself to her on the previous visit had nagged at Maisie, a slip of paper Nick had hidden somewhere . . . in the recesses of his leather chair? She had always trusted her intuition. She was blessed— and sometimes, she thought, cursed—with insight. Trust and skill had enhanced her ability to see where others were blind, and had led her time and time again to that which she was seeking.

She pushed her hands deep into the edges of the seat. Her fingers scraped against the frame and she felt a coin, a pen and a cork. *Blast!* Frustrated,

Maisie heaved the chair over to look underneath it. With a sudden thud, the chair landed on the wooden floorboards.

'Damn!' said Maisie, in anger as well as shock, for the last thing she wanted to do was to damage the carriage, and the weight of the chair had caused a floorboard to push up. She knelt to inspect it, but as she leaned closer, she realised that the piece of wood had merely become dislodged, because it wasn't a full-length floorboard. It was a shorter fragment which was already loose. She hadn't noticed it before, because it was covered by the chair. Taking hold of the torch, she shone the light into the dark, narrow recess below. When she reached in, her fingers brushed against a piece of paper. Extending her hand further, she pulled out an envelope of some weight.

Sitting back, Maisie turned the envelope to reveal the words FOR GEORGINA. She bit her lip, considering the question of integrity, then shook her head and opened the envelope. A key wrapped in a piece of paper fell out, with an address in southeast London. She breathed out a deep sigh. *Intuition was all very well, but luck held the trump card!*

After completing a quick repair of the floorboard and setting the chair on top so that the damage was not immediately visible, Maisie packed up her belongings. For the last time, she checked the cottage to ensure that she had left it as she had found it. It was just as she was about to leave, her hand on the doorknob, that she set down her baggage and returned to the wardrobe in the vestibule. There was no logical explanation for her actions, but she opened the door and pulled out the army greatcoat. With the sound of waves crashing onto the beach outside, and gulls whooping overhead, Maisie buried her head in the folds of rough wool, breathing in the musty smell that took her back to another time and place.

There was much she understood about Nick Bassington-Hope, even though they had never met. Having lived through death, he had discovered life again, but with war's horror still so present, he had searched for peace of mind. Maisie understood that Nick had seen his message clearly, and that he had been able to touch the canvas with his most potent images. And though she had never met the artist, she knew that this case, like so many before, contained a gift, a lesson that she would draw to her as surely as the coat she now held to her heart.

Carefully replacing the garment in the wardrobe, Maisie smiled. She patted the material one last time, acknowledging an essence as if the fibres had absorbed every feeling, every sensation experienced by the owner.

NOLLY BASSINGTON-HOPE was surprised but nevertheless extended a warm welcome to Maisie when she arrived at the house unannounced. She explained that her mother and father were out walking, sketchbooks in hand, making the most of a bright day, even though the cold snap continued.

'They may be getting on a bit, but it's their habit, and the walk does them good. They'll be back soon.' She showed Maisie into the drawing room, then excused herself for a moment to speak to the staff.

Maisie wandered round the room, grateful for time alone, time that allowed her to reflect upon how the house must have been before the war, with colourful, buoyant gatherings of artists and intellectuals drawn like moths to the bright light of Piers and Emma. She imagined gregarious friends of Nick's and Georgina's voicing opinions at the dinner table, encouraged by the free-thinking elders. There would be swimming in the river, picnics alongside the mill, perhaps with the boy Harry and his trumpet entertaining the group.

And Nolly? What about Nolly? She was left with an incomplete picture of the eldest sibling. Now she must add colour to her outline.

A sideboard bore a collection of family photographs in frames of silver, wood and tortoiseshell. Maisie was drawn to them, for there was much to learn from facial expressions. Her attention darted from one frame to another, for she knew Nolly would return shortly. One—of a young couple on their wedding day—caught her attention. Maisie picked up the photograph and, looking into the eyes of Nolly and her fresh-faced husband, saw joy and hope. She replaced the silver frame just in time.

'I bet you wish you hadn't taken on this assignment from my sister, don't you?'

'On the contrary, it's led me into some interesting places.'

Nolly held out her hand to a labrador, who heaved himself up and came to his mistress. 'Ah, you must have been out in search of Harry again. That would have taken you to some interesting places.'

Maisie laughed. 'Oh, they're certainly entertaining, those places where your Harry performs.'

Nolly softened and laughed along with Maisie. 'He's actually quite good, isn't he?'

'You've been to see him?'

'Curiosity, you know.' Nolly sighed. 'Is Harry in trouble again? Is that why you came?'

'I came because I've been to Nick's cottage a second time, and I have some questions, if you don't mind.'

They were interrupted by the housekeeper, who brought a tray with tea, biscuits and cake. Nolly continued, after pouring a cup for Maisie, 'How can I help?'

'I understand that three people went to the cottage after Nick died. I assume the visitors were you, Georgina and your father.'

Nolly nodded. 'Yes, that's right. Frankly, it was so upsetting that we only stayed for a short time. We thought we'd go back again in a few weeks. The cottage will be sold, obviously, but Emma just wants everything left as it was, for now.' She leaned forward to set her cup on the tray. 'If it were up to me, I would have everything sold immediately.'

Maisie nodded, acknowledging the practicality of Nolly's approach. 'So, the cottage was left as you found it, then?'

'For the most part. Piers looked round more than I, to tell you the truth. Nick was quite a tidy person, liked a certain order. Of course, the army does that for you. Godfrey was the same, though I only saw him on one leave before he was killed, but I noticed it, that order, so to speak.'

Maisie saw that when she spoke of her husband, Nolly's jaw tightened. She put her cup down and waited for Nolly to continue.

'Piers began to go through some of the sketchbooks, but found it too hard, though he did take a couple or three with him.'

'Your father took Nick's sketchbooks?'

The woman nodded. 'Yes, though I couldn't tell you where he's put them—probably in the studio.' She paused. 'Is it important?'

Maisie shrugged, an air of nonchalance belying her instinct. 'No, I doubt it, though it would be interesting to see them. Your brother's art is compelling, to say the least.'

Nolly gave a half laugh. 'Yes, as you've seen, my brother touched a fuse every time he lifted his brush or wielded a charcoal. If you saw his work, you saw what he was thinking, how he saw the world. He wasn't afraid.'

'I know. But were there others who *were* afraid?'

'Yes, others were afraid, Miss Dobbs.' She took a biscuit from the tray. 'I have seen people come to Nick's shows, only to reveal absolute relief not to see their own faces on a canvas. On the other hand, look at his landscapes, the mural work. I admired him enormously—and make no mistake, I admire my sister as well. Georgina is terribly brave, though we don't always agree.

But she should never have come to you. This dredging up of the past can only prevent us from coming to terms with the fact that he's gone.'

'Yes, of course, but—'

'Oh, look, here's Piers.' Nolly went quickly to the doors that led into the garden and opened them for her father to enter. Maisie had not seen the patriarch alone with his eldest daughter before, and was struck by the affection demonstrated between them. As Nolly took her father's coat and handed him a much-worn cardigan that had been draped across the corner of a chair, she understood the place that each held in the other's world. Piers loved all his children, of that there was no doubt, but it was Nolly, sensible Nolly, whom he had taken under his wing.

Was it her father who had comforted her when she learned of her widowhood? Maisie imagined his suffering as he held the grief-stricken young daughter whose hand he had placed into that of the kindly Godfrey Grant, with the words 'Who giveth this woman?' echoing in his ears. Had Piers stepped forward as Nolly's protector, even as she pushed despair to one side to care for the injured Nick when he came home from France?

'Lovely to see you again, Maisie, my dear. Emma has stayed in the studio, a pressing need to immerse herself in her work.' Piers turned to Nolly as she passed a cup of tea to him with one hand. 'Thank you, Nolly.'

'I hope you don't mind me dropping in to see you. I was passing through town,' Maisie explained.

Piers leaned back. 'Remember, our children's friends are always welcome, Maisie, though I do wish Georgie hadn't got you involved in questioning Nick's accident.'

'That's what I said.' Nolly offered cake to Piers, who helped himself to a slice. She placed a plate on his knee. 'Though I am sure Maisie has come to the same conclusion as the police, that Nick's death was an accident . . .'

Maisie turned to Piers. 'Nolly said you took two or three sketchbooks from Nick's cottage. I'm fascinated by his work, I'd love to see them.'

'I—I—good heavens, I have no idea where I put them.' Piers reached forward to set his plate on the tray, his hand shaking. 'That's the trouble with age, one forgets.' He smiled at Maisie, but Piers was unsettled and Nolly sat forward, her body language indicating concern for her father.

Maisie softened her tone. 'Well, I would love to see them, when you find them. I have come to hold your son's work in some regard.'

Nolly stood up, so Maisie reached for her shoulder bag. 'I really must be on my way. My father is expecting me this evening, and I'm sure he has cooked me a wonderful supper.'

'You must forgive me for not enquiring before, but is your father alone, Maisie?' Leaning on the arm of the settee, Piers rose to his feet.

'Yes. My mother died when I was a girl, so there's only the two of us.'

'I'm sorry.' He smiled, reaching for her hand.

Maisie returned the affectionate squeezing of her hand. 'It was a long time ago, though we still miss her very much.'

She bade farewell to Piers and Nolly, asking to be remembered to Emma. As she drove away, she glanced in the mirror to see father and daughter standing together for one final wave. Then Nolly put her arm round her father's shoulders and they turned back into the house.

Another piece of the puzzle had slipped into place. With or without the sketchbooks taken from Nick's cottage, she believed she knew why Piers Bassington-Hope might have wanted them out of harm's way.

The time with her father brought surprising news, though it explained Sandra's visit to her office. The Comptons, Sandra's former employers, had decided to close their Belgravia house completely. According to Frankie, events had progressed with speed. The Belgravia household staff had been offered new positions at the Chelstone estate, though only two had accepted. Eric and Sandra were engaged, so Sandra had declined the job in Kent, deciding to stay in London. No one knew what she was going to do for board or living until the wedding in June, when she, too, would live in the one-room flat above the garage. Now Maisie understood that Sandra had likely come to her for advice.

Pulling into Fitzroy Street, Maisie parked the MG, and as she looked up at the office window, she saw the light, indicating that Billy was there.

'Mornin', Miss. Well, I 'ope?' Billy stood up from his desk and came to Maisie to take her coat as she entered.

'Yes, thank you, Billy. I've a lot to tell you. Everything all right here?' Maisie didn't enquire after Doreen, or the other children, knowing that there would be time for them to speak of the family. Asking the question as soon as she walked into the office would pressure Billy in a certain way; she had decided it was better to wait until he had warmed to the day.

'Right as rain, Miss. Shouldn't say that, should I? Looks like it's fit to pour down out there.' He turned from an inspection of the sky outside the window back to Maisie. 'Need a cuppa, Miss?'

'No, not at the moment. Let's get down to work. Fish the case map out of the chimney—though I have to tell you, here's the old one!' Maisie held up the crumbled wad of paper returned by Customs and Excise.

Billy grinned. 'Where'd you get that, Miss?'

'I'll explain everything. Come on, let's get set up over at the table.'

Five minutes later, Maisie and her assistant were seated in front of both the old and new case maps, pencils in hand.

'So you say that Nick B-H and 'is mates were all in this smugglin' lark?'

'Alex Courtman was probably not involved, though I don't know why. Could be because he met them later at the Slade, and therefore wasn't part of that earlier camaraderie. Let's keep an open mind about that one.'

Billy nodded. 'What do we do next?'

Maisie looked down at their original case map. She picked up a pencil and struck a line through words and scribbled ideas that pertained to the smuggling operation, then she circled the notes remaining, looping them together with a red pencil. Billy joined her and ran his finger along the new lines that charted the progress of her thinking.

'I would never 'ave guessed that, Miss.'

Maisie frowned, her voice low as she responded. 'No, neither would I, Billy. Not at first, anyway. But I won't be able to prove this without more legwork.' She walked to the door and reached for her mackintosh. 'Oh, I didn't tell you, did I? I know where the lockup is. We're going there now, then we'll go to see Svenson again.'

Billy helped her into her mackintosh, took his coat and hat from the hook and opened the door. 'Why do we need to see 'im again?'

'Corroboration, Billy. And, if I'm right, to organise a special exhibition.'

THE LOCKUP was in what Maisie would have called an 'in-between' area. It was neither a slum nor was it considered a desirable neighbourhood. Built a century before on the south side of the river by a wealthy merchant class, the houses had been grand in their day, but in more recent years many had been divided into flats and bed-sitting rooms. Pubs and corner shops were still well frequented, and people on the street did not seem as down-at-heel and needy as those in the neighbourhood where Billy lived.

They saw only one other motor car, a sure sign that they had left the West

End. A rag-and-bone man went by atop his horse-drawn cart, calling out the contents of his load as he passed.

Slowing the MG to a crawl, Maisie squinted to read the street names on the right, while Billy, clutching a piece of paper with the address they were seeking, looked out on the left.

'It should be along here, Billy.'

''Old up, what's this?'

They had just passed a corner pub, and the next house, a one-storey brick building with double doors at the front, was partially hidden behind grass and brambles. A number had been painted on the wall.

'Yes, this is it.' Maisie drew the MG to a halt and looked around.

'Let's park the old jam jar back there, nearer where we made that first turn. Little red motor like this stands out a bit round 'ere.'

Maisie drove to the spot suggested by Billy, then they walked back to the lockup. She opened her black document case, removed the envelope she had found under the railway-carriage floorboard and took out the key. She leaned closer to the lock in one of the doors and pressed the key home.

'Got it, Miss?'

She nodded. Together they pulled back the double doors, entered the lockup and closed the doors behind them again.

'I imagined it would be darker in here.'

Maisie shook her head. 'I didn't. The man needed light. And I doubt if that skylight was there when he rented the place—it seems quite new and must have cost a penny or two.'

They both spent a moment inspecting the skylight, which ran the full length of the lockup—a not insignificant thirty-odd feet.

'In fact, I would say he put quite a bit of money into this place and intended to use it for a long time.' She pointed to indicate her observations. 'Look over there, the way the crates are stacked and held back. And the shelving for canvases and paints. This was his workshop—that's a drafting table, look, with plans for exhibits. If Dungeness was his coastal retreat, then this was his factory, where it was all put together.'

Maisie took off her gloves and surveyed the room again. 'Right, I want to search every nook and cranny. We've good light, thanks to that'—she pointed to the skylight—'and I've brought my torch with me. I'm anxious to see if my suspicions are right about those crates over there.'

They walked over to a series of crates of differing widths, though each was approximately eight inches deep.

'Let's see how many there are first.' Maisie nodded to Billy, who already had his notebook in hand.

'Right you are.' Billy nodded, then touched a number on the top of a crate. 'What d'you reckon these are for?'

Maisie scrutinised the numbers, which were marked 1/6, 2/6 and so on until the final crate, which was marked 6/6. 'This has to be the main piece for the exhibit and the numerals suggest that it comprises six pieces.'

'Are we goin' to open all of them?'

'Perhaps. Then we must search this place for anything pertaining to the placement. There must be a master plan here somewhere . . . and there has to be a cache of sketchbooks that contain the preliminary drawings.'

'What about all those books you saw down in Dungeness?' Billy asked.

'The sketchbooks were revealing in that I could see his progress from his early days as an artist. But I think there are books, somewhere, that pertain to this collection.'

Billy was studying a tool rack. 'Crowbar, Miss?'

'That'll do, but take care.'

Billy shimmied the crowbar between two slats of wood in the first crate. With each crack as a nail came free, both Maisie and her assistant stopped all movement and listened. Finally, the crate was opened, and Maisie reached to pull out a painting that had been packed in a similar manner to those she had seen unloaded by the smugglers. Billy helped her stand the work against another crate before removing a hopsack covering, followed by a clean linen cloth, which, when pulled back, revealed the painting.

In a plain wooden frame, the piece appeared to be a horizontal panel measuring approximately eight foot by three foot.

'Blimey.'

Maisie said nothing, feeling the breath catch in her throat.

'It's got me right 'ere, Miss.' Billy touched his chest.

'Me too, Billy.'

The panoramic scene depicted two armies marching towards each other, with every last detail so clearly visible that Maisie felt that she could focus on the face of each soldier and see into his soul. Across the barbed wire they ran forward to meet the enemy, then, to both left and right, men began falling, with wounds to head, to leg, arm and heart taking them down. In the mural, the foot soldiers had become stretcher-bearers, running to their wounded, caring for the dying, burying their dead. Ants in khaki going about the business of war. The work suggested no victor and no vanquished, no right or wrong side, just two battalions moving towards each other with the terrible consequence of death. Blending skill with passion, Nick Bassington-Hope had revealed the landscape of war in all its darkness and terror—the sky lit by shellfire, mud dragging down those who remained unfelled.

'If that's just one of 'em, I'm not sure I can look at the rest.'

Maisie whispered, as if to speak aloud would dishonour the dead. 'I just need to see one or two others, then we'll pack them all up again.'

'All right, Miss.' Billy lifted the crowbar and began to open the next crate.

THE TASK COMPLETED, Maisie and Billy leaned against some shelving to rest.

'Does anyone know what Mr B-H wanted to call this 'ere masterpiece?'

'Because he was so interested in the triptych form while in Belgium before the war, people assumed that's what it was.'

'I reckon I don't ever want to 'ear the word "triptych" again, not after this.'

'I don't think I do, either. Now, if you search through those shelves over there, Billy, I'll attack this chest of drawers.'

Both began work in silence. Taking up some rough sketches, Maisie looked over at her assistant, who was pulling out a collection of completed but unwrapped canvases. 'Will your boys be home soon, Billy?'

'Reckon by the weekend. The 'ospital talked about convalescence somewhere on the coast—you know, fresh air to clear the lungs. Costs money, does that. But the boys will be all right, you'll see.' He hesitated, just for a second. 'Of course, they know about their sister now.'

'I see,' Maisie said as she pulled some sketchbooks from a drawer. They were each numbered in the same manner as the crates. 'Oh, look . . . one, two, three, four . . .' She leafed through each one in turn. 'These are the sketchbooks where Nick did his preparatory work for the pieces, but—'

'What is it, Miss?'

'Two are missing.'

'P'raps Mr B-H took them down to 'is cottage in Dungeness. Do you remember seein' them?'

'No, but—'

Billy was silent, and Maisie knew his thoughts had kept pace with her own. She set the sketchbooks to one side. 'Those are coming with us. I think we can go now.'

They ensured that everything in the lockup was left as they had found it, then secured the doors and walked back to the MG. Billy glanced sideways at Maisie and cleared his throat, ready to ask a question.

She responded before he uttered a word, her eyes filled with tears. 'I'm all right, Billy. It's just those paintings . . .'

Chapter Twelve

It was midafternoon before Maisie and Billy arrived at Svenson's Gallery, opening the main door to a flurry of activity as the Guthrie collection was in the midst of being taken down and packed for shipping. Svenson was ever dapper in another well-cut suit set off by a rich blue cravat and bright-white silk shirt. He called across to Arthur Levitt, instructing him to oversee the movement of one particular piece, and as the visitors stood to one side waiting for him to notice them, he reprimanded a young man for having 'fingers like sausages and a grip like a wet fish'.

'Excuse me, Mr Svenson!' Maisie raised her hand.

'Ah, Miss . . . er, Miss . . .?' He turned and smiled.

'It's Miss Dobbs, and this is my colleague, Mr Beale.'

'Delighted to see you again, and to make your acquaintance, Mr Beale.' He inclined his head. 'How may I be of service to you, Miss Dobbs? I trust that all is well with our friend Georgina?'

Maisie nodded. 'Quite well, though it's still early days, isn't it?'

'Yes, poor Nicholas's death hit Georgie particularly hard.' He paused. 'Forgive me, Miss Dobbs, but is there something I can assist you with?'

'May we speak in private?'

'Of course.' Svenson held out his hand in the direction of his office, then called to Levitt. 'Make sure those gorillas are careful with that portrait!'

The office was, like the gallery, a bright room with white walls and furniture constructed of dark oak and shiny chrome. There was a cocktail cabinet in one corner, a system of filing cabinets in another and, in the centre, a large desk. Though there were two chairs in front of the desk, Svenson directed his guests to the right of the door, where a coffee table was surrounded by a matching settee and two chairs in black leather.

'So, what can I do for you, Miss Dobbs?'

'First, I have to make a confession. My first visit to your gallery was not in the context of my friendship with Georgina. We were, indeed, both at Girton, but I am a private enquiry agent, an investigator—'

'But—' The colour rose in Svenson's cheeks.

Maisie smiled. 'Let me finish, Mr Svenson, there is no cause for alarm.' She waited for a second or two. 'Georgina came to me several weeks after Nick's death, essentially because she felt, in her heart, that his passing was not the result of a simple, unfortunate accident. She wanted me to make some enquiries, and to see whether there might be any reason for doubt.

Svenson nodded. 'I wish she had confided in me; I could have helped her, poor girl.'

Billy stole a glance at Maisie and raised his eyebrows. Maisie nodded in reply, then continued speaking to Svenson.

'Please, do not take this as an indication of my suspicions or findings, but I do have some questions for you. I understand that you came back to the gallery later in the day that Nick died, to speak to him—is that so?'

Svenson sighed. 'Yes, I did. I came back.'

'But you did not tell the police?'

He shrugged, waved his hand to one side. 'To tell you the truth, no one asked me. When Mr Levitt found the body . . .' He rubbed a hand across his mouth. 'Levitt summoned the police first, then placed a telephone call to my home. I reached the gallery shortly after the detective, Inspector Stratton. The pathologist made an initial examination and away they all went, taking Nick with them.' He held out his arms. 'A man dead and his legacy all around us—it was unbearably strange, such a vacuum.'

'But you saw Nick on the evening of his death, didn't you?'

Svenson sighed again. 'Yes, I did. There was something of a contretemps between Mr Bradley—who as you know was Nick's most fervent supporter— and Nick, here in the gallery, earlier in the day. It was in connection with the triptych, a piece that Nick had announced would not be put up for sale, but would be given to the Tate or some other national museum. Their words were fierce and heated.'

He had been rubbing his hands together as he spoke, but now he looked up at Maisie, then Billy. 'I returned with the express purpose of cooling the eruption, so to speak. It was crucial that the two men remained able to do business, that there was respect on both sides, each for the other. Of course, the budding liaison between Georgie and Bradley did not help matters. Nick was furious with his sister.'

'Did you enter by the front or back door?'

'I entered by the front.'

'Did you lock the door upon leaving?'

'I . . . I . . .' Svenson frowned. 'I do not recall turning the key in the lock but it is something I do all the time, it is a habit.'

She pressed on. 'Did you see anyone lingering outside, as you departed the gallery?'

Svenson closed his eyes, as if trying to remember the details. 'I closed the door . . . raised my umbrella to summon a taxicab that had just turned into the street. It was a fortuitous arrival, since it had started to rain, and—I didn't take a second glance at the passenger alighting on the other side of the car. I remember thinking that I was glad he or she had stepped via the left-hand door so I could just dive in and be on my way, and—I have now recalled—oh, my dear. . . . I may not have locked the door.'

Maisie placed a hand on Svenson's forearm. 'Don't worry, Mr Svenson. If someone wanted access to the gallery, they would have found it whether the door was open or not.'

'But . . . do you think Nick was *murdered*?'

Maisie and Billy exchanged glances again. 'Mr Svenson, I'm also here with some news—news that, for the moment, we must keep between just we three. In addition, I have a proposal for you, and I need your help.'

Svenson shrugged. 'My help? How?'

'I know where the masterwork is, and I want to exhibit it here. I—'

'You know where the triptych is?'

'It's not a triptych. And, yes, I know where it is. Let me finish, Mr Svenson. I want informal invitations sent to a select group of people—Nick's friends from Dungeness, his family, Mr Bradley, perhaps a representative from each of the national museums.'

'Oh my God, we must make arrangements. I must see the work . . .'

Maisie shook her head. 'No, Mr Svenson. I have to make a request I hope very much that you will grant. Not only do I require you to keep the arrangements confidential, only releasing information in the manner I stipulate, but I want just men of my choosing to assist with mounting the pieces. There will be a timetable to follow, a specific period during which—to all intents and purposes—the gallery will appear to be unattended. I cannot emphasise enough that my instructions must be followed to the letter.'

'What about Georgie? Will she be told?'

'I will see her this afternoon. As my client she understands that I cannot be expected to inform her of every decision, if I am to be successful.'

'You ask much of me, Miss Dobbs.'

'I know. But you, in turn, asked much of Nick, and your reputation has increased a thousandfold as a result. I think you owe him this, don't you?'

The man was silent for a few moments, then regarded Maisie again. 'Tell me exactly what you want me to do.'

GEORGINA BASSINGTON-HOPE WAS, fortuitously, at home when Maisie arrived. When informed by the housekeeper that Miss Dobbs was waiting in the drawing room, Georgina emerged from her study with the now-familiar ink-stained fingers.

'My apologies if I have disturbed you while working, Georgina.'

'It's the curse of the writer, Maisie: I am both annoyed and relieved upon being interrupted.' She smiled, pulled a handkerchief from her pocket and rubbed the stains. 'Tell me, have you news?'

'I think we should sit down.'

Georgina sat down on the armchair, continuing to clean her fingers with a handkerchief, though now her hands shook. She looked at Maisie, who had taken a seat on the chesterfield at the end closest to her. 'Go on.'

'First of all, Georgina, I want to ask you about the painting above your cocktail cabinet; the one that belongs to Mr Stein.'

'Maisie, I told you, I'm just—'

'Georgina! Please do not lie to me. You must have known that my work on your behalf would lead me to unearth the truth of what has been going on down in Dungeness.'

Georgina stood up and began to pace. 'I didn't think it had anything to do with the investigation. I just knew Nick's involvement had no link to—'

Maisie stood up to face her client. 'That is as may be, Georgina, but I had to follow the lead I discovered and that has taken valuable time before I was able to conclude that it was of no import regarding Nick's death.'

'I—I'm terribly sorry. But what they're doing *is* all in a good cause.'

'Yes, I know that. But you realise that Harry is in deep water, and Nick must have been at risk too.'

'And you don't think it had anything to do with Nick's death?'

'No, Georgina, I don't.' Maisie sighed. 'But I do have some news for you.'

'About Nick's death?'

'Not exactly. I have located the lockup where Nick kept much of his art, including the missing work.'

Georgina reached out to touch Maisie's arm. 'You've found the triptych?'

'There are six pieces, actually.'

Georgina faced Maisie squarely. 'Then let's go, I want to see it.'

Maisie shook her head. 'There are other plans already in motion, Georgina; plans that I request you to follow.'

Georgina's tone was short. 'What gives you the right to execute "other plans" without first requesting my express permission?'

'Georgina, please!' Maisie reached out and clasped both the woman's hands in her own. 'Be calm, and listen.'

The woman nodded, snatching back her hands and crossing her arms.

'You are absolutely right to be put out, and right to want to see your brother's work,' continued Maisie. 'However, in the interests of developments in my investigation, I had to move with some speed.'

'But I'm your client! I'm the one paying your fees!'

'Yes, but there are times in my work when my allegiance has to be to the dead, and this is one of them. I have thought long and hard about what to do in this case, and I must ask for your trust and your blessing.'

There was silence in the room. Georgina Bassington-Hope tapped her right foot several times, then gave a final deep sigh. 'Maisie, I don't know why you are acting in this manner, or what has inspired your "plan", but . . . but, against my better judgment, I trust you.'

'Thank you.' Maisie smiled at her client. 'My work does not end when a solution to a given case is found. It ends only when those affected by my work are at peace with the outcome.'

Georgina stared into the fire for some moments, then turned to Maisie. 'You'd better tell me your plans.'

MAISIE LEFT THE FLAT just as it was getting dark. Having stopped at a telephone kiosk to leave a message at Scotland Yard for Detective Inspector Stratton, it was no surprise to see his Invicta waiting upon her return to the office. She tapped on the window as she passed, whereupon Stratton stepped from the car and followed her up the stairs.

'I do hope you have something I can use, Miss Dobbs.'

'I've some more information for you, Inspector; however, I need some assistance in return. I think you'll find it a fair exchange.'

Stratton sighed. 'I know I won't hear a word unless I agree, so, you have my word.'

Maisie pulled two chairs in front of the gas fire and ignited the jets. When they were both settled, she began.

'Let me start at the beginning. The three artists, Nick Bassington-Hope, Duncan Haywood and Quentin Trayner, have all been involved in the smuggling operation on the coast. They were helped in their quest by three fishermen—two from Hastings and one from Dungeness, an older man with, I am sure, a knowledge both deep and broad when it comes to the coves along the coast.'

'Go on.' Stratton did not take his gaze from Maisie.

'Now, the thing about this operation is that there was nothing strictly illegal, so to speak. Of course, this is conjecture on my part, gleaned from various sources and a sense of the mission—and I mean exactly that— taken on by the artists.' Maisie paused to see how her words were being received. 'As you may know, the most valued art collections here in Britain and across the Continent are being plundered by a select group of American buyers who are keen to take advantage of an aristocracy weakened by war and economic disaster. So a lot of valuable and beloved works of art are making their way across the Atlantic, since our museums can only afford to save so many. Then you have people like the artists who have seen an exodus of the paintings that inspired them as young men. Nick, especially, was angered by what was happening. And that's not all.' She paused, assessing Stratton's interest. 'There are others who have good reason to fear for the future of their property.' Maisie pressed her lips together, choosing her words with care. 'As you know, politics in Germany have become increasingly influenced by the new party, the one led by Adolf Hitler. There are those who predict that their property will be taken from them. And there are others who want to help. I have discovered that valuable works of art are being distributed throughout Europe, taken to safety until such a time as they can be returned in confidence to their owners. The artists have two contacts, one in France, one in Germany, and possibly more, who receive and prepare the items for evacuation. Once in safe hands, the valuables are then placed with sympathisers who will keep them hidden until claimed by their rightful owners when this unsettled time has passed.'

'That's all very well, Miss Dobbs, but the men we're after aren't interested in paintings.' Stratton held out his hands towards the fire.

'I know, but they are interested in diamonds, aren't they?' Maisie replied as she leaned down to turn up the jets.

Stratton was silent.

'As I said, much of what I have gleaned came from a comment here, an overheard conversation there, but here's what I think happened to interest the men you're looking for.'

'Go on.' Stratton pulled his hands back and pushed them into his pockets.

'Harry Bassington-Hope was in trouble—'

'For goodness sake, we know that!'

'Bear with me, Inspector,' continued Maisie. 'Harry was in trouble. His back against the wall, he revealed a secret that, at some point, his brother must have confided in him: that the artists were moving paintings from the Continent across the Channel for safekeeping. Such things are of little consequence to criminals who prefer to trade in what they already know, but one thing they do know is the market in precious stones, particularly diamonds. Bringing in the gems from their own overseas contacts therefore became a much easier proposition—lean on Nick Bassington-Hope, make it clear that his brother will suffer if he doesn't play the game, and you have a leader who will see that his partners acquiesce. In short, Nick had already created the means to traffic valuables, so your criminal element simply piggybacked on the scheme—and the threat to Harry Bassington-Hope's life ensured that mouths remained shut.'

'Assuming you're right, Miss Dobbs—and that remains to be proven—how the hell did you discover all this?'

'I paid close attention, and of course, I was lucky in places—being in Dungeness at the right time, seeing the operation first-hand. And my assistant and I have spent hours at the Tate, learning about art.' Maisie paused, smiling. 'And of course, I saw the diamonds being removed from the back of a painting, so I knew what was happening. And so did the Excise, though—as far as I know—they haven't yet caught your criminals. I should add that I was questioned in some detail by your fellow government servants, and I think I may have told them just about everything I've told you.'

Stratton was silent for a moment, then he turned to Maisie. 'Anything else, Miss Dobbs?'

'One more thing.' She paused. 'When I speak to Nick Bassington-Hope's friends, I will press them to see you as soon as possible. I trust that their willingness to assist you will result in a tempered view of their activities.'

'Dealing with me is one thing. When the villains get wind of this, those men will likely need some sort of protection.'

'I've thought about that. They were pressured into collaboration, Harry Bassington-Hope's life being the bartering point. With Nick dead and Harry owing money left, right and centre, both Haywood and Trayner were ready to throw in the towel.' Maisie shook her head. 'I know it's a stumbling block, but surely if they help you to make arrests . . .'

Stratton sighed. 'I'll do what I can.' He looked down at his hands, then back to Maisie. 'How do you want me to help you?'

'I think what I have in mind will help you too.' Maisie spoke quietly. 'This must be handled with the utmost care, Inspector.'

SVENSON ARRANGED for scaffolding to be erected at the far end of the gallery on Saturday, while, for her part, Maisie gathered the men—and one woman—who would assist her on Sunday afternoon when construction had been completed. Though the original layout plans were not available, and she did not want to request assistance from Duncan Haywood and Alex Courtman, Maisie had been able to sketch a layout for her helpers to follow.

Meanwhile, per her instructions, Svenson had prepared letters bearing news that the 'triptych' had been discovered and that, following work on the exhibition throughout Sunday, a preliminary viewing would take place during the following week. Formal notification of the reception would be sent shortly. The decision to have a reception for a limited, select group to honour the artist was impromptu and presented an opportunity for the gallery to pay respects to a man of uncommon depth. It was also noted that representatives would be invited from London's leading museums.

At her request, Maisie was handed the letters to post. They would have been received on Saturday morning by each member of the Bassington-Hope family. Envelopes were also prepared for Quentin Trayner, Duncan Haywood and Alex Courtman, and it was anticipated that the letter would be on Randolph Bradley's breakfast tray when it was delivered to his suite on Saturday morning.

Maisie and Billy spent most of Saturday assembling the people and equipment they would need to execute their part of the production. Svenson had stepped forward to cover all costs involved in setting up the exhibition. Billy's brother-in-law Jim would be working for the first time in months, and Eric had been given use of Reg Martin's van from the garage. Sandra assisted Maisie with procurement of all manner of nails, screws and hooks. The plans were falling into place. Sunday loomed almost too quickly.

MAISIE, BILLY, ERIC, Jim and Sandra entered the gallery as the men put final touches to the construction of wooden struts and trestles. Arthur Levitt had acted as foreman.

'That's all for now, Mr Levitt. We can manage from here.'

Levitt nodded. 'You'll need the keys.'

As soon as they heard the caretaker leave, Billy ensured the back entrance was secure and the front door was locked. 'Ready for us to unload the van, Miss?'

'Ready, Billy.'

Maisie and Sandra opened a box they had brought in with them and took out tools they would need for the next part of the plan. The men returned with six panels, which they laid out before returning to the van for more equipment. In the meantime, the women set to work.

Some three hours later, Maisie checked her watch and caught Billy's eye. 'Time to let Stratton in, Miss?'

'Yes, it's time. Then you go up to the landing.'

As Maisie took up her place behind a screen, she felt a churning in her stomach. There was always the chance that she would be wrong.

AT HALF PAST NINE, according to Maisie's watch, illuminated for just a second with her torch, she heard the rumble of a car in the alley, followed by the sound of a latch at the back of the gallery being rattled. Deliberate steps echoed, as if the person entering the gallery were carrying a heavy load. Soon there was a distinct creaking noise as the door leading into the gallery was opened, and the steps came ever closer. Then a pause. The intruder's breath came heavy and fast.

There was a deep sigh and a metallic sound echoed into the air. And something else, a distinct smell. *Oil. Paraffin.* Back and forth, the footsteps moved faster now, the sound of the inflammable liquid slopping across the floor beneath the pieces that Maisie and her helpers had worked so hard to install on the wall. The scaffolding would ignite in a second, though she could not make her move yet. She knew she had to wait, had to linger long enough to hear the interloper speak. There would be a declaration—at least she hoped she was correct in her sense that such destruction would be accompanied by words spoken to Nick Bassington-Hope, as if the artist were in the room himself. Finally, as the fuel's vapour became overwhelming, a voice spoke loud and clear.

'You disappointed me, Nick. I pleaded with you, dear boy. I did all I could to prevent this.' The can rattled with the dregs of paraffin, and Maisie heard a second can being opened. 'I couldn't believe you wouldn't listen. I didn't mean to hurt you, Nick, didn't mean for this . . . but you couldn't be allowed to do it, couldn't be allowed to dishonour your own flesh and blood . . .' The words drifted into a whisper as the man set down the can, then fumbled with a matchbox drawn from his coat pocket.

'Damn!' The match failed to ignite, and as he tried to take out another match, the box fell to the ground, its contents scattered in the toxic liquid. 'Damn you, Nick. Even dead you're trying to save that monstrosity.'

Maisie stood up and began to walk towards the man who had come to destroy the work of his beloved son.

'Piers . . .'

Now partially illuminated in a shaft of light from the streetlamp outside, the man frowned. 'What the hell?'

She could wait no longer; the risk was too great. 'Billy, Stratton!'

Soon the gallery was filled with movement as Stratton's men rushed in.

'It was his fault, you know, it was Nick. I didn't mean it to happen—'

'You can save that for the station, sir,' instructed Stratton. He nodded to a sergeant, who pulled the older man's arms behind him, the loud click of a handcuff lock echoing in Maisie's ears as the killer of Nick Bassington-Hope was led away.

'I—I wanted to talk to him, I—' Maisie looked around. The fire brigade had been summoned to secure the gallery.

'It's too dangerous here and there's no need for you to remain anyway, Miss Dobbs. You'll have to come down to the station, of course.'

'Yes, indeed—but I'll have to telephone Svenson first. I don't think either of us expected this sort of damage.'

Stratton looked up at the painting. 'Pity he didn't get rid of that thing.'

Billy, who had been talking to both the police and fire brigade, joined them at that moment.

'You talking about that valuable work of art there, Inspector?'

'I am indeed.'

Maisie rolled her eyes. 'Let us just say, gentlemen, that my endeavours with paint might have saved a great work of art this evening.'

They all turned to look at the six pieces of plywood that Sandra had whitewashed earlier, and that Maisie had proceeded to use as a background for her own masterpiece.

'Thank heavens he came without a torch!'

MAISIE FELT HEAVY in body and soul as she drove back to her flat in the early hours of the morning. Piers Bassington-Hope had trusted that one beloved child would understand the plea he'd made on behalf of another. He had not considered, as Maisie had, that the child he cared for so deeply might be strong enough to endure any depiction of life or death created by her brother.

Chapter Thirteen

The next day, instead of driving to Scotland Yard following the arrest, Maisie had gone immediately to Georgina Bassington-Hope's flat, where she broke the news that her father had been taken into police custody in connection with the death of her brother.

'Georgina, I am sure you want to be with him. I'll take you now, if you wish.'

'Yes, yes, of course.' Georgina placed a hand on her brow. 'No good talking to anyone before I've seen Daddy, and Inspector Stratton. Nolly will have a fit if I don't have every last detail at my fingertips.' Georgina gave a half laugh, then looked at Maisie, her eyes dark, her skin ashen. 'Fine mess I've got the family into, eh?'

'I'll get your coat, Georgina.' Maisie summoned the housekeeper, who left, then returned with her employer's coat, hat, gloves and handbag. Maisie opened the door for her client, steadying her as she descended the steps to the waiting car.

GEORGINA BASSINGTON-HOPE fell into her father's embrace upon entering the interview room at Scotland Yard, her sobs matching his own as they held each other. Maisie turned to leave, only to hear Georgina call to her.

'No, please, Maisie—stay!'

Maisie looked to Stratton standing behind Piers Bassington-Hope, who gave a single nod. She could remain in the room.

Piers repeatedly cleared his throat and ran his hands back through his silver hair as he recounted the events that led to his son's death. 'I'd driven to Nick's cottage, must have been early in November. We hadn't had much time to . . . to talk, as father and son, alone, for ages.' He swallowed. 'Nick had gone to fill the kettle with water, so I sat down—next to a pile of sketchbooks. I began leafing through them—as always, stunned by your brother's work.' He paused. 'I—I recognised the subject of the work immediately, no mistaking it. And I asked him what the hell he thought he was doing. How could he do that, how could my son . . . do that? He told me that the piece was the most ambitious undertaking of his life, that he could not compromise. Georgina, I begged him to choose an unknown model, but Nick declined, saying that in his work he must honour truth. I tried to make him understand, tried to make him see—but he just waved me away.' Piers clenched his teeth, trying to stem the tears. He held out his hand to Georgina. 'I came again over the following weeks, came to ask him to reconsider, to petition him to stop, to think again, to . . . to be kind in his work. But he wouldn't give an inch.'

Piers began to describe the final bid to change his son's mind. He had come to the gallery on the eve of the exhibition when everyone had left, knowing that he was the only person who had any knowledge of the paintings. Entering by the front door—left open by Stig Svenson—Piers saw his son was on the trestle and, wanting to face him, rather than look up at him, he went to the stairs leading to the landing. Still agile, Piers had climbed over the railing and onto the scaffolding so that he could press home the importance of his request. Nick began to turn his back on his father, going about his work as if he were not there.

Piers Bassington-Hope sobbed as he continued. 'I had seen, then, the cold refusal in Nick's eyes. How could he be so indifferent, so oblivious to what he was doing? I could not help myself, I could not—'

Georgina handed her father a fresh handkerchief, which he pressed to his eyes. 'I am so terribly sorry.' He shook his head, then went on. 'I raised my hand and struck him across the cheek. I struck my own son.' He swallowed deeply. 'The trestle began to move. We both became unsteady, barely able to stand upright, then . . . then . . . Nick turned round and swore at me, and I—I lost control of my senses. A welter of anger exploded in my head. I felt my hand connect with the side of Nick's face. I reached out to grab hold of the scaffolding, anything to steady myself. Then Nick was gone. It happened before I could stop it.' Piers looked directly at Stratton. 'I had never raised a hand to any of my children, Inspector. Never.' He was silent for a moment. 'Before I could reach out, he was gone, the barrier broken as he fell. And I heard a terrible thud as he hit the stone floor.' Piers Bassington-Hope leaned sideways, moaning.

'When did you know your son was dead, Mr Bassington-Hope?' Stratton spoke with a steady voice, neither soft nor confrontational.

Piers looked up. 'I rushed to his side and I . . . I knew he was dead, could see the life gone from his eyes. So I held my son in my arms until . . . until his body was cold.' He explained that it was only as dawn broke that he panicked, his thoughts now of his wife and daughters and the anguish they would feel upon learning that Nick was dead. 'He was my son, Inspector, *my son*. And I loved him.'

NICK BASSINGTON-HOPE'S final exhibition at Svenson's Gallery took place in early February 1931, with a select group of family and friends invited to preview an event that was also a memorial to the artist. There were those who were surprised to see Piers Bassington-Hope escort his wife from the Invicta that drew up outside the gallery, and as guests entered, Harry Bassington-Hope, at first tentatively, then with more confidence, lift his trumpet to play the heart-rending lament he'd composed after first seeing the work his brother had named *No Man's Land*.

Duncan and Quentin arrived together, furtively nodding an acknowledgment towards Maisie, who had helped broker their freedom with a full description of the events she had witnessed at the barn on Romney Marsh. Alex Courtman stepped into the gallery and joined his two friends. He saw

Maisie, raised his hand to greet her, only to have his attention drawn to the door: Randolph Bradley had arrived, his shining Du Pont Merrimac Town Car eliciting gasps from onlookers as it pulled up alongside the gallery.

Soon Harry leaned back, pressing his lips into a piercing final note and the low murmur of those gathered ceased as Stig Svenson climbed the steps onto a plinth, beside which was the cord that, when pulled, would reveal the completed *No Man's Land*. Svenson pressed a white handkerchief to his eyes as he stood behind the lectern to address the guests, who edged forward to hear him speak.

'Thank you, all of you, for coming today. As those closest to Nick, I know you would not have missed this opportunity to view *No Man's Land* before the work is available to a broader audience. It was no secret that Nick's most fervent wish was for a bequest to a public institution, and I am proud to announce that Mr Randolph Bradley has most generously purchased *No Man's Land* as a gift to the Imperial War Museum, in perpetuity.' There was a round of applause.

'We all knew Nick. We all knew that he journeyed to the very edge of convention in his quest to tell the truth of what he saw. He was a man of and beyond his time, a man of sensitivity almost crushed by the weight of his experience in the years 1914 to 1918. This piece is, perhaps, his most telling. Be prepared to hate it, be prepared to love it, but do not expect to leave untouched by the message of Nicholas Bassington-Hope.'

It seemed as if everyone in the room held their breath at the moment when Svenson drew back the curtains concealing the masterpiece. As silence followed the collective gasp, Maisie opened her eyes, for she had closed them when Svenson reached for the cord. No one uttered a sound.

The segment that had stemmed Billy's desire to see more when they first visited the lockup formed the base of the exhibit. Each and every face was clear and distinct. Three large pieces—the anticipated triptych—formed the next level, and were deliberately shaped to resemble the stained-glass windows of a grand cathedral. The column to the left mirrored part of the scene below, the soldiers' expressions even clearer, filled with fear, terror and determination as they marched forward. Then the magnificent giant centrepiece that had every person in the gallery transfixed.

The scene required no explanation. A cease-fire had been called, and, as was the custom, stretcher-bearers from both sides had been sent forth to bring back the living, while others toiled with shovels to bury the dead.

Soldiers brushed shoulders with those against whom they had fought, and every man knew that it was not uncommon for friend to help foe commit a countryman to the earth. Nick Bassington-Hope had recorded the instant when two infantrymen, one British, one German, had come upon their own, the dead having fallen to the ground next to each other. With mud and blood smeared across their faces, exhaustion writ large in eyes that had looked into the furnace of hell, the soldiers had reacted with instinct and, instead of taking up arms, in that terrible moment had reached towards each other for comfort. The men were kneeling, locked in a raw embrace, one clutching the other, as if holding on to that other human being was to hold on to life itself. The artist had caught, in eyes, in mouths, in lines across foreheads, a depth of grief, a futility that came when man recognised man, not as an enemy with a gun, but as a reflection of himself. And it was clear to anyone who knew the family that the British soldier offering succour to the German was the dead war hero Godfrey Grant.

Nolly stood in front of the painting, recognising now why Piers had sought to protect her. Maisie remained with the woman, as her eyes moved from the centre panel to the one on the right, the panel that spoke the truth of her husband's death. Nick Bassington-Hope could never tell his sister that her husband was tortured, then shot, by the very men with whom he had served. The gentle Godfrey, who had turned to his enemy and seen, instead, his brother, had made his way back to the British front line, to a silence in the trench that was broken only by taunting. He stood next to men who, afraid of what it meant to see the enemy as human, instead saw a foe in their fellow man. His life ended with the letters LMF scrawled in blood across his forehead: LOW MORAL FIBRE.

While some moved forward to study the pieces in detail, others, including Piers and Emma Bassington-Hope, moved back to view the work as a whole. No one spoke, there was no discussion of light or depth, of a brushstroke here, the use of a palette knife there. Maisie recalled something that the expert who had been so helpful at the Tate had said: 'With a true masterpiece, there are no words required, only the message for all to see.'

Maisie remained in the gallery for just a few moments longer, then left to return to her office, for she wanted to complete final notes on the written report she would hand to Georgina Bassington-Hope when the time was right, along with her bill. She said good night to the two policemen in plain clothes who waited by the door to escort Piers Bassington-Hope back to the cell where he awaited trial on a charge of manslaughter. As Maisie emerged from the gallery into the freezing night and made her way towards the MG, she realised she was glad to be leaving.

MAISIE TRAVELLED to Dungeness the following day, parking the motor car close to the railway carriages that had been Nick Bassington-Hope's home. Already a 'For Sale' sign had been set up, nailed into a thick stake that had been hammered into the ground.

The sun shone, though the air was crisp, and as she was dressed for a meander along the beach, with a woollen thigh-length coat atop walking skirt and boots, gloved hands and a cloche set well down to protect her ears, she set off. She turned away from the carriages and tramped along towards the lighthouse, pebbles scrunching underfoot as she made her way past fishing boats pulled up onto the shingle. With the sting of salt on her cheeks, her eyes smarting against the chill wind, Maisie was glad she had decided to walk, for she loved the water, loved to be here, at the boundary of sea and land. She stopped, drawn to the water's edge, so that waves almost, though not quite, reached her shoes as they crashed into the shore.

The sea lapped even closer, though Maisie remained in place, her hands holding her collar to protect her neck. *It's because it's the beginning, and also the end.* That was what she loved about the place where the water met the land—the promise of something fresh, a suggestion that, even if what is happening now is to be suffered, there is an end and a beginning. I could sail away on that beginning, thought Maisie, as she turned to leave.

IT WAS LATE FEBRUARY before Maisie made an appointment to visit Georgina Bassington-Hope at her home in Kensington. Arriving at the flat, she was surprised to see Nick's motorcycle standing outside.

As she waited while Georgina was informed that her visitor had arrived, Maisie heard the unmistakable rat-tat-tat-tat-tat of typewriter keys. The journalist was having a productive day. The housekeeper left Georgina's study, beckoning Maisie to enter. The book-lined room resembled a bee-hive, such was the level of energy generated by the woman. Maisie was still until, finally, with a forefinger resting on a key, Georgina turned to her.

'One second, just one second while I finish this thought . . .'

Maisie took a seat next to the desk. Finally, Georgina rolled out the sheet of paper and added it to a manuscript alongside the typewriter.

'Maisie, how are you?' She reached out and grasped Maisie's hand. 'Come along, let's sit by the fire.'

The two women moved to chairs set beside the blazing coals.

'I'm well, but more to the point, how are *you*?'

Drawing back her thick copper hair, Georgina wound the waves into a chignon at the nape of her neck, and secured it with a pencil. 'I thought I'd never climb out of the hole I'd dug for myself, to tell you the truth. What with the terrible, terrible outcome of your investigation—and I'm not blaming you, no, I blame myself—I thought it would be best if I just went away, take a leaf out of Nick's book and go off to America or something.'

Maisie's expression betrayed her thoughts.

'Oh, you are just like Nolly! You'll be delighted to hear that it's all over with Randolph Bradley. I'll get to that in a minute. However, you must know that Piers is expected home in just a few months. What with the verdict of manslaughter, and considering his age, and the circumstances of the crime, he'll be home by the autumn, according to the solicitors.'

'I'm glad. Are you all coping? What about Emma and Nolly?'

Georgina sighed. 'We're making progress, patching things up, you know. Nolly's been a great help, an absolute brick. She's done wonders with Piers and Emma. And with me—and she's sorted out Harry, come to that.'

Georgina paused to gaze into the fire before she spoke again. 'Piers was the only one who realised that Nolly's wall of tweedy organisation was all that stood between her and the tide of sadness that came with Godfrey's death. When she went on about him being a war hero, it was herself she was trying to convince, and I think that none of us really understood her. It was so easy to think that Nolly was all right, you know, "Good old Noll!"' She sighed. 'But what Piers didn't grasp was that Nolly might be better than any of us when it came to dealing with the truth, that even though she was devastated when she first saw the paintings, it was as if she understood right there and then why Nick had chosen to use Godfrey as the subject.'

'Yes, I can see that.'

'She's both worried and delighted about Harry.'

'And what's he going to do?' Maisie was warmed by the conversation and by Georgina's unexpectedly buoyant mood.

'You'll never believe this, but Harry has joined a shipboard band, entertaining passengers on their way from Southampton to New York.' She shrugged her shoulders. 'I just hope that staff are banned from the gaming tables!. Seriously, he said he'd wanted to go to New York for ages, that it's where his kind of music was born, and that's where he should be.'

'And what about you, Georgina?' Maisie gestured towards the type-writer. 'You seem to have found your muse.'

'My muse is Nick. Come along, I'll show you.' Georgina returned to her desk, followed by Maisie. She reached for a series of large black-and-white sketches that had been laid out for her to view as she worked.

'Oh, my . . .'

'Only sketches, but brilliant, aren't they? So detailed.'

Maisie nodded, pulling a lamp across so that she could better see the work. Nick Bassington-Hope had depicted everyday life on the streets that were home to those who knew only want. Scruffy street urchins, lines of men waiting for work, women struggling to wash laundry at a cold-water street pump—the forgotten of London seen through the eyes of the artist.

Maisie lifted her gaze from the sketches and looked at Georgina. 'What are you going to do with them?'

Georgina began to speak quickly, her excitement mounting. 'After you gave me the keys to the lockup, I went over on my own to have a look. That's when I found these, the sketches. I just sat there and wept.' She swallowed, looking at Maisie intently. 'You were right, Maisie, *this* is war, *this* is a battlefield, and I have to do something about it. But I have only one real gift, and that is my skill with words.' She pulled the pencil from the chignon and held it up to emphasise her point, her unclasped hair cascading across her shoulders. 'So, here's my plan. I not only have the promise of an exhi-bition from Stig, but I have a contract from my publisher!' Georgina splayed the sketches across the desk. 'There's a story in each of these, a history, a person whose life others will want to read about—someone who I will *make* them want to read about. And I'm not going to stop there.' She was speaking faster now. 'These are all of London, with some of rural poverty in Kent, but Nick hadn't finished. I'm going to travel across Britain, from London to Birmingham, to Newcastle, Leeds, Sheffield, up to Scot-land, and I'm going to tell the story of what's happened since the start of the Great Depression.'

'Is that why you ended the liaison with Bradley?' Maisie risked the impertinent question.

Georgina shrugged. 'It began to end almost as soon as it started.' With her hands still resting upon her brother's sketches, Georgina looked out of the window. 'I took such huge chances out there during the war, but—oh, it is so hard to explain—there was this thrill, this feeling that what I was doing was right, that it was a gamble for a good reason.' Her words began to slow, and she shrugged her shoulders. 'I missed that feeling, and I think I tried to get it back by having an affair. But it was never right. You see'—she turned so that she and Maisie were face to face—'you see, I realised that even though there was a risk, the thrill of an affair with a married man—it was completely false. There was no . . . no . . . no truth, no solid, meaningful reason to play with that particular fire. Do you understand?'

'I do, yes; I do understand.'

'So now, with this work, with Nick's sketches there to challenge me, I've found that reason again, that old voice saying, 'Do it, it's worth it.'

Georgina spoke for some moments longer, while Maisie encouraged her with a ready smile. Then having submitted her written report, Maisie gathered her belongings, ready to leave, but Georgina touched her on the arm.

'I've something for you. Call it a gift from Nick.' She held out a parcel wrapped in brown paper and string. 'No prizes for guessing, it's a painting. But one you will find quite extraordinary, I think.'

'A painting, for me?'

'Yes. I found it in the lockup. A completed watercolour. He had rolled a note along with it, explaining the subject. It reminded me of you, so I had it framed for you. Of course, if it isn't to your liking, you can give it away.'

MAISIE UNLOCKED the front door of her flat and called out. 'Anyone home?'

Sandra emerged from the box room, a duster in her hand.

'Settling in, Sandra?'

'Yes, Miss. I can't thank you enough. I hope me being here won't be too much of an imposition.'

'Not at all. We can't have you living in a hostel until your wedding.'

Sandra smiled, beckoning to Maisie. 'Come and have a look. Eric helped me move a bed and dressing table in. Got them cheap at a house sale.'

Maisie looked into the room that had already been made cosy by the new lodger.

'And now that I've got a job in that dress shop, I can do night classes as well—typewriting's the thing, you know. I was just about to go and sign up.'

'Right you are, Sandra. I'll see you later.' Maisie smiled as the younger woman gathered her coat and hat and left the flat. Though she had wondered about her decision to extend the offer to Sandra to live with her until her marriage, she was delighted to lend a helping hand, just as others had in turn helped her in the past.

LATER, AFTER SHE HAD HUNG the painting on the wall above the fireplace, Maisie dragged one of her two Queen Anne armchairs closer to the fire. Sipping tea from a mug, she read the note that Nick Bassington-Hope had left with the painting he'd completed a year before.

Winter, but you would think it's the first day of spring. The sun is shining, and everything has that look of readiness for rebirth. I had just returned from Lydd when I saw the subject for this painting. Despite the cold, she walked along the beach and stopped to look out across the Channel, almost as if she were looking into the future. I had the feeling that this was a woman on the brink of something fresh, something new, a woman leaving the past behind. So, what with the promise of spring in the air, I came back to the cottage and began to work.

Maisie wondered what Nick had seen on that day, for the picture could well have been a photograph taken on her last visit to Dungeness, as she walked on the shingle and looked out to sea. She finished her tea and sat for some time, studying the painting, thinking about the man who had caught a moment of reflection. Her moment of reflection. She read the note again and closed her eyes. *Readiness for rebirth.* Winter warming to spring; the land new again after battles have raged. It was time to move on, to dance with life again.

JACQUELINE WINSPEAR

Home: California
Former profession: academic publishing
Born: Pembury, Kent, April 30, 1955

RD: What took you to the States to live?
JW: I had been to the US many times on holiday and on business. However, in 1990 I decided to take a longer break—a 'sabbatical' if you like. I'd had a car accident in 1987 and had finally received modest damages, and it seemed a good opportunity to reappraise where I wanted to go in life and work—I was in my mid-thirties, so it was not a light decision. I was offered a publishing job several months later and ended up staying here, in California.

RD: How does life in America compare with that in the UK?
JW: You know, I've been here for so long now that I don't consciously notice differences any more. One of the overriding aspects of American life is that there is still that 'can-do' attitude. If you want to strike out on something new, people will encourage you rather than predict doom—which was something of a tendency when I left the UK, although things have changed a lot in the sixteen years I've been away.

RD: What was your childhood in England like?
JW: I look back at my childhood with such great affection. I grew up in rural Kent and was very much the country kid—even going to London was a major cultural shock. Most of our neighbours were elderly, so, until I was about twelve, because of the way they interacted with me, I think my childhood had more in common with that of an Edwardian child than any of my London cousins.

RD: When and why did you start writing?
JW: I began writing professionally after I came to the US. Having started a new life, I realised that I wanted to make a dream come true, if I could. I started by writing articles and essays—concentrating on nonfiction as I didn't think I would be able to break into fiction. Eventually, though, circumstances led me to begin *Maisie Dobbs*. I was one third of the way into it, writing in the evenings and any spare moment, when I had a really bad riding accident that was very nearly limb-threatening. Following major surgery, I was told that I was looking at a year or so of rehabilitation, and would be lucky to regain seventy-five per cent of my arm's range of motion and strength. I continued work on *Maisie*

Dobbs so that I would have something to show for myself at the end of it all. After three months, I not only had a complete manuscript, but also eighty-five per cent of my arm back in working order.

RD: What inspired your interest in the Great War, which casts its shadow over the period in which the Maisie Dobbs books are set?

JW: I was always asking, as a child, why my grandfather wheezed when he breathed, why he limped, and so on. The response was always, 'It was his war wounds, from the Great War.' It was that word, 'wound' that did it, I think. It spoke of something deeper than injury or hurt, for example. It suggested a pain to the very soul of a person. He passed away at the age of seventy-seven, when I was ten, and until he died bits of the shrapnel that had peppered his body when he was wounded at the Somme in 1916, were still breaking through his skin. As I grew up, that childhood curiosity matured, and I came to realise that it is not dates, generals and military strategy that interest me so much as the experiences of ordinary people.

RD: Your admiration for Maisie comes through very strongly in the books . . .

One of the things I wanted to do was to honour the spirit of that generation of women in Britain, the first in modern times to go into war-related work. So that men could be released for the battlefield, women were recruited to fill their jobs—there was barely a field of endeavour untouched by a woman's hand. They built ships and aircraft, drove trains and buses, worked on the land and in construction—everything. The sad thing is that the 1921 census revealed that there were two million 'surplus' women of marriageable age in Britain. Having lost sweethearts, young husbands, brothers and fathers, they had to become financially independent, build community and friendships, and prepare for growing old alone. They were extraordinary.

RD: You've spent part of your career as a life coach. Do you still do that?

JW: Not currently. But I am able to bring that work to various other endeavours, such as workshops to encourage new writers. It is always a privilege to see clients moving in the direction of something new, taking brave steps towards changing their futures.

RD: Have you had coaching yourself and, if so, how did it help you?

JW: Yes, I have had coaching. It helped me focus on what was possible in my life, and to see ways in which I could diminish the seemingly insurmountable peaks that stood between me and the life I wanted to live. It encouraged me to take more risks.

RD: Would you recommend it for everyone?

JW: Anyone who wants to achieve something bigger in life, might find it useful. As with anything, the time has to be right. I believe in the saying, 'If you can see a thing, you can make it so.' Coaching helps you envision the reality that you want to create. And, surprisingly, it doesn't take winning the lottery to breathe life into that vision.

MICHAEL CONNELLY
ECHO PARK

In 1993, Marie Gesto disappeared after leaving a Hollywood supermarket. No trace of her or her body was found, and the case has haunted Detective Harry Bosch ever since.

When, thirteen years later, a killer called Raynard Waits confesses to Marie's murder, many in the Los Angeles Police Department are convinced they've got their man.

Bosch thinks otherwise.

PROLOGUE: THE HIGH TOWER

1993

It was the car they had been looking for. The licence plate was gone but Harry Bosch could tell. A 1987 Honda Accord, its maroon paint long faded by the sun. It had been updated in '92 with the green Clinton bumper sticker and now even that was faded. The sticker had been made with cheap ink, not meant to last. Back when the election was a long shot. The car was parked in a single-car garage so narrow it made Bosch wonder how the driver had been able to get out. He knew he would have to tell the Forensics people to be extra diligent while checking for prints on the outside of the car and the garage's inner wall. They would bristle at being told this but he would become anxious if he didn't.

The garage had a pull-down door with an aluminium handle. Not good for prints, but Bosch would point that out to Forensics as well.

'Who found it?' he asked the patrol officers.

They had just strung the yellow tape across the mouth of the cul-de-sac, which was made by the two rows of individual garages on either side of the street and the entrance of the High Tower apartment complex.

'The landlord,' the senior officer replied. 'The garage goes with an apartment he's got vacant, so it's supposed to be empty. A couple of days ago he opens it up to store furniture and he sees the car. Thinks maybe it's somebody visiting a tenant, but the car stays put, so he starts asking his tenants about it. Nobody knows whose it is. He starts thinking it might be stolen because of the missing plates, so he calls us. Me and my partner have the Gesto bulletin on the visor. Once we got here we put it together pretty fast.'

Bosch stepped closer and breathed in deeply. Marie Gesto had been missing ten days now. If she was in the trunk he would smell it.

His partner, Jerry Edgar, joined him. 'Anything?' he asked.

'I don't think so.'

'Good. I don't like trunk cases.'

'At least we'd have the victim to work with.'

Bosch's eyes roamed over the car, looking for anything that would help them. Seeing nothing, he took a pair of latex gloves out of his coat pocket, blew them up like balloons to stretch the rubber, then pulled them onto his hands. He turned sideways and slid into the garage.

He borrowed the patrol officer's Maglite and shone its beam through the windows. The riding boots and helmet were on the back seat, next to a small plastic Mayfair supermarket bag. He couldn't tell what was in the bag.

He moved forward. On the front passenger seat was a small stack of neatly folded clothing on top of a pair of running shoes. He recognised the blue jeans and T-shirt that Marie Gesto had been wearing when last seen by witnesses as she was heading to Beachwood Canyon to ride. On top of the shirt were carefully folded socks, panties and bra. Bosch felt the dull thud of dread in his chest. Not because he took the clothing as confirmation that Marie was dead. In his gut he already knew that. Everybody knew it, even the parents who pleaded on TV for her return.

It was her clothes that got to Bosch. The way they were folded neatly. Did she do that? Or had it been the one who took her from this world? It was the little questions that always bothered him.

After surveying the rest of the car through the glass, Bosch carefully worked his way out of the garage.

'Anything?' Edgar asked again.

'Her clothes. The riding equipment. Maybe some groceries. There's a Mayfair at the bottom of Beachwood. She could have stopped on her way up to the stables.'

Edgar nodded. A new place to look for witnesses.

Bosch looked up at the High Tower apartment complex. Of Streamline Moderne design, and built into the extruded granite of the hills behind the Hollywood Bowl, the apartments were all linked at the centre by the slim elevator structure—the high tower from which the complex took its name.

'Where's the manager?' he asked the patrol officer with two stripes on his sleeves.

'He went back up. He said take the elevator to the top and his place is the first one across the walkway.'

'OK, we're going up. You wait for SID and the OPG. Don't let the tow guys touch the car until Forensics take a look.'

'You got it.'

The elevator in the tower was a small cube that bounced with their weight as they stepped in. Bosch pushed the button and the car lurched upwards. It was a small space, with enough room for four people at the most.

'Nobody in this place has a piano, that's for sure,' Edgar said.

'Brilliant deduction, Watson,' Bosch said.

They stepped out onto a concrete runway suspended between the tower and the apartments. The view took in almost all of Hollywood and had the mountain breeze to go with it.

'Here we go,' Edgar said, pointing to one of the apartment doors.

There was a sign that said MANAGER below a doorbell. The door was opened before they got to it by a thin man with a white beard. He introduced himself as Milano Kay, the manager of the apartment complex. After they badged him, Bosch and Edgar asked if they could see the vacant apartment. Kay led the way.

He opened the door, and signalled Bosch and Edgar in first. The apartment was small. There was a living room, a kitchen and a bedroom with an attached bathroom. A curving wall of windows looked out on the same view of Hollywood that they had seen from the walkway. A glass door led to a porch that followed the curve of glass.

'How long has this apartment been vacant?' Bosch asked.

'Five weeks,' Kay answered.

'I didn't see a FOR RENT sign down there.'

'I never need to put up signs,' Kay said. 'Word gets out. A lot of people want to live in this place. Besides, I've been getting it ready, repainting.'

'Who would have known that garage was empty?'

'Quite a few people. The residents here, of course, and in the last five weeks I've shown the place to several interested parties.'

'The garage is left unlocked?'

'There's nothing in it to steal. The new tenant will put a padlock on it.'

'Did you keep records on who you showed the apartment to?'

'Not really. I might have a few call-back numbers.'

Bosch nodded. It was going to be a tough angle to follow. 'What about the former tenant?' he asked.

'She lived here five years, trying to make it as an actress,' Kay said. 'She finally gave up and went home to Austin, Texas.'

Bosch nodded. 'She live here alone?'

'She had a boyfriend who visited a lot, but I think that ended.'

'We'll need that address in Texas from you.'

Kay nodded. 'The officers said the car belonged to a missing girl.'

'A young woman,' Bosch said.

He reached into his jacket and pulled out a photograph of Marie Gesto. Kay said he didn't recognise her as someone who'd looked at the apartment.

'She went missing Tuesday the 9th,' Bosch said. 'You remember anything unusual around here back then?'

Kay shook his head. 'I was on vacation in Italy.'

Bosch smiled. 'I love Italy. Where'd you go?'

Kay's face brightened. 'I went up to Lake Como and then over to a small hill town called Asolo. It's where Robert Browning lived.'

Bosch nodded, like he knew the places and who Robert Browning was.

'We've got company,' Edgar said.

Bosch followed his partner's gaze down to the cul-de-sac. A television truck had pulled up to the yellow tape. He looked back at the landlord.

'Mr Kay, see what numbers or names you can find of people who called about the apartment. We'll also need the name and address of the tenant who moved back to Texas. And we'll need to talk to the other tenants.'

'No problem.'

They left the apartment and walked with Kay back to the elevator. They said goodbye to the manager and went down, the steel cube lurching again before smoothing out on the descent.

'Harry, I didn't know you loved Italy,' Edgar said.

'I've never been.'

Edgar nodded. 'You thinking about him?'

'Not really. Besides, if it was him, why call the car in?'

'Yeah. But maybe he's outsmarting us, Harry. Maybe the girl came to look at the place and things went wrong. He knows he can't move that car so he calls it in like it might be stolen.'

'Then maybe you should run his Italian alibi down, Watson.'

'Why am I Watson? Why can't I be Holmes?'

'Because Watson is the one who talks too much.'

'What's bothering you, Harry?'

Bosch thought of the clothing neatly folded on the front seat of the Honda. He felt that pressure on his insides again. Like his body was wrapped in wire being tightened from behind.

'What's bothering me is that I've got a bad feeling about this one.'

'What kind of bad feeling?'

'The kind that tells me we're never going to find her. And if we never find her, then we never find him.'

'The killer?'

The elevator jerked to a hard stop. Bosch pulled open the doors.

'Yeah,' he said. 'The killer.'

1

The call came in while Harry Bosch and his partner, Kiz Rider, were sitting at their desks in the Open-Unsolved Unit, finishing the paperwork on the Matarese filing. The day before, they had spent six hours in an interview room with Victor Matarese discussing the 1996 murder of a prostitute named Charisse Witherspoon. DNA that had been extracted from semen found in the victim and stored for ten years had been matched to Matarese. It was a cold hit. His DNA profile had been banked in 2002 after a rape conviction. It has taken another four years before Bosch and Rider came along and reopened the Witherspoon case, pulled the DNA and sent it to the state lab on a blind run.

But because Charisse Witherspoon had been an active prostitute, the DNA wasn't an automatic slam dunk. The case didn't come down to the science but to the interview room. The first five hours were gruelling. In the sixth, Matarese finally gave it all up, admitting to killing Witherspoon and three more prostitutes in South Florida before coming to LA.

When Bosch heard his name called for line one, he thought it was Miami calling him back. 'Bosch,' he said, grabbing the phone.

'Freddy Olivas. Northeast Division Homicide. I'm over in Archives looking for a file and they say you've already got it signed out.'

Bosch was silent a moment while his mind dropped out of the Matarese case. He didn't know Olivas but the name sounded familiar. As far as signed-out files went, it was his job to review old cases and look for ways to use forensic advances to solve them.

'I pull a lot of files from Archives. Which one are we talking about?'

'Gesto. Marie Gesto. It's a '93 case.'

Bosch felt his insides tighten. They always did when he thought about Gesto, even thirteen years later. 'Yeah, I've got the file. What's happening?'

He noticed Rider look up from her work at the change in his voice. Their desks were in an alcove and faced each other.

'It's kind of a delicate matter,' Olivas said. 'Eyes only. Relates to an ongoing case I've got and the prosecutor just wants to review the file. Could I hop on by there and grab it from you?'

'Do you have a suspect, Olivas?'

Olivas didn't answer.

'Who's the prosecutor?'

Again no answer. Bosch decided not to give in.

'Look, the case is active, Olivas. I'm working it and I have a suspect. If you've got something, I'm part of it. Otherwise, have a nice day, OK?'

'Tell you what, let me make a phone call. I'll call you right back.' Olivas hung up without a goodbye.

Bosch looked at Rider. 'Marie Gesto,' he said. 'The DA wants the file.'

'That's your own case. Who was calling?'

'A guy from Northeast. Freddy Olivas. Know him?'

'I've heard of him. He's lead on the Raynard Waits case.'

Now Bosch placed the name. The Waits case was high-profile. Olivas probably viewed it as his ticket to the show. The Los Angeles Police Department was split into nineteen geographic divisions, each with a police station and its own detective bureau. Divisional Homicide units worked the less complicated cases and the positions were viewed as stepping-stones to the elite Robbery-Homicide Division squads working out of police headquarters at Parker Center. That was the show. And one of those squads was the Open-Unsolved Unit. Bosch knew that if Olivas's interest in the Gesto file was even remotely tied to the Waits case then he would jealously guard his position from RHD encroachment.

'He didn't say what he has going?' Rider asked.

'He wouldn't even tell me which prosecutor he's working with.'

'Rick O'Shea. He's on the Waits case. They just finished the prelim on that and are heading to trial.'

Bosch considered the possibilities. O'Shea ran the Special Prosecutions Section of the DA's office. He was a hotshot and was getting hotter. Following the announcement that the sitting district attorney had decided against seeking re-election, O'Shea was one of a handful of prosecutors and outside attorneys who filed as candidates for the job. He had come through the primary with the most votes but not quite a majority. The run-off was shaping up as a tighter race. O'Shea had the backing of the outgoing DA and had a track record as a prosecutor who won big cases. His opponent, a former prosecutor named Gabriel Williams, had spent the last two decades in private practice, focusing on civil-rights cases. He was running on the promise of reforming the county's law-enforcement practices, and it was clear that his platform and his outsider stance were taking hold in the polls.

The election stories that ran almost daily in the *Times* had kept Bosch up to date on the O'Shea–Williams fight. The prosecutor was bolstering his candidacy with high-profile prosecutions. He had parlayed the preliminary hearing in the Raynard Waits case into daily headlines. The accused double murderer had been pulled over in Echo Park on a late-night traffic stop. Officers spied trash bags leaking blood on the floor of his van. A subsequent search found body parts from two women. If ever there was a safe, slam-bang case for a prosecutor-candidate to use to grab media attention, the Echo Park Bagman case appeared to be it.

The catch was that Waits was bound over for trial at the end of the preliminary hearing and, since it was a death-penalty case, that trial was months off and well after the election. O'Shea needed something to keep momentum going. Bosch had to wonder what he was up to with the Gesto case.

The phone rang 'Open-Unsolved. This is Detective Bosch.'

'Olivas. Bring the file over to the sixteenth floor at eleven o'clock. You'll meet with Richard O'Shea.'

'We'll be there.'

'Wait a minute. What's this *we*? I said *you*, you be there with the file.'

'I have a partner, Olivas. I'll be with her.' Bosch hung up and looked across at Rider. 'We're in at eleven.'

'What about Matarese?'

'We'll figure it out.'

He got up and went to the locked filing cabinet behind his desk. He pulled the Gesto file and brought it back to his spot. Since returning to the job from retirement the year before, he had checked the file out of Archives three times. Each time, he read through it, made calls and visits and talked to a few of the individuals who had come up in the investigation thirteen years before. But nothing came of the effort.

Bosch had plenty of unsolved cases in his history. As any Homicide man would admit, you can't clear them all. But the Gesto case stuck with him. Each time he would work the case for a week or so, hit a wall and think he had done all that could be done. The absolution lasted only a few months, then there he was at the counter filling out the file-request form again.

'Bosch,' one of the other detectives called out. 'Miami on two.'

Bosch hadn't even heard the phone ring in the squad room.

'I'll take it,' Rider said. 'Your head's somewhere else.'

She picked up the phone, and once more Bosch opened the Gesto file.

BOSCH AND RIDER were ten minutes late because of the back-up of people waiting for elevators. He hated coming to the Criminal Courts Building because of the elevators. The wait and jostling for position put a layer of anxiety on him that he could live without.

In reception in the DA's office on the sixteenth floor they were told to wait for an escort back to O'Shea's office. After a few minutes, a man stepped through the doorway and pointed to the briefcase Bosch was holding.

'You got it?' he asked.

He was a dark-complexioned Latino in a grey suit. Bosch didn't recognise him.

'Olivas?'

'Yeah. You brought the file?'

'I brought the file.'

'Then come on back.'

They followed Olivas down a long corridor to O'Shea's office. Most of the time prosecutors shared offices, two or four to a room, but O'Shea's office was double-sized with a piano-crate desk and a seating area. Being the head of Special Prosecutions obviously had its perks.

O'Shea welcomed them from his desk, standing up to shake hands. He was about forty and handsome with jet-black hair. He was short, and Bosch liked short prosecutors. They were always trying to make up for something and usually it was the defendant who ended up paying the price.

Everybody took seats, Bosch and Rider in front of O'Shea and Olivas in front of a stack of O'SHEA ALL THE WAY posters leaning against the wall.

'Thank you for coming in, Detectives,' O'Shea said. 'Let's get down to business.' He put his hand above a thick accordion file open on his desk. 'Are you familiar with the Raynard Waits prosecution?'

'It's hard to miss,' Bosch said.

O'Shea offered a slight smile. 'Yes, we have pushed it out in front of the cameras. The guy's a butcher. Now, before I explain what we have going, let me ask about your investigation of the Gesto case. Freddy said you've had the file out of Archives three times in the past year. Is there something active?'

Bosch decided to give and then receive. 'You could say I've had the case for thirteen years. I caught it back in '93 when she went missing.'

'But nothing ever came of it?'

Bosch shook his head. 'We had no body. All we ever found was her car. We couldn't make connections so nobody rose to the level of active suspect. Then I retired in 2002 and it went into Archives.'

Bosch didn't think it was necessary to tell O'Shea that he had copied the file, along with several other open cases, when he left his badge behind.

'Since I came back on the job last year, I've pulled the file whenever I've had the time,' he continued. 'But there's no DNA, no latents. There's only legwork. I've talked to everyone I could find. There's one guy I always felt could be the guy, but I never could make anything out of it.'

'Who is it?'

'Anthony Garland. He comes from Hancock Park money. His father is Thomas Rex Garland, the oil man, or T. Rex, as he is known.'

O'Shea nodded. 'What's Anthony's connection to Gesto?'

'"Connection" might be too strong a word. Marie Gesto's car was found in a single garage attached to a Hollywood apartment building. We thought whoever hid the car there knew the corresponding apartment was vacant. Garland's former girlfriend had lived there and moved back to Texas.'

'That's pretty thin. That's all you had?'

'We thought it was thin, too, but then we pulled the ex-girlfriend's DMV mug and it turned out she and Marie looked a lot alike. We started to think that maybe Marie had been some sort of replacement victim. He couldn't get to his ex-girlfriend because she'd left, so he got to Marie instead.'

'Did you go to Texas?'

'Twice. The ex told us she split with Garland because of his temper.'

'Was he violent with her?'

'She said no. She said she left before it got to that point.'

'Does he have any kind of criminal record before or after Gesto?'

'He hasn't been a very productive member of society—he lives off his old man's handouts, as near as I can tell. He runs security for his father and his various enterprises. But there's never been anything criminal.'

'What was your next move going to be?'

'I don't know. Maybe talk to some of Garland's more recent friends, see if he ever mentioned Marie Gesto or anything about her.'

O'Shea cleared his throat. 'Did the name Ray or Raynard Waits ever come up in all those years?'

Bosch looked at him. 'No, it didn't. Should it have come up?'

O'Shea pulled a folder out of the accordion file and opened it. He lifted a letter from the top. 'We've made it public that we're going for the death penalty on Waits,' he said. 'After the prelim I think he realised the writing was on the wall. So he and his lawyer responded last week with this. Before I show it to you, I have to know that you understand this is a proffer from an attorney. No matter what happens, the information is off the record. If we choose to ignore the offer, no investigation can come from the information.'

Rider nodded. Bosch didn't.

'Detective Bosch,' O'Shea prompted.

Bosch finally nodded. 'OK,' he said.

O'Shea slid the paper across the desk and Bosch and Rider leaned forward to read it together.

Sept. 12, 2006

Richard O'Shea, Assistant District Attorney
Los Angeles County District Attorney's Office
210 West Temple Street, Los Angeles, CA 90012-3210

Re: *California v. Raynard Waits*

Dear Mr O'Shea,

This letter is intended to open discussions regarding a disposition in the above-referenced case. All statements about these discussions are made with the understanding that they are inadmissible under California Evidence Code §1153, California Penal Code §1192.4 and *People v. Tanner*, 45 Cal. App.3d 345, 350, 119 Cal. Rptr. 407 (1975).

Mr Waits would be willing, on terms and conditions outlined

below, to share with you and investigators of your choice information regarding nine homicides, excluding the two in the above-referenced case, and to plead guilty to the charges in the above-referenced case, in exchange for the People's agreement not to seek the death penalty on the instant homicide charges, or to file charges in regard to the homicides about which he would provide information.

Furthermore, you must agree that any statements by Mr Waits, and any information derived therefrom, will not be used against him in any criminal case; no information may be divulged to any other law-enforcement agencies unless those agencies agree to be bound by the terms of this agreement; no information provided by Mr Waits during any 'off-the-record' discussion may be used against him.

Mr Waits offers to provide information in regard to nine known and unknown homicides between 1992 and 2003. As an initial offer of credibility and good faith, he suggests that investigators review the investigation into the death of Daniel Fitzpatrick, 63, who was burned to death in his Hollywood Boulevard pawnshop on April 30, 1992. Investigative files will reveal that Mr Fitzpatrick was set afire by an assailant using lighter fluid and a butane lighter. A can of EasyLight lighter fluid was left behind, standing upright in front of the store security fence. This information was never made public.

Further, Mr Waits suggests that police investigative files in regard to the September 1993 disappearance of Marie Gesto will reveal that Ms Gesto's car, located in a garage at a Hollywood apartment complex, contained a grocery bag containing a one-pound bag of carrots. Ms Gesto intended to use the carrots to feed the horses she groomed in exchange for riding time at the Sunset Ranch stables. Again, this information was never made public.

I would suggest that an agreement of disposition, if achieved, would fall within the exceptions to California's prohibition against plea bargaining serious felonies inasmuch as there is insufficient evidence to prove the People's case in regard to these nine homicides.

Please contact me if the foregoing is acceptable.
Sincerely,
Maurice Swann, PA

Bosch realised he had read almost the entire letter without taking a breath. He gulped down some air, but it did not displace the tightness in his chest.

'You're not going to agree to this, are you?'

O'Shea held his gaze for a moment. 'We may get eleven solved murders.'

And you'll get more headlines in time for the election, Bosch thought but didn't say.

'But he still walks?' he asked.

'No, Detective, he doesn't walk. He never sees the light of day again. Have you ever been up to Pelican Bay, the place they send sex offenders? It only sounds like a nice place.'

'But no death penalty. You're giving him that.'

'Yes,' O'Shea said. 'But first we need to make damn sure he is good for those nine. This could all be a trick to avoid the needle or it could be the real thing. I want you two to work with Freddy in finding out which it is. I'll make the calls and you will be cut loose. That will be the assignment.'

Neither Bosch nor Rider responded. O'Shea pressed on.

'Freddy confirmed the Fitzpatrick thing. He was burned to death during the riots after the Rodney King verdict came in. He was heavily armed and what is not clear is how his killer got close enough to set him on fire. The can of EasyLight was found in front of the security fence, just like Waits said. The Gesto mention we could not confirm because you've got the file, Detective Bosch. Did he get that right about the bag of carrots?'

Bosch reluctantly nodded. 'Nobody knew about that except me, my partner at the time and the evidence tech. We held it back because that's where we ended up thinking she crossed his path. The carrots came from a Mayfair Supermarket at the bottom of Beachwood Canyon. Turned out it was her routine to stop there before going to the stables. She came out with the carrots and probably her killer as a trailer. We found witnesses who put her in the store. Nothing else after that.'

O'Shea pointed to the letter. 'Then this is looking good.'

'No, it's not,' Bosch said. 'Don't make the deal. If he killed Marie Gesto and eight other people, they ought to strap him down, put the juice in him and send him on down the hole to where he belongs.'

'What about all of those open cases?' O'Shea countered. 'We have a responsibility to provide answers to the families. Also, you have to remember that we are *seeking* the death penalty. We have to go to trial and win and *then* get the jury to recommend death. It only takes one juror to stop that. And one soft judge to ignore the jury's recommendation, anyway.'

Bosch didn't respond. He knew how the system could be manipulated and how nothing was a sure thing. Still, it bothered him. A life sentence didn't always mean a life sentence.

O'Shea picked up a pen and drummed it lightly on his desk. 'Detective Bosch, did Gesto have family?'

'She had parents up in Bakersfield. They had a lot of dreams for her.'

'Think about them. And the other families. We can't tell them that Waits was the one unless we know for sure. My guess is that they will want to know and that they would trade that knowledge for his life.'

Bosch said nothing. He had registered his objection.

'What is the time frame on this?' Rider asked.

'I want to move quickly,' O'Shea said. 'If this is legit, I want to clean it up and get it done.'

'Gotta get it in before the election, right?' Bosch asked.

O'Shea's lips formed a tight line. 'Detective,' he said. 'I will give you that I'm running for election, and clearing eleven murders would be helpful. But every night those parents go to bed not knowing what happened to their daughter is a night of terrible pain as far as I'm concerned. So keep your speculations to yourself.'

'Fine,' Bosch said. 'When do we talk to this guy?'

O'Shea looked at Olivas and then back at Bosch. 'Well, I think you should come up to speed on Waits, and I'd like Freddy to familiarise himself with Gesto. What about tomorrow?'

'Tomorrow's fine.'

'Did you bring the Gesto records?'

Bosch opened his briefcase on his lap and took out the investigation file, contained in a three-inch-thick binder generally known as a murder book. He handed it to O'Shea, who turned and gave it to Olivas.

'And I will give you this in return.' O'Shea handed the accordion folder across the desk. 'Happy reading. Are you sure about tomorrow?'

Bosch looked at Rider. They needed to walk the Matarese filing to the DA, but the work was mostly finished. Rider said nothing.

'We'll be ready,' he said.

'Then I will call Maury Swann and set it up.'

'What about the other seven?' Bosch asked. 'Are there any files?'

'The proffer indicates that these were women who were never reported missing. Waits is willing to lead us to them but there's no prep work we can do for them.' O'Shea looked at them both. 'I know I am repeating myself, but nothing in that file or anything that he tells you can ever be used to make a case against him, even if this falls apart. Is that clearly understood?'

'It's clear,' Rider said.

'There is one exception that I have negotiated. If he lies, if you catch him at any time in a lie or if any piece of information he gives you during this process proves to be knowingly false, all bets are off and we can go after him for all of it. He has been made quite aware of this too.'

Bosch nodded. He stood up. Rider did, too.

'Do you need me to call someone to free you two up?' O'Shea asked. 'I can flex a muscle if needed.'

Rider shook her head. 'I don't think so. The seven women might be unknown victims but there's got to be a file in Archives on the man in the pawnshop. It all cuts Open-Unsolved in. We can handle our supervisor.'

'OK, then. As soon as I have the interview set up, I will call.' O'Shea stood up. 'Detectives,' he said, 'I hope you are on my side on this.'

Bosch shook his hand. 'If Waits can help me bring Marie Gesto home to her parents, then I'm on your side.'

It wasn't a completely accurate summation of his feelings, but it got him out of the office.

BACK AT OPEN-UNSOLVED, they sat in their supervisor's office and brought him up to date on the day's developments. Abel Pratt was three weeks away from retirement after twenty-five years on the job. He was attentive to them but not overly so. On the side of his desk was a stack of Fodor's guidebooks for Caribbean islands. His plan was to pull the pin, leave the city and find an island to live on with his family. It was a common retirement dream among law-enforcement officers—to pull back from all the darkness witnessed for so long on the job. The reality, however, was that after about six months on the beach the island got pretty boring.

A detective from RHD named David Lambkin was set to be the squad's 'top' after Pratt split. A nationally recognised sex-crimes expert, he had been chosen for the job because so many of the cold cases they were working on were sexually motivated. Bosch would have liked to be briefing him instead. But one of the positive things about Pratt was that he'd give them free rein until he was out the door. He just didn't want any waves.

After hearing their briefing, Pratt gave his approval for them to work with O'Shea, and only became animated when recalling Raynard Waits's attorney.

'Let me tell you about Maury Swann,' he said. 'Whatever you do when you meet him, do not shake his hand.'

'Why not?' Rider asked.

'I had a case with him once, a gangbanger on a one-eighty-seven. Every day when we started court, Maury made a big deal of shaking my hand and then the prosecutor's.'

'So?'

'So after his guy was convicted he tried to snitch out the others involved in the murder to get a reduced sentence. He told me during the debriefing that he thought I was dirty. He said that during the trial Maury told him he could buy all of us. So the banger had his homegirl get cash, and Maury told him that every time he shook our hands he was paying us off. You know, passing the cash palm to palm. He always did those two-handed shakes.'

'Holy shit!' Rider said. 'Didn't you guys work up a case on him?'

Pratt dismissed the idea with a wave. 'It was after the fact; it wouldn't have gone anywhere—not with Maury being a member of the bar in good standing. But when you get in that room with him, don't shake his hand.'

They left Pratt's office, smiling at the story, and returned to their own workstation. The division of labour had been worked out on their walk back from the courthouse. Rider would take Fitzpatrick, and would also finish the Matarese filing. This meant Bosch was cleared to study full-time the world of Raynard Waits.

After pulling out the Fitzpatrick file for Rider, Bosch chose to take the accordion folder O'Shea had given them down to the cafeteria. He knew the lunch crowd would be thinning out and he would be able to work without the constantly ringing phones and chatter of the squad room. He had to use a napkin to clean a table in the corner, then settled into his review.

There were three files on Waits. The LAPD murder book compiled by Olivas and his partner Ted Colbert, a file on a prior arrest, and O'Shea's prosecution file. Bosch decided to read the murder book first.

Raynard Waits was thirty-four years old and lived in a ground-floor apartment on Sweetzer Avenue in West Hollywood. He wasn't a large man, standing five foot six and weighing 142 pounds. He was the owner-operator of a window-cleaning company, ClearView Residential Glass Cleaners. According to the police reports, he came to the attention of two patrol officers, a boot named Arnolfo Gonzalez and his training officer, Ted Fennel, at 1.50 a.m. on May 11. The officers were assigned to a Crime Response Team watching a hillside neighbourhood in Echo Park because of a recent rash of burglaries on the nights of Dodgers home games. Gonzalez and Fennel were in an unmarked cruiser at the remote edge of the Dodger Stadium complex, near the intersection of Stadium Way and Chavez Ravine Place, following a standard CRT strategy: to stay out on the perimeter of the target neighbourhood and follow in any vehicle or persons that looked out of place.

According to their report, Gonzalez and Fennel grew suspicious as to why a van with signs that said ClearView Residential Glass Cleaners was out and about at two in the morning. They followed at a distance and Gonzalez entered the van's plate number into a mobile digital terminal. The computer kicked back a flag. The plate was registered to a Ford Mustang out in Claremont. Believing that the licence plate was stolen, Fennel stopped the van on Figueroa Terrace.

'The driver of the vehicle appeared agitated and leaned out of the van's window to talk to Officer Gonzalez, in an effort to block a visual survey of the interior,' the arrest summary read. 'Officer Fennel approached the passenger side and beamed his flashlight into the van. He noticed some black plastic trash bags on the floor in the passenger footwell. A substance appearing to be blood could be seen leaking from the cinched mouth of one of the bags.'

According to the report, 'The driver was asked if it was blood, and he stated that he had cut himself earlier in the day when a plate-glass window shattered, and he had used rags to clean up the blood. When asked to show where he was cut, the driver made a move to restart the vehicle. Officer Gonzalez reached through the window to restrain him. After a short struggle, the driver was handcuffed and moved to the back seat of the unmarked car. Officer Fennel opened the bag to find human body parts.'

The driver's licence identified the man as Raynard Waits. He was booked into the holding tank at Northeast Division while an investigation of his van was carried on through the night on Figueroa Terrace. Only after Detectives Olivas and Colbert, the on-call team that night, retraced the steps taken by Gonzalez and Fennel was it learned that the rookie officer had entered the wrong licence plate number into the MDT, typing an F for an E.

The next morning, Olivas and Colbert obtained a search warrant for the apartment on Sweetzer. A four-hour search produced samples of human hair and blood taken from the washbasin and bathtub traps, and a space beneath the floor containing Polaroid photos of nude young women who appeared unconscious or dead. In a utility room was an empty upright freezer.

Meanwhile, the coroner's office had found that the three plastic bags contained the body parts of two young women. The parts from one of the bodies showed indications of having been thawed after being frozen.

The reports detailed efforts to identify the other women in the Polaroids as well as the two bodies. Fingerprints taken from one of the dismembered women drew a hit on the FBI's latent data base. She was identified as a seventeen-year-old runaway from Davenport, Iowa, and photos supplied by her mother were recognised by youth counsellors at Hollywood shelters. She had been using various names to avoid being sent home. There were indications she was involved in drug use and street prostitution.

The shelter counsellors were also shown the Polaroid photographs found in Waits's apartment and were able to provide a variety of different names for at least three of the women. Their stories were similar. They were runaways possibly engaged in prostitution to earn money for drugs.

It was clear to Bosch from the gathered evidence and information that Waits was a serial killer who targeted young women unaccounted for by society, fringe dwellers who were not missed when they disappeared.

The Polaroids were in the file, encased in plastic sheets. As Bosch studied the women's faces, he remembered one of his teachers in Homicide, who had a special sympathy for the ones he called 'murder's nobodies'. He had taught Bosch early on that in society all victims are not created equal, but to the true detective they must be.

At the end of Bosch's review of the investigation and prosecution files, two questions came to mind. First, why was there no photo of Gesto in Waits's apartment? But Bosch knew that killers evolved. Waits could have learned from the Gesto killing that he needed reminders of his work. The second question was more troubling. Waits lived in West Hollywood. What was he doing in Echo Park?

There was nothing in the file that dealt with this question. It was thought simply that Waits had been on his way to get rid of the bodies, possibly to bury them in the parklands around Dodger Stadium. No further investigation of this was contemplated. But to Bosch it was something to consider. Echo Park would have been a half-hour away by car from Waits's apartment in West Hollywood. That was a long time to be driving with body parts in bags. Griffith Park, which was larger and had more pockets of isolated terrain, was far closer to the West Hollywood apartment. To Bosch, this meant that Waits must have had a specific destination in mind in Echo Park.

No psychological study of the defendant had been conducted, and Bosch was mildly surprised by this. Perhaps, he thought, it had been a strategic decision by the prosecution. O'Shea wouldn't want to open a door to a possible insanity defence. Still, a psychological study could have been useful and should have been done. Whether the subject was cooperative or not, a profile could have been drawn from the crimes themselves as well as from what was known about Waits through his history, appearance, the findings in his apartment and interviews conducted with those he knew and worked for. Such a profile might have also given O'Shea an edge against any move by the defence to claim insanity.

Now it was too late. The department had a small psych staff and there would be no way for Bosch to get anything done before the interview with Waits the next day. Farming it out to the FBI would take two months at best.

Bosch suddenly had an idea about that but decided to grind it over for a little while. He picked up the last file, the investigation related to Waits's 1993 prowling arrest, the only blip on the radar involving him until his arrest with the body parts thirteen years later.

The reports said that Waits was arrested in the Fairfax District after a woman with insomnia happened to glance out of her window and saw a man looking in the rear windows of the house next door. She woke her sleeping husband and he jumped the man and held him until police arrived. The man was found in possession of a screwdriver and charged with prowling. He carried no identification and gave the name Robert Saxon to the arresting officers. He said he was only seventeen. But his ruse crumbled and he was identified as Raynard Waits, twenty-one, when a thumbprint taken during the booking process scored a match in DMV records to a driver's licence issued nine months earlier to Raynard Waits. That licence carried the same day and month of birth, but it said that Raynard Waits was four years older than he had claimed to be as Robert Saxon.

During questioning, Waits admitted to police that he had been seeking a home to burgle. However, it was noted that the window he had been looking through corresponded to the bedroom of a fifteen-year-old girl. Still, Waits avoided a sex-offender jacket in a plea agreement and was sentenced to eighteen months' probation, which he completed with high marks.

Bosch worked the dates, and realised that while Waits was successfully completing probation he was also graduating from prowler to murderer. Marie Gesto was taken before he cleared his tail.

'Howzit going?'

Bosch looked up. Rider had come down to get coffee.

'Almost done,' he said. 'How about you?'

'I'm done with what O'Shea gave us. I called Evidence Archives for the box on Fitzpatrick.'

'What's in there?'

'I don't know for sure. Did you eat lunch?'

'Forgot. What did you see in the Fitzpatrick file?'

She sat down opposite Bosch. 'The case was handled by the short-lived Riot Crimes Task Force. They had a clearance rate of like ten per cent. Basically, anybody who did anything during those three days got away with it unless they were caught on camera.'

Bosch remembered that there had been more than fifty deaths during the riots in 1992. It had been a free-for-all, a lawless time in the city. He remembered walking down the middle of Hollywood Boulevard and seeing flaming buildings on both sides of the street. One of those buildings probably contained Fitzpatrick's pawnshop.

'It was an impossible task,' he said.

'I know,' Rider said. 'Putting together cases out of that chaos. I can tell from the Fitzpatrick file that they didn't spend a lot of time with it. The whole thing was pretty quickly written off as random violence.'

'Look, do you have time to do an AutoTrack run on Waits?'

The division of labour in their partnership had her doing most of the computer work. AutoTrack was a computer data base that could provide an individual's address history through utility and cable hookups, DMV records and other sources. It was tremendously useful.

'I think I can swing it,' said Rider.

'I just want to see where he's lived. I can't figure out why he was in Echo Park, and it looks like nobody else has given it much thought. He lived closer to Griffith Park, and that would probably have been a better place to dump the bodies. I think he was going somewhere he knew.'

'Maybe he thought the farther away from him the better.'

Bosch wasn't convinced. 'I think I'm going to ride over there.'

'And what? You think you'll find where he was going to bury those bags? You turning psychic on me now, Harry?'

'Not yet. I just want to see if I can get a feel for Waits before we actually talk to the guy.' Saying the name made Bosch grimace and shake his head.

'What?' Rider asked.

'You know what we're doing here? We're helping to keep this guy alive. A guy who cuts women up.'

Rider frowned. 'I know how you feel, Harry, but I kind of come down on O'Shea's side on this. I think it's better that all the families know. It's like with my sister. We wanted to know.'

When Rider was a teenager her older sister was murdered in a drive-by shooting. The case was cleared and three bangers went away for it. It was the main reason she became a cop.

'It's probably like you with your mother, too,' she added.

Bosch looked up at her. His mother had been murdered when he was a boy. More than three decades later he solved the crime himself because he wanted to know.

'You're right,' he said. 'But it just doesn't sit right, that's all.'

He started closing the files and putting them away.

2

In the shadows of downtown's spires and under the glow of lights from Dodger Stadium, Echo Park was one of LA's oldest and ever-changing neighbourhoods. Over the decades it had been the destination of the city's immigrant underclass—the Italians first, then the Mexicans, the Chinese, the Cubans, Ukrainians and all the others. By day a walk down the main drag of Sunset Boulevard might require skills in five languages to read all the storefronts. By night it was the only place in the city where the air could be split by the sound of gang gunfire, the cheers for a home-run ball and the baying of the hillside coyotes—all in the same hour.

These days Echo Park was also a favoured destination of another class of newcomer—the young and hip. Artists, musicians and writers were moving in. Cafés and vintage-clothing shops were squeezing in next to the bodegas and *mariscos* stands. A wave of gentrification was washing across the flats and up the hillsides. The character of the place was changing. Real-estate prices were going up, pushing out the working class and the gangs.

As Bosch drove past Echo Lake he saw the statue known as the *Lady of the Lake* watching over the water lilies. As a boy he had lived for a year with his mother in the apartments across from the lake, but it had been a bad time for her and him and the memory was all but erased. He vaguely remembered that statue but nothing else.

At Sunset he turned right down to Beaudry. From there he drove up the hillside to Figueroa Terrace. For the most part the houses were postwar concrete-block construction with gated yards and barred windows. He pulled over and put the car in park. He wondered again why Waits had been on this street. After a few moments he opened his cellphone and called his partner.

'You run that AutoTrack yet?' he asked.

'Just did. Where are you?'

'Echo Park. Anything come up near here?'

'Uh-uh, I was just looking. The furthest east it puts him is the Montecito Apartments on Franklin.'

Bosch knew that the Montecito wasn't near Echo Park but it wasn't far from the High Tower Apartments, where Marie Gesto's car had been found.

'When was he at the Montecito?'

'After Gesto. In '99. A one-year stay.'

'Anything else worth mentioning?'

'No, Harry. The guy moved houses every one or two years. Didn't like staying put, I guess. You coming back to the office?'

'In a little while. Thanks, Kiz.'

He closed the phone and drove off. He took a left on Chavez Ravine Place and in a few moments he came to Stadium Way, and the spot where Waits had first drawn the attention of the CRT patrol. At the stop sign he surveyed the intersection. Stadium Way was the feeder line to the stadium's huge parking lots. For Waits to have come into Echo Park this way, he would have to have come in from downtown, the stadium, or the Pasadena Freeway. This would not have been the way in from West Hollywood.

Bosch realised that there was much about Waits he didn't know and it bothered him that he would come face to face with the killer the next day. He felt unprepared. Once again he considered the idea he'd had earlier, but this time he didn't hesitate. He opened his phone and called the FBI field office in Westwood, asking for an agent named Rachel Walling.

His call was transferred and picked up and a male voice said, 'Tactical.'

'Agent Walling, please.'

'Hold one.'

Bosch heard the click, and then he heard Rachel Walling's voice for the first time in a year. He hesitated and she almost hung up.

'Rachel, it's Harry Bosch.'

Now she hesitated before responding. 'Harry . . .'

'So what's "Tactical" mean?'

'It's just the squad designation.'

He understood. She didn't answer because it was eyes-only stuff, and the line was probably on tape somewhere.

'Why are you calling, Harry?'

'Because I need a favour. I could use your help, actually.'

'With what? I'm sort of in the middle of something here.'

'Then don't worry about it. I thought maybe you'd . . . well, never mind, Rachel. It's no big deal. I can handle it.'

'You sure?'

'Yeah, I'm sure. You take care.'

Bosch closed the phone and tried not to let her voice and the memory it conjured distract him. He was hungry now, having missed lunch. He decided to cross over the freeway into Chinatown to grab a takeout.

He pulled back onto the street, and was debating whether to call the squad room to see if anybody wanted anything from Chinese Friends when his cell rang. He saw the ID was blocked. He answered anyway.

'It's me.'

'Rachel.'

'I wanted to switch to my cell. How have you been, Harry?'

'I've been fine.'

'So you did like you said you were going to do. You went back to the cops. I read about you with that case up in the Valley.'

'Yeah, my first case back. Everything's been below the radar since then. Until this thing I've got working now.'

'And that's why you called me?'

Bosch noted the tone in her voice. It had been more than twelve months since they had spoken. And that was at the end of an intense week when they had crossed paths on a case, Bosch working on a private ticket before coming back to the department and Walling working from the LA field office after she had been a profiler at Quantico.

'I called because I thought maybe you'd be interested in putting your old skills to work again,' he said.

'You mean a profile?'

'Sort of. Tomorrow I have to go head to head with a serial killer and I don't know the first thing about what makes him tick. This guy wants to confess to nine murders in a deal to avoid the needle. I've got a couple of crime scenes and forensics. I've got his apartment inventory and photos. I was wondering if I could show you this stuff, maybe get some ideas on how to handle him.'

There was a long silence. 'Where are you, Harry?' she finally asked.

'Right now? Right now I'm heading into Chinatown to pick up some shrimp fried rice. I missed lunch.'

'I'm in downtown. I could meet you. I missed lunch, too.'

'You know where Chinese Friends is?'

'Of course. How about a half-hour?'

'I'll order before you get there.'

Bosch closed the phone and felt a thrill he knew came from something other than the idea that Rachel Walling might be able to help him. Their last encounter had ended badly but the sting had eroded over time. What was left in his memory was the night they had made love in a Las Vegas motel room and he had believed he had connected with a kindred soul.

In Chinatown he pulled to the kerb outside the restaurant and looked at his watch. He had time to call Marie Gesto's parents. His habit had always been to call them every time he pulled the file. He thought it was some comfort for them to know he had not given up.

The missing woman's mother answered the phone.

'Irene, it's Harry Bosch.'

'Oh!'

There was always that initial note of hope. 'Nothing yet, Irene,' he responded quickly. 'I just have a question for you and Dan.'

'Of course. It's just good to hear from you. What's your question, Harry?'

'It's a name, actually. Do you remember Marie mentioning someone named Ray Waits? Maybe Raynard Waits?'

He heard her breath catch and immediately knew he had made a mistake. The arrest and court hearings had made it into the media in Bakersfield.

'Irene, it's not what you think. I'm just running some checks on this guy.'

'Of course. Those poor young girls. Ending up like that. I . . .'

'Can you think back before you saw him on the news? The name?'

'No, I don't remember it, thank God.'

'Is your husband there? Can you check with him?'

'He's not here. He's still at work.'

Dan Gesto had given everything of himself to the search for his missing daughter. When he had nothing left, spiritually, physically or financially, he went home to Bakersfield and went back to work at a John Deere franchise.

'Can you ask when he comes home?'

'I will, Harry.'

'One other thing, Irene. Marie's apartment had that tall window in the living room. You remember that?'

'Of course. That first year we came down for Christmas. Dan put up the tree in that window. You could see its lights up and down the block.'

'Yes. Do you know if she ever hired a window cleaner?'

'I don't remember, Harry. I'm sorry.'

'It's OK, Irene. When you and Dan took everything from the apartment, did you keep all the bills and stuff we gave you when we were finished?'

'Yes,' she said in a strangled voice. 'It's in her room.'

'I need you to look through that box, Irene. For a receipt from a window cleaner. Go through her chequebooks and look for a company called ClearView Residential Glass Cleaners. Call me if you find anything. OK?'

'OK, Harry,' Irene said.

'Thank you. I'm going to go now. Give your husband my best.'

'I will. How's your daughter, Harry?'

He paused. Over the years it seemed like he had told them everything about himself. It was a way of keeping solid the bond and his promise to find their daughter. 'She's fine. She's great.'

'What grade now?'

'Third, but I don't get to see her that much. She's living in Hong Kong with her mother. I went over last month.'

'It must be very special when you are with her.'

'Yes. She is sending me emails now. She's better at it than me.' It was awkward speaking about one's daughter to a woman who had lost her own.

'I hope she comes back soon,' Irene Gesto said. 'Bye, Harry. Good luck.'

BOSCH DIDN'T SEE the closed sign until he got to the door of Chinese Friends. It was only then that he realised the restaurant closed in the late afternoon before the dinner rush started. He opened his phone to call Rachel Walling but remembered she had blocked her number. With nothing to do he bought a *Times* out of a box at the kerb and scanned the headlines. A brief item reported that Gabriel Williams and Rick O'Shea would be appearing the next night at a candidate forum.

As Bosch lowered the paper, an unmarked federal cruiser pulled in front of his car. He watched Rachel Walling step out. She was dressed in black slacks and blazer with a cream-coloured blouse. Her dark brown hair was down to her shoulders now. Bosch jumped back to that night in Vegas.

'Rachel,' he said, smiling.

'Harry.'

He walked towards her. It was an awkward moment. He didn't know whether to hug her or just shake her hand. There was that night in Vegas but it had been followed by that day in LA, on the back deck of his house, when everything had come apart and things had ended before they really started.

She saved him from making a choice by reaching out and touching him lightly on the arm. 'I thought you were going to go in and order food.'

'For some reason they're closed. They don't open up for dinner until five. You want to wait or go somewhere else?'

'Where?'

'I don't know. There's Philippe's.'

She shook her head. 'I'm tired of Philippe's. We eat there all the time. In fact, I didn't eat lunch today because everyone in the squad was going there.'

'Tactical, huh?' If she was tired of a downtown place she wasn't working out in Westwood. 'I know a place. I'll drive and you can look at the files.'

He opened the door of his car. He had to grab the files so she could get in, handed them to her and walked to the driver's side.

'Wow, this is so Steve McQueen,' she said of Bosch's new Mustang. 'What happened to the SUV?'

Bosch shrugged. 'Just needed a change.'

He revved the engine to humour her, went down to Sunset and turned towards Silver Lake.

'So what exactly do you want from me, Harry?'

'I want you to take a look and then tell me your impressions.'

She opened the top file and started reading. 'I've heard about this guy. He's the Echo Park Butcher, right?'

'Actually, they call him the Bagman. I have a previous connection to the case. Back in '93 I was working out of Hollywood Division. I caught a case involving a missing girl named Marie Gesto. She was never found. It was big at the time. This Raynard Waits says that's one of the cases he'll trade us.'

She looked over at him then back at the file. 'Knowing how you take a case straight to heart, I wonder if it's wise for you to deal with this man.'

'I'm fine. It's still my case. And taking it straight to heart is the way of the true detective. The only way.'

He glanced over in time to see her roll her eyes. 'Spoken like the Zen master of Homicide. Where are we going?'

'A place called Duffy's in Silver Lake. You'll love it. So, are you working out of the federal courthouse?'

She answered while turning pages. 'No, we're off campus.'

'One of those secret federal locations, huh?'

'You know the story. If I told you I'd have to kill you.'

Bosch nodded at the joke. 'That mean you can't tell me what Tactical is?'

'It's nothing. Short for Tactical Intelligence. We're gatherers. We analyse raw data we pull off the Internet, cell transmissions, satellite feeds. It's actually quite boring.'

'But is it legal?'

'For now.'

'Sounds like a terrorism gig.'

'Except more often than not we end up feeding leads to the DEA. Anyway, let me concentrate on this.'

'Yes, sorry. Have a look at it.'

He drove silently for the last few minutes, then pulled to a stop in front of the restaurant. He brought the newspaper in with him. When the waiter came, Bosch ordered an omelette and Rachel ordered a turkey sandwich.

'My warning is that my take is going to be very superficial,' she said when they were left alone. 'There obviously isn't going to be enough time for me to do a full psychological. I'll only be scratching the surface.'

'I know that,' Bosch said. 'I'll take whatever you can give me.'

She went back to the files. Bosch glanced at the sports pages but wasn't that interested. He used the newspaper mostly as a blind so that he could appear to be reading while he was actually looking at Rachel. Other than the longer hair, she had changed little. Still vibrantly attractive with an intangible sense of damage about her. It was in the eyes. They weren't the hardened cop's eyes he had seen in so many other faces, including his own.

'Why are you staring at me?' she suddenly said.

'What?'

'You're so obvious.'

'I was just—'

He was saved by the waiter, who appeared and put down plates of food. Walling moved the files aside and he detected a small smile on her face. They continued their silence as they ate.

'This is good,' she finally said. 'I'm starving.'

'Yeah, me too.'

'So what were you looking for?'

'When?'

'When you were acting like you were reading the newspaper but you really weren't.'

'Um, I . . . I guess I was trying to see if you were really interested in looking at this. It sounds like you have a lot going.'

'I hate my job, OK? Or rather, I hate what I am doing right now. But it will get better. Another year and it will be better.'

'Fine. And this? This is OK?' He pointed to the files.

'Yes, but there is too much. I can't even begin to help you. Why can't you delay the interview?'

'It's not mine to delay. And the prosecutor is running for DA. He needs headlines. He's not going to wait for me to get up to speed.'

She nodded. 'All the way with Rick O'Shea.' She put her hand on top of the stack of files. 'Let me keep them. I'll finish work, clock out and come give you what I've got tonight. Everything.'

He stared at her, looking for the hidden meaning. 'When?'

'I don't know. Nine o'clock at the latest. Will that work?'

He nodded. He wasn't expecting this.

'Do you still live in that house up on the hill?' she asked.

'Yeah. I'm there. Woodrow Wilson Drive.'

'Good. My place is down off Beverly, not too far. I'll come up to your place. I remember the view.'

Bosch wasn't sure what he had just invited into his life.

'Can I give you something to think about until then?' she asked. 'The name, is that his real name?'

Bosch frowned. 'I assume so. His fingerprints matched a previous arrest. That time he tried to give a false name but a DMV thumbprint made him as Waits. Why?'

'Do you know what a reynard is? Reynard spelled R-E-Y not R-A-Y?'

'No, what is it?'

'It's a name for a young male fox. The female is a vixen and the male is a reynard. I studied European folklore in college. There are medieval French stories about a fox named Reynard. He's a trickster. He's appeared through the centuries in children's books. You take it in context of the full name and—'

'The fox waits,' Bosch said. 'The trickster waits.'

She went back to eating and Bosch went back to watching her.

AS SOON AS Bosch dropped Rachel at her car, he called his partner. Rider reported that she was finishing up the paperwork on the Matarese case and they would be able to file charges at the DA's office the following day.

'Good,' said Bosch. 'Anything else?'

'I got the box on Fitzpatrick from Evidence Archives and it turned out to be two boxes. Mostly of old pawn records I can tell were never even looked at. They were sopping wet back then from when the fire was put out. The guys from Riot Crimes put them in plastic tubs and they've been mouldering ever since. Man, do they stink.'

Bosch computed this. It was a dead end and it didn't matter. An uncoerced confession is a royal flush. It beats everything.

'Have you heard from Olivas or O'Shea?' Rider asked.

'Not yet. I was going to call Olivas but wanted to talk to you first. Do you know anybody in city licensing?'

'No, but if you want I can call over there in the morning. They're closed now. What are you looking for?'

'I was thinking we should run Waits's business and see how long he's had it, whether there were ever complaints, that sort of thing. Olivas and his partner should have done it but there's nothing in the files about it.'

'You think that could have been the connection to the High Tower?'

'Or maybe to Marie. She had a big picture window in her apartment. It isn't something I remember coming up back then. But maybe we missed it.'

'Harry, you never miss a thing, but I'll get on it first thing.'

'The other thing is the guy's name. It could be phoney.'

'How so?'

He told her about asking Rachel Walling to look at the files. This was initially met with resounding silence, because Bosch had crossed one of those invisible LAPD lines by inviting the FBI into the case without command approval. But when Bosch told Rider about Reynard the Fox she dropped her silence and became sceptical.

'You think our window-washing serial killer was up on medieval folklore?'

'Doesn't matter,' he said. 'There is enough there that I think we've got to look at birth certificates. When he was popped for prowling in '93, he was booked under Robert Saxon—the name he gave—but they got Raynard Waits when his thumbprint hit the DMV computer.'

'What are you seeing there, Harry? If they had his thumb on file, I'm thinking the name isn't phoney.'

'Maybe. But you know it isn't impossible to get a driver's licence with a false name in this state. What if Saxon actually was his real name but the computer spit out his alias and he went with it?'

'Then why keep the name after? He had a record under Waits.'

'Good question. I don't know. But we've got to check it out.'

'Well, we've got him whatever his name is. I'll Google *Raynard the Fox* right now.'

'Spell it with an *e*.'

He waited and could hear her fingers on the computer keyboard.

'Got it,' she finally said. 'There's a lot about Reynard the Fox.' There was silence for a long moment. 'Says here part of the legend is that Reynard had a secret castle nobody could find. He used all kinds of trickery to draw his victims close. Then he would take them back to the castle and eat them.'

That hung out there untouched for a while. Finally Bosch spoke.

'Do you have time to run an AutoTrack on Robert Saxon?'

'Sure. Read me his DOB off the arrest report.'

'I can't. I don't have it here. I gave the files to Agent Walling. I'll get them back tonight. You'll have to pull the arrest report.'

'Harry, those are official investigative files. You know you shouldn't have parted with them. And we're going to need them tomorrow. I gotta tell you, partner, you're doing the cowboy thing again and I don't like it very much.'

'Kiz, I'm just trying to keep things moving. I want to be ready for this guy. What Walling is giving me will give us an edge.'

'Fine. I trust you. Maybe at some point you'll trust me enough to ask my opinion before you make decisions that affect both of us.'

Bosch felt his cheeks flare hot, mostly because he knew she was right. He didn't say anything because he knew that apologising for leaving her out of the loop wasn't going to cut it.

'Call me back if Olivas gives us a time for tomorrow,' she said.

'You got it.'

After closing the phone, Bosch thought about things for a moment. He tried to move on from his embarrassment. He focused on the case and what he had left out of the investigation so far. After a few minutes he called Olivas and asked if a time and place had been set for the Waits interview.

'Tomorrow morning, ten o'clock,' Olivas said. 'Don't be late.'

'Were you going to tell me, or was I supposed to pick it up telepathically?'

'I just found out myself. You called before I could call you.'

Bosch ignored his excuse. 'Where?'

'The DA's office. We'll set him up in an interview room.'

'Anything else I should know, Olivas?'

'Matter of fact, there is one more thing. Sort of a delicate thing, you could say. I've been talking to Rick about it.'

'What's that?'

'Well, take a guess at what I'm looking at here.'

Bosch blew out his breath. 'I have no idea, Olivas. What?'

'Your fifty-ones from Gesto.'

He was referring to the Investigative Chronology, a master listing kept by date and time of all aspects of a case, ranging from an accounting of detectives' movements to notations on routine phone calls to media enquiries and tips from citizens. Usually these were handwritten, with all manner of shorthand and abbreviations, as they were updated throughout each day. Then, when a page became full, it was typed up on a form called a 51, which would be complete and legible when and if the case moved into the courts.

'What about them?' Bosch asked.

'I'm looking at the last line on page fourteen, for September 29th, 1993 at six forty p.m. Must've been quitting time. The initials on the entry are JE.'

'That would've been my partner, Jerry Edgar. What's it say, Olivas?'

'It says, "Robert Saxon DOB Nov. 3 '71. Saw *Times* story. Was at Mayfair and saw MG alone. Nobody following." It gives Saxon's phone number. You know what that means?'

Bosch did. He had just given the name Robert Saxon to Kiz Rider to background. That name on the 51 meant that thirteen years ago Bosch and Edgar had a shot at Waits/Saxon, and for some reason never took it.

At last he found his voice. 'That's the only mention in the murder book?'

'That I've seen,' Olivas said. 'I missed it the first time through. Then the second time I said, "Hey, I know that name." It's an alias Waits used back in the nineties. It should be in the files you have.

'I know. I saw it.'

'He called you guys, Bosch, and you and your partner blew it. Nobody even ran his name through the box. You had the killer's alias and a phone number and didn't do anything. 'Course, you didn't know he was the killer. Just some citizen calling in about what he'd seen. He must've been trying to play you guys in some way, trying to find out about the case. Only Edgar didn't play. It was late and he probably wanted to get to that first martini.'

Bosch said nothing.

'Too bad, you know? Maybe this whole thing could've ended right then. I guess we'll ask Waits about it in the morning.'

The petty barbs couldn't penetrate the thick, dark cloud already coming down on Bosch. He knew that if the name Robert Saxon had been routinely run through the computer, it would have scored a match in the alias data base and taken them to Raynard Waits and his prior arrest for prowling. It was an oversight that had probably cost the lives of nine women.

'Olivas?' Bosch said. 'Make sure you bring the book tomorrow. I want to see the fifty-ones.'

He closed his phone without another word. His back felt hot against the car seat and he was starting to sweat. He opened the windows.

It was every detective's nightmare. A lead ignored or bungled, allowing something awful to be loose in the world. Something dark and evil, destroying life after life as it moved through the shadows.

He pulled out from the kerb and into traffic to get air moving through the windows. Then he made a screeching U-turn and headed home.

3

From the rear deck of his house, Bosch watched the sky dim. He lived up in a cantilevered house that clung to the side of the hill like a cartoon character hanging on to the edge of a cliff. Sometimes Bosch felt like that character. Like on this night. He was drinking vodka sprinkled liberally over ice, the first time he'd gone with hard liquor since coming back on the job. The vodka made his throat feel as though he had swallowed a torch, but that was OK. He was trying to burn away his thoughts.

Bosch considered himself a true detective, one who took it all inside and cared. Everybody counts or nobody counts. It made him good at the job but it also made him vulnerable. The mistakes could get to him and this was the worst of all mistakes.

He shook the ice and vodka and took another deep drink until he finished the glass. How could anything so cold burn so intensely hot? He walked back in to put more vodka on the ice. In the kitchen, with fresh drink in hand, he picked up the phone and called Jerry Edgar's cellphone.

Edgar answered and Bosch could hear TV noise in the background.

'Jerry, it's me. I gotta ask you something.'

'Harry? Where are you?'

'Home, man. But I'm working on one of our old ones.'

'Oh, well, let's go down the list of Harry Bosch obsessions . . . Fernandez?'

'No.'

'That kid, Spike whatever-her-name-was?'

'Nope.'

'I give up, man. You've got too many ghosts for me to keep track of.'

'Gesto.'

'Shit, I should've gone with her first. What's the question?'

'There's an entry in the fifty-ones. It's got your initials on it. Says a guy named Robert Saxon called and said he saw her in the Mayfair. You remember talking to the guy?'

'Harry, I don't remember entries in cases I worked last month. That's why we have the fifty-ones. Who is Saxon?'

Bosch took a drink before answering. 'He's the guy . . . I think.'

'You've got the killer, Harry?'

'Pretty sure. We could've had him back then. Maybe.'

'I don't remember anybody named Saxon. He must've been trying to get his rocks off, calling us. Harry, are you drunk?'

'Gettin' there.'

'That means something's wrong. What's wrong, man? What am I missing?'

'What's wrong is that Marie Gesto wasn't the last.'

Edgar was silent as it registered. Then he spoke in the weak voice of a child asking what his punishment will be. 'How many came after?'

'Looks like nine. I'll probably know more tomorrow.'

'Jesus,' Edgar whispered.

Bosch nodded. Part of him wanted to blame Edgar for everything. But the other part said partners shared the good and the bad. Those 51s were in the murder book for both of them to read and react to.

'So you don't remember the call?'

'No, nothing. All I can say is if there was no follow-up, then the call didn't sound legit or I got all there was to get from the caller. If he was the killer, he was probably just messing with us.'

'Yeah, but we didn't put the name in the box. It would have drawn a match in the alias files. Maybe that's what he wanted.'

They were both silent as their minds sifted the sands of disaster.

'Harry, did you come up with this? Who knows about it?'

'A homicide guy from Northeast came up with it. He has the Gesto file. He knows and a DA working the suspect knows.'

'Who is the DA?' Edgar asked. 'Can this be contained?'

'I doubt it,' Bosch said. 'And I don't really care. We should have been onto this guy in '93 but we missed it and he's been out there cutting up women ever since.'

'What are you talking about, cutting up? Is this the Echo Park Bagman you're talking about? What's his name, Waits? *He* was our guy?'

Bosch held the cold glass against his temple. 'That's right. He's going to confess tomorrow. Eventually it will get out because Rick O'Shea is going to run with it. And some smart reporter is going to ask whether Waits ever came up way back when in the Gesto case.'

'So we say no, because that's the truth. Waits's name never came up. It was an alias and we don't need to tell them about that. You have to make O'Shea see that, Harry. I'm up for one of the D-two slots in RHD. This thing will screw up any chance I have if it gets out.'

Bosch now regretted making the call. He had wanted Edgar to share the burden of guilt with him, not figure out a way to avoid blame.

'I'll do what I can, Jerry. But you know, sometimes when you screw up you have to take the consequences.'

'Not this time, partner. Not now.'

It angered Bosch that Edgar pulled the old 'partner act', calling on Bosch to protect him out of loyalty and the unwritten rule that the bond is stronger than even a marriage. 'I'll do what I can,' he told Edgar. 'I have to go now, *partner*.' He hung the phone on the wall.

Before returning to the back deck he educated the ice in his glass once more with vodka. Outside, he went to the rail and leaned his elbows on it.

The freeway noise far down the hill was a steady hiss. He looked up at the sky and saw that the sunset was a dirty pink.

Bosch heard a knock and started into the house. He opened the front door and Rachel Walling was standing there holding the files.

Since she had been in his home before, she didn't bother looking around. She put the files down on a table in the dining area and looked at Bosch.

'What's wrong?' she said. 'Are you all right?'

'I'm fine. I sort of forgot you were coming by.'

'I can leave if—'

'No, I'm glad you're here. Did you find time to look at the stuff?'

'A little bit. I have some notes. And if you want me to be there, I can make arrangements to be there—unofficially.'

Bosch shook his head. 'This is Rick O'Shea's ticket, and if I bring an FBI agent into it, then that will be my ticket out.' He gestured to the table so that she could sit down. 'Do you want something to drink?'

'What are you having?'

'I was having vodka. I think I'm going to switch to coffee now.'

'Hard-core Harry. I'll have coffee.'

He went into the kitchen to get a pot brewing. He heard her pull out a chair at the table. When he came back he saw she had spread the files out.

'Did you do anything about the name yet?' she asked.

'I'll go by the Hall of Records early tomorrow. Hopefully we'll know something before we get in the room at ten.' He sat down across from her.

She leaned forward and looked at her notes. 'Whatever his name is, he's obviously smart and manipulative,' she said. 'Look at his size. Short and slightly built. It is unlikely he used physical force to get these victims to go with him. He's too small for that. Instead, he employed charm and cunning. Even a girl just off the bus on Hollywood Boulevard is going to have some measure of street smarts. He was smarter.'

'The trickster,' Bosch said. 'What about a weapon? Or money? He could have just flashed the green. These girls would have gone for money.'

'To use either a weapon or money you still need to get close.'

Bosch nodded and wrote a few notes on a page of a notebook he had grabbed off a shelf. 'What else?' he asked.

'Do you know how long he's had his business?'

'No, but we'll know tomorrow morning. Why?'

'Well, it allowed him to be mobile and to travel throughout the city. It allowed him inside people's homes. I'm curious as to whether he started the job to help him fulfil his fantasies—the killings—or already had the business before he began acting on these impulses.'

Bosch made more notes. He had questions that ran along the same lines.

'I know I don't need to tell you this, Harry, but you are going to have to be careful and cautious with him. Obviously this is a rushed response to a lot of material, but something doesn't fit right about what I see here.'

'What?'

'You have to remember that until those officers found the bags in his van, Waits had been flying below the radar for years. He wasn't sending notes to the police. He wasn't displaying his victims as an affront to society. He was quiet. And he chose victims, with the exception of the first two, who could be pulled under without a ripple. You see what I mean?'

Bosch hesitated for a moment.

'What?'

He didn't answer.

'Harry, I don't want to be spinning my wheels here. If there is something I need to know, then tell me, or I might as well get up and go.'

'Just hold on until I get the coffee. I hope you like it black.'

He went to the kitchen, poured coffee into two mugs and brought them out.

'OK,' Rachel said after the first sip. 'What aren't you telling me?'

'My partner and I made a mistake back when we worked this in '93. I don't know if it contradicts what you just said about Waits staying beneath the radar, but it looks like he called us back then. About three weeks into the case. He used an alias. At least we think it was an alias, but maybe he used his real name. Anyway, we blew it. We never checked him out.'

'What do you mean?'

Reluctantly, he told her about the call from Olivas and his finding of Waits's alias in the 51. She cast her eyes down at the table as he told it.

'And the rest is history,' he said. 'He kept right on killing people.'

'When did you find this out?' she asked.

'Right after I left you today.'

She nodded. 'Which explains why you were hitting the vodka.'

'I guess so.'

'I thought . . . never mind what I thought.'

'No, it wasn't because of seeing you, Rachel. Seeing you was—I mean, is—actually very nice.'

She took up her mug and drank from it, then seemed to steel herself to move on. 'Well, it does seem out of character for him to have made contact, but the Gesto case took place in the early stages of his formation. There are a number of aspects that don't fit with the rest. But with the other cases he was getting his satisfaction in the work. He didn't need attention.'

'So then, what bothers you?'

She looked up at him. 'It's just that his profile doesn't support someone who would cooperate at this stage of the game, who would tell you about the other crimes. What I see here is someone who would never admit to it. I guess what I'm trying to say is that from his point of view, there is a higher goal. A plan. This whole confession thing is indicative of manipulation.'

'Sure. He's manipulating O'Shea and the system to avoid the needle.'

'But there may be other motives as well. Be careful.'

'Don't worry, I will,' Bosch said.

She ran down her sheet of notes. 'Have they determined where he was going when they pulled him over?'

He shrugged. 'Not really. The assumption was that he was going to bury the bags somewhere around the stadium, but that doesn't really work because they saw him drive off Stadium Way and into a neighbourhood. It seems to me that if he was going to bury them he would have gone deep into the park, where there was less chance of being noticed.'

'Exactly.' She glanced at some other documents.

'What?' Bosch asked.

'Well, this Reynard the Fox thing might have nothing to do with all of this. It may all be coincidence.'

'But in the epic Reynard had a castle that was his secret hideaway.'

She raised her eyebrows. 'I didn't think you had a computer, let alone knew how to research online.'

'I don't. My partner did the search. But I gotta tell you, I was over in the neighbourhood today. I didn't see any castle.'

She shook her head. 'Don't take everything so literally.'

Bosch took her in a new direction. 'How do the first two fit in? He went from the riots and a big media splash to diving beneath the surface.'

'Every serial killer's MO changes. The simple answer is that he was on a learning curve. I think the first killing—with the male victim—was opportunistic. He'd thought about killing but wasn't sure he could do it. He found himself in a situation where he could test himself and get away with it.'

Bosch nodded. 'And then we come to Marie Gesto.'

'He was still learning,' she said. 'He knew he could kill and now he wanted to go out and hunt. She crossed his path, something about her fitted his fantasy and she simply became prey. At that time his focus was on victim acquisition and self-protection. In that he chose badly. He chose a woman who would be missed, whose disappearance would draw an immediate response, but he learned from the heat he brought upon himself. After Gesto he added a third element: victim backgrounding. He chose victims whose comings and goings would not be cause for notice, let alone alarm.'

'And he went beneath the surface.'

'Exactly. He went under and stayed there. Until we got lucky in Echo Park.'

'It makes you wonder, doesn't it? About how many of these guys are out there. The under-the-surface killers.'

Walling nodded. 'Yes. Sometimes it scares me to death.' She held his eyes for a moment. 'Harry, you've got to give yourself a break on that phone call. You can't let it bring you down. The work ahead is too important.'

Bosch nodded insincerely. That was easy for her to say. She wouldn't have to live with the ghosts of all the women Waits would be telling them about.

'Don't just nod it off like that,' Rachel said. 'Do you know how many cases I worked in Behavioral where the guy kept killing? How many times we got calls and notes from these creeps but still couldn't get to them before the next victim was dead?'

'I know, I know.'

'How many murders have you solved, Harry?'

'I don't know. I don't keep track.'

'You're way ahead in the long run. Think about that.'

He nodded again. This time he meant it. 'OK.'

'I hope I've helped,' Rachel said.

'I think you did. I think I'll know better who and what I am dealing with when I go into the room with him tomorrow.'

She stood up from the table. 'I meant about the other thing.'

Bosch stood. 'That, too. You've helped a lot.'

'Be careful, Harry.'

'I know. You said that. But you don't have to worry. I will.'

It was time to go to the door but she was hesitating. She looked down at the file and then at Bosch. 'I was hoping you would call me sometime,' she said. 'But not about a case.'

'I thought because of what I said—what we said—that . . .'

He wasn't sure what he was trying to say. She reached up and put her hand lightly on his chest. He took a step closer, coming into her space, then put his arms round her and pulled her close.

LATER, after they had made love, Bosch and Rachel remained in bed, talking about anything they could think of except what they had just done. Eventually they came back round to the case and the next morning's interview.

'I can't believe that after all this time I'm going to sit down face to face with her killer,' Bosch said. 'It's kind of like a dream. I actually have dreamed of catching the guy. I mean, it was never Waits in the dream but I dreamed about closing out the case.'

'Who was it in the dream?' she asked.

Her head was resting on his chest. He couldn't see her face but he could smell her hair. Under the sheets she had one leg over one of his.

'It was this guy I always thought could be good for it. But I never had anything on him. I guess because he was an asshole, I wanted it to be him.'

'Well, did he have any connection to Gesto?'

Bosch tried to shrug but it was difficult with their bodies so entwined. 'He knew about the garage where we found the car and had an ex-girlfriend who was a ringer for Gesto. And he had anger-management issues. No real evidence. I just thought it was him. I followed him once during the first year of the investigation. He was working as a security guard up in the oil fields behind Baldwin Hills. You know where that is?'

'You mean where you see the oil pumps when you're coming in on La Cienega from the airport?'

'Yeah, that's the place. Well, this kid's family owned a chunk of those fields, and his old man was trying to straighten him out, I guess. You know, make him work for a living even though they had money. So he was working security up there and I was watching him one day. He came across these kids who were trespassing and fooling around up there. They were just kids, maybe thirteen. Two boys from the nearby neighbourhood.'

'What did he do to them?'

'He drew a gun on them, then handcuffed them to one of the pumps. And got back in his pick-up and drove away.'

'He just left them there?'

'That's what I thought he was doing. I was watching with binoculars from a ridge all the way across La Cienega and I could see the whole oil field. He had another guy with him and they drove over to this shack where I guess they kept samples of the oil they were pumping. They went in there and came out with two buckets of this stuff, put 'em in the back of the pickup and drove back. They then dumped that shit all over the two kids.'

Rachel got up on one elbow. 'And you just watched this happen?'

'I told you, I was clear across La Cienega. If he went any further I was going to try to intervene somehow, but then he let them go.'

She nodded. 'He just let them go?'

'He uncuffed them, kicked one of them in the butt and let them go. I could tell they were crying and scared.'

Rachel shook her head in disgust. 'What's this guy's name?'

'Anthony Garland. His father is Thomas Rex Garland. You might have heard of him.'

She shook her head. 'Well, Anthony might not have been Gesto's killer but he sounds like a complete asshole.'

'He is. You want to see him?'

'What do you mean?'

'I've got a "greatest hits" video. I've had him in an interview room three times in thirteen years. Each interview was on tape. I had them copied onto one tape, and I brought it home to watch the last time I worked the case.'

Rachel seemed to consider this. 'Then let's take a look.'

Bosch got out of bed, slipped on his boxer shorts and turned on the lamp. He went out to the living room and brought back a VHS tape. He had a television with a built-in VCR on the bureau. He turned it on, slid in the tape and sat on the edge of the bed with the remote.

Rachel reached a foot towards him and tapped her toes on his back. 'Is this what you do with all the girls you bring here? Show them your interrogation techniques?'

Bosch glanced back at her. 'Rachel, I think you're the only person in the world I could do this with.'

She smiled. 'I think I get you, Harry Bosch.'

He looked back at the screen and hit the mute with the remote. 'This first one is March 11th of '94. It's six months after Gesto disappeared and we were grasping for anything. I was able to convince him to come into the station to give a statement. He thought he was just going to talk about the apartment where his ex-girlfriend had lived.'

On the screen was a grainy picture of a small room with a table at which two men sat. One was a much younger-looking Harry Bosch and the other was a man in his early twenties with wavy surfer-white hair wearing a T-shirt that said *Lakers* across the chest. The sleeves were tight on his arms, and a black tattoo of barbed wire was visible on his left biceps.

Bosch brought up the sound. On the screen, Garland was looking all around the room with a slight smile on his face.

'So this is where it happens, huh?'

'Where what happens?' Bosch asked.

'You know, you break the bad guys down and they confess to all the crimes.' He smiled coyly.

'Sometimes,' Bosch said. 'But let's talk about Marie Gesto.'

'I told you I didn't know her. Never saw her in my life.'

'So if somebody told me you knew her, they'd be lying.'

'Right. Who told you that shit?'

'But you knew about the empty garage at the High Tower, right?'

'Yeah, well, my girlfriend had just moved out and so I knew. That doesn't mean I stashed the car in there. Look, you asked me all this at the house. Am I under arrest or something?'

'No, Anthony, you are not under arrest. I just wanted you to come down so we could go over some of this stuff.'

'I've already gone over it with you.'

'That was before we knew some other things about you and about her.'

Garland's face seemed to momentarily contort in anger. 'What things? What are you talking about? I had nothing to do with this. I've told you that at least twice now. Why aren't you out looking for the person who did it?'

Bosch paused. 'Because maybe I think I'm with the person who did it.'

'Fuck you, man. I've told you from day one, I'm not the guy!'

Bosch leaned across the table. 'I know what you told me. But that was before I went to Austin and talked to your girlfriend. She told me some things about you, Anthony, that require me to pay a little more attention.'

'Fuck her. She's a whore!'

'Yeah? Then why'd you get angry when she left you? Why did she have to run from you? Why didn't you just let her go?'

'Because nobody leaves me. I leave them. OK?'

'OK. So tell me what you did on September 9th of last year.'

Using the remote, Bosch started fast-forwarding the tape. 'He didn't have an alibi for the time we believed Marie was grabbed outside the supermarket, but we can skip ahead because that part of the interview took for ever.'

Rachel was now sitting up in the bed with the sheet wrapped round her.

'This is two years later,' Bosch continued. 'The lawyers from his daddy's firm slapped a temporary restraining order on me and I could only interview the kid if he had counsel present. So there's nothing much here, but there's one thing I want you to see.'

He slowed the fast-forward down to normal and the audio came back up. It was the lawyer doing the talking.

'My client has fully cooperated but you continue to harass him with questions that have not one ounce of evidentiary support.'

'I'm working on that, Counsellor,' Bosch said. 'And when I get it, there won't be a lawyer in the world who can help him.'

'Fuck you, Bosch!' Garland said. 'You better hope you never come for me alone, man. I'll put you down in the dirt.'

The lawyer put a calming hand on Garland's arm. Bosch was silent for a few moments before responding.

'You want to threaten me now, Anthony? You think I'm like one of those teenagers you cuff out in the oil fields and dump crude on? You think I'm going to go away with my tail between my legs?'

Garland's face pinched together and turned dark. His eyes looked like frozen black marbles.

Bosch hit the pause button. 'There.' He pointed at the screen with the remote. 'That's what I wanted you to see. Look at his face. Pure, perfect rage. That's why I thought it was him.'

Walling didn't respond. Bosch hit the fast-forward button again.

'Now we jump to last April. I grabbed him when he came out of lunch at Kate Mantilini's. He probably thought I was long gone from his life.'

He played the tape. On the screen Garland looked older and wider. His now-thinning hair was cropped short. He wore a white shirt with a tie. This time he sat in an interview room at Parker Center.

'If I'm not under arrest, then I should be free to go,' he said.

'I was hoping you'd answer a few questions first,' Bosch replied.

'I answered all your questions years ago. This is a vendetta, Bosch. You will not give up. Am I free to go or not?'

'Where did you hide her body?'

Garland shook his head. 'This is unbelievable. When will this end?'

476 | MICHAEL CONNELLY

'It will never end, Garland. Not until I find her and lock you up.'

'This is crazy! You're crazy, Bosch. What can I say to make you believe me? What can—?'

Bosch suddenly killed the TV with the remote. For the first time, he realised how case-blind he had been, going after Garland so relentlessly, unaware that right in front of him in the murder book was the clue to the real killer. Watching the tape with Walling had heaped humiliation upon humiliation. He had thought she would see why he had focused on Garland, and absolve him of his mistake. But now he couldn't absolve himself.

Rachel leaned towards him. 'It happens to all of us,' she said.

Bosch nodded. Not to me, he thought. 'I guess when this is all over I'm going to have to find him and apologise.'

'I wouldn't bother. He's still an asshole.'

Bosch smiled. She was trying to make it easy. 'You think?'

She pulled the elastic waistband on his boxers and snapped them against his back. 'I think I have at least another hour before I should be thinking about getting home.'

Bosch turned to look at her and she smiled.

THE NEXT MORNING Bosch and Rider walked from the Hall of Records to the Criminal Courts Building and, despite the wait for an elevator, got to the DA's office early. O'Shea and Olivas were ready for them.

As he sat down, Bosch saw the Gesto murder book on O'Shea's desk. He took it without asking and combed through the 51s until he found the page for September 29, 1993. The entry was the last of the day. Bosch felt the deep sense of regret tug at him all over again.

'Detective Bosch, we all make mistakes,' O'Shea said. 'Let's just move on from it and do the best we can today.'

Bosch closed the book and put it back on the desk. O'Shea continued.

'I am told that Maury Swann is in the interview room with Mr Waits. I want to take each case in order. We start with Fitzpatrick and, when we are satisfied by the confession, we move on to the Gesto case and so on.'

Everybody nodded except for Bosch.

'I am not going to be satisfied until we have her remains,' he said.

O'Shea lifted a document off his desk. 'I understand that. If you can locate the victim based on the statements from Waits, then fine. If it is a matter of him leading us to the body, I have a release order ready to go to the judge. If we take this man out of lockup, the security should be extraordinary. There will be a lot riding on this.' He looked from detective to detective to make sure they understood the gravity of the situation.

'We'll be ready for anything,' Olivas said.

The look of concern on O'Shea's face didn't change. 'You're going to have a uniformed presence, right?'

'If you want it we'll have it,' Olivas said. 'We'll either get a car from Metro to go with us or a couple of deputies from the jail.'

O'Shea nodded his approval. 'Then, are we ready to start?'

'There's one thing,' Bosch said. 'We're not sure who that is waiting for us in the interview room, but we're pretty sure his name isn't Raynard Waits.'

A look of surprise played off O'Shea's face. Olivas dropped his mouth an inch and leaned forward.

'We made him on fingerprints,' Olivas protested. 'On the prior.'

Bosch nodded. 'Yes, the prior. As you know, when he was popped thirteen years ago for prowling, he first gave the name Robert Saxon, with a birth date of November 3rd, '75. But when they matched his thumbprint to the DL of Raynard Waits, with a birth date of November 3rd, '71, they confronted him with it, and he said he had given the false name and year because he was hoping to be handled as a juvenile. This is all in the file.'

'But where does all of it go?' O'Shea said impatiently.

'Just let me finish. He got probation for the prowling because it was a first offence. In the probation report bio he said he was born and raised in LA. We just came from the Hall of Records. There is no record of Raynard Waits being born in LA on that date or any other. There have been a lot of Robert Saxons born in LA, but none on November 3rd of either '71 or '75.'

O'Shea stood up and paced around his office. 'So what are you saying, that the DMV had the wrong prints on file or there was some mix-up?'

'I'm saying that this guy, whoever he really is, could have gone to the DMV to set up a false ID. What do you need to get a driver's licence? Proof of age. Back then, you could buy phoney birth certificates on Hollywood Boulevard, no problem. The point is, there is no record of him being born here in LA as he said he was. That puts all the rest in doubt.'

'So are you saying he changed his name and continued to use it, after he had an arrest tail on it?' Olivas asked. 'That doesn't make sense to me.'

'Doesn't make a lot of sense to me, either. But we don't know the story behind it yet.'

'OK, so what are you suggesting we do?' O'Shea asked.

'Not much,' Bosch said. 'I'm just bringing it up. But I do think we ought to go on the record with it up there. You know, ask him to state his name, DOB and place of birth, as if it's routine. If he gives us Waits, then we might be able to catch him in the lie down the road and prosecute him for everything. You said that was the deal: if he lies, he fries.'

O'Shea nodded. 'I don't see where it could hurt,' he said.

Bosch looked at Rider. 'You'll be asking the question.'

'Fine,' she said.

O'Shea pushed back from his desk. 'OK, then,' he said. 'Are we ready? It's time to go. I'll stay as long as my schedule allows. Don't be offended if I jump in from time to time with a question.'

Bosch stood up. 'One last thing,' he said. 'We picked up a Maury Swann story that maybe you guys ought to know.'

4

Two uniformed sheriff's deputies stood at the door to the interview room. They stepped aside and allowed the prosecutorial entourage to enter. Waits and Maury Swann were sitting on one side of a long table. Only Swann stood up. Waits was held to the arms of his chair with plastic snap cuffs. Swann, a thin man with black-framed glasses and a luxurious mane of silver hair, offered his hand but no one shook it.

Rider took the chair directly across the table from Waits, and Bosch and O'Shea sat on either side of her. Olivas took the chair next to the door.

O'Shea handled the introductions. Waits was in an orange jumpsuit that had black letters stencilled across the chest: LA COUNTY JAIL, and beneath it, KEEP AWAY. The second line meant that Waits was housed by himself and not allowed into the general jail population, a protective measure both for himself and the other inmates.

As Bosch studied the man he had been hunting for thirteen years, he realised that the most frightening thing about Waits was how ordinary he looked. Slightly built, with soft features and short dark hair, he was the epitome of normality. The only hint of the evil that lay within was found in the eyes. Dark brown and deeply set, they carried an emptiness Bosch recognised from other killers he had sat face to face with. Nothing there. Just a hollowness that could never be filled, no matter how many lives he stole.

Rider turned on the tape recorder on the table. 'As was probably explained to you, we are going to record each session and turn the tapes over to your attorney, who will hold them until we have a completed agreement. Is that understood and approved by you?'

'Yes, it is,' Waits said.

'Good,' Rider said. 'Then let's begin with an easy one. Can you state your name, birth date and place of birth for the record?'

Waits leaned forward. 'Raynard Waits,' he said impatiently. 'Born November 3rd, 1971, in Los Angeles.'

'Thank you. Your first name is unusual. Could you spell it for the tape?'

Waits complied. Bosch felt an enormous sense of relief. He believed they had already caught Waits in a lie that might spring a fatal trap on him.

'We want to take these in order,' Rider said. 'Your attorney's proffer suggests your first homicide was the death of Daniel Fitzpatrick on April 13th, 1992. Is that correct?'

'Yes, I burned him alive behind his security cage,' Waits answered coldly. 'It turned out he wasn't so secure back there. Not even with all his guns.'

'Why did you do that?'

'Because I wanted to see if I could. I had been thinking about it for a long time and I just wanted to "prove myself".'

'What do you mean by "prove yourself", Mr Waits?' Rider said.

'I mean there is a line out there that everybody thinks about but not many have the guts to cross. I wanted to see if I could cross it.'

'When you say you had been thinking about it for a long time, had you been thinking about Mr Fitzpatrick in particular?'

Annoyance flared in Waits's eyes. 'No,' he replied calmly. 'I had been thinking about killing someone. All my life I had wanted to do it.'

'Why did you choose Daniel Fitzpatrick? Why did you choose that night?'

'Well, because I was watching TV and I saw the whole city coming apart. It was chaos out there and I knew the police couldn't do anything. People were doing just what they wanted. I saw a guy talking about Hollywood Boulevard and how places were burning and I decided to go see for myself.'

'Did you drive there?'

'Back then I lived on Fountain near La Brea. I walked up.'

Rider glanced down at the Fitzpatrick file for a moment, which gave O'Shea the opportunity to jump in.

'Where did the lighter fluid come from? Did you take it with you?'

Waits looked at O'Shea. 'I thought the dyke was asking the questions.'

'We're all asking the questions,' O'Shea said. 'Could you please keep the personal attacks out of your responses?'

'Not you, Mr District Attorney. I don't want to talk to you. Only her. And them.' He pointed to Bosch and Olivas.

'Let me just back up a bit before we get to the lighter fluid,' Rider said, smoothly pushing O'Shea to the side. 'You said you walked up to Hollywood Boulevard. Where did you go and what did you see?'

Waits shifted his focus back towards her. 'I saw the city burning, that's what I saw.' He smiled. 'It was like a Hieronymus Bosch painting.'

He turned to Bosch, who froze for a moment. How did he know?

Waits nodded towards Bosch's chest. 'It's on your ID card.'

Bosch had forgotten they'd had to clip their IDs on in the DA's office.

Rider moved in quickly with the next question. 'OK, which way did you walk once you got to Hollywood Boulevard?'

'I took a right and headed east. The bigger fires were down that way.'

'What was in your pockets?'

The question seemed to give him pause. 'I don't know. I don't remember. My keys, I guess. Cigarettes and a lighter, that was all.'

'Did you have your wallet?'

'No, I didn't want to have ID with me. In case the police stopped me.'

'Did you already have the lighter fluid with you?'

'That's right, I did. I thought I might join in the fun, help burn the city to the ground. Then I walked by that pawnshop and got a better idea.'

'You saw Mr Fitzpatrick?'

'Yeah, I saw him standing inside his security fence holding a shotgun.'

'Describe the pawnshop.'

Waits shrugged. 'A small place. It was called Irish Pawn. It had this neon sign that flashed a green three-leaf clover and then the three balls, you know. Fitzpatrick was watching me when I passed by.'

'And you kept walking?'

'At first I did. Then I thought about the challenge. How to get to him without getting shot by that bazooka he was holding.'

'What did you do?'

'I took the can of EasyLight out of my jacket pocket and filled my mouth with it. Squirted it right in, like those flame-breathers do on the Venice boardwalk. Then I put the can away and got out a cigarette and my lighter. I went back to the shop alcove in front of the fence and acted like I was looking for a blind to light my smoke. It was windy that night, you understand?'

'Yes.'

'So he started yelling at me to get away. He came right up to the fence to yell at me. I was counting on that.' He smiled. 'When he was about two feet away I got a flame on the lighter and looked him right in the eyes. I took the cigarette out of my mouth and spit lighter fluid in his face. Of course, it hit the lighter on the way, and he had a face full of flames before he knew what hit him. He dropped the shotty pretty fast so he could try to slap at the flames. But his clothes went up and pretty soon he was one crispy critter.'

After a long measure of silence, Rider asked a question. 'When did you place the lighter fluid in front of the store?'

'Oh, that was when I was walking away. I just took it out, wiped it off and put it down.'

'Did Mr Fitzpatrick call out for help at any time?'

Waits paused as if to ponder the question. 'He was yelling something, but I'm not sure it was for help. He kind of sounded like an animal to me.'

'What were you thinking as you were walking home?'

'I was thinking, Far out! I finally did it! And I knew I was going to get away with it, too. I felt pretty goddamn invincible, if you want the truth.'

'Did you ever think about the man you burned to death?'

'No, not really. He was just there. Like the rest of them that came after. It was like they were there for me.'

Rider spent another forty minutes questioning him, eliciting smaller details that nonetheless matched those contained in the investigative reports. Finally, at 11.15, she turned to Bosch and O'Shea.

'I have enough for the moment,' she said. 'Let's take a short break.'

She turned off the tape, and the investigators and O'Shea stepped out in the hallway to confer.

'What do you think?' O'Shea asked Rider.

She nodded. 'I'm satisfied. He solved the mystery of how he got to him. I don't think he's telling us everything, but he either did it or he was there.'

O'Shea looked at Bosch. 'Should we move on?'

Bosch dreaded what he would hear next but he was ready to hear it.

'Let's do it,' he said.

They all moved back into the room. Bosch took the seat across from Waits and turned the recorder back on. Rider and O'Shea took the wing positions and Olivas sat again by the door. Bosch had the Gesto file in front of him on the table.

'We're going to move on to the Marie Gesto case,' he said.

'Ah, sweet Marie,' Waits said. He had a brightness in his eyes.

'Your attorney's proffer suggests that you know what happened when Marie Gesto disappeared in '93. Is that true?'

Waits frowned. 'I'm afraid so,' he said with mock sincerity.

Here it was, the moment Bosch had waited on for thirteen years.

'She's dead, isn't she?'

Waits looked at him. 'Yes, she's dead.'

'Do you know the location of her remains?'

'Yes, I do.'

'Where is she?'

Waits broke into a broad smile. 'She's right here, detective,' he said. 'She's right here with me. Just like all the others. Right here with me.'

His smile turned into a laugh and Bosch almost went across the table at him. But Rider put her hand on his leg under the table. It calmed him.

'Hold on a second,' O'Shea said. 'Let's step out again, and this time I would like you to join us, Maury.'

Charging into the hallway before the others, O'Shea instructed the deputies to keep an eye on Waits. The door was closed.

'What the fuck, Maury?' O'Shea barked. 'We're not going to spend our time laying the groundwork for an insanity defence for you.'

Swann turned his palms up. 'The guy obviously has issues.'

'Bullshit. He's a stone-cold killer and he's in there vamping like Hannibal Lecter. This isn't a movie, Maury. This is real. You hear what he said about Fitzpatrick? So I'll tell you what, you go back and set him straight or we walk away from this and everybody takes their chances.'

Bosch was unconsciously nodding. He liked the anger in O'Shea's voice. He also liked the way this was going.

'I'll see what I can do,' Swann said. He went back into the interview room and the deputies came back.

'Sorry about that,' O'Shea said to no one in particular. 'But I'm not going to let them control this thing.'

'They already are,' Bosch said. 'Waits is, at least. The bottom line is, we're all engaged in an effort to save his life—at his own request.'

O'Shea shook his head. 'I'm not going back and forth on that again, Bosch. If you're not on board, Freddy will handle your part of the interview.'

Bosch waited a beat. 'Gesto is my case and I'll see it through.'

'Nice to hear it,' O'Shea said. 'Too bad you weren't so attentive in '93.'

He reached over and knocked harshly on the interview-room door. Bosch stared at his back with anger welling up from some place deep inside.

Swann let them in. After everyone retook their seats, and the recorder was turned back on, Bosch shook off his anger and locked eyes with Waits again.

'Where is she?'

Waits smirked slightly. 'Buried up in the hills.'

'Where in the hills?'

'Up near the stables. That's where I got her.'

'Exactly where is she buried?'

'I would have to show you. You go in the woods and then off the path. Way off the path. There's a lot of territory up there. You remember, they searched up there but they never found her.'

'And after thirteen years you could lead us to this spot?'

'It hasn't been thirteen years, Detective. I visited her there quite often. So I can certainly lead you there.'

Bosch took out a pen and wrote a note on the inside flap of the Gesto file. It gave him a moment to disengage from the emotions that were coming up.

'Did you know Marie Gesto before September 1993?' he said.

'No, I didn't.'

'Had you ever seen her before the day you abducted her?'

'Not that I remember.'

'Where did you first cross paths with her?'

'At the Mayfair. I saw her in there shopping and she was just my type. I followed her car up Beachwood Canyon. When she parked in the gravel lot below the stables, there was no one around, so I decided to take her.'

'It wasn't planned before you saw her in the store?'

'No, I went there to buy some Gatorade. It was a hot day.'

'You approached her in the lot below the stables?'

He nodded. 'I pulled in next to her in my van. She didn't think a thing about it. There was no one around, no one who could see. It was perfect.'

'What did you do?'

'I stepped out through the sliding door on the side where she was. I had a knife and told her to get in. She did. She was no trouble at all.'

'Then what?' Bosch asked.

'I asked her to remove her clothes and she told me she would do whatever I wanted as long as I didn't hurt her. She folded her clothes very nicely. As if she thought she would get the chance to put them back on again.'

Bosch rubbed a hand over his mouth. 'Go on,' he said.

'Well, you know the rest. We had sex. I did what I had to do.'

'Which was what?'

Waits locked eyes with Bosch. 'I killed her, Detective. I put my hands round her neck and I squeezed hard and I watched her eyes go still.'

Bosch stared at him. 'Waits,' he said. 'You are a worthless piece of trash.'

Waits put the smirk back on his face. 'If that is your best shot, Detective Bosch, you'll have to do much better. Because I took her soul and no one will ever get that back from me.'

Bosch looked down at the open file in front of him but did not see the words printed on the documents

'Let's move on,' he finally said. 'What did you do next?'

'I tidied up the van. I always had plastic drop sheets in the back. I wrapped her up for burial. Then I got out and locked the van. I took her things to her car. I had her keys, and I got in and drove it away, to throw the police off.'

'Where did you go?'

'You know where, Detective. The High Tower. A week or so before, I'd gone to look for work there and the manager happened to mention there was an open apartment. He showed it to me because I acted like I was interested.'

'He showed you the garage, too?'

'No, just pointed it out. I noticed that there was no lock.'

'So you drove Marie Gesto's car there and stashed it in the garage.'

'That's right.'

'Did anyone see you? Did you see anyone?'

'No and no. I was very careful. Remember, I'd just killed someone.'

'What about your van? When did you go back to get it?'

'I waited until night. I had some digging to do.'

'Was this van painted with the name of your business?'

'No, not then. I didn't have a city licence yet. That was thirteen years ago. I've gotten a new van since then.'

'How did you get back up to get your van?'

'I had a cab drop me at the stables. When there was no one around I found a nice private spot to plant my little flower.'

'And you dug a hole. What did you use to dig it?'

'I had a shovel.'

'You always carried a shovel in your window-washing van?'

'No, actually. I found it leaning against the barn up at the stables.'

'You put it back when you were finished?'

'Of course, Detective. I steal souls, not shovels.'

Bosch looked at the file in front of him. 'When was the last time you were at the place where you buried Marie Gesto?'

'Mmmm, a little over a year ago. I usually made the trip every September 9th, to celebrate our anniversary. This year I was a bit tied up, as you know.' He smiled good-naturedly.

'The media paid a lot of attention to Marie Gesto's disappearance,' Bosch said. 'Do you remember that?'

'Of course. That taught me a good lesson. I never acted so impulsively again. I was more careful about the flowers I picked after that.'

'You called the investigators on the case, didn't you?'

'As a matter of fact I did. I remember that. I called and told them I had seen her in the Mayfair store and she hadn't been with anybody.'

'Why did you call?'

Waits shrugged. 'I don't know. I just thought it would be fun. To actually talk to one of the men hunting me. Was it you?'

'My partner.'

'Yes, I thought I might be able to shift the focus away from the Mayfair. After all, who knows, maybe someone could describe me.'

'You gave the name Robert Saxon when you called. Why?'

'It was just a name I used from time to time.'

'It's not your real name?'

'No, Detective, you know my real name.'

'What if I told you I don't believe a word you've said here today?'

'I'd say, take me to Beachwood Canyon and I'll prove every word.'

Bosch pushed back his chair and told the others he would like to confer with them. Leaving Waits and Swann behind, they stepped out of the room into the cooler air of the hallway.

'What now, Bosch?' O'Shea asked.

'"What now" is that I don't believe him.'

'Why not?'

'Because he knows every answer. And some of them don't work. We spent a week with every cab company in the city going over records. Nobody made a drop-off up there that day or night.'

Olivas stepped up next to O'Shea. 'Bosch, that's not a hundred per cent and you know it,' he said. 'A cabby could've given him a ride off the books. They do it all the time. There's also gypsy cabs.'

'I still don't buy his stories. The shovel just happens to be leaning against the barn. How was he going to bury her if he didn't happen to see it?'

O'Shea spread his arms. 'There's one way to test him,' he said. 'We take him out on a field trip, and if he leads us to that girl's body the details aren't going to matter. On the other hand, if there's no body then there's no deal.'

'When do we go?' Bosch asked.

'I'll go see the judge today. We'll go tomorrow if you want.'

'Wait a minute,' Olivas said. 'What about the other seven? We still have a lot to talk to this bastard about.'

'Let's make Gesto the test case. Then we'll go from there.' O'Shea looked at Bosch. 'You going to be ready for this?'

Bosch nodded. 'I've been ready for thirteen years.'

THAT NIGHT, Rachel brought dinner up to the house, after calling first to see if Bosch was home. Bosch put some music on the stereo, and Rachel laid plates out on the dining-room table. The dinner was pot roast with creamed corn. She'd brought a bottle of Merlot, too, and it took Bosch five minutes to find a corkscrew. They didn't talk about the case until they were sitting across from each other at the table.

'So,' she said, 'how did it go today?'

'It went OK. Your take on everything was very helpful. Tomorrow's the field trip, and in Rick O'Shea's words, it will be put-up or shut-up time.'

'Field trip? Where to?'

'The top of Beachwood Canyon. He says that's where he buried her. I drove up there and looked around—couldn't find anything. The woods are thick but he says he can find the spot.'

'Do you believe he's the guy?'

'It looks like it. He's convinced everybody else and there's that call he made to us back then. That's pretty convincing.'

'But what?'

'I don't know. Maybe it's my ego not being ready to accept I was so wrong. No one wants to face that, I guess.' Bosch chased a mouthful of pot roast with some wine. 'Man, this stuff is great. Where'd you get it?'

She smiled. 'A restaurant off Beverly near my place. Harry, are you changing the subject or are you going to tell me about what happened?'

'I'm getting to it.' He looked at her eyes for a moment, then started telling her about Waits's confession.

'He's lying,' she said when he was finished. 'He tells you he just saw her in the Mayfair, followed her and grabbed her. I don't buy that. The whole thing doesn't feel like a spur-of-the-moment thing.'

Bosch nodded. 'We'll know tomorrow, I guess.'

'I wish I could be there.'

He shook his head. 'I can't make a federal case out of this. Besides, your own people wouldn't let you go, even if you were invited.'

'I know. I can still wish.'

Bosch got up and started clearing the plates. They worked side by side at the sink and after everything was put away they took the bottle of wine out on the deck to have a final glass. The evening chill drew them close as they stood at the railing and looked down at the lights in the Cahuenga Pass.

'Are you staying tonight?' Bosch asked.

'Yes.'

'You don't have to call, you know. I'll give you a key. Just come up.'

She turned and looked at him. He put his arm round her waist. 'That fast? Are you saying all is forgiven?'

'There's nothing to forgive. The past is past and life's too short. You know, all of those clichés.'

She smiled and they sealed it with a kiss. They finished their wine and went in to the bedroom. They made love slowly and quietly. At one point Bosch opened his eyes and looked at her and lost his rhythm. She noticed.

'What?' she whispered.

'Nothing. It's just that you keep your eyes open.'

'I'm looking at you.'

'No, you're not.'

She smiled and turned her face away from him. 'This is sort of an awkward time for a discussion,' she said.

He used his hand to turn her face to his. He kissed her and they both kept their eyes open. Halfway through the kiss they started laughing.

5

It seemed to Bosch to take for ever to amass the motorcade, but by 10.30 Wednesday morning the entourage was finally pulling out of the basement garage of the Criminal Courts Building.

The first car was unmarked. It was driven by Olivas. A sheriff's deputy from the jail division was riding shotgun, while Bosch and Rider were in the back on either side of Raynard Waits. The prisoner wore an orange jumpsuit, and the manacles on his wrists were secured to a chain round his waist.

Another unmarked car, driven by Rick O'Shea and carrying Maury Swann and a DA's office evidence videographer, was second in the motorcade. It was followed by two vans, one from the LAPD's Scientific Investigation Division and the other from the coroner's office.

It was a perfect day for a field trip. A brief overnight rain shower had cleared the sky and it was a brilliant blue with just the last wisps of clouds in view. The streets were still wet and shiny.

The vehicles stayed in a tight formation as they made their way onto the northbound 101 Freeway. Traffic was moving slowly because of the wet streets. Bosch asked Olivas to crack a window. It was apparent that the killer had not been allowed a shower or issued a laundered jumpsuit that morning.

'Why don't you go ahead and light up, Detective?' Waits said.

Bosch turned to look at him. 'I want the window open because of you, Waits. You stink. I haven't had a smoke in five years.'

'I'm sure.'

'Why do you think you know me, Waits? We've never met.'

'I know your type. You have an addictive personality, Detective. Murder cases, cigarettes, maybe even the alcohol I smell coming out of your pores.'

Waits smiled and Bosch looked away. He thought about things for a moment before speaking again.

'Who are you?' he asked.

'Are you talking to me?' Waits asked.

'Yes, I'm talking to you. I want to know. Who are you?'

'Bosch,' Olivas interjected from the front. 'The deal is, we don't question him without Maury Swann being present.'

'This isn't an interrogation. I'm just making conversation.'

'Yeah, well, I don't care what you want to call it. Don't.'

Bosch could see Olivas looking at him in the rearview mirror. They held each other's stare until Olivas had to put his eyes back on the road. Bosch leaned forward so he could turn and look past Waits over at Rider. She rolled her eyes at him. It was her don't-make-trouble look.

'Maury Swann,' Bosch said. 'Yeah, he's a damn good lawyer, all right. Got this man the deal of a lifetime.'

'Bosch!' Olivas said.

'I'm not talking to him. I'm talking to my partner.'

The manacles clinked as Waits tried to adjust his position. 'You didn't have to take the deal, Detective,' he said quietly.

'It wasn't my choice,' Bosch said without looking at him.

'You're an eye-for-an-eye man. The kind of man who would—'

'Waits,' Olivas said sharply. 'Just keep your mouth shut.'

They were cutting through Hollywood now, and Olivas signalled for Gower Avenue. Bosch turned round to look out through the back window. The group remained intact, but he could now see a helicopter trailing above the motorcade. It had a large number 4 on its white underbelly.

Bosch jerked back round. 'Who called out the media, Olivas? Was that you or your boss?'

'My boss? I don't know what you're talking about.'

Olivas glanced at him in the rearview then quickly back at the road. It was too furtive a move. Bosch knew he was lying.

'Yeah, right. What's in this for you? O'Shea's going to make you chief of investigations after he wins? Is that it?'

Now Olivas held his eyes in the mirror. 'Fuck you, Bosch.'

'Gentlemen, gentlemen,' Waits said. 'Can't we all get along?'

'Shut up, Waits,' Bosch said. 'Olivas, pull over. I want to talk to O'Shea.'

Olivas shook his head. 'No way. Not with a custody in the car.'

As they came to the light at Franklin it turned green, and they crossed Franklin and started up Beachwood Drive. Bosch pulled out his cellphone and called the number O'Shea had given everyone that morning.

'O'Shea.'

'It's Bosch. I don't think it was smart to call the media out on this.'

'They're at a safe distance. They're in the air.'

'And who's going to be waiting at the top of Beachwood?'

'No one, Bosch. I was very specific. They could track us from the air but anyone on the ground would compromise the operation. No need to worry.'

'Whatever.' Bosch jammed his phone closed.

'You need to calm down, Detective,' Waits said.

'And Waits, you need to shut up.'

Beachwood Canyon was a quiet neighbourhood on the slope of the Santa Monica Mountains. As they ascended, the Hollywood sign atop Mount Lee was in view through the windshield. A stone gateway halfway up Beachwood led to a small village circle with shops. At the dead-end at the top was the Sunset Ranch Stables, the starting point of miles of horse trails that stretched over the mountains. This was where the grim motorcade of investigators, body-recovery experts and a manacled killer finally came to a stop.

The Sunset Ranch parking lot was merely a level clearing on the slope below the ranch itself. Gravel had been dumped and spread. Visitors to the ranch had to park here and then leg it up to the stables at the top. The parking lot was isolated and surrounded by dense woods.

Bosch waited impatiently in the car until Olivas disabled the rear locks. He then got out and closed the door, making sure it was locked. The plan was to leave Waits inside until everyone was sure the area was secure.

O'Shea and Olivas convened everyone except Waits in a circle in the gravel parking lot. In addition to the lawyers, investigators and the sheriff's deputy, there were two body-recovery experts and a forensic archaeologist named Kathy Kohl, an LAPD forensic tech, as well as the videographer from the DA's office. Bosch had worked with all of them before.

O'Shea waited until the videographer had his camera going before he addressed the troops. 'OK, people, we are here on a grim duty, to find and collect the remains of Marie Gesto,' he said sombrely. 'Our primary concern is the security of the suspect and your safety. Be careful and be alert. Four of us are armed. Mr Waits will be manacled and under the watchful eyes of the detectives and Deputy Doolan. I would like the video and the gas probe to go along with us. When we find the body we can secure Mr Waits and all of you will come to the location. OK, let's do this.'

Olivas and Deputy Doolan went to retrieve Waits. Bosch heard the noise of the circling helicopter getting louder as the news crew came down for a better angle and a closer look with their camera.

After Waits was helped up out of the car, his manacles were checked by Olivas and he was led to the group. The deputy stayed six feet behind him with the shotgun up and ready. Olivas kept a grip on Waits's upper left arm.

'Mr Waits, fair warning,' O'Shea said. 'If you attempt to run, these officers will shoot you down. Do you understand that?'

'Of course,' Waits said. 'And they would do it gladly, I'm sure.'

'Then we understand each other. Lead the way.'

Waits led them towards a dirt path that fed off the lower end of the lot. It disappeared beneath a canopy of acacia trees, white oaks and heavy brush. He walked without hesitation, like he knew just where he was going.

'Not too much farther,' he said, as though he were a nature guide leading them to a secluded waterfall.

The path became narrower as the trees and brush encroached and the trail evolved from the well trodden to the seldom used. Olivas had to change position from holding Waits by the arm and walking next to him to following the killer, with a hand grasping the waist chain. Olivas was clearly not going to let go, but this new position blocked everybody else's shot if Waits tried to run. Bosch kept his eyes focused on the two men in front of him.

The terrain grew more difficult as the path followed the downslope of the mountain. The soil was soft and moist from the overnight rain. In some places, Bosch felt his hiking boots sink and catch. Progress was slow, and they had to stop at the edge of a steep drop-off where the weight of pooled water had caused a small mudslide. The ground had sheared away next to an oak tree, exposing half its root system. The drop was almost ten feet.

'Well, this wasn't here last time I came,' Waits said in a tone that indicated he was put out by the inconvenience.

'Is that the way?' Olivas asked, pointing to the bottom.

'Yes,' Waits confirmed. 'We go down there.'

'All right.' Olivas turned to Bosch. 'Why don't you go first,' he said.

Bosch nodded and moved past them. He grabbed one of the lower branches of the oak for balance as he tested the slope.

'No good,' he said. 'This is going to be like a sliding board going down. And once we get down, how do we get back up?'

Olivas blew out his breath in frustration. 'Then what do—?'

'There was a ladder on top of one of the vans,' Waits suggested.

'He's right. Forensics has a lightweight aluminium ladder,' Rider said. 'We put it on the incline and go up and down like stairs. Simple.'

'Simple,' Swann said, 'except my client is not going up and down a ladder with his hands chained to his waist.'

After a momentary pause, everyone looked at O'Shea.

'I think we can work something out,' he said.

'Wait a minute,' Olivas said. 'We're not taking the—'

'Then he's not going down there,' Swann said. 'I'm not allowing you to endanger him. He's my client and—'

O'Shea held his hands up. 'Maury makes a point. If Mr Waits falls going down the ladder without being able to use his hands, then we're responsible. I am sure that with all of you people holding guns and shotguns, we can control this situation for the ten seconds it will take.'

'I'll go get the ladder,' said the forensic tech. 'Can you hold this?'

Her name was Carolyn Cafarelli and Bosch knew that most people called her Cal. She handed the gas probe, a yellow T-shaped device, to Bosch and started back through the woods. They waited in silence.

When Cafarelli returned with the ladder, Bosch helped her slide it down the slope and steady it. When he turned back to the group, he saw that Olivas had uncuffed one of Waits's hands from the waist chain.

'The other hand, Detective,' Swann said.

'He can climb with one hand free,' Olivas insisted.

'I am sorry, Detective, but I am not going to allow that. He has to be able to break a fall if he happens to slip.'

'He can do that with one hand.'

While the posturing and debate continued, Bosch swung himself onto the ladder and went down the slope backwards. At the bottom, he looked around and realised that the trail to Marie Gesto's body was not as obvious as it had been above. He looked back up at the others and waited.

'Freddy, just do it,' O'Shea instructed. 'Deputy, you go down first with that shotgun in case Mr Waits gets any ideas. Detective Rider, you have my permission to unholster your weapon.'

Bosch climbed back up a few steps on the ladder so that Deputy Doolan could hand him the shotgun. He then stepped back down and the uniformed man came down the ladder. Bosch gave him back the weapon.

'Toss me the cuffs,' he called up to Olivas.

Bosch caught the cuffs and Waits began to go down while the videographer recorded his descent. When Waits was three rungs from the bottom Bosch grabbed the waist chain to guide him the rest of the way.

'This is it, Ray,' Bosch whispered in his ear from behind. 'Your only chance. You sure you don't want to make a run for it?'

Safely at the bottom, Waits stepped off the ladder and held his hands up for the cuffs. 'No, Detective, I like living too much.'

'I thought so.' Bosch cuffed his hands to the chain and looked back up the slope at the others. 'OK, we're secure.'

One by one they came down the ladder, then they regrouped.

O'Shea looked around. 'OK, which way?' he said to Waits.

Waits turned in a half circle as if seeing the area for the first time. 'Um . . .'

Olivas almost lost it. 'You better not be pulling—'

'That way,' Waits said coyly, nodding to the right of the slope. 'Lost my bearings there for a second.'

The group moved off through the brush with Waits leading, Olivas clinging to the chain and the shotgun never more than five feet behind. The ground on this level was softer and muddier. In five minutes they came to a clearing shaded by a tall oak. Bosch saw Waits looking up and followed his eyes. A yellowish white hairband hung limply from an overhead branch.

'It's funny,' Waits said. 'It used to be blue.'

Bosch knew that at the time of Marie Gesto's disappearance she was believed to have had her hair tied back with a blue band known as a scrunchie. The scrunchie was not found with the clothing neatly folded in her car.

Bosch lowered his eyes and Waits was waiting with a smile.

'We're here, Detective. You've finally found Marie.'

'Where?'

Waits's smile broadened. 'You're standing on her.'

Bosch abruptly stepped back and Waits laughed.

'Don't worry, I don't think she minds. What was it the great man wrote about sleeping the big sleep? About not caring where you fell?'

Bosch looked at him, wondering about the window cleaner's literary airs.

Waits seemed to read him. 'I've been in jail since May, Detective. I've done a lot of reading.'

'Step back,' Bosch said.

Waits stepped towards the oak. Bosch looked at the ground. He had left footprints in the mud, but it looked like there was another, recent disturbance, as though an animal had been digging. Bosch signalled Cafarelli forward with the gas probe and pointed directly below the colourless hairband. The tech pushed the probe into the earth, clicked on the reader and began studying the electronic display. Bosch knew that the probe measured the level of methane in the soil. A buried body releases methane as it decomposes.

'We're getting a read,' she said. 'We're above normal levels.'

Bosch felt strange, out of sorts. He looked at Waits. 'How far down is she?'

'Not too far,' Waits replied. 'Back in '93 we were in drought, remember? The ground was hard and I wore my ass out digging a hole. I was lucky she was just a little thing.'

Bosch looked back at Cafarelli, who was taking another probe reading. They all watched the grim work silently. After taking several readings in a grid pattern, Cafarelli dragged the point of the probe in the dirt to mark out a rectangle about six feet by two feet. A small grave for a small victim.

'OK,' O'Shea said. 'Let's get Mr Waits back and secured in the car and then bring in the excavation group.'

Cafarelli stayed at the site so there would be no issues about crime-scene integrity. The rest of the group headed back towards the ladder. Bosch was last in line, his mind deep in thought about the ground they were traversing. There was something sacred about it. It was hallowed ground.

At the ladder, Rider and Olivas went up first. Bosch then walked Waits to the ladder, uncuffed him and started him up.

As the killer climbed, the deputy trained the shotgun on his back. Bosch looked up at the top of the sheer face, and noticed that Rider was holding her weapon at her side. As Waits got to the top of the ladder, he was welcomed by Olivas with opened arms.

'Hands,' Olivas said.

'Certainly, Detective.'

From Bosch's angle below, he could see only Waits's back. He could tell by his posture that Waits had brought his hands together at his front for recuffing to the waist chain.

But then there was a sudden movement. A quick twist in the prisoner's posture as he leaned too far into Olivas. Bosch instinctively knew that something was wrong. Waits was going for the gun holstered on Olivas's hip.

'Hey!' Olivas shouted in panic. 'Hey!'

Before Bosch or anyone else could react, Waits used his hold and leverage on Olivas to spin their bodies so that the detective's back was now at the top of the ladder. The deputy had no angle for a shot. Neither did Bosch. With a pistonlike move, Waits raised his knee and drove it twice into Olivas's crotch. Olivas started to collapse, and there were two quick gunshots, muffled by his body. Waits pushed the detective off the edge and Olivas came crashing down the ladder onto Bosch.

Waits then disappeared from view.

Olivas's weight took Bosch down hard into the mud. As he struggled to pull his weapon, Bosch heard two more shots from above. Behind him he heard shouts of panic and the sound of running. Waits appeared at the edge of the precipice, calmly holding a gun. He fired down at them, and Bosch felt two impacts on Olivas's body.

The blast of the deputy's shotgun split the air but the slug thwacked into the trunk of an oak tree to the left of Waits. Waits returned fire at the same moment, and Bosch heard the deputy go down like a dropped suitcase.

'Run, you coward!' Waits yelled. 'How's your bullshit deal looking now?'

He fired twice more indiscriminately into the woods below. Bosch managed to free his gun and fire up the ladder at Waits.

Waits ducked out of sight, using his free hand to yank the ladder up the embankment. Bosch pushed Olivas's body off and got up, his gun aimed and ready for Waits to show again. But then he heard the sound of running from above and he knew Waits was gone.

'Kiz!' Bosch yelled.

There was no reply. Bosch quickly checked both Olivas and the deputy but saw they were both dead. He holstered his weapon and scrambled up the incline, using exposed roots as handholds. As he crawled over the edge, he saw Waits moving off through the trees in the direction of the parking lot. Bosch pulled his gun and fired five more shots but Waits never slowed.

Bosch got up, ready to give chase. But then he saw his partner's body lying crumpled and bloody in the nearby brush.

Kiz Rider was face up, clutching her neck with one hand while the other lay limp at her side. Her eyes were wide and searching but not focusing. It was as if she were blind. It took a moment for Bosch to spot the bullet wound in the palm of her limp hand. It was a through-and-through shot but he knew it wasn't as serious as the neck wound. Blood was steadily seeping between her fingers. The bullet must have hit the carotid artery, and Bosch knew that blood loss could kill his partner in minutes.

'OK, Kiz,' he said as he knelt next to her. 'I'm here.'

Her left hand was creating insufficient pressure on the right side of her neck. She was losing strength.

'Let me take over,' he said. He moved his hand under hers and pressed against what he now realised were two wounds, bullet entry and exit. He could feel the blood pulsing against his palm. 'O'Shea!' he shouted.

'Bosch?' O'Shea called back from below. 'Where is he? Did you kill him?'

'He's gone. Get on Doolan's rover and get a medevac. Now!'

'Doolan's shot! So is Freddy!'

'They're dead, O'Shea. Get on the radio. Rider is alive and we need—'

In the distance there were two gunshots, followed by a shout. It was a female voice and Bosch thought about Kathy Kohl and the people up at the parking lot. There were two more shots and Bosch heard the news helicopter banking away. Waits was shooting at it.

'Come on, O'Shea!' he shouted. 'We're running out of time.'

When he heard nothing in response, he brought Rider's hand back up against the wounds. 'Press hard, Kiz. I'll be right back.'

Bosch lowered the ladder back into place and climbed down. O'Shea was on his knees next to Olivas's body. The prosecutor's eyes were as wide and as blank as those of the dead cop. Swann was standing next to him with a dazed look on his face. Cafarelli was on her knees, trying to turn Doolan over to get to the radio. The deputy had fallen chest down.

'Cal, let me do it,' Bosch ordered. 'You go up and help Kiz. We've got to stop the bleeding from her neck.'

The Forensics tech scurried up the ladder. Bosch turned Doolan over and saw that he had been hit in the forehead. Bosch grabbed the radio off Doolan's belt and made the 'officer down' call. Once he was assured that a medevac chopper and paramedics were on the way, he reported that an armed murder suspect had escaped custody. He gave a description of Waits, shoved the radio into his belt, then went to the ladder. As he climbed back up, he called to O'Shea, Swann and the videographer, who was still recording the scene.

'All of you get up here. We need to carry her to the parking lot.'

He turned back to Rider. Cafarelli was holding her neck but Bosch could see time was growing short. The life was leaving his partner's eyes.

Bosch bent down and held her unhurt hand. 'Come on, Kiz, hang in there. We've got an airship coming and we're going to get you out of here.'

He looked around to see what was available to them and got an idea as he saw Maury Swann come up the ladder. He quickly moved to the edge. O'Shea was coming up behind him and the videographer was waiting his turn.

'Leave the camera,' Bosch ordered.

'I can't. I'm response—'

'You bring it up and I'm going to throw it as far as I can.'

The cameraman reluctantly put his equipment on the ground, popped out the digital tape and put it in a pocket of his cargo pants. Once everyone was on top, Bosch pulled the ladder up and carried it over to Rider.

'OK, we're going to use the ladder as a stretcher. Two men on each side and, Cal, I need you to walk beside us and keep that pressure on her neck.'

'Got it,' she said.

'OK, let's put her on.'

They took positions at Rider's legs and shoulders and carefully lifted her onto the ladder. Cafarelli kept her hands in place on Rider's neck. Then they raised the ladder and started moving back up the trail. Two times Swann slipped, and the makeshift stretcher almost went over. Each time Cafarelli literally hugged Rider to the ladder and kept her in place.

It took less than ten minutes to get to the parking lot. The coroner's van was missing, but Kathy Kohl and her two assistants were standing unharmed by the SID van. Bosch scanned the sky for a helicopter but saw none. With one hand hooked under the ladder, he used his free hand to operate the radio.

'Where's my airship?' he yelled at the dispatcher.

The response was that it was on the way with a one-minute ETA. They softly lowered the ladder to the ground. Behind him Bosch heard O'Shea interrogating Kohl.

'What happened? Where did Waits go?'

'He came out of the woods and shot at the news helicopter. Then he took our van and headed down the hill.'

'Did the chopper follow him?'

'We don't know. I don't think so. It flew away when he started shooting.'

Bosch heard the sound of an approaching helicopter and hoped it wasn't the news team coming back. He walked to the most open area of the lot and waited. In a few moments, a silver-skinned medevac chopper crested the mountain top, and he started waving it down.

Two paramedics jumped from the aircraft, carrying an equipment case and a folding stretcher. They knelt on either side of Rider, put a breathing mask over her face and examined her wounds. To himself Bosch repeated the mantra, *Come on, Kiz, come on, Kiz, come on, Kiz . . .*

One of the paramedics turned towards the chopper and gestured to the pilot, spinning an upraised finger in the air. Bosch knew it meant that they had to get going. The chopper's engine started to rev higher. Bosch helped move Rider onto the stretcher, then took one of the handles and helped them carry it to the waiting helicopter.

'Can I go?' he yelled loudly as they moved towards the open door.

'No, sir. We need room to work on her,' yelled one of the paramedics.

Bosch nodded. 'Where are you taking her?'

'St Joe's.'

St Joseph's was in Burbank, five minutes' flying time at most. By car it would be a lengthy drive round the mountain and through the Cahuenga Pass.

Bosch wanted to yell something to his partner but he couldn't come up with any words. He decided that if Kiz was conscious she would know what he had wanted to say. The helicopter took off as he was moving backwards, wondering if he would ever see her again.

Just as the aircraft banked away, a patrol car came roaring up the hill to the parking lot, its blue lights flashing. Two uniforms out of Hollywood Division jumped out. One pointed his gun at Bosch. Covered with mud and blood, Bosch understood why.

'I'm a police officer! My shield's in my back pocket.'

'Then let's see it,' said the man with the gun. 'Slowly!'

Bosch pulled out his badge case and flipped it open. It passed inspection and the gun was lowered.

'Get back in the car,' Bosch ordered. 'We have to go!'

He ran to the rear door and the two officers piled in.

'Take me to St Joe's,' he told them. 'My partner was in that airship.'

'You got it. Code three, baby.'

The driver hit the siren and pinned the accelerator. The car U-turned in a screech of tyres and a spray of gravel, then headed downhill. It swerved dangerously round the curves on the way down. Halfway down the hill, the driver slowed as they passed through the crowded shopping area.

'Stop!' Bosch yelled.

The driver complied with screeching efficiency on the brakes.

'Back it up. I just saw the van.'

'What van?'

'Just back it up!'

The patrol car reversed past the neighbourhood supermarket. There in the side lot Bosch saw the pale blue coroner's van parked in the back row.

'Our custody got loose and got a gun. He took that van.'

They got out with their weapons drawn, and searched and cleared the parking lot quickly. The coroner's van was unlocked and empty, but Bosch found an orange jail-issue jumpsuit on the floor in the back. Waits had either been wearing a set of clothes beneath the jumpsuit, or he had found clothes to change into in the van.

'He could be wearing anything,' Bosch announced. 'Stay close to me. I know what he looks like.'

In a tight formation they moved into the store through the automatic doors. Once inside, Bosch quickly realised they were too late. A man with a manager's tag on his shirt was consoling a woman who was crying hysterically. The manager saw the two uniforms and signalled them over.

'Mrs Shelton here just got carjacked,' the manager said.

'OK, listen,' Bosch said to the officers. 'One of you stays here, gets a description of what he's wearing and the car out on the air. The other leaves now and gets me to St Joe's. Let's go.'

The driver took Bosch and the other patrolman stayed behind. In another three minutes they came screeching out of Beachwood Canyon. On the radio they heard a BOLO—be-on-the-lookout—broadcast for a silver BMW 540 wanted in connection with a 187 LEO—murder of a law enforcement officer. The suspect was described as wearing a baggy white jumpsuit, which Bosch knew he had found in the Forensics van.

The siren was clearing a path for them but Bosch estimated that they were still fifteen minutes from the hospital. He had a bad feeling about it. He had a bad feeling about everything. He tried to think about Kiz Rider alive and smiling and scolding him the way she always did. And when they got to the freeway, he concentrated on scanning all eight lanes of northbound traffic for a carjacked silver BMW with a killer at the wheel.

6

Bosch strode through the emergency-room entrance with his badge out. An intake receptionist sat behind a counter.

'The police officer who was brought in on a medevac?' he said.

'I have no information, sir,' the woman said. 'If you'll take—'

'Where can I get information? Where's the doctor?'

'The doctor is with the patient, sir.'

'Then she's still alive?'

'Sir, I can't give out any information at this time. If you'll—'

Bosch walked away from the counter and over to a set of double doors. He pushed a button on the wall that automatically swung them open. Behind him he heard the desk woman yelling to him. He didn't stop. He stepped through the doors into the emergency treatment area. There were eight curtained patient bays, four on each side, and the nurses' and physicians' stations were in the middle. The place was abuzz. Outside a bay on the right Bosch saw one of the paramedics from the helicopter. He went to him.

'How is she?'

'She's holding on. She lost a lot of blood and—' He stopped when he turned and saw that it was Bosch next to him. 'I'm not sure you're supposed to be in here, Officer. I think you better step out to the waiting room and—'

'She's my partner and I want to know what is happening.'

'She's got one of the best ER attendants in the city trying to keep her alive. But you can't stand here and watch.'

'Sir?' A guard in a security uniform was approaching. 'Sir, come with me, please.' He put his hand on Bosch's arm.

Bosch shrugged it off. 'I'm a police detective. You don't need to touch me. I just want to know what is happening with my partner.'

'Sir, you will be told in good time. If you will please come—'

The guard made the mistake of attempting to take Bosch by the arm again. This time Bosch didn't shrug it off. He slapped the man's hand away.

'I said don't—'

'Hold on, hold on,' said the paramedic. 'Tell you what, Detective, let's go to the machines and get a coffee, and I'll tell you what's happening, OK?'

Bosch said nothing. The paramedic sweetened the offer.

'I'll even get you some clean scrubs so you can get out of those muddy and bloody clothes. Sound good?'

Bosch relented, the security man nodded his approval and the paramedic led the way, first to a supply closet, then down a hallway to the nurses' break room, where there were coin-operated machines serving coffee, sodas and snacks. Bosch took a black coffee. He had no change but the paramedic did.

'You want to clean up and change first? You can use the lav over there.'

'Just tell me what you know first.'

They sat at a round table across from each other.

The paramedic reached his hand across the table. 'Dale Dillon.'

Bosch shook his hand. 'Harry Bosch.'

'Good to meet you, Detective Bosch. The first thing I need to do is thank you for your efforts out there. You probably saved your partner's life. She lost a lot of blood but she's a fighter.'

'How bad is it?'

'It's bad, but it's one of those cases where they won't know until she stabilises. The bullet hit one of her carotid arteries. That's what they are working on now—repairing the artery. Since she lost a lot of blood, the risk right now is stroke. So she's not out of the woods yet, but if she avoids going into stroke she should come out OK, with a lot of rehab ahead of her.'

Bosch nodded. 'When will I be able to see her?'

'I have no idea, man. I just bring 'em in here. I told you all I know and that was probably too much. If you're going to wait around, I suggest you wash your face and change out of those clothes.' Dillon stood up.

'I will,' Bosch said. 'Thanks, Dale.'

After the paramedic left, Bosch went into the lavatory and stripped off his sweatshirt. Because there were no pockets in the surgical clothes for his weapon, badge and phone, he decided to leave his dirty jeans on. He spent the next five minutes washing the blood and dirt from his face and hands.

Bosch walked back to the ER reception area and now found it crowded with police, both uniformed and not. His supervisor, Abel Pratt, was there among the suits, looking drained. He saw Bosch and came over.

'Harry, how is she?'

'They're not giving me anything official. The paramedic who brought her in said it looks like she'll be OK.'

'Thank Christ! What happened up there?'

'I'm not sure. Waits got a gun and started shooting. Anything on whether they've got a bead on him?'

'He dumped the car he jacked by the Red Line station on Hollywood Boulevard. They don't know where the hell he is.'

Bosch thought about that. On the Red Line, Waits could have gone anywhere from North Hollywood to downtown. The downtown line had a stop near Echo Park.

'Are they looking in Echo Park?'

'They're looking everywhere. OIS is sending a team here to talk to you. I didn't think you'd be willing to leave to go to Parker.'

'Right.'

The Officer Involved Shooting squad would not be a problem. As far as

Bosch could see he had not done anything wrong in the handling of Waits. OIS was a rubber-stamp squad, anyway.

'They'll be a while,' Pratt said. 'They're up at Sunset Ranch interviewing the others. How the fuck did he get a gun?'

Bosch shook his head. 'Olivas got too close while Waits was coming up a ladder. He grabbed it and started shooting. I was down below them.'

'Jesus Christ!'

'He wasn't cuffed,' Bosch said in a low voice. 'We had to take off the cuffs so he could go up the ladder. The cuffs were going to be off for thirty seconds at the max, and that's when he made his move.'

Pratt looked stunned. 'You took the cuffs off?'

'O'Shea told us to.'

'Good. They can blame him. I don't want any blowback on Open-Unsolved. I don't want any on me. It's not the way to go out after almost thirty years.'

'What about Kiz? You're not going to cut her loose, are you?'

'No, I'm not. I'll stand behind Kiz but I'm not standing behind O'Shea.'

Bosch's phone vibrated and he took it out of his pocket. The screen said 'Unknown Number.' He answered it anyway to get away from Pratt's questions. It was Rachel.

'Harry, we just got the BOLO on Waits. What happened?'

Bosch excused himself and stepped into an alcove. As concisely as possible he told her what had happened and what the situation was with Rider. Rachel offered to come to the ER but he talked her out of it, saying he would probably be taken into a private interview with OIS investigators.

'Will I see you tonight?' she asked.

'If I get done with everything and Kiz is stable.'

'I'm going to your place. Call to let me know what you know.'

'I will.'

Bosch stepped out of the alcove and saw that the ER waiting room was beginning to fill with media now as well as cops. He guessed this meant the chief of police was on his way. He walked up to Pratt, who was standing with his boss, Captain Norona, the head of the Robbery-Homicide Division.

'What's going to happen with the excavation?' he asked them both.

'I've got Rick Jackson and Tim Marcia headed up there,' Pratt said. 'They'll handle it.'

'It's my case,' Bosch said, a mild protest in his voice.

'Not any more,' Norona said. 'You're with OIS until they finish this thing up. You're the only one with a badge who was up there and is still able to talk about it.'

There was a commotion at the ER entrance as several men with TV cameras on their shoulders jostled for position on either side of the double doors. When the doors opened, an entourage entered with the chief of police at the centre. The chief strode to the reception desk, where he was met by Norona. They spoke to the same woman who had rejected Bosch earlier. This time she immediately picked up a phone and made a call.

Inside three minutes the hospital's chief surgeon came through the ER doors and invited the chief back for a private consultation. As they moved through the doors, Bosch hitched a ride, joining the group of commanders and assistants in the chief's wake.

'Excuse me, Dr Kim,' a voice from behind the group called.

They all stopped and turned. It was the desk woman.

She pointed at Bosch. 'He's not with that group.'

The chief noticed Bosch for the first time and corrected her. 'He most certainly is,' he said in a voice that invited no disagreement.

The woman looked chastened. The group moved forward and Dr Kim ushered them into an unused ER patient bay.

'Is she going to make it?' the chief asked bluntly.

'We think so, yes,' said Dr Kim. 'The real question is about permanent damage, and we won't know that for some time. One of the bullets damaged one of the carotid arteries, which deliver blood and oxygen to the brain. We don't yet know what damage might have occurred, but we are seeing routine brain activity at this time. That is very good news so far.'

'Is she able to talk?'

'Not at this time. She was anaesthetised during surgery and it will be several hours before she comes out of it.'

The chief nodded. 'Thank you, Dr Kim.' In a low voice, he added, 'At one time this detective worked directly for me. I don't want to lose her.'

'We're doing our very best, Chief. We won't lose her.'

The police chief nodded again. As the group shuffled back towards the waiting room, the chief grasped Bosch's shoulder and pulled him aside.

'Detective Bosch, thank you for getting her here so quickly. But I want to know what happened on that mountain. How did things go so wrong?'

'That's a good question, Chief,' Bosch replied.

Once again, he began to tell his story.

LITTLE BY LITTLE the media and the police left the ER waiting room. In a way, Kiz Rider was a disappointment. If she had died, everything would have been an immediate sound bite. Get in, go live, then move on. But she hung on and people couldn't wait around. As the hours went by, the numbers in the waiting room got smaller until only Bosch was left.

Shortly before 5 p.m. Dr Kim came through the double doors looking for someone in uniform. He had to settle for Bosch.

'She's doing well. She's conscious, and nonverbal communication skills are good. She's not talking because of the trauma to the neck and we have her intubated, but the initial indications are all positive. No stroke, no infection.'

Bosch felt relief flood through him. 'Can I see her?'

'For a few minutes. As I said, she's not talking. Come with me.'

Bosch followed the chief surgeon through the ER to the intensive-care unit. Kiz was in the second room on the right. Her body seemed small in the bed, surrounded with all the equipment and monitors and tubes. Her eyes were at half-mast. She was conscious but just barely.

'Kiz,' Bosch said. 'How are ya, partner?' He grabbed her good hand. 'Don't try to answer. The chief surgeon told me you're going to be OK. You'll have some rehab, but you'll be good as new.'

A high-pitched sigh came from her mouth. Bosch couldn't read it as relief or anguish or anything in between. He felt her squeeze his hand, though, and he took that as something good.

He pulled a chair over from the wall and sat down. Over the next half-hour he said very little. He just held her hand.

At 5.30 a nurse entered the room and told Bosch that two men had asked for him in the ER waiting room. Bosch gave Rider's hand a squeeze and told her he would be back in the morning.

The two men were OIS investigators Randolph and Osani. They took him out to their car. With a tape recorder on the seat next to him, he told his story. When he began recounting that morning's field trip, they asked questions obviously designed to elicit answers that went with the department's preconceived plan for dealing with the disaster. It was clear they wanted to establish that the important decisions came through Rick O'Shea.

So when Bosch recounted the momentary disagreement over whether Waits should be uncuffed to descend the ladder, Randolph pressed him for exact quotes. They presumably had already talked to Cal Cafarelli, Maury Swann and O'Shea and his videographer.

'Have you looked at the video?' Bosch asked when he was finished telling his view of things. 'It should have everything on it. I think the guy was rolling video when the shooting started.'

'Corvin says he lost the tape in the woods,' Randolph said.

'Corvin's the camera guy?'

'Right. Says it must've come out of his pocket when you people were carrying Rider on the ladder. We haven't found it.'

'Corvin's lying,' Bosch said. 'He was wearing the kind of pants with all the pockets. Cargo pants. I definitely saw him put the tape in one of those pockets with the flap. It wouldn't have fallen out.'

Randolph nodded, as though being lied to was just par for the course.

'The tape's got O'Shea telling Olivas to take off the cuffs,' Bosch said. 'That's not the kind of video O'Shea would want on the news.'

Randolph didn't even bother nodding. 'OK, let's go over it all once more from the top and then we can get you out of here.'

'Sure,' Bosch said. 'Whatever you need.'

Bosch finished the second run-through and asked Randolph and Osani if he could ride with them back to Parker Center so he could retrieve his car. On the ride back, the OIS men did not discuss the investigation. Randolph turned on the radio and they listened to the media version of the events in Beachwood Canyon and the latest update on the search for Raynard Waits.

A third report was on the growing political fallout. Everyone from city council candidates to Rick O'Shea's opponent weighed in with criticism of the way the LAPD and district attorney's office had handled the fatal field trip. O'Shea sought to distance himself from the catastrophe by releasing a statement that characterised him as merely an observer who relied on the LAPD for all decisions. The report concluded with a mention of O'Shea's bravery in helping to save a wounded police detective while the armed fugitive was at large in the wooded canyon.

'That guy O'Shea?' Bosch said when Randolph had turned off the radio. 'He's got it down. He's going to make a great DA.'

'No doubt,' Randolph said.

Bosch said good night to the OIS men in the garage behind Parker Center, then walked to a pay lot where he kept a parking space reserved to retrieve his car. He was drained from the day but there was an hour of daylight left. He headed back up the freeway, plugged his dead cellphone into its charger and called Rachel. She was already at his house.

'It will be a while,' he said. 'I'm going back up to Beachwood.'

'Why?'

'Because it's my case and they're up there working it.'

'Right. You should be there.'

He didn't respond. He just listened to the silence. It was comforting.

'I'll get home as soon as I can,' he finally said.

Near the top of Beachwood Drive, Bosch passed a pair of vans on their way down, a body wagon followed by the SID van with the ladder on top. He felt a space open up in his chest. He knew they had come from the excavation. Marie Gesto was in that front van.

When he got to the parking lot he saw Tim Marcia and Rick Jackson, the two detectives who had been assigned to take over the excavation, peeling off the white jumpsuits they had worn over their clothes. Bosch parked next to them and got out.

'Harry, how's Kiz?' Marcia asked immediately.

'They say she's going to be OK.'

'Thank goodness.'

'What a mess, huh?' Jackson said.

Bosch just nodded. 'What did you find?'

'We found a body,' Marcia said. 'You've got dental records, right?'

'In the file on my desk.'

'We'll get it and take it over to the coroner's office. You doing all right?'

'Long day,' Bosch said. He knew they wanted to know how it could have happened, but he was tired of telling the story. 'Listen,' he said, 'If you get the ID I'd appreciate it if you'd let me make the call to the parents. I've been talking to them for thirteen years. They'll want it to come from me. I want it to come from me.'

'You got it, Harry,' Marcia said.

They spoke for another few moments and then Bosch looked up and appraised the dying light of the day. He asked if they had a flashlight.

'I'll bring it back tomorrow,' he promised, though they all knew he might not be back the following day.

'Harry, there's no ladder,' Marcia said. 'SID took it with them.'

Bosch shrugged and looked down at his mud-caked boots and pants. 'I might get a little dirty,' he said.

Marcia gave him a Maglite. 'You want us to stick around?'

'No, I'll be fine. I've got my cell, anyway.'

Bosch stood by while they got into their car and drove off. He headed down the path to the drop-off and turned on the flashlight. The place had been trampled by the coroner's people, OIS investigators and Forensics techs. He slid down the incline using the tree root, and in two minutes came to the clearing, now delineated by yellow police-line tape. In the centre was a rectangular excavation hole about four feet deep.

Bosch ducked under the tape and entered the hallowed ground.

7

In the morning Bosch was making coffee for Rachel and himself when he got the call. It was his boss, Abel Pratt.

'Harry, you're not coming in. I just got the word.'

Bosch had half expected it. 'From who?'

'The sixth floor. OIS hasn't wrapped it up, and because the thing is so hot with the media they want you to cool it on the sidelines for a few days until they see how it's going to go.'

Bosch didn't say anything. The sixth floor was where the department administration was located, and 'they' were a collective of groupthink commanders who froze whenever a case hit big on TV or in politics. This one had hit both. Bosch wasn't surprised by the call, just disappointed.

'The way I would read this thing is that they want to go by the numbers and nail it down tight,' Pratt said. 'So enjoy home duty and stay in touch.'

'Yeah, and what do you hear about Kiz?'

'Well, they don't have to worry about home duty with her. She's not going anywhere.'

'That's not what I mean.'

'I know what you mean.'

'And?' It was like peeling a label off a beer bottle. It never came all at once.

'And I think Kiz could be in some trouble. She was up on top with Olivas when Waits made his move. The question is, why didn't she take Waits out when she had the chance. It looks like she froze, Harry, and that means she could get hurt in this thing.'

Bosch nodded. Pratt's take on the situation seemed right on target. It made Bosch feel bad. Right now Rider had to fight to stay alive. Later she'd have to fight to keep her job. He would stand beside her the whole way.

'OK,' he said. 'Anything on Waits?'

'Nothing, man. He's in the wind. Probably in Mexico by now. If that guy knows what's best for him, he'll never raise his head above sea level again.'

Bosch wasn't so sure about that. Some instinct told him that Waits had not gone far. He thought about the Red Line subway Waits had disappeared into. He remembered the legend of Reynard the Fox and the secret castle.

'Harry, I gotta go,' Pratt said. 'You cool?'

'Yeah, right, cool. Thanks for running it down for me, Top.'

'All right, man. Technically, you're supposed to check in with me every day until we get the word you're back on active.'

'You got it.'

Bosch hung up the phone. A few minutes later, when Rachel came into the kitchen, he poured coffee into an insulated cup she had brought in with her the night before. She was dressed and ready for work.

'I don't have anything here for breakfast,' he said. 'We could go down the hill to Du-par's if you have time.'

'No, that's OK. I need to get going.' She tore open a pink packet of sugar substitute and dumped it into the coffee. 'What was the call you just got?'

'My boss. I just got sidelined while all of this is going on.'

'Oh, baby . . .' She came over and hugged him.

'In a way it's routine. The media and politics of the case make it a necessity. I'm on home duty until the OIS clears me of wrongdoing.'

'You going to be OK? What are you going to do?'

'I don't know. Home duty doesn't mean I have to stay home. So I'm going to the hospital to see if they'll let me hang with my partner for a while.'

'Want to have lunch?'

'Yeah, sure, that sounds good.'

They had quickly slipped into a domestic comfort that Bosch liked. It was almost as though they didn't have to talk.

'Look, I'm fine,' he said. 'You go to work. I'll call you.'

'OK.' She kissed him on the cheek before leaving.

Bosch drank a cup of coffee on the back deck while looking over the Cahuenga Pass. The skies were clear. It would be another beautiful day in paradise. He decided to go to Du-par's to eat breakfast on his own. He could pick up the papers, then take them to Kiz, maybe read them to her.

He decided to leave on the suit and tie he had dressed in before getting the call from Pratt. Home duty or not, he was going to act and look like a detective. He went to the bedroom closet and from a shelf he pulled down the box of case-file copies he had made when he had retired. He looked through the stacks until he found the copy of the Marie Gesto murder book.

He drove down the hill and up to Ventura Boulevard and followed it into Studio City. At Du-par's he bought copies of the *Los Angeles Times* and the *Daily News* out of racks in front of the restaurant, then went in and ordered French toast and coffee at the counter.

The Beachwood Canyon story was on the front page of both papers. Both displayed colour booking photos of Raynard Waits, and played up the hunt for the mad killer. The articles contained very few details about what had actually happened. According to the stories, information was being jealously guarded by those in charge. The short bios of the two cops killed in the shooting and the wounded detective were sketchy at best.

On the inside pages of both papers, sidebar stories quoted local pundits, who mostly said it was too early to tell whether the incident would help or hinder Rick O'Shea's candidacy. His opponent Gabriel Williams was quoted liberally, calling the incident a disgrace and laying all blame at O'Shea's feet. The papers said Bosch was under investigation by the department's OIS squad and could not be reached for comment. Neither noted that the OIS routinely investigated every shooting that involved a police officer.

Bosch finished his coffee and French toast, and left money for the bill and tip on the counter. Then he got in his car and drove to the hospital.

BOSCH KNOCKED ONCE on Kiz Rider's door and went in. His partner looked much better than before but still not even close to a hundred per cent. She was alert, and her eyes tracked him to the side of her bed. There was no longer a tube in her mouth but the right side of her face drooped, and Bosch immediately feared she had suffered a stroke during the night.

'Don't worry,' she said in slow, slurred words. 'They've made my neck numb and it's working on half of my face, too.'

He squeezed her hand. 'Other than that, how do you feel?'

'Not so good. It hurts, Harry. It really hurts.'

He nodded. 'Yeah, but you're on the road to recovery.'

'I hope so.'

She sounded depressed, and Bosch didn't know what to say. Fourteen years earlier, when he had been about her age, Bosch had woken up in the hospital after taking a bullet in his left shoulder. He still remembered the screaming pain every time the morphine wore off.

'I brought the papers. Want me to read 'em to you?'

'Yeah. Nothing good, I suppose.'

'No, nothing good.'

He held the *Times* front page up so she could see the mugshot of Waits. He then read the lead story and then the sidebar. When he was finished he looked over at her. She looked distressed.

'You OK?'

'You should've left me, Harry, and gone after him. You could've gotten him. Instead you saved me. Now look at the shit you're in.'

'It comes with the territory, Kiz. The only thing I could think about out there was getting you to the hospital. I feel really guilty about everything.'

'What exactly do you have to feel guilty about?'

'A lot. When I came out of retirement last year I made you leave the chief's office and partner me again. You wouldn't have been there yesterday if I—'

'Oh, please! Would you shut your mouth!' she said. 'No more of that. What else did you bring me?'

Bosch held up the copy of the Gesto murder book. 'Oh, nothing. I brought this to read if you were asleep. It's the copy of the Gesto file I made back when I retired the first time.'

'So what are you going to do with that?'

'Like I said, I was just going to read it. I keep thinking there's something I missed, something that's in here and I'm the only one who can find it.'

'Good luck. Why don't you sit on that chair and read your file. I think I'm going to go to sleep for a while.'

'OK, Kiz. I'll be quiet.'

He pulled the chair closer to the bed. As he sat down she spoke again.

'I'm not coming back, Harry.'

He looked at her. It was not what he wanted to hear but he wouldn't object. Not now, at least. 'Whatever you want, Kiz.'

'I shouldn't be a cop. I proved that yesterday.'

'What are you talking about? You're one of the best cops I know.'

He saw a tear roll down her cheek. 'I froze out there, Harry. I froze and I let him . . . just shoot me.'

'Don't do this to yourself, Kiz.'

'Those men are dead because of me. When he grabbed Olivas, I couldn't move. I just watched. I should have put him down, but I just stood there.'

'No, Kiz. You didn't have an angle on him. If you had fired you might have hit Olivas. After that it was too late.' He hoped she understood he was telling her what to say to the OIS.

'No, I have to own up to it. I—'

'Kiz, you want to quit, that's fine. I'll back you one hundred per cent. But I won't back you on this other shit. You understand?'

She tried to turn her face away from him but the bandages on her neck prevented her from turning. 'OK,' she said. More tears came down. 'You know, you should have gone up top.'

'What are you talking about?'

'If you had been up top, none of this would've happened. Because you wouldn't have hesitated, Harry. You would have blown him away.'

Bosch shook his head. 'Nobody knows how they're going to react in a situation until they're in that situation.'

'I froze.'

'Look, go to sleep. Get better and then make your decision. If you don't come back I will understand. But I'm always going to be your back-up, Kiz. No matter what happens and where you go.'

She used her left hand to wipe her face. 'Thanks, Harry.'

She closed her eyes and he watched as she finally gave it up. She mumbled something he couldn't understand and then was asleep. Bosch watched her for a while and thought about not having her as a partner any more. They had worked well together, like family. He would miss it.

He didn't want to think about the future right now. He opened the murder book and started with the initial crime report. He was about to turn to the witness reports when his phone vibrated in his pocket. He walked out into the hallway to take the call. It was Lieutenant Randolph from the OIS Unit.

'Sorry we're holding you off active while we take our time with this thing,' he said.

'It's all right. What can I do for you, Lieutenant?'

'I was hoping maybe you'd take a ride down here to Parker Center and look at this videotape we've got.'

'You have the tape from O'Shea's cameraman?'

There was a pause before Randolph answered. 'We have *a* tape from him, yes. I'm not sure it's a complete tape and that's what I want you to look at.'

'I'll be there in forty-five minutes.'

'Good. I'll be waiting. How's your partner?'

'She's still hanging in. I'm at the hospital now but she's still out of it.'

He hoped to delay Rider's OIS interview for as long as possible. In a few days, once she was off the painkillers and clear of mind, maybe she'd think better of volunteering that she had frozen when Waits made his move.

'We're waiting to hear when we can interview her,' Randolph said.

'Probably be a few days, I would think.'

'Probably. Anyway, see you soon. Thanks for coming in.'

Bosch closed the phone and went back into the room. Rider was still asleep. He picked the murder book up off the chair and left the room quietly.

He made good time on the drive in and called Rachel to tell her that lunch looked good, since he was already going to be downtown. She said she would make a reservation at the Water Grill for noon.

The OIS squad was on the third floor at Parker Center. Randolph had a private office with video equipment. He was sitting behind the desk while Osani got the tape ready. Randolph motioned Bosch to the only other seat.

'When did you get the tape?' Bosch asked.

'It was delivered this morning. It took Corvin twenty-four hours to remember he'd put it in one of those cargo pockets you mentioned. Of course, this was after I told him I had a witness who saw the tape go in the pocket.'

'And you think it's been doctored?'

'We'll know for sure after I give it to SID but, yeah, it's been edited. We found his camera at the crime scene, and Osani here was bright enough to write down the number on the counter. When you roll this tape the counter doesn't match. About two minutes of tape are missing.'

Osani started the tape, and Bosch watched as it began in the Sunset Ranch parking lot. There was an uninterrupted flow of raw video footage, which seemed to keep O'Shea at centre, until they all stopped at the top of the drop-off. Then there was a cut where it was presumed Corvin had turned the camera off. There was no discussion on the tape of whether Waits's handcuffs should be removed. The video cut from Rider saying they could use the SID ladder to Cafarelli returning with the ladder.

Osani stopped the tape so they could discuss it.

'It's likely that he did stop the camera while we waited for the ladder,' Bosch said. 'That would have taken ten minutes max. But he probably didn't stop it until after the back and forth about the cuffs.'

'Are you sure?'

'No, I'm just assuming. I wasn't watching Corvin. I was watching Waits. Did any of the other witnesses back me on this?'

'Cafarelli heard it. Corvin said he didn't and O'Shea said it never happened. So you got two from the LAPD saying yes and two from the DA's office saying no. Classic pissing match.'

'What about Maury Swann?'

'He says it is in his client's best interest to remain mute.'

Osani started the video again and it took them through to the clearing where Cafarelli used the gas probe to mark the location of the body. The shot was interrupted. The tape then documented the group's return to the ladder. Rider and Olivas went up to the top and Waits was uncuffed by Bosch. The prisoner climbed up, but the tape cut off just as he reached the upper rungs and Olivas was leaning down to grab him.

'That's it?' Bosch asked.

'That's it,' Randolph said.

'I remember after the shooting, when I told Corvin to leave the camera and come help with Kiz, he had it on his shoulder. He was rolling.'

'Yeah, well, he claimed he thought he was going to run short on tape. He wanted to keep some for when the diggers came in and excavated the body. So he turned the camera off while Waits was going up the ladder.'

'That make sense to you?' Bosch said.

'I don't know. You?'

'Nope. I think that's bullshit. He had the whole thing on tape.'

'That's just an opinion.'

'Whatever. The question is why cut the tape at this point? What was on it?'

'You tell me. You were there.'

'I told you everything I could remember.'

'Well, you better remember more. You're not in such good shape here. There's no discussion on the tape of whether the man should or shouldn't be cuffed. What is on the tape is you uncuffing him for the climb back up.'

Bosch realised that Randolph was right, and that the tape made him look like he had uncuffed Waits without discussing it with the others.

'O'Shea's setting me up.'

'Let me ask you something. When Waits grabbed the gun and started shooting, do you remember seeing O'Shea at that point?'

Bosch shook his head. 'I ended up on the ground with Olivas on top of me. I was worried about where Waits was. I don't know where O'Shea was, but he wasn't in my picture. He was behind me somewhere.'

'Maybe that's what Corvin had on the tape. O'Shea running like a coward.'

The word *coward* sparked something in Bosch. From the top of the drop-off, Waits had called someone a coward. Bosch remembered hearing the sound of running behind him. O'Shea had no weapon with which to protect himself, but for a candidate for top prosecutor in the county, running away under any circumstances would not look so good on the six o'clock news.

'I remember now,' he said. 'Waits called somebody a coward for running. It must've been O'Shea.'

'Mystery solved,' Randolph said.

Bosch turned back to the monitor. 'Can we back it up and look at that last part again?' he asked. 'Just before it cuts off, I mean.'

Osani worked the video and they watched it silently from the moment Waits was uncuffed for the second time. Bosch tried to use the images on the monitor to carry him into his own memory of what happened when Waits got to the top of the ladder. He remembered looking up and watching Olivas being swung round so that there was no clear shot at Waits. Then there were shots and Olivas was falling down the ladder. On the ground with Olivas on top of him, Bosch heard more shots and then the yelling.

The yelling. Forgotten in all the rush and panic. Waits had called O'Shea a coward for running. But he had said more than that.

Run you coward! How's your bullshit deal looking now?

Bosch had forgotten the taunt in the commotion and confusion. What was Waits saying by calling the agreement a 'bullshit deal'?

'What is it?' Randolph asked.

Bosch looked at him. 'Nothing. I was trying to concentrate.'

'It looked like you remembered something.'

'I just remembered how close I came to getting killed.' Bosch wanted to get out of there to work his discovery—to grind it down and analyse it under the microscope. 'Lieutenant, you have anything else for me right now?'

'Not right now. You call me when you remember what you can't remember.' Randolph gave Bosch a knowing look.

Bosch looked away. 'Right.'

He left the OIS office and went out to the elevator. He should have left the building then. But instead he pushed the button to go up.

REMEMBERING WHAT WAITS had yelled changed things. To Bosch it meant that something had been going on in Beachwood Canyon and it was something he'd had no clue about. His first thought now was to retreat and consider everything before making a move. But he planned to make the most of being in Parker Center before leaving.

He entered room 503, the offices of the Open-Unsolved Unit, and headed towards his desk. The squad room was almost vacant. Bosch had to walk by Abel Pratt's office, so he decided to be up-front. He stuck his head in the open door and saw his boss at his desk, eating raisins out of a little red box.

'Harry, what are you doing here?' Pratt asked.

'OIS called me down to look at the video O'Shea's guy took.'

'He's got the shooting on it?'

'Not quite. He claimed the camera was off.'

Pratt's eyebrows arched. 'Randolph doesn't believe him?'

'Hard to tell. Randolph's going to have SID check it. Anyway, listen, I thought I'd take a bunch of files and stuff back to Archives so it's not all lying around. Kiz had some files out, too.'

'That's probably a good idea,' Pratt said. 'Hey, I just heard from Tim and Rick. The autopsy was this morning and they got the ID. Marie Gesto, confirmed. They got it on the dental.'

Bosch nodded as he considered the finality of this news. The search for Marie Gesto was over.

'I guess that's it, then.'

'They said you were going to make the next-of-kin call on it.'

'Yeah. But I'll probably wait until tonight, when Dan Gesto comes home from work. It'll be better if both parents are together.'

'However you want to handle it. I'll call the ME and tell them not to put it out until tomorrow.'

'Thanks. Did Tim or Rick tell you if they got a cause of death?'

'Looks like manual strangulation. Hyoid was fractured.'

He touched the front of his neck in case Bosch didn't remember where the fragile hyoid bone was located. Bosch had worked only about a hundred cases in his time, but he didn't bother saying anything.

'Sorry, Harry. I know you're close to this one.'

Bosch nodded, more to himself than to Pratt. He went to his desk, remembering how thirteen years earlier he had been all but convinced that Marie Gesto would never be found. It was strange how things turned out.

He started gathering all the files associated with the Waits investigation. Then he walked round to his partner's desk to gather the files she had on Daniel Fitzpatrick, and saw two big plastic cartons on the floor. He opened one, and found that it contained the records salvaged from the burned-out pawnshop. He decided he would take these as well, but that would mean two trips past Pratt's open door, which would give his boss two opportunities to become curious about what he was really up to.

But then Bosch got lucky. Pratt stepped out of his office.

'I don't know who decided raisins are a good snack food,' he said. 'You want anything from downstairs, Harry? A doughnut or something?'

'No thanks, I'm fine.' Bosch noticed that Pratt was holding one of his West Indies guidebooks. 'Doing some research?' he asked.

'Yeah, checking things out. Says here you can buy an old sugar mill on eight acres for less than four hundred. Hell, I'll clear that on my house alone.'

It was probably true. Bosch had never been to Pratt's home but knew that he owned a property up in Sun Valley big enough to keep a couple of horses on. He'd lived there twenty years and was sitting on a real-estate gold mine.

'You want to make sugar?' Bosch asked.

'No, man, it's just what the property was used for at one time. Now you'd fix it up and make it a bed-and-breakfast or something.'

Pratt left the office and Bosch waited thirty seconds for him to get the elevator. He then put a stack of files on one of the cartons and carried it all down to his car. He was able to get back before Pratt returned, then took the second carton and left. No one questioned what he was doing.

After pulling out of the pay lot, Bosch checked his watch and saw that he had an hour to kill before lunch. The city's main library was in the same block as the restaurant, so he decided to go there and do some file work.

He parked in the garage beneath the building, then carried the Gesto murder book with him into the elevator. Once inside the sprawling library, he found a cubicle in a reference room and finished his review. Moving through the book in order, he didn't reach the Investigative Chronology until the end. Nothing about the investigative moves made or the calls received struck him as any more important than they had done originally.

Then suddenly he was struck by what he had not seen. He flipped back the pages until he came to the 51 for September 29, 1993, and looked for the entry on the call that Jerry Edgar had taken from Robert Saxon.

It wasn't there.

Bosch leaned forward to read the document more clearly. This made no sense. In the official murder book the entry was there. Raynard Waits's alias, Robert Saxon. The call was at 6.40 p.m., September 29, 1993. Bosch had seen it clear as day in O'Shea's office. He had studied it, knowing it was an error that had allowed Waits another thirteen years of freedom to kill.

But the entry was not in Bosch's copy of the murder book.

What the hell?

At first Bosch couldn't put it together. The copy in front of him had been made four years earlier, when Bosch had decided to retire. He had secretly copied murder books from a handful of open cases that still gnawed at his insides. They were his retirement cases. His plan had been to solve them at his leisure, before finally letting the mission go and sitting on a beach in Mexico with a fishing pole in one hand and a Corona in the other.

But Bosch had learned that the mission was best served with a badge, and he came back to the job. After he was assigned to the Open-Unsolved Unit, one of the first murder books he pulled out of Archives was the Gesto case, the live record updated each time anybody worked it. What he had in front of him was a copy that had not been updated in four years. Even so, how could one have a notation entered in 1993 while the other one didn't?

Logic dictated only one answer. The official record had been tampered with. The Saxon notation had been added after Bosch made his copy. That left a four-year window during which the false notation could have been added, but common sense told Bosch he was dealing with days, not years.

Just a few days earlier, Freddy Olivas had taken possession of the murder book. It was Olivas who had brought the Robert Saxon entry to light.

Bosch flipped through the chronology again. Almost all the pages were filled in completely. Only the page marked September 29 had space at the bottom. Olivas could have removed the page, typed in the Saxon entry, then put it back. Back in 1993 Bosch and Edgar did the 51s on a typewriter in the Hollywood squad room. It was all done on computer now but there were still typewriters around most squad rooms for the old-school cops.

Bosch felt a mixture of relief and anger start to overtake him. The burden of guilt over the mistake he and Edgar had supposedly made was lifting. But he couldn't embrace the feeling—not yet—because of the growing rage he felt at being victimised by Olivas. He stood up and walked from the cubicle into the library's main rotunda. He felt like yelling, exorcising the demon, but he kept quiet. A security guard walked across the floor of the cavernous structure. Bosch watched him go, then went back to the cubicle.

He tried to think through what had happened. Olivas had typed a two-line entry into the 51, which said that Robert Saxon had called to report seeing Marie Gesto at the Mayfair supermarket on the afternoon she had disappeared. That was all. It wasn't the content of the call that was important to Olivas. It was the caller. Olivas had wanted to get Raynard Waits into the murder book somehow. Why? Because he needed to tie Waits to Gesto? But Waits was about to admit he murdered Gesto, and there could be no stronger tie. He was even going to lead the authorities to the body.

Ultimately, Bosch was confounded by the risk Olivas had taken. He had tampered with the official record of the murder investigation for seemingly little reason or gain. Now he was dead and could not be confronted. There was no one to answer why.

Except maybe Raynard Waits.

'How's your bullshit deal looking now?'

And maybe Rick O'Shea.

In a moment it came together. Bosch suddenly knew why Olivas had put the spectre of Raynard Waits into the Marie Gesto murder book. He saw it with a clarity that left him no room for doubt.

Raynard Waits didn't kill Marie Gesto.

He jumped up, gathered up the files and hurried through the rotunda towards the exit. His footfalls echoed behind him in the great room like a crowd of people chasing him. He looked back but there was nobody there.

8

Bosch had lost track of time in the library. He was late. Rachel was already seated and waiting for him. She was holding a large menu that obscured the look of annoyance on her face as Bosch was led to the table by a waiter.

'Sorry,' Bosch said as he sat down.

'It's OK,' she replied. 'But I already ordered for myself. I didn't know if you were going to show or not.' She handed the menu across to him.

He handed it to the waiter. 'I'll have what she's having,' he said.

The waiter hurried away. Rachel smiled at him, but not in a nice way.

'You're not going to like it. You'd better call him back.'

'Why? I like seafood.'

'I ordered the sashimi. You told me you like your seafood cooked.'

He decided he deserved to pay for arriving late. 'It all goes to the same place. Forget about it. We need to talk. I need your help, Rachel.'

'With what? What's wrong?'

'I don't think Raynard Waits killed Marie Gesto.'

'What do you mean? He led you to her body. Or was it not Marie?'

'It was definitely her. ID was confirmed at the autopsy today.'

'So if he confessed, and led you to her, how can he not be the killer?'

'Because something is going on that we don't know about. Olivas and O'Shea had some sort of play going with him. I'm not sure what it was but it all went to hell in Beachwood Canyon.'

She held up her hands in a hold-it-right-there gesture. 'Why don't you start at the beginning. Only tell me facts. No theory, no conjecture.'

He told her everything, starting with the tampering with the murder book by Olivas. He told her what Waits had yelled at O'Shea in Beachwood Canyon and what had been edited out of the field-trip video. During the fifteen minutes it took him, their lunch was served. Bosch felt lucky to be the one doing all the talking. It gave him a ready excuse not to eat the raw fish.

Rachel's mind had clearly gone to work on everything. 'It doesn't make sense,' she said. 'Waits is already connected to the case through his confession and leading you to the body. So why bother with the murder book?'

Bosch leaned across the table. 'Two things. One, it put me in a position of being preconditioned to believe the confession. But it was also about knocking me off my game.'

She looked at him. 'You'd better explain that.'

'Olivas put that line in the chronology and then threw it in my face. He knew that if I believed it, then I would believe that my partner and I had horribly messed up in '93. The weight of all those women Waits had killed would be on me. And it would bring things to a raw edge when I finally came face to face with the guy. It would distract me.'

'From what?'

'From the fact that Waits didn't kill her. He confessed, but he didn't kill her. He made some sort of deal with Olivas and probably O'Shea to take the fall for it because he was already going down for all the others. I was so overcome with hatred for him that I didn't have my eyes on the prize.'

'But if he didn't kill her, how did he lead you right to her body?'

'It could have been done. He could have been schooled in his cell by Olivas. It could have been a Hansel and Gretel trick, a trail marked in a way that only he would notice. I'm going back up to Beachwood this afternoon.'

Bosch reached over and took her empty plate and exchanged it with his untouched plate. She didn't object.

'But how did Olivas know the details to give Waits?' she asked. 'How did he know where she was buried? Are you saying Olivas killed Marie Gesto?'

Bosch shook his head emphatically. 'No, I'm saying that Olivas was gotten to by the killer. He and O'Shea. The real killer came to them and made some sort of a deal. It sounds a little far-fetched I know, but—'

'More than a little. Harry, this just . . .'

She didn't finish. She pushed the sashimi on her plate around with her chop sticks but ate very little.

The waiter approached the table. 'You didn't like your sashimi?'

'No, I . . . I guess I wasn't very hungry.'

'She doesn't know what she's missing,' Bosch said, smiling. 'I thought it was great.'

The waiter took the plates and said he would be back with dessert menus.

'"I thought it was great",' Walling said in a mocking voice. 'You jerk.'

'Sorry.'

The waiter brought the dessert menus and they handed them back and ordered coffee. Walling remained quiet, and Bosch decided to wait her out.

'Why now?' she finally asked.

Bosch shook his head. 'I don't know exactly.'

'When was the last time you actively worked on the case?'

'About five months ago. The last video I showed you the other night— that was the last time I worked it.'

'What did you do besides pull Garland in again?'

'Everything. I talked to everybody. I knocked on all the same doors again. I only brought Garland in at the end.'

'You think it was Garland who got to Olivas?'

'For Olivas and maybe O'Shea to make a deal, it would have had to be somebody with juice. Lots of money and power. The Garlands have both.'

She shook her head as the waiter came with their coffee. He saw the doubt creep back into her eyes.

'What?' he said when the waiter had left.

'I don't know, it's just . . . it's such a long shot. Look at it from Waits's view of things. Why would he confess to a murder he didn't commit?'

Bosch made a dismissive gesture with his hands. 'Because he had nothing to lose. He was already going down as the Echo Park Bagman. His only shot at living was to confess to his crime, and if, say, the investigator and the prosecutor wanted him to add another killing in for good measure, what was Waits going to say? No deal? Don't kid yourself. They had the leverage.'

She nodded.

'And there was something else,' Bosch added. 'He knew there'd be a field trip, and I bet that gave him hope that he might get a shot at an escape.'

She nodded again. They were silent for a long moment. The waiter came with the bill. Lunch was over. Despite Rachel's protestations, Bosch paid. It had to have been the most expensive lunch he had never eaten.

'So what are you going to do?' she asked as they walked to the door.

'Like I told you, next stop Beachwood Canyon to look for markers.'

'Well, good luck. I think you're going to need it.'

'Thanks, Rachel. Will I see you tonight?'

'If I'm not held up. There's word of a case coming our way from Washington headquarters. How about if I call you?'

BOSCH DROVE HOME to change from his suit into jeans and a pullover. He called Jerry Edgar to tell him about the doctored 51 in the Gesto murder file. The conversation was brief but he could hear the anger and relief in Edgar's voice. Then he drove over to Beachwood Canyon.

The parking lot below Sunset Ranch was empty. He got out of his car and pulled out a coiled thirty-foot length of rope from the trunk. He guessed that if there were markers for a Hansel and Gretel trail, they would be at the bottom of the mudslide embankment. He headed that way.

At the top of the precipice, he looped the rope round the trunk of the oak and rappelled down. He left the rope in place and started walking towards the grave site, looking for carvings in the trunks of the trees, anything that Waits might have used to lead the way. Bosch got to the site without seeing a single indication of a marked trail. But he thought it was possible that whatever markings had been there had been trampled over and obliterated by investigators and technicians the day before.

Refusing to give up, he made his way back to the embankment, then turned and looked towards the grave site. He tried to put his mind into the position Waits was in. He had never been to the spot before, yet he had to choose a direction quickly while everyone else watched. *How did he do it?*

Bosch stood motionless, thinking and looking off into the woods. After five minutes he had the answer.

In the middle distance, on the sight line to the grave site, was a tall eucalyptus tree, split at ground level into two fully mature trunks. In the split, about ten feet off the ground, a fallen branch had become lodged horizontally between the trunks, creating a clearly recognisable inverted *A*.

When Bosch reached the eucalyptus, he scanned again until he picked up on another obvious anomaly. It was a young California oak, its natural symmetry lost because one of the lower limbs was missing. Bosch walked over to it, pulled himself up into the tree and examined the break. Someone had sawn across the top of the branch, then pulled down on it to break it.

Bosch dropped to the ground and looked in the direction of the final clearing. He was less than twenty yards away and he was easily able to pick out what he believed to be the last marker. High up in the oak tree that shaded the grave site was a nest that looked like the home of a large bird.

He walked to the clearing and looked up. The hair scrunchie that Waits had said marked the spot had been removed by the Forensics team. Bosch could not see the nest from directly beneath.

As his eyes dropped to the open grave, he remembered the disturbance in the soil he had noticed the day before. He had credited it to animals foraging. Now he believed it had been left after the first digging into the soil to confirm the grave. Olivas had been out here before any of them. He had either been told where to find the grave or had been led to it by the real killer.

Bosch had been putting the scenario together for several seconds before he realised he was hearing voices, two men in conversation. They were coming from the same direction Bosch had come from.

He moved quickly across the clearing, and picked his way back through the brush. He got to the eucalyptus and saw Osani and another man he assumed was from OIS. There was a ladder on the facing now, and Bosch realised that the men were cleaning up the official report. They were taking distance measurements that had been forgotten or deemed unnecessary the day before. Today, in light of the political fallout, everything was necessary. It looked as though they were measuring various lengths from the spot where Bosch had been to the positions where Waits, Olivas and Rider had been.

A cellphone rang where the men were working. Bosch peeked round the tree and saw Osani take a phone off his belt. He listened to the caller and then took a sweeping look around the woods. Bosch ducked back.

'No, Lieutenant,' Osani said. 'We don't see him. The car's in the lot but we don't see anybody out here.'

Osani listened some more and said yes several times before closing the phone. He went back to work, and within another minute or so they had what they needed. The two OIS men climbed the ladder, then pulled it up the embankment. It was at that moment that Osani noticed the rope looped round the oak. He pulled it from the trunk, and a few minutes later they were gone, loudly trudging through the woods. Bosch went to the embankment but waited until he could no longer hear them to climb up.

When he got to the parking lot, there was no sign of them. Bosch's phone started vibrating. He recognised the number as an Open-Unsolved line.

He took the call. 'This is Bosch.'

'Harry, where are you?' It was Abel Pratt. There was urgency in his voice.

'Nowhere. Why?'

'Where *are* you?'

Something told Bosch that Pratt knew exactly where he was. 'I'm in Beachwood Canyon. What's going on?'

The urgent tone was replaced with one of annoyance. 'I just got a call from Lieutenant Randolph at OIS. He says there's a Mustang registered to you in the lot up there. I tell him that's strange, because Harry Bosch is supposed to be a million miles away from the investigation in Beachwood Canyon.'

Bosch thought quickly. 'Look, I'm not investigating anything. I lost my challenge coin out here yesterday. I'm looking for it.'

'What?'

'My RHD chip. It must have come out of my pocket when I was sliding down the embankment. I got home last night and it wasn't in my pocket.'

As he spoke, Bosch reached into his pocket and pulled out the heavy metal coin he was claiming to have lost. Called a challenge coin or chip, it was a carry-over from the practice of elite military units. Upon acceptance into the unit, a soldier is given a challenge coin and is expected to carry it always. At any time a fellow unit member can ask to see the coin. In a bar or canteen, if the soldier fails to be carrying it, then he picks up the tab. The tradition had been observed for several years in the Robbery-Homicide Division. Bosch had been given his coin upon returning from retirement.

'Forget the coin, Harry,' Pratt said angrily. 'You can replace it for ten bucks. Go home and *stay away* from the investigation. Am I clear?'

'You're clear.'

'Besides, if you lost your coin out there Forensics would have found it already. They went out there with a metal detector looking for cartridges.'

'Yeah, I sort of forgot about that, Top,' Bosch said. 'I was bored and decided to come look for it. I saw Randolph's people and decided to keep my head down. I just didn't think they'd call in my plate.'

'Well, they did. Then I got the call. I don't like blowback like this, Harry.'

'I'm going home right now.'

'Good. Stay there.'

Pratt clicked off and Bosch closed his phone. He flipped the heavy coin into the air, caught it in his palm and pocketed it. He then walked to his car.

SOMETHING ABOUT BEING TOLD to go home made Bosch not go home. After leaving Beachwood Canyon he made a stop at St Joe's to check in on Kiz Rider. She was now out of the ICU. She didn't have a private room but the other bed in the room was empty. They often did that for cops.

Speaking was still difficult for her and her depression had not lifted. Bosch didn't stay long. He finally went home as instructed, hauling the cartons and files he had collected earlier from Open-Unsolved.

He put the cartons on the dining-room floor and spread the files out on the table. He knew there was enough to occupy him for at least a couple of days. First and foremost was the copy of the investigative record in the current Waits case, turned over by Olivas but not studied closely because the Fitzpatrick and Gesto cases were priorities. Bosch also had the Fitzpatrick murder book, his secret copy of the Gesto murder book, and the two plastic cartons containing salvaged pawn records.

Bosch found himself a pen and a legal pad. After twenty minutes, his freeform thoughts had filled less than half a page.

>   / arrest
> Echo Park
>   \ escape (Red Line)
> Who is Waits? Where is the castle? (destination: Echo Park)
> Beachwood Canyon—set up, false confession
> Who benefits? Why now?

Bosch looked at the last two questions, then reversed their order. *Why now?* He had to believe the entire Beachwood Canyon plan had come about because he'd knocked too hard on someone's door.

This conclusion led to the answer to the other question, *Who benefits?*

Bosch wrote: *Anthony Garland—Hancock Park oil.*

But there was no evidence directly connecting Garland to the murder. Bosch hadn't been made privy to the evidence developed during the autopsy, but he doubted that after thirteen years there would be anything usable—DNA or forensics that could tie the killer to the body.

Garland was a suspect under the 'replacement victim' theory. That is, his rage towards the woman who had dropped him led him to kill a woman who reminded him of her. The shrinks would call it a long-shot theory, but Bosch now moved it front and centre. Garland was the son of a wealthy oil baron. O'Shea was in a highly contested election battle, and money was the gasoline that kept a campaign engine running. It was not inconceivable that a quiet approach had been made to T. Rex Garland, and a deal struck. O'Shea gets the money he needs to win the election, Olivas gets the head investigator nod, and Waits takes the fall while Garland takes a ride.

It was said that LA was a sunny place for shady people.

'Run, you coward! How's your bullshit deal looking now?'

He just had to find the angle from which to work it. He picked up the file marked WAITS—BACKGROUND and started to read.

FROM THE STANDPOINT of law enforcement, Raynard Waits was a rarity as a murder suspect. When his van was pulled over in Echo Park, the LAPD in effect had captured a killer the department wasn't even looking for. In fact, Waits was a killer no department or agency was looking for. The case came to Freddy Olivas and his partner, Ted Colbert, with a momentum that simply dragged them towards prosecution. It was a slam dunk, and that precluded the need to know exactly who they had in custody and what had brought him to be in that van on that street at that time.

Consequently, little in the file helped Bosch. The background data on Waits was either provided by the suspect himself or culled by Olivas and Colbert during routine computer searches. Bosch completed his read-through in twenty minutes. When he was finished, he again had less than half a page of notes on his pad. He had constructed a short timeline that charted the suspect's arrests, admissions and use of names.

Apr. 30 '92 —Daniel Fitzpatrick murdered, Hollywood
May 18 '92 —Raynard Waits, DOB Nov. 3 '71, DL issued, Hollywood
Feb. 1 '93 —Robert Saxon, DOB Nov. 3 '75—arrested, prowling
—DL thumbprint ID'd as Raynard Waits, DOB Nov 3 '71
Sep. 9 '93 —Marie Gesto abducted, Hollywood
May 11 '05—Raynard Waits, DOB Nov 3 '71, arrested Echo Park

Bosch noticed that Waits always gave the same month and day of birth, and while he once offered 1975 as his birth year in an attempt to be considered a juvenile, he uniformly gave 1971 at other times. Bosch knew that people switching identities often changed their name but kept some details the same to avoid forgetting basic information—an obvious giveaway.

He also knew from earlier in the week that there was no birth record of Raynard Waits or Robert Saxon with the November 3 birth date in Los Angeles County. He had concluded from this that both names were false, but now he considered that maybe Waits, or whoever he was, kept his real date of birth as he changed his name.

Bosch looked at the close proximity between the date of the Fitzpatrick murder and the date of issue of Waits's driver's licence. It was less than a month. According to the records, Waits did not apply for the licence until he was twenty. Bosch thought it unlikely that a boy growing up in the auto-topia of LA would wait until he was twenty to get his driver's licence. It was yet one more indication that Raynard Waits was not his real name

Bosch started to feel it. Like a surfer waiting for the right swell, he felt his wave coming in. He thought that what he was looking at was the birth of a new identity. Eighteen days after he murdered Daniel Fitzpatrick under cover of the riots, the man who killed him had walked into a DMV office and applied for a driver's licence, under a false name and using a phoney birth certificate. Something about the murder caused him to change his identity. In his confession, Waits had characterised it as a thrill kill, depicting Fitzpatrick as chosen at random. But if the killer had no previous connection to the victim, then why did he act almost immediately to reinvent himself? Within eighteen days, Raynard Waits had been born.

To Bosch, the conclusion was obvious. Fitzpatrick could, in fact, be linked in some way to his killer. And that was why his killer changed his name.

Bosch needed to stay up on the wave. He went to the stereo and put in the jazz masterpiece *Kind of Blue*. It never failed to give him a charge. 'All

Blues' was the first song out of the shuffle, and it was like being dealt black-jack at a twenty-five-dollar table. It was his favourite and he let it ride.

Back at the table he opened the Fitzpatrick murder book and started to read, looking for the hidden connection. The investigation of Fitzpatrick's death had been cursory. No witnesses were located, and no forensic evidence found other than the can of lighter fluid, which had been wiped clean. Most of the shop's records had been destroyed by fire or water. What was left was put in two cartons and ignored. The murder book was so thin that Bosch finished his read-through in less than twenty minutes. He had taken no notes, got no ideas. He felt the tide ebbing.

He thought about getting a beer out of the refrigerator and attacking the case again the next day. Then the front door opened and Rachel Walling walked in, carrying takeout cartons from Chinese Friends. Bosch stacked the reports on the dining-room table so there would be room to eat. Rachel brought plates from the kitchen and opened the cartons. Bosch got out two Anchor Steams, happy he'd gone high end the last time he bought beer.

They small-talked for a while and then he told her what he had been doing since lunch. He could tell she wasn't convinced by his description of the trail he'd found in Beachwood Canyon. But when he showed her the timeline, she readily agreed about the killer's changing of ID after Fitzpatrick. She also agreed they might have his real birth date.

Bosch looked down at the two plastic cartons on the floor. 'Then I guess it's worth the shot,' he said.

She leaned over to see what he was looking at. 'What are those?'

'Pawn slips mostly. Nobody's ever looked through them all.'

'Is that what we're doing tonight, Harry?'

He looked up at her and smiled. He nodded.

After they had finished eating, Bosch lugged the cartons onto the back deck and got two empty cardboard boxes from the carport. They sat down in deck chairs and began the work.

Bosch took the top off his carton and used it to wave away the fumes that came out. Pink pawn slips and 3 x 5 cards had been put in haphazardly as if with a shovel. Many of the slips had stuck together while wet, and the ink on others was smeared and unreadable. Bosch looked over at Rachel.

'This is bad, Harry,' she said.

'I know. Just do the best you can. It might be our last hope.'

Bosch brought wads of slips up to his lap and started going through them, attempting to make out the name, address and birth date of each customer. Each time he looked at a slip, he checked the top corner with a red pencil and dropped it into the box on the other side of his chair.

They were at it a solid half-hour, working without conversation, when Bosch heard the phone in the kitchen ring. Knowing it might be a call from his daughter in Hong Kong, he got up.

'I didn't even know you had a land line,' Walling said.

'Not many people do.' He grabbed the phone on the eighth ring. It wasn't his daughter. It was Abel Pratt.

'Just checking on you,' Pratt said. 'I figure if I get you on the house line, then you're really home.'

'Look, home duty does not mean I have to be at home twenty-four-seven. I checked with the union.'

'I know, I know. What are you doing?'

'I'm sitting on the back deck with a friend. We're having a beer and enjoying the night air. Is that OK with you, Top?'

'Anybody I know?'

'I doubt it. She doesn't like cops.'

Pratt laughed and it seemed that Bosch had finally put him at ease. 'Then I'll let you get back to it. Good night, Harry.'

Bosch hung up, checked the refrigerator for beer and returned to the deck empty-handed. Rachel was waiting for him with a water-stained 3 x 5 card attached to a pawn slip with a paperclip.

'Got it,' she said, handing it to him.

Bosch read the card. Its smeared blue ink was still legible.

Unsatisfied Customer—Feb. 12 '92
Customer complained property sold before 90-day period expired.
Shown pawn slip and corrected. Customer complained 90 days
should not include weekends and holidays. Cursed/slammed door.

The pawn slip carried the name Robert Foxworth, the date of birth November 3, 1971, and an address on Fountain in Hollywood. The item pawned on October 8, 1991, for eighty dollars, was listed as an 'heirloom medallion'.

'The DOB matches,' Rachel said. 'Plus the name connects on two levels.'

'What do you mean?'

'Well, he took Robert forward when he used Robert Saxon and he took the fox in Foxworth forward when he used Raynard.'

'Maybe we just found another alias.'

'Maybe. But at least it's something you didn't have before.'

She was right. Bosch pulled out his phone, called central dispatch and ran the name and birth date. Then he thanked the operator and hung up.

'Nothing,' he said. 'Not even a driver's licence.'

'But that's good,' Rachel said. 'Don't you see? Robert Foxworth would be about to turn thirty-five right now. If there's no history or current licence, then that's further confirmation that he's either dead or he became someone else. Is there a way to check defunct driver's licences? If he got a licence when he turned sixteen, it would have expired when he switched identities.'

Bosch considered this. He knew that the state did not start requiring a thumbprint for licensed drivers until the early nineties. So Foxworth could have got a driver's licence in the late eighties and there would be no way to connect him to his new identity as Raynard Waits.

'I could check with the DMV in the morning,' he said.

'What do you think about this medallion he pawned?'

'I have no idea.'

'The fact that he wanted to get it back is interesting. Makes me think maybe it wasn't stolen. Maybe it belonged to someone in his family.'

Bosch nodded, then yawned, and all at once realised how tired he was. He'd been running all day just to get to this name. Rachel noticed.

'Harry, I say we quit while we're ahead and have another beer,' she said.

'I don't know how far ahead we are but I could use another beer,' Bosch said. 'There's only one problem with that.'

'What?'

'No more beer.'

'Harry, you invite a girl over to do your dirty work and all you give her is one beer? What's wrong with you? What about wine?'

Bosch shook his head sadly. 'But I'm on my way to the store.'

'Good. I'm on my way to the bedroom. I'll wait for you there.'

'Then I won't delay.'

'Make mine a red wine, will you?'

'I'm on it.'

Bosch hurried from the house. He had parked at the kerb so that Rachel could use the carport if she came over. As he walked out of the front door, he noticed a silver SUV at the opposite kerb two houses down. It suddenly took off without its lights on. It sped north round the bend and disappeared.

Bosch jumped in his car and headed after it. He drove as fast as he could safely go. Within two minutes he had followed the curving street to the four-way stop at Mulholland Drive. There was no sign of the SUV.

'Shit!'

Bosch sat at the intersection for a long moment. He decided that it either meant nothing or it meant someone was watching his house. But at the moment there was nothing he could do. He turned left and drove down Mulholland at a safe speed. There was a liquor store near Lankershim. He headed there, checking the rearview mirror the whole way.

HOME DUTY or not, Bosch dressed in a suit the next morning before heading out. He knew it would give him an aura of authority and confidence while dealing with government bureaucrats. And by twenty minutes after nine it had paid off. He had a solid lead. The Department of Motor Vehicles' archives had produced a licence issued to a Robert Foxworth on November 3, 1987, the day he turned sixteen. It was never renewed.

The address on the licence was the lead. It listed Foxworth's residence as the Los Angeles County Department of Children and Family Services, 3075 Wilshire Blvd. In 1987 he had been a juvenile ward of the county. He either had no parents or they had been declared unfit to raise him, and he was either housed in one of the department's youth halls or in foster care. Bosch knew all of this because he, too, had been a ward of the county.

As Bosch stepped out of the DMV offices, his cellphone vibrated and he answered it without looking at the screen, hoping that it would be Rachel and that he'd be able to share the good news.

'Harry, where are you? No one answered the home line.'

It was Pratt. Bosch was getting tired of his constant checking up on him.

'I'm on my way to visit Kiz. Is that all right?'

'Sure, except you're supposed to check in with me every day.'

'It's not even ten o'clock!'

'I'm just trying to look out for you, Harry. You heard the latest, I take it.'

Bosch stopped in his tracks. 'They caught Waits?'

'No, I wish. Some girl got snatched off the street last night, pulled into a van on Hollywood Boulevard. One of the new street cameras caught part of the abduction. I haven't seen it but they say it's Waits. There's a press conference at eleven and they're going to show the tape.'

Bosch felt a dull thud pound in his chest. He had been right about Waits not leaving town. He wished now he had been wrong. As he had these thoughts, he realised that he still thought of the killer as Raynard Waits, and always would, even if he was truly Robert Foxworth.

'Did they get a plate off the van?' Bosch asked.

'No, it was covered. All they put out was that it was a white Econoline van. Like the other one he used but older. Look, I've gotta go. Hopefully, this is the last day. OIS will finish up and you'll be back in the unit.'

'Yeah, that would be good. But listen, in his confession Waits said he had a different van in the nineties. Maybe the task force should get somebody to look through old DMV registrations under his name.'

'I'll tell them. Stay close to home, and give Kiz my regards.'

Bosch closed the phone, happy he'd come up with the Kiz line on the spot. But he was becoming a good liar with Pratt, and that didn't make him happy.

He got into his car and drove to Wilshire Boulevard with an increased sense of urgency. Waits had abducted another woman, but she might still be alive.

The DCFS offices were crowded. He waited at a records counter for fifteen minutes before a clerk told him there was indeed a juvenile file relating to Robert Foxworth, DOB November 3, 1971, but that to see it he would need a court order authorising his search.

Bosch just smiled, too excited to be upset by one more frustration. As he stepped back out into the sunlight, he knew he was at a crossroads. If he applied for a search warrant seeking the DCFS records without departmental approval he would be completely going off the reservation, conducting a rogue investigation and committing a fireable offence.

He figured he could take what he had to Randolph at OIS, or he could go the rogue route and accept the consequences. Since coming back from retirement, Bosch had felt less constricted by departmental rules. He pulled out his phone and made the one call he knew might save him from making a choice between bad options. Rachel answered on the second ring.

'So what's happening over there in Tactical?' he asked.

'Oh, we always have something happening. How did it go downtown? Did you hear Waits abducted another woman?'

Bosch told her he had heard, then related his morning activities.

'So what are you going to do?' she asked.

'Well, I'm thinking about seeing if the FBI might join the case.'

'And what would carry it across the federal threshold?'

'You know, corruption of public officials, campaign finance violations, cats and dogs living together—the usual stuff.'

She stayed serious. 'I don't know, Harry. You open that door and there's no telling where it will go.'

'Look, I need a search warrant. If I go off the reservation to get one I probably won't be able to come back on again. It will be the last straw with Pratt, that's for sure. But if I can say I was brought into a federal investigation, that would give me a valid explanation. It would give me an out. All I want is Foxworth's DCFS file. I think it will lead us to whatever is in Echo Park.'

She was quiet for a long moment. 'Where are you now?'

'I'm still at DCFS.'

'Go get a doughnut or something. I'll be there as soon as I can.'

'You sure?'

'No, but that's what we're going to do.' She hung up.

Bosch closed his phone. Instead of a doughnut, he went to a newspaper box and got the morning edition of the *Times*. He took a seat on the planter that ran along the length of the building and looked through the paper.

There was no story on the abduction on Hollywood Boulevard because that had occurred during the night. The Waits coverage had moved off the front page but it was still extensive. The most prominent report was on the nationwide search for the escaped serial killer. Most of the information had been rendered obsolete by the events of the night.

Bosch finished reading the stories and there was still no sign of Rachel. He started pacing in front of the building, feeling anxious. She finally pulled up in a federal cruiser. He crossed the sidewalk as she was getting out.

'What's the plan?' he said by way of greeting.

'What, no "How are you doing?" or "Thanks for coming"?'

'Thanks for coming. What's the plan?'

They walked into the building.

'The plan is the federal plan. I go in and draw down on the man in charge the full force and weight of the government of this great country. I raise the spectre of terrorism and he gives us the file.'

'You call that a plan?'

'It's worked pretty well for us for more than fifty years. Which way?'

He pointed straight ahead. 'I didn't wait forty minutes for this, Rachel.'

'You have a better idea?'

'I *had* a better idea. A federal search warrant, remember?'

'That was a nonstarter, Bosch. This is better. In and out.'

She was two paces in front of him now, moving with federal momentum. Bosch secretly started to believe. She moved through the double doors that said RECORDS with an authority that could not be questioned.

The clerk Bosch had dealt with was speaking with another citizen. In one smooth move, Walling stepped up to the counter and drew her credentials.

'FBI. I need to see your office manager in regard to a matter of urgency.'

The clerk looked at her. 'I will be with you as soon as I—'

'You're with me now, honey. Go get your boss or I'll go get him.'

The woman made a face that seemed to indicate she had never encountered such rudeness. Without a word, she walked to a door behind a row of cubicles. In less than a minute she stepped back out, followed by a man.

He came over to Rachel. 'I'm Mr Osborne. Over this way, please.'

A swing door at the far end of the counter was buzzed open and they followed Osborne to his office. Rachel showed him her credentials.

'Mr Osborne, I work for the Tactical Intelligence Unit here in Los Angeles. And this is Detective Harry Bosch of the LAPD. We've learned that a file exists pertaining to a Robert Foxworth, date of birth November 3, '71. It is vitally important we review that file immediately.'

'The records of our juvenile wards are not open to the public without—'

'Sir, Robert Foxworth is no longer a juvenile. He is thirty-four years old. The file might contain information that will lead us to the containment of a very grave threat to this city.'

'But you have to understand that we are not—'

'I understand that if we don't see that file now, we could be talking about a loss of human life. You don't want that on your conscience, Mr Osborne. That's why we are on the same team. I'll make a deal with you, sir. We will review the file with you watching. In the meantime, I will instruct a team member at Tactical to see that a search warrant is signed by a judge today.'

'Well . . . I'd have to call it up from Archives personally.'

'Thank you, Mr Osborne. We don't have a lot of time, sir.'

As the man left the office, Rachel looked at Bosch with a slight smile. 'Now let's hope he doesn't change his mind.'

They waited for nearly fifteen minutes. Osborne came back carrying a file nearly an inch thick. He presented it to Walling as she was standing up.

'We'll get this back to you soon,' she said. 'Thank you, Mr Osborne.'

'Wait a minute! You said you were going to look at it here.'

Rachel was gathering that momentum again. 'There's no longer time, Mr Osborne. We have to move. You'll have the file tomorrow morning.'

She was already through the office door. Bosch followed, closing it behind him on Osborne's final words: 'What about the court ord—?'

As they passed behind the clerk, Walling asked her to buzz them out, keeping a two-pace lead on Bosch. He liked walking behind her and admired how she handled herself. Commanding presence in spades.

Out on the sidewalk they walked east to a tiny luncheonette. They went in, sat side by side at the counter and opened the file. By the time Bosch had ordered two coffees, Rachel had a one-page lead on him.

The first document was a copy of Foxworth's birth certificate. He was born at Queen of Angels Hospital. The mother was listed as Rosemary Foxworth, DOB June 21, 1954, Philadelphia, and the father as unknown. The mother's address was an apartment on Orchid Avenue, in the middle of what was now Hollywood's Kodak Center, all glitz and glass and red carpets, but in 1971 the neighbourhood would have been patrolled by streetwalkers and hypes.

Rachel passed Bosch more documents. Robert was removed from his mother's custody at age two and taken into the DCFS system. For the next sixteen years he was in and out of foster homes and youth halls. Among the facilities he had lived in was the McLaren Youth Hall in El Monte, a place where Bosch himself had spent a number of years as a child.

The file was replete with psychiatric evaluations conducted as Foxworth floated from place to place. He had no real home or family. In total the file charted the journey of a broken life. The pages brought up memories in Bosch. Two decades before Foxworth's journey through the system, Bosch had charted his own path, surviving with his own set of scars.

Rachel handed him a copy of a death certificate. Rosemary Foxworth had died March 5, 1986, of complications stemming from drug use and hepatitis C, at County-USC Medical Center. Robert would have been fourteen.

'Here we go,' Rachel suddenly said. 'His longest stay in any foster home was in Echo Park. And the people he stayed with? Harlan and Janet Saxon.'

'What's the address?'

'Number 710 Figueroa Lane. From 1983 to '87. Almost four years. He must have liked them and I guess they liked him back.'

Bosch leaned over to look. 'He was on Figueroa Terrace, only a couple of blocks from there, when he got pulled over with the bodies. It's got to be where he was going!' He stood up. He was ready to make a move.

Walling closed the file. 'So what now?' she asked.

Bosch looked at her. 'Echo Park,' he said.

'What about back-up?'

'I'm going to check it out first, then call back-up.'

She nodded. 'I'm going with you.'

9

Bosch and Walling drove to Echo Park in Bosch's Mustang but did not approach the Saxon house at 710 Figueroa Lane. There was a problem. Figueroa Lane was a short turnaround street that extended for a block off the end of Figueroa Terrace and curved up along the ridge below Chavez Ravine. There was no cruising past it without being obvious. If Waits was there, he would have the advantage of seeing them first.

Bosch stopped the car at the intersection of Beaudry and Figueroa Terrace. 'He picked a good place for the secret castle,' he said.

Looking to his left towards downtown, he saw the tall buildings rising over the roofs of the homes on Figueroa Terrace. One of the closest was the Department of Water and Power headquarters, directly across the freeway.

'I've got an idea,' Bosch said.

They drove to the DWP garage and parked in one of the visitor slots. Bosch popped the trunk, went to the surveillance kit he always kept in the car and got out a pair of high-powered binoculars and a surveillance camera.

When they reached the lobby, Bosch went to an information desk, showed his badge and credentials and asked to see a security supervisor. In less than two minutes a tall black man in a navy blazer and tie came through a door. This time Bosch and Walling both showed their creds.

'Hieronymus,' the man said, reading Bosch's ID. 'Do you go by Harry?'

'That's right.'

The man put out his hand and smiled. 'Jason Edgar. I believe you and my cousin Jerry were partners once.'

Bosch smiled and shook his hand. 'That's right. Nice to meet you.'

'Likewise, man. What do we have here if the FBI's involved?'

'Jason, we're just looking for a place where we can see a neighbourhood in Echo Park. There's a house we can't get close to without being obvious. We were thinking that maybe from one of the offices here or from the roof we could get an angle, and just see what's happening over there.'

'I've got just the spot,' Edgar said without hesitation. 'Follow me.'

He led them to the elevators and had to use a key to get the fifteenth-floor button to light. On the way up he explained that the building was being renovated floor by floor, and the fifteenth was gutted and empty.

'You can pick any angle you want,' he said.

The elevator doors opened and they stepped out onto a floor that was wide open from glass exterior to glass exterior. Edgar led them towards the glass wall that would look down on Echo Park.

'There's something else you could help us with,' Walling said. 'Could you run the address through your computers and tell us who pays for utilities?'

'Not a problem. Let me just get you situated first.'

At the glass wall at the north of the building, Bosch and Walling looked down and across the 101 Freeway at Echo Park. They were further away than Bosch had thought they'd be, but still had a good vantage point.

'There's Fig Terrace,' he said. 'Those three houses above are on Fig Lane.'

Rachel nodded. 'Which one is seven-ten?'

'Good question.' Bosch raised the binoculars. He finally zeroed in on a black trash can sitting out front of the house in the middle. Someone had painted 712 on the can in large white numerals. Bosch knew the address numbers would rise away from downtown. 'The one on the right,' he said.

'So that's the address?' Edgar asked. 'Seven-ten Fig Lane?'

'Figueroa Lane,' Bosch said.

'Got it. Let me go see what I can find.'

'Thanks, Jason.'

Bosch looked back at the house. It was of similar design to the other two on Figueroa Lane: built high on the hillside with steps down to a street-front garage cut into the embankment. But while the other houses were neatly cared for, its pink paint had faded, its front yard overrun with weeds.

Bosch moved the field glasses from window to window. Next to him Walling was using the surveillance camera. He noticed a small metal platform at the top of the garage steps, and guide rails.

'There's a lift,' he said. 'Whoever's living there is in a wheelchair.'

He dropped his focus to the garage. It had a pedestrian entrance door and double garage doors that had once been painted pink but were now grey.

One had closed at an uneven angle to the pavement, and didn't look operational. Across the top panel of each garage door was a row of small square windows, but the reflected sunlight prevented Bosch from seeing in.

Bosch heard the elevator ding. He turned and saw Jason Edgar.

'Services to that address are billed to a Janet Saxon,' Edgar said, 'and have been for twenty-one years.'

'Thank you,' Rachel said. 'You've been a great help.'

'Good luck. Hope you get your man.'

Everybody shook hands and Edgar returned to the elevator. Twenty minutes went by with no movement at the house. Bosch was training his focus on the heavy brush on the ridgeline, looking for another observation position, when Walling spoke excitedly.

'Harry, the garage.'

Bosch lowered his glasses. The sun had moved behind a cloud and the glare had dropped off. Through the windows of the garage door that appeared to be still functional, he could see the back of a white van.

'A white van,' Walling said. 'It's part of the BOLO.'

'That's it!' Bosch shouted. 'He's in there with the girl. Rachel, we gotta go!'

They got up and hurried to the elevator.

THEY DEBATED BACK-UP as they sped out of the DWP garage.

'Look,' Bosch said, 'she might be in that house, but he might not be. If we storm in there with the troops, we could lose him. All I want is to check it out up close. We can call for back-up if we need it.'

'And what if he *is* in there? The two of us could be walking into an ambush. We need at least one back-up team to do this safely.'

'We'll call them when we get there.'

'That will be too late. I know what you're doing,' Walling said. 'You want this guy for yourself and you're willing to risk that girl—and us—to get it.'

'You want me to drop you off, Rachel?'

'No, I don't want you to drop me off, Harry.'

'Good. I want you to be there.'

Decision made, they drove to where Figueroa Terrace ended and Figueroa Lane curved up the hillside. Bosch pulled up to the kerb.

'We walk up, staying close to the line of garages until we get to 710,' he said. 'He won't have an angle from the house.'

'What if he's isn't in the house. What if he's in the garage?'

'We clear the garage first, then go up the stairs to the house. Let's go.'

Bosch got out and started trotting up the sidewalk. He pulled out his phone and turned it off. Rachel was right behind him. They got to 710 quickly and Bosch went to the window panels in one of the garage doors. Cupping his hands against the glass, he looked in and saw that the interior was crowded by the van and stacks of boxes and junk. A door at the back was closed.

He checked the knob to the pedestrian door. 'Locked,' he whispered.

Rachel was leaning close to the far pull-up door to listen for sounds. She shook her head. Nothing. There was a handle at the bottom of each door but no exterior lock. Bosch tried to pull one open. It came up about an inch, then stopped. The second door did the same. Bosch guessed that they were padlocked inside. He shook his head at Rachel and pointed up at the house.

They moved to the concrete steps and started up. Bosch crouched down four steps from the top. He looked at Rachel. He knew he was winging it. There was no way to approach the house but to go directly to the front door.

He studied the windows one by one. He saw no movement, but thought he could hear a radio. He pulled his gun and held it at his side as he crossed the porch. He put his hand on the front doorknob and turned.

As Bosch pushed the door open, the sound of the radio became louder. An evangelical station, a man talking about the impending rapture.

They stepped into the entry area. To the right it opened into a living room with a dining area to the back. Directly ahead, through an arched opening, was the kitchen. A hallway to the left led to the rest of the house.

Bosch stepped forward and pointed to the right. As he reached the archway, he glanced at Rachel and saw her moving through the living room, weapon up in a two-handed grip. He stepped into the kitchen, which was clean and neat. The radio was on the counter. Another archway led to the dining room. Rachel came through it, pointed her gun up and shook her head. Nothing.

Bosch turned and went back to the entry area. He was startled to see an old woman sitting in a wheelchair in the threshold to the hallway. On her lap she was holding a long-barrel revolver.

'Who's there?' she said forcefully.

Her head was turned at an angle. Though her eyes were open, they were focused on the floor instead of on Bosch. It was her ear that was trained towards him and he knew she was blind.

He pointed his gun at her. 'Mrs Saxon? Take it easy. My name is Harry Bosch. I'm just looking for Robert.'

A look of puzzlement played on her features. 'Who?'

'Robert Foxworth. Is he here?'

'Bobby uses the garage. I don't let him use the house. All those chemicals, it smells awful.'

Bosch started edging towards her. 'I'm sorry, Mrs Saxon. I thought he was here. Has he been here lately?'

'He comes and goes. He comes up here to give me the rent for the garage, that's all. What do you want him for? Are you his friend?'

He was getting closer. 'I just want to talk to him.' Bosch reached down and took the gun out of her hand.

'Hey! That's my protection.'

'It's all right, Mrs Saxon. I'll give it back. I think it needs to be cleaned. I'm going to get Bobby to oil it, then I'll bring it back.'

'You better. I need it.'

Bosch checked the gun. It was loaded and appeared operational. He put it into the waistband at the back of his pants and looked round at Rachel. She made a movement with her hand, pantomiming turning a key.

'Do you have a key to the garage, Mrs Saxon?' he asked.

'No. Bobby came and got the extra key.'

'OK, Mrs Saxon. I'll check with him.'

He moved towards the front door. Rachel joined him and they went out. Halfway down the steps to the garage she grabbed his arm.

'We have to call back-up. Now!' she whispered.

'Go ahead and call but I'm going in. We can't wait.'

He shook off her grip and continued down. When he got to the garage he looked again through the top windows and saw no movement inside. The door on the rear wall was still closed.

He moved over to the pedestrian door, opened a small folding knife attached to his key ring, and went to work on the lock. He got the blade across the tongue and pulled the door. It didn't open. He pulled again hard.

'There's an inside lock,' he whispered. 'All the doors are locked from the inside. It means he's in there.'

Rachel nodded. 'What do we do?' she whispered back.

He thought for a moment, then handed her his keys. 'Go get the car. Park it with the rear end right here, then pop the trunk.'

'What are you—?'

'Just do it. Go!'

She ran down the sidewalk. Bosch moved towards the pull-up door that looked out of alignment. He heard the Mustang's big engine before he saw his car come over the hill. Rachel turned in the street, then backed towards the garage. The trunk was popped and Bosch reached in for the rope he kept in the back. It was gone. He then remembered that Osani had taken it after discovering it tied round the tree in Beachwood Canyon.

'Shit!'

He quickly looked through the trunk and found a short length of clothesline he had used once to tie down the trunk lid while moving furniture. He tied one end to a steel towing loop underneath the car's bumper and the other to the handle at the bottom of the garage door.

Rachel had got out of the car. 'What are you doing?'

'We're going to pull it open. Get in the car. Go forward, slowly.'

Without a word she got back in the car and started driving forward. She watched in the rearview and he rolled a finger to keep her moving. The cord pulled taut and the garage door groaned. He stepped back and drew his gun.

All at once the door popped up and out three feet. Rachel stopped, and Bosch moved forward quickly, ducking and rolling under the door. He came up inside the garage with his gun up and ready. He swept the space but saw no one. Keeping his eyes on the rear door, he stepped over to the van. He jerked one of the side doors open and checked the interior. It was empty.

Bosch moved towards the back wall round an obstacle course of barrels, rolls of plastic, bales of towels and squeegee blades and other window-washing equipment. There was a strong smell of ammonia and other chemicals, and his eyes started watering.

The hinges on the door at the rear wall were visible and Bosch knew it would swing towards him when he opened it.

'FBI!' Walling yelled from outside. 'Coming in!'

'Clear!' Bosch yelled back.

He heard her scrabble under the garage door but kept his attention on the door on the back wall. Taking a position to one side of it, Bosch turned the doorknob. It was unlocked. He looked back at Rachel. She was in a combat stance at an angle from the door. She nodded, and he flung it open.

The room was dark and windowless and he saw no one. As he quickly sidestepped into the room, he saw a string overhead and yanked on it. The light came on. He was in a crowded workroom about ten feet deep.

'Clear!'

Rachel entered and they stood scanning the room. A bench cluttered with old paint cans, tools and flashlights was on the right. Rusting bikes were stacked against the left wall, with folding chairs and collapsed cardboard boxes. The back wall was concrete block. Hung on it was a dusty old flag. On the floor was a stand-up electric fan caked with dust. At one time somebody had tried to blow the fetid, damp smell out of the room.

Bosch lowered his gun and walked back into the garage. He didn't understand. Were they too late? Were they following the wrong lead?

'Check the van,' he said to Rachel. 'See if there's any sign of the girl.'

Bosch went to the pedestrian door. There was a dead bolt on it. He was right, too, about the garage doors: they had padlocks on interior slide locks. Either someone was inside the garage or there was an exit point he hadn't identified yet. But this seemed impossible. The garage was dug directly into the hillside. There was no possibility of a rear exit.

He was checking the ceiling, wondering if it was possible that there was a passageway up to the house when Rachel called from inside the van.

'I've got a roll of duct tape,' she said. 'And strips of it on the floor with hair.'

Bosch stepped to the open side door of the van. He pulled out his phone. He noticed the wheelchair lift in the van. 'I'll call for back-up and Forensics,' he said. 'We missed him.'

While he waited for the phone to boot up he realised that the fan in the back wasn't pointed towards the garage doors. If you were going to air the room out, you'd point the fan towards the door.

He punched in a number and told the dispatcher to connect him with the Raynard Waits Fugitive Task Force. An officer picked up.

'This is Detective Harry Bosch. I have—'

'Harry! Gun!'

Time slowed. All in a second, Bosch looked at Rachel in the side doorway, her eyes focused over his shoulder. Without thinking, he jumped forward, pulling his arms round her and taking her to the floor of the van in a crushing tackle. Four shots came from behind him, followed by the sound of glass breaking. Bosch came up gun in hand and caught a glimpse of a figure ducking into the rear room. He fired six shots through the doorway.

'Rachel, OK?'

'I'm OK. Are you hit?'

'I don't think so!'

'It was him! Waits! Did you hit him?'

'I don't think so.'

'I thought we cleared that room.'

'I thought we did too.' Bosch stood up, keeping his aim on the door to the rear room. He noticed the light from within was now off. 'I dropped my phone,' he whispered. 'Call for back-up.' He moved towards the door.

'Harry, wait. He could—'

'Call for back-up! And remember to tell them I'm in there.'

He cut to his left and approached the door from an angle that would give him the widest vision of the interior, but the room was cast in shadows and he could see no movement. He started taking small steps using his right foot first and maintaining a firing position. Behind him he heard Rachel on her phone asking for a transfer to LAPD dispatch.

Bosch got to the threshold, swung the gun across his body and side-stepped in to the right. There was no sign of Waits. The room was empty. He looked at the fan and confirmed his mistake. It was pointed towards the flag hanging on the back wall. It had not been used to blow damp air out. The fan had been used to blow air in.

He reached the flag, grabbed it by the edge and ripped it down.

In the wall, three feet off the ground, was a tunnel entrance. A dozen concrete blocks had been removed to create an opening four feet square. Bosch crouched to look into it from the right side. The tunnel was deep and dark, but he saw a glimmer of light coming from round a turn thirty feet in.

Bosch leaned close and realised he could hear a low whimpering sound. It was a terrible sound but it was beautiful just the same.

He reached back over to the bench and picked up a flashlight. He flashed the weak beam into the tunnel and confirmed that the first leg was clear.

'Harry, wait!'

He turned and saw Rachel in the doorway.

'Back-up's on the way!' she whispered.

Bosch shook his head. 'She's in there. She's alive.'

He flashed the light into the tunnel once more, then turned it off to conserve it. He glanced back at Rachel, then stepped into the darkness.

BOSCH HESITATED a moment in the mouth of the tunnel to let his eyes adjust. He then started moving in a crouch. Flashlight in his right hand and gun up in his left, he kept his eyes on the dim light ahead. The sound of the woman crying grew louder as he moved forward.

Ten feet in, the musty smell turned into the deeper stench of decay. Bosch knew that he was headed towards something horrific, that the missing victims of Raynard Waits were ahead somewhere in the tunnel. This had been the destination on the night Waits was pulled over.

Bosch's thigh muscles burned from the strain of moving in a crouched position. Sweat began to sting his eyes. And as he got closer to the turn, he saw the light changing and rechanging, and knew that this was caused by the undulation of a flame. Candlelight.

Five feet from the turn, Bosch slowed to a stop. Behind him, he thought he could hear sirens. Back-up on the way. Ahead there was only the intermittent sound of crying. He started forward again. Almost immediately the light went out and the whimpering took on a new urgency.

Bosch froze. He heard nervous laughter from ahead, followed by the familiar voice of Raynard Waits.

'Is that you, Detective Bosch? Welcome to my foxhole.'

'Waits? Let her go. Send her out.'

'No, Bosch, she's with me now. Anybody comes in, I'll kill her on the spot. I'll save the last bullet for myself.'

'Waits, no. Listen. Just let her come out and I will come in. We'll trade.'

'No, Bosch. I like the situation the way it is.'

'You need to save yourself. There's not a lot of time. Send the girl out.'

The voice came out of the darkness. 'Save myself for what?'

Bosch's muscles were on the verge of cramping. He lowered himself to a seated position against the right side of the tunnel, sure the candlelight had come from the left. He kept his gun up, bracing it with the flashlight.

'There's no way out,' he said. 'Give it up and come out. Your deal is still in play. You don't have to die. Neither does the girl.'

'I don't care about dying, Bosch. That's why I'm here. Because I don't care. I just want it to be on my own terms.'

Bosch noticed that the woman had gone silent.

'Waits, what's wrong? Is she all right?'

'She passed out. Too much excitement, I guess.' He laughed.

Bosch decided that he needed to keep Waits talking, distracted from the woman. 'I know who you are,' he said quietly.

Waits didn't take the bait. Bosch tried again.

'Robert Foxworth. Son of Rosemary Foxworth. Raised by the county. Foster homes, youth halls. You lived here with the Saxons. For a time you lived at the McLaren Youth Hall out in El Monte. So did I, Robert.'

Bosch was met with a long silence. But then the voice came quietly out of the darkness. 'I'm not Robert Foxworth any more.'

'I understand.'

'I hated that place. McLaren. I hated them all.'

'They closed it down a couple of years ago. After some kid died in there.'

'Fuck them. How did you find Robert Foxworth?'

Bosch felt a rhythm building in the conversation. He understood the cue Waits was giving by speaking of Robert Foxworth as someone other than himself. He was Raynard Waits now.

'It wasn't that hard,' Bosch answered. 'We figured it out through the Fitzpatrick case. We found the pawn slip in the records and matched dates. What was the heirloom medallion?'

'It was Rosemary's. It was all he had from her. He had to pawn it, and when he went back to get it that pig Fitzpatrick had already sold it.'

There wasn't a lot of time. Bosch decided to jump to the present.

'Raynard. Tell me about the set-up. Tell me about Olivas and O'Shea.'

There was only silence. Bosch tried again.

'They used you. O'Shea used you and he's just going to walk away from it. Is that what you want? You die here in this hole and O'Shea walks away?'

'I can't give you O'Shea or Olivas,' Waits said in the darkness.

Bosch didn't get it. Was he wrong? He doubled back in his head and started at the beginning. 'Did you kill Marie Gesto?'

There was a long silence. 'No, I didn't,' Waits finally said.

'Then how was this set up? How could you know where—?'

'Think about it, Bosch. They're not stupid. They would not directly communicate with me.'

Bosch nodded. He understood. 'Maury Swann. He brokered the deal?

'He said you were bothering the wrong people and had to be convinced.'

'What people?'

'He didn't tell me that. And he went to them without my knowledge. If he'd asked me I'd have said, don't bother. I'd rather take the needle than forty years in a cell. You understand, Bosch. You're an eye-for-an-eye guy. I like that about you, believe it or not.'

'So then what happened?'

'One night in the jail, I was taken to the attorney room and Maury told me there was a deal on the table. But he said it would only work if I threw in a freebie. Admit to one I didn't do. He told me there would be a field trip and I would have to lead a certain detective to the body. This detective had to be convinced, and leading him to the body would be the only way to do it. That detective was you, Bosch.'

'And you said yes.'

'When he said there would be a field trip, I said yes. That was the only reason. It meant daylight. I saw a chance at daylight.'

'And you were led to believe this offer came from Olivas and O'Shea?'

'Maury said it came directly from them.'

'How did you get the details you gave during the confession?'

'Swann. He got them from them. He said they had the records from the original investigation.'

'And he told you how to find the body up there in the woods?'

'Swann told me there were markers in the woods. He showed me pictures and told me how to lead everybody there. It was easy.'

Bosch thought about how easily he had been led down the path. He had wanted something so badly and for so long that it had made him blind.

He looked down the tunnel in the direction of the garage. He could see nothing but he knew that there would be people there. They had blacked out that end to prevent backlighting. They would be coming at any moment.

'What about your escape?' Bosch asked in order to keep the dialogue going. 'Was that planned or were you just improvising?'

'A little of both. Swann told me about how the markers would begin after we came to where there had been a mudslide and we'd have to climb down. That's when I knew I might have a chance. So I told him I wouldn't follow through on the deal if I had to climb with my hands cuffed.'

Bosch remembered O'Shea overruling Olivas and telling him to take the cuffs off. Olivas's reluctance, like everything else, had been a play for Bosch's benefit, and he had been played perfectly.

Bosch heard the sound of men crawling behind him in the tunnel. He turned the flashlight on and saw the SWAT team. Black Kevlar, automatic rifles, night-vision goggles. Any moment they would launch a flash-bang grenade and start coming. He turned the light out. He thought about the woman. He knew Waits would kill her the moment they made the move.

'Were you really at McLaren?' Waits asked.

'I was there. It was before your time but I was there. I was in B dorm. It was closest to the ball fields so we always got the best equipment.'

'Maybe you were there, Bosch. And look at us now. You went your way and I went mine. I guess I fed the wrong dog.'

'What do you mean? What dog?'

'You don't remember. At McLaren they used to pass around that saying about every man having two dogs inside. One good and one bad. They fight all the time because only one can be the alpha dog, the one in charge.'

'And?'

'And the one that wins is always the dog you chose to feed. I fed the wrong one. You fed the right one.'

Bosch didn't know what to say. He heard a click behind him. They were going to launch the grenade. He quickly stood up, hopeful that they would not shoot him in the back.

'Waits, I'm coming in.'

'No, Bosch.'

'I'll give you my gun. Watch the light. I'll give you my gun.'

He switched on the flashlight and played its beam on the turn in the tunnel ahead. He moved forward and extended his left hand into the light. He held his gun by the barrel. 'I'm coming in now.'

Bosch took the turn and entered the final chamber. It was at least twelve feet wide but still not tall enough to stand in. He swept it with his light. The dim beam revealed a ghastly sight of bones and skulls and decaying flesh and hair. The stench was overpowering and he held himself from gagging.

The beam came to the face of the man Bosch had known as Raynard Waits. He was propped against the far wall of his foxhole, sitting on what looked like a throne carved into rock and clay. The woman he had abducted lay naked and unconscious on a blanket. Waits held Olivas's gun to her temple.

'Easy now,' Bosch said. 'I'll give you my gun. Just don't hurt her any more.'

Waits smiled, 'Bosch, you are a fool to the end.'

Bosch tossed the gun to the right side of the throne. As Waits reached down to grab it he lifted the muzzle of the other gun off the woman. Bosch dropped the flashlight and reached behind him at the same time, his hand finding the grip of the revolver he had taken from the blind woman.

The long barrel made his aim true. He fired twice, hitting Waits in the centre of the chest with both rounds.

Waits was knocked back against the wall. Bosch saw his eyes go wide, then they lost that light that separates life from death. His chin dropped and his head tilted forward.

Bosch crawled to the woman and checked her for a pulse. She was alive. He covered her with the blanket, then called out, 'This is Bosch—RHD! It's clear! We are clear! Waits is dead!'

A bright light flashed on round the corner.

He felt safe now. He slowly moved towards the light.

10

After emerging from the tunnel, Bosch was led out of the garage by two SWAT officers wearing gas masks. He was delivered to the waiting members of the Fugitive Task Force and others associated with the case. Randolph and Osani from OIS were on hand, as well as Abel Pratt. Bosch looked around for Rachel Walling but didn't see her anywhere.

Next out of the tunnel was Waits's last victim. The young woman was carried to a waiting ambulance and immediately transported to County-USC Medical Center for assessment and treatment.

The task-force leader wanted Bosch to sit in a van and tell his story, but Bosch didn't want to be in a closed space. Even out in the open air on Figueroa Lane he couldn't get the smell of the tunnel out of his nose, and he noticed that everyone who had crowded round him at first had now taken a step or two back. He saw a garden hose alongside the stairway of the house next to 710. He went over, turned it on and ran the water through his hair, on his face and down his neck. It pretty much soaked his clothes but it washed away a good deal of the dirt and sweat and stench.

The task-force top was a sergeant named Bob McDonald from Hollywood Division. Luckily, Bosch knew him from past days and that set the stage for a cordial debriefing.

'Where's the FBI agent?' Bosch asked. 'Where's Rachel Walling?'

'She's being interviewed,' McDonald said.

'And the old lady upstairs in the house?'

McDonald nodded. 'She's fine,' he said.

Bosch told his story, giving the step-by-step playback of his moves after discovering the connection between Waits and Fitzpatrick. There were no questions. Not yet. They simply listened. It took him twenty minutes, and then McDonald said they should take a break. As the group around Bosch splintered, Pratt walked up. He looked anxious.

'Well, Harry, what did he tell you in there?'

Bosch was surprised that Pratt wasn't jumping all over him for acting on his own, without authority.

'He told me it was all orchestrated through Swann,' Bosch said. 'Swann took the deal from Olivas and O'Shea to Waits. Waits didn't kill Gesto but agreed to take the fall for her.'

'That's it? Why would Olivas and O'Shea do this?'

'The oldest reasons in the book. Money and power. And the Garland family has plenty of both.'

'Anthony Garland was the person of interest on Gesto, right? The guy who got the court orders keeping you away.'

'Yeah, until Olivas and O'Shea used Waits to convince me otherwise.'

'You think McDonald will go after Swann for this?'

Bosch thought a moment. 'Not a chance. Whatever was said between them was privileged information. Besides, nobody would go after him based on the word of a dead madman like Waits.'

Pratt kicked the ground. He had nothing else to say or ask.

'Look, Top, I'm sorry about this,' Bosch said. 'About not being up-front with you on what I was doing, the home duty and everything.'

Pratt waved it off. 'It's OK, man. You got lucky. You took out the bad guy. What am I going to say to that?'

Bosch nodded his thanks.

'Besides, I'm coasting,' Pratt continued. 'Another three weeks and you'll be someone else's problem. He can decide what to do with you.'

Whether Kiz Rider came back or not, Bosch didn't want to leave the unit. He hoped he'd still be part of Open-Unsolved when all this shook out.

'Holy shit!' Pratt whispered.

Bosch followed his eyes to a car that had just parked near where the media trucks and the reporters were setting up for sound bites. Rick O'Shea was getting out. Bosch felt the bile rise in his throat.

Pratt caught his arm. 'Harry, take it easy.'

'What the hell is he doing here?'

'It's his case. He can come if he wants. You better play it cool. Don't show your hand or you might never be able to get to him.'

'And what, meantime he turns this into another campaign commercial?'

Bosch broke free of Pratt's grasp and leaned against one of the police cars. He folded his arms and kept his head down. He knew Pratt was right.

'Just keep him away from me,' he said.

'That will be kind of hard because he's coming right to you.'

Bosch looked up just as O'Shea and the two men that made up his entourage got to him.

'Detective Bosch, are you OK?'

'Never better.'

'Thank you for what you have done here today. Thank you for saving the young woman.'

Bosch just nodded while looking down at the ground.

O'Shea turned to Pratt. 'Could I speak to Detective Bosch alone?'

His minions walked off. Pratt hesitated until Bosch nodded to him, telling him everything was cool. Bosch and O'Shea were left to themselves.

'Detective, I have been briefed on what Waits—or, I should say, Foxworth—revealed to you in the tunnel. I hope you do not give credence to what a confirmed serial killer would say about the men prosecuting him, especially one who cannot even be here to defend himself?'

Bosch stepped away from the car. His hands were balled into fists at his sides. 'You're talking about Olivas?'

'Yes, I am. And I can tell you actually believe what Foxworth told you. But you're wrong, Bosch. He was lying.'

'He was confirming what I already knew before I even went into that tunnel. Olivas was dirty. He put the entry in the murder book that falsely tied Waits to Gesto. He marked a trail for Waits to follow and lead us to the body. And he wouldn't have done it without somebody telling him to do it. He wasn't that kind of guy. He wasn't smart enough.'

O'Shea stared at him. 'I can't dissuade you from this crap, can I?'

'Dissuade? Not a chance. And I don't care what it does or doesn't do for the campaign, Mr Prosecutor.'

'Then, I guess I'll have to appeal to a higher authority.'

Bosch took a step closer. 'You smell that? That's the putrid smell of death. I've got it all over me, O'Shea, but at least I can wash it off.'

'What is that supposed to mean?'

'Whatever you want it to mean. Who's your higher authority? You going to call T. Rex Garland up in his shiny office?'

O'Shea took a deep breath and shook his head in confusion. 'Detective, I don't know what happened in that tunnel but you aren't making much sense.'

Bosch nodded. 'Yeah, well, it will make sense soon enough. Before the election, for sure. Somehow, some way, I'm going to take down you and the Garlands and everybody else who had a part in this. Count on it.'

'Are you saying that I did this, that I set all this up, for T. Rex Garland?'

Bosch started laughing. O'Shea was the consummate actor to the end. 'You're good,' he said. 'I'll give you that.'

'I have never spoken to either of the Garlands. T. Rex Garland is a valid contributor to my campaign. Up-front and legal. So what? The guy spreads money through every election in the county.'

'You are so full of shit. You—'

'There is no connection, Bosch. Take your best shot and we'll see who comes out standing.'

He walked away, barking an order to his men for a telephone with a secured line. Bosch wondered who the first call would go to, T. Rex Garland or the chief of police.

He turned away and saw Rachel Walling walking towards the yellow tape that marked the perimeter of the crime scene. There was a federal cruiser there and a man in a suit and sunglasses was waiting for her. She had apparently called for a ride.

Bosch trotted towards the tape, calling her name. She stopped and waited.

'Harry,' she said. 'Are you all right?'

'I am now. How about you, Rachel?'

'I'm fine. What happened to you?' She indicated his wet clothes.

'I had to hose off. It was bad. Are you leaving?'

'Yes. They're done with me for the time being.'

Bosch nodded towards the man in the sunglasses ten feet behind her. 'Are you in trouble?' he asked quietly.

'I don't know yet. I should be all right. You got the bad guy and saved the girl. How can that be a bad thing?'

'*We* got the bad guy and saved the girl,' Bosch corrected. 'But there are people in every institution and bureaucracy who can find a way to turn something good into garbage.'

She looked him in the eyes and nodded. 'I know,' she said.

Her look froze him and he knew they were now different.

'Are you mad at me, Rachel?'

'Mad? No. Look, I have to go.'

'Will you call me, then?'

'When I can. Goodbye, Harry.' She took two steps then turned. 'That was O'Shea you were talking to, wasn't it?'

'Yeah.'

'Be careful, Harry. If you let your emotions run you the way they did today, O'Shea could put you in a world of pain.'

'You know what they say about pain, don't you?' Bosch smiled slightly. 'Pain is weakness leaving the body.'

She shook her head. 'Well "they" are full of shit. Don't put it to the test unless you have to. Goodbye, Harry.'

'I'll see you, Rachel.'

He watched as the man in sunglasses held the tape up for her. She got into the passenger seat and the man drove off. Bosch knew that something had changed in the way she saw him. His actions in the garage and going into the tunnel had made her change her mind about him. He guessed he might never see her again. It would be one more thing he would blame on O'Shea.

He turned back to the crime scene, where Randolph and Osani were standing waiting for him. 'You two again,' Bosch said.

'Gettin' to be like déjà vu all over again, isn't it?' Randolph said. 'We need to take you to Parker Center, Detective, this time for a formal interview.'

Bosch nodded. He knew the drill. This time he had killed somebody.

'I'm ready to go,' he said.

BOSCH WAS SEATED in an interview room in the Officer Involved Shooting Unit. Randolph had allowed him to shower and he'd changed into blue jeans and a black sweatshirt, clothing he kept in a locker for times he needed to fly below the radar. He had dumped his contaminated suit into a trash can.

The tape recorder on the table was turned on, and Osani read him his constitutional rights as well as the police officer's bill of rights. But Bosch knew that, when push came to shove, in these rooms neither would do much to protect him. At Randolph's request he once more told the story of the shooting of Robert Foxworth, aka Raynard Waits.

Randolph asked many detailed questions about the moves in the garage and the tunnel. More than once he asked Bosch why he didn't listen to the cautioning words of FBI agent Rachel Walling. This told Bosch that Rachel had not said things particularly favourable to his case, which disappointed him greatly. But he tried to keep his feelings about her out of the interview room. To Randolph he repeated a mantra he believed would ultimately win the day for him, no matter what Randolph or Rachel or anyone else thought of his actions and procedures.

'It was a life-or-death situation. A woman was in jeopardy and we had been fired upon. I felt I could not wait around for back-up. I used as much caution as I could and used deadly force only when necessary.'

Randolph asked Bosch what he was thinking when Foxworth revealed that Bosch had been set up. He asked what he was thinking when he saw the remains of Foxworth's victims. He asked what he was thinking when he pulled the trigger. Bosch patiently answered each question but something was off-kilter. It was almost as if Randolph were working from a script.

'What's going on here?' Bosch finally asked. 'I'm sitting here telling you people everything. What aren't you telling me?'

Randolph leaned towards the tape recorder, and held his fingers on the buttons. 'Detective Osani, could you go get us a couple of bottles of water? All this talking and my voice is about to go. We'll hold up until you get back.'

Osani got up to leave and Randolph turned off the recorder.

'The thing is, Detective,' he said when the door had closed, 'we only have your word on what happened in that tunnel. The female was unconscious.'

'That's right. Are you saying my word is not acceptable?'

'I'm saying Forensics might come in with a description of events that varies from your statement. It can get messy very quickly. Things can be left open to public and political misinterpretation.'

'So what?' Bosch said. 'I don't care what the public or politicians think. Waits pushed the action in that tunnel. I did what I had to do.'

'But there is no witness to your description of events. Agent Walling didn't go into the tunnel. She warned you not to go in.'

'You know, there's a woman at County-USC who probably wouldn't be alive right now if I hadn't gone in. What is going on here, Lieutenant?'

Randolph looked like a man with a distaste for what his duty called on him to do. 'That's probably enough for today,' he said. 'You've been through a lot. We'll keep things open for a few days while we wait for the forensics to come in. You'll continue on home duty. Once we have everything in order, I'll bring you in to read and sign your statement.'

'This is about Olivas, isn't it, Lieutenant? The funeral's set for tomorrow, and you want to keep Olivas a hero killed in the line of duty.'

'Nobody is going to bend over backwards if Olivas was dirty.'

'Then it's about O'Shea. He reached out to a higher authority. He told me he would. That authority then reached out to you.'

Randolph leaned back in his chair and seemed to search the ceiling for a reply. 'There are a great number of people in this department who believe that Rick O'Shea would make a fine district attorney. They also believe he would be a good friend to the LAPD.'

Bosch closed his eyes. He couldn't believe what he was hearing.

Randolph continued. 'Gabriel Williams has allied himself with an anti-law-enforcement constituency. It would not be a good day for the LAPD if he were to be elected.'

Bosch opened his eyes and stared at Randolph. 'You're going to let this guy skate because you think he could be a friend to the department?'

Randolph shook his head. 'I don't know what you are talking about, Detective. I'm simply making a political observation. But I do know this. There is no evidence of this conspiracy you speak of. If you think Foxworth's attorney will do anything other than deny the conversation you outlined, then you're a fool. Be wise. Keep it to yourself.'

'How high up did O'Shea reach? Who told you to knock me down?'

'Detective, I have no idea what you are talking about.'

'Right. Of course not.' Bosch stood up. 'I guess you'll write it up the way you've been told and I'll either sign it or I won't.'

Randolph nodded but said nothing.

Bosch leaned down and put both hands on the table. 'You going to Deputy Doolan's funeral, Lieutenant? Remember him, the one Waits shot in the face? I thought maybe you'd go to explain to his family about how the man behind that bullet could be a friend to the department.'

Randolph stared at the wall. Bosch pulled open the door, startling Osani standing just outside. He wasn't holding any water bottles. Bosch pushed past him and left the squad room.

In the elevator he pushed the button for the fifth floor. The Open-Unsolved Unit was deserted when he got there. It was just after four and most detectives worked seven-to-four shifts that put them on the road home before rush hour. The only one still around was Abel Pratt, because as a supervisor he had to work till five. Bosch waved as he walked by his door.

He dropped into his chair, exhausted by the day's events. He looked down and saw that his desk was littered with pink phone message slips, most from colleagues in different divisions and stations. They were all call-backs.

Bosch knew they wanted to say 'Nice shooting' or words to that effect. Anytime anybody got a clean kill the phones lit up.

There were also several messages from reporters. And there was a message from the Gestos. Bosch had called the night before to tell them their daughter had been found and the ID confirmed. He put that slip in his pocket. With the autopsy completed, the body would be released. He could not tell them that their daughter's killer had been brought to justice, but at least he could help them get her home.

There was also a message from Jerry Edgar. Whoever took it had written *Says it's important* on the slip. Bosch noted that the call had come in before the shooting, so Edgar had not been calling to congratulate him. Bosch put that message in his pocket, and the others in a desk drawer.

'I just got the word.'

Bosch looked up. Pratt was standing in the doorway of his office. He was in shirtsleeves, his tie loose at his neck.

'What word?'

'From OIS. You haven't cleared home duty, Harry. I gotta send you home.'

Bosch looked down at his desk. 'So what's new? I'm leaving.'

Pratt paused. 'Everything OK?' he asked tentatively.

'When the fix is in, everything's not OK. Not by a long shot.'

'They're going to cover up Olivas and O'Shea?'

Bosch looked up at him. 'I don't think I should talk to you about it, Top. It could put you in a spot. You wouldn't want the blowback.'

'They're that serious about it, huh?'

'They're serious. They're willing to jam me up if I don't play the game.'

Bosch stopped there. He didn't want to be having this conversation. Pratt had to play the game until the buzzer sounded.

'My cell is part of the crime scene,' he said, reaching for the phone. 'I just came in to make a call and I'm out of here.'

'I was wondering about your phone,' Pratt said. 'Some of the guys have been trying to call you. They wanted to take you out for a drink at Nat's. They might still be heading over there.'

Nat's was a dive off Hollywood Boulevard. It wasn't a cop bar but a fair number of off-duty cops passed through there on any given night.

'You going?' Bosch asked Pratt.

'Maybe later. I've got something to do first.'

Bosch nodded. 'I don't think I feel like it. I'm going to pass.'

'Suit yourself. They'll understand.'

Pratt didn't move, so Bosch picked up his phone. He called Jerry Edgar's number just so he could follow through on the lie he'd told. But Pratt remained in the doorway. Edgar answered the call.

'It's Bosch. You called?'

'Yeah, man, I called. Nice shooting today, partner. You OK?'

'Yeah, fine. What were you calling about?'

'Something I thought you might want to know. I don't know if it matters any more. My cousin Jason called me. He said you saw him today.'

'Yeah, nice guy. He helped a lot.'

'Yeah, well, he said you didn't give him a business card or anything. He said that about five minutes after you and the FBI agent left, another cop came and asked at the lobby desk for the guy who was just helping the cops.'

Bosch leaned forward at his desk. He was suddenly very interested.

'He said this guy showed a badge, said he was monitoring your investigation and asked what you had wanted. Jason took him up to the floor you people had gone to and they were looking down on Echo Park when you and the lady agent showed up there. They watched you go into the house.'

Bosch leaned forward at his desk. 'Then what happened?'

'The guy ran out of there.'

'Did he get a name off this guy?'

'Yeah, Detective Smith. When he held up his ID he sort of had his fingers over his name. White guy, about six feet and one-eighty, short grey hair. Let's see, mid-fifties, and he was wearing a blue suit, white shirt and a striped tie. He had an American flag on the lapel.'

The description matched about 50,000 men in the immediate vicinity of downtown. And Bosch was looking at one of them. Abel Pratt was staring at Bosch with raised eyebrows. He wasn't wearing his suit jacket but it hung on the door behind him. There was an American flag pinned to the lapel.

Bosch looked down at his desk. 'How late does he work to?'

'Normally, I think he stays till five. But there's a bunch of people hanging up there, watching the scene in Echo Park.'

'OK, thanks for the tip. I'll call you later.' Bosch hung up before Edgar could say anything else.

'What was that?' Pratt asked.

'Oh, just something on the Matarese case. We might have a witness after all. But it'll hold until I get back from home duty.'

'Good. Glad to hear it.' Pratt stepped back into his office.

Bosch said goodbye and headed towards the door of the squad room. The Open-Unsolved Unit had three cars assigned to its eight detectives and one supervisor, and the keys hung on hooks next to the door. The procedure was for a detective taking a car to write his or her name and the estimated time of return on an erasable white board below the keys. When Bosch got to the door he opened it wide to block the view from Pratt's office. There were two sets of keys on the hooks. Bosch grabbed one and left.

A few minutes later, he pulled out of the garage and headed towards the DWP building. The mad rush to empty downtown by sunset was only just beginning and he made it the seven blocks in quick time. He parked illegally in front of the DWP entrance and jumped out of his car. He checked his watch as he approached the door. It was twenty minutes to five.

A uniformed security guard came through the doors. Bosch showed him his badge and asked him to radio Jason Edgar.

Bosch turned and headed back to his car. He waited five minutes before he saw Jason Edgar come through the glass doors. When he got to the car he opened the passenger door to look in.

'What's up, Harry?'

'I got your message. Get in.'

Edgar got in reluctantly. Bosch pulled away from the kerb.

'Wait a minute. Where are we going? I can't just leave.'

'This should only take a few minutes,' said Bosch.

'Where are we going?'

'Parker Center. We won't even get out of the car.'

'I have to let them know.' Edgar took a small two-way off his belt and called in. 'What are we doing at Parker Center?'

'Making an ID of the cop who talked to you after I left today.'

Traffic had already got worse. Bosch finally pulled back into the police garage at ten to five. He found a parking space in the first row. The garage was an open-air structure with a view of San Pedro Street, which ran between Parker Center and the garage.

'Somebody is going to leave at five,' Bosch said, 'and when he does he'll cross the street right there. I want to see if he's the guy who told you he was monitoring my investigation.'

'Is he Internal Affairs?'

'No. He's my boss.'

Bosch slapped the visor down as a precaution, though they were parked a good thirty yards from the crosswalk. Edgar asked questions about the Echo Park shooting and Bosch answered them in short sentences. He didn't want to talk about it but he had just yanked the guy off post. It was only being courteous. At 5.01 he saw Pratt come down the ramp by the jail's intake doors. He walked out to San Pedro with four other detective supervisors.

'OK,' Bosch said, cutting Edgar off mid-question. 'See those guys crossing the street. Which one came to DWP today?'

Edgar studied the pack crossing the street. 'Yeah, the last guy,' he said without hesitation. 'The one puttin' on the shades.'

Pratt, at the back of the group, had just put on his Ray-Bans. Bosch felt a deep pressure in his chest, like the worst case of heartburn he'd ever had.

'Now what? You going to follow him?'

Bosch remembered Pratt saying he had something to do after work. 'I want to but I can't. I've got to shoot you back to DWP.'

'Don't worry about it, man. I can walk. Probably be faster with this traffic, anyway. I don't know what's going on, but good luck, Harry.'

'Thanks, Jason. Hope to see you again.'

After Edgar was clear, Bosch left the garage. He took San Pedro in the direction of the freeway, crossed Temple and pulled to the kerb in a red zone.

In two minutes he saw a silver Jeep Commander come out of the garage with Pratt behind the wheel. Its dimensions and colour matched those of the mystery SUV Bosch had seen the night before near his house.

Bosch leaned down across the seat as the Commander approached Temple. He heard it make the turn and got back up. Pratt was on Temple up at the light, turning right onto Los Angeles Street. Bosch waited until he had completed the turn, then took off to follow.

Pratt entered the northbound 101 Freeway and joined the crawl of rush-hour traffic. Bosch pushed into the line of cars about six vehicles behind the Jeep. Luckily, Pratt's vehicle had a white ball atop the radio antenna, which allowed Bosch to track it without getting too close. His unmarked Crown Vic might as well have had a neon sign that flashed POLICE! Slowly Pratt made his way north. When the freeway cut past Echo Park, Bosch looked up to the ridgeline and saw the crime scene still in full swing. He counted two media choppers. He wondered if his car would be towed from the scene.

As he drove, Bosch tried to piece together what he had on Pratt. It was not feasible to think that he'd been following Bosch simply to see if he was abiding by the rules of home duty. There had to be another reason and Bosch could think of only one thing. The case.

Once he'd made this assumption, other things only served to stoke the fire burning in his chest. Pratt had told the story about Maury Swann earlier in the week, and that made it clear they knew each other. It was a negative story, but that could have been an attempt to distance himself from someone he was actually close to and working with. Pratt was also aware that Bosch regarded Anthony Garland as a person of interest in the Gesto case. Perhaps most important, Pratt had access to the Gesto murder book. It could have been Pratt who put in the phoney connection to Robert Saxon so that Olivas would discover it.

Bosch realised that the whole plan could have originated with Pratt. He was in a perfect position as a go-between who could monitor all parties. And with Swann involved, Pratt wouldn't need Olivas or O'Shea. All Swann had to do was tell Waits that the prosecutor and investigator were behind it and he would have planted a false trail for Bosch to follow.

A hot flash of guilt started to burn at the back of Bosch's neck, as he realised that he could be wrong about everything he had been thinking until a half-hour before. Maybe Olivas had been used as skilfully as Bosch had been used himself, and maybe O'Shea was guilty of nothing more than political manoeuvring. O'Shea could have called for the department fix simply because Bosch's accusations would be damaging, not because they were true.

Bosch thought this new theory through again and it held up. The only thing missing was motive. Why would a guy who was looking at imminent retirement risk it on a scheme like this? How could a guy who had spent twenty-five years chasing bad guys let a killer go free?

From working a thousand murders, Bosch knew that motive was often the most elusive component of crime. Obviously, money could motivate, but it couldn't readily explain why Abel Pratt had broken across the line.

Bosch banged his hand hard on the steering wheel, embarrassed and angry with himself. Pratt had played him perfectly and the betrayal was deep and painful. Pratt was his boss. They had eaten together, worked cases together, told jokes and talked about their kids together. Pratt was heading towards a retirement no one in the department believed was anything other than well deserved. Everybody was shooting for that blue heaven, and no one begrudged it. It was the policeman's dream.

But now Bosch saw through it. 'It's all bullshit,' he said aloud in the car.

11

Thirty minutes into the drive, Pratt exited the freeway and took Barham Boulevard into Burbank. The traffic was still thick and Bosch had no trouble maintaining his distance and cover. Pratt drove past Universal and Warner Bros., made a few turns and pulled to the kerb in front of a row of town houses on Catalina. Bosch drove on by, took his first right and then another and another. Taking one more right, he pulled to the kerb half a block behind Pratt's SUV and slid down in his seat.

He could see Pratt standing in the street, looking both ways before crossing. But he was taking too long. The street was clear but Pratt kept looking back and forth. He was looking for someone or checking to see if he had been followed. Bosch slouched down lower in the car.

Finally, Pratt crossed the street, then turned and surveyed the area in both directions. His eyes held on Bosch's car for a long moment.

Bosch froze. He didn't think Pratt had seen him, but he might have recognised the car as an unmarked police cruiser. Pratt started walking down the street towards it. Bosch grabbed the door handle, ready to bail out towards Verdugo, where there would be traffic and people.

But suddenly Pratt stopped, his attention drawn to something behind him. He turned round and looked up the steps of a town house. The front door was partially open and a woman was calling out and smiling. Pratt signalled her back inside. She put a pout on her face and disappeared from the door. Bosch recognised the woman and she wasn't Pratt's wife—whom Bosch had met at the squad-room party when Pratt announced his retirement.

Pratt looked towards Bosch's car again, but turned back to the town house. He strode up the steps, went through the open door and shut it behind him.

Bosch immediately started the car and made a U-turn. He took a right on Verdugo and headed to the Burbank Airport. Bosch figured he could dump the Crown Vic at the airport, pick up a rental car and be back at the town house in less than half an hour.

As he drove, he managed to place the woman he had seen. She was an attractive, young civilian employee who worked down the hall from Open-Unsolved, in a personnel office known by the rank and file as Hiring & Firing.

BOSCH GOT BACK to Catalina Street in thirty-five minutes. He drove his rented Taurus past Pratt's Jeep and this time found a spot on the north side of the town house. While he slouched down in the car and watched for activity, he turned on the car's cellphone. He called Rachel Walling but got her voicemail. He ended the call without leaving a message.

Pratt didn't come out until it was dark outside. He looked up and down the street, then went to his Commander and soon pulled away from the kerb. He made a U-turn and headed south to Verdugo, then turned right.

Bosch went north a block, turned and gunned the car's weak engine to California Street and took a quick left. He was playing a hunch.

Just as he got to Verdugo he saw Pratt's Commander go by in front of him. He had obviously delayed, watching for a follower. Bosch let him get some distance, then turned right to follow.

Pratt stayed on Verdugo into North Hollywood, then turned south on Cahuenga. Bosch guessed that Pratt was planning to join the squad members at Nat's, but halfway through the Cahuenga Pass he turned onto Woodrow Wilson Drive, and Bosch felt his pulse kick up a notch. Pratt was now heading towards Bosch's own house.

Woodrow Wilson wound up the side of the Santa Monica Mountains, one deep curve after another. It was a lonely street and the only way to follow a vehicle was without headlights. Bosch could make the drive half asleep—which he had done on occasion. He tried to stay two curves back but never lost sight of Pratt's lights for long.

When he was two curves away from his house, Bosch started to coast, and the rental eventually came to a stop. He got out quietly and edged round a hedge until he could see Pratt's SUV at the kerb ahead. Pratt's lights were off and he seemed to be just sitting there watching the house.

Bosch looked up at his house and saw lights on behind his dining-room windows. He could see the tail end of a car protruding from his carport and recognised Rachel's Lexus. Even as he was buoyed by the prospect of her being there, he was concerned about what Pratt was up to.

Bosch heard a car coming behind him. He started back to his car as if he were on an evening walk. The car drove by slowly and, as it came up behind Pratt's Jeep, Pratt sped away.

Bosch ran back to his rental car. As he pulled away from the kerb, he hit redial on the phone. This time Rachel answered.

'Rachel, it's Harry. Are you in my house?'

'Yes, I've been wait—'

'Come outside. I'm going to pick you up. Hurry.'

'Harry, what is—?'

'Just come out and bring your gun. Right now.'

He clicked off and pulled to a stop in front of his house. Rachel was coming out. She pulled the door shut and hurried to the car.

'Get in. Hurry!'

She jumped in and Bosch took off before she had closed the door.

'What is going on?'

He gave her the shorthand as he sped through the curves on the way up to Mulholland. He told her he'd be able to prove it all later.

'Your phone rang, right before you called my cell. I didn't answer it.'

'It was probably him. Something's going on.'

They came round the last bend to the four-way stop at Mulholland. Bosch saw taillights just as they disappeared to the right. The car that had made Pratt move on was going straight through the intersection.

Bosch got to the stop and turned right. Mulholland followed the crest line of the mountains across the city. Its curves were not as deep as Woodrow Wilson's. It was also busier. He quickly caught up to the vehicle and confirmed that it was Pratt's Commander, then dropped back. For the next ten minutes the sparkling lights of the Valley sprawled below.

'I was waiting at your house to say goodbye,' Rachel suddenly said.

'I know. I understand.'

'I don't think you do.'

'You didn't like the way I was today, the way I went after Waits. I'm not the man you thought I was. I've heard it before, Rachel.'

'It's not that, Harry. Nobody is ever the man you think they are. I can live with that. But a woman has to feel safe with a man. And that includes when they are not together. How can I feel safe when I've seen first-hand how you work? I'd wonder every night if it's the night you won't be coming home.'

'It's a dangerous job,' Bosch said. 'You know that more than anybody.'

'I do. I do. But I don't want to have to worry about someone who is reckless. There's enough to worry about without that.'

Bosch blew out his breath. He gestured towards the red lights. 'Let's talk about it later. Let's just concentrate on this tonight.'

As if on cue, Pratt hooked a left onto Coldwater Canyon Drive and started dropping towards Beverly Hills. Bosch made the same turn.

'Well, I'm still glad I've got you with me,' he said.

'Why?' Rachel asked.

'Because if he ends up in Beverly Hills I won't need to call the locals because I'm with a fed. You have your gun with you?'

'Always. You don't have yours?'

'It was part of the crime scene. That's the second gun they've taken from me this week. It's gotta be a record—the most guns lost during reckless gunplay.' He looked over to see if he was getting under her skin.

She showed nothing. 'He's turning,' she said.

Pratt made the turn and Bosch went on by. He used the next street down to turn round in and headed back up.

'Do you know where he could be going?' Rachel asked.

'No idea. Another girlfriend's place, for all I know.'

They were on another curving mountain drive, but the homes here ran a minimum seven figures, easy, and all had manicured lawns and hedges. Bosch drove looking for the silver Jeep Commander.

'There,' Rachel said.

She pointed at a Jeep parked in the driveway of a mansion with a French provincial design. Bosch parked two houses away. They walked back.

The gate was open. The cast-iron mailbox had no name on it. Bosch looked inside. They were in luck. There was mail, and he angled the top envelope towards a streetlight to read it.

'"Maurice"'—it's Maury Swann's place.'

'Nice,' Rachel said. 'I guess I should have been a defence attorney.'

A loud voice came from behind a tall hedge running along the far side of the turnaround. 'I said get in there!' There was a splash.

Bosch and Walling headed towards the sound. Bosch searched the hedge with his eyes, looking for an opening. There didn't appear to be one. Wordlessly he signalled Rachel to follow the hedge to the right while he went left. He noticed that she was carrying her weapon down at her side.

The hedge was at least ten feet high and thick, but as Bosch moved along it he heard the close sound of voices.

'Please, I can't swim. I can't touch the bottom!'

'Then what d'you have a swimming pool for? Keep paddling.'

'Please . . . Why would I tell a soul about . . .? Please!'

'I'm telling you, if I get even a hint that you're playing an angle on me, next time it'll be the Pacific Ocean.'

Bosch came to an alcove where the pool's filter pump and heater were located on a concrete pad. There was also a small opening in the hedge for a pool maintenance man to squeeze through. He slipped into the opening and stepped onto the tiles surrounding a large oval pool. He was twenty feet behind Abel Pratt, who was standing at the edge, looking down at a man in the water. Pratt held a long blue pole with a curved extension. Each time the man grabbed at it, Pratt jerked it away.

It was hard to identify the man in the water as Maury Swann. His glasses were gone and his hairpiece had slipped to the back of his gleaming scalp.

The sound of the pool filter gave Bosch cover. He was able to walk unnoticed to within six feet of Pratt.

'What's happening, Top?'

Pratt quickly lowered the pole so that Swann could grab it. 'Hang on, Maury!' he yelled. 'You're all right.' He started pulling Swann towards the side of the pool.

'Don't bother with the lifeguard act,' Bosch said. 'I heard it all.'

Pratt paused and looked down at Swann. 'In that case,' he said. He let go of the pole and whipped his hand behind his back to the belt line.

'Don't!' It was Walling. She was on the other side of the pool, pointing her weapon at Pratt.

Pratt froze. Bosch moved in and yanked out the gun.

'Harry!' Rachel called. 'I've got him. Get the lawyer.'

Swann was sinking. The pole was going down with him. Bosch grabbed it and pulled him to the surface. Coughing and spitting, the lawyer held tight. Bosch walked him down to the shallow end.

Maury Swann was naked. He came up the steps, went to a pile of clothes by a bench and started getting dressed while still soaking wet.

'So what was going on here, Maury?' Bosch asked.

'Nothing that concerns you.'

Bosch nodded. 'A guy puts you in the pool to watch you drown and you don't want anybody concerned about it.'

'It was a disagreement, that's all. He was scaring me, not drowning me.'

'Why was he scaring you?'

'I don't have to answer your questions.'

'You know what I think? I think that with Waits dead, there's only one person who can link him to the Garlands. I think your partner there was getting rid of that link because he was getting scared.'

'I'm finished talking. You can leave my property now.'

'Not yet, Maury. Why don't you join us at the deep end.'

At the other end of the pool, Pratt was now handcuffed and sitting on a concrete bench. Swann walked over to join them, his clothes sticking to his wet body. Bosch pointed Swann to a spot next to Pratt.

'Sit down, Maury,' he said. 'You're under arrest.'

'For *what?*' Swann said indignantly.

'Double murder. Both of you are under arrest.'

Swann laughed. 'And what murders would these be?'

'Detective Fred Olivas and Deputy Derek Doolan.'

'I'm assuming these charges fall under the felony-homicide rule, since there's ample evidence we did not pull the trigger. That rule comes into play only when someone is killed during the commission of a serious crime. What serious crime have I conspired to commit?'

Bosch thought for a moment. 'How about suborning perjury and obstruction of justice? We could start there and move up to corruption of a public official, maybe aiding and abetting an escape from lawful custody.'

'I was representing my client. You have not a shred of evidence, and if you arrest me it will simply prove your undoing.'

'I'll leave that to the prosecutors to decide, Maury.'

Pratt sat with a slight smile on his face. 'Harry, I think Maury makes a good point. Maybe you should think about this before doing anything rash.'

Bosch shook his head. 'You aren't walking away from this. I know you're the set-up man. You made the deal with the Garlands, then you went to Maury, who took it to Waits. You doctored the murder book after Waits gave you an alias to stick in it. There's more than enough for obstruction. That means no island and no pension, Top. That means you go down in flames.'

Pratt's eyes dropped to the dark waters of the pool.

'I want the Garlands. You can give them to me,' Bosch said.

Pratt shook his head without turning his eyes from the water.

'Then have it your way,' Bosch said. 'Let's go.'

He signalled Pratt and Swann to stand up. They complied. As Bosch cuffed Swann he looked over at Pratt. 'After we book you, who're you going to call about bail, your wife or the girl from Hiring & Firing?'

Pratt immediately sat back down as if hit by a sucker punch.

Bosch kept the pressure on. 'Which one was going to go with you to the sugar plantation? My guess is it was what's-her-name.'

'Her name is Jessie Templeton, OK. And I made your tail.'

'And I made you making me. But tell me, how much does she know?'

'Bosch, she doesn't know anything. Leave her out of it. Leave my wife and kids out of it, too.'

Bosch shook his head. 'Doesn't work that way. You know that. We're going to turn everything upside-down and see what falls out. I'm going to find the money the Garlands paid you and I'll tie it back to everybody. I just hope you didn't use your girlfriend to hide it, or she'll go down too.'

Pratt leaned forward on the bench. Bosch got the impression that if his hands hadn't been cuffed behind his back, he'd have been using them to hold his head and hide his face from the world.

Bosch walked Swann over to Rachel, then turned back to Pratt. 'You fed the wrong dog,' he said.

'What's that supposed to mean?'

'Everybody's got choices and you made the wrong one. Problem is, we don't pay for our mistakes alone. We take people down with us.'

Bosch walked to the edge of the pool. The water shimmered on top but was impenetrably dark beneath the surface.

'Jessie doesn't need to be part of this, and my wife doesn't need to know about her,' Pratt said.

It was an opening offer. Pratt was going to talk. Bosch kicked his foot on the tile edging and turned back to face him.

'I'm not a prosecutor, but I'll bet something could be worked out.'

'Pratt, you are making a big mistake!' Swann said urgently.

Bosch reached down to Pratt and patted his pockets. He pulled out the keys to the Commander. 'Rachel, take Mr Swann to Detective Pratt's car. We'll be right there.' He threw her the keys.

She walked Swann to the opening in the hedge, and pushed him through. Bosch waited until he heard the car door close. Then he stood in front of Pratt and noticed that sweat was dripping down his face.

'I don't want Jessie or my family involved,' Pratt said. 'And I want a deal. No jail time and I'm allowed to retire and keep my pension.'

'You want a lot for somebody who got two people killed,' Bosch said. 'What are you giving back?'

'I can give you the Garlands, easy,' Pratt said desperately. 'Anthony took me up there two weeks ago and led me to the girl's body. And I can give you Maury Swann on a platter. The guy's as dirty as . . .' He didn't finish.

'You?'

Pratt lowered his eyes and slowly nodded his head.

Bosch didn't know whether he'd be able to sell the deal to a prosecutor. He didn't know if he could even sell it to himself. But in that moment, he was willing to try if it meant he'd finally get the man who killed Marie Gesto.

'No promises,' he said. 'We'll go see a prosecutor. What about O'Shea and Olivas?'

Pratt shook his head once. 'They were clean on this. That wasn't the only thing you got wrong, Harry.'

'Yeah, what else?'

'You said I went to the Garlands with this thing. I didn't. They came to me.'

Bosch shook his head. He didn't believe Pratt for the simple reason that if the Garlands had had the idea to buy off a cop, their first overture would have been to the source of their problem: Bosch.

Pratt stood up and came face to face with Bosch. 'Harry, nobody was supposed to get hurt, OK? It was a perfect plan with nobody getting hurt. If Waits had just done what he'd been told, everybody would be alive and you'd have solved the Gesto case. That's how it was supposed to be.'

Bosch had to work to hold back his anger. 'Keep telling yourself that one,' he said. 'You might actually be able to live with it one day.'

He took Pratt roughly by the arm and led him to the opening in the hedge.

12

At 10 a.m. on Monday morning Abel Pratt walked from his car across the green lawn of Echo Park to a bench where an old man was sitting beneath the protective arms of the *Lady of the Lake*. There were five pigeons resting on her outstretched arms and one on her head.

Pratt shoved a newspaper into the full trash can by the statue and sat next to the old man. He looked out at the smooth waters of the lake.

The old man, who held a cane and wore a tan business suit, spoke first. 'I remember when you could take your family here on a Sunday and not worry about being shot up by gangbangers.'

Pratt cleared his throat. 'Is that what you're worried about, Mr Garland?

The gangbangers? Well, I'll give you a little tip. Most of your gangbangers don't roll out of bed until the afternoon. That's why whenever we go out with warrants we go in the morning.'

Garland nodded approvingly. 'That's good to know. But that's not what I am worried about. I'm worried about you, Detective Pratt. Our business was concluded. I was not expecting to hear from you again.'

Pratt leaned forward and studied the tables on the other side of the lake, where the old men played dominoes. His eyes then moved along the cars parked at the kerb that edged the park. 'Where's Anthony?' he asked.

'He's taking precautions,' Garland said. 'I don't like this place. It's full of ugly people, and that includes you. Why are we here?'

'Wait,' a voice said from behind them. 'Don't say another word, Dad.'

Anthony Garland had approached from their blind side. He came round the statue to the bench and signalled for Pratt to stand up.

'What is this?' Pratt protested mildly.

'Up,' he said. 'Just stand up.'

Pratt did as he was asked and Anthony Garland produced a small electronic wand from his pocket. He moved it up and down in front of Pratt from head to toe.

'If you're transmitting an RF signal this will tell me.' Then he ran his hands over Pratt's body.

'That's my gun,' Pratt said. 'And my cellphone.'

Garland went down both legs, and when he was satisfied he told Pratt to sit down. The detective returned to his seat. Anthony Garland remained standing, his back to the lake, his arms folded across his chest.

'He's clean,' he said.

'OK, then,' T. Rex Garland said. 'What's this about, Detective Pratt? I thought it was made clear to you: You don't call us. You don't threaten us.'

'If I hadn't threatened you, would you have come?'

Neither of the Garlands answered.

Pratt smiled smugly. 'I rest my case.'

'Why are we here?' the old man asked. 'I made it quite clear before. I don't want my son touched by any of this.'

'Well, I sort of missed him since our little walk in the woods. I mean, a guy leads you to a body, I'd say normally they'd stay pretty tight. But I haven't heard from Anthony since.'

'You don't talk to my son,' T. Rex Garland said, his eyes cast towards the lake. 'You're bought and paid for, Detective. I call you. You don't call me.'

'Yeah, all that was fine, but things have changed,' Pratt said.

The old man put both palms on the polished gold dragon's head at the top of his cane. 'And whose fault is that? You told us that you and the lawyer could keep Raynard Waits in line. You called it a clean operation.'

'No matter whose fault it is, I now need more money.'

'You were paid one million dollars,' T. Rex Garland said.

'The fee was based on everything working smoothly,' Pratt responded. 'Now there are complications. You know who paid me a visit on Friday night? Harry Bosch, and he had an FBI agent with him. They took me to a little meeting with Mr Rick O'Shea. Turns out that before Bosch capped Waits the little bastard told him that he didn't kill Marie Gesto. So that puts Bosch back on your ass, Junior. And it puts all of them on mine. They've damn near worked the whole story out—connecting me and Maury Swann. They just need somebody to fill in the blanks, and since they can't get to Swann they want that somebody to be me. They're starting to apply the pressure.'

Anthony Garland groaned and kicked at the ground with his expensive loafers. 'Goddammit! I knew this weasel would—'

His father put a hand up for quiet. 'Bosch and the FBI don't matter, and O'Shea is bought and paid for. He doesn't know it yet, but once I apprise him of his situation he will do what I tell him, if he wants to be district attorney. I took care of O'Shea. Detective, you take care of Bosch. Let's go, son.'

The old man started to get up, using the cane to push up on. His son stepped over to help him.

'Wait a minute,' Pratt said. 'I'll take care of Bosch, but then I need to disappear. I said I want more money and I'm serious.'

Anthony Garland angrily pointed down at him. 'You goddamn piece of shit,' he said. 'You were the one who came to us. This whole thing is your plan from start to finish. You get two people killed, and you have the balls to come back to us for more money?'

Pratt shrugged and spread his hands. 'I'm looking at a choice here, same as you. I could sit tight with the way things are and see how close they come to me. Or I could disappear right now. The thing you should know is that they always make deals with the little fish to get to the bigger fish. I'm little fish, Anthony. The big fish? That would be you.' He turned to the old man. 'And the biggest fish? That would be you.'

T. Rex Garland nodded. He now seemed to understand the gravity of the situation. 'How much?' he asked. 'How much to disappear?'

'I want another million dollars and it will be well worth it to you to give it to me. The price is non-negotiable. Anything less and it is not worth it for me to run. I'll make a deal and take my chances.'

'What about Bosch?' the old man asked.

Pratt stood up. 'I'll take care of him before I split. I'll throw that in for free.' He reached into his pocket and took out a piece of paper. He slid it across the bench. 'There's the bank account and wiring code. I'm going over to the boathouse to take a leak. When I come back I'll need an answer.'

Pratt walked past Anthony, coming close, each man holding the other's eyes in a hard stare of hatred.

HARRY BOSCH studied the monitors in the surveillance van. The FBI had worked through the night setting cameras in the park. One whole side of the van interior was covered with digital screens that showed a multitude of angles on the bench where T. Rex Garland sat and his son stood waiting for Abel Pratt to return. The cameras were located in path lights, in flowerbeds, in the mock lighthouse atop the boathouse and in the fake pigeon perched on the *Lady of the Lake*'s head.

Added to this, the bureau techs had set up microwave sound receivers triangulated on the bench, aided by mikes located in the fake pigeon, a flowerbed and the folded newspaper Pratt had placed in the trash can. A tech named Jerry Hooten sat in the van and manipulated the audio feeds. Bosch and the others had been able to watch Pratt and the Garlands and hear their conversation word for word.

The others were Rachel Walling and Rick O'Shea. The prosecutor was sitting front and centre, the video screens spread before him. It was his show. He pulled off his earphones, and so did Rachel and Bosch.

'He's going to call,' O'Shea said. 'What do I tell him?'

Three of the screens showed Pratt about to enter the park's restroom. According to the plan, he would wait until the room was clear and then call the surveillance van's number on his cellphone.

'I don't know,' Rachel said. 'It's your call, but we don't have much of an admission from the son in regard to Gesto.'

'That's what I was thinking,' O'Shea responded. 'We need more.'

Bosch nodded. It had been decided on Saturday morning that Pratt's word was not going to be good enough to build a solid prosecution on. He was a crooked cop, and building a case on his testimony was too risky in an age when juries were highly suspicious of police integrity.

A low-level buzzing sound indicated an incoming call. O'Shea raised a finger over the console, looking for the right button to push.

'Here,' Hooten said. He punched a button that opened the cell line.

'This is the van,' O'Shea said. 'You're on speaker.'

'How'd I do?' Pratt said.

'It's a start,' O'Shea said. 'What took you so long to call?'

'I actually did have to take a leak.'

While O'Shea talked to Pratt about trying once more for an admission, Bosch slipped his earphones back on to hear the conversation taking place at the bench. From the visuals it looked like Anthony Garland was arguing with his father. Bosch picked it up in the middle.

'It's our only out,' Anthony Garland said.

'I said no!' the old man commanded. 'You will *not* do this.'

On the screen, Anthony stepped away from his father, then stepped back, like he was on an invisible leash. He bent down close and spoke so low the FBI microphones picked up only a mumble.

'Jerry,' Bosch said. 'Can you work on this?'

Hooten went to work on the audio dials, but it was too late. Anthony had straightened up and was looking across the lake.

Bosch leaned back so that he could see the screen from one of the path lights at the water's edge. It was the only one that showed Anthony's face. Bosch saw the rage in his eyes. He had seen it before.

Anthony set his jaw tightly and turned back to his father. 'Sorry, Dad.'

With that he started walking towards the boathouse. Bosch saw his hand go inside his blazer.

He slapped off his earphones. 'Anthony's headed to the men's room! I think he's got a gun!' Bosch jumped up and shoved past Hooten to the door.

Behind him he heard O'Shea barking commands into the radio mike. 'Everybody move in! Move in! Suspect is armed. Repeat, suspect is armed!'

Bosch ran towards the boathouse. There was no sign of Anthony Garland. He was already inside. Bosch was more than a hundred yards away. Other agents deployed closer were running with weapons out. Just as the first man got to the doorway, the sound of gunfire echoed from the restroom. Four quick shots.

Bosch knew that Pratt's weapon was dry. It was a prop. He had needed to have a gun in case the Garlands checked him. But Pratt was in custody and facing charges. They had taken away his bullets.

As he watched, the agent at the doorway dropped into a combat stance, shouted 'FBI!' and entered. Almost immediately, there were more shots. The agent stepped out, radio to his mouth. 'We have two down. Scene is secured.'

Winded from his run, Bosch gulped some air and walked to the door.

'Detective, that's a crime scene in there,' the agent said. He put his hand up in front of Bosch's chest.

Bosch pushed it aside. 'I don't care.'

He entered the restroom and saw the bodies on the dirty concrete floor. Pratt had been shot twice in the face and twice in the chest. Garland had taken three chest shots. The fingers of Pratt's right hand were touching the sleeve of Garland's blazer.

Bosch stepped out of the boathouse and looked over at the bench. The old man sat leaning forward with his face in his hands. The cane with the polished dragon's head had dropped to the grass.

THE ENTIRETY OF Echo Park was closed for the investigation. For the third time in a week, Bosch was interviewed about a shooting, only this time it was the feds doing the questioning and his part was peripheral because he had not fired a weapon. When he was finished he walked over to a *mariscos* truck that was parked at the kerb and open for business to the onlookers outside the yellow tape. He ordered a shrimp taco and a Dr Pepper and took them over to one of the nearby federal cruisers. He was leaning on the front fender eating his lunch when Rachel Walling approached.

'Turns out Anthony Garland had a concealed-weapon permit,' she said. 'His security job required it.' She leaned next to him on the fender.

Bosch nodded. 'I guess we should have checked.' He took his last bite, wiped his mouth with a napkin, then balled it up in the aluminium foil.

'I remembered your story about Garland rousting those kids in the oil field,' she said. 'You said he drew a gun on them.'

'That's right.'

She didn't say anything. She looked out at the lake. Bosch shook his head like he wasn't sure what was going on. She finally spoke.

'You knew about the permit and you knew Anthony would be carrying, didn't you?' It was a question but she meant it as a statement.

'Rachel, what are you saying?'

'I'm saying you knew. You knew from way back that Anthony carried a gun. You knew what could happen today.'

Bosch spread his hands wide. 'Look, that thing with the kids was twelve years ago. How would I know that he would have a gun today?'

She got off the fender and turned to face him. 'How many times did you talk to Anthony over the years? How many times did you shake him down?'

Bosch squeezed the ball of foil tighter. 'Look, I never—'

'Are you telling me that in all those times you never once checked permits? That you didn't know there was a high probability he'd bring a gun—and his uncontrolled rage—to a meeting like this? If we'd known this guy carried a gun, we'd never have set this thing up in the first place.'

Bosch smiled unpleasantly and shook his head in a disbelieving sort of way.

She stared pointedly at him. 'What was it you said the other day? About being a true detective?'

'Rachel, there was no way anybody could have predicted this.'

'Predicted, hoped, accidentally set in motion—what's the difference? You remember what you said to Pratt the other night by the pool?'

'I said a lot of things to him.'

Her voice took on a tone of sadness. 'You told him about the choices we all make.' She pointed at the boathouse. 'And, well, Harry, I guess this is the dog you chose to feed. I hope you're happy with it. And I hope it fits in perfectly well with the way of the true detective.'

She turned and walked back towards the boathouse. Bosch let her go. For a long time he didn't move. Her words had gone through him like the sounds of a roller coaster. Low rumbling and high shrieks. He squeezed the ball of foil in his hand and shot it towards a trash can by the *mariscos* truck.

He missed by a mile.

KIZ RIDER CAME THROUGH the double doors in a wheelchair. Bosch was waiting for her with a smile and a bouquet of flowers he had bought from a vendor at the freeway exit near the hospital. As soon as she was allowed by the nurse, she got out of the chair. She tentatively hugged Bosch as though she felt fragile, and thanked him for coming to take her home.

'I'm right out front,' he said.

With his arm across her back he walked her out to the Mustang. He helped her get in, then put a bag of cards and gifts she had received into the trunk and came round to the driver's side.

'You want to go anywhere first?' he asked once he was in the car.

'No, just home. I can't wait to sleep in my own bed.'

'I hear you.'

He started the car and pulled out. They drove silently. When he got back to the freeway the flower vendor was still there. Rider looked down at the bouquet in her hand, realised that Bosch had got them as an afterthought, and started laughing. Bosch joined in.

'Ow, that hurts!' she said, touching her hand to her neck.

'Sorry.'

'It's all right, Harry. I need to laugh.'

Bosch nodded his agreement. They lapsed back into silence.

'Harry, I took your advice,' Rider said after a few minutes.

'What was that?'

'I told them I didn't have a shot. I told them I didn't want to hit Olivas.'

'That's good, Kiz.' He thought about things for a few moments. 'Does that mean you're going to keep your badge?'

'Yes, Harry, I'm keeping the badge . . . but not my partner.'

Bosch looked over at her.

'I talked to the chief,' Rider said. 'After I finish rehab I'm going to go back to work in his office, Harry. I hope that will be all right with you.'

'Whatever you want to do is all right with me. You know that. I'm glad you're staying.'

'Me too.'

A few more minutes went by and when she spoke again it was as if the conversation had never lagged.

'Besides, up there on the sixth floor, I'll be able to watch out for you, Harry. Maybe keep you out of all the politics and bureaucratic scrapping. Lord knows you're still going to need me from time to time.'

Bosch smiled broadly. He couldn't help it. He liked the idea of her being up there one floor above him. Watching out and watching over.

'I like it,' he said. 'I don't think I've ever had a guardian angel before.'

MICHAEL CONNELLY

Detective novels published: 17
Advice to budding writers: 'Write every day, even if it's just a paragraph.'

Michael Connelly, who went to university in Florida to study engineering, but ended up graduating in journalism and creative writing, reckons he might have become a builder, like his father and grand-father, if he hadn't become utterly hooked on the detective novels of Raymond Chandler. They made him realise that he wanted to write and, luckily, his parents were supportive. 'My father was an unfulfilled artist who, after being accepted into the Philadelphia Institute of Art, had to drop out because he was married with a child on the way. He had to make a living. So, from the background of that unfilfilment, when I came to him and told him I wanted to become a writer, he was all for it.'

Like his literary hero, Connelly wanted to become a crime novelist, and he believed that working as a journalist would be the best form of preparation. At the age of twenty-nine, while employed as a crime reporter on the *Orlando Sun-Sentinel*, he was nominated for a Pulitzer Prize in feature writing. One of the biggest newspapers in America, the *Los Angeles Times,* quickly snapped him up for their crime desk and, at the same time, Connelly began to write fiction at night and at weekends. Three years later, in 1992, *Black Echo* was published, introducing the LAPD detective Hieronymous 'Harry' Bosch to the world. By 1994, with two more best-selling novels about the maverick detective under his belt, Connelly felt confident enough to give up his day job.

Echo Park is Bosch's twelfth outing, and once again sees him working in the Open-Unsolved Unit of the LA Police Department. 'I got in kind of tight with the LAPD cold case squad a few years ago,' Connelly explains, 'and I have this exposure to what the real guys and women are doing. It's a squad of eight detectives—five men and three women—and they're all very open for me. Two years ago, when I was hanging out with them, a couple of detectives were preparing to take a confession from some guy in jail in California. He was convicted of murder and was there for life. He claimed to have gotten religion and a guilty conscience, and he contacted the police and said, "I want to tell you about some other murders I committed and clear it all up." As an outsider, I thought the detectives would just get in the car and drive up to the prison. Instead they went through all this research about the cases, and about the guy who was going to confess. They were very thorough in preparing for that interview and it really inspired me. I thought: Some day I want to do a story about that.'

In two earlier novels, Connelly tried turning Harry into a private investigator, but after *Lost Light* and *The Narrows*, his detective was back inside the LAPD. 'Private eye novels are repetitive. There are only so many variations . . . And that was also at the time my relationship with the cold case squad suddenly blossomed. I thought, Why am I writing about a PI when I could be writing about someone doing cold case work? How do I get him back into the police department? I reckoned I'd have to make something up, but then the LAPD got a new police chief who started a programme of hiring back police. So it's based on accuracy, on the real world. They helped breath new life into Bosch.'

Does Connelly have a favourite among his own novels? 'I like *Lost Light* because Harry meets his daughter and finds out he's a father. He's built his world so he has no one close to him, so he cannot be gotten to, and then he realises that this person in his life is the most important thing, and it changes him. For me that was a big shift in the series.'

CRACKING THE CASE

A scene from the popular BBC TV series, *New Tricks*, features Amanda Redman and Alun Armstrong (pictured right), in a cold case unit similar to the LA Police Department in which Michael Connelly's Detective Bosch works. One UK real-life equivalent is the Murder Review Group within London's Metropolitan Police. The unit consists of both serving and retired detectives who undertake detailed reviews of unsolved major crimes. Their work is greatly assisted by access to a computerised DNA database and by improved means of recovering forensic evidence. Convictions are often obtained several years after previous inquiries proved inconclusive.